THE ARMSTRONGS

The History of a Riding Family... 1040-1650

Derek James Stewart

AMERICAN ACADEMIC PRESS

AMERICAN ACADEMIC PRESS

By AMERICAN ACADEMIC PRESS

2038 S 1500 E   8345 NW 66 ST #A3869

Salt Lake City   MIAMI

UT 84105 USA   FL 33166 USA

Email manu@AcademicPress.us

Visit us at http://www.AcademicPress.us

All photographs are author's and the Pont's Map - belongs to the National Library of Scotland - Edinburgh which the author has the permission to reproduce for this book.

ISBN: 978-1-63181-830-1

Distributed to the trade by National Book Network Suite 200, 4501 Forbes Boulevard, Lanham, MD 20706

10 9 8 7 6 5 4 3 2 1

To my parents – Alistair & Doreen Stewart

CONTENTS

GAZETTEER

Armstrong Country

See gazetteer for key

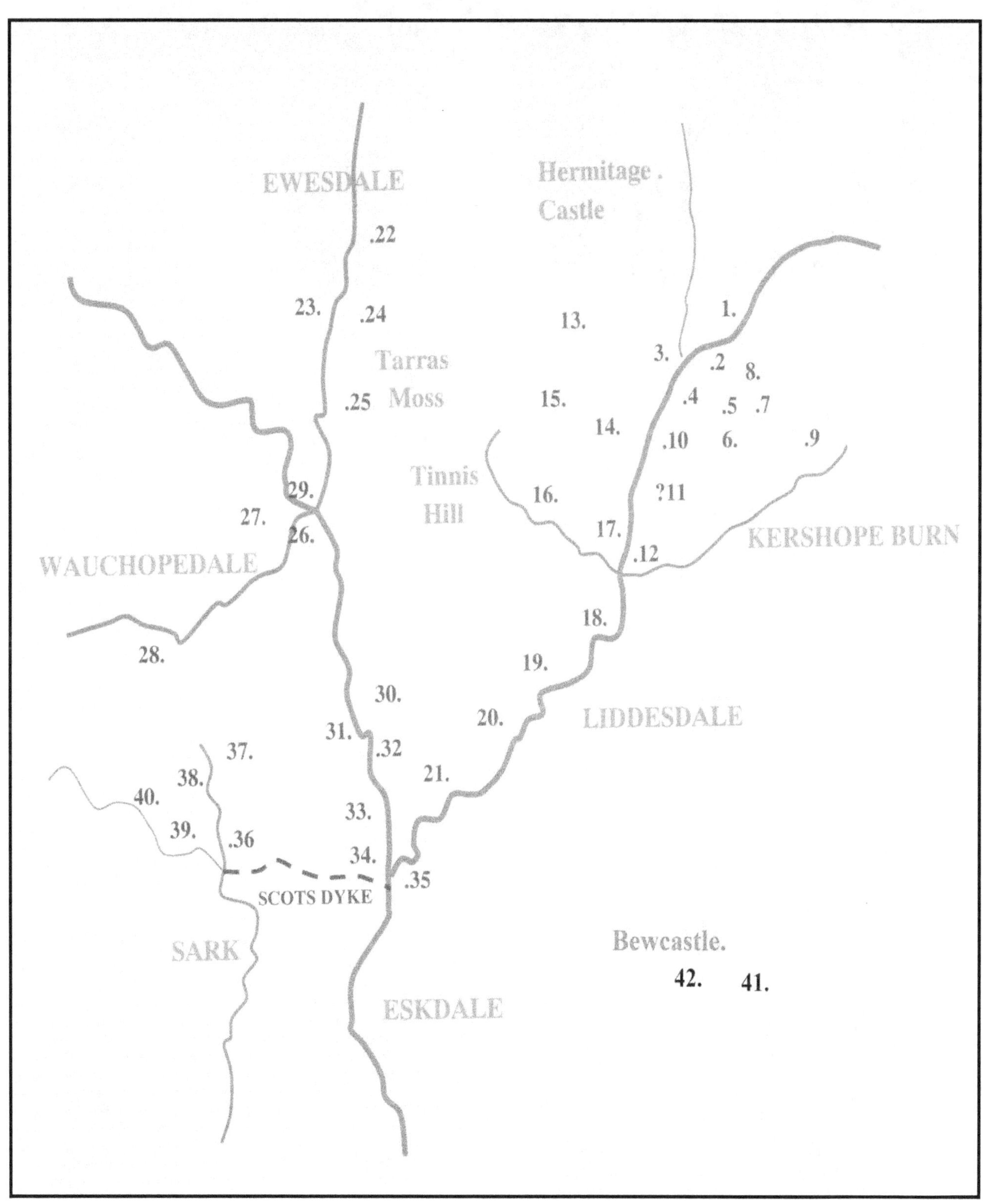

1. Mangerton Tower, the chief seat of the Armstrongs

2. Milnholm Cross – standing guard over Ettleton cemetery

3. Site of Roan Tower

4. Whithaugh Farm, built over the tower with the same name

5. Tarras Water – A place of refuge for the Armstrongs

6. Bewcastle Castle... Location of the first Scotland v England international football match

7. The Gingles, with Near Jingle Sike to the right

8. The Gingles on the horizon with the Tweeden Burn to the right

9. Site of the Hillhouse on the appropriately named Castle Hill

10. The site of Potterlamport village within Newcastleton Forest

11. View of Liddesdale from the top of Tinnis Hill

12. The Side – on the southern side of Kirk Hill

13. All that remains of Puddingburn Tower, turned into a sheepfold

14. Site of Whisgills village, with Tinnis Hill in the background

15. Kershopefoot – The meeting of the Kershope Burn with the Liddel Water

16. Tourney Holme, one of the many Truce Day sites on the Border

17. Site of Harelaw Tower and the origin of the term "to take Hector's cloak"

18. Site of Munkhurst Tower

19. Statue of Lang Sandy Armstrong in Rowanburn

20. Stubholm, home of Archie Armstrong, the fool to the wisest fool

21. View from the site of Calfhill Tower, on the southern slope of Naze Hill

22. Langholm Castle, on the confluence of the River Esk and the Ewes Water

23. The mass grave of Johnnie Armstrong and his followers at Carlenrig

24. The site of Gilnockie Castle on the east bank of the River Esk

25. Hollows Tower, the best preserved of all the Armstrong's towers

26. Site of Barngleish Tower

27. Site of Woodhouselees, opposite the confluence of the Esk and the Liddel Water

28. Site of Morton Tower, with Tower-of-Sark farm behind

29. The postern gate of Carlisle Castle, through which Kinmont Willie Armstrong was rescued

30. Sark graveyard, where the body of William Armstrong of Kinmont lies

31. Raes Knowe, location of the murder of Sir John Carmichael in 1600

32. One of the last raids by the reivers was to the Leaplish in 1611

Chapter 1. Introduction

The Armstrongs were originally an English family, and would have been one of many living out a quiet life, conforming to society and kings – making ends meet as best they could. The Armstrongs however, rose to an unusual status of notoriety in the 14th century, when a branch of the family was gifted land in the Scottish Borders. At borders, society is often at its most strained, where military friction and political tension are at their most sensitive, with strife and conflict never far away. It does not have to be the Berlin Wall or the Great Wall of China, any border has the capacity to arouse and exhilarate. The Anglo/Scots Border was no exception; and here amongst the melancholy hills, under a hodden grey sky, the dramas of the Border reivers where played out. Reiver were mounted raiders – and the Armstrongs came to be their greatest exponent.

The Border itself needs to be understood in order to put the Armstrongs into context. The frontier runs for sixty miles as the crow flies, but due to landmarks, and local and international politics, the Border twists and turns for 110 miles. Many of the deviations on the line seem to make no sense, shaped by centuries of dispute now long forgotten. The Border runs roughly between its main two towns, Berwick to Carlisle, in a south west direction, and follows were possible the main landmarks – the River Tweed and the Cheviot Hills. The frontier in its current form was laid down during the reign of King Malcolm III, in around 1090 – and became agreed upon and enshrined in laws and Marches in 1249. The Border reiver was a unique figure in British history, born out of fire and steel they were a curse on the frontier for three centuries. He was a hard fighting man, a skilled guerrilla soldier and an expert in weapon handling and riding – to whom the arts of theft, raid, tracking and ambush were second nature. He was a highly organised professional gangster who invented and perfected the protection racket – and it is from his lawless activities that we have the words blackmail and bereaved in the English language. Reivers were found at every social level and could range from a labourer to gentleman farmer – and even up to a lord.

It was the Wars of Independence (1296 – 1328) which created the Border reivers. When Edward I of England crossed the Border in 1296, a 300 year war was kicked off and in this crucible of conflict and destruction the reiver was forged. The Borderlands were in the forefront of these attacks and soon became devastated, a wasteland as armies fought back and forth. To the people who farmed the land; why plant crops when armies could trample them – why graze cattle when they could be stolen? What alternative did people have; to move away, do nothing and starve, or build a tower and fight back? With crops burned and the cattle stolen, the Borderer had little back up plans for help, if any at all. The seats of government were too far away and did not care anyway, with local lords squabbling amongst themselves for power, and who were often a part of the problem in causing the wars in the first place. Famine and destitution were real every day worries, with many having an early grave. Self help became the order of the day, with an easy and instant solution to the food issue at hand; to thieve what you wanted from your neighbour. The wars deprived the farmer from farming and gaining his own food-stuffs by honest toil; and at the same time militarised society, hardening it to the brutal realties of winner takes all. These two factors combined to the ill-fortune of both Scotland and England, into manufacturing the reiver. Many chose to stay in their valleys and fortify themselves, making up for the losses in food by theft; and a whole society developed from stealing. The Armstrongs rose out of this unique mixture of landscape, politics and culture to become the worst of the worst – a label which they themselves would have been proud of. Like wolves living amongst hyenas, the Armstrongs did more than just survive in this world of casual murder and constant theft – they thrived.

Way of Life

It was the horse which allowed the Border hill farmers to survive in this harsh environment, enabling them to cross into more fertile valleys and take what they wanted, and then safely navigate home in one piece. Ironically, the same Wars of Independence which brought about a lack of food on the Border also provided the method to obtain a replacement source, in the form of the mounted horseman. During the wars both Scots and English sought light cavalry in their armies, seeking to fill a tactical gap. The Scots especially sought light cavalry, as there was a lack of even basic horsemen in the Scots army in the first place, and all mounted units were eagerly welcomed. Light cavalry were never a match for the war horse of the English, with their mighty destriers, but they were never designed to take them on. Light cavalry developed in 13th century Ireland, in the form of the hobelar. These were highly mobile horsemen and excelled in scouting, reconnaissance and patrols. The hobelars rode the Irish hobby (now extinct), represented today by the Connemara pony. They were ideal at picking their way through the bogs and woods, which the heavier mailed knight never could, and aided the rider in many a tight scrape. The hobelar's success and adaptability was obvious from the instant they were observed, and became the proto-type to emulate. The Borderlands with its hills and bogs were an ideal environment for the light horseman to operate, and the reiver had his means of transport. The reivers later became known as the best light cavalry in Europe, with a renowned reputation for stamina and courage.

When King Robert the Bruce gained the Scottish throne in 1306, he desired light cavalry to bring the war to the England, and his eyes fell upon the Border hill farmers. The Armstrongs would have entered the service of Robert when he obtained the allegiance of William de Soules of Hermitage Castle within Elliot country, after the Scots victory at Bannockburn in 1314, seeking to unify Scotland and obtain more soldiers. De Soulis was previously in the service of England, and his switch gave Bruce access to the Liddesdale riders. De Soulis was rewarded with honours, he was made the Butler of Scotland in 1318, and in 1320 he put his signature to the Declaration of Arbroath. Robert for his efforts recruited the Armstrongs to his cause desiring to employ their skills in horsemanship, and these early troopers became the very first Armstrong reivers.

Out of all the Riding families (families which raided by horseback – numbering around 89 in total) along the Anglo-Scottish frontier, the Armstrongs were the most dangerous and feared – a mighty boast considering the rapacious nature of the reivers. They probably did more damage than any other single family along the Border. There was rarely a piece of Border intrigue that they were not involved with. They commanded a notorious reputation unlike any other family, one which was well earned and became the epitome of the Border reiver. The Armstrongs were also arguably the largest and most powerful of the Riding surnames. At the height of their power, the Armstrongs could put more riders in the saddle than any other family, and were the most effective clan at plundering the English countryside. It is said in Johnnie Armstrong's day c.1528 (see page 264), that the Armstrongs could put 3,000 men in the saddle; a vast number which illustrates the level of danger and intimidation that the Armstrongs potentially possessed. This figure of 3,000 does not mean that every rider was an Armstrong, but was the total that came about under the complex system of alliances and family allegiances connected to the Armstrongs – an impressive figure and enough to put fear into all but the monarch. Through marriages, bonds and clan alliances, the Armstrongs could put together international gangs in huge numbers that amounted to a small army. In the Armstrongs heyday they would have been virtually unstoppable.

In order to administer and police this Borderland, the area was divided up into three areas called Marches for both Scotland and England, each overseen by a warden. This added up to six March Wardens along the frontier – an extra seventh was required however, just for Liddesdale (based at Hermitage Castle), such was the criminality of this single valley that it needed its own watchkeeper. Wardens were responsible for keeping the law within the Marches, and became very familiar figures with the Armstrongs. Wardens were probably the most accomplished trouble shooters in British history. They had to be a mixture of soldier, judge, lawyer, fighting man, lawyer, diplomat, politician, rough rider, detective and administrator. He had to guard the frontier, supervise strongholds, pursue fugitives, hold domestic courts, muster the March for defence and confer with his opposite warden. The wardens were often corrupt and as crooked as the reivers that they pursued. There was an element of setting a thief to catch a thief. If they could not keep order – who could? Due to the unique geo-politics on the frontier, unique laws were needed. "Hot Trods" (the pursuit of stolen goods straight after a crime) – "Warden's Rodes" (punishment raids) – and "Truce Days" (outdoor meeting to resolve cross-border conflicts) – all aided the warden in his days work.

The reivers can be viewed as farmers who were not very good at farming. They were a rural society who lived mainly in the high country, building their strongholds within the glens and cleuchs – secluded lairs from which they could mount their missions and hide away from reprisals. The reiver's way of life was shaped by family allegiance and the constant need to be ready for war – loyalty to family came before nation. Living depended on livestock rather than crops though they did plant oats, rye and barley. In spring, the cattle and sheep were moved up to the high ground for pasturing. Summer was devoted to planting crops. Then in autumn the livestock was moved back down into the valleys and all food was harvested, and made ready for the winter months. Any gaps in the food stocks for the winter months were filled in by raiding. You could call it a semi-nomadic horse culture. Reivers lived mostly on broth with a little beef or mutton, milk and boiled barley as staple diet. Bread was rare, being replaced with oat cakes. Beer and wine is rarely recorded, and may have been uncommon except for in the towns, or was a regular feature and not worth documenting.

The Border reiver built strong houses for themselves; a living by crime required a defensive home base. The peel (pele) tower was the deluxe stronghold of choice for the thieves, becoming to symbolize the very essence of their society. Strong, solid and dour, these were fortified keeps, fireproof and usually with commanding views of the landscape. The name derives from the Anglo-Norman French word "*pel*," and the Latin "*palus*," which means a stake / palisade / enclosure. The peels were originally built along the frontier to act as watch towers against the raiders. An act of parliament in England in 1455 demanded that all the towers had an iron basket placed on their roofs to function as a warning beacon (balefire) to alert on approaching marauders.

With irony, the same peels and balefires became adopted by the reivers as their own homes. These iconic buildings were unique to the Border, and became the personal homes of the lairds and headsmen. Peel towers were of a standard design; they had 3-4 floors; a barrel vaulted ground floor which was used as a store room, great hall on the first floor, the laird's bedroom on the second, third floor for the rest of the family, and servants in the rooftop garret. A large wall called a barmkin surrounded the peel, which gave a basic protection to the locals and their livestock who could run to the tower for temporary refuge during minor attacks. A statute in Scotland from 1535 obliged all lairds to build barmkins onto their towers at a regulation size of over two feet thick and 7-8 feet high.

A more common type of accommodation though was the bastle house. The word bastle is derived from the French word "*bastille*," meaning a fortified place. Bastles were all of a similar design consisting of a long single barrel vaulted room on the ground floor, where cattle could be kept safe – and above was another single room which served as the living quarters. The first floor was entered either through a small trap door from the barrel vaulted room or by a staircase from the outside. Bastles were built in small groups for mutual protection, and were strong enough to resist the average hit and run raid. An alternative to the bastle was the blockhouse. These were built from long baulks of oak which were bound hard together, and had turf piled up around them to make the structure fireproof. The overall residence sounds dark and smoky inside. Going down the social ladder, the average followers of the headsman would have lived in a simple hut. These had a turf or thatched roof, with walls made from whatever was around; if burned down, it was of no loss as a replacement could be built the following day. Seasonal dwellings called shielings were built high up in the hills; dry-stone shelters to watch the cattle from, which contained only the basics for life.

Tools of the trade

The most important item of the reiver's equipment was his horse, without it reiving could not exist. The reivers used the Galloway pony (nag) as their horse of choice and was central to their way of life. Today these hardy animals are now sadly extinct. They were small, agile and sure footed and had great stamina, were easy to look after, good natured and easily trained. They stood about 14 hands high with a shaggy brown coat, black legs and a small head and neck. When ridden, the rider's legs almost touched the ground. A Galloway could carry a fully armed man on round trips of anything up to 100 miles – and this being over difficult rough moorland and at night almost by instinct – an amazing task. This ability made the reiver a dangerous adversary, who could strike at any location and time of day with little or no warning.

The preferred weapon of the reiver was the lance, 8-12 feet long, which was used as a thrusting spear, and could be reversed and used for herding cattle. As a secondary weapon, swords were carried from a shoulder belt. Other weapons included the pistol ("dag"), crossbow, longbow and dagger. Body armour mainly consisted of the metal breastplate and quilted jack. The quilted jack was preferred over the breastplate; made from 2 inch square plates of metal and coated in wool it provided the same protection as a steel breastplate but had the advantage in being flexible, more comfortable to wear and gave essential warmth on a cold night. On the head was worn the steel bonnet; either a burgonet, cabasset or morion. These were all light weight helmets and gave good visibility, designed to deflect sword blows away from the wearer.

The Scots reivers would look no different from their English counterparts, apart from the wearing on occasion of the blue bonnet by the Scots. In an age before the Agricultural Revolution, the landscape was much boggier than today. Fields were not as enclosed, with no wire fences criss-crossing the landscape and no dense conifer plantations to avoid. Traversing the hill tops with a mounted armed host of family and friends, with no barriers in sight – master of all they surveyed – gave the reiver a unique freedom and an authority very much of their own making.

Chapter 2. The origin of the name

The Armstrong's have the most suited surname for a Border reiver clan out of all the Riding families. Strong of arm, they more than lived up to their name – strong in courage, manpower and horseflesh, they came to be a dominant power and ride the Marches with a saddle for a throne.

It is worth looking into the source of the Armstrong name, as it went towards forming the clan's character and gave it a sense of pride. The Armstrong origins are surrounded in mystery, with more than one story on how the family came about. The most popular origin of the Armstrongs go back to Siward (Sigurd) Bjornsson – nicknamed "*Digri*" (Norse for the Stout – meaning strong) – a Viking noble. Siward was an important and powerful figure within English society and the Armstrongs claim him as the first Armstrong; however there is no archival evidence linking Siward to the House of Armstrong.

Siward (c.995 – 1055) was a Danish Viking and cousin to Earl Ulf, the *Earl of Denmark* who married King Cnut's sister Estrith. The surname of Siward, son of Bjorn/Beorn comes from the Norwegian name for bear. Bears feature extensively in the Nordic legends of the Fairy Bear or Fay Bairn, from which later developed into the surname of Fairbairn. Tradition places the name "Fairbairn of the Strong Arm" onto Siward, although there is no historical evidence that he was ever called this. Siward was the cliché Viking, described as being fair haired and bearded, and having blue eyes; a giant of a man who possessed an incredible strength. He also possessed a great wit and wisdom, skilled in diplomacy as well as the sword.

The life of Siward has a lot of legends attached, which makes it difficult to dissect the Armstrong connections. The legend despite having an obvious flaw in its accuracy is still important to the Armstrong story as the tales would have permeated up into Liddesdale, and influenced all who heard them. Mystery is added to the clan's roots, entering realms of the heroic. Norse sagas portray Siward initially arriving from his native Denmark to land at the Shetland Islands, where he proceeded to slay heroically a dragon in single combat. Siward then sails to Northumbria in search of further serpents to cut down. Failing to find any, he heads for London where the king welcomes him and he settles down, becoming the Earl of Northumbria.

Removing the myths, Siward came to England from Denmark in the wake of King Cnut (c.995 – d.1035), hoping to benefit from the aftermath of the Scandinavian conquest. Siward did well, gaining an earldom and rising to become a sub-ruler of most of northern England. He is recorded in 1033 as in control of southern Northumbria, and gaining the north by 1041. Between 1042 and 1055, Siward took control of Cumbria south of the Solway (which was a part of Scotland), an action which was probably prompted by troubles in Scotland, caused by upheavals during the reign of Macbeth (c.1005 – 1057). Siward enters international fame in 1054 courtesy of William Shakespeare and his play "Macbeth," when he led an expedition into Scotland. The purpose of this invasion is unclear, but was probably in support of Malcolm's (later to be King Malcolm III) civil war against Macbeth. Siward was related to Malcolm, his daughter Sybil ("Suthen" in Gaelic – died 1070) was married to King Duncan (c.1001 – 1040), who was Malcolm's father.

Siward marched to join in the war against Macbeth, but his progress was hampered when a year later his health failed him. In 1055 he looked death in the face. Siward had dysentery; this was not in the script for the death of a son of Odin, this was not how his life should end. Siward had led a valiant life, and it should be valiant to the grave. Faced with the ignoble death of the bloody flux, Siward sought a more suitable entry to Heaven/Valhalla. Siward is reported as saying *"How shameful it is that I, who could not die in so many battles, should have been saved for the ignominious death of a cow! At least clothe me in my impenetrable breastplate, gird me with my sword, place my helmet on my head, my shield in my left hand, my gilded battle-axe in my right, that I, the bravest of soldiers, may die like a soldier."* And armed as he had requested, he gave up his spirit with honour.

Siward was buried at St Olave's Church at Galmanho, York. One of his last acts in life was to order this church to be built and consecrated, York being his main residence. St. Olaf (995 – 29 July 1030) was Olaf II Haraldsson, the King of Norway – who became Norway's patron saint; his tomb at Nidaros Cathedral in Trondheim was a cult focus for pilgrims, with various miracles associated to him. Siward's building is the earliest date for a church dedicated to St. Olaf anywhere. The dedication to St Olaf illustrates Siward's Scandinavian sentiments, despite being a Christian he was still a Viking at heart.

Siward had at least two sons, Osbeorn *"Bulax"* (pole axe) and Waltheof, both of whom met violent ends. Osbeorn was killed in the Battle of the Seven Sleepers (also known as the Battle of Dunsinane) in 1054. Siward was not present at the battle where Osbeorn was slain, which some sources place at the hands of Macbeth. In Shakespeare's play "Macbeth," the character of Osbeorn is renamed as "young Siward." The historian Henry of Huntingdon (c.1088 – c.1157), would later comment – *"And when they reported to his father that he had been slain in battle,* [Siward] *said, 'Did he receive the mortal wound in front of his body, or behind?' The messengers said, 'In front'. And he replied: 'I rejoice wholly, for I would deem myself or my son worthy of no meaner death'."*

And Waltheof was beheaded at Winchester in 1076, for his part in the Revolt of the Earls, against William the Conqueror in 1075. Waltheof was buried in Croyland (Crowland) Abbey, where he was given the status of martyr. Miracles became attributed to his tomb, attracting pilgrims with their prayers and ailments.

Siward's dynasty lived on though, despite the brutal deaths of his two sons. Waltheof had no sons, but a daughter Maud / Matilda (c.1074 – 1130/31), married King David I, entering the Scottish royal family line. Osbeorn is said to have had two sons according to the *"Chronicles of the Armstrongs,"* named Siward Barn the Red and Siward Barn the White (Fairbeorn), though this claim lacks evidence and is widely debateable. Osbeorn had good relations with Scotland and Malcolm III (c.1031 – 1093), as his sister was the mother of Malcolm. He was possibly responsible for Malcolm regaining Cumbria in 1061, judging by his lack of loyalty to William the Conqueror and family ties. There is little known about Siward the Red, but Siward Barn the White is claimed to have fled to Scotland to find refuge after the invasion of William the Conqueror (c.1028 – 1087) in 1066. It is from Siward Barn that the Armstrongs of Mangerton claim to be descended from. The new Norman overlords of England would have looked with mistrust at the Anglo-Danish lineage of Siward, fearing that they became figureheads for an "English" uprising.

Norman fears became a reality in 1068, when a revolt broke out in the north of England. Siward Barn played a prominent part in this, teaming up with his uncle Waltheof and Edgar the Ætheling. Siward Barn spent a short time in Scotland in 1070, where he received a warm reception from Malcolm. He then returned to England by ship in the following year, to meet up with Hereward the Wake, and was captured by King William. Siward Barn was lucky to escape being executed, and was dispossessed of much of his lands. He was finally released after William's death in 1087, with little record of what happened to him next – though according to some historians, he became a mercenary fighting for the Byzantine Empire, perhaps joining the Varangian Guard and settling down as a colonist.

The story and legend does not end here, in 1138 another named source rises to provide the originator of the Mangerton line – Fairbairn. Fairbairn as his name suggests had a Norse link. He was the armourer of King David I and if tradition is believed, became the first Liddesdale Armstrong, although there is no written source to confirm this. In 1138 Fairbairn accompanied David when he led an army into England seeking to expand his kingdom and support his niece's (Mathilda) claim to the throne of England. At Cowton Moor near Northallerton, David's army ran into the English force under the command of William Le Gros, Count of Aumale, on 22 August. Here, the Battle of the Standard was fought, a fierce engagement in which English archers played a prominent roll. During the fighting, the king had his horse killed from under him, and Fairbairn came to David's rescue. Fairbairn passed his left arm around the king's thigh, and lifted him up onto his own horse saving his life. He then fought his way to safety through the disintegrating army. Fairbairn was rewarded for his courageous act by the monarch, given a knighthood and land in Liddesdale at "Merieton" (Mangerton). He was also allowed to display the crest of an armoured arm and hand holding an armoured leg and foot. Legend accords Fairbairn and Siward Barn as being the same person; and from that time on, he is referred to as the Sword of the Strong Arm – or Armstrong. The Armstrong family from that day would forever be associated with bravery and strength, and reminded of their Norse ancestor's heroic deeds.

Problems enter the narrative however when looking at the time logistics which make it impossible for Siward Barn to be also the Fairbairn who fought at the Battle of the Standard. This would place Siward Barn's age at around ninety, plus having an armour bearer's roll would be too lowly for a descendant of the great Earl of Northumbria. The event though may be in part correct, with Fairbairn either being a separate character, or Siward Barn was from a different time period, or more probable Siward himself.

When looking at the legend which mentions the battle, oddly it does not give the name of the conflict. This is a puzzle considering the occasion should have been of huge significance to the Armstrongs. And the name of the monarch is not given, the text merely stating *"an ancient king of Scotland."* The king is not necessarily David and was more likely Malcolm III, his father. In all probability, the action of the king awarding Mangerton to an Armstrong probably happened nearly a century earlier, when King Malcolm presented the land to Siward as a reward for his help at the Battle of Dunsinane. This earlier date for the event makes sense when evidence is looked for. Siward had just lost a son, it would have been sentimentally appropriate for Malcolm to both award and compensate Siward with the gift of an estate. Another clue is the Armstrong emblem of an oak tree. The oak tree is a distinct and early Armstrong heraldic device, and it came from the Battle of Dunsinane. This battle must have been important amongst the Armstrongs in order to have a reminder of it placed upon their flags and shields. It takes little stretch of the imagination to view Mangerton as having an association to the oak and the battle – if the land was presented as a reward to Siward and his strong arm for the victory.

The first named Armstrong

Having established the name of Armstrong in 1138 at the very latest, it can be expected that the Armstrongs would begin to be found within the archives after that date, however there is silence for nearly one hundred years. The first reference to the Armstrongs comes from a Carlisle court record of 1235, where Adam Armstrong was pardoned for killing a man. Adam Armstrang de Ulvesby (Ousby, near Penrith) was a verderer and worked the great Cumbrian Royal Forest of Inglewood. This tract of wild wood measured sixty miles in circuit stretching from Penrith to Carlisle and was well stocked with wild boar, red deer and fallow deer for the hunt. Adam held a position of responsibility within Ousby, holding a moiety (half share) in the village. He was related to Patrick de Ulvesby, a major figure in the region, either through blood or marriage. Patrick of Ulvesby was of Flemish descent, as were other families from the surrounding villages, suggesting another source for the Armstrong surname. Adam and his kinsmen operated as forest officials and clerks within the woodlands, administering forest law.

Frustratingly, researchers have found no ties between Adam Armstrong of Ousby and Siward however the name of the forest raises some interesting questions. Inglewood means the wood of the English or the Angles. The area was not Norman and was an area heavily influenced by the Danish and Anglo Saxons. Adam could have been one in a long line of verderers, a family dynasty who served the king. And the area may have been the birthplace of the Armstrongs. Safe within their woodland fastness, Siward and his progeny and followers may have taken up the name of the strong arm, forming a new surname to hide their Norse origins, and display a new courageous and strong future. The forest became the haunt of outlaws and such figures as Adam Bell, who led a Robin Hood type life. The next named Armstrong dates to 1274, "William Armestrangh," recorded in Carlisle serving on an inquisition.

When Siward/Siward Ban/Fairbairn was given the land in Liddesdale, he did not immediately settle at Mangerton. He occupied another estate in Tynedale, leaving it for later generations to build a castle. There is no mention of an Armstrong chief until the first Laird of Mangerton in the early 1300s. The fortalice of Maingertoun was constructed later, probably around 1240, at the same time as the motte and bailey castle at Hermitage built by Nicholas de Soulis.

There are other sources for the Armstrong name. A separate possible origin may come from the Norman surname of "Fortenbras," assumed from a personal attribute to strength of arm. Yet another interpretation of Armstrong may come from the surname Armiston (pre Norman Conquest) in Berwickshire. The name could have morphed into Armstrong gradually, or become double barrelled on the marriage to a "Strang/Strong" surname. "Strang/Strong" was a surname used in the Borders and northern England, originally given as a nickname to one who possessed great physical strength.

The Strong Arm

The Armstrong surname's progenitor has indeed caused great discussion and controversy. The most plausible candidate has to be Siward, the Earl of Northumbria. Siward's nickname of *"Digri"* may have been enough on its own to originate the Armstrong family. Those around Siward may have taken up the name of Strong, and it's not a far stretch for Strong Arm to develop. It is possible that Siward called his own extended family the Armstrongs. Siward could have had a troop of mounted bodyguards, a retinue and called them the Strong Arms – a job title and a privilege which over time became a surname. It is possible that Siward was at the Battle of Dunsinane and it was Malcolm, the future king of Scotland and not David who fell from his dying horse, to be rescued by Siward. It would then have been Siward receiving the land in Liddesdale, in recognition of his strength and bravery. Siward and his family possibly became known as Armstrongs from as early as 1054. From a heartland in Inglewood, the Armstrongs became an established family. From there his descendants moved into Liddesdale, whether at invitation, land grant or by force is open to question.

Everything would change though when the Border moved further north in the late 12th century. Carlisle became English together with many Armstrongs in Cumbria, creating a national divide. And in 1296 when Edward I invaded Scotland, relationships between Scotland and England were poisoned, which would rumble on for the next 300 years and make reivers of the Armstrongs. It was the war with England that probably instigated the forming of a laird at Mangerton, and the subsequent wars that forced the strong arms of the Armstrongs into extreme action – to live by raiding.

Chapter 3. Armstrong Country

The Armstrongs were truly an international Border family, with branches both in Scotland and England. The Scottish Armstrongs were located in the West and Middle Marches within the valleys of Liddesdale, Ewesdale, Eskdale and Wauchopedale; with a branch extending into Annandale who kept to themsevles. In England the Armstrongs resided in the West March around Bewcastle and Gilsland – with a branch entering South Tynedale in the Middle March from Scotland in the 17th century. The Scottish Armstrongs were originally based within the Liddesdale Valley in Roxburghshire, where their chief seat was at Mangerton. They occupied the southern half of the valley, with the Elliots, Crosers (Croziers) and Nixons in the upper. The valley takes its name from the Liddel Water, which was originally called the "Hlyde," an Old English word for loud. Liddesdale is not the most fertile of valleys, but the valley floor is well watered and has good grazing. The surrounding hills were covered with a blanket heather moorland and moss, with pockets of dense scrub woods – scarred with deep sikes and cleuchs. Off road travelling was slow and tiresome.

The high surrounding hills gave the Armstrongs excellent vantage points from which to observe approaching danger, such as Watch Hill 5km to the NW of Newcastleton and Watch Knowe 6.5km to the NE of the same town. During daylight, the Armstrongs used a white sheet to signal down warnings to the valleys below. The sheet was spread over a prominent bush or sloping hillside, and was faster to operate than lighting a beacon. At night beacons were employed, with the watchers of the horizon well stocked with wood and kindling, ready to strike flint onto iron. The towers of the Armstrongs, like many others across the Border, had a balefire fixed to the roof, which could signal for help and alert a defensive force. The owners of these strongholds were actually obliged to light their beacons on discovering any raid, with a penalty set at a fine of 3s 4d for those who failed to alert others.

If the going became too hot for the Armstrongs and the thick walls of their strongholds was not enough to keep them safe, families could always hideaway in the Tarras Valley until the danger passed. The Tarras Valley, named after the Tarras Water which passes through it, runs in-between and parallel to the Ewes Valley and Liddesdale. The river starts on the slopes of Hartsgarth Fell, and then meanders 17km SW to meet the Esk just below Langholm. Sir Walter Scott the author described the place as a "*desolate and horrible marsh,*" no right minded traveller would ever set foot in the place. Sir Robert Carey (1560-1639) the English West March Warden, described the valley in his memoirs, "*was of that strength, and so surrounded by bogges and marshi ground, with thicke bushes and shrubbes, that they fear no force nor power of England or Scotland.*" The Tarras had secret access routes into it, and paths that crossed the wettest areas allowing swift and easy passage. Those new to the area would have become lost; their progress slowed up and even halted by the soft moss, marsh reeds, waist high ferns, dense birch scrub and various thorns.

From this base the family moved south west towards the frontier, giving alarm to the English. Population growth, food pressures and the chance to obtain more land pushed the family into new pastures. Oddly the Scottish Armstrongs never seemed to have met up with their English brethren, who kept to the legal side of life as farmers, tradesmen and shop keepers. It was not unheard of, for the Scottish Armstrongs to have raided the English Armstrongs. Families lived in graynes (branches), and unless they were allied to each other, with bonds of loyalty and marriages, then any family was fair game for plundering or exacting blackmail from. The English Armstrongs appear not to have copied their Scottish cousins and become reivers, with the one notable exception of the Armstrongs of Williava.

Population growth

Life must have been good to the Armstrongs in their new home, as their population began to grow rapidly. Looking at the number of sons some of the Mangerton laird's produced, at 7-10 per family they were a very fertile and long living lot. Families must have been huge, in addition to these sons, daughters have to be added and other children who died young (25% of children died before they were five years old). Fed on a diet of beef, oats and milk the sons would have grown up big, healthy and strong. The Armstrongs having their trade based in theft and extortion were immune from the seasonal fluctuations of the weather, and its influences on the harvest. A bad harvest brought hard times and worse to farming communities everywhere, but the Armstrongs and other Riding families could avoid the lack of food by simply stealing it from others. The targets of the Armstrongs though would have been thrown into extreme poverty and starvation when crops failed; with the Armstrongs being the straw that broke the camel's back when thieving away the little that they had left. The reiving society had the happy fortune to be self supporting and not based on the success of the harvest. As the population grew, it was a case of thieving more to cope with the new mouths. Normal farming communities needed to put more land under the plough to feed more people, but reiving homesteads just required more lances. The standard Malthusian theory of balances and checks on population growth were not appropriate to the Armstrongs, as they could side track famine with the use of the armed foray and extortion racket.

The Armstrong lairds who avoided the gallows appear to have had long lives, bucking the trend of the average life expectancy of 35 years. The wives of the lairds had a life of child rearing, needlework and food preparation, being in almost a state of permanent pregnancy for fifteen years. Death in child birth was a common fear for all women, and was arguably the biggest cause of female mortality, claiming one in three of all deaths. Other diseases such as the bloody flux (dysentery), influenza, pneumonia, scarlatina (scarlet fever), smallpox, and whooping cough could all cut life short, with 40% of all children failing to reach adulthood. Life was healthier in the rural communities than in the towns, with their often overcrowded and unsanitary conditions. Here, outbreaks of typhus, smallpox, tuberculosis and bubonic plague were common. Despite all the various ways, in which life could be cut short, the population grew in Liddesdale and the family desired new land.

The custom of gavelkind added to the problem of an expanding population; this was a form of inheritance were a farmer shared out his land equally to all of his sons. This system sounds fair in theory, but if a laird had 100 acres and ten sons, each would get 10 acres – but then if they all had ten sons each, the subsequent farms would give the second generation of farmers an unliveable plot to farm. Thieving would become an attractive alternative to starving or moving away from the protection of the family group.

Debatable Land

From there Liddesdale origins, the Armstrongs spilled over into Eskdale and the Debateable Land in around 1518. This came in the aftermath of the death of King James IV in 1513. With rising population and the removal of a firm government to be replaced with a child king (James V), the Armstrongs sought new territory. The Debateable Land was the epitome of the Border frontier. A small strip of land 6km wide by about 20km long, it made up in drama and chaos for what it lost in size. As its name suggests, the Border was disputed here, becoming a thorn in the flesh for both Scotland and England as legal arguments happened, and the worst of the reivers settled within its confines. The land was excellent pasture for livestock being flat and well watered; it lacked obvious features to define a border, and contained one of the main routes across the frontier. Neither Scotland nor England would admit to owning this strip of land and by default would not take responsibility for it. This made the Debateable Land a magnet for broken men and career criminals – and the Armstrongs.

The Armstrongs, more than any of the other Border clans, milked the nationality factor. When living in the Debateable Land, they were always prepared to debate whether the land and themselves were either Scots or English. The Armstrongs became experts at playing one side off against another. The Armstrongs would claim to be English when approached by the Scots March Warden to answer for crimes in Scotland, and the same Armstrongs suddenly became Scottish when approached by the English March Warden. They used the undefined Border to tie the legal system up in knots, and avoided being made accountable for many of their crimes.

A method employed to keep the Debateable Land free of the reivers, was to occasionally devastate it all of human habitation. This only had a temporary effect, as the Armstrongs would pull back, and then return the next day to rebuild their houses. The dwellings in the Debateable Land due to the nature of the politics were mostly make-shift huts, quick to build and of no loss if burned down. Block houses were also popular, made from logs and covered in earth to make them fireproof. Stone towers were always at risk of being torn down, seen as too much of a threat and as a base camp for crime. For a short period, just after the "Rough Wooing" had ended, it was agreed that anyone could thieve, burn and kill within the Debateable Land and not be charged, on the hope that it would discourage people to live there. And to lead an example on how to carry this out, Lord Maxwell, the Scottish West March Warden, led a force on a foray in 1551, destroying every household that they came across. The problem of the Debateable Land was partly solved in 1552, when commissioners aided by a French ambassador finally agreed on where the border should be. A trench and embankment was dug in an east-west direction, which became known as the "Scots Dike." The Debateable Land was no longer debateable and the Armstrongs were all now officially Scottish. The area continued to be called the Debateable Land, but the long arm of administration could now at least stretch in and deal with the many outlaws.

The Armstrongs were not the only family moving into the Debateable Land, in around 1516 a family of Grahams from Moskesso (or Maskesswra) in Hutton Parish arrived. William, "Lang Will" Graham was banished from his land for collecting tithes from the church that he was not entitled to. An outrage which resulted in him being put to the horn, and seeking as many broken men before him – he fled to the Debateable Land. By luck at this time, there was land vacant for the Grahams to settle. The Storeys had recently upset Lord Dacre when they betrayed him by giving warning of a planned warden's rode to its target, which resulted in an ambush and subsequent mauling for Dacre and his men. The Storeys fearing reprisals, sensibly vacated the area. Lang Will then set up home at Stuble, near Longtown, with his eight sons and established a new strong branch of the Grahams.

It would be expected for the two families to be natural enemies, competing for the same resources along the same River Esk, but to both Scotland and England's dismay, they actually got along really well. The families had more in common than in difference. Overall there was more collaboration than conflict. The Armstrongs new neighbours had Scottish roots, and as both families were geo-politically aligned strategically along the Border, alliances formed naturally and were often sealed with marriages. In being friendly with the Grahams, the Armstrongs gained advance warnings on raids coming their way, and in return the Armstrongs promised not to raid the Grahams. To the annoyance of both governments, the live and let live Border relationship between the two families aided the criminal activities in the area. It suited both countries to have both families permanently at each other's throats – fighting each other rather ran coming together and ravaging their neighbours. The Grahams and the Armstrongs would come to dominate the Debateable Land, a constant thorn in the flesh of both Scotland and England.

Carlisle

The Armstrongs had strong links with England and especially Carlisle. Within their Liddesdale lair, the Armstrongs lived nearer to the English seat of rule than the Scottish. The Armstrongs regularly visited Carlisle on outings of both business and pleasure. Their presence in the town would have thrown up many tense encounters with the seat of Border Law and the March Warden's castle, only a stone throws away. Such visits to Carlisle illustrates the dual irony of life on the Border, how criminal, victim and law enforcer could all pass by each other peaceably at the market, in the street or drinking in a tavern. The Armstrongs probably exchanged greetings by day with people, who by night they would be robbing – and given a knowing glance at troopers and officials that could easily be later pursuing them and bringing the Queen's justice to bear. The various Riding families would have met up socially, exchanged gossip and done their shopping, brushing past the locals whose opinion on the visitors can only be guessed at. Carlisle was a microcosm of the Border community, with every layer of society all co-existing cheek by jowl. It has to be wondered how some individuals kept their restraint and composure at times, when they passed those who had previously robbed them, demanded black mail, or murdered a relative. The written and unwritten code of Border Law was at its most used and tested within the walls of Carlisle.

From Carlisle market cross the Armstrongs learned about news both local and wider, from proclamations read out and pinned up. Trade was also important in Carlisle, other towns such as Hawick and Jedburgh had markets also, but Carlisle had the addition of a horse market. The Armstrongs had their eyes on fine English horse flesh, seeking horses which were taller and faster than their usual Galloway nags; horses which could be used in the great reiver pastime of horse racing – or for out running an adversary during a foray. It was illegal to trade in horses without permission across the Border, but the Armstrongs could easily get over this law by claiming to be English and not taking the horses into Scotland.

Despite the Armstrongs obvious criminal and often murderous actions, they were freely allowed to visit Carlisle. This presence was grudged by many, as the Armstrongs flaunted their wealth and power strutting along the cobbled streets. The tensions can be imagined, with the obvious illogical nature of having the Border thieves at liberty in the town. Arguments breaking out and worse was a regular feature of market days, when the victims of theft met face to face with their adversaries. The Armstrongs were seen to be rubbing in their superiority and strength, going about the town like an untouchable mob of 1920s American gangsters.

The madness of the situation fell at the hands of William, 3rd Baron Dacre, and English West March Warden, to resolve in 1528. Dacre was accused of giving the Armstrongs a license to the Armstrongs to attend the weekly markets at Carlisle market, paperwork which allowed the Armstrongs to attend the market without hindrance. The Armstrongs were then protected by law from any animosity against them, a situation which angered many. The Armstrongs could undertake safe and happy trading, rubbing shoulders with their victims and also the warden, in a unique mix of enforced tolerance. Dacre was also accused of dealing lightly with the Armstrongs. The Armstrongs and their adherents, *"great thieves and murderers, who numbered upwards of three hundred men,"* had long been a problem within the English West March. It was noted that when any robbery or felony was committed by the Armstrongs in the West March, redress was made, but for crimes in the other Marches there was never any punishment.

Dacre of course had some well thought out replies to the charges, and managed to defuse any ill feelings away from him. Dacre stated that the license the Armstrongs had from him to enter Carlisle was extended to them, as with many other Scottish subjects, on his authority as warden – and not given by him personally. A document was quoted from 17 July 1518 which stated that the Armstrongs were licensed, with an agreement by the English authorities, allowing them to keep their market daily with England. Regarding the non-punishment of the Armstrongs, Dacre answered that in times of peace the Armstrongs had redressed injuries committed within the West March as other Scottish subjects had done. And as for the East and Middle Marches, this was the responsibility of the Scottish Middle March Warden, who had been called on to answer for the said Armstrongs, but had failed in his attempt to obtain redress. Dacre was stating that he could not influence law and order within other parts of the Border Marches, and could only address issues within his own West March.

Chapter 4. Mottos & Crests

As with other surnames of the period, Armstrong was spelled in numerous different ways – *"Airmestrang"*, *"Airmistrayng"*, *"Armistronge"* – and everything in between. Literacy rates were low, and people wrote how they spoke with little standardisation in words. Whichever way it was spelled, the name took on a meaning and symbolism all of its own as the family expanded. It became almost a metaphor for an armed outlaw; a name which gave pride to those who bore it, and fear to those who heard it.

Out of all the Riding names, Armstrong sounds the most appropriate for a reiving family. The very name itself was a war cry, and can be imagined to have struck dread and panic into all those on the receiving end, a psychological weapon to invoke obedience and subjugation. It would have taken a brave soul to rise to tackle the Armstrongs, especially at night and when lurking amongst the mosses and peat hags. Farms and villages across the English Marches dreaded the news of a gang of Armstrongs approaching. The name was associated to blackmail and theft – and mounted raiders in the night. The Armstrong name when shouted out inspired a flight or fight response. Many farmers spent worried days and nights scanning the horizon, listening for the beat of a hoof and glint of spear – signs to get the cattle inside and bolt the door, and sit tight until the danger had gone away.

✳✳✳

The family motto of the Armstrongs is *'Invictus maneo'* (I remain unvanquished), a stubborn boast which was no idle threat. The Armstrong lairds would have done their best to live up to the standard set by the motto. Crests and emblems were important for all land owning families in Medieval Britain, and the Armstrongs were no exception. The emblem of the Armstrongs comes as no surprise, in being a strong arm. A raised bent right arm with clenched fist; defiantly armed and aimed at all who would challenge their independence. The Armstrongs though were unusual among the Border families in having more than their own share of heraldic devices.

The earliest Armstrong emblems contain a sword, arm with hand, and an oak tree – either as individual forms or in different combinations together. The sword links back to the Norse god of the sword Odin, and makes the connection on how Siward was a true son of Odin. The arm is the strong arm of Siward from his nickname of *"Digri."* The oak tree though is less obvious in its meaning, and refers to the Battle of Dunsinane where Osbeorn fought against Macbeth and helped to "move" Birnam wood. The oak tree was also prominent in Norse mythology, where the tree was sacred and features in such works as the "Story of the Volsung of the Norse Edda." Acorns were also used to illustrate symbolically Birnam wood; a stone carved keystone at Whithaugh Tower dated 1559 has three acorns upon it. Sometimes the arm with hand is depicted holding the sword or the tree, reinforcing the symbolism. A curious offshoot is the hand holding a broken branch, which refers to a tale of the king riding through a forest trail and having his passage blocked by a tree bough. To prevent the king from dismounting, a man named as Fairbairn came forward and snapped off the offending branch. The incident is also put forward as a possible source for the name of Armstrong.

The Armstrongs for their emblems chose those subjects that were most precious to their ancestors. Together, the emblems sought to link the Armstrongs with Siward's strength and heroic deeds. By maintaining the oak tree and the sword, the Armstrongs were not only perpetuating the names and achievements of their forefathers, but were also displaying a new confidence and power. Across the Scottish Borders, many gravestones of Armstrongs portray carved the "strong arm," on occasions three were depicted together. The sword and oak tree feature also in various combinations of design. One of the oldest Armstrong carvings is the Milnholm Cross dating to 1320 (see page 161), which shows a single sword proudly commemorating the first Laird of Mangerton, summoning a link to Siward.

Moving into the 16th century, the emblems evolved to take into account the new generations, but still held a link to the past. The oak tree of Birnam wood was given four roots, and then later seven branches were added. The roots referred to the four children of the 5th Laird of Mangerton, and the branches to the seven children of the 6th Laird of Mangerton. Each of the children would go on to form their own grayne of Armstrongs, building towers and expanding Armstrong power in every direction. The oak tree then became symbolically to stand for the House of Armstrong, with deep roots and strong boughs.

Chapter 5. Organisation

Clan structure

The Armstrongs, as with all other Riding families were divided up into graynes/grains. These were family branches, each with their own tower and land. They operated with their own independence, but came under the overall watch of the clan chieftain. The Armstrongs main seat was at Mangerton in the Liddesdale Valley, whose laird was traditionally the chief of the whole clan. The lairds of Mangerton ran the families forays and blackmail enterprises, spreading their influence south into Eskdale and the Debateable Land.

An interesting observation can be made when reading the various court cases in the archives that the Mangertons do not appear the most often – that destructive honour applies to the Whithaugh grayne. Judging from the number of times that they feature in official correspondence, it was the lairds of Whithaugh who were the big trouble makers in Liddesdale. The Armstrongs of Whithaugh were arguably the worst of the Armstrongs; the worst lot from the worst family on the frontier. They must have been a despicable mob indeed. It is easy to imagine the Whitehaugh Armstrongs being responsible for the famous quote written about the Border reivers – that *If Jesus Christ where amongst them, they would deceive him.*

It is not known how structured the Armstrong's raids were. Whether they all came under the planning of the chieftain, or were a more random affair based around when the family pot was empty. The Laird of Mangerton though probably had the main say in the operations. Meetings would be held before any raid, choosing the target and who would go on the foray. Often the members of a raid came from different locations and a rendezvous ("tryst") had to be made to enable all of those taking part to gather safely before setting off. Opposite Mangerton there is a stream called the Trysting Sike, perhaps this was a gathering area prior to a raid. These meeting places were usually well known landmarks, such as the Kielder Stone. Here the fine tuning of a raid would be done, last minute planning undertaken with checks and double checking on the route to be travelled. Sometimes notes were left at the tryst for those who were late on arriving, or an arrow was laid out in stones informing the direction of the foray. After a raid, a place was organised for the dividing up of the spoils, where the livestock was counted and the "heidsman" could decide what share of the plunder the various graynes and gang members received.

A raid averaged between twelve and fifty in its members, although they could be as small as a single rider. In the case of the Armstrongs, two-three hundred was common and on occasion when the gangs came together, two-three thousand was achieved. There was a reiving season, from Michaelmas (29 Sept) to Martinmas (11 Nov), when the cattle were at their fattest, though a raid could happen at any time of year. The night was the preferred time to ride out, for the obvious factor of concealment and a sleeping target. A full moon was also desired, which gave a useful light for navigation. Such full moons during the Riding season became to be known as a "Reiver's Moon" – a sight which put a dreaded fear into the farmer and villager alike.

Gangs

The Armstrongs organised themselves into groups of armed riders called gangs to carry out their raiding, as with other Riding families. Each gang came under the command of a "heidsman/hedesman," the term literally meant head-man. The "heidsman" could be the local laird, or one of his sons, they were very much extended family affairs, leading to strong bonds of camaraderie. Several gangs could combine together for a raid, and form small armies which were virtually unstoppable. Allied families could also help out, those families linked through marriage (such as the Grahams), and smaller families (such as the Nixons and Crosers) who wanted the protection of the Armstrongs. Gangs were often named after their headsman, such as "Kinmont's Bairns." There is a fascinating court case from March 1536, involving Finlay Johnestoune who was convicted of common theft of old and new. He was charged "*ITEM, of art and part of treasonably bringing the surnames of GRAHAMIS and ARMSTRANGIS, Englishmen, DIK THE DEVILLIS BAIRNIS, common thieves and traitors, within Scotland, committing slaughters, murders, fire-raising, and Hereschips upon the King's poor lieges.*" It has to be wondered who Dick of the Devil's Bairns was – an Armstrong or Graham? A more apt name for a gang of Armstrongs could never be found. Finlay was found guilty for his crime, with the sentence passed – "*To be drawn to the gallows and HANGED thereupon as a traitor; and all his goods to be escheated.*"

Musgrave's list of 1583

A good historical source to understand the network of Armstrong families is from a report compiled by Thomas Musgrave to William Cecil, Lord Burghley (principal advisor to Queen Elizabeth I), on the Border Riders in December 1583. Musgrave was the Captain of Bewcastle, which held a garrison of forty government troopers who had the daunting task of policing the English West March. He was an experienced officer in affairs on the Border, one of the best and knew the area intimately. He explains in the document the reason why he was making the report – "*Because I understand that your honour is not well acquainted with the names of the waters and the dwelling places of the riders and ill doers both of England and Scotland, I beinge animated by your lordshipes late curtesyes and inquisitions, have made boulde to present this platt both of theire names, dwellynges and allyaunces, one with another, trusting your lordship will accepte my dutye towarde your selfe and good will to my cuntrey.*" Burghley was not well acquainted with the area or its geography and Musgrave took it upon himself to list the area valley by valley, and list all of its troublesome families. He played special attention to marriages which went across the Border, as these could produce particular problems of alliances.

Musgrave's research into the subject was not without its dangers, he states – "*I have spente a great parte of my tyme, not without the losse of my bloode, and manye troblesome travels and dangers, but with the losse of my deare frendes and companyons which have bene cruelly murdered by the rebellyous Scottes.*" The result though gives an excellent time capsule of the period, presenting the main Riding families and where they lived. An interesting side line was on marriages, Musgrave was careful to record cross Border marriages, as these produced extended family bonds. Being forewarned of these could prevent difficulties in the future, enabling the complex web of alliances to be worked out. Knowing who could be trusted, and more importantly, who could not – was often a matter of life and death on the frontier.

Musgrave describes the river valleys and the various families that inhabited them. On Liddesdale he writes – *"Maye it please therefore your lordship to understand, that the ryver called Lyddall, is a fayre ryver, and hath her course doune Lyddisdall, soe as the dale hath the name of the ryver. The ryver is all Scottishe, untill it come to Kyrsopp foote, planted with Ellotes untill it come neare Wheatoughe towre, then the Armestronges inhabit it on bothe sydes, untill it come to Kyrsopp foote, where it takes the dyvysion of the realmes from Kyrsopp – then the Armestronges have the one syde, and the Englishe Fosters the other syde, soe it desendes by the Harlowe on the one syde and the Haythawyt on the other, and runeth into the ryver called Eske."*

Musgrave continues to describe the Esk and its feeding tributaries into England and the sea:- *"Eske is a fayre ryver, and cometh throughe Esdall, and is Scottishe, inhabyted with Battesons of Esdell, untill it come neare a placed called the Langhalme castill and meateth with the water called Use, which waters and dales are bothe my Lorde Maxwells untill it come to Canonby kyrke, and then the Armestronges and Scottishe Graymes have it untill it meete the ryver of Lydall at the Mote skore, where Fargus Grayme his howse standes. Then it taketh the devysyon of the realmes untill it come to a place called Morton rigge where Will of Kinmont dwelleth; then there is a mere dyke that goeth to a ryver called Sarke, then is Eske Englishe on bothe sydes, and Sarke ryver devydes, and there are Graymes on both sydes, the one English, the other Scottishe untill it come to Gretnay, where it meteth Eske and both rune to Bownus, and soe take the sea."*

Musgrave then goes on to list the various graynes of Armstrongs, which is worth quoting in full, giving a snap shot of the various families, their power structure and inter relationships. He begins with the principal Armstrong family, that of Mangerton and works outwards.

✳✳✳

The Lord of Mangerton and his frendes, and theire allyaunces with England:-

1. Seme Armestronge lord of Mangerton marryed John Fosters daughter of Kyrsope foot, and hath by her issue.

2. Joke Armestronge called the Lordes Joke dwelleth under Denyshill besydes Kyrsope in Denisborne, and maryed Anton Armestronges daughter of Wylyave in Gilsland.

3. John Armestronge called the lordes John, marryet Rytche Graymes sister called Meadope, and he bathe two sonnes ryders in England.

4. Joke his eldest sonne marryed Hobbe Fosters daughter of Kersope alyes.

5. Thome Armestronge called the lordes Tome, dwelleth on a place called Hyghe Morgarton, not marryed with Englande.

6. Runyon Armestronge called the lordes Runyon, dwelleth in a place called the Thornythaite.

7. Rowye Armestronge called the lordes Rowye, dwelleth in Tarrassyde, and marryed oulde Archer Graymes doughter.

8. *Seme Armestronge called yonge Seme, dwelleth on the Flates nere Margerton, and marryed Rowye Fosters doughter called Robins Rowye.*

9. *Dik Armestronge of Dryup, dwelleth nere Hyghe Morgarton, and his wyfe is a Scottishe woamen.*

10. *Thom Armestronge called Sims Thom, dwelleth in the Demayne Holme by Lendall syde, and maryed Wat Storyes daughter of Eske, called Wat of the Hove ende.*

11. *Joke Armestronge of the Caufeld dwelleth on the Cawfeld, not marryed in England.*

12. *Gorthe Armestronge of the Bygams dwelleth on the Bygams, and marryed Will of Carl(i)lles daughter.*

The Armestronges of the howse of Whetaughe towre:-

1. *Lance Armestronge the olde lord of Whetaughe.*

2. *Sime Armestronge the yonge lord his Sonne.*

3. *Andrewe Armestronge called the ladyes Andrewe.*

4. *Arche Armestronge his brother.*

5. *Frauncis Armestronge his brother.*

6. *John Armestronge, called John of Whetaugh.*

7. *Hobbe Armestronge his sonne, marryed Jeme Fosters daughter of the Stangerth syde.*

8. *Joke Armestronge his brother.*

9. *Rynyon Armestronge called Gaudee.*

10. *Rynyon Armestronge called Rynyon of Twedon.*

11. *Hector Armestronge of the same.*

12. *Joke Armestronge of the same.*

Hector Armstrong of the Harlawe and his friends and allies:-

1. *Hector Armestronge called ould Hector.*

2. *Hector his sonne called yonge Hector, marryed Fargus Graymes daughter.*

3. *Wille Armestronge called Hectors Wille.*

4. *Thome Armestronge called Hectors Tome.*

5. *Andrewe Armestronge of the Harlawe.*

6. *Patton Armestronge of the Harlawe.*

7. *Alexander Armestronge called the Gatwarde, marryed Gawins Wille Fosters daughter.*

***

The Armstrongs of Melyonton quarter and their allies with England:-

1. *Arche Armestronge called Rynyons Arche.*

2. *Gorthe Armestronge sonne to Rynyon.*

3. *Sime Armestronge, called Whetlesyd, marryed two English women – the fyrst was Robin Fosters daughter, the other Thome Graymes daughter called little Thome.*

4. *Aby Armestronge sonne to Rynyon.*

5. *Will Armestronge called Will of Powter-lampert.*

6. *Gorthe Armestronge called yonge Gorthe of Arkyldon, marryed Will of Radhall doughter.*

7. *Rynyon Armestronge his brother.*

8. *Martyn Armestronge his brother.*

9. *Dave Armestronge of Whetlesyd.*

10. *Andrewe Armestronge of Kyrkton.*

11. *Hector Armestronge of Chengles.*

12. *Thome Armestronge his brother marryed Gourth Routlishe daughter of Shetbelt.*

13. *Elle Armestronge his brother, marryed John Fosters daughter of Krakrop.*

14. *Eme Armestronge his brother.*

15. *Arche Armestronge his brother.*

16. *Riche Armestronge called Carhand.*

17. *Thome Armestronge called old Thome of Chengles.*

18. *Abye Armestronge called Thoms Abye.*

19. *Arche Armestronge his brother.*

20. *Rynyon Armestronge his brother.*

✸✸✸

The Armstrongs of Langholm and their allies with England:-

1. *Creste Armestronge goodman of the Langholme castell, marryed Robbye Graymes sister called Robbe of the Feild.*

2. *John Armestronge of the Hollus, marryed Walter Graymes sister of Netherby.*

3. *Creste Armestronge of Borngles marryed Gorthe Grames daughter called Thomas Gorthe of Eske.*

4. *Hector Armestronge of the Stobham.*

5. *Rich Armestronge called Ekkes Riche.*

Offspring of "ill Wills Sandy":-

1. *Ebye Armestronge the goodman of Waddusles.*

2. *Wille Armestronge his eldest sonne dwelleth in England, and enjoyeth that land that Kinge Henry the Eight gave old Sand Armestronge.*

3. *Dave Armestronge his brother.*

4. *Sande Armestronge his brother.*

5. *Creste Armestronge called Sandes Creste.*

6. *Creste Armestronge his sonne, and other two sonnes whose names I knowe not.*

7. *Wille Armestronge called Kynmont, marryed Hotchane Grames daughter, sister to Hot(c)hans Ritche.*

8. *Joke Armestronge his sonne.*

9. *Gorthe Armestronge his brother.*

10. *Frauncis Armestronge his brother.*

11. *Thome Armestronge his brother.*

12. *Rynon Armestronge called Sandes Rynyon.*

13. *Thome Armestronge his sonne.*

14. *John Armestronge called Skinabake.*

15. *Forge Armestronge called Sandes Forge.*

16. *Joke Armestronge called Castills.*

17. *Joke Armestrouge, called Walls.*

18. *Arche Armestronge, called Sandes Arche.*

19. *Dave Armestronge, called Dave of Kannonby, marryed Patyes Gorthes Grams doughter.*

20. *Wille Armestronge his brother.*

21. *Jeme his brother.*

22. *Thome Armestronge of Rowenborne.*

23. *Gorthe Armestronge of the same, marryed Jeme Taylors daughter of Harper hill.*

Inter family marriages

Marriages across the frontier between the Scots and English, without the permission of the warden was illegal and termed as March Treason. Treason as the name suggests, was taken very seriously, and at its most extreme level carried the death penalty. This severe punishment for an act of romance hints at the seriousness of the problem of Borderers falling in love, and the warden's determination to stamp it out.

Despite the harsh cost, inter family marriages across the Border was a must for the Armstrongs. Marriage within reiver society was very important, as they strengthened family bonds and often created alliances. Marriage was one of the best means to heal a family feud and the Armstrongs were the experts at causing feuds. What better way to deal with outlaws, than to make them your in-laws. Being located geographically on a debateable part of the Border and surrounded by other Riding families, the Armstrongs needed all the friends that they could get. Musgrave commented in December 1583 on the problem, which could very well sum up the Armstrongs, *"they are a people that will be Scottishe when they will, and Englishe at theire pleasure."*

The Armstrongs made a point of frequently marrying their immediate neighbours in England; their most common partners were the Grahams and the Forsters. With the help of cross Border marriages, the Armstrongs grew to get along fine with those that could do them harm. The Grahams despite being officially English, had a Scottish ancestry, the Armstrongs were the opposite. Perhaps the mixture of desperados, thieves and broken men, all square pegs in a round hole, found a common ground which bound all together. The Armstrong's friendship with the Grahams paid dividends in 1528, when an invading forces commanded by Lord Wharton entered Armstrong territory, and the Grahams tipped off the Armstrongs allowing them to take action (see page 265). The Grahams were at friendly terms with Johnnie Armstrong of Gilnockie, with some Graham "heidsmen" being noted amongst those hung at Carlenrig in 1530.

In 1580 it was noted when looking at seventy nine Armstrong marriages, twenty one of these were between a Scots Armstrong and an English woman. These marriages produced a headache for the authorities as alliances between the Riding families were created. At least toleration occurred between the families, and at worse cooperation in raids. The families bonded by marriage turned blind eyes to each other's raiding, providing safe houses to hide out in and helped to sell on stolen goods. Having the Grahams and Forsters territory as safe ground, the Armstrongs were to a high degree able to approach almost up to the walls of Carlisle and Bewcastle, unchallenged and unreported. This placed them in a prime position for making a sweep across an unsuspecting country, before returning home along the same route they had just followed.

The phenomenon was known in England, and even tolerated by certain officials. The main culprit in this was the English Middle March Warden, Sir John Forster (c.1520 – 1602), whose blatant and often open disregard for the law brought an investigation into his corrupt practices. The issue was noted in a report compiled by Lord Eure on 31 January 1596, for the attention of Burghley, in an attempt to bring the notable rogue to some form of justice. Eure wrote about the *"Marriages tolerated betwixt the gentlemen of the March and thieves and English fugitives, who plunder nightly on the Tyne, - and intermarriage with Scots a principal annoyance, viz... Reade with Armestronge of Liddesdale."*

Musgrave in his same 1583 report to Burghley also mentions some of the routes taken by the reivers, two of which refer to the riders of Liddesdale, and would have been used by the Armstrongs regularly. In the first example the Fenwicks were the target, with a route which skirted the edge of Bewcastle Fells before descending into Tynedale – *"When Leddisdall people make anie invacions to the Fenwickes, they goe without Bewcastell x or xii myles, and goe by the Perlfell without the Horse heade nere Kelder, and so alonge abone Chepchase."* Another route is described – *"When they goe to the water of Tyne, they goe by Kyrsopp* [Kershope] *head, and without the Gele Crage and by Tarnbek and Bogells Gar and so alonge by the Spye Crage, and the Lampert, and come that waye."*

Chapter 6. The Bloody Feud

Being the most belligerent of the Riding families, it comes as no surprise to find the Armstrongs getting into numerous deadly blood feuds with their neighbours and beyond. A phenomenon of Border life was feuding between the families, lairds and even towns. Feuds were commented on by the author George MacDonald Fraser as *"the great cancer of the Borders."* They tore at the very fabric of society and made an already precarious existence that much more hazardous.

Feuds were caused when members of one family killed those of another, or on the theft of an important item. Family came first with the Riding clans, and this fact added fuel to the forming of inter-family vendettas. When a family had one of its members murdered, the death was treated by all as very personal. The extended families took the loss to heart and would often seek tribal revenge rather than report the killing. With a natural mistrust of authority, on occasion the warden was by-passed when seeking justice. And even when the warden was brought in, sometimes the verdict given did not satisfy those offended, and a more personalised form of justice was sought. The Riding families had their own morality, and when this was broken, pride and honour drove the clan to obtain their own version of law, and settle scores on their terms.

Feuds could escalate beyond their initial offence, such as the stabbing of a clan chief, and become full scale wars. It was often difficult to define the winner, within this tit-for-tat war of ever shifting goals. Lord Burghley commented – *"deadly foed, the word of enmytie on the Borders, implacable without the blood and whole family destroyed."* The "Chorographia" (or Survey of Newcastle), 1549, contained within "The Border Antiquities of England and Scotland," 1814, by Sir Walter Scott, has some interesting observations to make on the subject of feuds...

"The people of this countrey hath had one barbarous custome amongst them: if any two be displeased, they expect no lawe, but bang it out bravely, one and his kindred against the other and his; they will subject themselves to no justice, but in an inhumane and barbarous manner fight and kill one another... This fighting they call their feids, or deadly feides, a word so barbarous that I cannot express it in any other tongue."

The murder of a single individual could result in the whole family of that person wanting to seek pay-back for the loss. The revenge inevitably was an eye for an eye, with a hit party sent out to cut down those who had caused the death. Sometimes the pay-back was done with interest and more people were slain than were initially killed in the first offence. This was done as a warning and to settle the score. The seeking of revenge and especially inflicting greater head tolls of death was a way to end a feud, but such blood baths often failed to have their desired effect and only escalated the problem with the new killings demanding retaliation. A chain reaction effect of killing and counter revenge killing developed, with no obvious check to halt the misery. Feuds went on in this fashion lasting years and even decades, with the family quarrel often passed down over the generations, keeping alive grudges well after those responsible for the original offence had died. The vendetta was not always aimed at the person responsible for the initial killing. Thomas Musgrave observed, *"they are grown soe to seeke blood, for they will make a quarrel for the death of there grandfather, and kill any of the name*." When a feud was declared, it could be open killing season on all people who shared the same surname. In order to stop feuds spilling over and harming innocent bystanders, drastic measures by the warden could be put in place. For example when Liddesdale and Teviotdale families were at feud, the Liddesdale clans were ordered to keep out of Hawick and Jedburgh.

The pain and loss caused by feuds had the obvious effect of making people reluctant to bring one down upon their family. This had the effect of making the average law abiding person frightened to fight back against the reivers to protect their property. Robert Carey observed – "*The country dare not kill such thieves for fear of feud.*" This resulted in the reivers mounting their forays into farmsteads and villages with impunity, and taking what they wanted. With no resistance, the Borders fell further into a state of decay and chaos towards the end of the 16th century. It was thought better to be raided and hide away and survive with all your possessions stolen, than to fight back and risk a return raid and have all of your family slaughtered. The larger families with their greater man power had less chance of having a feud declared upon them; and on the same parameter, the large families were more eager to declare a feud. The Armstrongs with their confederate allies and subsequent strength would have been a family that all others thought twice to tangle with. The Armstrongs themselves held the opposite view and could unleash with little thinking a vendetta on almost anyone they chose.

Family feuds did not always involve every individual of that surname. On occasion it was kept to an exact valley. In 1579 for example the Armstrongs were at feud with the Elliots of Ewesdale. The Armstrong protagonists were careful to keep their quarrel confined to Ewesdale, and not to take their anger out on the Liddesdale Elliots. In the same year the Armstrongs of the Debateable Land were at feud with the Turnbulls of Bedrule, it can be supposed that their fellow clansmen of Liddesdale kept out of the quarrel.

1583 was a very belligerent year for the Armstrongs. Thomas Musgrave in 1583, within his list of the Border Riders, also records the feuds that were in progress at that time. And as expected the Armstrongs are listed, and were unsurprisingly involved in no less than three feuds simultaneously that year – "*The crose frendes and varyaunces, one surname with an other:- the Armestronges, Grames, and Urwens with the Musgraves... the Armestronges with the Robsons of Tendall... the Taylors with the Armestronges.*" It is interesting to see the Armstrongs teaming up with the Grahams and the Irvines to tackle the Musgraves. The Musgraves would have had a real bitter fight on their hands that year. Another point worth noting is how the Armstrongs were at feud with the Robsons of Tyndale, a distinct Riding family, and quite separate from their Scottish cousins the Robsons of Teviotdale.

To round the century off, in 1597 the Armstrongs declared a vendetta against the Bells of Gilsland. This occurred when two Bells on the orders of the March Warden arrested an Armstrong. The feud was very much one sided, resulting in severe depredations to the Bells and a need to swiftly have the quarrel settled, which meant allowing the Armstrongs to equal the score, plus have their usual revenge pay-back.

The Grahams

When the Armstrongs moved south in around 1518 and into the Debatable Land, they were always going to become embroiled with the Graham family in an argument over land at some point. The Grahams were also new to the area, eager to carve out a living space and lay claim to the land. The relationship was initially amiable, with the Grahams sharing a common Scottish root, but on the Border family came first, making friendships brittle.

The feud that grew between these two families came about by their own successes, and competition for resources. In the Debateable Land the Armstrongs and the Grahams became jealous of each other's strength. Arguments occurred over the large force of broken men which sought sanctuary in this lawless zone, who were looking for a gang to ride with. Both families wanted to recruit the same freebooters and friction arose. Going into the 1530s relations with the Grahams broke down. The reason may have been the rise in Graham strength, perhaps brought on by the murder of Johnnie Armstrong of Gilnockie and his main supporters. The Grahams were known for their extortion racket, less for mounting raids. The Grahams would become the Borders greatest blackmailers under the watchful eye of Richie Graham of Brackenhill in the 1580/90s. There must have been a clash of interests at times with the Armstrongs over the blackmail trade, and it is easy to imagine with Johnnie Armstrong gone in 1530, the Grahams taking advantage of the power vacuum, and expanding their blackmail business with the competition eliminated.

Another reason for the breakdown in relations was the desire by both the Crowns in 1537 to clear the Debatable Land of malefactors. A proclamation was submitted which allowed all Englishmen and Scotsmen to freely rob, burn, spoil, slay, murder and destroy all and every item/person that they came across, without any redress being made. It was free game to claim all bodies, buildings, goods and cattle upon the land as their own, if found out with the hours of sunrise and sundown. When enacted, this resulted in the movement of families to escape the clamp down, which caused disruption and at times friction as the land in places became overcrowded. Many of those displaced were "broken men" with little to lose, and added another factor to the heated mix. Tempers were stretched and a full blown feud erupted in 1541.

King James V recorded the beginning of the feud when he wrote on 29 May 1541, complaining that six sons of "Lang Will" Graham (Fergus, Hutcheon, John, Richard, Thomas, Will), rode into the Parish of Kirkpatrick along with fifty others, and ran an open day foray upon Auchinbadrig, in the lands of Logane. The gang murdered the three sons of David Armstrong – Rolland, Thomas, and William Armstrong. No thieving or damage to property is mentioned, which suggests the raid was undertaken purely for revenge. The outrage rightly demanded a trial. The accused were requested to attend a Day of Truce on the Scottish West March the following Tuesday, to establish guilt and punishment. The Grahams with utter contempt for the process of law, and perhaps feeling they would get no fair trial, brazenly appeared before Lord Maxwell, the Scottish West March Warden and his English counterpart Sir Thomas Wharton, with the blood of the slain still on their hands, faces, and clothes. Maxwell asked for redress from the Grahams, and was bluntly rejected. Despite their obvious guilt and caught red handed, the Grahams avoided the death penalty.

The deaths of the three Armstrong brothers were only the start of the killing and raids. The Grahams had become emboldened, and undertook a series of daytime summer forays, which were in stark contrast to the typical raids that usually took place during the winter months and at night. The goals were not to thieve or be hidden, but to destroy property and lives, and to be seen doing so. The Grahams wanted the Armstrongs to know who was responsible for their misery. On 24 July Lang Will's sons were out again on the war path, their previous run in with the warden had done little to cool their ardour. Taking an armed gang, the brothers rode into Ewesdale where they cut down Bartholomew Bell, Willie Thompson, and Roger Wauch. A number of horses were also spirited away. Two days later a gang of Grahams burned the houses of Kirkhill, Stanegill and Whisgills, belonging to Christopher, Jenkin and Simon Armstrong. Before the month was out, the Grahams made another day raid, crashing into Eddleton parish and killed David Turner.

Both sides were determined to battle it out for a bloody conclusion. All hopes of a peaceful settlement had been abandoned, with the death toll mounting. Perhaps out of frustration, or to end the feud quickly, the Armstrongs came up with the idea of a duel and challenged the whole clan of Grahams to mortal combat in true medieval style. The Scottish king was contacted, who gave his consent, seeing that it was probably the only way to settle their deadly quarrel. The English authorities also found out about the planned duel. Directions were sent by the Privy Council of England to Sir Thomas Wharton, Warden of the English West March, stating: *"And as touching the challenge made by the Armstrongs against the Grames, his Highness is contented that the same shall be performed so as his Majesty be first advertised of the circumstances thereof, and that it be done in an indifferent place before the Wardens of both Marches."*
On receipt of the Royal sanction, the two families gathered up their ablest fighting men, preparing teams to take part in what amounted to a trial of their strength. The two families probably signed up to agree on the outcome of the contest. The victor would gain control of the area around Canonbie. Duels came with rules; normally they were not to the death, but on the first person to draw blood. This duel however, was being fought as part of a blood feud, so may have thrown the rule book literary away. The combatants would have worn all the armour that they could get their hands upon, and be bristling with secondary weapons, rapier, daggers and axes, to use after the primary lance was dispensed with. The day, time and place were set, with the location on the banks of the Esk, near Hollows Tower chosen for the show down.

There are two versions of what happened next, which sounds more like a heroic episode from Homer's Iliad. One narrative has a brutal and prolonged battle being engaged, with many slain on both sides. Victory conditions were set, and whatever they were, the Armstrongs met them. The Grahams kept their honour to the results, and vacated the area, moving further down Eskdale. The second version is a lot less exciting. There is no documented evidence that the fight took place, so it is possible an amicable settlement was found before blows were struck. Sir Thomas Wharton wrote to King Henry VIII on 2 September 1541, forwarding his thoughts on the duel – *"where there was great repreifes borne by the Grahams Englishmen and the Armstrongs Scotishmen upon Friday the 26th of August last before the Lord Maxwell and me at our meeting, the same day as I did advertise you by one of my deputies, I had knowledge that the Armstrongs would send a challenge into England thereupon, and I devised with the Grahams that the Armstrongs would be challenged at the same present. Whereupon such writings passed as ye may perceive by the very same writing sent from the Armstrongs and by the copy sent from the Grayms hereinclosed. The Armstrongs haith maide no answer."*

In October 1541 the deputy warden Thomas Dacre, led a series of warden raids into Liddesdale, adding to the tension in the valley. Livestock was lifted and crops were burned – and houses at *"Quhisgillis, Dalferno, Dalquhairney holme, Myddlee, Flatt, Cristyhill, Mangerton, and Copshawholm,"* were set on fire. One casualty was recorded, with Andro Armstrong noted as slain. The Armstrongs demanded redress seeking compensation the legal method, holding back on retaliating with violence. They had taken a loss of food stuffs and with winter approaching they required at the very least a replacement in victuals.

The redress was not obtained, which suggests that the Armstrongs did not have the legal protection of their own warden or government. The Armstrongs would have to rely on themselves in this instance, as the normal proper legal channels had failed. To horse – Archibalde, Ringen, Symon and Jenkyn Armstrong, all brothers, plus other Scotsmen rode across the Border where they *"cruelly slewe and murdured Arthure Grame, Inglishman."* News of the death caused King James great concern with worries over war with England. In order to placate King Henry, his uncle, James led a force into Liddesdale in person intent on punishing the Armstrongs.

The Armstrong/Graham feud was to end soon after the king's intervention, suggesting that the monarch brought both protagonists to a peaceful solution. The Armstrongs and the Grahams were soon after mingling again in friendship. Inter family marriages were to follow, which was the best way to secure an ending to a feud. Marriages helped to break down the barriers of hostility and mistrust between opposing families. Prominent Armstrong's from Mangerton, Whithaugh, Barngleish and Harelaw all married Grahams.

1. A daughter of George Graham of the Fauld married Christopher of Barngleish.

2. A son of George Graham of the Fauld married a daughter of a Harelaw Armstrong.

3. A grandson of George Graham of the Fauld married a daughter of the Laird of Whithaugh.

4. A son (William) of Richard of Netherby married the daughter of Thomas Armstrong, Laird of Mangerton.

The marital arrangements networked together the main branches of the Armstrongs with the descendants of "Lang Will" Graham. There were to be no more vendettas – peace was restored between two families, but few would have celebrated. The two families came to dominate the Debateable Land, and a shared understanding developed. The alliance was to cause many headaches for the Border officials for the rest of the century.

Ridley Feud

The cause of the Ridley feud is not known, but judging by its greatest protagonist, the Armstrongs of Whithaugh, the Armstrongs can be considered as the chief culprit. The feud with the Ridley's was in progress at least in 1599, when William Ridley of Willimoteswick records the murder of several of his friends to the Scots. He planned his revenge on 13 May of that year, seeking to ambush a football team made up of Liddesdale riders after their match, however in practice everything went horribly wrong and he paid with his life (see page 58). What had probably began as a pay-back revenge exercise against the Armstrongs, ended up the opposite. The Ridleys had the option to halt the feud there and then, to accept that the vendetta was settled – or to hit back at the Armstrongs twice as hard.

The death of William Ridley was never going to be the last drop of blood spilt on the feud. The Ridleys were snubbed and bloodied, seemingly well put back into their place – but a smouldering hatred would linger, waiting and hoping for a chance to strike back. The green light for a revenge attack came in 1601 when James VI, feeling exasperated at the lack of success in his own officers ability at keeping justice on the Border, invited any willing English officer to tackle the problem. Sir Robert Carey the English warden could now cross the Border legally and sort out the Scottish reivers at their source. The Armstrongs would get a shock when they next came raiding, finding out that they could not simply dodge back into Liddesdale and be safe.

The opportunity for revenge by the Ridleys came in May 1601, when a raid led by Simon Armstrong of Calfhill struck deep setting a village on light and sped away taking four or five prisoners to hold for ransom (see page 241). The barefaced audacity of it all demanded a reaction by the authorities. Sir Robert Carey sprang into an eager action and organised a proactive response. By the time notice of the raid had gone out, the trail was no longer hot. Carey however was determined that the raiders should be punished; he knew who was responsible and sent out a warden's rode under Henry Woodrington. The ensuing rode resulted in the death of Simon of Calfhill, slain by a Ridley who by chance was a member of Woodrington's posse. The rode was a great success, but it had ironically added an extra cycle to the vendetta.

The feud was finally brought to an end when Carey captured some principle Armstrongs after his venture in the Tarras Valley in July of that year and forced the peace conditions upon the Armstrongs as part of their bonds for release.

Johnstone feud

The Johnstone feud came about during the period that the Lisles were guests of the Armstrongs in Liddesdale. The vendetta was caused by the cruel murder of a boy called "*Meickle*" Sym Armstrong, which resulted in John, Andrew and Roland Bell, William and Mathew Johnstone, and John Johnstone of that ilk facing charges on 14 October 1527. It has to be wondered on what reason did these six individuals find to slay a young lad, but it was reported that Lord Maxwell, had encouraged them in their dark deed. The accused did not turn up for their trial, despite James Douglas of Drumlanrig acting as their pledge. The absence of the six men was seen as admission of their guilt; they were denounced as rebels and had their estates taken as legal possession for a period of four years. The Armstrongs took the blow to the core; perhaps the boy's youth made the killing a greater outrage, and would later demand revenge.

Vengeance would come twenty years later, when the Armstrongs joined the army of Sir Thomas Carleton of Carleton Hall (not to be confused with Thomas Carlton from 1580s – Constable of Carlisle) on an invasion into Dumfriesshire under the English Crown's orders in February 1547. This was during the Rough Wooing; King Henry VIII had recently died, but the plan to marry his son Edward VI, to Mary, Queen of Scots, still lived on. Many Armstrongs were hired as mercenaries to help, eager to share in the spoils that no doubt would follow. The campaign would also give them the chance to settle old scores with the Johnstones; such was the nature of feuds were a grudge could last decades. The invasion went well, with Dumfries taken and used as a base camp for operations. During the campaign, "Ill Will's" Sandy Armstrong (see page 280) suggested that Lochwood Castle would be a suitable target to take and garrison. This was the chief seat of the Johnstones, and the taking of this stronghold was thought to amount to a suitable revenge. The tower was undermanned, and was easily stormed in an early morning surprise assault. Carleton and the Armstrongs lorded it up for the remainder of that year, with a mixed Molotov cocktail crew of English, Scots and broken men – who randomly raided and stashed away all that they could before the army was recalled back into England in 1551 after the Treaty of Norham. The Armstrongs did very well out of the escapade.

The Armstrongs were clashing again with the Johnstones in the early 1580s when they helped out the Maxwells in their own feud with the Johnstones. Several Armstrong lairds held their land under the tenancy of Lord Maxwell, and owed a bond of help – and it was always good to keep in with the strongest power in the March. The Maxwells and Johnstones hold the record for the longest family feud on the Border, fuelled by jealousy over the possession of the title of West March Warden.

In 1581 John Johnstone lost his seat as the West March Warden, to be replaced by John, 8th Lord Maxwell. The change brought disgruntled raiders into his property, with Langholm being burned and spoiled, which would have annoyed the Armstrongs. Maxwell only lasted one year in his new post, being dismissed for inactivity, with Johnstone resuming the warden's role again. Maxwell was enraged at the power shift, and ordered his followers not to recognise Johnstone as the warden. Johnstone with his authority undermined, felt threatened and contacted the king to ask for military support. The air was brewing for a scrap, with a contingent of Armstrongs supporting the Maxwells. In early 1585 the Maxwells together with 400 Armstrongs, Beatties, Littles and Scotts in support descended upon Lochwood Castle and broke in. The castle and its outhouses were all put to the flame, and it was claimed *"that Lady Johnstone might have a light to put on her hood."*

Henry, Lord Scrope reported from Carlisle the developments to Walsingham in two letters...
1. 7 April 1585
"By my late letters I signified that Robert Maxwell bastard brother to the Earl of Morton, had come to the Borders to stir up the Armstrongs against Johnston. Now I hear that the said Robert with his friends, and the Armestrongs and others to the number of 400, the night last past, have ridden upon the Johnstons owne landes tenantes and speciall freindes, even at and abowt his cheiff house called the Loughwoode, and there have slayne one of the Johnstons, taken foure more prisoners, and brent the Lardes owne howse, and his provisyon of victuales, with the spoyle of a great deale of insight of the said house and others his freindes abowt yt. I fear dangerous trouble therefore, as no surname of account on that Border but is a party therein. The Laird is not yet returned from Court or any order taken. I shall report what falls out."

2. 27 April 1585

"The troubles of the opposite borders doe still contynue and encrease, for even of late, Robert Maxwell with Kynmontes and their complices, have brent almoste foure skore howses of the Larde Johnstons his tenauntes and freindes, and have made spoyle of a great deals of victuall, catle, and insight. And albeyt the same was done xx myles within Scotlande, yet was there not any parson that made resistance. It is thought the Lord Maxwell would not act thus, without the privity of some of the other noblemen of Scotland. Johnston is not yet returned, and when he does, it is like enough he will ask my help to suppress disobedience; wherein I pray you to procure her Majesty's pleasure and direction."

This was a heavy blow for the Johnstones, more devastation of Johnstone property occurred that year, with warnings from the king to halt his attacks. The Johnstones struck back, as the laws of feuding expected, raiding the Maxwell village of Duncow. In return this demanded a counter raid, as the cycle of destruction spun out of control. Robert Maxwell (bastard brother to Lord Maxwell) led his Armstrong supporters in a raid along the Dryfe valley, which they gleaned of all Johnstone cattle and finished the foray off by burning Lockerbie. Scrope describes the event in a letter to Walsingham on 1 May 1585...

"Since my last of 27th ultimo, [letter on 27 April] *the yong Larde Johnston and his freindes have come to the towne of Dunkowe being the Erle of Mortons heritadge, and there setting in fyer have brent some parte of the same towne, to the reskewe whereof the Maxwelles and their complices came, and drove the Johnstons from thence, slewe one man and hurte dyverse. And for a further revendge the Erle of Morton him selff in propre person, with a good nombre both of horsemen and footmen, with dromme, and banners displayed, dyd burne the towne of Brommell inhabited by the Johnstons their tenauntes and servauntes, and spoyled the towne of Thornythwate, being also the Johnstons boundes. And the same daye at the same tyme, Robert Maxwell brother to the Erle, with a great number of the Armestranges, Batysons, Litles, Carrudders, and other the surnames of the Borders, runne a forraye six myles to the water of Dryeffe and Dryefdale, perteyning speciallie to the Johnstons, and there made great spoyle bothe of nolte and sheepe and brent somme parte of the towne of Lockerbye, and somme other onsettes thereabout – all which was done without resistance or contradiccion of any parson."*

In the summer of 1585 the Armstrongs set off on a foray targeting Crawford, and cut down several of Johnstone's troopers. By the end of the year, Maxwell was the undisputed master of the Scottish West March. Again Scrope gave a testimony to the proceedings, in a letter to Walsingham on 30 July 1585...

"I am credible advertised that uppon Thursdays at nighte last past, the Belles, and the Armestronges ran a forrey uppon Crayford More, from whence they broughte to the nomber of xii score kyne and oxen. In which forrey Capten Crayforde sett uppon them, to have rescued the goodes, which not withstandinge, they brought awaye with them, slue two of Crayfordes men, hurte three, and tooke twelve, bringeinge them awaye as prisoners."

A generation later the falling out had all been forgotten about, with the Armstrongs allied to the Johnstones. At the Battle of Dryfe Sands in 1593, the Armstrongs took the Johnstone's side in their feud with the Maxwells and aided them to a spectacular victory.

Chapter 7. Sport & Pastimes

Life for the Armstrongs was not of course all spent in the saddle. By way of recreation they participated in hawking, hunting and fishing; robust activities for this energetic society. For the indoors and especially during the cold and dark months of the year, music and poetry was enjoyed. The Armstrongs gathered around the hearth and in the great halls of the lairds, to hear and sing traditional ballads – poems handed from generation to generation. Tales of romance, tragedy, and the supernatural, played to the harp or small pipes. Looking at the ballads that have come down into the present, among all of the Riding families, the Armstrongs are the family which features most within the verses. They sung about their own exploits, celebrating and commemorating events of daring and tragedy. At times the Armstrongs echoed the great Norse sagas from which they believed came from their Danish Viking roots. A pride in the ballads was natural, where the deeds of the reivers mirrored an already ancient heroic past.

Gambling was a great passion of the reivers, and the Armstrongs certainly indulged in the vice. Card games, dice and backgammon were routinely played. And bets made on the outcomes of cock-fighting and horse races were common. High stakes for the games added to the excitement, were stolen coins, jewellery and even animals would be gambled as stakes. The stigma of losing would not have affected the Armstrongs to a large degree, as the loser could always go out and loot back his losses, and return the next day to the gambling table.

Horse racing

Horse racing though was the most popular recreation of the reivers, which comes as no surprise. The reivers were a horse based society, with all the men being able to ride from a young age. Horses were in the blood, with life lived in and around horses on a daily basis. The Armstrongs obtained great fulfilment in watching and admiring the animals perform. In an occupation such as reiving, the speed and stamina of a horse could make all the difference between life and death. The horse assumed an importance amongst the Riding families beyond that of any usual farming community. Horse racing was a natural extension of the equine passion.

Horse racing brought together the two big loves of the reivers, horses and gambling. Many thrilling days out were spent by the track, on placing bets and watching the horses compete. Race meetings were also important places of business, for socialising, and catching up with the gossip in the next valley. Market stalls were set up, with food and beer brought in for sale. The prizes won at the races were not cups as expected, but bells, being presented to the lucky owner as trophies. Horse racing took place at many venues, with tracks at Berwick, Selkirk, Hawick, Langholm and elsewhere. The Armstrongs even had their own course along the west bank of the Liddel Water, where the village of Newcastleton sits today. Race courses in the West March of England were also popular with the Armstrongs – at such places as Langwathby Moor (Langanby) near Penrith and the King's Moor at Carlisle. They would have rubbed shoulders regularly with the English March Wardens, and even struck up friendships with them.

The authorities disliked these race meets however, as they attracted large crowds and suspected that raids and deeds of no-good were being planned amongst the multitudes. The authorities were correct to fear such gatherings, as the breakout from Carlisle Castle of Kinmont Willie (see page 298), was launched from Langholm race track. Racehorses were greatly prized, obtaining a status symbol amongst the Riding society. Every reiver watching a race would have naturally desired to own one of the fine animals, but such international trade was banned by Border Law. The Armstrongs had to be content to just watch the spectacle, to place their bets and cheer on the horses – but since when did the Armstrong obey any laws?

The typical reiver's horse, the Galloway nag, was not fast, built for trotting over moorlands not running over flat fields. Owning a thoroughbred horse would have elevated a Border laird above his neighbours, something to behold and respect – and as such many lairds were on the lookout for fine horse flesh. Selling horses across the Border was illegal, but this Border law was sometimes sidetracked using the race meetings as a cover for illegal horse trafficking. In 1585 for example Humfrey Musgrave sold a fine horse to the Laird of Mangerton and Kinmont Willie bought another from Lancelot Carleton, actions which were forbidden.

The reivers interest in horse racing descends into the present day, existing in the form of the "Flapping" – flat horse racing meets held annually at various towns across the Scottish Borders.

Football

Football was another sport greatly enjoyed – with games that could last all day, with no apparent rules or restrictions in numbers. The game suited the reivers, providing a robust and healthy activity that appealed to their warlike nature. Amongst the Riding families, the Armstrongs of Liddesdale stick out most as being the biggest football enthusiasts on the Border. The Armstrongs can even be credited as taking part in the very first Scotland V England international football game.

The playing of football has a long history in Scotland. The English claim they invented the game in 1848 when a group of students from Cambridge had the bright idea to draw up a definitive set of rules, however evidence is around for an earlier date. A manuscript from the reign of King James IV shows he paid two shillings for a bag of *"fut ballis"* in April 1497. An actual leather football dating to 1540 was found in 1981 stuck in the roof of the Queen's Chamber at Stirling Castle, making it the oldest in the world. From the same period, accounts exist of small football matches taking place in the grounds of castles, which suggests that the game was well organised and structured at a much earlier date than officially documented. One of the game's earliest recorded spectators was that icon of Scottish history Mary, Queen of Scots – becoming also the first monarch to watch the "beautiful game." In 1568 while staying at Carlisle Castle in Cumbria as a prisoner, she observed twenty of her retinue playing a two hour game outside the walls on Bitts Park. According to her custodian Sir Francis Knollys, all played *"very strongly, nimbly and skilfully, without any foul play offered."* The pitch was 50 metres long (half the length of today's pitches) with trees planted at either end used as goal posts.

Football in Scotland was enjoyed by all classes, providing a useful safety valve for energies, and to burn up aggression that could easily have erupted elsewhere in a more destructive form. The game was even played by the ruling classes; for example Francis Stewart, the 5th Earl of Bothwell was a considerable expert of the game. Bothwell was reported as playing dirty on occasion. Robert Bowes wrote on 29 May 1583 concerning a quarrel *"betwixt Bothwell and the Master of Marishal upon a stroke given at football on Bothwell's leg by the Master, after that the Master had received a sore fall by Bothwell."* Basically Bothwell had committed a foul by tripping up an opponent – it took James VI some time to reconcile them. A top player of the family was Walter Armstrong (The Laird's Wat, see page 168). His sporting career was cut short when he was struck by an arrow which went through his steel helmet and into his head. In June 1600 the Armstrongs used the cover of watching a football match to meet up and plan the murder of Sir John Carmichael, the Scottish West March Warden (see page 320).

The game was not universally liked and was actually banned on occasions. King James I decreed that *"Na man play at the fut ball"* in the Football Act of 1424; and a further act of parliament was passed in 1457 which banned both football and golf. The reason for this was that it interfered with archery practice which was compulsory to undertake every Sunday.

The Scotland-England football game is the oldest international fixture in the world – first played at the West of Scotland Cricket Club's ground at Hamilton Crescent in Partick, Glasgow in Scotland on 30 November 1872. The gathered crowd of 4,000 watched, as a draw was played out at 0-0. There was however another game recorded from an earlier time between these two countries in 1599, which can arguably claim this accolade – and the final result then was far from different. The honour for organising the football match in 1599 goes to Thomas Musgrave, the Captain of Bewcastle in Cumbria. Thomas's job was to keep peace on the Border and seems like an odd character to be behind the game; why would he entertain reivers on his home turf? This was a similar situation to having a police officer socializing with criminals. The reason behind this lies with Thomas having family connection to the Armstrongs. He had an illegitimate daughter who was married to Sim Armstrong of Whithaugh (see page 136), one of the most notorious of the Border thieves. Thomas held a game planning meeting with Sim and Robyn Elwood (Elliot), and agreed on the matches date and team members. The location of the game was probably chosen by Musgrave, to be played in England and at Bewcastle; a windswept village in the middle of bleak moorland, which was well familiar to the Armstrongs from their forays.

The match was played on 13 May 1599 between six locals from Bewcastle and six from Liddesdale. The names of the team members are not known, but can be guessed at based on later football players who rose to international stardom in the 1960/70s, such as Bobby Robson, Jack Charlton and Bobby Charlton for England. The Scottish team was made up mostly of Armstrongs from Whithaugh (with possibly Sim amongst them) and an Elliot or two. Travelling to the game, the Armstrongs probably followed a main route, with no need to be concealed; today was a tranquil ride with lances discarded. Here, the Armstrongs found themselves in the unusual circumstances of being in Bewcastle legally, a situation which must have amused them. The locals for once enjoyed a peaceful night from the thieves. Sim travelled down with the party and stayed in Thomas's house being entertained as a guest on the night before the big game. What would the neighbours have thought?

The game was played on a field adjacent to the castle. There is no record on how the game went; looking at other such games, it can be guessed that there were plenty of thumps, bumps, scuffles and fights. The game could have lasted from dawn to dusk, or anywhere in between, and was played with the minimum of rules. Amongst the spectators watching was William Ridley of Willimoteswick (mentioned earlier on page 49); he had heard *"that certain Scotsmen to the number of 12 were to come to a tryst in the West March of England,"* not an unusual matter of facts, but these certain Scotsmen so happened to be Armstrongs. William observed their arrival, noting their low numbers and vulnerability to attack with sinister pleasure. William had a personal deep grudge against the Armstrongs having had friends *"murdered downe bye the sayd Scotes men."* The temptation was too much, here was a readymade target given to him on a plate. Vengeance was in mind; he sent word by horse messenger and organised a party of forty of his friends and fellow tenants with a plan *"to apprehend them on English ground."* To take on the Armstrongs when in Scotland would be breaking March Law, but to ambush them in England, especially when he outnumbered them, would definitely be worth the attempt. Then he could have his pay-back with interest on this voracious family.

William's best laid plans however became unravelled, with *"the Scots having intelligence of his design."* During the game, word of his devious plot leaked out, Francis Forster of Kershope Foot had overheard the plotters and persuaded two women to take a warning message to the Armstrong's home base. A rider travelled hot-hoofed over the waste-land and into Liddesdale to muster a swift counter attack to save the Scots football team from being cut down and murdered. When word reached Liddesdale, the Armstrongs had a well rehearsed method of gathering armed troopers with their militarised society, raising men quickly was second nature to them. Perhaps beacons were lit or white blankets were unfolded, the effect was the same; quickly a force of two hundred riders was assembled, and a rescue party was on the way. They rode to the Border armed with lance and sword in great determination – with those in their way making themselves scarce and glad that the Riders had a final destination further away.

When the game was over, both sides went *"drynkyng hard at Bewcastle house."* Some things have never changed with sport, with alcohol an essential part of the game. This also illustrates the friendliness between the Borderers of both nationalities, socialising with each other, their guards well and truly down. This is also a rare example of reivers drinking. There is an image of reivers being hard living and hard drinking, but there is no record of reivers labelled as being drunk. Perhaps it never happened, or the opposite – it was so common and thought not worth reporting. Alcohol was mostly associated to the towns and not the rural areas. Heavy drinking was the order, before hitting the saddle for the ride home on the same night. The Armstrong football team probably knew the dubious fate that awaited them, as they tucked into several ales and socialised with their opposite side. Faith in their rescue party's ability to help gave them the courage to act without suspicion, and to ride into the jaws of the trap without letting on. In their intoxicated state, a fearless bravado may have permeated the group as they took to the moors on their Border nags, placing their lives in the hands of their colleagues. With the reivers, family came first before king and nationality – and a bonding trust.

William, with mischief and murder in mind, must have smiled with evil glee as he took his party to a concealed hollow in the moorland to await the Armstrongs returning home. Meanwhile the Scots rescue party with no qualms entered England fully armed, with fighting in their minds. This was their day job, and with arrogance and confidence they crossed the frontier. When they were three-four miles into England they came across William and his gathered host. The look upon his face must have been priceless when the ambushers became the ambushed. The English were stationary at the time that they saw the Armstrongs, and no doubt felt a terrible dread as the Armstrongs lowered their lances and broke into a trot. A charge occurred followed by a chase, with the English having no stomach for the combat. Before the charge made contact, some if not all of the English had fled the area. The fight was brief. The impression is of a running skirmish, with the English routing with little resistance and the Scots taking prisoners on every hand. The Armstrongs captured twenty six men and thirty two horses, the horses complete *"with all ther spoyle and furniter."* The English had volunteered to apprehend a small group of men with no bloodshed, not to engage in a full battle and risk life and limb.

Casualties were light, with three of the English party killed which included William Ridley, the man responsible for this entire affair. The manner of Ridley's death suggests that he was captured and later executed in cold blood. He had his throat cut alongside Nychol Welton. The Armstrongs singled out who they saw as the ring leaders for the ambush. No mercy was granted, for this was a case of dishonour and deceit – a betrayal of friendly intentions. Ridley had behaved in an unsporting manner on this day of sport, and was dealt with according to reiver justice. A Robson was also slain *"and many sore hurt, especially John Whytfeild whose bowells came out, but are sowed up agayne, and is thought shall hardly escape, but as yet lyveth."* The Scots losses were probably nil. Judging by the death toll on Ridley's men, killing the enemy was not the target, but a double dealing Ridley was another matter completely.

The Armstrongs came out on top after the six-a-side match, with a physical and moral victory over the English. Though sadly in all the excitement, the actual result of the international game was never recorded – lost to posterity.

The incident reached the authorities, with a report draughted up and signed by witnesses...

John Whitfeild   *Frauncis Whitfeild* ... (Names signed – reminder signed by their mark)
James Rydlie of the Waltoune   *Uswalde Rydlie of the Waltoune*
Hew Rydlie of Plenmeller   *Nicholas Rydley of the Hardridinge*
Christofer Rydley of Unthanke   *Thomas Rydley of Milbredge*
John Rydley of Henshaughe   *Nicholas Snawdon of Plenmeller*
Marmaduke Rydley (sonne the foresayde William Rydley)

The fracas and killings were probably prompted by the feud between the Armstrongs and the Ridleys. The Border officials had little to say on the matter, with the slaying of a potential murderer. It would make little sense bringing to trial those who had killed those who had tried to murder innocent football players. The case was dropped – justice had been done reiver style.

Chapter 8. Religion

Scotland at the start of the 16th century was a Roman Catholic country. This changed in 1560 on the Reformation, when Scotland embraced a strict Calvinistic Presbyterianism. The break with the papacy was sought with the National Kirk, and a protestant revolution to end corruption and begin a new relationship with God. Some families such as the Maxwells clung onto the old Catholic faith, risking persecution and monitoring. How the changes filtered into the wild valleys of Liddesdale is not known, but the Armstrongs were not known for their toleration of Christianity at the best of times, and a new variation would have gone over their heads. Religion was at the centre of Medieval / Renaissance life, providing a moral compass to society and ceremonies to celebrate throughout the year. The big events of life came under the Church's guidance, from Christenings at birth, to marriage blessings, the last rites and burial in consecrated ground. The Church provided more than spiritual needs, being the centre for education and medical care. It would be an extreme act of folly to ignore, or worse, to attack a church – but on occasions the Armstrongs did exactly this.

There is a traditional story of a traveller passing through Liddesdale, and noticed the unusual absence of churches, there was not a single chapel to be seen. He was puzzled and enquired on the subject, asking *"Are there any Christians here?"* A gruff blunt reply rang out – *"Na, we're a' Elliots and Armstrangs!"*

The Armstrongs had no respect for the Church judging by their regular habit of burning them down. Within the State Papers of Henry VIII, there is a document by the emissary Thomas Magnus, Archdeacon of the East Riding, dated on 13 February 1529 to Thomas Wolsey, on the subject of *"the gretteste theves upon the borders, called Armestrongges."* Magnus in an aggrieved testament, writes – *"the Armstrongs of Liddesdale had presumptuously said that they would not be ordered, neither by the King of Scots, their sovereign lord, nor by the King of England ... that the said Armstrongs had boasted that they had been the destruction of two and fifty parish churches in Scotland besides the unlawful and ungracious attempts by them committed within England."* The destruction of fifty two churches would go a long way to explain the lack of religious buildings in Liddesdale. It is easy to imagine the anger and pain felt by these two men of the Church, at the disrespect and destruction of all they held Holy.

The Church did fight back against the reivers for their lack of Christian virtue. Gavin Dunbar, the Archbishop of Glasgow, in October 1525 issued his "Monition of Cursing" against the Border Riders, in an attempt to halt their evil ways. The Archbishop could not retaliate with an army, but he could undertake a spiritual assault. The composition is over 1500 words, a flowing verbal attack which barely lets up for breath in a no holds barred tirade of venom. This piece of fascinating verbose, was aimed at all of the Border reivers, but could well have been inspired directly by the Armstrongs. The curse was ordered to be read from every pulpit in the diocese and to be circulated throughout all of the Borders. A portion of the script is worth quoting to gain a flavour of the prose, a literal assault on every inch of the reiver's physical body and beyond:-

I curse thair heid and all the haris of thair heid; I curse thair face, thair ene, thair mouth, thair neise, thair toung, thair teith, thair crag, thair schulderis, thair breist, thair hert, thair stomok, thair bak, thair wame, thair armes, thair leggis, thair handis, thair feit, and everilk part of thair body, frae the top of thair heid to the soill of thair feit, befoir and behind, within and without.

I curse them gangand, and I curse them rydand, I curse thaim standand, and I curse thaim sittand; I curse them etand, I curse thaim drinkand, I curse thaim walkland, I curse thaim sleepand, I curse thaim rysand, I curse thaim lyand; I curse thaim at hame, I curse thaim fra hame, I curse them within the house, I curse thaim without the house, I curse thair wiffis, thair barnis, and thair servandis participand with thaim in thair deides.

I wary thair cornys, thair catales, thair woll, thair scheip, thair horse, thair swyne, thair geise, thair hennys, and all thair quyk gude. I wary thair hallis, thair chalmeris, thair kechingis, thair stanillis, thair barnys, thair biris, thair bernyardis, thair cailyardis, thair plewis, thair harrowis, and the gudis and housis that is necessair for their sustentatioun and weilfair.

I FORBID all cristin man or woman till have ony company with thaime, etand, drynkand, spekand, prayand, lyand, standand, or in any uther deid doand, under the paine of deadly syn.

And, finally, I CONDEMN thaim perpetualie to the deip pit of hell, to remain with Lucifer and all his fallowis, and thair bodies to the gallowis of the Burrow Mure, first to be hangit, syne revin and ruggit with doggis, swine, and utheris wyld beists, abhominable to all the warld.

Clearly something had riled up the Archbishop, what exactly this was is not made clear. Besides being the Archbishop of Glasgow, Dunbar also held the position of Prior of Whithorn, and was preceptor to King James V from 1518. Whithorn was a place of pilgrimage; Dunbar may have come across wearied souls wanting salvation from the reivers, praying for a miracle. The beggared villagers, poor from black mail and raids perhaps approached Dunbar for charity, and told him tales of fire and slaughter. And at James's court, the latest news of Border atrocities was a common concern. Judging by the length and ferocity of Dunbar's curse, he must have had a run in with the reivers himself. And it can be assumed that he was reived by them, having his horse, money and jewellery all taken from him on at least one occasion.

The curse was designed to excommunicate the reivers and condemn them to an eternal Hell. It sadly did not work. Excommunication was a serious matter for the medieval mind; those suffering this sentence were in for more than a well meaning verbal attack. This was intended to put the fear of God into the outlaws and make them think twice and stop their thieving; not only would the reiver be cut off from the Church, but also cut off from society. The essential rituals of life could not be undertaken, sins could not be heard or God's Kingdom entered. A bigger concern was on marriages not being performed which held property advancement and family security. The sacrament was denied, and the numerous Christian feasts and festivals could not be participated in. To be excommunicated was to be a pariah, with an afterlife spent in purgatory awaiting a torturous Hell. This threat was enough to make any medieval subject, from peasant to king, be terrified to the core and take all actions possible to make amends. The reivers however were beyond such intimidation. They never had much affection for kings and queens at the best of times, and even less for the priest. A Christian burial was denied, but was not a real threat when many ended their days on the gallows and a shallow unmarked grave. Ignoring the threat of purgatory was a professional necessity, when livelihood was based on the sin of theft. The Archbishop's voice was seen as the growl of a toothless lion, a futile gesture which all would ignore.

The Armstrongs may have been secure in the belief of avoiding purgatory, as they had an "unblessed hand." There was a tradition amongst the Riding families of when christening boys the right hand was excluded from the ceremony. This omission allowed the men once adult, to strike "unhallowed" blows upon the enemy, a useful function when a family feud occurred. Slaying an opponent with an unblessed hand was free from sin, allowing the reiver to kill guilt free.

It has to be wondered at the Armstrongs lack of faith in an age of faith. Did the harsh realities of life on the frontier, with theft and murder always at your doorstep, rob the Armstrong's of their faith in humanity? The lack of religion in the reiver's lives was placed as a possible cause to the unruly nature of the Armstrongs. Lord Eure wrote to the queen on 17 April 1596, a report on the state of the Border, prompted by the escape of Kinmont Willie from Carlisle Castle, which he saw as proof in the weakening fall in law on the Marches, stating... *"Another most grievous decay is want of knowledge of God whereby the better sort forget oath and duty, let malefactors go against evidence, and favour a partie belonging to them or their friends. The churches mostly mined to the ground, ministers and preachers comforthles to com and remaine where such heathenish people are, so there are neither teachers nor taught."* It was a vicious circle. The reivers had no morals due to there being no churches, and there were no churches due to the reivers.

Chapter 9. Before Flodden

From small acorns in the 13th century, by the 16th century the Armstrongs were the most numerous family in Liddesdale. Becoming a major nuisance, the Armstrongs could muster what amounted to small armies, and were at times able to strike and raid almost anywhere they chose. Riding the tops of the hill ranges, the Armstrongs had a free spirit life, master of all they saw and servant to none.

The late 16th century is considered to be the peak hey-day of the Border Riders however the Armstrongs had a head start in the mayhem. A letter was issued on 14 June 1501 summoning seventy Armstrongs to appear at Selkirk on 21 June, to be charged for the slaughter of John Blackburn. Failure to attend would result in the named Armstrongs being denounced as the King's rebels, and put to the horn. Needless to say, none of the Armstrongs showed face, defying the royal command. Sitting safe in their Border valley, far away from the seat of power, the Armstrongs recognised no rule but their own. King James IV was having none of this, a truly renaissance king, and full of energy, he set about bringing the Armstrongs and the Border into line. That same summer he sent a letter to Patrick Hepburn, the 1st Earl of Bothwell with orders demanding that he set upon the Armstrongs as his office of the King's Lieutenant required – *"To raise the kings lieges for to pass upoune saidis Armestrangis, rebellis, thar assistaris, parte- takaris, and resettaris, and to persewe thame to deid, and to tak thare gudis, as eschete."*

The first named Armstrong reivers appear on 31 October 1502, documented at a justice aire held at Jedburgh; Archibald and Ninian Armstrong from Liddesdale. They were accused of burning and plundering Cragend of Minto and Syntoune where they killed two persons. The guilt of the Armstrongs was questionable, as David Scott of Stirkshaws produced a remission for the treasonable bringing in of the pair. Richard Armstrong also attended and was charged for plundering Fechane. It was noted that the three named Armstrongs had been unusually active that year, and in previous raids had captured some *"400 oxen and cows, 104 horses, 200 sheep, with a large amount of goods and money."*

James himself was in the Borders in November 1502 attending a court assize at Jedburgh – and then again on 2 September 1503, where James despatched a messenger to the Armstrongs commanding them to appear before him. The outcome of the summons is not known, and whether they submitted and received a pardon for their offences. Further action was taken in the summer of 1504, when accompanied by Thomas, Lord Dacre, the English warden; James led a raid into Eskdale hanging all those he thought as outlaws. A royal progress was made into Ewesdale, Liddesdale and Annandale with much feasting and fanfare. Dacre's time spent with the king, in hawking, feasting and hanging criminals, would later come in useful, when after the Battle of Flodden he was brought in to identify James's body, as it lay half naked amongst thousands of others.

James was determined to have a peaceful kingdom, and to have a pacified and unified Scotland from the Borders to the Highlands. He wanted to use soft tactics were possible, and persuade the Armstrongs were their loyalties should land.

The king fined Adam Hepburn, 2nd Earl of Bothwell (who had taken over the title from his father in 1508) in 1510, in his capacity as the Lord of Liddesdale, £10 for his lack of action, and set about putting his own ideas into operation. James granted a respite to the Armstrongs on 26 May, 1510, inviting the main chieftains to Edinburgh under letters of safe conduct, showing the greatest of courtesy to encourage their attendance. He permitted the Armstrongs to visit any *"burrows"* that they pleased and purchase whatever *"necessaries"* they desired. The king declared that he would take the Armstrongs and their goods under his special protection, and when in Edinburgh they would not come to harm or be punished for any manner of crime or offense in the past.

James wanted to bring the Armstrongs and other Border clans onboard in a genuine, fair and conciliatory manner. He granted remissions and invited the Border chieftains to attend his council meetings, where they would be consulted on how to better rule their own land. James's policies were exactly what the Borders needed to bring about a workable peace, and were a far cry from the severe measures that his later successors would inflict. James's velvet glove worked, which induced many of the Liddesdale riders to give up their evil practices and make peace with the Crown. The Border was never fully pacified though, but loyalty to the king had been developed with many of the Border lairds now accepting James as their sovereign liege. All looked well for the future, however a spanner in the works was not far off, which derailed the excellent progress off track, and would remain so for the rest of the century.

The loyalty of the Border clans to King James IV would come to cost many their lives, when three years later on a sodden Branxton Hill, the flowers of the forest were cut down alongside their monarch. James in his popularity attracted the biggest muster of soldiers that Scotland has ever known. The highest estimate of James's army was put at 40,000 men on its initial gathering. There is no record if the Armstrongs attended the calling, but they probably did – together with their neighbours the Elliots. If the unruly Elliot family were moved enough to fight for King James and Scotland, it makes sense to assume that the Armstrongs did likewise. The men of Liddesdale met up with the Earl of Bothwell and swapped their *"lang speirs"* for the pike – and more reluctantly, dismounted from their nags and formed into foot companies. The Scots had been promised by the French that the pike would bring the Scot's victory. Forty French captains trained the Scottish army in the use of the pike, with the Armstrongs joining rank and learning the drill which they believed would defeat the English.

The Battle of Flodden was the outcome on 9 September 1513, in which the Armstrongs were arrayed within the vanguard pike block of Alexander Home, 3rd Lord Home. After enduring an afternoon of rain, stationary awaiting the English to attack – the battle began at 4pm with an artillery duel, the first of its kind in British history. The terror of cannon balls ripping through the massed ranks can be imagined, ploughing through several soldiers at a time. When the guns fell silent, James ordered his three pike blocks to attack, with the vanguard leading in echelon. As practiced, Home's pike block marched down the hill in silence, and through a hail storm of arrows which normally meant the end of the Scots. The English archers for once failed in their attempt to defeat the Scots. After two hundred years of combating the English longbow, the Scots had finally found the solution – employing the pavise (a long shield) and excellent body armour. At last the Scots finally reached the English line intact. The pikes were levelled horizontally, and it was time to put the wonder weapon to its test and defeat the English.

As the pike far outranged the English bill, there would be little hand-to-hand combat at this stage, the English were impaled at a safe long range and pushed back as promised. Edmund Howard's billmen gave way – Victory. The moment of triumph against the "auld enemy" brought an intense joy. The pikemen now had only to turn 90 degrees, and the whole English army would be rolled up from the flank and pushed off the field in rout. This was sadly not to be, as a hidden formation of English cavalry under Lord Dacre was hovering to strike.

Dacre commanded 1,500 riders; these included many English reivers recruited from Bamboroughshire, Tynemouth and other parts of Northumberland, expert "prickers" skilled with the lance. Dacre's Border Horse plugged the gap left by Howard, and charged into Home's phalanx. This was not in the plans for the Scots, many pikes had been dropped and ranks had become disordered, allowing the light horse to carve a swathe into the massed block. The frustration of the Armstrongs can be felt; to be on foot and with a pike – and have a reiver bearing down with lance levelled must have been un-nerving. The Armstrongs as a unit all wished that they were mounted. This static warfare of the pike block was not for them. A bloody clash ensued, with the Scots coming off the worse. Home pulled back the vanguard to a safe distance, leaving many behind killed and wounded by the prickers.

The vanguard would play no further part in the battle, and stood by as the remainder of the Scots army fought valiantly, and were cut down as they stood. The Armstrongs survived the encounter with no losses noted, but the Elliots lost their chieftain, Robert Elliot of Redheugh, and Bothwell was also killed. The day had been costly with the death of the king and the flowers of the forest slain, with implications that would echo badly for years to come.

Chapter 10. The Lords of Misrule

Scotland breathed a sigh of relief as the victorious English army was disbanded soon after their amazing victory at Flodden, and did not attempt their own counter invasion. All was not peaceful however, Thomas, Lord Dacre, Warden of the English West March, reaped a destructive swath across Liddesdale, Ewesdale and Teviotdale – burning and thieving as he went. In one raid undertaken by Dacre's brother Christopher Dacre, 4,000 cattle were lifted, indicating the scale of the loss to the Borders. Many Border families were left destitute, with their only chance of survival placed at having to mount their own retaliation raids to obtain sufficient food. The momentum of goodwill between the monarch and the Riding families stalled with the death of James. His son James V inherited the throne but at only seventeen months in age, a regency had to be put in place. With James IV gone and a burning Border, the Armstrongs drifted back into their law-less ways.

As a method of self preservation, the Armstrongs sided with the "Auld Enemy." A letter dated 21 June 1517 from Dacre to Wolsey, contains the passage, *"As for the Armstrongs and oder evill disposed personnes, their adherents, the king's highness shall not be charged with none assistance for them, but only myself."* In the wake of the military and political upheaval in Scotland, the Armstrongs were building up their powerbase. Scotland lacking a strong ruling monarch, allowed the Armstrongs to find the protection they desired for life on the frontier – which ended up being themselves. John Stewart, Duke of Albany granted respite to several of the Riding clans, including the Elliots and the Nixons, with the Armstrongs strangely rejecting the offer. This action makes sense when it is thought possible that the Armstrongs were in the pay of Dacre, subsidised to disrupt the fragile peace on the Scottish Border, and hopefully distract thoughts on any further Scottish invasions.

The Armstrongs and their allies were exceedingly troublesome during 1518-19, requiring measures to limit the damage they were inflicting. On 12 March 1518 the regent and council directed that a proclamation should be made and read out at the market crosses of Jedburgh and Selkirk against the Armstrongs. The Armstrongs were not directly attacked; the focus of the diatribe was aimed at the town's inhabitants. The proclamation forbade the town's people to provide *"the thevis and traitouris of Liddesdale, with ony maner of vittales, undir the pane of tynsale of lif, landis and gudis."* This implies that the locals were actively supplying food and other market products to the outlaws, and tolerating the thieves. This live and let live attitude can be expected, building a relationship with the reivers would be beneficial, resulting in the trade of stolen goods and hopefully prevent raids on the town.

Patrick Hepburn, 3rd Earl of Bothwell, should have been responsible for Liddesdale and the Armstrongs, having succeeded to the Lordship of Liddesdale in 1513 on the death of his father. However due to his young age (born in 1512), a relative, Patrick Hepburn, Master of Hailes (second son to the 1st Earl of Bothwell), stepped in to undertake the roll. A letter by the Master of Hailes to James, Bishop of Moray, on 17 July 1518, describes a recent successful expedition into Liddesdale and is worth quoting – *"As for the Armstrangis thai ar in the Debatable landis, and agreit with Ingland, and kepis thare markat daily in Ingland, nochttheles I am laborand and traistis to gett thare plegis."* It is interesting to note that the Armstrongs are established in the Debateable Land at this stage, 1518 being the earliest record. The Armstrongs are noted making inroads into England, which involved regular visits to Carlisle on market day to spend their ill-gotten money. The Armstrongs would later claim to be English on occasion, and this link to markets in England lends substance to their stance. Two days later the Master of Hailes was ordered by the council to do his utmost to get pledges from the Armstrongs.

The English were part to blame for the damage done, when gangs of Armstrongs under English assurance made forays against Scottish targets. One of these raids took place on 20 March 1520, which resulted in *"The towne of Mynchame of the larde of Mynchames landis brent: One slayne and tenne hurte in peril of dathe, x prisoners, xiiii horse and naggis, xi oxen and kyen."* The obtaining of pledges by the Master of Hailes was hoped to end these incursions.

Moving into the 1520s, the rise of the Armstrongs began in earnest. The family had spread south out of Liddesdale and into the Esk and the Debateable Land. From this territory right on the English Border, the Armstrongs could fully exploit the loop-holes over the Border Law. Were the Armstrongs English or Scottish? The family could play one country off over another, and basically avoid trial by confusing their national identity. From their new base along the Esk, an empire of extortion was extorted across the frontier, which brought wealth and status to the new robber barons.

The Mangerton branch of the Armstrongs not surprisingly was the most troublesome of the family. They became such a menace to England, that a national war could have easily been provoked. Extending their blackmail racket was highly lucrative and friendships developed with many of the English outlaws. The Armstrongs developed alliances with many of the Riding families in the Tynedale valley, especially amongst the Charltons and Dodds. The English authorities found this a most dangerous development, recording in early 1524 – *"the Armstrongs and the theiffs of Ewysdaill were joined with the rebells of Tyndaill, and were comyn untoe theym and kepet all company togedders."* The increase in the number of day forays being mounted was a sign in the strength of the outlaws growing and in the weakness of the government to prevent it. Reiving was normally carried out under the cover of darkness, making these day time raids setting a new deadly trend. During this period the reivers had grown contemptuous of the law, and displayed their power with a sense of raised arrogance and audacity. They were operating in groups larger than before, with various gangs co-operating and coming together for a single raid. Normally reivers would never display banners, a situation which was reserved for the battle field where recognizing who was who was not only important but life depending – but on this occasion flags were regularly flown. Why would a reiver advertise the fact they were an Armstrong or an Elliot? As this would be like giving a postcard address of where to find the culprit and aim a hot trod towards – surely not a good idea. The Riders were carrying with them various family crests and mottos, proudly stating who they were, an act which was pointless and counter-productive within the context of an average raid. This illustrates the security with which the Riders felt, thinking themselves immune from any counterattack raid and legal prosecution and on the weakness of the authorities to keep the peace. Proudly stating their family name was a two fingered gesture to authority, and symbolically displayed who really ruled in this part of the Kingdom.

The situation could not go on, and had been allowed to fester for as long as Scotland lacked an adult monarch at the hand of the tiller. In February 1525 Archibald Douglas, 6th Earl of Angus (estranged husband to Margaret Tudor, Queen of King James IV) was made a Lord of the Articles, and with a place in the Council of Regency, he wanted to show he was a man of action and the material of holding a key office in Scotland. Angus held great ambition, with designs on becoming regent, sorting out the Border would be a good start on his progress to power. That same year, Angus made a venture into the Borders eager to sort out the problem were others had failed, descending in a style that only he knew, rapid and severe. Angus targeted the Armstrongs as they had developed alliances with the Tynedale outlaws, he wanted to make an example of them and end their dangerous friendships. He entered Liddesdale *"sodeinly upon the gretteste theves upon the bordours, called Armstrongges, being the gretteste maynteners of the theves of Tyndaill"* – and landed by surprise some of the main Armstrong leaders. Angus captured twelve Armstrongs, two were the most important captains of the chieftain at Mangerton, Sym the Laird of Whithaugh and Davy "the Lady" his brother (see page 123/124). As punishment Angus stole around 4,000 head of livestock and many horses. Then after setting fire to numerous houses, returned well satisfied in his mission.

Angus took away a number of Armstrongs to Edinburgh to act as assurances for the family's good behaviour, and for a limited time a peace of sorts was brought to the Border. The Armstrongs taken were not kept in prison, but were paroled in Edinburgh, having men attending them night and day to all of their needs. The Armstrong's hospitable treatment was observed by Thomas Magnus the English ambassador to Scotland in October of that year, who saw James Beaton, Archbishop of Glasgow (and Lord Chancellor of Scotland) arguing and falling out with Angus over the Armstrongs. With so many known thieves and cut throats in the hands of the officials, Beaton wanted several of them executed, but this would have negated the whole purpose of having them taken captive in the first place.

The Armstrongs had their pledges extracted however, but the promise for good behaviour was only extended to the Scottish side of the Border. Angus was keen to keep the Armstrongs in his favour; he wanted to punish them but at the same time retain their loyalty to Scotland. In his need to not displease the Borderers, he left the door open for the Armstrongs thieving, with the pledges not covering raids into England. The Armstrongs were given the green light to continue with their forays – they would be tolerated just as long as they did not go plundering in Scotland. Ultimately the expedition by Angus was punitive and counter-productive, as the victims of the raids had to recoup their losses – and surprise surprise, would go off reiving at the first opportunity. The Riding family societies were based around theft and extortion, the very core of this required to be addressed rather than using brute force and further theft to solve. By thieving from reivers, it could only end in the encouragement of further thieving, and not less. More lawlessness was inevitable, which fed the vicious circle of trouble, with a solution lost to all and seemingly impossible to pin down.

The raiding did not let up, in 1525 a force of 400 Scottish riders, many of which were Armstrongs, together with their Tynedale allies, went foraying in England spoiling all that they came across – burning and killing indiscriminately, and returning with *"55 horss and presoners."* Another raid followed two weeks later, with presumably the same riders as before and were gathered in even greater strength. The target on this occasion was the English garrisons in Tynedale, a similar toll of plunder was achieved, with forty prisoners and as many horses taken, leaving a trail of several men killed in its wake. Complaints rightly were made by English officials to the Scottish court, with envoys from King Henry noting the flaw in Angus's pledges on peace with the Armstrongs. The envoys had always feared that the pledges made by the Armstrongs would only apply to Scotland and their fears were correct. They noted with bitterness that Angus had not even imprisoned the Armstrongs, and had them under house arrest, with *"men attending daye and night upon theym, having gret favourers."* A pledge was not the same as a prisoner, they were kept captive but not for any crime, and as such the experience was not meant to be a punishment.

The Armstrongs and their confederate gangs should have been kept in check by Robert, 5th Lord Maxwell, the Scottish West March Warden, but the reverse was the reality. The Armstrongs were enjoying the protection of Maxwell, and in return the Armstrongs aided in his family's feud with the Johnstones. Maxwell had a prickly relationship with Angus, hostile to his rule, making Maxwell's support of the Armstrongs a rebellious signal on his disregard for Angus's authority. Sir William Eure, English deputy warden, complained in his report on 13 May 1526 that some Charletons and Dodds of Tynedale and Redesdale had fled to Liddesdale, and had been welcomed by the Armstrongs. Eure noted that the renegades had since been returning into England on forays, and were carrying away many prisoners. This addition of English reivers to the Armstrong gangs was alarming news to the authorities. There were periods of sporadic peace and quiet, to be punctuated by such events as a joint Liddesdale-Tynedale attack on Tarset Hall in the English Middle March, setting it on fire. Scotland and England made attempts at making an agreement to deny outlaws from either side in finding refuge in their opposite countries. And another idea was to allow English assistance across the Border into Scotland, in order to help the Scottish wardens' track down the outlaws. The ideas looked good on paper, but broke down in practice. Liddesdale became a law to its own, with the Armstrongs, Elliots, Crosers and Nixons operating outside of the legal system and doing exactly what they pleased. Neither Scotland nor England could obtain redress, with violence the only way to bring about a temporary rethink.

On 20 May 1527, the Scottish government decided on another mission of subjection into the Borders. Angus, together with the king and a force numbering 6000, made a rapid descent into Liddesdale, on an expedition to shock and awe. The surprise was complete with Liddesdale's warning system failing and many reivers were caught at home unprepared. A score were cut down where they stood and another thirteen were strung up as a warning and left dangling over a bridge. Eleven were taken back to Edinburgh as hostages, with a plan to sign them up as pledges to guarantee the good behaviour of their kinsmen. The idea of having hostages was an effective method to obtain peace, however on this occasion the relatives of the prisoners were not playing ball. Nothing was signed or agreed upon, and the Liddesdale riders were soon off raiding again, ignoring the plight of their family members. Henry de Clifford, 1st Earl of Cumberland, Warden of the West March complained on 21 June 1527 that the Armstrongs had run a day foray and were receiving the Nixons who were English. On 4 July an interesting answer was forwarded from Edinburgh on the problem of the Armstrongs. It was proposed by the council that the wardens of both countries should take the wives and children of the Armstrongs and ship them to Ireland or to other places, and not permit them to return – an idea which pre-dates what would occur sixty years later. The whole point of holding the hostages had failed. The question now arose, what to do with the hostages? As they were either reivers or the relatives of reivers, and guilty of some crime for sure, directly or by association – Angus had them all executed.

In 1527 a new gang came onto the block, when the Lisles of Northumberland approached the Armstrongs with the offer of an alliance, which the Armstrongs accepted. The Lisles based themselves in the Debateable Land, where a core of broken men formed around them. The Lisles formed a large and intimidating gang, which made itself a major nuisance within England. Many Armstrongs rode alongside to share in the plunder, adding to the decay and fear within the English West March. The Lisles though had a limited life span, as the authorities could never tolerate the level of raiding and focused their efforts to eliminate the gang.

A number of Armstrongs and Lisles were incarcerated in Newcastle prison that same year and were rescued by a joint Scots/English mission. The Lisles as a result threw themselves into the reiving business and recruited a large gang which operated from the Scottish side of the Border on the fringes of Armstrong territory. A confederation of families mustered, which had dozens of Armstrongs amongst its ranks, who then burned and plundered at will in England. This power block of outlaws was a dangerous cancer which had to be removed, and in January 1528, Henry Percy, Earl of Northumberland, thwarted two forays capturing and hanging many of the gang. Within weeks the confederacy was no more, with the ring leaders surrendering (and executed) and the remainder melting back into the valleys.

The tide was appearing to be turning against the reivers, and encouraged by the new trend, William Lord Dacre, Warden of the West March, put in his penny's worth and made an advance against the Armstrongs who had taken root in the Debateable Lands and fortified themselves. He mustered a large force of 2,000 and crossed the Border hoping to catch such outlaws as Johnnie Armstrong and Sim the Laird, but ran into stiff opposition and was sent packing after a severe thrashing (see page 125). Dacre was back in March 1528 having taking his slight personally he declared a one man war with the outlaws of the Debateable Land and Liddesdale. In a letter to Cardinal Wolsey, Dacre stated his goals, *"I woll neithr suffer the said Armistranges to inhabit upon the Debateable grounde, nor yet suffer theim or any Scottisman of evill name or fame to com to Carlisle market."* Dacre proceeded to systematically pull down all the strongholds that he came across, and then banned anyone who lived in Liddesdale from attending the market at Carlisle. Wolsey was appalled at this free interaction with the outlaws. He never understood the Border spirit, or could get his head around its complex balance and weave of family relationships. The Armstrongs would be denied their weekly jaunt to Carlisle market and to the horse sales, and perhaps a greater loss – the entering of the town's inns, steeped in music, bawdy humour, stories and ale – all of this would come to an end. The Armstrongs were obviously furious at this disruption to their social life. How the ban was implemented is open to question and if it was ever workable in the first place. The actions aggravated further the tense relationship between Dacre and Liddesdale, not the most intelligent of responses to take.

1528 was a happy hunting time for the Armstrongs, with great opulence entering many of the households. The family mounted raid after raid, with a regular monotony into England – and to have corresponding warden rodes made into the Debateable Land in return. In one such raid, the Armstrongs teamed up with the Irvines in May, and burned a swathe across Cumbria. Eight villages lay in their path, with the gang setting on fire and destroying at least sixty houses and an uncounted number of outhouses. Another Armstrong raid followed rapidly, raking in the embers of the first foray between Esk and Leven. The raiders felt untouchable, riding boldly in broad daylight. At around noon they struck and lifted away seventy livestock, leaving behind eight people dead who dared to resist their will. The response from England came in the form of a rode by Christopher Dacre, the deputy warden (for his brother William), who targeted the Routleges, causing a mass escape into the Tarras Moss, removing their herds and rounded off the venture with a foray into Armstrong territory, burning several dwellings in an attempt to even the score.

Power politics were changing in that same year, when King James V turned sixteen and took over the reins of kingship, casting Angus aside and into exile. The reivers and especially the Armstrongs were glad to see Angus get the push. Angus had made at least six raids against the Armstrongs between 1525 and 1528; however they did not foresee what would be replacing Angus. Angus was ambitious and zealous in his actions, but he was not cruel, James on the other hand had a ruthless streak, which was about to be unleashed. James had a desire *"to put gude ordoure and reule apoun thame, and to stanche thiftis and rubberis committit be theiffis and tratouris,"* and his methods would be fire, steel and the rope. The Armstrongs were in for a bumpy time ahead; their happy hunting days were to be halted.

James did not instantly pounce on the Borders once he was properly on the throne; it took him a while to get the wheels of government running smoothly. As James was putting together his new policy for the Borders, the Armstrongs and their confederates were preparing a knock-out blow against Dacre. The Armstrongs wanted to colonise the Debateable Land, and Dacre was making life there impossible. A permanent solution to Dacre was needed; something had to give, and the Armstrongs were determined it would not be themselves. King James and his lords added their own part to the Armstrongs saga on 14 July 1528, when they ordained all those dwelling within Liddesdale to be as free in market and church as any other of His Majesty's subjects. The Armstrongs now had the monarch's blessing to attend market day in Carlisle and if they so wished, to visit the church also – but this was stretching their requirements too far.

A new power came into the block at the same time on 14 July 1528 when Patrick Hepburn, 3rd Earl of Bothwell, at the tender age of 16 appeared before the equally young King James V and the Lords, and took upon himself the rule of Liddesdale. Sir Ralph Sadler (Secretary of State and ambassador to Scotland) wrote in 1543 *"as to the Earl of Bothwell, who hath rule of Liddisdale, I think him the most vain and insolent man in the world, full of pride and folly, and here nothing at all esteemed."* Bothwell claimed to answer for any unlawful attempts made within the lordship, and it comes as no wonder to hear about him becoming involved in the feuds that often plagued the Marches a few months after. In the following year he was imprisoned for two years for protecting the Border freebooters, and released after six months on the payment of twenty thousand pounds by his friends.

The Armstrongs apart from insisting they could enter freely enter into Carlisle at will, also claimed a right from medieval times to hunt, sport, and market in Cumberland. They thought nothing of it to cross into England to gather wood and hunt deer, and then return back to Scotland. They enjoyed hunting in Cumberland, something which they were reluctant to give up. In their own minds, the Armstrongs were breaking no laws, but the legal world was closing in on them.

The domestic life of the Armstrongs was about to take a rock, when in the summer of 1528 Wolsey ordered Dacre, in his office as the English warden to withdraw some privileges from the Armstrongs. The Liddesdale Armstrongs were livid when they received the news that they could no longer hunt or go sporting across the Border – and worse of all, a ban from the Carlisle market. This was viewed as an attack on the Armstrong's ancient rights. The affront added to the family's annoyance of Dacre, whom they blamed for the bans. Adding to this, Dacre's recent attempts at driving the Armstrongs from the Debateable Land, the Armstrongs had every reason to be mounting on the war path.

The Armstrongs were determined to obtain revenge, and in early August of 1528 mustered a mixed force of Armstrongs, Elliots, Nixons and Crosers to strike back at the heart of the problem. The party numbered over three hundred and set off at night into Cumberland. The Liddesdale riders developed a simple trap to take Dacre out, built around the good old fashioned classic ambush. Every trap needs some tasty bait, which took the form of about thirty riders who entered England at Bewcastle and targeted Thirlwall. The gang was under the instructions to lift some livestock and provoke a hot trod, tempting Dacre and his troopers into Scotland and the jaws of a well timed trap. The gang herded up a small number of cattle as planned, and then to ensure that Dacre would bite at the bait, they kidnapped one of his tenants. Dacre recalls the event in a letter to Wolsey on 3 August 1528... *"certein Scottis men, as Elwaldes, Nyksons, Crosers, with other their adherentis, Liddisdale men, to the number of xxx personnes, upon Thuresdaye at night last, cam into this realme by Beawcastell, and Thirlwall in Northumbrlaund, iii myles above my hous, and ther tooke one John Bell, a tenant of myne, and certein of his cattell."*

The raiders wanted to be pursued, and turned around in no great haste for the journey home. Word of the foray spread out quickly, and as hoped reached the capable hands of Dacre who immediately mustered a hot trod... *"And I caused my householde servantis to goo furth with the countrey."* The raiders returned by the same route which they had can come in by, with the trod not far behind. Dacre was not present on the trod, his household servants though were well furnished and felt confident in their pursuit; they were a strong force and had learned that they outnumbered their quarry. When the trod reached Bewcastle, the trail of the Liddesdale riders became clear, and pulled in at the castle for a short break. The castle at Bewcastle held a small permanent garrison, whose duty it was to protect the Border, placed tactically at the junction of the busiest of all the reiving routes. Strangely, the soldiers refused to join the trod, an inaction which should have sent the alarm bells ringing into over-drive. Not only was it illegal to refuse to join a hot trod, but it was the actual job of the soldiers to help out in the chase. The garrison was probably bribed to not react to any trod and turn a blind eye to the raiders. The many alliances and contacts of the Liddesdale families had seemingly stretched into Bewcastle and effectively silenced one of the main counter measures/deterrent against the outlaws. Arguments must have occurred between the garrison and the trod, with the soldiers trying their best to fob off an excuse at their lack of action. Perhaps they blamed the absence of horses, or some defect in their equipment which prevented the soldiers from mounting up. The trod was in too much of hurry to linger long, and having sufficient men for their task, they spurred on before the trail went cold.

Within a mile of the Scottish Border (*"thys side of Kirssop"* – Kershope), the trod came within eyesight of the raiders as they lumbered along prodding the lifted cattle before them. Lowering lances and bunching up, the warden's household servants closed in for the kill, cantering in eagerly as the gap closed. Before the ground was covered to the clash of arms, unexpectedly out of the surrounding scrub and moss, the riders of Liddesdale sprung their trap. Dacre relates later how an *"abushement"* was lying in wait, kin and friends of the raiders – consisting *"of the Elwaldes, Nyksons, Armistrangis, and Crosers, to the nombr of ccc personnes, as well on hors as foote."* From left and right, emerging from their hiding places Liddesdale would have its revenge and charged in on the now outnumbered trod. The Liddesdale riders were out to do as much damage as possible, with level lances and slashing rapiers, the trod was engulfed in a torrent of jabs and blows. Forty prisoners were taken, with an unknown number managing to extricate themselves from the melee and scamper for home. It would have come as a disappointment to the Armstrongs to discover that Dacre was not amongst the trod. Denied their vengeance on Dacre, the personal followers of Dacre's were looked for amongst the prisoners – with thirty being pointed out. The process at which this was achieved can only be guessed at. Did the Liddesdale men know these riders personally, or made threats or even torture, in order to obtain what they wanted to know? The prisoners must have been gripped with terror, as the outlaws sought their brand of suitable justice to apply. Eager to have their revenge on Dacre, and to act as a warning to prevent further constraints on Liddesdale and the Armstrongs – eleven of the prisoners were callously cut down in cold blood where they stood. Acts like this have to be remembered today when judging the reivers – to not view them through rose-tinted glasses, as bold horseman riding against a tyrannical government, but on occasions as just plain murderers. The remaining prisoners were led into Liddesdale, to be sold back at a later date for a suitable ransom. Dacre recorded the atrocity, stating:-

"And unbekest about my said servantis, and suche of the countrey as was with theim, and ther tooke XL personnes, whereof XXX of theim was of my housholde servantis. And after thay were taken and their swordes and wepins givin frome theim, and holdin, thay cruelly and shamfully murdered and slewe XI of my said householde servantis, and the residue tooke, like as your grace may percieve by a cedull herein inclosed who was slaine and who was taken."

Dacre was determined to bring the culprits to justice. He finished off his letter to Wolsey by saying:-

"Pleas it your grace also that seing this cruell murdour and shamfull slaughter is done upon my servantis in following of their laufull trodde, according to the article of the trux takin betwixt thes two realmes, the like therof haith not bene sene, it woll pleas your grace that I maye knowe the kingis highnes pleasour, and your gracis, howe I shall ordur me in this behalve, considring as I staund the kingis wardein, and maye nothing do to the violation or breche of the treux. The said slaughter is done unto me bicause that I woll neithr suffer the said Armistranges, Nyksons and Crosers to inhabit upon the Debatable grounde, or yet suffer theim or any Scottisman of evill name or fame to com to Carlisle market, or have any recurs within myne office of wardenry, according to your gracis instructions and commaundment to me gevin."

There surely would be a loud and very public fall-out on this outrage, and a demand for some form of redress. The *"fraudulent great bushement"* motivated King Henry to step in and endeavour to obtain redress for the complaints of Dacre and others. Commissioners from Scotland and England were appointed and came together on 8 November 1528 to think up a workable solution to the problem. On investigation it was discovered that with one or two exceptions, the problems were all committed by the same persons – riders from Liddesdale. The representatives of Scotland stated that they could not answer for the Armstrongs, hoping to deflect having any responsibility for the area. The Scots authorities were basically implying that they could not control Liddesdale. The English commissioners were not tolerating any excuses from the Scots, and played their ace card – denying Scotland the signing of a three year peace treaty which King James sorely desired. Liddesdale's raiding was then elevated to becoming a barrier to peace between the two Kingdoms. The English commissioners put forward their proposal, yes they would sign the treaty, but only if they were permitted to pursue the Armstrong raiders into Scotland without breaking the peace. The Scottish commissioners considered the request and found it reasonable. This was a solution to the problem, but the Scots could not give a full answer until the king was informed and the agreement was made official. The proposal was a humiliation for James as he had to openly admit that Liddesdale could not be controlled. Liddesdale was to be written into the new peace treaty otherwise England would never sign it.

Another meeting was held on 12 December 1528, were James had to give into his pride and accept the earlier proposal that was put forward. It was agreed that the King of England, in the case of the excesses of the Liddesdale freebooters not being duly redressed, could enter into Scotland and pursue their own justice. The English were at liberty to issue letters of reprisal to King James's subjects in Liddesdale who raided across the Border. They were also granted the power to invade the said inhabitants of Liddesdale, *"to their slaughter, burning, herships, reifing, despoiling, and destruction, and go to continue the same at his grace's pleasure."* Both sides got what they wanted and Liddesdale was effectively placed into a no man's land. England would be allowed to invade Liddesdale and burn and thieve at will, all legally approved by the Scots under the label of keeping the peace. It was open hunting season on the Liddesdale riders. The opinions of the Armstrongs were never asked for during the discussions, stoking the fires of alienation. The bond of loyalty between the Liddesdale folk to Scotland took yet another stretch, with King James failing to win them over as his illustrious father had once done. The Scottish government had lost their power to control Liddesdale, despite their promises to destroy the outlaws. The sabre rattling and punitive raids by the authorities caused an openly contemptuous attitude to develop back in response by the Armstrongs. The Liddesdale riders were soon causing mischief again, as the dust from the Dacre ambush was settling, but on this occasion the foray did not go how they had planned. On crossing into the English Middle March they ran into the very able Sir Ralph Fenwick, who was prepared with his troopers and struck a decisive blow against the raiders, repelling them back to their starting point.

The Armstrongs had the attitude that King James could not keep the peace in Scotland, which was not far away from the truth when regarding the Border. James had sold them out, and feeling abandoned the Armstrongs sensed the need to form a treaty of their own, and looked towards England for justice. The Armstrongs attempted a separate peace with the Earl of Northumberland, hoping to almost create a state within a state and have their own form of self rule. Northumberland wrote to Bryan Tuke, Treasurer of the Chamber on 20 December 1528 stating that the Armstrongs could muster three thousand horsemen. He proclaimed that the men of Gilnockie, Mangerton, and Whithaugh were the enemies of both the King of England and Scotland – described as traitors, fugitives and felons. The Armstrongs were engaging in power politics, playing one side against the other. Forever to be Armstrong's first and Scottish or even English a long way back in second. In an emergency the Armstrongs could cast aside their Scottish nationality and assume the red-cross to become temporary English subjects. Together with the Elliot-Croser-Nixon confederation, no other Scottish families collaborated so often, closely and eagerly with England. It can be suggested that the Armstrongs were driven to help England due to the attitude of the Scottish government; but to a greater extent, it was because it suited them. The Armstrongs at one time claimed to be independent of the laws of both countries. An interesting observation was made by Thomas Magnus in 1529. He heard that *"the Armestronges of Liddesdail reported presumptuously that they would not be ordered neither by the King of Scots, their sovereign Lord, nor by the King of England, but after such manner as their fathers have used before them."* This was an incredible boast, and one that would surely bring about a reaction from either the Scots or English monarch. It comes as no wonder that a year later, James was on the war path, determined to deliver a knockout blow and bring the family to heal.

Safe in their moorland fastness, the Armstrongs had little reason to listen to the views of their inland fellow subjects. Edinburgh was another world away, the word of the monarch was at best ignored, if it penetrated at all. The life at court was a different planet to that by the Liddel Water, the Armstrongs often looked north with derision at the will of kings. The harder monarchy tried to bring law upon the Armstrongs, the more they lost respect. At one stage the Armstrongs referred to King James V as the King of Fife and Lothian, implying that he held no sway within the Borders. They could not look upon James as their king. The Armstrongs always had problems respecting the power of the Crown. During the 16th century, it was only James IV who gained a working relationship with the clan. Other monarchs tried and tried, but ultimately failed.

The King strikes back

The process was two way, in the breaking down of trust between James and the Armstrongs. In August 1528 James broke free from the suppressive rule of Angus and the House of Douglas. For the first time in his reign, James could rule fully and independently. James laid much of the blame on the rise of the reivers onto Angus. Angus from his new home in England was accused by James of having maintained the thieves and broken men of the Scottish Border, allowing them to gain in riches and numbers as to be difficult to destroy. The numbers of robberies had increased, with great portions of the king's realm being laid waste. Further information came from Thomas Magnus, who reported from Berwick to James on 13 February 1529, stating that *"the Armestrongges of Liddersdaill had reapoorted presumptuously that thay woode not be ordoured, naither by the king of Scottes, thair soveraine lorde, nor by the king of Einglande, but after suche maner as thaire faders had used afore thayme."* He added that *"the said Armestrongges had avaunted thaymselves to be the destruction of twoe and fifty parisshe churches in Scotteland."* The information would have further lowered James's opinion of the Armstrongs, which was at rock bottom to start with. Here was proof of the Armstrongs utter contempt towards the authority of everyone, including Gods. Rightly or wrongly, James laid the blame upon Angus on the rise of the Armstrongs and other offenders, who he asserted had granted many remissions and pardons to, and bound *"them to doe unto hym service whenne he shulde call upon thaym."* The tension was building up for a stand off between the monarch and the Armstrongs. It could only go one way.

At the best of times, the Armstrongs had a thin veneer of loyalty to King James, and a variable shred of Scottish patriotism. This would all be successfully killed off over the next two years, when the monarch decided that enough was enough with the Armstrong elite. James began to flex his new found power, determined to proceed to the sharp and rigorous task of punishing all transgression upon the Border. James initiated his policy by calling together the Border lairds for a meeting, and sent his March Wardens to meet their English counterparts. Communication and understanding was the way forward, to establish new relationships on both sides of the frontier. In the summer of 1529 he travelled to the Borders and held courts, taking assurances in the process. Numerous lairds and "heidsmen" gave bonds for themselves and their followers, pledges for good behaviour which was hoped would end the raiding. The Armstrongs however still refused to submit to anyone, stubbornly accepting no one's authority but their own. The Border was observed as being unusually calm that year, even the Armstrongs were quiet. It appeared that James's non-violent policy and patience was paying off. The summer gave way to the autumn, and the reiving season, this would be the ultimate test to see if the Armstrongs had been reined in.

November came and the temptation was too much, food was needed and Liddesdale mustered; shaking loose the Border it was business as usual. One hundred riders ran a day foray against Birkshawes on 19 November 1529, causing the English March defences to spring into action with a reciprocal hot trod. Nicholas Ridley, acting under the Warden-General led the pursuit, and ran straight into another Armstrong ambush. If it is not broken then don't fix it, the Armstrongs repeated their earlier tactics which had brought success, and history repeated itself. Ridley had learned nothing from Dacre's debacle the previous year, perhaps lulled into a false sense of security thinking that the Armstrongs were less able to use force. On this occasion nineteen prisoners were taken, and led into Liddesdale. Four servants of the English warden were also taken, and cruelly murdered in cold blood, illustrating the dangers that could occur from taking part in a hot trod. News of the atrocity spread, with Henry Percy, 6th Earl of Northumberland reporting to King James that he had difficulty in keeping his people from seeking revenge.

This second ambush and its crop of murders as expected brought howls of outrage from England. Moving into winter, and perhaps prompted by this raid, James decided to change tact on the outlaws taking off the velvet glove, his patience finally stretched by a foray too far. James had been observing the misrule of his kingdom over the years as a youth, and now having grown into his full power, he would crack the royal whip. The king began his proactive plans on 20 March 1530, when he appointed his half brother James Stewart, 1st Earl of Moray (c.1500 – d.1544, illegitimate son of James IV) into the office of lieutenant over the three wardenries. On the same day Bothwell appeared before the king and council, recently released from prison for harbouring robbers, and on discussing the problem of the reivers, he took up the task to bring proper rule to Liddesdale. Moray took to his new job enthusiastically, but protested as Bothwell was now in charge of Liddesdale, that he would not be answerable for any crimes committed there.

Moray led the expedition which entered the Borders in early May (there is no evidence that King James was present), taking bonds and making summary executions. Moray was the power house behind the venture, acting with energy making the rounds of the worst offenders. He collected up Adam Scott of Tushielaw and William Cockburn of Henderland; arresting both Moray took them back to Edinburgh for a show trial, pleased with a job well done.

Cockburn in the presence of James, was tried and beheaded on 16 May, Scott followed the same fate two days later. The trials of Cockburn and Scott (and probably untold others), brought out the state of the Border to James, illustrating the level of lawlessness and the stubborn turbulence of its chiefs and inhabitants. It was clear that nothing short of the strongest coercive measures was likely to be of the least service towards restoring a better state of society among the Borderers. James decided a follow up action was necessary and began to put together a second progress into the Borders. On this occasion, James would take part in the expedition, deeming his presence as necessary for establishing tranquillity. He decided it was time for himself to pacify the country into his own hands, and put together a force which amounted to a small army of around 4-6,000. The king had little confidence in his nobles, having had a life time of dealing with the constant squabbling and jealousies from the lords and barons. James was tired and frustrated by the lack of success in bringing the reiver fraternities to heel, this should have been the job of his Border lords and they had so obviously failed in their task, to the shambolic ruin of the country. To ensure the smooth running of the expedition, James desired to remove were possible the obstacles in his path, which basically meant the imprisoning of many of his nobles. This drastic action illustrates both James's seriousness to tackle the problem, and the cause of the problem.

On the day after Cockburn's execution, James summoned some his Border nobles to Edinburgh Castle for a meeting. James reprimanded those present, criticising them for their failure to keep order, and added a further condemnation in the lords committing some of the outrages themselves, and protecting criminals. Much of James's disapproval was aimed at Patrick Hepburn, 3rd Earl of Bothwell, who had the difficult job of having responsibility for keeping the peace in Liddesdale. What followed next had little precedent within Border history, with James taking a radical move to shake his nobles into becoming a more effective force. With little ceremony Bothwell, Buccleuch, Ferniehirst, Johnstone, Robert Lord Maxwell, Mark Ker, and George Lord Hume, were called forward. They were abruptly detained, and in a disciplinary clean sweep to the calls for justice, were all led to prison and warded in Edinburgh Castle.

On 18 May a list of Roxburghshire and Berwickshire lairds was published, naming those who had to enter surety before the Justice to underlie the law for any crimes imputed to them. Another batch of nobles were taken and warded at Blackness and Dumbarton castles. On the day after, a similar procedure was undertaken for a list of Berwickshire lairds and barons. With this temporary purge complete, the Border clans were now leaderless and without the direction of their lords, making them easier meat for James's royal progress. With the Border barons in check, the king had another meeting on 19 May in which it was arranged that the true barons and lieges of James, should ride in accompaniment, and bring the strong arm of the law to quell the frontier.

James then led a second royal progress into the Borders, with hunting and entertainment along the way. The purpose of the mission was to bring forward the Riding families to give their bonds, with sureties under heavy penalties to "*keip gud reule within their respective boundis*." The fine details of the venture is not known, however one incident came to overtake the whole expedition. James knew his targets, with Liddesdale the end destination. Approaching Armstrong country, a memorable meeting occurred, which has gone down as probably the most famous incident in Border history, and has been captured numerous times in works of prose and ballad form. This of course was the meeting of Johnnie

Armstrong of Gilnockie and King James V in July 1530 (see page 268). The outcome was the hanging of the Armstrongs without a trial, and a tarnished Royal name. If the king could not be trusted, then what could be said about other government officials? The little scrap of loyalty that the Armstrongs had to the Crown evaporated, as word on the fate of Johnnie and his gallant followers spread. James would eventually come to regret his quick temper on that day, and the Armstrongs had their distrust of authority confirmed once again, and looked more towards self determination – reivers first and reivers all.

The removing of Gilnockie and several other Armstrong chiefs had a short term effect in blunting the raids, lacking leaders and shocking the remaining chiefs into a temporary paralysis. Life on the Border could be short and brutal, with the Armstrong elite being its latest victims. Violent and unexpected deaths were a part of reiver society, and would not have seriously set back the Armstrong's raiding. Reivers had been hung before and many would later follow, Johnnie had been unfortunate enough to have paid the ultimate price for his chosen career. His hanging may have been expected, but the method of his demise, in lacking a trial and being tricked by the monarch was not. New chiefs and headsmen were appointed to replace those executed, and the cycle of raids would soon continue.

In 1541 a new mischief broke loose, when an English Armstrong, named Anton led a gang which savaged Bewcastle, setting on fire the house of Jack Musgrave and several barns, slaughtering seven Fenwicks in the process who were unluckily enough to get in their way. The outrage induced great rage from King Henry, especially since Thomas Wharton had recently sent him assurances (based on his spy network) that the Borders were "*very qwyett*," and that James V "*intendithe no warre*" with England. The Border was in a very "*tickle*" state, with full scale war on the cards. Henry held all the motives to take military action against the Scots, with Wharton and other leading English Lords straining at the bit to give the Liddesdale riders a bloody nose and to avenge the massacre of the Fenwicks. The tinder for English action was the Scot's occupation of the Debateable Land, and the spark was Lord Maxwell, who had been reported by the spies of Wharton as having recently had a meeting with the leading Armstrongs, Crosers and Elliots. Trouble was afoot, and it was expected to be launched from the Debateable Land. What to do? It was thought the best type of action was a pre-emptive strike, rather than await the inevitable Liddesdale foray, and its crop of murders and kidnappings.

A fiendish plan was then hatched by Wharton; the Debateable Land would be targeted in which the Armstrongs living there were to have their homes burned and livestock driven off. The raid, though fine in its own right, was secondary to the main plan, used as the bait to trap the Liddesdale Armstrongs and their allies. It was hoped that seeing the plight of their kinsmen would tease out the Armstrong's from their secret glens and mosses, and then once lured into England, Wharton would spring a carefully laid ambush. This was the classic tactic of the reivers put into practice by their adversaries. As the idea was being discussed and fine tuned, King Henry's commissioners at Alnwick were plotting "*by whate meanes the Tynedale and Redesdale men might beste be inducede to enterprise the slaughter of some of the Liddesdale men.*" This second and independent attack on Liddesdale was hoped to stem the raiding, and at the same time prepare the way for invasion and international conflict. Pressure was placed on the English riding families to mount up, and go raiding into Liddesdale. Reivers were the best light cavalry in the country; governments would be hard pressed to find any better horsemen to tackle the outlaws. It made sense to use reivers to fight reivers. Some of the English families, such as the Charltons, Dodds, and Milburns refused to make forays into Liddesdale, and could not be persuaded even when money was made available. Over the decade, the Armstrongs and their confederates had built up a net work of friends, allies and safe houses across the English Border, and many English reivers were fully signed up as accomplices with the Armstrongs in their forays.

Before any English raid could be undertaken, Liddesdale shook loose the Border in an impressive demonstration of bravado and power. The Armstrongs aided by their usual bedfellows of cut throats, the Crosers and the Elliots, descended upon Haughton Castle (Humshaugh) on the North Tyne; and using scaling ladders, they successfully stormed the walls. Once inside, the garrison was mauled into submission, allowing the Scots to make a swift plunder on what they could lay their hands on and away to a safe exit. The Liddesdale men stole nine horses and £40 worth of plate. With this show of strength, the Armstrongs were demonstrating that they were more deadly than ever – a dangerous foe to try and attack. The riders of Redesdale and Tynedale were adamant that they would not tangle with Liddesdale, but West Teviotdale was another matter. The commissioners agreed with this new seemingly softer target and forays went forward in November 1541. The plan backfired, with a hard hitting retaliation launched, with the Kerrs raiding out along the Coquet Valley.

In the same period Archie Elliot of Thorlieshope led a Liddesdale gang on a foray to Halton, where they spoiled the property of William Carnaby. On the journey back home with their "*riven kye*," the gang made sure that they avoided pursuit by taking a route which would not be expected – following the "tops" along the watershed between Redesdale and Tynedale. The high ridges were the preferred route of the reiver, avoiding the obvious valleys which had guarded fords and chained bridges, and tracks that could easily be followed. As a double safeguard to being caught and having to answer for complaints, the raid was led by only the youngest riders from Liddesdale. If things went wrong, the Armstrongs could try and fob off the authorities by saying that the raid was done unofficially by some junior hot-heads, and was not the work of the senior chieftains. And by that excuse they hoped to avoid any repercussions and revenge warden's rode. To ensure this story would stick, the main Liddesdale "heidsmen" went into Hawick to establish alibis, doing their best to be seen going about town on the same night as the raid. If push came to shove, they could call upon the Hawick locals to vouch for their peaceable activities during the crime spree of their siblings. The Hawick plan was not required however, as the raiders returned safely and all was fine on the high moorland trails.

The Armstrongs did not get away Scot free however, as King Henry's commissioners at last began to make headway in their negotiations with the English riding families. The Fenwicks were at last persuaded to enact their revenge, and together with John Heron and "*the beste of Redesdale and Tyndale*," a reprisal raid was planned. The plan was devised around the burning of an old house belonging to Heron, which would serve the dual purpose of signalling the start of the English raid, and in giving it a reason for occurring. Heron and his riders would pretend that the house on fire had been spoiled by the Scots, providing the ideal excuse for the party to arm up and charge in a threatening manner into Liddesdale.

The plan was put into action, with Heron making all haste for Liddesdale, concerned that his force potentially contained English allies of the Scots, who could ride ahead and give the game away – resulting in an ambush on his troopers. Heron's plotting and speed paid off with a successful attack. Thirteen houses were destroyed, which included Archie Elliot's and a great herd of cattle was carried away.

Solway Moss

The scale of raiding increased in 1542, with Robert Bowes, the English East March Warden, when leading a reprisal raid against the Scots, numbering around 3,000 riders. Teviotdale was the target, where Heron again led the Redesdale and Tynedale horsemen, leaving behind a swathe of burning villages as they progressed across the country. King Henry was determined to have his war with Scotland, with an army being raised, and the Scots obliged by doing likewise. A clash occurred on 24 August at Haddon Rigg; an English defeat that added fuel to Henry's rage, which had been building up steadily against the Scots. On the same day as the battle, Henry's intentions to invade Scotland were announced by the Privy Council, and an army of 20,000 was mustered at York under Thomas Howard, the Duke of Norfolk (previously was the Earl of Surrey). Liddesdale held its breath to see which direction the mighty forces would march and fight. Armies marched with their stomachs and did not care what property they destroyed along the way. A country's crops and livestock were all a target of war, armies could easily torch a field or slaughter cattle, and a ravaged land reduced a population to beggarly destitution. It was such scorched earth policies during the Wars of Independence which gave birth to the reivers in the first place. And now 250 years on, the Borderers knew exactly how to live with a repeat threat. Norfolk led his forces into Scotland on 21 October; the war had properly begun.

The invaders burned and devastated towns and villages along the Teviot and Tweed, with the Scots shadowing at a safe distance. After seven days of ravaging the Border, Norfolk's army became low in provisions and went to Berwick to restock. With the pressure off, James put his energy into raising his own army, and planned a counter invasion; two could play at that game. James's army was impressive indeed, numbering around 15,000–18,000, under the command of Lord Maxwell, Warden of the West March. The Armstrongs were requested to muster their strength to follow on, but for obvious reasons snubbed the offer. Lord Maxwell was amongst the Scots and possibly encouraged the Armstrongs to change their view, but too much bad blood had been spilt by the Stewart dynasty to amend any loyalty. James cleverly fed false information to the English, giving the impression that he intended to take his forces into the East March, whilst all the time planning to go by the West March. The rouse worked, with the army avoiding Suffolk's forces – the king would have his revenge.

The Armstrongs shadowed the Scots army from a safe distance as they passed south through Langholm and Eskdale to the English Border. Marching armies were always a problem on the Border; they required to be fed and often just took what they wanted. Crops could be crushed, houses dismantled for fire wood and cattle slaughtered for beef – it made sense to keep an eye on what they were up to. The progress of the Scots was also observed by Sir Thomas Wharton, scouting at the head of 300 riders. Wharton had mustered by beacons 3,000 men hastily to protect the frontier, and valiantly prepared to halt the invasion.

The Scots crossed the Esk at Longtown on 24 November 1542 in the early morning, fording the river at Sandy Ford by Arthuret mill dam. All was going fine so far, but on touching English soil the dynamics of the army changed. Oliver Sinclair announced that he held the King's commission to command, demanding that he now held control of the army (James was not present, remaining behind at Lochmaben). The switch in power caused arguments and alienation amongst the officers, unsure on whose authority they had to obey. The consequent confusion could not have come at the worst possible time, as the Scots marched onto uneven and boggy ground to be confronted by Wharton's full army. In theory battle should never have commenced between Wharton and the Scots, as his force was vastly outnumbered six to one. Wharton should have withdrawn his forces back into Carlisle, prepared for a siege, and the raiding of the Scots baggage train if they bypassed the town. Wharton however was made of sterner stuff, an experienced and skilled leader he spotted a weakness in the Scots deployment, and felt confident at sending in an attack. From a column, the Scots had to deploy into a pike block, a manoeuvre which was tricky enough on a level field, but on the moss with its ditches and pools, was totally impossible. The battle when it broke out was one of the most unusual in British history, as the number of combatants fighting at any one time was so few compared to the armies overall size. The Scots could not put up much of a battle frontage, lacking cohesion due to a discord in who was in command. The reassuring calm of an officer who knew what they were doing was soundly lacking. The average soldier was floundering in the mud, unsure whether to march on or form up. The English occupied the area around Arthuret Howes, high ground from which they could survey their enemy and the problems they were having. The Scots now found themselves penned in, with their backs to the Esk and the Moss on all sides. Having a river in the rear was a tactical nightmare if things went wrong, and for the Scots this scenario was about to become true. The English would strike.

Wharton's army contained a unit of mounted "prickers," light horsemen armed with lances who were to all intents and purposes, English reivers. The prickers numbered around 7-800 and were under the command of William Musgrave, mounted on their small sturdy ponies, ideal transport for the broken terrain. True to their name, the prickers went into action jabbing and thrusting their lances into the flanks of the Scots. The attack was well timed, catching the Scots before they could form up properly. The Scots were also ill prepared from a command point of view, as Sinclair in his demands to be in control of the army, caused a breakdown in communication and obedience. Confusion over who held authority occurred, and with no head to supply a backbone, concern developed into worry, and this led to panic. The prickers were in their element; this was a situation in which they excelled at. Like a pack of hyenas taking on a poor wildebeest, the lancers made repeated charges into the unformed mass of Scots. Those in the centre of the Scots were blind to what was happening, with fear rising, and those at the back non-discretely turned around and headed back for the safety of the north side of the Esk. The melting away of the Scots army caused the panic to spread, and with the prickers pushing the Scots into a further confined bottleneck, a rout occurred. Reivers using reiver tactics were not only holding the frontier against a national army, but were pushing it back. This illustrates the effectiveness of the reivers in military combat, and the boast of the reivers as being the best light cavalry in Europe. Wharton would have been both surprised and proud as the battle began to go his way. Wharton commented later "*our prickers... gatt theym in a shake all the waye*," on observing the chaotic scene.

The Battle of Solway Moss did not last long, through skilful use of troops and topography, Wharton had pulled off a surprise victory. The battle was over rather quickly, with the reported casualties giving a clue to the flow of the fighting. One estimate puts those killed as twenty Scots and seven English. These figures sound incredibly low, but possibly several hundred Scots may have drowned in the marshes and river as they fled north. The toll of prisoners though gives a better indication on the defeat, with 1200 rounded up (including Lord Maxwell, who surrendered to Edward Aglionby) and ten field guns. The battle was more of a running chase once the moral of the Scots was broken.

The Armstrongs were passive observers to the pain and panic of the Scottish army, watching the events unfold from the north bank of the Esk. The Armstrongs were to add their own brand of insult to the proceedings. If the Scots had not been humiliated enough by their defeat, the Armstrongs were waiting to thieve from the Scottish soldiers as they scrambled up the river bank to safety. Here was a chance for not only profit, but to get revenge against King James V for the death of Johnnie Armstrong a dozen years before. The soldiers were surrendering to anyone in there masses with one rider taking up to five Scots captive at a time, even women took prisoners. The soldiers were often stripped of their clothes and allowed to go free in just their underwear. Boots, spurs, weapons, armour, horses, hats, and doublets – were all gleaned from the once proud army and the stripped soldiers sent packing north in a sorry state of disarray. The defeat can be considered the greatest military embarrassments for the Scots, and for the English as a great victory. When considering the Scots were beaten by only a third of the English army, it added to the scale of the English triumph.

James at his Lochmaben base heard with heavy news the crushing defeat, his plans for invasion was no more. James withdrew to Falkland Palace where a fever engulfed him. Feeling humiliated, and on hearing that his wife had just gave birth to a daughter and not the hoped for son and heir, he fell into a deep despair. Three weeks later on 14 December 1542, James V died, leaving the two week old Mary as queen.

Chapter 11. The Rough Wooing

With the infant Mary on the throne, Scotland had to endure another set of regents and divided weak governments, something which was music to the reivers ears. The Armstrongs would have happy hunting times again, and were elevated to a new scale by an unexpected source – King Henry VIII.

With James dead, Henry saw a way to obtain power over Scotland by using non violent means to marry his five year old son Edward, to the new born Queen Mary. And when Edward became king, Scotland would become ruled by England, an ideal solution to wars and invasions with the "auld enemy," and an expansion of territory. The Scots of course would never agree to such an arrangement and refused the offer. Henry then decided to use some force to entice the Scots into the betrothal agreement, and this plunged the Scottish Borders into a period named by historians as "The Rough Wooing," in which a swath of indiscriminate burning and slaughter was carried out, not seen on a scale since the days of Edward I.

Assured Scots

In the wake of the changing political scene, the Earl of Angus and his brother Sir George Douglas returned from exile in England, keen to regain their lost influence. Robert Maxwell, 5th Lord Maxwell came back also, released from English captivity, providing a command structure for the newly recruited assured Scots. Angus married the daughter of Maxwell in 1543 forming family bonds that was hoped would bring power and stability. Armed forces were picking their sides and lining up awaiting their orders. The Border of Scotland was about to enter yet another dark and chaotic period, and on this occasion many of those involved in the destruction was the Scots themselves.

Wharton began the process of forcing the Scots to agree to Henry's wishes almost as soon as James was laid to rest, by using the Scots to fight each other (signing them up as "assured Scots"). He would pay the Scots reivers to raid and burn targets he selected; why risk English lives when there were armed Scots around to do the same job? Using threats and bribes, Wharton persuaded the Armstrongs to make destructive forays against the Kerrs and the Scotts. The Kerrs and Scotts were strong and influential families in the Scots Middle March, and having their power reduced would be a bonus to the English. The Armstrongs jumped at the chance, as they were already at feud with the two families. Wharton was playing a careful Machiavellian game, selecting one family against the other were he saw disputes and discord already in progress. The Armstrongs saw the offer as manna from reiver heaven. They would actually be getting paid to reive, an amazing concept. The Armstrongs were not only to gain plunder from the raids, but also obtain payment afterwards from Henry's war chests. This was a win-win situation, and by helping the English, the Armstrongs themselves escaped the wrath of King Henry. The Armstrongs enemies would be reduced in power, and feuds ended to their advantage. The clan eagerly signed up to do Wharton's bidding.

At one typical signing on 6 September 1543, sixteen Liddesdale men came personally before Sir Thomas Wharton, deputy Warden of the West Marches, and took solemn oaths on *"their sons, kin, friends and clannes whose names are expressed in a schedule unto this present bond annexed,"* to henceforth serve the king and his officers of the Marches. The names signed were as follows...

Thomas Armstrang laird of Mayngerton	*Chr. Armstrang called Braide Crystell*
Paton Armstrang	*Archibald Armstrang*
Sym Armstrang called Reide Sym	*Ector Armstrang*
Renyan Armstrang	*Wyll Armstrang called Wyll of ye Gyngles,*
Davy Armstrang called Davy ye Lady	*Sym Armstrang Whyntyn son*
Yngrye Armstrang	*Joke Routlege*
Cristy Armstrang John son	*Arche Armstrang Hew son*
George Forster of Grenow	*Cristy Armstrang Whyntyn son*

In March 1543, the Armstrongs were amongst a party of Liddesdale riders who attacked Hexham, burning and slaying as they went and taking prisoners for ransom. On the journey home, the raiders were ambushed and lost around a dozen killed. Wharton was eager to put this destructive power to a more useful task. Wharton brought the Armstrongs and Crosers to *"spoil under Henry's wing"* in September of that year with further payments undertaken to sign up more assured Scots. Wharton now had these two families under his wing, acting like foreign mercenaries, who turned against their fellow Scots. In that same month 150 Armstrongs from Liddesdale plundered two villages belonging to the Scotts, lifting 250 livestock. In October of that year it was the turn of the Kerrs to be targeted by the Armstrongs, descending upon Ferniehirst to plunder corn, cattle and insight, slaying one of the laird's men who put up a brave defence. Other families were also hired by Wharton, with the Storeys taking part in their own foray, an unsuccessful fire raid on Selkirk, and a joint Elliot / Nixon raid on a village near Jedburgh. Wharton contributed to the mayhem also, with a foray on Bonjedworth. The Armstrongs rounded 1543 with another attack on the Scotts, burning two more villages and looting two towers belonging Buccleuch. The usual insight and prisoners were taken, the standard product of reiving; and for this service King Henry gave further rewards.

An illustration into the Armstrong's involvement during the "Rough Wooing" can be found in the British Museum. Within the Harleian Collection, a manuscript (No.1757) details a long list of damages done by the Scots under English assurance. It is worth quoting some extracts of the pillaging committed by the Armstrongs, to get an idea of the scale and frequency of the destruction...

1543

9 Sept – *"At Awtrick, a towne of the lordes Buckclugh, of his own goodes: 30 kene and oxen, 200 shepe, one horse."*

14 Sept – *"At Herihugh the lorde of Cliffurthes landez: 24 oxen and kene, 30 shepe, 2 prisoners, muche insight of howsolde stuff."*

15 Sept – *"At Hellmburn the yong larde of Crymstons landes: 11 oxen and kene, 6 horses and mares, all the insight in six houss there."*

16 Sept – *"The townes of Kirkhop with the gates of the towne there brent, ballioles and shaves: 40 nolte, 12 shepe, all the horses and insightz within the same townes."*

21 Sept – *"At Midsop and Firleston of the Scottes landes: 102 oxen and kene, 20 horss and mares 5 prisoners, all the insight in the sayde towne."*

6 Oct – *"The towne of Rowley with the... of Deynsyde brent: one prysoner, 12 horss and mares, naggis, 11 oxen and kene, all the insight there, one slayne, 30 prysoners."*

9 Oct – *"The townes of Ormiston and Orthatche brent: 30 oxen and kene 24 shepe, muche insight, sundrye hurte."*

31 Oct – *"The graunge of Farnehurst, all the houss of the onsettis with much corne and catell of the lorde of Farnehurst brent: one slayne."*

12 Nov – *"The towne of Borthickesheilz fyred and spoyled: 6 prisoners, 9 oxen and kene, 10 horss and naggis, all the insight, sundrye hurte."*

7 Nov – *"The towne of Alsop: 9 nolte, 200 shepe and gotes brent, 4 prisoners, 20 kene, one horss, much insight."*

11 Nov – *"Towre of Howpaslet spoyled belonging to the lorde of Howpaslet, and the keys of the gate brought to Mr. Wharton: 16 kene, all the stuff, 6 prysners, 4 hurte to deathe."*

21 Nov – *"The townes of Over and Nether Crisshopp with muche wheate brent: 4 horss, 11 oxen and kene, and muche insight."*

1544

5 Jan – *"The manour of Abniton belonging to the erle of Arreyn with all the come there brent. Two prysoners, one slayne."*

17 Feb – *"The towne of Laduppe, with fourtye nolte, brent belonging to the lord of Howpasley: four horses, with insight."*

20 Mar – *"The towne of Mynchame of the larde of Mynchames landis brent: One slayne and tenne hurte in peril of dathe, 10 prisoners, 14 horse and naggis, 11 oxen and kyen."*

21 Mar – *"The townes of Mykkel Kydston, Maislandis and Eshellis brent: 9 prysoniers with muche goodis."*

Wharton was fighting many little wars rather than one large knockout blow. This type of warfare was death by a thousand cuts, and was more intimidating to the population than a large marching army. The unseen raider in the night was being used for national aims, with Scots fighting Scots. More families would be signed up as assured Scots in 1544, with Wharton approaching the Middle March, increasing his campaign to destroy the power of the Kerrs, and in the East March to reduce the Humes.

The scale of destruction was increased in 1544 to an unprecedented scale when Henry ordered a full invasion under the command of Edward Seymour, Earl of Hertford. The "Rough Wooing" began proper when 10,000 soldiers landed at Granton on 4 May and marched on Edinburgh with orders to raze the Scots capital and to slaughter any who resisted, including women and children. 4,000 Borderers joined in with the English, many of whom were Armstrongs, attracted by the opportunity of plunder. Leith and Edinburgh were sacked, and then the army turned south burning Dunbar on its route to Berwick. At the same time along the Border, English reivers and assured Scots made their own raids adding to the destruction. The Armstrongs along with many other Scottish families sewed on the St. George cross onto their doublets, and joined in with the harrying of their fellow countrymen. The Armstrongs put family first, and during the "Rough Wooing", this was at its most blatant. By taking sides with Henry, the Armstrongs were not only making a profit, but also protecting themselves from the same destructive forces which they were supporting. It was a case of join in with the raiding, or become a victim of it. William, Lord Eure, the English East March Warden, led a force along the Tweed during the summer, carving a swath of scorched earth carnage, which left nothing standing. The hit list of ruin included 192 towns, towers, steadings, bastles and churches – plundering away 10,386 cattle, 12,492 sheep, 1296 horses, and an enormous amount of insight and corn. 816 prisoners were taken, and 403 Scots were slain, struck down forming a brave resistance when protecting their families. The Scottish Border was left a smoking wasteland, with the population left destitute and homeless. These figures were just for a five month period, illustrating the scale of devastation which was inflicted over the years.

The archives capture some of these raids in detail for 1544. An Archibald Armstrong acting under the command of Lord Wharton is recorded committing *"an onset"* upon Temple Hall on the *"water of Rowll"* (Rule Water). The building was burnt, lifting away *"xl [40] kene and oxen, lx [60] shepe and gotes, thre prysoniers."*

An undated document from 1544 lists the greater scale of the pillaging...
Townes onsettz, graunges and hamlettis spoyled and burnt... 124
Oxen and kene brought awaye... 3285
Horss and naggis brought awaye... 332

Shepe and gete brought awaye... 4710

Prysoners taken...   408

Menne slayne...   35

And how...

"Grete quantite of insight brought awaye, over and besydes a grete quantite of corne and insight, and a greate nombre of all sortes of catail burned in the townes and howss, and is not nombred in the lettres, and menye menne also hurt."

Lord Wharton himself describes in several letters, raids in which the Armstrongs took part in.

1. 10 July1544

"The Armestrongis of Ledisdaill ran two forays, the one to the lorde of Grestones place, the other to the lorde of Cardonyes place, and slew there two Scottis and brought awaye 12 prisoners, 100 nolte, 60 shepe, certayne horse and naggis, with much insight geare."

2. 17 July 1544

"The Armestrangis ran a forraye to the towne of Ladope of the larde of Howpaslettis landis called Scott, brent the towne and brought away 50 cattail, one horse, with much insight and 4 prysoners and burnt much wool in the sayd towne."

3. 1 October 1544

"One hundred of the Armstrangs of Lyddysdayll brent two townes in Dryvisdayll, in Scotland, called Over-hawhill and Nather-hawhill of the lard of Applegurthes lands, and brought away 6 prisoners, 30 nolt, 6 horses or naggs, 50 shepe, with all the insight in both the said townes."

4. 27 October 1544

"Certen of the Armestrangs of Lyddesdaill wan and spoylcd the tower of Langhope [Langholm], *brought away all the goods in the same, and 4 prisoners."*

5. 7 November 1544

"The Armestrongs of Lyddesdaill brent a place called Hall-roul, with a mylne and a town thereunto adjoyning, and ther slew a Scott, and, in ther return, burnt a town called the Wyndes [Weens]*, and brought away 80 shepe, 40 nolt, 12 horse and mares; 1 Scott slayn."*

Wharton wrote to Lord Shrewsbury on 14 February 1545, stating *"that he had placed a body of foot and a troop of fifty horse in Langholm Tower belonging to the Armstrongs."* This would have been in response to the earlier raid on the tower. By being a part of the process, Liddesdale avoided the scorched earth policy of Henry. The Armstrongs took a pragmatic approach to the problem, along with many other riding families, and it did not take much pushing to join in with the burnings and trashing of their neighbour's lands and properties.

Ancrum Moor

The English and their assured Scots did not have everything go their way however, when Archibald Douglas, 6th Earl of Angus in February 1545 decided to wage a campaign against those Scots who supported England. Sir Ralph Eure, Warden of the English Middle March on hearing this news led a force into Scotland on 25 February to counteract the threat against England's allies. Eure was accompanied by Sir Brian Laiton, Governor of Norham Castle, leading a force that numbered 1,500 English, 3,000 foreign mercenaries, and 700 assured Scots. Jedburgh was reached on the first day, and put on fire together with its abbey, setting the tone for what was about to be inflicted upon the rest of the Border. Eure learned that Angus was not far away at Melrose with just 300 riders. Eure saw an opportunity to take out Angus's force, and protect the assured Scots, and rode out that night to catch the Scots unaware. Angus was on the ball fortunately with piquets out, and had advanced warning of the danger. Before any attack could be made, he led his small army north across the Tweed and into the hills, and lived to fight another day.

When day break came, the English army resumed their mission of destruction, and plundered Melrose abbey and the immediate vicinity. The Armstrongs were probably involved in the plundering that happened, some of which was wanton vandalism. The abbey held the tomb's of several leading Douglas lords and the shrine of King Robert the Bruce's heart – all of which were smashed up. This desecration of graves and the Bruce's shrine would have hit Angus personally and enraged him to boiling point. He was deeply hurt on numerous levels and swore vengeance on all those responsible. It is hoped that the Armstrongs and the other assured Scots were not involved in this sacrilegious act, but as often was the case, the Scots could be their own worst enemies. The abbey held significant meaning to the Douglases. The chief Douglases wanted to be buried close to the Bruce's heart to link themselves to the "Good Sir James Douglas," who was trusted with taking the heart to Jerusalem in 1329. That same heart became added to the family's heraldry, and was a symbol of their loyalty to the Crown and their courage. The blow to the Douglas pride ran deep and personal. There was only the one positive respite in the destruction; the Bruce's heart was luckily spirited away by some keen minded monks, to be returned later into the Chapter House once the danger had gone.

Eure polished off his spate of ravaging by setting on fire Broomhouse Tower, and burned alive its occupants of an old lady and her family. The English, glutted with cruelty then headed back for Jedburgh along the Roman road of Dere Street on 27 February, laden down with plunder and cattle happy in their day's excursion. Unknown to Eure, Angus had been shadowing his exploits and was now reinforced by James Hamilton, 2nd Earl of Arran, Scott of Buccleuch, and 700 Fife cavalry; the English and their allies would soon have a fight on their hands.

The Scots timed their strike well, following from the north out of sight, observing the English as they crossed Ancrum Moor, 7km short of their destination of Jedburgh. The English were strung out in a marching column, ladened with plunder and not expecting any resistance. At this point the road narrowed at a *"Sandy causeway,"* which resulted in only two riders passing through at a time, causing a delay that enabled the Scots to approach unseen and deploy within striking distance. With the English bottlenecked at Lilliardsedge, the Scots instead of approaching on the same route, marched south-west and used the undulating landscape to conceal their numbers and to form up into an attacking block on the English flank. The Scots were outnumbered, having no more than 2,500, but planned to use the land to work for them and the element of surprise. On spotting the Scots, the English formed into two "battles" – a vanguard which led the attack under Laiton, comprising of 1,000 spearmen with a right wing of 500 hagbutters and a left of 500 archers. And a second main battle under Eure which had 1,000 spearmen in the centre, and wings of 1,000 hagbutters and 1,000 archers. The forthcoming clash is interesting from a military historian's perspective, noted as the earliest battle in Britain to see the arquebus (hagbut) play a major part. Cavalry played little part in the battle as the English combatants dismounted, probably as a precaution to avoid injuring the horses against the Scots pikes. The Scots meanwhile formed into a large pike block out of sight of the English behind a low hill, and a second unit advanced to the higher ground to set up their artillery.

The battle began in possibly two ways; either the Scots sent in a false attack by the lancers in order to lure the English into a counterattack and straight onto the awaiting pike block – or the English spotted the Scots artillery setting up and a mounted unit riding off, and mistakenly thought the Scots to be retreating. The end result for both theories was the same, the English advanced first and onto an enemy that they thought was inferior and pulling back. The English advanced in their two battle units one behind the other, confident that they would be the victors. The geography of the battlefield went against the English. The land they crossed to get at the Scots was marshy, and in their haste the English ranks became disordered. The curve of the landscape and a setting Sun concealed the main Scots army awaiting in full array, which came as a shock to the English. The Scots opened fire with canons, arquebus and long bows; sending a blinding smoke into the faces of the English, which obscured the horizon. With their vision distorted and a hail of shot taking out the front ranks, the English charge was blunted and came to a halt. The Scots advanced to contact with levelled pikes and close combat was engaged. On this outing of the pike all went according to plan; a far cry from Flodden without the pikes becoming bogged down and entangled. The Scot's ranks locked together and in a push-of-pike formation, halted the English advance. Laiton's vanguard was forced to give ground, a manoeuvre that caused worry in the approaching main battle of Eure. The battle could have gone any way at this point; however disorder in the English ranks caused the assured Scots to swap sides. English contemporary accounts placed most of the blame on their defeat upon the assured men, who are described as treacherous when they tore off the red St. George's cross from their tunics as identifying them as English soldiers, and turned against their former employers. The English effectively had to fight an opponent from both the front and the rear. An English report records that the turncoats *"distressed and took many of our men and horses,"* which added to the chaos of battle and removed the armies fighting capabilities. The Scots saw red, with a blood lust stemming from revenge for the destruction at Melrose Abbey. Some accounts mention local men and women who were the victims of the English raiding, picking up weapons and joining the fracas to pick off stragglers, calling out the rallying cry *"Remember Broomhouse!,"* referring to the Broomhouse outrage.

As the battle became desperate, the foreign mercenaries stopped fighting. They were here for plunder, not to lose their lives; they were not fighting for a nationalist cause and had no grudge against the Scots. The Scots on the other hand had every reason to be fired up and motivated to fight to the last. The English contingent quickly found themselves the only men fighting, and it was they who were now outnumbered. The English became surrounded, with many surrendering as the hopeless situation became known. Eure and Laiton could expect no quarter. Both were marked men and died fighting, knowing that they could only sell their lives as dearly as possible.

When the fighting grounded to a halt, it was difficult to disentangle who was who. Arran was shown the body of Eure and commented *"God have mercy on him, for he was a fell cruel man."* English dead were reported as between 500 and 800, with around 1,000 prisoners taken. Scottish losses are not known, but one source says that they were very light. The battle was a significant defeat for the English, was well earned and came at a time when the Scots needed good news. Nothing was changed though politically or militarily, the raiding and killing would go on for another few years. An impact of the battle though was the arrival of 3,500 French troops into Scotland, sent by the French king who was impressed by the turn in Scotland's fortunes. The Armstrongs and other assured Scots possibly came out of the scrape unharmed, reluctant to fight their fellow Scots and only taking on the English to capture prisoners. They robbed their old paymasters and then discretely slipped away.

After the death of King Henry VIII

Life on the Border quietened in 1546, raiding continued but on a much smaller scale that before. 1547 began with Arran mounting a mission into the Borders and took Langholm Tower from the English, a stronghold which the Armstrongs had given over two years earlier. The normal cross Border raiding by the Scots was starting again, prompting Wharton to send Sir Thomas Carleton north with a reminder on what benefits could be had for keeping loyal to Henry. Carleton never got to make his journey, as on 28 January, Henry died at Whitehall Palace at the age of 55.

If the Scots thought Henry's death would ease their suffering, they were mistaken. The Scots were fortunate though in that the new monarch, Edward VI, was only 9 year old, and not of an independent mind to inflict any new wrath onto Scotland. Wharton wanted to continue and extend English influence in Scotland, and contacted many of the Riding families which included the Armstrongs. The Laird of Mangerton was approached and was found to be ever willing to serve the King's Majesty; he noted also that the Armstrongs were continually causing great displeasures to the enemy. It was business as usual for the Armstrongs, and now with a chance to gain extra money for doing what they were already doing. The Armstrongs signed up to Wharton's deal and served him well. The Armstrongs attended a campaign with Wharton into the Scot's West March later that year, where Archibald Armstrong, the son of Mangerton, captured the Laird of Johnstone after he was flushed out of Lochwood Castle by a ruse and taken prisoner after an ambush and a running skirmish.

To give an extent at the effectiveness of Wharton's campaign to sign up the Riding families to do England's bidding; lists compiled at the time contain the names of around 5,000 Scots. From the lists it can be estimated that one in three of all reivers from the West March had taken a pledge of oath on loyalty to England at this period. The Armstrongs were probably the most eager of families to become assured Scots. One list of Liddesdale riders names 300 Armstrongs, 74 Elwoods (Elliots) and 32 Nixons – all bound to England. And another list mentions 619 Armstrongs, 80 Elliots and

60 Nixons. On 28 September 1547 Wharton had 1900 Scottish Borderers signed up; and by 5 October the number he could count on was 2400, and it had risen again by 12 October to 2700. Wharton found plenty of work for his new employees. From Wharton's view point the reivers were behaving themselves and not a threat to England, how they treated their fellow Scots was not of his concern.

The suffering on the Scottish Borders continued into 1549, even after the object of it all Mary, Queen of Scots, had been shipped off on 7 August 1548 to France, and was betrothed to another suitor. Changes though were on the horizon, with French influence altering the power balance. Wharton reported to the Duke of Somerset (Edward Seymour, Earl of Hertford) in June 1548 on the subject of French financial support to the Scots war efforts, and how it was going towards the assured Scots, tempting them away from the English pay-chest. Wharton stated *many of the greatest thieves have had at one time in their purses both of His Majesty's and of the French king's.* It is easy to imagine the Armstrongs taking money from both the French and English at the same time, and choosing on a daily basis which employer to obey based on their own private needs. The number of Scots forays into England began to increase, with Wharton observing *there are more riots and misdemeanours within these two months than in three or four years before.* The "Rough Wooing" was coming to an end, with geo-politics and will power changing England's policies towards Scotland. Peace returned to the two nations in 1551 – but the damage had been done.

Chapter 12. Alarums & Excursions

The Armstrongs and other assured Scots had made a good life out of the suffering; with a hardnosed brutal pragmatism, strength and selfishness brought in family safety and a tidy profit. The down point of the raids and invasions was that it brutalised society. How could the Borderers disarm and adjust to peace after witnessing years of carnage? The lesson was learned well by the Borderer; Wolves survived whilst the sheep went under and a new generation of reivers were born.

The 1550s was a happy hunting time for the reivers, with the wardens stretched beyond their coping point. The post of Wardenship of the Marches went through a period of rapid turnover, giving the Scottish Middle March great problems in keeping stability of rule. The Debateable Land was filling up again with broken men, all desperate cut throats living off ill-gotten gains. The sheer quantity of raids and other crimes went past the capability of the courts to process them. In 1556 for example, within one warden's March, there were at least a thousand bills of complaint that went undressed. The Armstrongs were always at least one step ahead of the authorities – when Patrick Hepburn, 3rd Earl of Bothwell and Sir James Douglas of Drumlanrig mounted an expedition into Liddesdale to clamp down on the Armstrongs, they were easily pounced upon and sent packing the way they had just come. Bothwell would die later that year in Dumfries, to be replaced by his son James, as the 4th Earl of Bothwell. The new Bothwell on the block got off to a harsh start, as the Keeper of Liddesdale he fell straight into conflict with the Border outlaws. In 1557 he was defeated twice by the Armstrongs, having little effective power over the country.

A Regent's Rage

Scotland again was plagued by having regents ruling due to an infant queen. Mary was safely in France, which put a question on law and authority over the nation. Would Mary ever return to Scotland? Mary of course would arrive back as the Queen of Scots on 19 August 1561, and on occasion she brought the Royal hand of justice into the Border. She made her own expeditions south, such as to Jedburgh in October 1566; and sent Bothwell into Liddesdale to round up the worst offenders. This venture almost turned tragic for both Bothwell and Mary, when he was stabbed by "Little Jock" Elliot of the Park, and she caught a dangerous fever. James Stewart, 1st Earl of Moray, her half brother, had better luck with the reivers when he became Regent of Scotland in 1569, and set about his own campaign to enforce the Royal peace.

The state of the Borders had become intolerable, Moray found the Scottish Marches, especially the West, difficult to control. It was noted that the Liddesdale riders were committing *"innumerabil slauchteris, fyre raisingis, herschipps and detestabil enormities,"* and the call came for severe repressive measures to counteract the outrages. A memorandum was sent to the Privy Council, which declared the thieves of Liddesdale, Annandale, Ewesdale and Eskdale as enemies of the Scottish Middle and East Marches. The Armstrongs were listed amongst thirteen other clans, named to ostracise the Riding families, together with their wives and children. The list was signed by Alexander 5th

Lord Home, Scott of Buccleuch, Kerr of Ferniehirst, Ker of Cessford and others. Moray sought direct means to enforce the same result, and planned to employ less subtle actions by bringing fire and steel into Liddesdale.

Moray led three expeditions in 1569. The first was in March and took the shape of a warden's rode in which he led 2000 horse and foot to Jedburgh aimed at Liddesdale. The group rested a day at Jedburgh and was met by Home, Buccleuch, Ferniehirst, Cessford and a number of gentlemen and their followers. Hearing of the threat to burn Liddesdale, some of the leading Liddesdale chiefs and headsmen tried to halt the destruction and met with the regent, trying to negotiate a different solution to the anticipated violence and loss. It was proposed by the reivers that they give assurances and pledges for their future good behaviour to Moray, and in return to have their offences pardoned. The negotiations fell through; Moray was not happy with the sureties on offer, and was not swayed from his original goal to spoil Liddesdale.

The rode journeyed on to the Swirehead on the Wheel Causeway (the old Roman Road), and was joined by Sir John Foster and Heron of Chipchase with 300 horsemen. At the Swirehead the lairds of Ferniehirst and Buccleuch were given the task of burning the Liddel valley; and taking a troop of horse and 200 of the regent's footmen, they set off on their task. The remainder of the force stayed behind to follow on later, taking care to guard the supply line. Travelling down both sides of the Liddel Water, Ferniehirst and Buccleuch proceeded "*to burn and destroy as much as in them lay*," accompanied by Moray who superintended much of the destruction himself. Several light skirmishes with the Armstrongs were encountered, resulting in 8-9 foot soldiers slain and thirty horsemen taken prisoner. Moray was close to the action, with skirmishes daily. With surprise it was remarked that "*the Regent should put himself in such danger for so small an enterprise*," and was lucky to have returned at all.

On reaching the Armstrong's chief residence at Mangerton, Moray resisted the urge to rush on and tear down the tower. This was not a change of heart from Moray, but a planned delay to allow the Armstrongs to think over what was happening to their land, and to organise their reaction. He spent a hopeful night sleeping in Mangerton Tower, expecting the next morning to have the clan waiting outside to offer him their submissions. When quite the opposite happened, no one showed up, it was taken as a warning of their defiance; Moray must have despaired. He ordered Mangerton to be blown up and headed back for Jedburgh, setting alight Whithaugh Tower en route for good measure.

Having used violence as a deterrent, Moray put the soft option on the table and returned to Teviotdale in his second attempt to sort out the problem of the Armstrongs and Liddesdale. On 5 May, together with Scott of Buccleuch and other gentlemen, they took pledges of assurance in Hawick. The visit must not have been thought a success, as it was repeated later that autumn. Moray had done everything to make the exercise pay-off, with the whole Border under his control, but there was one notable exception, Liddesdale. Moray was experienced enough to know the nature of Liddesdale and would need to keep hitting the same target again and again to get his will across. In October Moray descended into Liddesdale once more and put down the pen for the sword, spreading more terror and fear into the inhabitants. The threats of fire, rope and steel brought results, it was noted that "*there was sic obedience maid be the said thevis, to the said Regent as the lyk was never done to na king in na man's dayes befoir*." On this occasion all of the "*Sir names' of Liddesdale and otherwise*" came in and gave pledges for their good obedience, arriving in Hawick on 20 October 1569. Reading the signs, there was little alternative for the Armstrongs, Elliots, Crosiers and Nixons – Moray had run a brutal campaign and for the time being they would have to concede to his wishes. Hawick was filled with a multitude of outlaws and broken men on that day, as names were signed and agreements made on which family kinsmen were to be led away into captivity. Those being warded were technically not prisoners having committed no crimes, their future accommodation could vary from the luxury of a nobleman's house to a bare jail cell within a tower or tollbooth. Their future safety depended on their relatives behaving themselves. Time limits were agreed upon, on the number of days spent locked up, and perhaps with other kinsmen lined up to rotate the pledges. It was a great inconvenience to be a pledge, but if the stated time was shared by more than one family member, then the system could be more agreeable.

Moray returned to Edinburgh with sixty (another source gives one hundred) pledges / hostages, who would be later distributed across the country – Dundee, St. Andrews and other places. The Armstrongs were amongst those who gave their pledges, and for a while were forced to give up their evil ways and become loyal subjects of the regent. Prudence was the order of the day; the reivers had met their match in Moray, a man to fear. The tide was turning against the outlaws. The Scottish Privy Council also joined in and wrote up new legislation which included a law against the Scots Middle March raiders – caught three times and you would be hanged.

To the Armstrong's great relief, the reign of Moray was not to last long. On 23 January 1570, Moray had the unfortunate honour to be the world's first recorded assassination victim by a firearm. He was shot by James Hamilton of Bothwelhaugh, a supporter of Mary, Queen of Scots, when passing through Linlithgow. Word of the slaying of Moray reached the Borders on the same day that it occurred, giving rise to the theory that the murder was planned in advance and was well known about. News of his death brought a renewed hope to the Queen's party, who sought to place her back on the Scottish throne, which had the Armstrongs on board as members. The Armstrongs on hearing the news mustered their riders to meet up with Buccleuch, Ferniehirst and other clans. The combined force then crossed into England and spread devastation along the frontier with unusual ferocity. Moray was a popular figure and his loss was much lamented, however the Armstrongs had a different view. Whilst Scotland had no controlling hand, the opportunity was taken to seek revenge for their captive queen, plundering all as they rode.

Raid of the Redeswire

The Armstrongs were present at the Reidswire Fray on 7 July 1575. The clash is known as the last battle between the Scots and the English, but was more of a skirmish – an argument that went out of control during a Truce Day, rather than a fully pitched fight. Sir John Forster attended the warden's meeting on the Carter Bar, travelling up the Rede valley with his deputy Sir George Heron of Ford. They met up with their opposite Scots party under Sir John Carmichael (k.1600), the Keeper of Liddesdale, and proceeded to get down to the business of Border Law. There was perhaps bad blood between Forster and Carmichael before the meeting even started, an unfinished argument – there is no proof of this, but relations quickly plummeted.

The day began quietly enough with the first few bills being read out and disposed of without incident, until the case of a notorious English thief named Farnstein appeared. Farnstein is not a Border name, conjuring up the image of a German mercenary, but refers to the village of Falstone – and a reiver called Harry Robson. Forster was asked to produce the offender for trial, who could not be found. Carmichael mistrusted Forster, and believing that Robson was being protected by Forster, demanded the thief to be handed over. Forster made up an excuse to move the proceedings on, saying that Robson had taken "*leg-bail*" and that he promised to bring him along at the next warden's meeting. Carmichael took offence and dug his heals in, refusing to allow the next bill to precede. Truce Days were famous for drinking and quickening tempers. Forster was not accepting being told what to do by the likes of Carmichael, a mere deputy warden, and pulled rank on him which inflamed the situation further. Carmichael responded with his own insults, and Forster let fly with personal remarks that Carmichael was his social inferior. Tempers flared with others joining in. Cat-calling spread amongst both parties, as Forster shouted at the Scots red faced – to be returned by a swift rebuke. Matters spiralled out of hand, resulting in the men of Tynedale snapping, who loosed a flight of arrows into the Scots. Battle was joined, and a fracas engulfed the encampment in which neither warden was capable of stopping. The Scots received the worst end of the encounter, driven back in disarray. The Scots would have lost the battle, but for the well timed arrival of horsemen from Jedburgh, who were late for the meeting, and instantly rode into the affray as reinforcements for the Scots. Shouting their war cry – "Jethart's here," the new force charged in and was enough to tip the balance in the Scots favour and bring the battle to a swift conclusion. Several Englishmen were killed in the ensuing scuffle, including Sir George Heron. When calm returned, Forster found himself a prisoner, together with his son-in-law Lord Francis Russell and Cuthbert Collingwood. The outcome was a complete victory for the Scots – calm returned to the field. For good measure, the Scots rode down into Redesdale and reived three hundred cattle. With the word of law pulled down, why not take full advantage of it. There were enough reivers on the Carter Bar to pull off a spontaneous raid. The Armstrongs would have taken more than their own share in the plunder. The unexpected battle became embarrassing for the Scots, due to the haul of prisoners (captured for their ransom value); with the hasty excuse made up that they were only taken in order to protect them from being slain in the heat of battle – which does sound a plausible reason. Forster was treated courteously as a prisoner and was released quickly with the others, packed off home ladened with gifts as a compensation and apology for the inconvenience. Elizabeth I was furious at the skirmish and breakdown of relations, she was anxious to avoid war, as were the Scots. A commission of inquiry was convened to find out the reasons for the battle, with the finger of blame pointed at Forster.

Musgrave's problem at Bewcastle

Bewcastle was probably the most reived place in all of the Borderlands, lying in the path of numerous Riding families who regularly criss-crossed the Bewcastle Waste on their raids. The Armstrongs were very familiar with Bewcastle, arriving unannounced on its doorstep was a regular habit, having circumnavigated their friendly neighbours the Graham's land unreported. From Bewcastle, the Armstrongs could travel south east down the Roman road and into the Irthing Valley, with the target of Gilsland available for rich pickings. Standing in the Armstrongs way was Sir Simon Musgrave, the Constable of Bewcastle, who had the unenviable job of trying to keep order amongst the turbulent hills, aided by his son Christopher, the Captain of Bewcastle. Inevitably they clashed numerous times with the Armstrongs, and developed a blood feud with the family. The Musgraves did their best to keep the Armstrongs in check with their limited resources. Bewcastle had a full time garrison of forty troopers, but there was never enough money or manpower to give an effective policing on the frontier. Outlaws were captured and imprisoned, with many being subsequently executed, but the flow of raids never stopped. Simon wrote to Sir Francis Walsingham (Secretary of State to Queen Elizabeth) from Bewcastle on 25 January 1583 describing his situation and hoping to obtain more reinforcements – stating:-

"Sens my sunne Christofer Musgrave dydde delyver into the Quenes Majestes jayole the iiiith notabyll theffs of the Armstrongs of Lyddesdayl, of whom thre was executytt, all dying to theyre deservings, - thare frendes the Armstrongs of Scotland, with thare complyses, have nott seassyt to mayk greatt incurtyons within thys offes of Bewcastell, and have murtheryd manye of the Quenes Majestes subjectes and utterlye spoylyd the sayd offes, so as the pore men are redy to departe forthe off the contrie."

Musgrave had previously asked Henry, Lord Scrope for assistance, and contacted King James VI on the problem of the Armstrongs, but all to no effect. Simon finishes off his letter by saying *"Wherfore my humble suit to her Majesty is to grant me 50 horsemen for defence, and send a reply with convenient speed, for there are few nights without some murder or robbery."* Scrope backed up Simon's request to Walsingham by writing his own letter from Carlisle on 28 January 1583 reminding him of Christopher Musgrave's actions in bringing in four notable thieves, three of whom were executed – in the hope that he saw the Musgraves as courageous officers and demanding of more help. Scrope recommended *"that Sir Symon be allowed 50 horse for two months, and, as the country is broad and wyde, that 50 foot of the bands of Berwick be also sent to lie there during her Majesty's pleasure, for the better defence of the March."*

In June 1583 an interesting document was produced reporting on the defences along the Border which were designed to combat the reivers. Bewcastle was included and was described as *"her Majesties owne, which hathe bene, and should be, the chiefe and onlie defence of that borders; but that yt is now allmoste broughte to ruyn, by reason that the chiefest and ableste borderers and tenantes therof are herede and slaine by the Scottishe theeves of Liddesdale, and can skarselie now in anie good time be broughte to the former estate and savetie therof againe, as yt hathe bene chiefly by reason of the deadlie foode [feud] and greate hatrede betwen the Greimes and the Musgraves not longe since fallen, who without greate maintenance of her Majestie, can not saulflie serve there."*

The problems facing Simon Musgrave at Bewcastle are made clear in the document, made worse with an ongoing feud with the Grahams. The document echoes Simon's request for more soldiers, and that his needs were well known and seen as an important addition to the security of the Border. The document suggests that the only amendment and remedy for Bewcastle and the frontier's safety was to have some of Her Majesties soldiers from Berwick stationed at both Bewcastle and *"Cressope foote"* (Kershopefoot). To be able to keep fifty troopers *"well horste and well furnishede to serve on horse backe with horsemens pecies, calivers and pistolls, not onlie to helpe to kepe the said watches, but also to ride and follow with the contry speares of that Borders, yet partelie in saftie."* An additional company of *"shott and pikes on foote*" was recommended to follow after them as a safeguard "*if anie repulse or overmatche happen.*" To have sufficient men to guard the mosses, marshes and fords upon the waters of Leven (River Lyne), Esk, Liddel, and Cressope (Kershope) – and to serve unto, and on occasion rise to defend the country "*from the Armestronges of Tunnes also Pudingborne, the Whitofes, and Mangertons, and also the Ellwods that joyne with them, leave their owne habitacions, and reve and steale in their owne cuntries, even to Edenborowe portes.*"

Bewcastle was still noted in a defenceless condition in 1584 within a memorandum on the Borders. The reason given for this predicament was "*owing to the feuds of the Graymes and Musgraves lately happened.*" The situation had improved though with the requested extra soldiers arriving from Berwick, with 100 foot to "*lie at Cresoppe, and assist to keep down the Armstronges of Tinnes alias Puddyborne, the Whithaches and Mangertouns, and Elwoods.*" The increase in manpower was helpful, but is questionable if it was sufficient for Musgrave's needs.

Assurances, Lists & Reports

1583 was a big year for reports and lists. In July 1583 the Armstrongs were listed as being surnames present within the Scottish Middle March, and the English East and West Marches – contained within a document on "*The Names of the Marches.*" In the same month of 1583, Scrope commented on the March's principal offenders, naming the Laird of Mangerton and the Laird of Whithaugh, plus "*yonge Robert Elwoods brother*" for Liddesdale. Under "*A note of the loose men in the Midle Marches,*" Scrope records – "*Lidisdale, 1000 horsmen and footemen – The Crosiers, the Nixons, the Armestrongs, the Ellwoodes.*" The family were noted as being at feud that same year, but not who with. Thomas Musgrave compiled his list of the Border Riders also in this year. The problem with the outlaws was worse than ever, but at least the names of the worst offenders and where they lived was now known to all.

The Liddesdale riders were of a voracious nuisance during this period. Scrope on 12 June 1584, records a typical raid – "*Yesterday very early the Liddesdales came to a place called Hethersgill and spoiled an honest man of 40 head of nolt. My deputy Humfrey Musgrave with my household servants, Mr Leighe, and Captain Pickman with the soldiers, followed the fray unto Liddisdale, where the thieves made a great shouting and assembly of their neighbours, to force my people to leave their trodde. But it so fell out that some of the principal thieves are taken, whom I have in prison, and one is slain.*" Scrope despite the odds was managing to gain some successes against the outlaws.

An effective way to bring the reivers to heal was to demand pledges from the main troublesome families. The handing over of assurances regularly happened at Truce Days, one such event occurred at Hermitage Castle on 15 December 1584, taken by the "*honourable lord Sir John Forster knight lord warden of the Middle Marches of England, for his wardenry, and likewise in the West Wardenry under the Lord Scroope's office.*" The day was attended mainly by the Elliots of Redheugh, who brought along various lairds and tenants to sign bonds to pledge that they would keep the peace. Amongst the Elliot names, were several Armstrongs; Thomas and Hector of the Gingles, Archibald and George of Arkleton, and "*Ecktor Armestrange for himself and his bairns in like manner.*" Another meeting was held five days later at Whithaugh, and this time it was the turn of the Armstrongs to make their assurances to Forster. Lance

Armstrong, the Laird of Whithaugh, appeared who arguably can be considered the most troublesome of the Armstrongs at this period; otherwise other family graynes would have been approached also. Whithaugh gave assurances for himself, followed by:-

Eckkie [Hector] *Armestrange of Twedden*
Syms Thome Armestrange and Reade Androwe Armestrange of Kirkhill
The Larde Ryngie dwellinge in Debaitable lande and his brother the Lards Rowye
Jocke Armestrange of Monckbehirst
Pawtons Cristie Armestrange and his three brothers
Johne Armestrange of Tornewynholme and his brother and tenants
Armestrange of Thornewhattie and his brother's sons William and George
The 'Lairds Jock', and his tenants and servants

Stirling raid

In 1586 the Armstrongs became involved in national politics when they accompanied Francis Stewart, the 5th Earl of Bothwell, Lord Maxwell (Earl of Morton), Lord Home, Ker of Cessford, and Buccleuch to Stirling on 2 November to remove the Earl of Arran from the King's Councils. The Armstrongs (see William of Kinmont, page 290) took full advantage of this excursion, using it as an opportunity for reiving, making it their furthest raid north. The king required to bring those responsible for the looting to justice, writing on 16 November 1586 to give instructions to Archibald, 8th Earl of Angus to gather up the principle broken men of the West March and bring them to speak with their monarch. The meeting took place on 10 May 1587, where Bothwell and other nobles (including George Armstrong of Arkleton, Thomas Armstrong of the Gingles, Christie Armstrong of Barngleish, William Armstrong of Kinmont, and Christie of "Auchingaall") protested their innocence over the raid on Stirling Castle. The king wisely accepted their oaths and declared them to be his *"honest and true servants."*

Termed as honest and true servants by the monarch, in 1592 Liddesdale was described in a report on the Borderlands as follows:-

"Lyddesdale is the most offensive countrie against both the West and Middle Marches. It is governed by a keeper who lyeth att Armytage the cheif strength of Liddesdale. The Lord Bodwell hath most land theire. The strength of this countrie consisteth in two surnames of Armestranges and Elwoodes. Theis people ride most into Gilsland, Aston more, and Northumberland."

Dryfe Sands

The Armstrongs were usually friendly with the Maxwells, the most powerful family in the Scots West March. The Maxwell often held the post of the West March Warden, and owned a lot of land – some of which was leased to the

Armstrongs. They were a family that the Armstrongs had to keep in with for sure. The Maxwells had a long standing feud with the Johnstones, which held infamy in being the longest family vendetta in British history. The falling out became hereditary, the grudge passed down from generation to generation.

In 1593, the feud entered a particularly vicious stage, were the very survival of the Johnstone family was at stake. Lord Maxwell, Warden of the West Marches, armed with royal authority took the family vendetta up a notch, and invaded Annandale at the head of 2,000 men determined to deliver a knockout blow to Johnstone power. The threat galvanised the Johnstones, seeking to rally their supporters in an act of self defence. The Armstrongs came to the assistance of the Johnstones, together with Buccleuch, the Elliots, the Irvines, and the Grahams. Although inferior in number at around 6-800, the Johnstones would employ wit and the lie of the land, to bring about their own attack on the Maxwells. Using a concealed force, on 7 December 1593 the Johnstones lured a group of Maxwell's army into an ambush. The surprise and shock sent this unit backwards crashing into the main body of the army. Maxwell's forces became disorganised with panic setting in and a running skirmish then followed. The Battle of Dryfe Sands, as it became to be known was more of a chase than a stand-to slug out. Maxwell's men were routed back into Lockerbie, where many became cut off and surrendered. Many of the Maxwells received a souvenir of the defeat in the form of a "Lockerbie Lick" – a nasty diagonal sword slash across the face. The Armstrongs would have taken their own fair share in administering this wound from the backs of their nags. Maxwell meanwhile, was lying dead by the river bank, in full armour and missing one hand (another source says it was the head) – cut off as a trophy to be sent back to the Laird of Johnstone for a reward of £5.

Kinmont rescue

The Armstrongs have to be thanked for producing the Border's most enduring and heroic incident – the rescue of Kinmont Willie Armstrong from Carlisle Castle in 1596. The rescue brought out all that was good within reiver society – team work, loyalty, planning, tactics, and courage. Having the chance to take a hit back at authority was something close to the heart of all Armstrongs, and finding recruits to carry out the mission would have been easy. The rescue plan was originated by a Graham and nurtured by the Carletons, under the watchful eye of a Scott, but the Armstrongs were its backbone. On Sunday 13 April 1596, the Armstrongs probably led the rescue party from Langholm on its secret journey to Carlisle. Having allies in Graham country, they had a trouble free ride along the Esk, acting as scouts in advance of the main body of riders. Around eighty riders set off, with only a small select crew going forward to do the actual breaking into the castle. A group of the riders were held back to form an ambush party should the rescuers be pursued once the mission was completed. This task was no doubt filled by the Armstrongs, being experts at the ambush. The skills of the Armstrongs were not required that day, as the raid went in like clockwork, and all returned to great joy back to Langholm, with a new ballad to be compiled on the night's heroics.

Thomas, Lord Scrope, Warden of the English West March, was responsible for the captivity of Kinmont, and therefore took the escape personally to heart. Scrope had a suspicious nature, to the level of paranoia, and the raid set his mind into overdrive. In a mixture of rage and shame, Scrope paced the halls of Carlisle Castle looking for a scapegoat and persons to blame. Scrope though would not have long to wait; fallout from the raid was quick to form, when a traitor came forth and issued the names of the culprits. On the day after Kinmont's rescue, Scrope documented the names of the principal assailants at the raid. Before scribing the list, Scrope noted "*These names were taken by the informer at the mouthe of one that was in person at the enforcinge of this castell.*" The name of the informer was possibly Andrew Graham, William ("Riches Will") Graham, or Thomas Armstrong. All three would later give evidence on the raid, no doubt encouraged with money and immunity from prosecution. Amongst the names, the following Armstrongs were included:-

The Laird of Mangerton
The young Laird of Whithaugh and his son
Three of the Calfhills
Jocke, Bighames, and one Ally, a bastard
Sandy Armestronge son to Hebbye
Kinmontes Jocke
Francie, Geordy, and Sandye, all bretheren, the sons of Kinmont
Three bretheren of Tweda
Young John of the Hollace and one of his brethren
Christie of Barneglish
And Roby of the Langholm

Scrope had been humiliated by the attack on his castle and by hook or by crook, he would claw back his revenge. The horse had bolted the stable, but Scrope would pursue his cold trod independently, sending his troopers out on regular reprisal raids. The Armstrongs were often the target of Scrope's wrath, with warden rodes sent out designed as acts of vengeance rather than to address the escape of Kinmont. Scrope had illegally imprisoned Kinmont so was on shaky legal legs in seeking justice, but he took the stance that the breaking into one of Her Majesty's castles was a crime in itself, which justified his forays.

One of the many raids came close to causing a serious international outcry, when Captain Carvell took Scrope's anger a stage too far. Carvell was an experienced officer and under Scrope's authority led 2000 men into the Debateable Land with orders to burn and thieve from the local population. Carvell's soldiers efficiently set fire to all the houses that they came across and lifted 700 livestock; and on a roll they took the raid into Liddesdale with an intention to repeat the process. With an advantage in numbers, Carvell could inflict any amount of damage that he chose with impunity. Twenty four buildings were burned down and over 3,000 beasts were rounded up. To add humiliation into the package and reinforce upon the Armstrongs never to mess with Lord Scrope again, sixty prisoners were taken and marched back into England. A successful warden's rode, well done and dusted – however the undertaking led to complaints over its methods. It was alleged by the Scots that the prisoners were stripped naked and tied in pairs, and led on leashes, many of them women and children, into England. It was claimed that many of the children died of exposure on the journey back to Carlisle; complaints were duly issued on this outrageous behaviour. The Scots may have been exaggerating the offences, but for a peace-time incident, Scrope would have a lot of sharp-witted explaining to do. Scrope began by stating "*I could not restrain her majesty's subjects from taking what amends they could get.*" This was an attempt to wash his hands of any blame and cleverly avoided the obvious point on why he failed in the task of restraining his soldiers. Scrope was ultimately to blame, as Carvell was following his orders. Scrope was charged for his part in causing harm to the civilians when they were stripped and left "*exposit to the injurie of wind and weather,*" and the resulting deaths of nine or ten infants.

Scrope in his defence declared that the fore-mentioned 2000 raiders in Carvell's party, numbered in reality only one hundred. Adding that the raid took place in the summer heat, removing the accusation of children dying of exposure. Scrope was trying to undermine the Scottish claims against him, to reveal them as lies and exaggerations. Scrope had help on his side, as those investigating the case were English commissioners, not Scots. The commissioners used an ancient March custom which required a warden to assist their opposite number when pursuing thieves. By default, Scrope was simply helping the Scottish officials when he sent Carvell into Liddesdale, aiding the Keeper of Liddesdale (Buccleuch) to keep the peace. Scrope added that his raid had expressly been ordered by the queen, and that Buccleuch far from being a keeper of the peace, was in fact responsible for much of the damage done in England, and was in league with all of the worst outlaws in his area. Scrope was implying, harsh though his methods may seem, he was only giving back to Liddesdale and the Armstrongs what they had done to him. He had no other means of achieving redress against such a cunning character as Buccleuch, other than to use warden rodes and a force of arms. Scrope was as slippery as Buccleuch and avoided the charges laid against him. He did not get off Scot free however; James VI was on his case, issuing a gentle warning. Another more severe rebuke came from Sir Robert Cecil, "*Your lordship should not too suddenly use that kind of force... that course would be kept for the last extremity.*" An eye had to be kept on the future; with an aging Queen Elizabeth it would be wise to keep sweet towards James and a new united kingdom.

The Carleton brothers

The Armstrongs had mixed relationships with the Carleton brothers, Lancelot and Thomas, who played major parts in the rescue of Kinmont Willie. The brothers formed one of the most corrupt double acts on the Border and belonged to a well established and influential family in Cumberland. Thomas was the Land Sergeant of the Barony of Gilsland and Constable of Carlisle Castle, and Lancelot was the Bailiff of Brampton – important offices which the brothers used to line their own pockets. Thomas in his line of duty came into contact with the Armstrongs on a regular basis. On one occasion he came across a gang of sixteen Armstrongs who were driving a herd of stolen cattle before them. Thomas was never a person to back down from a challenge, a man of courage and conviction. With only four followers, Thomas decided to attack and charged the gang – killing one and capturing two.

At some point the Carleton brothers befriended the Liddesdale Armstrongs; the bond was based on live and let live and financial gain. Thomas agreed to turn a blind eye to the raiding of the Armstrongs into the Barony of Gilsland, and in return he received a cut of the plunder. The arrangement seems difficult to believe, as Thomas was responsible for the safety of Gilsland; it would have been impossible for him to look his tenants in the eye. Thomas's intrigues were known to Scrope, he was accused of being an accomplice to the Liddesdale raids into Gilsland. He was not directly involved personally in the forays, but at the same time he did nothing to stop them. During this period, the Armstrongs were involved in a one sided feud with the Bells who lived in Gilsland, a family who became their favourite targets, to be hit again and again. Scrope wrote on 25 July 1597 to Burghley to report a raid *"upon Wednesday last"* which was committed by six hundred riders from Liddesdale, *"the chief frinds of Tho Carleton in Scotland."* The raiders were a mixture of Armstrongs and Elliots, friends and associates of the Carletons and Graham of Brackenhill. The Scots were guided to their target in England by Carleton's people – Will Tailler (known as Thomas Carleton's man), Gayfry Carleton and *"yong Heardhill."* The party *"ran a day foray on the Bells in Gilsland, taking 200 oxen and kye, 40 horses and nagges and a number of English prisoners."* Scrope mounted a hot trod in defence of the Gilsland Bells, which went cold. As an afterthought and to help out the Bells, the herds of Kinmont Willie were sought and taken, as compensation to be given to the Bells. The Bells would have been happy with Scrope's efforts, unfortunately on the return journey a gang of Grahams turned up and lifted the lot.

Two days later a repeat raid was made into Gilsland. Scrope wrote on 26 July 1597 to Cecil to report – *"The Scots made a great incursion on Friday last in Gilsland, taking 14 score cattle and nags and many prisoners."* Scrope ordered a reprisal raid into Liddesdale in an attempt to halt the forays against the Bells, as the raids were becoming a regular feature and throwing the Bells into destitution. Scrope planned a warden's rode and summoned the men of Greystoke to take part. The rode failed to materialise when during the night a visit was made by Gerrard Carleton (son of Thomas), John Grame alias "Allreames" (uncle to Will's Jock Grame), and a son of Will's Jocke called "Jocks Wattey" (servant to Lancelot Carleton). Intimidating threats were made, which put such fear into the troopers, that they abandoned their orders.

Scrope was concerned at the *"disorders, &c., daily increasing, the poor people forced to leave the country for want of redress from Buccleuch."* He requested from Burghley that forty horse troopers be sent from the Queen's garrison in Berwick to Gilsland, *"to imbolden the people to remain on their farmholds."* The sight of armed Border officials Scrope thought, would give the Bells hope that the Queen's justice prevailed, and that they would be safe to continue farming the land. Scrope's temper was at boiling point over Thomas Carleton's behaviour and wrote complaints and reports to the Privy Council. Lancelot stepped in to help his brother by stating the Bells, Elliots and Armstrongs had formed an alliance to kill Thomas, adding that recently a hundred Liddesdale riders had attempted to slay Thomas – a highly unlikely scenario.

The Bells were obviously concerned for their safety and with Scrope temporarily hobbled, Thomas and James Bell wrote to the Privy Council on 18 November 1597, to complain on behalf of their kinsmen about the *"great spoils by the Scots"* upon Gilsland. They reported eighty of their name *"utterlye beggerd and spoiled"* and another sixty taken prisoner; and blamed Thomas Carleton for their situation, whose *"hatred and malice towards them"* had directed the Scots down to fall upon them. The many incursions made by the Armstrongs was also said to have been the Carleton's responsibility, who accompanied *"after their brutish manner, a deadly feed."* The Bells of Gilsland (numbering 500) feared they would be driven to extinction *"unless some help is shortly provided."* The desperation of their plight is clear

– *"they pray for Godes cause to have some help."* Otherwise without help, the Bells of Gilsland would be *"cleane rooted out from those partes."* Thomas Carleton, as Machiavellian as ever, fobbed off the accusations as exaggerations, stating – *"it is untrue that there were 80 Bells beggard, &c., for there were never so many of the name in the country."* How could there be eighty Bells in poverty when Gilsland did not even contain eighty Bells? Thomas Carleton probably held back from helping the Armstrongs for a while, until the heat blew over. Thomas though would not survive much longer. To the relief of the Bells, he was shot through the head on 4 July 1598, when pursuing a party of Ogle raiders who had recently made a revenge assassination on David Elliot, known as the "Carlyne," for murdering one of their own family members.

Chapter 13. Decline & Fall

Moving into a new century, the signs were ominous for the future of the Armstrongs. There were seven branches to the Armstrong tree – in 1600 the roots were shaken, to be followed in the next year by the loss of the first branch (see Ninian of Auchinbedrig, page 324). Over the next decade three branches were to have a similar fate.

A major breakthrough in curbing the Border Riders came on 18 April 1601, when a document was issued which allowed Lord Scrope and Carey the authority to enter Scotland legally and deal with the Liddesdale outlaws themselves. The jurisdiction came from King James, who was displeased at Buccleuch's lack of progress at dealing with the outlaws. James wanted the Scottish reivers brought to heal and was getting nowhere, so outsourced the solution to England. Scrope and Carey were only too happy to help out, not only would they be helping to stop the raids into England, but also become known to King James as trust worthy subjects, a favourable occupation since he would soon be king of a joint united kingdom.

Carey watched with interest as the new policy of James went into operation for the first time in May of that year. His deputy Henry Woodrington had chased a Scots raiding party back to its base of Calfhill in May of that year and accomplished a great success. This gave Carey the idea to mount his own venture, which would be on a scale never attempted before and be focused solely on the Armstrongs. The Armstrongs had an excellent system to warn of danger approaching, as mentioned earlier, with a swift escape route out of Liddesdale and into the safety of the Tarras Valley until the heat was off. Carey though had a plan in mind which would counteract all of the Armstrong's cunning and set off in June of 1601 to cut off the raids at their source.

Carey was aiming for a knock-out blow on the Armstrongs, to sort them out once and for all and had the blessing of King James VI. Carey's force looked conventional as it approached Liddesdale, with 150 horse and some regular infantry. The Armstrongs received plenty of advanced warning of Carey, with the valley's inhabitants melting away into the Tarras wilderness and other side valleys as expected, until the threat moved on. This raid was different however, as the troopers did not move on. Carey was here for the long haul and downed tools pitching camp at the entrance to the Tarras Valley. Carey records in his memoirs how he established "*a pretty fort, and within it we all had cabines to lie in*" – and here he would remain until he had rounded up the Armstrongs. Provisions were brought to the make-shift fort, and further reinforcements as the garrison prepared for the autumn and the start of the Riding season.

The main lairds and headsmen of the Armstrongs, together with their valuables and followers, hid amongst the scrub trees and dense undergrowth playing the waiting game. The scene can be imagined; the Armstrongs watching Carey with bemusement as he constructed his fort, hearing the hammering of nails and sawing of wood echo through the valley. The Armstrongs were filled with a stubborn arrogance and could not sit quietly whilst this symbol of officialdom was on their very doorstep. It was against the principles of the Armstrongs to do nothing. Forced out of their homes, the Armstrongs were determined to put on a brave face and gain the upper hand in a psychological war, hoping to end Carey's campaign against them. Carey was contacted by the Armstrongs, by an individual who stealthily approached the fort and threw a letter over the palisade. Carey describes the communication – *"They sent me word that I was like the first puff of a haggis, hottest at the first, and bade me stay there as long as weather would give me leave, they would stay in Tarras-wood 'till I was weary of lying in the waste, and when I had had my time, and they no whit the worse, they would play their parts, which should keep me waking the next winter."* Carey's garrison believed that the Tarras was impregnable, doubting that their venture would be a success, and that winkling the Armstrongs out of the moss was impossible. Carey though did not share this pessimism, secure in his own belief for success and was determined to prove his troopers wrong.

Carey quietly made his preparations to net the Armstrongs on the night of 4 July, when he sent out in secret 150 troopers *"conveighed by a moffled man not known to any of the company."* The trooper's guide may have been a deserter from the Armstrongs, someone eager to cause the family harm – perhaps from a rival family or eager to settle a feud. No doubt money was exchanged, and the individual was more than anxious to keep his identity hidden. The Armstrongs only had their scouts on the hills to the south, overlooking Carey's fort and once the troopers had gained some distance north, they progressed unobserved. Carey's men encircled the Tarras Moss, with their guide pointing out the three main exits from the moss. The plan was to guard all of the exits and then to flush out the valley, catching what was evicted from the haul. A company of troopers was left behind at each exit as they circumnavigated the moss, blocking all three in the darkness with ambushes which were soon to be sprung.

The trap was set without being noticed. Carey with a great hope and sense of intrepidation mustered his garrison quietly and led them out at 4am in the maximum wee small hours to ensure the surprise was complete. His force contained 1000 infantry and 300 horse, acting like the beaters of a gamekeeper; they strived through the heather and bogs flushing the reivers out of their cover – or so they thought. Carey describes the scene – *"Our men brake down as fast as they could into the wood. The outlaws thought themselves safe, assuringe themselves at any time to escape, but they were so strongly set upon on the English side as they were forced to leave their goodes, and to betake themselves to their passages towards Scotland."*

The hiding Armstrongs fled the valley in an *"unrulye rout"* and straight into the ambushes. The traps were sprung and prisoners taken. The leaders of the Armstrongs were targeted, which allowed many of the clansmen and their families to escape back into the moss where *"our men durst not follow them, for fear of losing themselves."* There were no casualties recorded during the operation, which implies the Armstrongs put up limited resistance to being captured. The ambushes appear to have been well executed, with the Armstrongs emerging piecemeal into the traps, removing the danger of an organised counter attack.

With his net of notable Armstrongs, which included two sons of the Whithaugh chieftain, he was able to negotiate the release of some English prisoners and the submission of the remaining outlaws, who handed themselves in the next day. Assurances were taken for good behaviour and all of the prisoners were released. The mission had a limited goal and was carried out with precision. Carey had every right to be happy and with self congratulations felt confident that his

March was now *"freed from the hurt of Liddesdale."* The future looked bright on the Border, with this new power to go in after the reivers. Carey stated that he *"was never after troubled with this kind of people"* again; his venture into the Tarras Moss was a rare tactical success against the Armstrongs.

The end for the Border reivers was on the horizon and came on 24 March 1603 when Queen Elizabeth I passed away. Her death was immediately followed by the last great "hurrah" for the reivers – "Ill Week," in which every self respecting reiver would have dropped what they were doing, to take part in one last great raid before a united kingdom clamped down on such activities. The Armstrongs were probably the most active family during the week of thieving, netting the largest haul in the process. Once back safely in Liddesdale, the clan wondered and worried what the fallout would be. The country was entering a new era, and the reivers were certainly not a part of it. The newly crowned King James I of Great Britain would not tolerate the outlaws. The old way of life had been swept away overnight. The Armstrongs would have to change immediately; to put down the lance and pick up the plough – to become farmers, tradesmen and shop keepers. To resist would be a choice between the gallows or exile.

The pacification of the reivers took about seven years, with the first four breaking the back of the Riding society. The purging process began immediately in 1603; when thirty two reivers (a mixed batch of Armstrongs, Elliots, Batys and Johnstones) were hung, 15 banished and 140 outlawed. This was only the beginning, with Carlisle, Dumfries and Jedburgh seeing similar scenes over the next few years. In 1605 one group of reivers had a narrow escape from the gallows, when 29 out of 33 Armstrongs and Grahams, condemned prisoners in Carlisle Castle managed to break out.

In 1605 a Border Commission was set up consisting of five English and five Scots, based in Carlisle and appointed to enforce discipline. Under Henry Leigh on the English side and Sir William Cranston on the Scottish, patrols went out to make arrests. Old charges were brought out and arrests made. This was the time of *"Jethart Justice,"* when reivers were hanged first, and then questions were asked afterwards. By 1606 the number of declared outlaws was put at 300, with many of them Armstrongs. The number of fugitives had shrunk to sixty by 1611, as the last of the outlaws were finally brought under control.

In 1609 voluntary option of settlement in Ulster was made available to the Armstrongs. King James was keen to reinforce the Protestant population of the plantations, and what better supply could there be than the reivers. The Armstrongs also had the alternative choice to become foreign mercenaries and travel to the Low Countries where the Eighty Years War was in progress – helping the Dutch against an aggressive Spain. The Bold Buccleuch took a force of two hundred ex-reivers in 1604 across to the continent to become respected soldiers, and the Armstrongs must have decorated their ranks. Those who defied the exile and returned, often came back to find their lands gone, given to the Scotts and the Elliots.

It comes as no surprise to find the Armstrongs amongst the last of the reivers. The last recorded foray was in 1611 when a gang of Armstrongs and Elliots raided the Robsons of Leaplish in North Tyne. The raid was violent in its undertaking, reflecting the desperate times – *"Elizabeth Yearowe was shott with twoe bullettes through both her thighs, the right thighe broken asunder with the shott, and slaine. Mane Robson, wife to James Robson, called Blackhead is shott with five haileshott in her breastes*", and "*Elizabeth Robson … being great with childe, is hurte verie sore in the head with the stroke of a peece.*"

The Armstrongs had their chieftain executed in 1610, and with no new chief stepping forward, the family became a headless clan. The Armstrongs were now tamed, but old instincts would come out of the woodwork within a couple of generations when civil wars (1639-51) blighted the country; and the moss-troopers were born. The term is often wrongly applied to the reivers; the earliest recorded use of the term comes from the Scots Privy Council in the 1640s. The wars opened a niche in civil disorder which the Armstrongs were quick to exploit. The moss-trooper, also known as "Mossers," started life as highway robbers and progressed to thieving cattle – reaching at their high point, fighting as a unit two hundred strong at the Battle of Inverkeithing in 1651. The mossers came into their own during the English invasion of Scotland in 1650, when bands of irregular horsemen formed along the east coast of Scotland, and pricked at the flanks of Oliver Cromwell's army, destroying supply lines, killing messengers and slaughtering any stragglers lagging behind. One of the most famous moss-troopers was a German mercenary called Captain Augustine Hoffman, whose depredations upon Cromwell led him to view the mossers as common criminals. Cromwell, in despair wrote to the Scot's commander, General Leslie, wanting justice, complaining on the mosser's "*barbarous murders and inhuman acts.*"

Gazetteer

Liddesdale

1. Mains

Mains was a village on the west bank of the Liddel Water, 1km NE of Castleton. It is not known if the Mains had a tower, but must have had several bastle houses within the community.

✳✳✳

Thomas of the Mains – (c.1590)

Ingram of the Mains / Castleton – (c.1590)

Thomas and Ingram both lived in the same village of Mains. Ingram is also recorded as coming from Castleton, on the opposite bank of the Liddel. Castleton takes its name from Liddel Castle, a motte and bailey built by Ranulph de Soules on land granted to him by David I (ruled Scotland 1124-53). Only its impressive earthworks remain today.

Thomas and Ingram both appeared at the Bells Kirk (location for Truce Days – near Deadwater and source of the River North Tyne) on 13 April 1590 to answer for two charges put up against them for raids committed in 1589. William Fenwick the deputy Middle March Warden of England and Thomas Trotter the deputy Keeper of Liddesdale were redressing the bills on both sides.

1. *"The said John Heron and Richard Crawforde his man complain upon said 'Whyntins Arche'* [Archibald Croser], *'Adams John,' Ingram Armestrong and Thomas Armstrong of Maynes, for stealing 16 kye and oxen, insight to 13L. 'Englishe,' about Candlemas last."*

2. *"The said John Heron complains upon... 'Whyntin's Arche,' said Ingram and Thomas Armstrong of the Maynes, for stealing a black gelding to the vellowe of 20L. sterling, about Martinmas last."*

Ingram is contained within a third bill by himself in that same year on 16 March, having a complaint made upon him by John Heron of Chipchase and Agnes Heron late wife to Cuthbert Heron. Ingram was again accompanied by Archibald Croser (*"Whyntynes Arche"*), plus *"Renyon Armestronge of Twedon."* They were accused of *"stealing 7 score of yowes and wetheris, and 3 score of hoggis."*

✳✳✳

Simon (Sim) of the Mains – (ex.1598)

Sim is mentioned within John Monipennie's (Moneypenny) list of the Border clans from 1597. Under Liddesdale, the grayne of Whithaugh is listed as containing the Laird of Whithaugh, Johnnie of Whithaugh and *"Sym of the Maynes."* Sim must have been an important character amongst Armstrong society to have been named alongside such illustrious characters as the Whithaughs.

Most of what we know about the life of Sim comes from the ballad *"Hobbie Noble,"* a work of literature which would be thought invalid to extract factual data from. Ballads though can be useful to the historian, when treated cautiously they possibly contain elements of fact concealed within them and the barebones of real events. Robert "Hobbie" Noble was a real character who lived at the Crew, 3.2km north of Bewcastle. He was an active English reiver who often aided the Scots in their raids against his own countrymen. Eventually the activities of Noble became a great concern, with the tenants of Bewcastle feeling both angry and betrayed. Hobbie became a wanted man and feared for his life. Hobbie had many friends in Liddesdale, and decided to up-sticks and become a permanent member of an Armstrong gang. The ballad states that Hobbie was banished to Liddesdale, which suggests he was put to the horn and declared an outlaw, becoming a "broken man." Hobbie was a great asset to the Armstrongs, with his expert knowledge of the landscape and ability to lead forays through the Cumbrian wasteland. He had an inborn instinct to find his way across the bleakest of moors, and even in the darkest of nights.

Hobbie served the Armstrong family well on many raids, and even distinguished himself helping to rescue Jock Armstrong of the Side from Newcastle prison in the mid 1560s. Noble though was not liked by all of the Armstrongs, with Sim feeling a great hostility towards him. Perhaps Sim was jealous of Hobbie's popularity with the Laird of Mangerton, and felt threatened by his rise within the Armstrong ranks. The feeling of enmity grew within Sim, and when he got the chance to be rid of Hobbie, he jumped at it eagerly. Hobbie's whereabouts was known to the English authorities, but they were powerless to enter Liddesdale and physically apprehend him. Hobbie could easily hide himself away in the hundreds of cleuchs and peat hags, and never be seen. The authorities though would use the weakness of the reivers to winkle out Hobbie – money.

A bribe was forthcoming for Sim to betray Hobbie, and turn him over to the English authorities so that he could be tried. Sim accepted the transaction, he would be rid of Hobbie and be a few pounds sterling the richer. A win-win situation, or so he thought. Sim thought the best way to deliver Hobbie was to lure him over the Border in a false raid, a raid that would lead straight into the hands of the warden and his men. Sim was associated to the Armstrongs of Whithaugh, providing him with the necessary man power and authority to plan his own raid. Details on times, dates, targets and who was riding out were organised. For cash Sim was prepared to hand this information over, feeling confident that his betrayal would not be revealed.

Sim shared his hidden agenda with a select few; the last thing that he wanted was a fight on his hands. What happened next is related in the ballad which was published in Sir Walter Scott's book, the *"Minstrelsy of the Scottish Border"* in 1802. Sim eventually put the planned trap into action and organised a foray to Haltwhistle, hoping to ask Hobbie on board as the navigator. Sim met up with Hobbie and persuaded him to lead the raiders on the pretext that he knew the English ground better than anyone else, and made the offer of a fine horse as payment.

"Wilt thou with us into England ride,
And thy safe warrand we will be?
If we get a horse, worth a hundred pound,
Upon his back that thou shalt be."

Hobbie was concerned that he could be spotted and caught when on the raid, with Sim suggesting they headed out at night to avoid being recognised. Hobbie agreed to the plan, he had no reason to smell a rat and here was another chance to make some personal gain. It is interesting to note within the ballad that Sim is never referred to as an Armstrong, the act of his betrayal is enough to signify a family connection to the Armstrongs. Sim organised to meet up with Noble at Kershopefoot on the English Border, from where their raid would be launched. As the plans were sent to Hobbie, another message was relayed to the Keeper of Askerton, announcing that Hobbie would soon be back on English ground, and to have an ambush party ready. The ballad mentions the scene as follows:-

At Kershope foot the tryst was set,
Kershope of the lilye lee;
And there was traitor Sim o' the Mains,
And with him a private companie.

The marauders set off and without any mishap reached Foulbogshiel at the edge of the Bewcastle Waste, where Sim ordered a stop for a rest. They would undertake the raid at first light on the following day. Unknown to Hobbie, as he was sleeping Sim sent word to *"Willeva and Speir Edom* (Spadeadam)" to warn them of his approach. A warning was sent to Hartlie-burn also, to *"See they sharp their arrows on the wa',"* and for them all to meet him in the morning on the *"Rodric-haugh."* Sim rode ahead in the early morning to meet up with the English forces and guided them across onto *"Conscouthart-Green"* to find their prey. Hobbie had no chance when the English soldiers arrived, making their surprise advance. Despite the odds, Hobbie bravely yielded his sword in defence, but it was a one sided struggle:

They were beset by cruel men and keen,
That away brave Hobbie could not gae.

There was heaps o' men now Hobbie before,
And other heaps was him behin'.

Sim and his followers held back and voiced their allegiance to the English – Hobbie knew at once he had been betrayed for English gold. Hobbie eventually gave in to the inevitable; it would be death or capture. He had his hands bound with the string from his bow and was taken by horse south to Carlisle as a prisoner. The town was entered by the Rickergate, to the interest of on-looking women who remarked *"That's the man loosed Jock o' the Side!"* He was imprisoned within the keep of Carlisle Castle, inside its windowless dark and damp prison. Hobbie felt humiliation at the experience, but held onto his pride with great grace. When he came to be tried, Hobbie was told that he would be hanged the next day unless he confessed to stealing a horse belonging to Peter of Winfield. He denied the allegation, fully knowing what his decision meant. He held his dignity to the end and was hung to a watching crowd; many felt sympathy to this rogue who had risked his life to rescue Jock of the Side from a similar fate. The ballad states Hobbie's farewell, naming his betrayer as Sim of the Mains for all to hear, to let posterity know of his shameful deeds.

"And fare thee weel, sweet Liddesdale!
Baith the hie land and the law;
Keep ye weel frae the traitor Mains!
For goud and gear he'll sell ye a'."

"Yet I had rather be ca'd Hobbie Noble,
In Carlisle, where he suffers for his fau't,
Before I were ca'd the traitor Mains,
That eats and drinks o' the meal and maut."

Sim of the Mains returned to Liddesdale happy with his days work and thought his troubles were over. He imagined life returning back to normal before the arrival of Hobbie, but Sim had not taken into consideration the act that he had just committed – the betrayal of an Armstrong gang member. Sim was not to escape the consequences of his treachery, he had sold a friend of the Laird of Mangerton to the gallows, the chief of the Armstrongs; and the resentment would burn deep. Word leaked out on Sim's guilt, with probably one of his gang members coming forward to point the finger when the weight of the crime emerged. Mangerton was furious, an anger which Sim saw as life threatening and fled into England for refuge. Seeking shelter in England was not the best of avenues for Sim, but his options were limited. Sim was captured; and ironically met the same fate as Hobbie, hanged at Harraby on the outskirts of Carlisle – just two months after the execution of Noble. The gathering crowd would have shed no tears on this occasion; justice was seen to be done.

2. Westburnflat

Westburnflat sat on the southern side of the Liddel Water at its junction with the Hermitage. Sir Walter Scott used the location for one of his characters, "The Red Reiver of Westburnflat," in his novel "The Black Dwarf."

Archibald (Airchie) of Westburnflat – (fl.1597)

Archibald is recorded by John Monipennie in his 1597 list of Border principal chiefs. He is listed under the heading "*LIDDISDAIL – Merietoun quarter*," alongside "*Wanton Sym in quhitley side*" [Whitlawside] and "*Will of Powderlanpat.*" Archibald's inclusion within the list suggests he was an active reiver and a main troublemaker at that.

The stronghold was burned in 1599 by Gideon Murray of Elibank (who was the father of "Muckle mou'd Meg" – Big mouthed Agnes), Walter Scott of Harden and Gilbert Elliot of Horsleyhill. The raid was probably to punish Archibald for some theft or breaking March Law. The tower was owned later by Lancie Armstrong in 1632 and by John Armstrong until about 1683.

William (Willie) of Westburnflat – (ex.c.1700s)

One of the last owners of Westburnflat was William Armstrong, who is noted sometimes as being "the last reiver." This notorious acclaim though is incorrect, with William's crime taking place in the early 1700s. William was probably the last of the cattle thieves, living one hundred years away from the actual Riding period.

Willie was a farmer and not a contented one at that. Reiving was always about obtaining food for the pot; Willie must have gone through some lean times in Liddesdale to have turned to thieving. With generations of Armstrong reivers in his DNA, the temporary solution to his problem was not far away. In the remote Liddesdale Valley, it was easy for William not to think of the consequences of his actions, not to realise that the long arm of the law was capable of extending down towards him with full force. William put together a gang of ten to undertake their mission. And taking strength from their forefathers, they set off with a sense of adventure and energy, reliving the old skills and sampling for a short time a new pride and status.

The gang targeted a gentleman of property in West Teviotdale and stole twelve cows in the one night. They made their way successfully home however, the cattle's angry owner put together a posse and in the old tradition of a hot trod, was on the tail of the thieves. There was a sufficiently good trail to lead the posse directly to Westburnflat, where William was in his bed sleeping off the nights exertion. He was taken by complete surprise, bounded hand and foot, and was taken north to be handed over to the authorities at Selkirk.

William found himself in a circuit court in Selkirk together with his nine gang mates. The jury could not discover any direct evidence to convict the gang. Despite this they did not hesitate to bring down a verdict of guilty upon them, based on the weak evidence that their general character was as *"notour thieves and limmers."* William and his colleagues were probably well known thieves and guilty of previous crimes. The sentence when it came was for the death penalty. On hearing this, William was possessed by a fury and sprang to his feet lifting the heavy oak chair that he had previously been sitting on, and smashed it to the ground. The chair crumbled into several fragments, allowing William to select one strong leg, which he brandished like a weapon. He encouraged his comrades to do like-wise, to grab a piece of the chair and to join him in a fight out of the court. The nine gang members remained in their seats, accepting their fate unquestioningly. To William's mortification, his colleagues grabbed his hands preventing the escape, and cried out asking him to *"let them die like Christians."* Times had changed indeed. The Armstrongs were now fully fledged Christians, light years away from when they regularly burned down churches and taunted Bishops until they cursed.

There was no change of heart on the men's sentence. To die fighting was a better fate, but society had moved on from the brutal cycle of murder and revenge. All were duly hanged in Selkirk.

3. Roan (Ralton)

Roan Tower once stood on a high eminence on the west bank of Ryedale Burn, near to its confluence with Ralton Burn, which runs into the Liddel. Roan was initially called Ralton, taking its name from the Ralton Burn. It is marked on the Pont's map (Timothy Pont c.1583-1614, Scottish cartographer and topographer) of c.1595 as "*Renn.*" The Roan had the Elliots of Redheugh and Copshaw as their neighbours to the north and south, with the Armstrongs of Whithaugh and Greenshiels to the east and west. Nothing remains today of the tower, the site now a pasture field in front of the modern farm house. The name Ralton is said to have sprung from a Norman called Raoul (Ralph), who fought with Siward against Macbeth, the alleged originator of the Armstrong name. Interestingly, the Ralstons of Renfewshire bore three acorns upon their shield in a similar manner to the House of Whithaugh, sharing the tale of acorn trees and Birnam wood.

One of the earliest Armstrongs to live at Ralton was Ninian Armstrong ("Sandies Rinion"), the son of Alexander of the Chengils (Gingles), alias ill Will's Sandie. He represented the House of Ralton, which was also known as the Gingles. Ninian lived at Ralton for a number of years together with his brother Thomas, William (of Kinmont), and Robert. Ninian moved on to live at Auchinbedrig in the Debateable Land.

Simon (Sym) of the Rone – (c.1580/90s)

Simon was the son of Simon ("Sym the young / old laird") of Whithaugh (ex.1607). He had at least three brothers:-

1. Lance of the Flatts – (b.1580)   **2.** Archibald (Archie)   **3.** Alexander (Sandy) – (fl.1611)

His father was an active reiver having around two hundred men at his command, often riding with "Kinmont's Bairns," Simon probably rode alongside as a member of the gang.

4. Whithaugh

The House of Whithaugh originates from John Armstrong, a son of Thomas, 5th Laird of Mangerton (b.c.1425 – 1498). The Whithaugh grayne were the second most powerful of the Armstrongs, coming after Mangerton. On a thieving scale, they were probably worse than the Mangertons, making them arguably the Border's most destructive raiders, or most successful reivers – depending on your view point. Whithaugh probably means simply "the white haugh," and has changed its spelling widely over the centuries. Before the Armstrongs arrived at Whithaugh in 1376, it is recorded as "*Qwhythawlgh*." The first spelling as an Armstrong residence comes in 1541, when it is "*Whythauch*". No two spellings seem to be the same, varying over the years from "*Quhithauch*" (1576) to "*Whetaughe*" (1583).

Whithaugh Tower stood on the east bank of the Liddel Water, opposite Copshaw Tower (and modern Newcastleton), near the confluence of the Whithaugh Burn with the Liddel. It was said that from the tower parapet, a commanding view of the horse races could be seen which once took place on the flat land where Newcastleton would later be built (in 1793). Horse racing was a great sport amongst reiving society, combining the joys of gambling with the love of horses. Nothing remains of the tower today, it having been destroyed c.1770, with the stones reused in the building of a steading. A portion of an unvaulted cellar survives under the south wing of the modern mansion of Whithaugh. An armorial stone from the tower dated 1552 was saved and inserted above the entrance to the mansion, inscribed "*BIGIT B(E) LONSI ARMSTRONG.*" Known as "*The hous of Quhythauch in Liddisdaill*," the tower was a hive of reiving activity and was the target of many attacks in return. It was taken by the English in an escalade in 1582 and burned in 1599. The Whithaugh grayne as expected appear extensively within Thomas Musgrave's list of 1583 on the most troublesome familys, coming under the heading of "*The Armestronges of the howse of Whetaughe towre.*"

✳✳✳

John Armstrong of Whithaugh – (c.1451 – ex.1528)

John was the son of Thomas Armstrong, 5th Laird Mangerton, and was given the land of Whithaugh forming a new grayne which would go on to terrorise the frontier to new levels. The Whithaughs were a voracious family, and when teamed up with the Mangertons 3km to the south, were an unstoppable force.

In 1527 the Armstrongs entered into an alliance with the Lisles of Northumberland, with plans to do harm in England. They jointly invaded Hexhamshire expecting rich pickings however the inhabitants rose against them and succeeded in killing several and making many more prisoners. The prisoners that were taken included some high ranking Armstrongs, such as John's son, Sim of Whithaugh and various relatives of the Laird of Mangerton. They were all closely warded in Newcastle by Sir William Eure, with word of their captivity rapidly returned to Liddesdale. The capture of such high Armstrong leaders made it desirous to have them released, but how to proceed?

Sir William Lisle and his son, Humphrey, were also coincidentally in Newcastle at the same time, held on charges which had been brought against them by Sir William Ellerker, Sheriff of Northumberland. They were not in jail or under any close restraint and had a relative freedom to range within the town. An idea then began to be developed, to use Sir William's help to bust the Armstrongs out of Newcastle. A correspondence with John was opened up, were he became employed carrying letters to and from Sir William Lisle in Newcastle, making a secret arrangement to free his kinsmen. When all was ready, a joint party of Armstrongs and Lisles numbering around forty entered the town where they located the keeper of the castle, and using unsubtle threats of violence compelled him to deliver his keys. The party proceeded to open all of the cell doors and released nine prisoners in total, both Scots and English. The combined party escaped with the Armstrongs back to Liddesdale, mission accomplished.

The breakout was brought to the attention of King Henry VIII, who wrote to Angus on 7 August of that year desiring that a search should be made for the Lisles, and that when captured they should be handed over to his officers. The Lisles now living with the Armstrongs, having helped in the rescue of outlaws, decided that they had nothing left to lose and became a professional gang of reivers – broken men with only an allegiance to themselves. Sir William Lisle assumed the leadership of the outlaws, attracting other rebels to gather around him. Lisle's prime goal was to seek revenge on Sir William Ellerker, the person who was responsible for his warding in Newcastle. The Lisles and their allies once organised, entered again into England and robbed, burned, and spoiled the town of Holmeshaugh in Northumberland, a property of Ellerker. The raid caused Lisle and several members of his gang to became indicted for high treason, and were proclaimed rebels with large rewards offered for their apprehension.

The Lisles made another foray on a property belonging to Ellerker to reinforce their resentment, and carried off forty horses from Wilderington. A repeat visit was made to Wilderington, together with the support of the Armstrongs with possibly John in tow. King Henry was unhappy at this new arrangement and wrote to James stating that if the Scottish warden could not apprehend the Armstrongs and Lisles responsible, then he requested that English officers should be allowed to enter Scotland and sort out the problem. The tide was turning against the Lisles, with the Armstrongs caught in the middle.

In early January 1528 John set off on a raid into Northumberland to get in some late winter beef. Unknown to him, word had leaked out on his foray to the Earl of Northumberland, who passed the word onto Felton and a welcoming committee set off to ambush the raiders. John rode straight into Felton and was one of fourteen who were captured. The prisoners were taken to Alnwick for trial on 8 January, where John and six others were executed. Sir William Lisle realised that the game was up and dressed in a plain shirt and with a halter around his neck; he made the plea of a penitent man to Cardinal Wolsey hoping for mercy. Wolsey was not in a forgiving mood unfortunately and on 26 January 1528, Lisle was hanged, drawn and quartered. His son Humphrey was spared, seen as too young to be guilty of treason.

John had the following children:-
1. Simon – "Sym the Larde" – (ex. 1536)

2. David – "Davy the Lady" – (fl.1525)

3. Martin – (fl.1536)

✳✳✳

Simon ("Sym the Larde") of Whithaugh – (ex.1536)

Sim was the son of John of Whithaugh (son of the 5th Laird of Mangerton), and it was Sim who put the Whithaugh grayne firmly on the map. Sim was one of the most feared Border headsmen to have ever lived. Sim was no ordinary reiver; together with Johnnie Armstrong of Gilnockie, he raised the family to the zenith of their power. He was a major gang leader, perhaps the right hand man of Johnnie Armstrong and was able to command an equal size of lancers. Sim was feared across the English Border and was a thorn in the side of the March Warden. Sim had at least two brothers, Martin and David ("Davy the Lady Armstrong"), and at least three sons, Lancelot, Quentin and John. He inherited the title of Laird of Whithaugh from his father in 1528 after his execution, and propelled with wolfish energy the family into becoming the second strongest of the Armstrong graynes.

The period after the death of King James IV at Flodden was a busy raiding time for the Armstrongs, with Sim in the thick of it. With a new child monarch, Scotland often lacked the focus and will power to tackle its outlaws. There was infighting struggles amongst the nobles for power, with issues on the Border the farthest concern on their mind. The Armstrongs of Liddesdale were undergoing a dangerous phase in 1525 when they upped the scale of destruction by joining with the freebooters of Ewesdale and outlaws from Tynedale, to form one large raiding gang. This alliance put the fear into the English authorities, with the gang prophesising that before the year had passed, there would be many of the monarch's subjects becoming despoiled.

Sim did not have everything his way though, as the authorities were still capable of hitting back hard when they wanted to. In May 1525 Archibald Douglas, 6th Earl of Angus, who had just been appointed as Lieutenant of the Marches in March of that year, decided to make a surprise expedition into Liddesdale. Angus had new responsibilities within the Scottish government and wanted to show that he was an effective leader, with an eye on becoming the guardian of King James (which he achieved in July of that year). Angus prepared his expedition well and brought off a swift descent which netted twelve prisoners, two of those were Sim and his younger brother David. A good days work; Angus would have been proud of himself in capturing the worst reivers on the whole frontier. As a punitive act of revenge, Angus burned many of the outlaw's houses and as poetic justice he marched off with 600 nolt, 3000 sheep, 500 goats – and most importantly, the reiver's horses, without which their raiding ability was very much restricted. Angus was highly satisfied at teaching the reivers a lesson in loss, on what happens to those who thieve – you have your home destroyed. A harsh case of tasting your own medicine was delivered.

The captured Armstrongs were not sent to a prison to await trial as would be expected, but were paroled in Edinburgh. It was reported that the prisoners had men attending them night and day, and were given great favours. Thomas Magnus, the English ambassador to Scotland, wrote in October stating that James Beaton (Archbishop of St. Andrews and Lord Chancellor) and Angus had fallen out over the fate of the Armstrongs. Beaton wanted the Armstrongs executed, for whatever reasons Angus did not agree. Angus ironically became the unlikely saviour of Sim and David. They were able to walk away from Edinburgh and live to raid again.

The Armstrong's raiding had been given a check, but it could only ever be temporary. Such punitive raids actually made the problem worse, as the Armstrongs would now want replacement herds and the extraction of these added further deaths and caused houses to be burned down in the process. Using theft to halt theft was never going to work, it fed a vicious circle. The reivers of Whithaugh had to recoup their losses somehow and innocent farm steadings would be attacked that same winter to compensate.

In October 1525 Gavin Dunbar the Archbishop of Glasgow, delivered his famous "Bishop's curse," a full on verbal blast of vitriol and angst, which could well have been caused by the raiding of Simon. The Bishop certainly had a low opinion of the reivers. Out of the entire Riders active on the Border, Sim arguably generated the greatest damage and perhaps had a personal run in with the Archbishop in the flesh. The Archbishop's hatred fell on deaf ears; Sim did not care anything if his hair, eyes and teeth were cursed. Sim probably heard the curse read out, perhaps at the market crosses of Castleton, Carlisle or Hawick. And gave it little thought, excommunication was the worst thing that could happen to him. Sim would not lose any sleep over this; he had an unblessed sword hand and would not suffer in purgatory for those he had slain.

In 1527 the Lisles of Northumberland approached the Armstrongs with the offer an alliance, which the Armstrongs, including Sim took up. The English Middle March braced itself for the repercussions, meanwhile Whithaugh sharpened their lances. The new alliance however did not get off to a good start, when one of the group's early joint forays into Hexhamshire did not go according to plan. The raiders ran into armed opposition and were repulsed with several prisoners being taken, which included Sim. For the second time Sim was held captive, being warded in Newcastle by Sir William Eure. Luckily Sir William Lisle was also held captive in Newcastle and was sympathetic to the Armstrongs. Word got out on Sim's captivity and a rescue attempt was organised which rode into Newcastle and broke into the jail releasing nine prisoners – Sim was amongst them. Sir William Lisle threw in his lot with the Armstrongs and formed his own gang of outlaws, which began its own predatory forays into England. For a few months Lisle enjoyed some sweet revenge on his former captors, but a re-energized Henry Percy 6th Earl of Northumberland (recently taking over as earl from his father) broke up his gang in early January 1528, and had several of its members hung. Sim watched the rise and decline of the reiver gang-lord, and wonder when his turn would come for execution; the tide seemed to be turning against the outlaws.

As not to be outdone, a month later William, Lord Dacre, Earl of Cumberland, recently made the new warden of the English West March, began his job as he meant to go on, and moved robustly against the Armstrongs wanting to hit them hard and in their home ground. Dacre mustered a force of 2,000 in secret and had a plan to winkle the Armstrongs out of the Debateable Land, hoping to at least capture Sim and Johnnie Armstrong of Gilnockie, the worst offenders of the Border. There had been a new power shift on the Border which worried Dacre, the Armstrongs had recently been moving out of Liddesdale and down the Esk into the Debateable Land, building towers as they went. He wanted to stub this advance and push the family back into Liddesdale.

In February 1528 Dacre set off on his expedition, hoping to take the Armstrongs by surprise. Dacre unfortunately failed to take into consideration the Armstrong's fine web of alliances and warning beacons. The Armstrongs through marriages across the Border had built up a set of bonds and friendships which remained hidden to the authorities. As Dacre set off from Carlisle, they went observed by the English Storeys, who sent runners north to warn and muster Eskdale and beyond. On hearing the tip off Sim and Johnnie lit their beacons and gathered in their riders. Soon the hunters became the hunted and using the land to their advantage Dacre's force was attacked, and after a sound bludgeoning was driven off.

Later that year, *"Quyntyn,"* a son of Sim was taken prisoner by the English. Sim was determined to have Quentin released and contacted Sir Rauf Fenwick of Tynedale requesting that he arrange a meeting with themselves and the Earl of Northumberland. Sim gave the purpose of the talk as *"for reformacon of justice,"* though the key object was in having his son released. Fenwick was true to his word, and organised the council, with Sim being conducted to Alnwick Castle in late December, where he met with Northumberland (who was also the March Warden), Henry Tempest his cousin and other Border officials. Sim must have felt a shiver run up his spine at Alnwick, as earlier that year his father had been executed there. He was now the new Laird of Whithaugh and held a power that Northumberland was eager to keep in check.

Northumberland hoped to use the opportunity of the meeting to shape a realistic peace with Liddesdale. The interview which followed was instructive and would have been fascinating to observe – a meeting of two opposite poles. It has to be wondered what Northumberland made of Sim, a robber baron with self made power through theft and steel. Luckily for posterity, Northumberland wrote to Brian Tuke on 20 December, 1528 giving an account of the meeting. The document provides a fascinating insight on Sim's opinion of government and justice in Scotland, and on the condition of the frontier at this stage in King James V's reign. As Sim was one of the leading reivers, the document captures a unique moment in time and he spoke his mind openly, free of the court room and without any legal constraints. Northumberland questioned Sim on *"hys dutie of alegiaunce unto hys soverain lorde; unto whiche he awnswered, that he thought in hys tyme nevir to se kyng in Scotland, nor that realme to be kepit with justice, without the kyng, our soverain lorde, hade the governaunce thereof; for their kyng was all set uppon vicousnes, ande hys counsaill that were about hym was of no stabilite."*

Sim explained that Scotland had no justice as King James was currently controlled by vicious counsellors. This would refer to the Earl of Angus who was the king's guardian and pulled the monarch's strings. Sim did not realise an important power change had just occurred in August 1528 James had escaped the council of Angus and was now ruling in his own right. The lights had changed and Sim had not noticed. Sim said something unexpected to Northumberland, on his reason for wanting the meeting – *"Ande that hys commyng was oonly to mynystre justice, and to have justice out of England; for in the realme of Scotland he wold nevir looke to have justice kepit, seying.*" Basically Sim was looking to England for justice, as there was no hope in finding it in Scotland. As evidence on the lack of justice, with no sign of irony Sim used himself as an example on the state of affairs – *"that hymself ande hys adherentes have endway laid waiste in the saide realme LX myles, ande laide downe XXX parisshe churches; and that there is not oone in the realme of Scotland dar remedy the same.*" Sim was pointing out that his riders had devastated the land for sixty miles around and destroyed thirty churches, and no one dared to stop them. This destruction of churches explains why the Archbishop of Glasgow was angry at the reivers and Sim was probably the main individual responsible. Sim was pointing out the fact that the Scottish government was very poor and ineffective, as it could do nothing to curb his actions. Sim was both boasting on the power of the Armstrongs, and trying to gain respect for his clan with the English authorities as a separate entity to King James's Scotland. There is an impression that both Sim and Johnnie Armstrong saw themselves as petty rulers of the Borders, having their own kingdom within a kingdom. The Border poet W.H. Ogilvie (1869-1963) covers the situation very nicely within his poem, "The men of the Open Spaces," based on his life as a sheep ranger in Australia, but could easily refer to the Border reivers:-

"Who ride with a gallant bearing
where every saddle's a throne,
and each is an emperor sharing
an empire enough for his own."

Northumberland put an estimate on the number of lances available to Sim – *"the great power of the Armestranges with ther adherentes, whiche ys above iii thousand horsemen.*" Three thousand riders was a small army, putting the likes of Sim and Johnnie into the status of minor warlords. It would be wise for Northumberland to do a deal with Sim. Sim was eager for the prestige of being consulted with, and in bringing an end to the English attacks into Liddesdale, his son's release could be brought into the deal also. Northumberland mentions the conclusion to his meeting – *"I caused Sym to make suche articles as he wold be bounden unto; the whiche articles I send unto you herwith, praying you, goode Mr. Treasourer, to shew my lordes grace the same, ande that in convenyent haste I may have knowlege of hys gracious pleasour again.*" Sim signed the bond which Northumberland had draughted up. It has to be assumed that it contained a pledge of Sim not making any raids into Northumberland, and in good faith Quentin was released. A truce was concluded which was outside of the normal Scotland / England treaties, a direct deal between the Armstrongs and Northumberland. Sim was first an Armstrong; nationality did not come into the equation, he was happy to become bedfellows with anyone for the good of his family. Sim believed the Armstrongs were far too powerful for King James to deal with, and that he and Johnnie of Gilnockie were virtually untouchable within their Border valleys. A separate power that was immune from the vanities of kings. Sim and the Armstrongs though did not understand fully that James's lack of authority had come to an end, their arrogant assumption would soon be proven spectacularly wrong.

In 1530 King James took off the velvet glove and descended upon the Border in an unprecedented attempt to sort out the problem of the Border outlaws. The Armstrongs were at the head of his hit list, with an invitation going out to the main Armstrong lairds to meet the monarch as his guest, to dine and go on a hunting trip. Sim was on the guest list, but for some unknown reason did not attend. Perhaps Sim did not trust the king, as he had just taken Adam Scott of

Tushielaw and William Cockburne of Henderland prisoner and ushered them up to Edinburgh for a show trial followed by beheadings. Or perhaps it was the wishes of Johnnie Armstrong that Sim stayed behind to man the Border. With all the main chiefs away attending the king, a strong hand was needed to watch their backs. Sim was already on good terms with some of the English officials, so was the ideal person to try and halt any invasion – employing diplomacy rather than violence. The meeting between the Armstrong chieftains and the king took place at Carlenrig in July of that year. Sim indeed was a lucky man to have avoided this rendezvous; if he had gone along he would have been executed along with the entire party of Armstrongs and their allies. Sim had yet again dodged a date with the grim reaper. The Armstrongs took a heavy blow to their power and were temporarily stunned. With their main leaders cropped off, the remaining hierarchy including Sim were jolted into a new reality that they did not like. James had only been ruling in his own right for the past two years, if the monarch kept up this pressure on the Armstrongs over the next few years, the family would be broken down into a vassal status. A general five year peace treaty had been signed between Scotland and England in 1528, this attack on the Armstrongs went towards ensuring that they would keep to the treaty and not go off on their own personal wars across the Border and wreck the peace.

Sim found himself in trouble with King James in 1531, when he accompanied a contingent of English reivers from across the Border on a raiding expedition into Scotland. The incident was reported to James, who heard how Simon Armstrong, called *"the Laird,"* and Clement Crosar, *"two formidable borderers,"* were in company with a party of English, whom they led into the Scotland and had committed depredations. This group of English riders were not a group of broken men, but were led by Lord Dacre and the Earl of Northumberland, who commanded five hundred riders from Lillesland and Tyndale. This was a bad sign for King James; he certainly did not want Liddesdale allying themselves with English forces. The Armstrongs probably hosted the raid, taking the lead command. The Anglo-Scots force rode into Teviotdale burning selected targets, with Little Newtown noted as consumed in flames. Amongst the spoiling, Sim kidnapped Sir Walter Scott, Laird of Buccleuch, hoping to profit from a tidy ransom. Buccleuch, based at Branxholme, probably saw the destruction and rode out to protect the property, becoming outnumbered and forced into surrendering. Sim was not the main target of the king's anger, which was aimed at the English for having raided in Scotland. The Armstrongs were only the vehicle being the incident. A complaint had to be made; an ambassador of James was sent to report the outrage to King Henry and his Council to ask for redress.

Henry sent his herald-at-arms with the reply that he was not aware of this incident and would look into redress if the Earl of Northumberland should be found culpable, promising to take the necessary action to reform the abuses. Sim and Clement submitted themselves to King James, not seeing any other solution to the problem. James was in a lenient mood towards the Armstrongs and showed restraint upon his most unruly of subjects. In a document dated 26 January 1531, with the King's seal from Edinburgh attached, James ordained a remission on their crimes – the charges were for being *"in company with Englishmen,"* the *"treasonable inbringing"* of the English into Scotland, and the *"treasonable taking of Walter Scott of Branxhelm, knight."* Scott of Buccleuch was released, presumably Henry paid the redress and the matter was resolved. Perhaps James felt guilty at hanging the Armstrongs at Carlenrig, by offering an olive branch to the remaining Armstrong lairds. The Armstrongs were not totally silenced however; the Earl of Angus was back on the scene and living in England, eager to cause problems in Scotland he supplied cash payments to the outlaws to encourage their raiding. Sim and his gang were only too eager to oblige. King James would not make any repeat ventures into the Borders on the extent of 1530, which allowed Armstrong rebellion to recover. James could not be too harsh on the Armstrongs, as he needed a strong militaristic body of Scots on the frontier to deter English invasions, a bulwark to protect the rest of the country.

The thin peace came to an in 1535, when freebooters from Bewcastle under the command of a fellow called Taylor, rode into Liddesdale during the summer and targeted Whithaugh Tower. Sim was not present during the raid, as he was off visiting Eweshead with the bulk of his supporters, a summer time occupation. Whithaugh had only a minimal of guards and was easily taken by the Bewcastle raiders. The tower was plundered, with the raiders carrying off amongst the usual array of items, several documents which were valuable to Sim. Sim was outraged, he could replace stolen cattle but not these papers; they included the original deed of Whithaugh. Sim wanted the documents back and sent a messenger to Bewcastle requesting Taylor hand them over. Taylor was in no mood to be told what to do by the Armstrongs, he ordered the papers to be brought out and in open defiance before the eyes of the Armstrongs – he burned them. This act was more than fighting talk, Sim's anger boiled over, vengeance would be required. Sim had to bide his time to find the ideal moment to strike, when the garrison at Bewcastle were busy elsewhere and the night was long and dark enough to conceal the journey. The ideal conditions were not long in coming; Sim mustered his followers and stealthily approached the dwelling of Taylor. He managed complete surprise; carrying bundles of twigs the Armstrongs approached the strongholds of their intending victims and whickered up their doors. The twigs were then set on fire, to consume those inside with smoke and flame – the debt was paid.

On 30 October 1535, Sim was requested to appear on trial in Edinburgh for the crimes of cattle stealing, taking prisoners and *"stouthreif."* He was listed as *"Sym the Larde"* amongst a motley crew of cut-throats which included John Forster (*"schaik – buklar"*) and Thomas 7th Laird of Mangerton. Sixteen were named in total, accused of under the silence of night on 27 July, raiding the lands of Craik in Roxburghshire and lifting from *"John Cokburne of Ormistoune,"* seventy *"drawand oxin"* [oxen used for ploughing] and thirty cows. The gang also carried away three servants of John, removing from them their clothes, whingers (a short stabbing sword/long dagger), and money. None of the group showed up as demanded in Edinburgh, and *"were all denounced Rebels, and their whole goods, moveable and immoveable, to be escheated."*

Sim was a dangerous man and as such was doomed. He was captured in 1536 and this time his luck had run out, too dangerous to be freed, another trial was held in Edinburgh. On 21 February 1536 the same old charges from the raid at Craik were dragged out, plus some new charges were added, all in an attempt to have Sim despatched off for good. Five items were brought up against him...

ITEM 1. *"Convicted of art and part of the theft and concealment of two oxen from the Laird of Ormistoune, furth of the lands of Craik, and a black mare from Robert Scott of Howpaslot, furth of the lands of Wolcleuche; committed during the time he was in the King's Ward, about Lammas 1535."*

ITEM 2. *"Of art and part of the theft and concealment of five score of cows and oxen from the said Laird of Ormistoune, stolen furth of the said lands of Craik; committed by Alexander Armstrong, called Evil-Willit Sande, and his accomplices, in company with Thomas Armstrong, alias Greneschelis, and Robert Carutheris, servants of the said Symon, and certain Englishmen, at his command, common thieves and traitors, on July 27, 1535."*

ITEM 3. *"Of art and part of the traitorous FIRE-RAISING and BURNING OF THE TOWN* [farm town] *OF HOWPASLOT; and concealment the same time of sixty cows and oxen belonging to Robert Scot of Howpaslot and his servants; committed by Alexander Armstrong in company with Robert Henderson alias Cheys-wame* [Cheese belly], *Thomas Armstrong alias Grenescheles, his servants, and their accomplices, common thieves and traitors, of his causing and assistance, during the time he was within the King's ward, upon Oct 28 1535."*

ITEM 4. *"Of art and part of the Theft and concealment of certain sheep from John Hope and John Hall, the King's shepherds, furth of the lands of Braidlee in the forest* [Ettrick]; *committed during the time he was within the said ward."*

ITEM 5. *"For art and part of the treasonable assistance given to Alexander Armstrong, called Evill-willit Sandy, a sworn Englishman, and sundry other Englishmen his accomplices, of the names of Armestrangis, Niksounis, and Crosaris, in their treasonable acts."*

Simon had no chance in dodging the charges; the authorities were out to get him. The inevitable sentence was read out that day, for Simon *"To be drawn to the gallows and hanged thereupon: And that he shall forfeit his life, lands, possessions, and all his goods, moveable and immoveable, to the King, to be disposed of at his pleasure."*

✳✳✳

David – "Davy the Lady" – (fl.1525)

David was the younger brother of "Sim the Laird." David's nickname of "Lady" has to be wondered at; was he a transvestite, or perhaps gay – or was it a tease on his overtly male nature, being the opposite of his real character. Maybe he was a cultured gentleman, a refined soul who appreciated the Renaissance and enjoyed a glass of claret and fine music, standing out amongst his more belligerent neighbours.

David was captured in around May 1525, when the Earl of Angus mounted a pacification expedition into Liddesdale. Angus rounded up twelve prisoners, which included David and his brother Sim. David and his brother came close to being executed in Edinburgh on the will of the Scottish Lord Chancellor, but Angus acting as their surprise benefactor, having them released on parole.

Opposite Whithaugh on the other side of the Liddel, was Copshaw Park. Copshaw came within the bounds of Whithaugh and it was here that David's son, Herbert lived. David had perhaps three other sons. Within Thomas Musgrave's list of the Border Riders in 1583, under Whithaugh come possibly their names:-

✱✱✱

Lancelot (Lancie) – Laird of Whithaugh – (d.c.1599)

Lancelot's father was Sim, the Laird of Whithaugh, and took up the lairdship on his execution in 1536. Lancelot had at least five sons – Simon, Andrew, Archibald, Francis and John.

Lancelot was present at the Battle of Solway Moss in 1542, but not as a combatant. Lancelot was probably asked to join the king's army as a loyal Scottish subject, but the deaths of so many of his relatives at Carlenrig twelve years earlier had killed his patriotism. He observed with interest and concern the passing Scottish army, but kept out of its way distrusting King James. Lancelot was worried about the army pausing to plunder the Armstrong's livestock and ordered his herds to higher pastures for safety. His lancers were mustered and made vigilant, venturing out to discourage any foraging soldiers from trespassing onto Armstrong property. With relief, Lancelot watched the Scots army cross the Esk and then with curiosity paused to observe the outcome of the Scots army's fortunes when they ran head on into Wharton's soldiers. The Battle of Solway Moss unfolded on a flat plain out of view; its final stages though were played out in full sight of the Armstrongs. As the Scots army disintegrated and recrossed the Esk, with great satisfaction Lancelot led his riders like vultures to pick at the carcass of what was left of a once organised unit. Thieving anything that they could get their hands on – horses, gun powder and boots – the debris of a fleeing army was stolen away.

The services of Lancelot were required by the English in the following year, when Dacre signed up assured Scots to raid fellow Scots for cash during the "Rough Wooing." This was reiver heaven, getting paid for reiving. Lancelot did well out of the arrangement, raiding and burning his neighbours land for English gold. Lancelot was probably present at the Battle of Ancrum Moor in 1545 on the English side – and non-discretely changed sides as he saw the English losing. It was not the mercenary's job to die in a blaze of glory, it was to make money. It was no loss of face to betray the English and live to fight another day.

Trouble came to Whithaugh when James Hepburn, 4th Earl of Bothwell inherited his father's titles on his death in 1556 of the Lord of Liddesdale and Keeper of the Hermitage Castle onto his young and ambitious shoulders. A virtual war occurred between Bothwell and his new territory from 1557, with numerous encounters and skirmishes. Whithaugh Tower was damaged during the melees, but Bothwell had little effective power and was twice defeated by the Armstrongs. In 1559 Lancelot made repairs to the tower and added a carved stone with his initials inscribed to mark the work, surrounded in a shield design with the heraldic charges of a *chevronel couped* dividing three acorns.

On 22 September 1562 a bond was signed by Lancelot and other Armstrongs to enter one of their clan as a prisoner to the Laird of Ferniehirst; an action which was done to guarantee good behaviour of that particular grayne of the family. The bond was worded as follows – "*Be it kend tell all men be this present wryteng, that we, Lancie Armstrang, lard of Whithawche, Sanny Armstrang of Tenesburne... to enter Christy Armstaring, callit Chresty the bwll, to Thomas Ker of Farnyharst, knycht, heis heirs and assigns, upon the 1 St of January following, within the iron yettis of the Fernihirst, under pain of 500 angell nowbeles* [Angel Noble was an English gold coin worth 10 shillings]."

Lancelot had some secret dealings with Lord William Howard, the Warden of the English West March. Howard succeeded to Naworth Castle, but fell out of favour with Queen Elizabeth when his strong attachment to Mary, Queen of Scots became known. He was executed on 2 June 1562. Within his diary were found several Armstrong names, which included Lancelot – suggesting intrigues and Lance's pro Mary stance.

In 1566 Bothwell again made his power known in Armstrong country. Bothwell was now well favoured by Mary, Queen of Scots and was eager to show his loyalty to her and his skill at governing the Queen's Marches. He descended into Liddesdale in force and used Hermitage as his base camp from which he planned to organise sweeping forays and bring in the surrounding reivers for trial. Bothwell had good success in his September campaigning, capturing Lancelot and Archibald, 8th Laird of Mangerton, who were held captive in Hermitage. The numbers of reivers held prisoner grew; they were not held in the castle's dark pit-dungeon, but within a locked chamber. Bothwell would eventually hold a court of assize on his haul of outlaws, or may have transported the captives to Jedburgh where Mary was staying as a guest of Thomas Kerr of Ferniehirst – and hold the trials there before the queen. This was the plan anyway, to have the Royal justice to be seen to be done, but things did not go accordingly as Bothwell ran into a reiver that was too prickly to handle – "Little Jock" Elliot of the Park.

On 7 October, Lancelot and his fellow inmates managed to overpower their guards and escape their confinement. Arming themselves they took over the castle and barred the front door to avoid a counterattack. By coincidence, as Lancelot and Mangerton were preparing their escape, Bothwell was fighting for his life. Bothwell had come across "Little Jock" at Billhope Burn, 6km to the west of Hermitage and not attempting to take him prisoner, decided to just shoot Jock dead off his horse. Jock fell heavily to the ground, watched by a satisfied Bothwell. He had despatched the Queen's justice and saved the time of a trail into the bargain. To make sure Jock was dead, Bothwell dismounted and walked across to the corpse – and on bending over the body, Jock suddenly sprang to life and jabbed his sword several times into Bothwell. The roles were reversed, but Jock was too injured to linger and ran off as best he could to the safety of the moors. Bothwell collapsed at the loss of blood; this would be the last of his patrolling after the outlaws. He was too injured to ride back to Hermitage, with servants sent back to the castle to bring a mode of transport to help out. Speed was of the essence, a sled was produced and Bothwell was unceremoniously dragged bumpily back to the castle and the surgery that was needed to save his life. Lance and Mangerton watched the approaching Bothwell with high interest. Here the mighty earl was way-laid; they now held all the aces. Calling out through a high window, Lancelot and his companions announced their presence and their intentions. They were holding the castle as hostage and would not allow Bothwell to enter unless they were allowed to freely escape. Bothwell was in no condition to negotiate; the longer he was outside the castle, the longer he was denied medical treatment – with the imminent danger of dying at the very gates. Robert Ellot of the Shaws, who lived nearby observed the predicament and stepped in to be an intermediate. As an Elliot, the Armstrongs trusted him and a deal was soon struck. All the prisoners were enabled to safely exit the castle, with horses probably being made available and all returned home unpursued. Bothwell then regained his castle and had his wounds stitched up – living to rule another day.

Bothwell's venture was later turned into a poem by Professor William Aytoun, within his work *"Bothwell: a poem. In six parts,"* in 1856. Within the lines, Lancelot and Mangerton get a brief mention.

> *Saint Andrew! 'twas no easy task*
> *To hunt an Armstrong down.*
> *Or make a Johnstown yield his sword*
> *At summons from the Crown:*
> *Yet, ere a week had passed away,*
> *One half my work was done.*
> *And safe within my castle lay*
> *Whithaugh and Mangerton.*
> *I had them all but one,*
> *John Elliot of the Park,*
> *As stalwart and as bold a man,*
> *As ever rode by dark.*

In 1570 Lancelot was held in ward by Sir John Wemyss, with a letter from the Earl of Lennox instructing Wemyss *"to keip Lancy Armstrang of Quhithauch."* The authorities were keeping a close watch on him, seeking to halt his family's depredations on the Border. In 1578/9 twenty two Border lairds were summoned before the Privy Council, which included Lancelot. Alongside Simon, 9th Laird of Mangerton, the group were asked to deliver pledges, relatives who were to be handed over and act as assurances for good behaviour. Lancelot handed over his son Archibald, who was replaced by another son, Francis, a year later.

Lancelot's lack of concern for any law was more than an obvious statement, he even used the Border laws to his advantage when an easy plunder could be made. The hot trod was an important legal right on the Border, with those it passed by having an obligation to assist and it was certainly illegal to obstruct the trod. All this fell on deaf ears regarding Lancelot. A hot trod was as good and valid a target as any other. In August 1580 a hot trod of fifty Gladstones and Scotts rode past Lancelot's tower in pursuit of cattle stolen by English reivers from Whitlaw. The trod was led by Robert Elliot of Redheugh, who was the deputy Keeper of Liddesdale, and it was his job to organise just defence against the English Riders. When Lancelot saw the burning spear, he was reluctant to ride out. Lancelot though did saddle up, but not to aid in the trod, but as a hovering vulture, hoping to swoop down on any easy pickings. The

Gladstone/Scotts pursued their herd into Cumberland as far as "*Billieheid*" (Baileyhead), where the trail ran out. They "*rypit for the nowt*" (searched for the cattle), but drew a blank, the English outlaws having got clean away.

The Gladstone/Scotts then turned around and headed for home empty handed, riding past Lancelot and his rapacious gang. The Armstrongs were hoping to find cattle amongst the Gladstone/Scotts; cattle which they thought could easily be thieved away. After a long chase there would be little resistance in thieving from the trod. Lancelot ordered his riders out to surround the trod and were disappointed to find no booty, however the trod themselves was an excellent alternative prize. A brief skirmish ensued in which Walter Gladstone, the brother of James, Laird of Cocklaw was killed and another dozen were wounded, including Elliot of Redheugh and Walter Scott of Goldielands. After a spirited defence, all of the trod were taken prisoner. The prisoners were forced "*to make band and promise to Whithaugh*;" this was a bond of assistance, a promise to come to the aid of Whithaugh whenever he asked within eight days of being summoned. The Gladstone/Scotts kept to their bond apparently, with an honour among thieves; no one ever doubted the promise was hollow.

The attack on the hot trod was seen as an outrage, with a complaint being made by Elliot of Redheugh and James Gladstone of Cocklaw to the authorities. Lancelot and several other Armstrongs and Elliots were summoned to appear before the Lords of the Council, but all refused to show up. As a consequence, Lancelot and his colleagues in violence were all denounced as rebels and put to the horn. As rebels, Lancelot, his sons and nephews needed a temporary place to hold up in for a while. That sanctuary came from a close neighbour, Martin Elliot of Braidley. In 1580 Martin offered "reset" to the rebel Armstrongs, an action which was against March Law. Lancelot was grateful for the friendship and gave back a gesture of thanks by joining in with the Elliots when they raided the farm of Slaidhills. A request was made to Lancelot in 1581 to present various members of his clan, which included his son Francis, to answer for their crimes on raids which had been made on Eilrig, Bellendean and other farms. Again he failed to respond and was once more denounced as a rebel.

In June 1582 Lancelot took part in a raid alongside his son Simon, Jock of Copshawe and "*Sims Thom*" Armstrong of D'mainholme. The raid ran into some spirited defence by the locals and Martin Taylor was cut down defending his goods. A complaint was issued by Matthew Taylor and the poor widow of Martin, "*for 140 kie and oxen, 100 sheep, 20 gaits, and all the insight, L.200 Sterling.*"

Simon Armstrong, the 9th Laird of Mangerton was a regular companion with Lancelot on his raids. Lancelot rode out on 5 October 1583 together with Mangerton and Eamont Armstrong of Whisgills in a forty rider strong gang – and into Bewcastle where they lifted thirty cattle and all the insight of two steadings. It was noted that "*at this spoile soudry personnes were hurt in perill of death,*" resulting in Rowy and Dand Rowtlege lodging a complaint.

A day later Lancelot led the same gang on two forays, again into Bewcastledale and with the Routledges as the target. The famous quote of the Routledges being "*every man's prey*" would certainly be true for the Armstrongs in 1583. The first was against George Rowtlege of the Greinhilesh (Green Hill Ash) in Bewcastle, in which he had stolen "*x goates, xx yowes,"* and all of his insight. The raid was of a particularly violent nature; George and his son were recorded as *"hurt in perill of death."* That same night a second *"heirshipp"* occurred, with the Armstrongs not satisfied at their already ample plunder. Their target was again the Routledges of Bewcastle and in a violent attack they had reft from them twenty six cattle and all the insight from Anthonie Rowtlege of Nutticlughe (Nunscleugh). The raid again had a high level of violence, documenting Allan Rowtlege as slain, William Rowtlege, Thome Rowtlege, John Rowtledge and Thome of Toddholls, as *"all maymed and hurt in perill of death,"* and gorily with one of the injured as having his *"legge cutt off"* (another source says it was both legs).

Lancelot was named two months later in the list of Thomas Musgrave on the Border Riders, noted as *"Lance Armestronge the olde lord of Whetaughe."* Interestingly, it was noted that he had murdered Will Noble of the Crew – perhaps a relative of Hobbie Noble. Lancelot was a marked man, with the English authorities eager to get their hands onto him. In 1584 the Laird of Mangerton was captured by Humphrey Musgrave, the deputy of Lord Henry Scrope. Scrope proudly wrote to Walsingham on the 13 January 1584, feeling satisfied at having the chief *"evildoer"* on the Border safely out of the way, it only remained to capture Lancelot also. He wrote enthusiastically that he was *"next after the laird of Whithaugh, whom though I cannot well come by, yet I hope in time to grieve him and his."*

On 20 December 1584, Sir John Forster descended upon Whithaugh with his entourage of officers and guards, demanding assurances for the good behaviour of the Whithaugh grayne. Forster had previously obtained assurances from the Elliots of Redheugh at Hermitage Castle on 15 December. Lancelot wrote on the event – *"In the first I Lancey Armestrange of Whithawghe assures for my selfe and my howse and dependers upon me and my servands and suche lyke... bynds me by this my writinge to performe and keip the promyses of our said assurance, as the howse of Readhewghe."*

The fact of Lancelot not holding the deeds to his own tower must have preyed upon his mind. They had been burned in 1535 (see page 128) and he wanted a new set made up. Lancelot approached Francis Stewart, 5th Earl of Bothwell and had his lands re-granted to him on 9 October, 1586. The lands remained in possession of his descendants until about 1730.

At Martinmas 1587, the poor widow and inhabitants of the town of Temmon made a complaint upon the Laird of Whithaugh and the Laird of Mangerton, and their accomplices, for the murder of John Tweddel, Willie Tweddel and Davie Bell – for *"taking 100 kine and oxen, spoil of houses, writings, money, and insight 400L. sterling."* In the raid ten of the locals were kidnapped and taken back to Liddesdale to be ransomed later.

The exact date of Lancelot's death is not known. He was last recorded alive in a document from 1599, when he was named as *"Lancie Armestrang, elder of Quhithauch,"* in which he signed a bond with Walter Scott of Buccleuch at Branxholme Castle, promising to be held responsible for the inhabitants of Liddesdale should there be any complaints from England. A *"young Lancie Armestrang, sonne to Sym of Quhithauch"* is also named as signing the document, who presumably was his grandson. Lancelot died before 1601, as he is referred to as the *"auld laird of Whithaughe"* in a reference to his sons Andrew, Francis and John, who were listed as outlaws in an English document. Lancelot seems to have died in bed at an advanced age, which says a lot for the man's intelligence and courage – avoiding the gallows and death in combat from leading many a foray. He led the Whithaugh grayne with great skill and preserved his father's legacy well, building upon the acorns which he symbolically planted into the wall of his tower in 1559. His son Simon would take over as the next laird of Whithaugh.

John (Jock) of Whithaugh – (Ex.1588)

Jock was the brother of Lancelot. He had at least one daughter and two sons, Robert ("*Hobbe*") and John ("*Joke*"). He eventually came into the possession of Whisgills. Jock is recorded in Musgraves list of 1583 on the Border Riders, with a mention that his daughter was married to John Foster, the son of Will Foster of the Rone; And – "*Hobbe Armestronge his sonne, marryed Jeme Fosters daughter of the Stangerth side.*" Musgrave was very particular to note marriages across the Border, pointing out family allegiances and possible alliances.

In 1588 one of the King's lieutenants led an expedition through Liddesdale in an attempt to bring good rule to the Border. When passing through Tarras Burn they ran unexpectedly into Jock, who was as surprised as they were. His guard was down and was totally unprepared to take any evasive action. Liddesdale's normally vigilant watch towers and look-outs had failed that day. Jock was seized there and then, and having the King's authority the party decided to string Jock up from the nearest tree. Jock was an infamous reiver and it was thought no trial was necessary. Why go through all the hassle of taking Jock back to Edinburgh and a court session, when they could much easier and quicker do things here. The end result would be the same after all. Their kangaroo court lynching did not go according to plan however, a suitable tree to hang Jock from could not be found. There was of course the Tarras Burn only a few metres below them, a suitable alternative. Execution by drowning was a common sentence in the Borders, with named "drowning pools" in several rivers. Jock had his hands bound and was "*marched down to the rocky pool below the linn, stepping as lightly and briskly as though he were walking to his wedding.*" Jock knew his end had come, and he would die with courage. At a place which has since been named "Jock Armstrong's Pool," he was tilted into the water and held under by the butts of their spears. With no ceremony or afterthought, the party rode off down the valley and continued their expedition – leaving the corpse of Jock by the burn side, awaiting its sad discovery.

Simon ("Sym the young / old laird") of Whithaugh – (ex.1607)

Sim was the son of Lancelot Armstrong, the Laird of Whithaugh, and took over the title on his father's death in around 1599. Sim was known as the "young laird of Whithaugh" until his father's death, a common title for heir's of land in the Borders. Simon was married to the illegitimate daughter of Thomas Musgrave, the Captain of Bewcastle, a marriage that provided him great assistance in his forays and warnings of counter raids. Sir Robert Carey, the English

West March Warden, mentions Simon in his memoirs; "*He had five or six sons, as able men as the Borders had. This old man and his sons had not so few as two hundred at their commands, that were ever ready to ride with them to all actions at their beck.*"

Simon had the following sons:-

1. Lance of the Flatts – (b.1580)   **2.** Simon (Sym) of the Rone

3. Archibald (Archie)   **4.** Alexander (Sandy) – (fl.1611)

The first record of Sim comes in 1579, in a complaint made by Thomas and John Dod of Thorneborne, and Lyell Dod of the Blacklawe. It was brought upon "*William Armestronge of Kynmothe, Syme Armestronge younge Lard of Whithaughe, Rynione and Eckie Armestronge of Tweden, and other 400 men, who ran a day foray, took 40 score kye and oxen, a thousand sheep and 'gate,' and slew Uswold Dode, about Midsummer 1579.*" Sim was a reiving companion with Kinmont and they were probably good friends. Sim had his own gang of riders and was not a member of "Kinmont's Bairns," though teaming up with them on raids was certainly achieved and seems a regular partnership. The spoils were probably split equally amongst the headsmen.

A document from September 1583 records a complaint by Thomas Swynborne of Captheton, "*against Sym Armstrong of Whithaugh and other 24, for taking 80 kyne and oxen from Captheton Whithouse, on 6 August last.*" Later that year in December, he appears within Thomas Musgrave's list of the Border Riders and was named as "*Sime Armestronge the yonge lord,*" the son of Lancelot of Whithaugh.

On "*the Satterdaie after St Elen daie 1584,*" Sim together with old and young Thomas Armstrong of the Gingles, Thomas Armstrong ("Rowyes Thom") of Mangerton, Adie Ellott of the Shawes and others, ran a day foray to the "Slyme." Tristram Fenwicke and Sandie Hall made a complaint upon the raiders for "*taking sixteen score kye and oxen, 21 horses and meares, spoiling 30 sheiles, and ransoming 10 prisoners.*"

Sim was recorded again riding alongside with "Kinmont's Bairns" on 6 October 1587, when he was called to answer for a bill by the Commissioners at Berwick. William Maughen and Thomas Hynde put forward the complaint against Sim and Kinmont on behalf of themselves and forty three other persons from Her Majesty's tenants of Haddingbriggs and Rattenrawe. The raid was large scale, numbering six hundred men and was under the command of Sim, the Laird of Mangerton and John ("*Jokkie*") Armstrong of Kinmont (the eldest son of Willie). The raid was probably put together with three separate gangs and it made an unstoppable plundering machine that could do exactly what it pleased. The three "heidsmen" were charged "*for burning 15 houses, taking 24 prisoners – one had his hand cut off – reaving their chattels and insight gear, worth 900 L. sterling.*"

October 1587 was not a good month for the Armstrongs, with five raids against the family. One of the raids was undertaken by Captain Humphrey Musgrave and his soldiers, which implies an official sanction to the venture – and included a spot of opportunist reiving on the side. Musgrave lifted eight hundred sheep from Sim and further livestock from the Laird of Mangerton and Thomas of Tinnisburn. Complaints were launched to Lord Scrope, the Warden of the

English West March for redress and action was taken. Ten of the most noted leaders of the raids, which included Musgrave, were delivered to Scrope for trial.

With such losses to the Whithaugh livestock, compensation herds would be required the following year. Sim appeared at the Bells Kirk on 13 April 1590 to address for his crimes in 1588. William Fenwick, acting as the deputy warden of the English Middle March, and Thomas Trotter, the deputy Keeper of Liddesdale, were the principal officers who heard the bills on that day, attempting to bring redress on both sides of the Border. There were two bills read out against Sim – the first being for a raid on 27 November 1588, in which he rode alongside the lairds of Buccleuch and Chisholm, in a gang which totalled one hundred Scots. There oddly was no reported stolen plunder on that foray, with the gang targeting those keeping a lookout for the reivers. Lord Henry Scrope and Captain Steven Ellis testified to the Scots *"pretending some outrage in Bewcastle or Gilsland,"* to give them an excuse to launch an attack on a hill-top watch whose job it was to light a bale-fire and give warning of raids. Scrope continues on how the Scots *"by accident fell upon the watch set that night, killing Mr Rowden, Nicholas Twedell, Jeffrey Naitby, Edward Stanton."* The watch was deliberately targeted and taken out, which suggests the watch was in a strategic place and was guarding a location which the gang wanted to raid requiring the element of surprise. The second bill was for a raid on the following day when *"36 kye and oxen, 3 horses and mears, and insight worth 8L."* were stolen from Lord Scrope's tenants.

When Kinmont Willie Armstrong was captured and imprisoned in Carlisle Castle in March 1596, with no surprise Sim rose to the challenge to help in his rescue. After the raid had taken place to free Kinmont, Lord Scrope named *"the young Laird of Whithaugh and his son"* on 14 April 1596 as among the principal assailants. Confirming his suspicions, Scrope received an Anonymous letter (from "Richies Will" Graham) on 24 April 1596, which stated that from Langholm, Buccleuch had with him Mangerton and Whithaugh and eight of their followers.

Sim became enemy number one, with an assertive effort to curb his lawless ways. James was open to English suggestions, wanting to seem favourable to the English public with an eye to Queen Elizabeth's throne. The solution to the problem was to have Sim handed over as a pledge for the good behaviour of his grayne. This was achieved without any fuss when pledges were demanded by Scotland and England, to be delivered to Sir William Bowes, the Queen's ambassador at the west ford near Norham on the 25 June 1597 at 10 hours before noon. Simon's name was included within the list, coming under the pledges for Liddesdale and named as *"Symy Armstrong young laird of Whittasse."* Sim was sent to York Castle and was placed under the charge of Robert Redhead, the castle's keeper, together with twelve other Scots. The weekly bill for the Scots diet and lodgings was recorded at the rate of 10s. 4d. per week. A pledge was only a temporary state and those held were often swapped for other members of the same family, it was not the same as being a prisoner. The conditions that the pledges were kept in was often very pleasant, however on this occasion Sim and his fellow Scots were unhappy at their environment. Dissent grew after Christmas when the victual payment was stopped and they had to use their own money to buy food. The harsh treatment planted the seed on all of the Scots to escape – enough was enough.

A fellow prisoner Lawrence Canby was in jail for murder and had local knowledge and contacts. Canby was the ideal foil to plan an escape through and became employed by the Scots to act as the organiser for the breakout. Sim and Everton approached Canby and offered him a deal – *"if he took their letters to Scotland, he should be so well used he would not need to care for England."* A correspondence then began with Ker of Cessford, who would provide horses just outside of York for the escapees to use. Cessford offered Canby a horse as a reward for his help and enough gold to live better than he ever did in England. Canby was facing execution, so what did he have to lose? Canby jumped at the opportunity and agreed to be the guide for the escapees once out of the castle. All looked good for the attempt, however there was one major flaw in the plans, Canby turned into an informant – he went straight to the jailer and betrayed all of the plans.

Canby was hoping that at his forthcoming trial, the information he was providing would save his life. Initially eight of the pledges were going to escape, then another four were added on Tuesday 13 March on the orders of Sim, when it was agreed that their location in an outer chamber could be reached after breaking through a wall in the gallery and unbolting the door. James Dargon, a local, was asked to obtain horses and a boat to aid in the rescue. Horses were too impractical for him to organise, but a boat was a different matter. Dargon found a rowing boat and moored it on the River Ouse, ready to take the Scots to the other side of the bank and their awaiting horses from Cessford.

Those lined up for the escape were:-

1. William Hall	2. Dandy Pringle	3. James Young
4. Richard Rutherford	5. Raphe Bourne	6. William Tayte
7. Robert Fryssell	8. Richard Young	9. Simon Armstrong
10. Thomas Aynesley	11. William Elwood (young)	12. William Elwood (elder)

The break out began on Wednesday 14 March 1598, between 8 and 9pm after locking up – when Hall, Pringle, Young, and Rutherford burst through their chamber wall. They emerged into the main gallery and unbolted a door to release three captives. Another cell was approached which was locked, and using an iron bar, the bolt of the lock was wrenched back to reveal Sim. The gathering party moved onto the third and final chamber which was similarly broken into, releasing young Elwood, Bourne, Tayte and Young. Meanwhile as the break out was starting, the Council sent twenty men armed with bills (a type of pole-arm) to a place called St Georges, and another company under John Redmaine, a justice official, to take up their positions on the opposite side of the castle. All exit avenues for the breakout were covered.

In the early hours of the 15 March, all twelve escapees made it into the gallery. Here they found a barred window facing to the outside, which they hacked at the mortar with makeshift implements and broke free the iron bars of the window. It was a long drop to the ground; straw was found and thrown out to make a soft cushion to land upon. Six of the party then climbed out through the window, Sim and the remaining five chose a different route, not liking the long drop. They ran along the gallery and burst through two doors to come across a rear wall halting their progress, with freedom behind. The group climbed over the wall with the exception of young Elwood (*"William Ellwood the younger of Dinleybyer – a boy about 12 years of age*"), who did not have the reach due to his young age. No one had the insight to offer a leg-up and he was left behind. Sim had bad luck on his landing on the other side – *"the lard of Whitto in leaping downe from the castle wall, broke his legg beneath the knee."* Now down to eleven Scots, the party ran and limped to their rendezvous by the river and straight into the awaiting levelled bills of the castle guards. The game was up and the Scots knew it, all were caught without any fighting back. The Scots were soon back inside York Castle and this time they were well guarded, held in irons in the strongest places of the castle. There would be no repeat escape for Sim and his colleagues.

Sim's father died in 1599, which transported him from being the young laird to the old laird of Whithaugh. This advancement made Sim's potential for destruction increase, now that he was in the sole command of the whole grayne of Whithaugh and beyond. This factor did not go un-noticed in Carlisle with a concerned Lord Scrope seeking more than ever to hold onto Sim. The young laird was bad enough, what new horrors could be expected with his power fully installed?

Sim remained in captivity for another two years. On 24 April 1600 he appealed to the queen to be released, in an exchange for his son Lance. His offer was written out and endorsed by William Selby, junior, as Simon was illiterate:-

"The Lard of Whithaugh and William Ellott, who for more than 2 years have been prisoners in York castle, for bills fyled on them and their friends by the late commission, bind themselves to pay and satisfy the Englishmen owners of the same, if the Queen of England of her clemency grants them liberty to return to their country, viz., on delivery of Launcelott Armstrong eldest son of Whithaugh 20 years of age, and of Robert Ellott eldest son of William Ellott, of like age, to remain true prisoners in York city: and to lay in bonds of 4 English gentlemen of yearly revenue and inheritance of 300L. or 400L. sterling at the least, in sums to the full value of the bills, – to be forfeited if their sons break prison, or if they pay not the said bills within 3 months of their freedom: their sons to be freed on payment of the bills.
Signed:- Symon Armestronge lord of Whitaughe his marke, Will'm Ellott his marke."

In that same month of April 1600 a document on the Scottish pledges for Liddesdale lists, *"Symon Armstrong laird of Whitthawgh,"* together with William Ellott of Esk and William Ellott of Clintwood as being delivered by Buccleuch. Simon must have been released in order to obtain a new negotiation on pledges to be organised. It is interesting to note that only one Armstrong was required for the pledges and that it was Simon who was selected – and two Elliots. Lord Scrope knew who the main Liddesdale trouble makers were and target the heads of these households.

Simon was locked up in York Castle for a second session, which came as a great annoyance to him. He was not to remain there for long, with a second escape attempt about to be launched. Lord Eure wrote to Cecil on 23 October 1600, on the outcome of the venture – *"Your honor has heard by my lord president, of the escape of Ellott and Armstronge, two principal of the Scottish pledges. The guarding of them so negligent and careless as cannot be excused: I dare not judge the dishonour to the Queen, and forbear to relate the triumph of the base people at large leaving it to my lord president's report from myself and this council."* Robert Redhead the castle jailer was concerned that he would be blamed by the queen for the breakout and voiced his concerns to Eure, *"to escape punishment and procure pardon for his offences."* Sir Robert Carey had great concern on Sim's escape and wrote to Cecil on 27 October expressing:-

"But there will be trouble on these borders, for notwithstanding our good order, the late unhappy escape of the 2 Liddesdale pledges from York, now with their friends at home, will breed more disquiet than anything that has happened since my living in the north. One of them is Will of Hescottes an Ellwood, the other Sim of Whithaughe, an Armstronge. These two were the principal of their name, and only spoilers of the Middle March: and they defied their officer the Laird of Buccleuch, refusing to enter at his command, till by the strong hand and other means, he got beyond them, and delivered them whether they would or no. Now on their escape, they refuse him obedience, and proclaim openly that all fugitives Scots or English who join them, shall be aided and protected, respecting neither their King nor his officers, or any hurt that England can do them: so that all honest men will rue the time they came home."

Sim was free and more dangerous than ever. Attracting broken men to his gang and with Buccleuch unable or unwilling to control him; Sim was arguably the most troublesome outlaw on the Border. Sir Robert Carey recorded Simon in his memoirs as *"The chief of all these outlaws, was old Sim of Whittram."* Perhaps prompted by Sim's potential for mayhem and certainly by the Scot's poor attempts to curb him (Buccleuch), King James brought in a new piece of law which allowed English officials to cross the Border legally and come directly to the source of the problem. Sim of course was not aware of the new changes issued on 18 April 1601, this was something radical and he would get a nasty shock when out on his next foray.

Life would now heat up and become exceedingly dangerous, with Carey having his new cross Border power. The first probable incident that Sim and his clan ran into Carey's heavy policing occurred in May 1601, not long after Carey received the warrant. Simon of Calfhill had been slain a few weeks earlier in an expedition by Woodrington. The manner of Calfhill's death, slain by a Ridley, provoked Sim into action. The Ridley's were at feud with the Armstrongs and the incident caused extreme rankle amongst the Armstrong lairds. The Armstrongs *"vowed cruel revenge; and that before the next winter was ended, they would leave the whole country waste, that there should be none to resist them."* The Calfhill Armstrongs saddled up for a raid on Haltwhistle, with the Whithaughs lending their support, planning to do as much damage to Ridley property as possible. Simon may have ridden along also, accompanying his sons who were intent in helping to address an Armstrong grievance.

Luckily for posterity, Sir Robert Carey recorded the event in his memoirs (first published in 1759), providing a first hand testimony to these stirring times...*"Thither they came, and set many houses of the town on fire, and took away all their goods ; and as they were running up and down the streets with lights in their hands to set more houses on fire, there was one other of the Ridleys that was in a strong stone house that made a shot out amongst them, and it was his good hap to kill an Armstrong, one of the sons of the chiefest outlaw. The death of this young man wrought so deep an impression amongst them, as many vows were made, that before the end of next winter, they would lay the whole Border waste. This (the murder) was done about the end of May."* The Armstrong who was shot was a young son of Simon, possibly Simon or Archibald – another death that would have to be avenged.

Carey wrote about the incident on 1 June 1601 to Cecil, expecting more trouble to follow...

Sim's son was not the only casualty at Haltwhistle, Walter Armstrong (the Laird's Wat) a son of Thomas, 7th Laird of Mangerton was also slain. The two deaths of such prominent Armstrongs, as reiver society demanded could only be satisfied with further blood loss. Sim after mourning the loss, gathered together his brood of sons to plan their pay-back revenge on the Ridleys, a death would have to be returned and with interest. The cycle of kill and revenge was difficult to break on the Border, but the cycle had less than two years to run, when King James used the power of the pen to conquer the sword.

Sir Robert Carey was doing his best to halt the Armstrongs in their tracks and had a determination and authority that previous wardens lacked. In June of that year he entered Liddesdale to encounter the usual Armstrong reaction of the population fleeing to the Tarras Moss for safety. Sim had seen all of this before and watched with disinterest expecting Carey to do a token amout of damage and then retreat the way he had just come. On this occasion however, something was odd, something new was underfoot. Carey's force halted at the mouth of the Tarras Valley and downed tools; what could they be up to? Out came saws and hammers and the soldiers began to contruct a fort. This action was unprecedented, sending shocks of conern through the Armstrongs. Sim put out guards to watch those who were watching them, and sat back to play the waiting game. It was a case of see who could sit it out the longest. Sim hoped that Carey would either get bored, or lack supplies and pull his men back. Surely this would not drag on into the winter. There is an anecdote which tells that as Carey was besieging the outlaws in the Tarras, the Armstrongs sent a raiding party into England which plundered his own lands. On Carey's return home, the Armstrongs sent him one of his own cows, informing him that they feared he was low on provisions after his visit to Scotland and had taken the precaution of sending him some English beef.

The siege of the valley would not to last much longer. At 4am on 5 July, Sim was awoken to the sound of shouts; Carey was attacking, marching up the valley in an attempt to flush out the Armstrongs. It was time to vacate the valley, but unknown to the Armstrongs three ambush parties had been placed on exits to snare those escaping. Carey's plan worked well with five of the principal Armstrongs captured. Sim escaped, who presumably used a route that was not guarded. Carey commented in his memoirs, _"The principal of the five, that were taken, were two of the eldest sons of Sim of Whittram. These five they brought to me to the fort, and a number of goods, both of sheep and kine, which satisfied most part of the country, that they had stolen them from."_ Lance of the Flatts was among the five captured. As Simon's heir and oldest son, Carey had the best possible bargaining card to use against the Whithaugh Armstrongs. Carey continues the narrative in his memoirs..._"The five that were taken, were of great worth and value amongst them; insomuch, that, for their liberty, I should have what conditions I should demand, or desire. First, all English prisoners_ *were set at liberty. Then had I themselves, and most part of the gentlemen of the Scottish side, so strictly bound in bonds, to enter to me, in fifteen days warning, any offender, that they durst not, for their lives, break any covenant that I made with them; and so, upon these conditions, I set them at liberty, and was never after troubled with these kind of people. Thus God blessed me in bringing this great trouble to so quiet an end; we broke up our fort, and every man retired to his own house."* Sim because of his captured sons was forced to come to the negotiation table with Carey, and his clan were now hobbled. Strict bonds were brought in and probably an end to their feud with the Ridley's was also forced upon them. The writing was on the wall, the days of Whithaugh power was over.

Sim was not able to survive the harsh process of pacification on the Border after 1603. As the head of the second worst grayne of the worst of the Riding families, he was a targeted man. He was recorded in a list of *"Prisoners Taken by Lord Dunbar"* in 1607, *"Of Scottishmen: John Armstrong of Mangertoun; Syme Armstrong of Quhitehanche; Andrew Armstrong his brother."* Execution was not long to follow. On 23 February 1607, from Berwick, George Home, 1st Earl of Dunbar wrote to the Bishop of Carlisle and Sir Wilfrid Lawson, stating that *"Mangerton, Whithaugh, William Ellott, Andrew Armstrong, and Martin Ellot, are executed for very odious and criminal causes, and fourteen others for stealths and other punishable causes."* Andrew, his brother was also hanged, bringing an abrupt end to the Armstrong power in Liddesdale.

✷✷✷

Sons to Lancelot, Laird of Whithaugh (d.1599)

1. Simon (Sim) – (ex.1607)   **2.** Francis – "The Standard Bearer" – (c.1580s/1600s)
3. Andrew – (ex.1607)   **4.** John – (c.1580s/1600s)
5. Archibald (Arche) – (fl.1589)

Lancelot had at least five sons, who followed in their father's footsteps as reivers. Simon as the heir to the lairdship has already been mentioned, with his four brothers being no less troublesome. Judging by the entries in the Border Calendar Papers, Francis was the most destructive of the brothers, appearing eight times before the March Wardens. Francis had a son named after his father – Lance, who was hanged by Lord William Howard "Belted-Will" in 1612.

Francis is first recorded in 1581 when he led a gang into the Borthwick Valley and raided the farm of Eilrig, an action that resulted in him being declared a rebel. Larger raids were to follow in May 1584; in a list of complaints compiled by Sir John Forster, Francis is recorded taking part in a hundred rider open foray to the Slymefoote on the Middle Marches together with Robert Armstrong his cousin. Robert (Hob) was probably the son of John of Whithaugh (ex.1588), who was the brother of Lancelot of Whithaugh. Hob was married to the daughter of Jeme Foster of the Stonegarthside. Sandie Hall of Yerduppe (Yardhope – in the Coquet Valley) made the complaint against *"Frauncis Armstronge of Whittawghe, Hobbe Armstronge of Whittaughe,"* and a who's who of Border ruffians and cut throats – including a horde of Armstrongs of the Gingles – Emey, Willie, Eckie, Tom, Elley, and Ebbey, plus Dick Armstrong of Dryhope,

Edie Ellott of the Shawes, Eckie Armstrong of the Harelaw, Willie Ellott of Thorlieshope, Clemey Crosier (*"nebles Clemey"*), Davie Ellott (*"the Corlen"*) and Hobbie Ellott of the Burneheades. They were all charged for *"stealing 300 kie and oxen, 40 horses and meires, spoiling 30 sheles to the value of 100L. Englishe, and taking 20 prisoners."*

Three years later Andrew joined in on the family raiding. On 23 June 1587 Andrew rode out in a five hundred strong day foray which *"carried off 600 kye and oxen, 600 sheep, 35 prisoners and insight worth 40L. sterling."* The complaint was made by the Laird of Prendicke and Henrie Collingewood of Ryle and their tenants of Ingram and Reavelie – and was laid upon *"John Armestronge called 'the Lairds Jocke', Andro Armestronge of Whithaugh, Ecktor Armestrong of the Hilhouse, Jock Armestronge of Kynmoth, Georg Armestronge of Arcleton, John Bateson called 'John of the Score'."* Two months later Andrew was riding alongside his brothers Francis and Simon in a raid against the Laird of Bellister and his tenants. On 30 August 1587, a night foray was made by – *"Andro Armestrong and Frauncis, sons to the Laird of Whithaughe, and Syme of Whitthaughe their brother, Arche Armestronge called 'Alexanders Arche', servant to Syme of Whithaughe, Ekkye Armestronge of Tweden, Thom Ellot of Copshawe, William Ellott of Goddamburie and others who burned 25 houses and more, and carried off chattels and insight goods worth 1000L. sterling."*

On 13 April 1590, all of the Armstrong sons plus Robert their cousin were requested to attend a warden's Truce Day at the *"Belles Kyrk"* to hear Middle March bills against Liddesdale. The family appeared in four of the bills and faced questioning by Thomas Trotter, the deputy Keeper of Liddesdale, and his opposite number William Fenwick, deputy warden of the English Middle March.

1. 11 Nov (Martinmas) – 1588

"'Mertynmesse,' 1588. – Roger Watson and his neighbours of Rinyonhill, upon Arche Armestrong 'Andrews son', Francis and Andrew of Whithawgh, &c. for taking 24 kye and oxen, a 'lyrehorse', insight 10 L. sterling. Memorandum. – At this heirshipp Arche Armstrang horse was slayne and had therfore bestowed of him the sayd lyrehorse."

2. 22 Feb – 1589

"John Robinson and George Person of Todborne Steile complain upon Andrew and Francis Armstrong sons to the laird of Whythawgh, &c., for stealing 40 kye and oxen, 2 horses, insight value 20L., and maiming said John, Jerard Orde and others, damage 100L., 20 days after Candlemas last."

3. 8 Sept – 1589

"Edward Shaftoo of Bavington complains upon Hob 'the Taillour', Arche Armstrong son to the 'owld' laird of Whithaugh, Robine Armstrong of Whithaugh, Alexanders Arche Armstrong for stealing 18 oxen, a bull and 7 old kye, a horse and a meare, about 8th September last."

"Thomas Blenkesopp, Raiphe Walles, Georg Walles, Nicholas Tesdale, Robert Younger, Nicholas Tesdalle the elder, Henrie Johson, Henrie Smythe, John Smythe, Thomas Cowtart, John Harrison, William Tesdale, William Harrison, Henrie Parker, Richard Liddell, Henrie Lyddell, John Bell, Henrie Bell, Richard Gray, Robert Cowtarte, Henrie Ramshatt, and Robert Walles, &c., complain upon Andrew Armstrong son to the Larde of Whithawghe, Francys and John Armstrong his brothers, of Whithawghe, Arche Ellott of Clentwood, Hob Ellott, Gib Ellott his brother, Marting Ellott called 'Martinges Gib', James [ ], and old Will Elot of the Steile, George Simpson, John Ellott 'longe John', Andrew and 'red nebb' Hob Armstrong for about St. Luck's day 1589 coming to the Blackcluche in Kirkhawhe and reaving 40 yowes, 10 hogges, and taking the complainers prisoners following the lawful trode, with their horses and furniture and ransomed them for 180L. sterling."

It is not known if Francis, Andrew, John and Archibald attended the rescue mission of Kinmont Willie in April 1596. There is a good possibility as their brother Simon, the Laird of Whithaugh and the Laird of Mangerton were reported as having eight followers with them on the raid. On 28 April 1597, Lancelot and Francis Armstrong of Whithaugh, together with David Armstrong called *"bredsworde,"* surfaced at Carlisle for Middle March bills on Liddesdale. The Lancelot named was probably the nephew of Francis (Lancelot of the Flatts, the son of Simon) and not his father – who if he was even alive (he died in this year), would have been of an advanced age and infirm. A bill was put forward by Thomas Blackett of Burnefoote that was found *"quit on the said keeper's honor."*

In 18 April 1601 a document was issued by the Scottish king that passed over the authority to control a number of Scottish outlaws from the Laird of Buccleuch to Lord Scrope and Sir Robert Carey. James was unhappy and frustrated at the lack of progress at stopping the constant raids, which came as no surprise as Buccleuch was a part of the problem himself. The document contained a list of the outlaws that were to come under Scrope and Carey's observations. The names were in two groups, one for the West March and the other for Liddesdale. The list of Liddesdale outlaws is interesting as it contains a large proportion from the Whithaugh grayne, ten out of the seventeen, illustrating that the family were the main trouble makers in Liddesdale in 1601. Breaking the list down it contained:-

Three sons of Lancelot, the Laird of Whithaugh:-

1. Andrew   **2.** Francis   **3.** John

Three sons of Simon, the Laird of Whithaugh:-

4. Sym of the Rone   **5.** Archie   **6.** Sandy

Four brothers from the House of Whithaugh:-

7. Archie ("Whitehead")   **8.** John   **9.** Sym   **10.** "Alexander's Archie"

Various other names:-

11. Sym Armstrong of Calfield   **12.** Thom Rannik   **13.** Andrew Tayler

14. John Armstrong of the Whisgills   **15.** John Hill ("the Lordis Geordie")
16. John Armstrong of the Side   **17.** "Symis Archie"

Francis found himself in hot bother when on a raid to Cotehill, SE of Carlisle, when the locals rose to defend their property. Francis was a part of a gang of Scots thirty strong who harried most of the town of *"Coathill"* on a Thursday night with fire and sword. The Scots did not have things all of their own way; as they were raiding the warning beacons had been lit and a party of sixty men made up from Corby and other adjoining townships had been mustered to block the Scots route back home. Graham country lay between the Armstrongs and safety, and here they were tracked down by the Corby hot trod. The incident was documented in a letter by John Dalston (juror) to Lord Scrope on 15 January 1602, who described how in the ensuing encounter *"the Scots fought themselves away with all the goodes."* A running skirmish occurred, with the Armstrongs getting the best from it and managing to put some distance between their adversaries. The Scots had bad luck on the return journey, running into a "plumpe watch" of seventeen principal Grahams which halted their movement and allowed the Corby trod to catch up. Another melee ensued, with steadying resolve the trod fought with a new valour determined to teach the thieving Armstrongs a lesson. The Grahams were the tipping balance in the skirmish and the Scots received a bloodied nose. Seven prisoners were taken, *"Francie Whittow among them, and 20 horses, with their furniture."* The rest of the Scots managed to escape by fleeing to the wild country, getting *"verie hardlie away on foote in the mosse, where hardly either horse or man cold passe, els had they bine all taken."* Francis and his fellow prisoners were taken to Rockcliffe Castle to await Scrope's further pleasure.

Francis took part in the "Ill Week" of 1603, the last hurrah of the reivers. He is referred to as *"the Standard Bearer"* during the cross Border raiding – was this his normal nickname or a one-off for "Ill Week?" And carrying a standard; reivers did not carry flags as there was no point, wanting their identity to be anonymous. Why would a thief broadcast who he was, it could only lead to a self-conviction. "Ill Week" though was no ordinary raid and perhaps sensing the game was up, the Whithaugh Armstrongs decided to go out with a bang, and had Francis proudly bear the family coat-of-arms above the lances as they rode for one last time. The Whithaugh's wanted their targets to know exactly who they were and what better way than to have a standard fly before them. Francis accompanied Simon, the 9th Laird of Mangerton and his son Archibald, and together they numbered about two hundred. They penetrated as far as Penrith, the strong arm of Armstrong leading the fore. And safely back with a handsome haul of insight and livestock.

The ultimate fate of Francis is not known. Andrew was executed in 1607 alongside his older brother Simon.

5. Gingles

The Armstrongs of Gingles descend from William "Ill Will" Armstrong (b.c.1425 – ex.1530), who was a son of Thomas Armstrong, 5th Laird of Mangerton. The tower of Gingles stood halfway in between the two strongest Armstrong graynes, of Whithaugh and Mangerton, 1.5km away from both on the lower slope of Yethouse Hill. There is no sign of the tower today, but it stood close to the streams of the Near Jingle Sike and the Far Jingle Sike (perhaps between both), which flow into the Tweeden Burn. The House of Gingles takes its name from the French for dog – "Chien," and the Old English term "gill," for a deep ravine/narrow mountain stream. Having a stronghold between two gills would provide excellent defence and help to corral cattle within. The spelling of the House changed over time, merging from Jingles/Chingils into Gingles.

It was Ill Will's son, Sandy, who became known as the Father of House of Gingles. The Gingles grew to become a powerful family, with their progeny expanding beyond Liddesdale. A branch of the Gingles was set up in the Ewes Valley, with towers constructed at Glendivan and Kirkton. Having family bases in two different valleys makes it difficult to work out who was who within the family. The family headsmen and chiefs also moved around from stronghold to stronghold during the year, according to the season and social politics.

$$\ast\ast\ast$$

William – "Ill Will" – of the Gingles – (b.c.1449 – ex.1530)

William was the son of Thomas, 5th Laird of Mangerton and originated the House of the Chingils (Gingles), sometimes also called Raltoun (Ralton). William had at least two sons – Alexander ("*Ill Will's Sandie*") and Simon ("*Mickle Sym*"), and was the grandfather of Kinmont Willie Armstrong. It is an interesting exercise to work out what was "ill" about William for him to gain such a nickname. He lived to a grand old age, so could not have had any debilitating health problems. William was more probably named after an ill temper. It easy to visualise William becoming angry at dozens of tasks and individuals – and shouting his abuse at any peasant, merchant, reiver or lord who happened to displease him. He must have been a fearsome character and can be imagined bellowing his defiance across the moors.

In 1527 William's son Simon, was killed by the Johnstones. A death that progressed to a blood feud, which was led by William's other son Alexander. A dislike for the Johnstones would continue for the rest of the century, with the Armstrongs often aiding the Maxwells in their own separate feud with that family. As the Armstrongs grew in number and power, William moved out of Liddesdale and into the Debateable Land. William allied himself with Lord Maxwell, who was the overlord of Eskdale and lands across the Debateable Land. The association allowed William to lease lands at Morton Rig on the east bank of the River Sark, where he built a stronghold which became named as the Tower of Sark / Morton and later Kinmont's Tower. William's stronghold was the type of dwelling known as a blockhouse.

The tower's location gave problems to the English authorities; it was right in the middle of the Debateable Land, land which was impossible to be labelled as belonging to Scotland or England. This confusion was milked by William, who would commit crimes in England and then return home insisting that he was on Scottish land and immune from prosecution. William also pastured his cattle freely in England from sunrise to sunset, returning them each night to a Scottish byre. In March 1528 William, Lord Dacre decided to sort out this legal loophole and invaded the Debateable Land, targeting out William. Dacre had recently been made Warden of the West March in England in that year and was eager to show off his new power and put an end to Armstrong raiding. On Dacre's approach, William sensibly fled for the hills. Dacre described in a document on what his men faced; William's house was described as *"buylded after siche a maner that it couth not be brynt ne distroyed, unto it was cut downe with axes."* William's stronghold was left a smouldering ruin once the axes had done their work, he would have to find temporary accommodation until a new building – and axe-proof – could be constructed. The Armstrongs had enjoyed a long streak of weak opposition to their abuse of power since the Battle of Flodden, however the tide was about to change.

The Scottish king joined in on the clamp down on the outlaws in 1530, mounting large expeditions into the Borders. The Armstrongs were on his list to pacify and he sent a letter on ahead inviting the main Armstrong lairds to meet him as guests. The Armstrongs feared no one and had no reason to be worried about James V, as the Armstrongs were always careful to never raid in Scotland. They were a major nuisance to England, but Scotland had no reasons to have concerns. The Armstrongs though proved disastrously wrong in their judgement of the monarch. Johnnie Armstrong of Gilnockie organised the Armstrong party and invited William along. All gathered in their finest clothes; William was in his advanced years and would have looked splendid in the latest European fashion. The Armstrongs rode off to meet their monarch – full of pride and achievement... and straight into a trap. Only one came back.

✳✳✳

Thomas – (Old Thom) – (c.1583)

Thomas – (Young Thom) – (fl.1584)

Hector (Eckie) – (fl.1584)

Alie/Elley – (fl.1584)

Herbert (Ebbey) – (fl.1584)

Old Thom was the father of young Thom, Hector, Elley and Ebbey – and judging by the company they kept, resided in Liddesdale. The head of the family is first named on 22 August 1556, noted as *"Thom Armstrang of the Chengylls"*– when making a bond along with Hector Armstrong of the Hairlaw, George Armstrong of Powterlampet, Martin Elliott and Arche Nykson of the Steill – *"to enter Will Nyksoun within the iron gates of Fernyhirst to John Kerr."* With a second documentation in the 1583 list that Thomas Musgrave draughted up, and recorded as *"Thome Armestronge called old Thome of Chengles."*

At a Truce Day heard 3-19 May 1584, Sir John Forster viewed a series of complaints, one of which included several of the Gingles tribe. Four sons of Old Thomas were involved, together with another two families of the Gingles. It is difficult to work out who was exactly who, with the family being spread out in different locations. The complaint was made by Sandie Hall of Yerduppe, against the following groups of Gingles Armstrongs:-

1. *"Eckie, young Tom, Elley, and Ebbey Armstronges, all of the Gingells"*

2. *"Tom of Glendennengs son, his brother Christie the same Toms son"*

3. *"Emey Armstronge of the Gingells, Willie Armstronge of the Gingells"*

This collection of Gingles was probably made up of three separate families, and not all necessarily living in Liddesdale. The group were accompanied by Francis and Hobbe of Armstronge of Whithaugh, Eckie Armstronge of the Harlawe, Dickie Armstronge of Driauppe (Dryhope), Edie Ellott of the Shawes, Willie Ellott of Thorlieshope, Clemey Crosier (nebless Clem – a reiver with no nose), Davie Ellott the *"Corlen,"* Hobbie Ellott of the Burneheades and one hundred others. The combined gang ran *"an open foray at the Slymefoote on the Middle Marches, stealing 300 kie and oxen, 40 horses and meires, spoiling 30 sheles to the value of 100L. Englishe, and taking 20 prisoners."*

The family were recorded raiding in 1584 and in the same location as previous (the gang must have saw more easy pickings available), in a complaint made by Tristram Fenwicke and Sandie Hall. They named *"old Thom Armestronge of the Gyngles, younge Thom Armestronge of the same, Eckie his brother, Alie his brother"* – together with Syme and Hob Armstrong of Whithaugh, Thomas Armstrong (*"Rowyes Thom"*) of Mangerton, Adie Ellott of the Shawes and others – who ran a day foray on *"the Satterdaie after St Elen daie 1584"* [21 May]. The gang were charged for *"taking sixteen score kye and oxen, 21 horses and meares, spoiling 30 sheiles, and ransoming 10 prisoners at the Slyme"*.

✱✱✱

<u>Other members of the House of Gingles</u>

It is not known if the following Gingles were from Liddesdale or Ewesdale.

Alexander of the Gingles – (fl.1528)

Alexander was the son of ill Will's Sandie Armstrong. He is recorded on 23 April 1528 riding with Heby Armstrong, the Irwens (Irvines) and Clement Nykson, in a revengeful foray into England. The target was the home of Lang Will Graham, which they set on fire and slew many persons including Will Foster, before heading home with a large head of cattle. The cause of the raid has to be wondered at as the Grahams were good friends and allies of the Armstrongs.

✱✱✱

George – ("Richie's Geordie") – "Henharrow" of the Gingles – (b.c.1565)

George was named in a list delivered to the Bishop of Carlisle as one of the principal offenders who made incursions into Cumberland and Westmorland. In the list were also mentioned Archie, Jock and Emie of Gingles. He died in Bewcastle, England. George had at least one son Adam Armstrong, who was born in 1612 in Bewcastle and died 1672 in Canonbie.

Ninian (Renyon) of the Gyngills – (fl.1589)

At the "*Belles Kyrk*" on 13 April 1590, Ninian was summoned to appear before William Fenwick, deputy for the warden of the Middle March of England, and Thomas Trotter, deputy for the Lord Bothwell, Keeper of Liddesdale. Ninian was charged for taking part in a raid by the "*Larde of Varren John Snawdon of Lynbrigges, John Wilkenson of Dunsgren, George Gren of Allenton,*" alongside the rest of the town of Allenton and Linbriggs. Their complaint was made upon "*Will Ellott of Fidderton, Hobb Ellott larde of the Burne heades, Quintins Arche Croser, Renyon Armestrong of the Gyngills, and 200 others for reiving 100 kye and oxen, 20 horses and meares, spoiling the town, and taking 20 men prisoners, 23rd June 1589.*"

6. Catheugh

Catheugh was located on the south bank of the Tweeden Burn, opposite the Gingles.

✳✳✳

Lancelot (Lancie) – of Catheugh – (fl.1645)

Lancelot was not a reiver, as his reign of theft occurred well after the Union of Crowns; however he was a moss-trooper. These troopers were the last remnants of the reiving society – giving the Riding spirit a final release of life during the Great Civil War. The moss-troopers had reiving in their blood, their fathers having been the last generation to have brought fire and steel across the Border to fill the pot.

Many in Liddesdale took the breakdown in rule and disorder within the Kingdom caused by the wars to make a quick profit, and followed in their ancestors hoof prints. Lancelot was one of these restless souls, who perhaps put on his father's breastplate and helmet, and with a gang of marauders, rode south into England along the once common thieves' roads in 1645. He was accompanied by Geordie Rackesse of the Hillhouse, and several others, who silently slipped across the Border. The raiders of course would not be expected, with the bale-fire system of warnings now dismantled. The gang made a successful raid and lifted about eighty oxen, then returned for home on a Sunday forenoon. Interestingly, on heading back the gang met up with the owner of the cattle Roger Harbottle, who attempted to stop the theft by bargaining with Lancelot and Geordie. It is not recorded how Harbottle came to run into the gang, with the most probable reason he attempted a mounted rescue of the cattle. Harbottle must have lacked the men to enforce a hand over of the cattle and used negotiation instead. Harbottle began by asking for the return of the cattle as they belonged to him. Lancelot replied that he was taking the cattle as this was a business agreement; it was blackmail, payment due for the past unpaid forty odd years. He stated that his father and grandfather had formerly taken "protection-money" from this area, and that he was simply coming to collect the arrears that should be due to him. Lancelot of course was chancing his luck, as the payment of blackmail had not been in operation on the Border since 1603, a system which was both hated and illegal. Harbottle lived in an age of relative peace, safe from having to watch his livestock from the night time marauders. His father would have told him tales about the reivers, and he listened in amazement to their dangerous exploits, but felt safe at night as they were now no more. But suddenly on that single night in 1645, the fears of his ancestors came back to visit and became very much real.

Harbottle offered Lancelot eight shillings sterling for each of his cattle, which was a fair exchange, but without success. Lancelot was not in the mood for trade, feeling immunity from the punishment that the Civil War had brought. He hoped that this was the beginning of a return to the old reiving society, and the levying of this protection-money was only the beginning. Lancelot alleged that the Barony of Langlie, in which Harbottle was located, owed him thirty pounds sterling in arrears for services granted. He added with malice the threat of another raid.

The day of drama was not over. When driving the cattle past Chiffonberrie Craig, one of the victims of the raiders, a poor English curate was present, and noticed that his cattle were amongst the herd. The curate followed the raiders and desired them earnestly to let him have his *"twae or thrie beasts again, because he was a Kirkman."* Geordie laughed merrily and replied that he could have his beasts again if he would give his men a little preaching. The curate remarked back *"Oh! – good youths, this is a very unfit place for preaching; if you and I were together in church I would do my best to give you content."* Geordie was not happy at the arrangement and raised the stakes – *"Then, if you will not preach to us, yet you will give us a prayer, and we will learn you to be a moss-trooper."* The curate still refused, not wanting to compromise with thieves. Geordie accepted he was getting nowhere with his demand and changed tact, with good humour he stated – *"If you will neither preach nor pray to us, yet you will take some tobacco or sneisin* [snuff] *with us."* The curate was content at this, and agreed to join the snuff taking, but *"provyding they wald give him his beastes againe,"* which they accordingly agreed to. Snuff was taken and the curate received his cattle.

Lancelot for this short time was living out the life of his ancestors, savouring the power, freedom and profits of being the lord of all he surveyed. It was not to last however, he was summoned to court later that year to answer for his crimes. A civil society was soon to resume after the iron fist of Cromwell, a new era of elegance and stability under Charles II was approaching.

7. Hillhouse

The Hillhouse as the name suggests was a house on the hill, located 2km to the east of Newcastleton on a hillside overlooking the Liddel Water. The hill which gave the tower its name was Swarf Hill, and was built half way up its SW slope, providing excellent views down the Liddel Valley giving advanced warning of trouble. Their neighbours were the Armstrongs of the Gingles, 0.5km away down the valley at Tweeden Burn, and the Armstrongs of Tweeden.

Hector (Ecktor) of the Hillhouse – (c.1584)

Hector was first recorded on a raid in 1584 at Michaelmas. He was part of a 300 man day foray which included Davye Ellott ("*the Carlinge*"), Clement Croser ("*Nebles Cleme*"), Thomas Armstrong ("*Symes Thom*") of Demayne Holme and Will Armstrong called "*Kynmothe.*" The group took away a large haul, listed as "*forty score kye and oxen, three score horses and meares, 500 sheep, burned 60 houses, and spoiling the same to the value of 2000L. sterling and slaying 10 men.*" In total 1360 beasts were driven back into Liddesdale, the valley would be well supplied with beef and mutton that winter. Their targets on the other hand faced destitution and a grim hunger. A complaint was issued by Jenkyn Hunter, Bartie Milburne of the Keam, Jarrie Hunter, Mychaell Milburne and Lante Milburne of Tarset in Tyndale, in a hope that the authorities could get them compensation and have their livelihood restored.

Hector took part in a second raid on 23 June 1587, accompanied by John Armstrong ("*the Lairds Jocke*"), Andrew Armstrong of Whithaugh, Jock Armstrong of Kinmont, George Armstrong of Arkleton, John Bateson ("*John of the Score*") and another 500 men. This was a large scale raid containing the main Armstrong graynes; it would have been an unstoppable force. The group ran a day foray and "*carried off 600 kye and oxen, 600 sheep, 35 prisoners and insight worth 40L. sterling.*" A complaint was made on the raiders by the Laird of Prendicke and Henrie Collingewood of Ryle and their tenants of Ingram and Reavelie.

8. Potterlamport

Potterlamport was located 2km east of Whithaugh and 2km south of Castleton, on the east side of the Liddel Water. The site was situated on the east side of Pouterlampert Sike, a stream which flows between Priest Hill and Stell Knowe. There is no documentary evidence to support that Potterlamport had a tower, and may have been purely a domestic village.

William (Will) of Potterlamport – (c.1580s/90s)

William is first recorded in December 1583, when included within Thomas Musgrave's list of the Border Riders. He appears as *"Will Armestronge called Will of Powter-lampert,"* within the section of *"The Armstrongs of Melyonton quarter."* William is included in another list a few years later, compiled by John Monipennie in 1597 on the principal clans and chiefs of the Border. He is listed as *"Will of Powderlanpat,"* and named alongside Archibald of Westburnflat and *"Wanton Sym"* in Whitlawside. Simon and Archibald must have formed their own gang and raided as a unit. William was obviously an important Armstrong headsman; however there is no record on his activities and how he came to have gained his status.

***

9. Tweeden

Tweeden was located on the Tweeden Burn; the exact location is not known, but ranged from an area between Tweedenhead and the Tweeden Burn's confluence with the Liddel Water, with the Tweedenhead end being the most likely. Tweedenhead was where the Cadger Road met the Maiden's Way, a communication hub which would have brought trade to the area. The Maiden's Way is said to perhaps predate the Romans; the road ran south to Birdoswald Fort on Hadrian's Wall and north to Castleton and beyond. The Tweeden along its banks once had a cave (close to a powerful petrifying well) where the Armstrongs used to hide their plunder; a location which must have been thought safer than a tower house.

✳✳✳

Ninian (Rynyon) of Tweden – (c.1570s/1600s)

Hector (Ekkye) of Tweden – (c.1580s/1590s)

Ninian and Hector were brothers, a troublesome duo who chalked up a long list of crimes and misdemeanours. Ninian is the first of the two to reach the archives, when in 1576 an order was issued to allow him to be released from ward and detention by Sir David Wemyss. Ninian was held temporary by Wemyss as a pledge for *"the gang of Quhithauch,"* an action designed to ensure the good behaviour of the Whithaugh Armstrongs. This suggests that Ninian that was both an illustrious reiver and a member of the gang of Whithaugh.

The brothers are first recorded on a raid in around the Midsummer of 1579 when Ninian and Hector took part in a four hundred rider strong day foray into Northumberland. Thomas and John Dod of Thorneborne, and Lyell Dod of the Blacklawe, later made their complaints on the raid. The Armstrongs were in such numbers that they were unable to mount their own trod. The complaint was worded as against *"William Armestronge of Kynmothe, Syme Armestronge younge Lard of Whithaughe, Rynione and Eckie Armestronge of Tweden."* Hector and Ninian must have been important Armstrongs to have been named alongside the Laird of Whithaugh and Kinmont Willie Armstrong. The Armstrongs are reported as taking *"40 score kye and oxen, a thousand sheep and gate."* A huge haul which numbered 1,800 beasts – enough for every rider to have 4.5 animals each, more than enough beef and mutton for the winter. In the raid Uswold Dode was slain, a relative of those who made the complaint – there would always be winners and losers in this culture of thieving.

The Tweeden Armstrongs had strong connections with the Whithaugh Armstrongs, and raided together in the same gang. This connection brought Ninian and his Hector into armed combat with the Scotts and Gladstones in August 1580. The clash was caused when a party of fifty Scotts and Gladstones passed through Liddesdale on a hot trod mission to fetch back their stolen cattle from an English raid. The trod posed no threat to the Armstrongs, and by March Law Ninian and Hector should have actually joined the trod, but Lancelot Armstrong of Whithaugh had other thoughts. As mentioned earlier in the chapter on Lancelot of Whithaugh, the Armstrongs fell upon the trod for an easy profit, in which the brothers fought in the one sided skirmish which ensued. The fallout from ambushing a hot trod was treated seriously, as this attacked one of the key elements of Border Law challenging its very authority. Hector, named as *"Hecke Armstrang, callit Tweden,"* Ninian and several others were summoned to appear before the Lords of the Council to stand trial – and predictably none showed up. Those named were denounced as rebels and put to the horn, though how effective this action would be, was highly debateable.

Ninian was not deterred by being put to the horn, a year later he led a gang on a raid to Bellendean in Scott country, and stole sixty sheep. He was summoned to appear before a court alongside his servant on this charge, and again failed to attend. He was declared a rebel soon after for the second time. Ninian is named within Thomas Musgrave's document on the Border Riders produced in December 1583, listed as *"Rynyon Armestronge called Rynyon of Twedon,"* within the section titled *"Armestronges of the howse of Whetaughe towre."* To be so named within the document suggests that Ninian was the senior headsman at Tweeden. The brothers lived at the core of Armstrong power, between the graynes of Mangerton and Whithaugh. The following year Hector was required to sign an assurance for his guaranteed good behaviour on 20 December 1584 at Whithaugh Tower. The demand came from Sir John Forster, an order that he dare not challenge. Hector must have been singled out from the many other Armstrong Riders as a particular troublesome individual who needed to be hobbled. Lance Armstrong mentions Hector in a document, describing him as *"Eckkie Armestrange of Twedden, dwellinge benethe Twedden upon the Larde of Mangertons grounde, beinge one of my howse and beinge upon the grounde where skaithe was done."*

Another raid is recorded on the night of 30 August 1587, when the Laird of Bellister and his tenants made a complaint *"uppon Andro Armestrong and Frauncis, sons to the Laird of Whithaughe, and Syme of Whitthaughe their brother, Arche Armestronge called 'Alexanders Arche', servant to Syme of Whithaughe, Ekkye Armestronge of Tweden, Thom Ellot of Copshawe, William Ellott of Goddamburie and others who burned 25 houses and more, and carried off chattels and insight goods worth 1000L. sterling."*

Ninian was called to attend a Truce Day on 13 April 1590 at the Bells Kirk, coming before the English deputy Middle March Warden William Fenwick, and his opposite number Thomas Trotter, who was standing in for Francis Stewart, 5th Lord Bothwell, Keeper of Liddesdale. The two deputy's job was to attempt to redress bills on both sides of the Border, with Ninian on charges for three bills of Liddesdale...

1. William Loren made a complaint upon *"Robert Armstrong 'Robine the taillor', Rinion Armstrong of Tweeden, Mathew Armstrong, Adam Ellott son to Davie of Dunlies, 'Alexander's Arche' Armstrong,"* for coming into Trewhitt, near Morpeth on 26 January 1589 and *"taking away a black mare price 4L., money and insight 5 marks."* During the raid Robert Storie's house was broken into, and the poor Robert was abducted and carried back to Scotland as a prisoner.

2. John Heron of Chipchase esquire and Agnes Heron late wife to Cuthbert Heron, made a complaint upon *"Renyon Armestronge of Twedon, Ingram Armestronge of the Castleton, and Archebalde Croser alias 'Whyntynes Arche', for stealing 7 score of yowes and wetheris, and 3 score of hoggis about 16th March last."*

3. *"The said John Heron complains upon the said Renyon, John Croser, alias 'Adams John', 'Whyntons Arche' Croser, for stealing 9 horse and mears about Michaelmas last."*

Ninian took part in the Battle of Dryfe Sands on 7 December 1593, taking the side of the Johnstones. When Maxwell's army broke and fled down the Dryfe Water to the town of Lockerbie, Ninian chased after the panicking soldiers and probably inflicted many a "Lockerbie Lick," upon the unfortunate Maxwells. The battle caused an enquiry within the Scottish Government as it was a needless family feud and resulted in the death of a lord. The authorities sought out the names of those who were responsible for the slaughter, seeking to punish the worst offenders, and *"Niniane Armestrang of Tueden,"* was listed amongst the 180 pointed out. By the time a trial came along, the government's desire to press charges had cooled off and was dropped. In the following year respite was given to all those who had followed Sir James Johnstone, and for the killing of Lord Maxwell and others.

Hector was requested to attend a Liddesdale in-denture on 7 March 1594 at the *"Dayehohne in Cressoppe,"* held by Walter Scott (the cousin of Buccleuch) of *"Gowdelandes"* (Goldielands), and Thomas Carlton the constable of Carlisle Castle. During the proceedings, Umfray and Herrie Dobson brought a bill up against *"Eckye Armstrange of Tweden,"* – Hector living up to his usual reliability, failed to turn up. The authorities were not tolerating this lack of show; in Hector's place Will Armstrong of Tweeden was delivered instead. It was proposed for Will to stay within Carlisle until Lord Scrope or Mr Carlton gave him license to depart.

Hector is last recorded raiding within a series of Gilsland complaints against Liddesdale on 24 October 1595. Anthony Carleton raised the complaint for the *"hearshipp at Tredermayne the 12th September,"* naming *"Watt of Harden, John Henderson of Hoghyll, Andro Henderson, Hector Armstrong of Tweden, Andro Armstrong 'the bundgell', Gyb Ellott brother to Wyll of the Fawandeshe, Arche and Hobe Ellott sons to the said Wyll, and Hob Ellott the laird of the Burnheads,"* as those responsible. The gang stole *"60 kye and oxen, and 6 horses and mares."*

On 13 April 1596 the dramatic rescue of Kinmont Willie Armstrong took place at Carlisle Castle. The following day Lord Scrope drew up a document which named the principal assailants on the raid. The document mentions *"three bretheren of Tweda, Armstrongs;"* there is a high probability that Hector and Ninian were two of them.

Attempts were made to make the Tweeden brothers behave themselves. On 30 September 1599, Walter Scott of Buccleuch requested from Branxholme Castle, the presence of Ninian – alongside Sym Armstrong of Mangerton, Lancelot Armstrong (elder) of Whithaugh, young *"Lancie Armestrang, son to Sym of Quhithauch,"* and John Armstrong of Tinnis Burn alias the *"Lairdis Jok,"* to sign a bond to make the inhabitants of Liddesdale answerable to the king and his laws – and more importantly *"to be answerable to the Laird of Balcleuch."* The named Armstrongs were the worst offenders within Liddesdale, and having them under bond would go a long way to keeping the peace.

Ninian makes one last appearance in the records, when at trial on 7 March 1606 in Edinburgh. This was not for a reiving offence but murder. He was named as *"Niniane Airmestrang, callit Niniane of Tueidane,"* and was charged alongside Andrew Henderson, servant to the Laird of Mangerton, and Archibald Armstrong, called *"Fair Archie"* – for the *"Dilaitit of the Slauchter"* of *"Andro Smyth, and demembring of Thomas Tueidie* [of Dunsyre] *of his neise* [nose]." Gavin Elliot of Fiddleton was charged separately for cutting off Thomas Tweedie's nose.

10. Mangerton

The chief seat of the Scottish Armstrongs was at Mangerton, an area of low-lying level pastureland which was originally called Merieton / Myreton. The name Mangerton comes from the Old English *"mangera tun,"* meaning the farm of the merchants, and has no connection to mangers. Mangerton Tower was located on a flat plain on the east bank of the Liddel Water where the river bends outwards to Kirk Hill. The tower was in the shadow of Blinkbonny Height and Carby Hill, sentinels which fall away to the south and the English Border at Kershopefoot. The Armstrongs had a homeland well protected by hills, which had grazing excellent for livestock – ideally situated for a life of crime at the centre of a secluded valley with good trade links nearby.

In the cock-pit of Liddesdale, the Mangerton Armstrongs came to dominate the area. It was a case of the survival of the fittest, and the Mangertons were certainly fit. The Border Games of Liddesdale used to be held at Mangerton, an event which came about after the creation of the village of Newcastleton in 1793. In this sporting occasion athletes would compete with putting a 23lb ball, and the throwing of a 14lb hammer; all great reiver training. It is easy to imagine a similar event being enacted in the 16th century, with the different Riding families testing their strength for prizes and kudos. The first stronghold to be built at Mangerton was probably a wooden tower in around 1135. In 1244 the tower was ordered to be repaired by King Alexander II of Scotland, fearing a threat of invasion by Henry III of England. At around the same time, building work was begun on Hermitage Castle to give further protection. The Armstrongs had no chief at this moment, but with the outbreak of war with England in 1296, the Border would need new strong guardians. The Armstrongs fought for King Robert the Bruce, and it is probable through this association that the Armstrongs obtained their first chieftain – Alexander (the second of that name), who became the 1st Laird of Mangerton. The Armstrong's long reign of reiving had just been launched.

✳✳✳

Alexander – 1st Laird of Mangerton – (b.c.1292 – m.1320)

Children:-

1. Richard – (b.c.1281)

2. William – (b.c.1282)

3. Alexander – 2nd Laird of Mangerton – (b.c.1318 – d.1398)

Alexander was a loyal subject of Scotland and had excellent morals, far from what his later descendants became. He probably fought at the Battle of Bannockburn in 1314 and was friendly with King Robert the Bruce. Alexander arguably was the first of the Armstrong reivers. Robert could never face the might of the English in a field battle, and had to rely on the war of the hit and run. Robert wanted light cavalry, and Alexander could supply that demand – and the very first contingent of Armstrong lancers was born.

Alexander's life though was cut tragically short by his more powerful neighbour to the north, William de Soulis of Hermitage Castle (his father Nicholas built the castle). De Soulis, who if legend is believed, was a wizard and heavily involved in black magic, who kept a familiar called Robin Redcap, a Border bogle similar to a goblin. Redcaps traditionally lived in ruined castles along the Border, where they roamed the moors and preyed upon unwary travellers. They were so named as they dipped their caps in the blood of their victims. If the bloodstains dried on their cap, they died. They wore heavy iron bound boots, and carried a pike. The only way to escape a Redcap was to quote a passage from the Bible, whereupon the creature would be repulsed and lose a tooth. Robin Redcap was especially feared, who De Soulis was thought to summon regularly and committed many evil deeds around Hermitage.

De Soulis was a giant of a man thought to be in league with the Devil, and was loathed by his vassals. De Soulis took great pleasure in exploiting his power, and on inflicting pain and misery onto his people. On one such expedition in 1320, de Soulis sank his evil clutches into a young Armstrong lady to satisfy his passions, seeking to spirit her away to Hermitage Castle. He had done this numerous times before, bringing terror to the women of the valley. Riding back to Hermitage with his spoils, de Soulis encountered the lady's father who was determined to defend his daughter, despite his adversary being such a powerful figure. De Soulis had no time for such debate, and lashed out at the man for defying his authority, killing him. The incident did not go unnoticed; the local population had witnessed the murder and became infuriated. An angry mob soon gathered with a hateful vengeance in their minds. De Soulis was forced to abandon his Armstrong lady and flee for his life. Alexander hearing of the commotion went to investigate the scene, and managed to calm and restrain the crowd who were baying for de Soulis' blood. Alexander for sure saved the life of de Soulis, who then escorted him back to Hermitage and safety.

De Soulis should have felt eternal indebtedness towards Alexander for his actions; gratitude however was not the nature of the man. De Soulis was full of spite feeling snubbed at his social inferior who had more control of the local population than himself. Brooding over these destructive thoughts within the bowels of Hermitage, de Soulis thought that the only conclusive action to take was to have Alexander eliminated. He sent an invitation to Alexander, requesting his presence to a banquet at Hermitage in his honour, to thank him for saving his life and demonstrate his appreciation for his help. Alexander eagerly attended, but walked into a trap. One source states that Alexander was served up a black bull's head at the feast, the symbol of death – though this story was probably added later, copying an event from 1440 when King James II had two Douglas's executed at the "Black dinner" in Edinburgh Castle. They all agree that Alexander was lulled into a false sense of security, allowing de Soulis to plunge a dagger into his back.

Alexander's grieving friends received the body and bore it away back to Mangerton. Arriving at Ettleton in the dark, it was too late to bury the body, and rested the corpse by the roadside below the graveyard to await light on the following day to complete their sad task. The body was eventually interred in the family graveyard of Ettleton, after a climb up the eastern slope of Kirk Hill which overlooked the valley, establishing a traditional and sacred burial ground for the Mangertons.

According to folklore tradition, de Soulis would soon meet his comeuppance for his years of dastardly deeds. The murder of Alexander was a murder too far, and the news reached the Scottish king who cried out *"Soulis! Soulis! Go boil him in brew!"* What the king demanded, the king got. De Soulis was seized and taken to the Nine Stane Rig, a stone circle 3km to the NE of Hermitage Castle. Within the stone circle, a fire had been lit and on top a cauldron full of water was bubbling away. De Soulis was then plunged into the cauldron to be boiled alive. A version of this story has de Soulis being wrapped in lead to neutralise his magic powers before being boiled, this is a later addition from an 18th century ballad. It was thought that de Soulis could not be killed by normal means, and ties in with local superstition. The king on hearing that his words had been taken literally dispatched his officials to ride hastily into Liddesdale, and to halt the boiling. Tragically they appeared too late, arriving to find de Soulis *"supping his own broth."*

This story, however colourful, is probably just that – a tale. The real event was a lot less dramatic. In 1320 de Soulis took part in an English-inspired plot along with Sir David de Brechin to kill King Robert. Perhaps he wanted the Scottish throne for himself, but more probable de Soulis aimed to place Edward Balliol on the Scottish throne. The conspiracy was discovered, and de Soules was arrested in Berwick along with his followers. He was brought before parliament and confessed his treason. De Soulis was imprisoned in Dumbarton Castle, where he died on 20 April 1321, in mysterious circumstances.

A monument known as the Milnholm Cross was erected in the memory of Alexander and his treacherous murder by Lord de Soulis. The monument was thought to mark the actual grave of Alexander, but was raised to mark the site where Alexander's body was rested by his sorrowing attendants before the burial. The cross was in full view of Mangerton Tower, designed to remind the descendants of Alexander of their feud with de Soulis and the legacy of their first laird. The monument consists of an eight foot column of stone, with inscribed into its length a long two-handed sword with a rounded pommel and straight quillons, and the letters AA and MA. The letters are a later addition, covering the original AA II – the initials of the second Alexander Armstrong clan chief and the first Laird of Mangerton. The top of the cross has the Armstrong coat of arms displayed, three bent arms; another later adornment. The cross sits on a square base of stone, which interestingly may have once been a mill wheel, an appropriate material since Milnholm means the mill on the plain. Nearby was the village of Milnholm (now gone) – the area was once a hive of trade and activity.

✳✳✳

Alexander – 2nd Laird of Mangerton – (b.c.1318 – d.1376)

Alexander was only two years old when his father was murdered, requiring a stand-in chieftain until he was of age. He had the following children:-

1. Alexander – 3rd Laird of Mangerton – (b.c.1341 – d.1398)   **2.** John – (b.c.1342 – k.1388)
3. Gilbert – (b.c.1343 – d. 1375)   **4.** Adam – (b.c.1344)

A son of Alexander, John was said to have been the original inhabitant of the castle at Gilnockie. He was slain at the Battle of Otterburn in 1388. Gilbert rose to a high position within the Royal Household of King David II. He was the Master of the King's Horse and was the Canon of Moray from at least 1361. Gilbert was also an envoy to England, and had a role as a Commissioner to England in raising the ransom for the release of King David, who had been captured at the Battle of Neville's Cross in 1346. He helped to arrange payments from the Exchequer Rolls in 1364 and 1366.

✲✲✲

Alexander – 3rd Laird of Mangerton – (b.c.1341 – d.1398)

Alexander was accused of stealing cows in 1394/5, answering the charges at court in Jedburgh. He was a bondsman for the Earl of Douglas in 1398. He had the following children:-

1. Archibald – 4th Laird of Mangerton – (b.c.1370) **2.** David – (b.c.1371)
3. Geffery – (b.c.1371) **4.** Rouland – (b.c.1374)

✲✲✲

Archibald – 4th Laird of Mangerton – (b.c.1370)

Children:-
1. Thomas – 5th Laird of Mangerton – (b.c.1425 – 1498) **2.** David – (b.c.1427)

✲✲✲

Thomas – "Bell the cat" – 5th Laird of Mangerton – (b.c.1425 – 1498)

Thomas takes his nickname of "Bell the cat" from a popular medieval fable, which concerns a group of mice who debate plans to neutralize the threat of a marauding cat. One of the mice suggests placing a bell around its neck, so that they could hear the cat approaching and be warned. A great idea, which was applauded by the others, but who would actually risk the dangerous task of belling the cat? All of them made excuses, and no one volunteered. The moral of the tale was very appropriate to the Border reivers – to teach the wisdom of evaluating an impossibly difficult task, and agreeing on how to achieve the desired outcome. It is easy to imagine Thomas coming up will all sorts of dangerous missions / raids / rescues... and giving no thought on who would do them and how.

Children:-
1. Alexander – 6th Laird of Mangerton – (b.c.1445)
2. George – of Ailmure (Eizellie Muir/Aislie-moor) – (b.c.1447)
3. William – "Ill Will" – of Chingils (Gingles) – (b.c.1449 – ex.1530)
4. John – of Whithaugh – (b.c.1451 – ex.1528)

Thomas's offspring would go on to launch three new Houses of Armstrongs, whose descendants became the most notorious and destructive reivers to have ever ridden the frontier. The four sons of Thomas would appear symbolically as the four rays descending from the heraldic monogram of Thomas, and later on the family's crest as four roots of the oak tree. The four branches; Maingertoun, Whithaugh, Ailmure, and the Chingils were almost all adjoined to each other, providing a strong central power block for the Armstrongs. The roots would serve the Armstrongs well, forming the foundation for the family to take off in the 1500s; rising proudly to carry through the 16th century, establishing them as the Border's most dreaded and powerful clan.

It was William ("Ill Will") of Chingils who expanded the Armstrong's territory south, out of Liddesdale and into the Debateable Land, where he established a stronghold at Morton Rig. Another son, John began the grayne of Whithaugh, which grew to become the second most powerful of the Armstrong graynes, after Mangerton. Alexander would become the next laird of Mangerton, and be the father of the notorious Johnnie Armstrong of Gilnockie. George of Ailmure was the father of Hector of Harelaw, "with the Griefs and the Cuts," which began another branch of the Armstrongs. Ailmure was located just above Kirndean on the Liddel, between Harden Burn and Powet Sike. Ailmure should not be mistaken for Alemoor, which was further north and in the possession of Scott of Buccleuch. Ailmure was the furthest north possession in the Liddel Valley for the Armstrongs.

✼✼✼

Alexander (Sandy) – 6th Laird of Mangerton – (b.c.1445 – d.c.1510)

Alexander appeared before the justice court at Jedburgh on 28 February 1495, on a charge for stealing cows alongside several other Armstrongs, which included his son Thomas, and possibly William, George, Robert and Alexander also – plus William Armstrang called "*Slittrik*" (from the Slitrig Valley, a tributary of the Teviot). William of Slitrig made a pledge for good behaviour to Patrick, Earl of Bothwell in 1498, which implies he was a noted troublemaker. The gang of Armstrongs were noted as having recently engaged in a "*hereschip*" at "*Quitmur*," from which they had carried off a hundred cows and oxen and much other booty.

Alexander, accompanied by Robert Elliot of Redheugh and eight others from Liddesdale, journeyed to Edinburgh in 1510 and swore to keep the peace. There must have been heavy coercion from King James IV to have encouraged such a trip. James was a popular king, and was the last Scottish king to command respect from the reivers. Alexander died that same year and was buried in Ettleton Kirkyard, where his gravestone can be seen today in a fenced off area within the cemetery. Today there are no remains of the kirk or the associated community. Alexander had seven sons, a power base which he and future Armstrongs were proud of. The seven sons came to be represented symbolically on the Armstrong's shield and coat of arms from around 1500, in the form of seven branches on the oak tree.

Children:-

1. Thomas – 7th Laird of Mangerton – (b.c.1479 – d.1549)

2. John (Johnnie) – of Gilnockie – (b.c.1480 – ex.1530)

3. Alexander – of Kirktown (House of Gingles) – (b.1485)

4. George – (fl.1498)

5. Christopher – of Langholm – (fl.1498)

6. Robert – (ex.1530)

7. William – (d.c.1541)

Alexander's offspring became a thorn in the side of both Scotland and England. Two of his sons fell foul of King James V's rough justice in 1530, when Robert and Johnnie were hung at Carlenrig.

✻✻✻

Thomas – 7th Laird of Mangerton – (b.c.1479 – 1549)

Thomas, known as "*The Gude Laird,*" was the oldest son of Alexander 6th Laird of Mangerton. He had six brothers, one of which was Johnnie Armstrong of Gilnockie, an individual who would rise in status above that of Mangerton, and suffer for it. Thomas was extremely fortunate to have missed out on that fateful day in 1530 when Johnnie and his gallant company were invited to go hunting with King James V.

It is not known if Thomas took part in the Battle of Flodden, but the odds suggest that he led the Armstrong contingent and was present within the Earl of Home's pike block on Branxton Hill. The experience opened up a new level of raiding for the Armstrongs, with the king's steady hand gone. In the power vacuum Thomas was looked to as a figurehead to lead the family through these troubled times. At the heart of the Armstrong raiding business, Thomas first ran into trouble with the authorities when he was charged alongside sixteen others, for raiding the property of "*John Cokburne of Ormistoune*" at Craik in Roxburghshire on 27 July 1535 under the silence of night. The gang was indicted of thieving away seventy oxen and thirty cows, and kidnapping three men servants of the said John Cockburn. An extra charge was added for the treatment of the prisoners, as they had their money, swords, purses and clothes taken from them. When called to address their crimes, Thomas and his fellow raiders failed to appear. This was taken as a snub by the monarch; on 30 October 1535 the gang was accused of "*breaking of their Bonds made to the King,*" and all were put to the horn, with "*their whole goods, moveable and immoveable, to be escheated.*" Thomas was none the worse for having been made into a rebel. He was recorded on the Tax Roll for Liddesdale in 1541, as tenant of Billhope and held heritable lands at Hawthornside, Langlands, Millholm, Ragarth, Sorbie and Sorbietrees.

Thomas was very much pro-active during the chaotic and turbulent 1540s. He was probably requested to raise his clan and attend King James V on his invasion into England in 1542 – something that he was never going to do, casting his mind back to 1530 and the judicial murder of several of his relatives. Thomas raised his lances eventually, thinking it was better to keep an open eye on the Devil than risk a dagger in the back. He kept a watch on the Royal forces, which paid off after the defeat of Solway Moss, gaining a haul of looted provisions and armaments in great quantities, enough to furnish all of Liddesdale.

In the following year, Sir Thomas Wharton sought out Thomas with the offer of English gold to become an "assured" Scot. The news was reiver heaven to Thomas's ears – this was a win-win situation, what could possibly go wrong? Thomas led the Armstrongs during the "Rough Wooing," helping to devastate the Scottish Border land for English gold, causing trauma and great distress to his fellow countrymen. This was a happy hunting time during the years of 1543 and 1544, burning and thieving at will as part of a greater English force. 1545 began in the same mode as the previous two years, with the Armstrongs continuing to raid the Scottish Borders. In February Thomas accompanied Ralph Eure and his mixed force of 3,000 riders as they raided Teviotdale. Thomas took part in the sack of Melrose Abbey, after which the army headed south to Jedburgh with saddlebags full of loot. So far little resistance had been encountered on these raids, but all would change on 27 February when Angus and Buccleuch ambushed the English on Ancrum Moor. A desperate battle ensued, with Thomas reluctant to lead his men against whatever lay beyond the gun smoke, and held back until he had a better idea. The Scots attackers fought like lions, and broke up the English lines sending a concern into the Mangertons. Thomas hastily ordered his lancers to tear off their St. George's cross badges and to swap sides. The action probably saved Thomas and many of his follower's lives, who then sheepishly tried to exit the scene without any awkward questions asked.

Thomas is last heard of in 1549, in two letters dated 1 January and 1 February. Both were on the same subject, a bond to enter prisoners to Sir John Kerr of Ferniehirst. The first letter was for two prisoners, the second for a larger number of prisoners, which ended in the ominous note – "*By yours at all poor, Thom Armstrang, lard of Mangerton, with my hand at pen.*" Thomas was in poor health, there would be no third letter from him. His son Archibald was signing as the new "*young lard of Mayngertoun*" on 14 February.

Children:-
1. Archibald – 8th Laird of Mangerton – (b.c.1517 – 1578)
2. John – "Laird's Jock" – of Puddington – (b.c.1518 – 1599)
3. Richard (Dick) – of Dryup (Dryhope) – (b.c.1519 – d.c.1603)
4. Thomas – "Laird's Thome" – (b.c.1520)
5. Simon – of Tinnisburn – (b.c.1521)
6. Walter – "Laird's Wat" – (b.c.1522 – 1601)
7. Ninian (Runyon) – "Laird's Runyon" – (fl.1583)
8. Sybil – Mother of Jock and Christopher of the Side – (c.1560)

Thomas had secured the Armstrongs power and status on the Border. Like the oak tree which now adorned the family coat of arms, it was hoped the Armstrongs would continue to grow and be mighty. The strongest of the trees, combined

with a sword yielded by a strong arm; the combination would surely allow the Armstrongs to rule the Border one day –
and perhaps even their own kingdom.

Thomas's brood took after their father, becoming seasoned raiders in their own right. John, Thomas and Ninian were all documented together in December 1583 by Thomas Musgrave. Musgrave was careful to note the occasion of cross Border marriages, which was an area of concern to the wardens. Musgrave recorded the following information for Burghley's advantage, hoping to point out were trouble spots could break out:-

"**Joke Armestronge** *called the Lordes Joke dwelleth under Denyshill besydes Kyrsope in Denisborne, and maryed Anton Armestronges daughter of Wylyave in Gilsland.*"

"**Thome Armestronge** *called the lordes Tome, dwelleth on a place called Hyghe Morgarton, not marryed with Englande.*"

"**Runyon Armestronge** *called the lordes Runyon, dwelleth in a place called the Thornythaite. Rowye Armestronge called the lordes Rowye, dwelleth in Tarrassyde, and marryed oulde Archer Graymes doughter.*"

All of these marriages were across the Border; with English Grahams, Forsters and Armstrongs being sought for Armstrong brides. This would produce useful networks of cooperation for the Armstrongs.

✻✻✻

Walter – "Laird's Wat" – (b.c.1522 – k.1601)

Walter was a son of Thomas, 7th Laird of Mangerton. Walter has the unique honour in literature to appear in not one but three of the border ballads, "*Jock o' the Side,*" "*The Raid of the Reidswire,*" and "*The Fray o' Hautwessel.*" Literature is not the best source for historical fact but can lend to put flesh on the bare bones of dry dates and documents in a way that other media's often fail. The ballads show that Walter was not the bravest of reivers, but he had an energy and passion to match. He was also an excellent football player.

The ballad "*Jock o' the Side,*" describes the story of the rescue of John Armstrong of the Side from a prison cell in Newcastle. The news of Jock's capture came to Archibald, 8th Laird of Mangerton in around 1561-1567, resulting in great panic amongst the Armstrongs, causing a strong desire to set him free. Jock was a regular visitor to Mangerton and was the uncle of Walter. The laird put together a rescue party, which involved two of his sons, Walter and John (The Laird's Jock), plus Hobbie Noble. Walter mounted a white horse, and all disguised as cadgers (itinerant merchants), they rode off for Newcastle without any mishaps. The venture was a complete success, and not without its dramas. The ballad makes Walter out to be the coward in the tale, and his brother the hero; but this of course could be artistic license, to build the tension of the adventure. When the party returned home after rescuing Jock, their route was blocked by the flooded River Tyne, which filled Walter with dread. He refused to swim across. The ballad recounts...

Then up and spake the Laird's saft Wat,

The greatest coward in the companie;

"Now halt, now halt! we need na try't;

The day is come we a' maun die!"

The steadying encouragement of his brother was required to spur him on, who led by example...

"Poor faint-hearted thief!" quo' the Laird's Jock,

"There'll nae man die but he that's fie;

I'll lead ye a' right safely thro';

Lift ye the pris'ner on ahint me."

Walter was present at the last battle between the Scots and the English, when he led a contingent of Armstrongs to a Truce Day at Reidswire in July 1575. Walter was probably the most senior of the Armstrongs present, attending on the request of Sir John Carmichael. Walter can be imagined to have taken part in the unruly behaviour which erupted, probably full of ale and hurling insults at Sir John Forster. He was perhaps a major factor in provoking the English to fire the first shot. The story of the skirmish unfolds in the ballad *"The Raid of the Reidswire,"* which contains a mention of Walter within...

Carmichael was our warden then,

He caused the country to conveen;

And the Laird's Wat, that worthie man'

Brought in that sirname weil beseen;

The Armestranges that aye has been

A hardie house, but not a hail,

The Elliots' honours to maintaine,

Brought down the lave o' Liddesdale.

The third ballad was based from a real event which took place in May 1601, when Walter rode together with the Armstrongs of Whithaugh and Calfhill on a revenge raid to Haltwhistle. The raid was brought about when a Ridley had slain Simon Armstrong, the Laird of Calfhill two weeks earlier. The Armstrongs rode into Haltwhistle with a loud bravado, which must have made an alarming site with burning torches in their hands. The Armstrongs rode up and down the streets setting fire to as many houses as they could. The locals were no soft target; a Ridley from within a strong stone house, took aim with a musket and fired a shot which killed Simon, Laird of Whithaugh. Another two Armstrongs were injured, and Walter himself was knocked off his horse – killed outright. The deaths of these two Armstrong chieftains brought the foray to a premature end, forcing the raiders to retire after only burning ten outhouses and barns, and thieving little of value.

The two deaths wrought a deep impression amongst the Armstrongs with many vows being made to strike revenge and lay the whole frontier waste. The manner in which Walter was killed is not mentioned by Carey or in any other document however it is featured in literature form contained within the ballad *"The Fray o' Hautwessel."*

Then cam Wat Armstrang to the toun,

Wi' some three hundred chiel or mair,

And sweir that they wad bren it down,

A' clad in Jack, wi' bow and spear,

Harneist reet weel, I trow they were:

But we were aye prepared at need,

And dropt ere lang upon the rere

Amaingst them, like an angry gleed.

Then Alec Rydly he lette flee

A clothyard schaft, ahint the wa';

It struk Wat Armstrang in the ee',

Went thro' his steel cap, heed and a':

I wot it made him quickly fa',

He ca'd na rise, tho he essayed;

The best at thieve craft or the Ba',

He neer again shall ride a raid.

An arrow through the *"ee"* (eye) – ended the career of one of the best reivers and footballers on the Border.

✳✳✳

Archibald – 8th Laird of Mangerton – (b.c.1517 – d.1578)

Archibald shared in his father's adventures during the 1540s as a young man, taking part in the aftermath of the Battle Solway Moss and during the "Rough Wooing." After the Battle of Ancrum Moor, Archibald still held an ear out to helping the English for gold. Wharton's assured Scots had taken a rattle to the system, with many converting back their loyalty to Scotland. Archibald would have done likewise, however in 1547 a new opportunity came to make more money as an ally of King Henry.

During the "Rough Wooing," the Johnstone family managed to avoid the main spoiling of the Borderlands, and also avoided co-operating with Henry as an assured Scot. Perhaps the Laird of Johnstone thought Annandale was far enough away to avoid the English, or that he was safe within Lochwood's castle walls, surrounded by its impenetrable bog. He would lay low and bide his time, surely Henry could not keep up this raiding for much longer. Johnstone's optimistic hopes were dashed on the morning of Thursday 2 April 1547, when an English raiding force under Wharton arrived on his doorstep.

Archibald was with Wharton when they approached Lochwood, the tactics they chose to capture the castle was one of ambush. Wharton sent out a decoy force of *"fortye lyght horsmen of Langholme to burne a towne called Wamfraye halfe a mylle from his house of Loughwod, and appoynted the capitaign of Langholm with the rest of the garyson to lye in ambushe for the relefe of those."* This unit contained a number of Armstrongs, who completed their task well setting Wamphray alight. The rising smoke alarmed the Laird of Johnstone, who set out with his lancers from Lochwood to investigate and chased off the raiders. This was all going according to Wharton's plans; he could now spring his ambush.

Johnstone rode into Wamphray and caught the raiders red handed, or so he thought. His men lowered their lances and went into the charge, spiriting into the village – and straight into a force of concealed riders. A brief running skirmish developed, with Johnstone having the momentum to break through. Wharton was an experienced commander and had a second ambush prepared containing three hundred riders, which when released over-ran Johnstone and cornered his men. Archibald was involved in this battle, on horseback leading his men from the front. Johnstone was made of stern material and was not going to be taken without a struggle. Cased in armour Johnstone fought off at least three attackers, who broke their spears upon him. Johnstone eventually yielded when he took a wound in the upper part of the thigh, and surrendered to Archibald. Archibald was perhaps the individual who caused Johnstone's wound. The butcher's bill was low when the dust settled, with Wharton reporting eight Scots slain and many hurt. No English were killed with four wounded. There were large numbers of prisoners taken, so many that Lochwood Castle was now seriously undermanned, a situation which Wharton was seeking to achieve from the outbreak. The attention was then turned to Lochwood, with Sir Thomas Carleton leading a force which included Archibald, to complete the second part of the expedition. A small surprise party of twelve crept off under the cover of darkness, crossing a stretch of marshland to reach the barmkin unobserved. The walls were successfully scaled, but the party could go no further as the door into the main tower was bolted shut. But not to be deterred, they hid themselves within the outhouses of the courtyard and waited patiently until day break when the unsuspecting garrison would open up. Everything went almost according to plan, at dawn a man unlocked the main wooden door and outer iron yett – the signal for the awaiting raiders to make their move. The dozen men charged but their timing was a little too early and a watching lady servant managed to close the inner door on the attackers. A pushing struggle ensued, with the woman managing to hold out for a surprisingly long time. But eventually her strength gave way and the tower was entered. The garrison only consisted of two men, who put up no struggle. The tower was now in English hands. Carleton was well pleased with the morning's work. Once secured, Carleton departed for Carlisle to report his success to Wharton, leaving Alexander (Ill Will's Sandie) Armstrong in temporary charge of the castle. This element of trust suggests Archibald's high involvement in the expedition. He would have been highly rewarded for his help. Carleton eventually returned to Lochwood, where he was appointed as keeper of the castle, and used the stronghold as his base camp of operations for a few weeks. Archibald enjoyed his time at Lochwood, lording over the district and taking what he wanted from the surrounding countryside.

In October 1566 Archibald was captured by James Hepburn, 4th Earl of Bothwell, when he led an expedition into Liddesdale to round up and pacify the outlaws. Archibald found himself locked up in Hermitage Castle, alongside Lancelot Armstrong, Laird of Whithaugh and various other illustrious outlaws. The prisoners were to be tried, with an outcome of signing pledges for good behaviour and hostages taken, or execution. Not a good situation. However, before Bothwell could impose Border Law, his enforced house guests escaped on 7 October. The prisoners went on to successfully take over the castle, and add further drama to the story of Bothwell's wounding by "Little Jock" Elliot of the Park, with a life or death stalemate at the castle's gate.

In March 1569 the Regent Murray made an expedition to Liddesdale accompanied by Lord Home, Buccleuch, Cessford and Ferniehirst, plus 4,000 foot and horse. The regent was in a merciful mood and was content for the Liddesdale chiefs to make their pledges, agreeing to be dutiful subjects of the young King James VI. Murray was also joined by Sir John Forster, and together they progressed through the valley. Murray though became dissatisfied at the sureties given and his attitude hardened towards the chiefs. For some reason he abandoned the soft approach, and would now not leave a single house standing. On arriving at Mangerton he met Archibald and spent the Sunday night within the tower. It can be assumed that he was not an invited guest, but as the regent was accompanied by a large host, prudence would have made Archibald welcome Murray and put on a feast suitable for a king. Murray's steely opinion of the Armstrongs did not change during his stay; on the Monday morning as a parting gift to show his appreciation to Mangerton, he filled the tower full of gun powder and set the building on fire. The laird had to stand by helplessly as his tower was blown up. The harsh treatment should have brought the Armstrongs into line, however Forster had his doubts. He wrote later to Cecil – *"the Regent hath the whole border of Scotland in obedience at this time, saving only Liddesdale, who I am sure will seek to annoy both England and Scotland as far as in their power lies."* Pledges though would solve the matter. Archibald himself was requested as a pledge for his brother John (Laird's Jock), the Laird of Tinnisburn, but he declined. On 21 October 1569, it was agreed for seven Armstrongs to be received as pledges, who were to be relieved later by another twenty.

The assassination of the regent on 23 January 1570 would have brought Archibald great pleasure, seeing his death as poetic justice for destroying his home.

Archibald had the following children:-
1. John – "Laird's John" – (b.c.1548)
2. Simon – 9th Laird of Mangerton – (b.c.1550 – d.1603)
3. Ninian – "Laird's Ringan" – (b.c.1554 – d.1600)
4. Robert – "Laird's Robbie" – (fl.1597)
5. Roland – "Laird's Rowye" – (b.c.1560)

Archibald's son, John, the "Laird's John" is not to be confused with his uncle the Laird's Jock. John appears within Musgrave's list of the Border Riders in December 1583, documented as – *"John Armestronge called the lordes John, marryet Rytche Graymes sister called Meadope, and he bathe two sonnes ryders in England.*" Musgrave was careful to record any cross Border marriages, as these were potential trouble spots for alliances and plotting of misdemeanours. It is interesting to note that John had two sons living in England, a situation for concern. It was also noted by Musgrave that "*Joke his eldest sonne marryed Hobbe Fosters daughter of Kersope,*" another English connection. In 1587 a son of the "*Lardis Johnne,*" Archibald, was demanded and handed over to be held in ward as a pledge for both of the Mangerton and Whithaugh Armstrongs.

Roland is also listed within the 1583 document. Among the Lords of Mangerton he is named as – "*Rowye Armstronge called the lordes Rowye, dwelleth in Tarrassyde, and married ould Archie Graymes daughter.*" Ninian, the "*Laird's Ringan,*" was recorded as living at Thorniewhats near Canonbie in 1583, and was named within John Monipennie's publication on the principle chief men and surnames on the Border in 1597. Under the "*Debaitable Land,*" he noted a raiding squad of reivers called "*Lardis Rinzians gang,*" which contained the "*Lairdis Rinziane – Lairdis Robbie – Rinzian of Wauchop.*" The gang was named after Ninian, who would have been the "heidsman" for the group. The other leaders were Ninian's brother, the "*Laird's Robbie,*" and Ninian ("*Ringan*") of Wauchope. Ninian had at least one son, called "*Joke.*"

✳✳✳

Simon (Sym) – 9th Laird of Mangerton – (b.c1550 – d.1603)

Simon was known as "Sym of Tweeden," before taking up his role as the Laird of Mangerton. When Simon became the 9th Laird of Mangerton in 1578, he inherited a ruined family seat. Mangerton Tower had lain in ruins since 1569 when the Regent Murray had demolished it. Simon had the tower rebuilt in 1583, placing an escutcheon carved upon it which contained a two handed sword (belonging the hero Siward Bjornsson in the Armstrong tradition), and a chevronel couped dividing three roundles. Above the shield sat the date "1583" and the initials "SA – EF," referring to Simon and his wife Elizabeth Foster.

Simon first crops up in the records in 1578/9, when along with Lancelot, Laird of Whithaugh, made promises to the Privy Council that they would present them certain family and servants who "*offendit againis the subjectis of England or Scotland,*" as pledges to make the Armstrongs answerable for their crimes. The Privy Council gave Simon and Lancelot a time limit for their task, to deliver those requested within six days or face the pain of a 2000 merks fine. In total twenty two Border lairds were summoned to appear – but all refused to show up. Simon was probably alongside Lancelot again in 1580, when he led three hundred Liddesdale riders in an ambush on the Scotts and Gladstones who were engaged on a hot trod. The fallout for those involved was an order to appear before the Privy Council to answer the charges of killing and injuring several of the trod party. Again Simon failed to attend the summons. There was little the authorities could do beyond an armed invasion, to make the Armstrongs do as they were commanded.

Simon's list of crimes and misdemeanours begin in October 1582 when reported in a foray alongside his uncle John (The Laird's Jock). The bill was reported as – *"Sir Simon Musgrave, Knight, complains upon the Lard of Mangerton, Lards Jock, Sim's Thom and their complices, for burning of his barn, wheat, rye, oats, bigg, and peas, with L. 1000 sterling."* The raid would have given Simon an extra pleasure, taking a pot shot at authority by spoiling Musgrave's land as he was the Constable of Bewcastle. If Musgrave could not keep his own property safe from the reivers – then who could? The implication was that the Mangertons could raid anyone that they wanted to.

On 21 August 1583, Davy Bell of Overdenton made a complaint *"upon Larde of Mangerton and Bessies Andrewe* [for] *vi kyne and oxen."* In that same year Simon, together with the Laird of Whithaugh, and Eamont Armstronge of Whisgills, numbering forty in total, rode into Bewcastledale on 5 October and lifted thirty head of cattle and all the insight from two steadings belonging to Rowy Rowtlege of Bewcastle. The raid had a high level of violence attached, with several injured persons noted. More was to come from this gang, on the following night twin raids were carried out. On 6 October the gang lifted ten goats and twenty sheep, plus insight from George Rowtlege of Green Hill Ash, who was left badly hurt together with his son – they must have defended their property and came unstuck. The first raid may have not netted the reivers sufficient plunder; as they turned on a second target. On the second raid, the gang thieved away *"xvi kyne and oxen,"* and all the insight from Anthonie Rowtlege of Nunscleugh. The second foray was more violent than the first, with Allan Rowtlege being slain; plus William Rowtlege, Thome Rowtlege, John Rowtledge and Thome of Toddholls, all reported as maimed and in peril of death. Another casualty lost a leg.

In December 1583 Thomas Musgrave drew up his famous list of the Border Riders for the benefit of Burghley. As expected, Simon heads the list of the Armstrongs, coming under *"The Lord of Mangerton and his frendes, and theire allyaunces with England."* Musgrave was very particular in recording cross Border marriages amongst the outlaws. Simon's entry read as – *"Seme Armestronge lord of Mangerton marryed John Fosters daughter of Kyrsope foot, and hath by her issue."* He married an English Foster from Kershopefoot, right on the English Border just three km south, a useful ally to warn of approaching raiders. Simon would have married tactically and probably advised/chose all the partners for his children.

Simon has one of the rare statuses amongst the Border lairds, in that he was taken prisoner within his own house. Simon had only been a resident in his recently refurbished Mangerton Tower for a few months, when in 1584 Humphrey Musgrave, the deputy of Lord Scrope, made an expedition into Liddesdale and captured him. The Armstrongs had been causing mayhem in and around Bewcastle at this period with a blood feud in operation with the Musgraves, and Musgrave took the unusual measure of braving up to the threat and going straight into the jaws of that danger. He was accompanied by Henry Leigh (steward of Brughe) and Captain Pickman, who managed to penetrate undetected right up to the main seat of the Armstrongs with their soldiers on a Friday morning. The warning system of the Armstrongs had completely failed, with the intrusion being unobserved; no warning beacons burned or white sheets displayed from the hilltops. Musgrave took his soldiers directly into Mangerton, where Simon walked straight into his hands and was apprehended without any struggle. Simon was then taken back to Carlisle Castle, and was held in *"close warde to answere what shall be layd unto him."*

Lord Scrope wrote enthusiastically from Carlisle to Walsingham on 13 January 1584 on the achievement – *"This man is the chief and principal of his surname, and also the special evildoer and procurer in the spoils of this March, next after the laird of Whithaugh, whom though I cannot well come by, yet I hope in time to grieve him and his. His taking is greatly wondered at here, for it was never heard of that a laird of Mangerton was taken in his own house either in peace or war, without the hurt or loss of a man. Now I have him, I trust it will be to good effect and keep the others quiet, and I will provide against requital, so far as I can."*

Musgrave has to be congratulated at his courage in undertaking the mission, going straight to the source of the problem and removing it. Simon was not detained for long, being at leisure a few months later. Simon, in order to be released would have been required to sign bonds to keep the peace, and perhaps handed over a member of his own family as an assurance for that bond. But on the other hand, murkier activities may have occurred; with exchanges of cash and deals on passing on stolen goods and turning a blind eye to raids for a cut of the plunder. Musgrave and Simon got on very well together, despite being on the opposite poles of both nationality and a family feud. They can even be described as friends, and during Simon's short imprisonment, a further rapport developed. Both men had an interest in fine horses and horse racing; interests that were very particular to reiving society and Simon was a connoisseur in both.

In 1585 Musgrave entered one of his own horses, called Bay Sandforth, at a race meeting in Liddesdale for the sole purpose that Simon could view it and see if he liked the animal prior to buying it. The selling of horses across the Border was illegal; the last thing both Scotland and England wanted was the reivers to be charging around on fast thoroughbred Arabian stallions – impossible to catch. Bay Sandforth ran in three races and won all three prizes. Simon was very impressed and bought the horse. The sale illustrates ties of friendship across the frontier which over-rid boundaries and the wills of kings and queens. There is no record on how Simon employed his new purchase. Simon can be imagined out on future raids, and escaping the warden easily on hot trods, racing home on his fine fast new horse.

The Laird of Whithaugh was a good raiding companion of Simon, residing only two km to the north. On 6 October 1587, Simon together with *"the young Laird of Whithaugh and Jokkie Armestronge of Kynmett,"* and six hundred other riders went on a destructive foray upon Her Majesty's tenants of Haydon Bridge and Rattenrawe (Row-town row). The raiders were billed *"for burning 15 houses, taking 24 prisoners – one had his hand cut off – reaving their chattels and insight gear, worth 900 L. sterling."* The bill was found filed by the Commissioners at Berwick, and was made by William Maughen and Thomas Hynde on behalf of forty three persons who were at the receiving end of the Armstrongs.

At Martinmas 1587, the poor widow and inhabitants of the town of Temmon made a complaint upon the Laird of Mangerton and the Laird of Whithaugh, and their accomplices for the murder of John Tweddel, Willie Tweddel and Davie Bell – and *"taking 100 kine and oxen, spoil of houses, writings, money, and insight 400L. sterling."* Ten prisoners were also picked up and taken back to Liddesdale for ransoming.

In the winter of 1587, Simon took part in a large scale raid of 2,000 riders. This amounted to an unstoppable army. Ker of Cessford and Scott of Buccleuch were also involved, the raid being a revenge response to an earlier raid made by Sir Cuthbert Collingwood. Simon followed Cessford's contingent, who descended upon Eslington, the home of Collingwood, where the surrounding community was looted. A large scale skirmish took place around the house, as Collingwood and a band of English soldiers under Captain Bellas bravely defended themselves. Dozens were killed and wounded as a desperate running retreat took place to find defensive strongholds. Collingwood himself had to flee for his life and take refuge within his own fortified house, with one of his sons being caught in the chase. Bellas and about twenty foot soldiers were pushed back and had to take refuge in a ruined house upon a hill, as the Scots numbers grew. A vicious hand-to-hand struggle took place to winkle Bellas out, in which Simon was involved. The Scots dismounted to make themselves more difficult targets from musket shots, taking up their places for a siege. Bellas was twice given the offer to surrender but refused; despite being wounded he and his men continued to keep up a withering fire of shot. The Scots almost gave up their fight on Bellas, but a rider named Watty Turnbull whose brother had been killed in the battle, wanted revenge and rallied the men into one last all-out attack. The onslaught was from all directions and ran over the English defences, ending with the close combat clash of daggers and rapiers. Within the narrow confines, it was Simon who finally captured the intrepid Bellas.

The Scots could not lurk long after their plundering of Eslington, as a hot trod had been mustered and was on their way. Cuthbert regained his composure after the raid, and took the lead of the trod, eager to get back his kidnapped son and reived cattle. The Scots were strung out on their return journey, with those mounted away ahead in front, a bad tactical error. Those walking made an easy target, with the trod catching them up. After a brief one sided scuffle, 150 of the Scots were taken as prisoner. Simon rode back into Liddesdale safely; the venture had netted thirty cattle. Hunsdon, the East March Warden would later criticise Cuthbert for his trod, saying that if he had pursued it more energetically he could have captured all of the Scots. Hunsdon observed that the trod had been reluctant to kill any of the reivers when they were caught red-handed. This lack of aggression was caused by the fear of a reprisal raid. Hunsdon had no such reservations and promised to hang forty or fifty of the prisoners. The Scottish king demanded the release of Bellas and the son of Collingwood, the raiders listened and relinquished their prisoners. Bellas was recorded in February 1588 as drawing his pay of captain, proving that he had returned safely and was in relatively good shape despite the experience.

Simon was requested to appear before William Fenwick (gentleman and deputy warden of the Middle March of England) and Thomas Trotter (deputy Keeper of Liddesdale), at the *"Belles Kyrk the xiiith of Aprill 1590,"* to address Middle March bills for Liddesdale. At the hearing, the tenants of Langupp (Langhope – near Hexham) made a complaint *"upon the Laird of Mangerton &c. for stealing 23 kye and oxen, 5 horses and meares, 40 sheep, and insight of 4 houses, 10L. sterling on 9 November 1589."*

Simon was singled out in the "Act for the Borders" drawn up *"At Haliruidhous the sext day of Januar the yeir of God 1590 yeir"* by King James VI at a council meeting. Also present at the meeting, were Francis 5th Earl of Bothwell, John Lord Maxwell, Alexander Lord Hume and Sir John Carmichael. They personally promised His Majesty to *"deliver Syme Armstrong of Mangertoun* [and about 50 other Armstrongs, Elliots, Crosiers, Nixons, Baties and Scotts] *to abide the law by certain days fixed.*" Those named were *"to be delivered to the English wardens in relief of the King and his wardens, or allege reasonable cause to the contrary."* The act was draughted up after certain offenders failed to be delivered to answer justice before the commissioners at Berwick for six bills in February 1587, and for others in April 1589 at Jedburgh.

Simon could not help himself becoming involved in the rescue of Kinmont Willie from Carlisle Castle in April 1596. As the chieftain of the Armstrongs, his presence could almost be expected. He was named as one of the principal assailants at the raid by Lord Scrope on 14 April 1596. And was pointed out by an eye witness ("Richies Will" Graham) in an anonymous letter to Scrope on 24 April 1596, as riding along with Buccleuch on the raid – together with the Laird of Whithaugh and eight other men.

The last years of the 16th century saw what was known at the time as a period of "*decay*" on the Border. It was more than just an increase in raiding, a reign of chaos seeped deep into people's lives and a feeling of hopelessness grew as the downward spiral seemed impossible to halt. Lord Eure gives an excellent insight into this mind frame when writing to the queen on 17 April 1596 in the aftermath of Kinmont's rescue. The incident made Eure worry as this was evidence that the Scots knew the weaknesses of the Marches; otherwise the rescue attempt would never have been attempted. He blamed the lack of churches and ministers on the heathenish behaviour of the Scots. On how the Scottish Border was enriched with English sheep and cattle, and how the poor Englishman was powerless to steal them back lacking horses. Eure added, *"I fear this weakness is over all the Marches,"* and quoted the actions of Simon, *"Lard of Mangerton and other suche like,"* when he aided *"the Lard of Baclughe keeper of Lyddesdale,"* in freeing Kinmont as proof. Eure could not have chosen any better of an example as Simon, as a cause of this descent into anarchy.

Simon features with no surprise in John Monipennie's list from 1597 on *"The names of the principall Clannes, and surnames on the Borders."* Simon is recorded along with two other names...

LIDDISDAIL
1. *The Laird of Mangerton*
2. *The Lairds Jok*
3. *Chrystie of the Syde*

This group of three chiefs were all related and probably raided together within the same gang, or had gangs of their own each. After his Carlisle ventures, the need to have Simon reeled in grew. On 25 June 1597 *"Symy Armstrong laird of Mangerton"* was named as a pledge demanded by Scotland and England. He was to be delivered on that day at ten hours before noon, to Sir William Bowes at the west ford near Norham. The authorities had taken enough of Simon's raids and escapades; taking pledges would neutralise the Mangerton threat. From Norham, Simon was delivered to Carlisle together with John Scott (servant to Sir Walter Scott of Branxholme), where he was noticed and recorded in a letter on 15 August 1597, between Lord Scrope and Sir John Carmichael. They were described as having made their pledges, and were *"to remayne at free warde within the citie of Carliell... and not to departe without the sayd Lord*

Scroppes lycence." Lord Eure writing from Norham to Cecil on 30 September 1597, mentions *"Sim Armstrong who is now in Carlisle castle for Lord Scrope's bills."* There would be peace from Liddesdale for this short while.

Simon was a good friend of Hobbie Noble of the Crew, who was an English reiver skilled in the art of navigation. Hobbie sought sanctuary with the Armstrongs, and Simon employed his services on numerous occasions. Hobbie became a treasured part of the Mangerton's gang of thieves. Hobbie though came to a sticky end, when he was betrayed by Simon Armstrong of the Mains in 1598, and handed over to the English authorities and hung. Simon was grievously upset by this action, and took it upon himself to actively hunt down those responsible. Family was everything for the Armstrongs, and here was a blatant abuse of the Armstrong code of honour. Simon of the Mains was eventually tracked down, probably by Simon of Mangerton himself, and met a common thief's end on the same gallows that ended Hobbie's life.

The exact year of Simon's death is not known, but was probably in 1603, as he is referred to as the *"old laird"* of Mangerton during the "Ill Week" of March, and is not mentioned after that date. At "Ill Week" every self respecting reiver picked up their lance and was horse bound for one last hurrah. Simon was no exception and led the last great raid of the Armstrongs, together with his son Archibald ("The Young Laird"), Francis of Whithaugh ("The Standard Bearer"), Hingle and about 200 fellow Armstrong horsemen – who ran a week long foray into England dreading a uniting of the Crowns. The gang penetrated as far as Penrith, turning around when Sir William Selby, Captain of Berwick, detached a large force to bring the predators to order. Simon and Archibald would have netted a fine weight of plunder, but this was to be their last happy haul, the lights had now changed, and the hunters had just become the hunted.

On 23 July of that year, the young Laird of Mangerton was proclaimed an outlaw at Carlisle, which must have referred to Archibald, Simon's eldest son. There is no mention of Simon as an outlaw, which would be expected as both were guilty of the same crimes. It can be assumed that Simon was either dead or in exile in 1603. Simon's cause of death can be guessed at, with execution being the most likely, however there is evidence in literature of a totally different fate.

The ballad *"The Death of Simon Ninth Lord of Mangerton,"* though a work of fiction to an extent can provide a historical guide to the ultimate fate of Simon, and is worth a look at to glean any possible evidence. The ballad in this case, does seem entirely fictitious, being a retelling of the story of the 1st Laird of Mangerton and de Soulis. However, there may be an element of fact; some bare bones story of Simon causing jealousy over a young lady, or giving reset to a known criminal, and finding himself at the wrong end of a spiteful dagger.

The ballad begins by introducing Foster of Greenah, who had a *"daughter Fair"* who attracted countless suitors. One of these was Lord Douglas of Hermitage who arrived one morning calling at Foster's door...

"Where is your daughter dear?"
But Foster loudly did reply,

"My daughter is not here."

Foster had sent his daughter south to keep her safe, when Douglas heard this, he became angry...

Then vengeful Douglas sped
To aim a wound at Foster's heart,
And from his presence fled.

Foster fell dead to the ground, and Douglas had to flee the scene on his horse, pursued by the populace who rose in rage at the murder. Douglas fled *"To Mangerton's high lofty towers,"* with a mob tailing behind baying for his blood. Simon heard the approaching shouts and cries, and opened the tower gates to rescue Douglas from the *"tumultuous crowd of foes."* Douglas was relieved to say the least at Simon's help and remarked...

"To you I owe my life, my lord.
How shall I you repay?"

As a debt of gratitude Douglas offered Simon to visit him at Hermitage, to reward his help. Simon held the offer in his mind then eventually took it up, arriving as a guest. Mirroring what happened to Alexander Armstrong nearly three hundred years earlier, *"Mangerton was basely slain."* With Simon dead, Lord Douglas had to flee again with speed from the fury of Simon's friends. Jock of the Side was the main stalker of Douglas, who *"long did seek... Dress'd in a beggar's weed,"* pursuing relentlessly his quarry. The end was in sight.

At last he found out the retreat.
Where Douglas did reside;
He plung'd a dagger in his heart,
And there the tyrant died.

Simon married Elizabeth Foster in around 1565, and had the following children:-
1. Archibald – 10th Laird of Mangerton – (b.c1566 – ex.1610)
2. Ungle (Umqle) or Hingle – (b.c.1567)
3. Simon – of Rinch (or Runchback) – (b.c.1568)

Simon had at least one daughter, who was married to William Graham, the second son of *"old Riche,"* Richard Graham of Netherby. This marriage was likely arranged and achieved to gain strategic alliances and cross Border deals. The children of Simon are a puzzle to work out, who exactly was Hingle – referred to as a brother of the Laird of Mangertoun in 1607? The Musgrave list of 1583 on the Border Riders brings up – *"Seme Armestronge called yonge Seme, dwelleth on the Flates nere Margerton, and marryed Rowye Fosters doughter called Robins Rowye"*... another possible cousin or close relative of Simon.

✳✳✳

Archibald – 10th Laird of Mangerton – (b.c.1566 – ex.1610)

Archibald was the last laird of Mangerton. He took part in the last great raid of the Armstrongs, alongside his father Simon in March 1603 during "Ill Week." Archibald in his status as heir to the most powerful grayne of the Armstrongs can be considered to have taken a lead role in the raiding. The Armstrongs along with the other reivers thought that the rule of law was suspended until the new monarch was crowned in London, and that they were immune from persecution until then. They were part correct in their assumption, with mass of numbers they could raid freely for the time being, but King James was taking careful mental note, and there would be hell to pay for later. James back dated his revenge on the Armstrongs, with an agenda to punish all those who took part in the "Ill Week" raid, and planned to raise every Armstrong tower to the ground.

Archibald, following his spate of raiding during "Ill Week," known as the *"younger of Maingertoun,"* was proclaimed an outlaw on 23 July 1603, at Carlisle. Archibald would have felt at a loss on what to do next, as the Border no longer gave its usual protection. He fled south into England and laid low in a safe house, hoping that the "Ill Week" would soon be forgotten about, and he could return home safely. King James wanted Archibald and his ilk to turn the iron yetts (gates) of their tower's into ploughshares, and to betake themselves to agriculture. It was to be a battle on many fronts to enforce the Royal will. Those who did not halt their reiving would have their house pulled down – no idle threat. Archibald ignored the threat, which earmarked Mangerton Tower for demolition. Mangerton Tower was duly knocked down, with Archibald and his family having to move or build a simple farmhouse. This indeed was the end of an era, and the beginning of another. And Archibald did not like it one bit, finding the new life difficult to adjust to. Archibald had at least two sons, and he was concerned for their future.

Children:-

1. Archibald – (b.c.1596)   **2.** William – (b.c.1600)

Archibald sought a low profile life in England, probably with his Forster in-law relatives, hoping with time life could settle. His tower had been laid waste, making him homeless, the future looked grim. From all around, he was hearing horror stories of his followers, friends and relatives being hung on gibbets at Dumfries, Carlisle and Jedburgh. "Jedburgh Justice" was in full action, hanging first, and then asking questions afterwards. Old crimes were being dug up and used to try the outlaws, and now the penalty for reiving was not a fine, but execution. In 1607 Archibald's participation in "Ill Week" was wheeled up and used to put him to the horn, an outcast from society.

Archibald was safe for the moment in England with a small core of relatives and clansmen, but food was getting low. Deprived of the ability to reive and access to his own lands, there was the real risk of starvation. An idea was at hand to relieve the situation, to ride back into Liddesdale, and take what he wanted. Surely the authorities would not classify this as reiving, stealing from himself. The Armstrongs then prepared for their last mission, *"all bodin in feir of weir, with swordis, gantillatis, plait slevis and utheris wappinis, and with jackis, lances, hagbutis, and pistolletis."* They set off on 10 January 1610, the final raid of *"Archibald Armestrang the elder, and tenth lord of Maingertoun"* was now in progress. Archibald was accompanied by twenty-four persons, their target was his ancestral lands of Grena and Holme, where they hoped to find easily lifted stores of food. Being January, the cattle would be in the byres, crops all harvested and indoors. Entering Liddesdale, the gang came across standing stacks of corn, a lucky find, and carried off 240 *"thravis"* of the corn. This would keep the clan going during the winter; unfortunately their theft did not go unseen. Archibald was spotted and recognised, with his name passed onto the authorities. Archibald was ordered to appear before the council on 1 March to answer for his conduct, an action that he was never likely to do. He failed to turn up and was denounced as a rebel and put to the horn for the second time.

Archibald, declared as a rebel was deprived of his lands, the hunt was on to capture him. He was tracked down later that year and taken to Edinburgh for trial where his fate was already decided, and was executed. His sons were present and witnessed the tragic show trial. They were traumatised by the whole experience, and of what befell many of the inhabitants of Liddesdale, and refused to carry on the Mangerton hereditary claim of chieftainship. The oldest son Archibald, should have become the 11th Laird of Mangerton on his father's death, however he kept his head low, disappearing into the hills and probably lived out his days as a farmer or may have took exile in Ireland. Archibald can't be blamed for turning his back on his birthright; at fourteen years old it would have been too much for him to take in. The Armstrongs were now a "headless" clan, and they would remain that way to the current day.

11. Dryhope

The location and nature of Dryhope is a puzzle, as there is no tower marked on any maps within Liddesdale of this name and no landmarks. There is however a Dryhope Tower within the Yarrow Valley some 40km away to the north, the property of the Scotts. But what would an Armstrong be doing so far from home? There are two solutions to this problem; either there was a second tower called Dryhope by coincidence and located in Liddesdale, or the title was inherited by the Armstrongs through marriage to a Scott.

Richard ("Dick") of Driupp (Dryhope) – (b.c.1519 – d.c.1603)

Dick was the third oldest son of Thomas Armstrong, 7th Laird of Mangerton. Dick is mentioned within the 1583 list on the Border Riders made by Thomas Musgrave. His entry reads – "*Dik Armestronge of Dryup, dwelleth nere Hyghe Morgarton, and his wyfe is a Scottishe woamen.*" He is listed as living at High Mangerton, which was at the heart of the Armstrong's power structure. Musgrave was particular to note who was married to whom, especially when it was a cross-Border marriage. Dick was married to a Scottish lady, which made the union of no threat to Border security. The name of his wife though is frustratingly not known. If Dick's wife was a Scott of Dryhope, then this would explain the Dryhope title which he held.

Dick was a particular ruthless reiver, having no morals or thoughts for his victims. He is first recorded in the archives coming within a list of complaints heard by Lord Forster from 3-19 May 1584. Dick had taken part in a large scale open foray to Slymefoote in the Middle Marches. He rode with one hundred riders, which included the Armstrongs of Whithaugh, Gingles and Harelaw, plus their Elliot and Crosier allies. The gang stole "*300 kie and oxen, 40 horses and meires, spoiling 30 'sheles' to the value of 100L. 'Englishe,' and taking 20 prisoners.*"

A month later Dick found himself in a very narrow scrape which almost cost him his life, when a raid he was leading went wrong. On the morning of 11 June 1584, he ran a dawn raid from Liddesdale on Hethersgill and "*spoiled an honest man of 40 head of nolt.*" A hot trod followed which was led by Henry Scrope's deputy Humfrey Musgrave and contained several of Scrope's household servants, plus some soldiers led by Mr Leighe and Captain Pickman. The trod followed the fray back into Liddesdale, a risky business as a cornered rat could always turn and bite. The Liddesdale men back on home turf decided to turn tables on the trod, and at least attempt to scare it off so that they could divide up their spoils in peace and return to their homes. Scrope records what happened next in a letter to Walsingham on 12 June – "*the thieves made a great shouting and assembly of their neighbours, to force my people to leave their trodde.*" The reivers must have lacked the numbers to attempt an assault on the trod, relying on bluster and bravado to halt their advance. Musgrave was an experienced Border officer, and was not deterred. He signalled the charge and his men went in. A brief fight broke out in which a reiver named "Howloose" was slain, and four were captured. Scrope lists those taken prisoner – "*Dick Armestrange alias Dick of Driupp a head theife, two brethren of the Whisgills that was before here executed, and one Stokoe an English rebell and fugitive are taken and in safe ward."* Musgrave emerged out of the hornet's nest with no casualties; the trod was a success, with the prisoners taken back to Carlisle Castle. Scrope recommended that the Council give thanks to three gentlemen (Musgrave, Leigh and Pickman) for their services. He requested *"to remit the disposal of these four thieves to himself which will be to good purpose,"* the four of which languished in the dank airless prison within the keep of Carlisle Castle, mulling over their fate. Dick was lucky to avoid an immediate execution.

Dick and his fellow prisoners were probably released after a Truce Day meeting. Scrope in a letter to Davison written on 12 June states – *"In case the King* [James VI] *think himself grieved... if his grace will direct his officer of Liddesdale to meet me for redress, which has not been done for 5 years past, I shall be ready to answer for my office."* And to oil the wheels of officialdom, Scrope sent Davison the gift of *"a handsome gelding."* Dick would have paid a fine as redress at a wardens meeting or in Carlisle Castle, and was free to return home – and steal again.

Far from being deterred, Dick did not let his experience within a Carlisle jail keep him from his chosen reiving career. In July 1586 Thomas Musgrave, the deputy Warden of Bewcastle made a complaint upon the *"laird's Jock, Dick of Dryupp and their complices,"* for thieving *"400 kine and oxen, taken in open forrie from the Drysike in Bewcastle."* The Laird's Jock was Dick's brother, and must have been a common companion on his forays. They are recorded again together in September 1587 when they rode with Lancie of Whisgills and their accomplices on a raid upon Andrew Rootledge of the Nuke. They were billed for stealing fifty head of cattle. They also burned Andrew's house and corn, before exiting with insight to the value of £100 sterling.

The autumn of 1588 was a busy season for Dick, getting in the beef ready for the winter. On 22 September 1588 Adam Storie and Will Storie of the Peilehill, made a complaint upon *"Dick of Driupp, the Whisgills, and 100 men"* for a destructive raid upon their property. The raiders burned the mill and murdered the miller, John Tailor, and William of the Park. Another twelve houses were also put to flames, before the gang departed taking *"100 nolt"* with them. Another raid was made with the same gang on 24 September, who descended upon Hecky (Hector) Noble, and *"burnyng to dede his sonne John, and his wief great with child."* This was a particularly brutal raid, in which the *"said Dick and other 100 Scots,"* set on fire nine houses, and burned alive John Noble and his pregnant wife. Two hundred *"nolt"* were then rounded up and driven back to Liddesdale. To round the year off, in November 1588 Margaret Forster of Allergarth, Bewcastle, made a complaint against *"Pawtie of Harlawe, Wille of Biggams, Wille Kang, Dick of Dryupp, Jock of Calfhills, &c., for 18 kye and oxen and her insight, 5L. sterling."*

On 13 April of 1590, Dick attended a Warden's Day meeting on orders to address a bill made on a complaint by Raphe Anderson of Davisheile. The March bills were read out at the Bells Kirk before William Fenwick and Thomas Trotter. Anderson's grievance was personal, and against *"Robert Armestronge, called 'Hob the taillour,' Clement Croser of Borneheades, Rychard Armstronge called 'Dick of Dryupp,' Rynione Armestronge his brother, and others."* The gang not only stole six oxen, but also rode away with John Anderson as a prisoner, who presumably was a relative of Raphe.

John's ransom was paid the *"morrow after St Luke's day 1589,"* a sum which Raphe would seek to obtain back at the trial.

Dick's last appears in the archives is within a "Liddesdale Indenture," listing bills to be charged at a later date. Dick for a change was the victim of reivers, an ironic twist. The indenture was taken on 7 March 1594 at Dayholme, Kershope, heard by Walter Scott of Goldielands and Thomas Carleton. When three bills came up for crimes at Bewcastle, Dick was noted *"alleged not to be within Liddesdale."*

Dick is mentioned in the *"Ballad of Kinmont Willie,"* one of the most stirring and romantic of all the Border ballads. The ballad recalls the daring rescue of William Armstrong of Kinmont from Carlisle Castle in April 1596 by the "Bold Buccleuch" and a party of forty riders. Dick appears within two verses, and plays a principal character in the narrative as the slayer of the *"fause Sakelde."*

"Where be ye gaun, ye broken men?"
Quo' fause Sakelde; "come tell to me!"
Now Dickie of Dryhope led that band,
And the never a word o' lear had he.

"Why trespass ye on the English side?
Row-footed outlaws, stand!" quo' he;
The never a word had Dickie to say,
Sae he thrust the lance thro his fause bodie.

The *"fause* [false] *Sakelde,"* alias Thomas Salkeld, the Deputy Warden of the English Middle March, was the figure responsible for causing the whole dramatic Kinmont affair in the first place. He was the individual who initially captured Kinmont and began the chain of events which led to his sudden rescue.

Salkeld ran into William of Kinmont at a Truce Day at Dayholme on 17 March 1596, and on the return journey home, he could not resist the tempting target of such a high ranking reiver being so close. Salkeld had clearly broken March Law, as his *"fause"* nickname suggests, all those who attended a Truce Day were free of prosecution for that day. It is not known if Salkeld ordered the capture of Kinmont, or gave the action a nod and a wink, but the capture was strictly illegal and he was guilty of not following the proper protocols. To the Scots, Salkeld became the big hate figure, with Lord Scrope adding a stubborn incompetence to the mix. This dislike of Salkeld all feeds into the *"Ballad of Kinmont Willie,"* when near to the end of the action Salkeld gets his just deserve, when Dick of Dryhope runs him through with a lance – killing him dead – Hurrah!

The truth though behind the ballad is very different, proving that the works of literacy are just that. The historian has to be aware when using literature for evidence of the past. Regarding the *"Ballad of Kinmont Willie,"* the event of the death of Salkeld is totally made up. No one was actually killed during the raid; the inclusion was probably down to Sir Walter Scott's imagination. The death of Salkeld would be a mark of moral justice, adding to the adventure and drama of the ballad. Truth and righteousness is the victor over lies and deceit. Salkeld got what he deserved slain for his false ways, but in reality he was never harmed and lived for a good forty years more (1567 – 1639).

And another disappointment to the narrative, there is no evidence that Dick even took part in the rescue. There is no mention of Dick contained within a letter sent by Scrope to Burghley on 14 April 1596, listing those who took part in the raid. The list was taken from the mouth of an informer who was present at the enforcing of the castle, and can be taken as accurate. The Laird of Mangerton was included, but his third son Dick is nowhere to be seen. Dick's absence has to be wondered about, he no longer appears in the archives, was he still alive?

12. The Flatt

The Flatt was located 2km south of Mangerton, on the East bank of the Liddel Water, opposite D'mainholm. Just 0.7km away to the south was the Border at Kershopefoot and Tourneyholm were truce days and single combats were held. The land as the name suggests was flat, good pasture land and well watered from Carby Hill to the east.

Lancelot of the Flatts – (b.1580)

Lance was the eldest son of Simon, the Laird of Whithaugh and was named after his grandfather. At the tender age of sixteen Lance rode with his father on the rescue of Kinmont Willie Armstrong in April 1596. In the summer of 1601 he was captured by Sir Robert Carey when hiding out in the Tarras Moss. He was released that same summer after Carey had agreed bonds for good behaviour with Lance's father. Lance was brought up to inherit one of the most powerful of the Riding families; however the death of Queen Elizabeth changed all this. With the Union of Crowns in 1603 the Armstrongs refused to play ball, and in 1607 Lance's father was hung. Lance would now be the new laird of Whithaugh and with no surprise was reluctant to step into his father's old riding boots.

Lance managed to avoid the fate of his father and many of his relatives in the executions of 1607, but the experience must have been a traumatic jolt for the family. Lance carefully held onto his life and property, and for a while played by the rules of the new United Kingdom. It was clear what would happen to those who did not give up reiving, with the Armstrongs having to turn their iron yetts into plough shares. It can be wondered at how Lance adjusted to the new life. Now a sheep/cattle farmer, he no longer had the excitement of the night raid to look forward to and the group camaraderie of riding the open moors as part of a gang. Despite the obvious dangers of mounting a reive after 1603, the venture was never far from his mind, he would have been hard tempted to mount up and cross the moors to make the occasional low key foray to fill the pot.

Lance took part in what was probably the very last foray on the Border in 1611. The raid was most likely Lance's idea, and at the time no one present would have realised the significance of their actions – the last recorded reive. The raid in question was against the Robsons of Leaplish in North Tyne, where Lance led a gang of seventy armed Scotts, Elliots, Armstrongs, and others on 26 May down onto a community which must have thought the reivers were all dead and buried. The gang was of a surprisingly large size, considering the brutal pacification of the previous eight years. The raid was of a particular brutal nature, and reflects the character of these final mounted desperados. Surprise was complete; the scene of chaos can be imagined, with people fleeing and others trying to protect their homes. The raiders were well armed and used their firearms to shock the population into submission. During the fracas, Elizabeth Yarrow was hit twice in the legs with musket shot, one of which broke her right thigh. She later bled to death. Mane Robson ("Blackhead"), wife to James Robson, was hit in the chest with hail-shot. And Elizabeth Robson, who was heavily pregnant, took a painful knock on the head with the butt end of a musket.

The Earl of Cumberland sent a complaint to Salisbury on 28 May, which listed the slain, wounded, and some of the offenders from the Leaplish raid, including: *"Lancelot Armestrong of Whithaugh called the young Larde, Alexander of the Roane his brother, Francis of Whithaugh and his son Lancelot."* The outcome of the eventual trial is not recorded, but can only have led to the gallows or exile for Lance.

A Lancie Armstrong is documented as the owner of Whithaugh in the 1630s. He was probably the son of Lance of the Flatts, or the Lancelot who accompanied his father Francis (brother of Sim the Laird of Whithaugh), on the Leaplish raid. In around 1730 the site was bought by William Elliot for his eldest son John.

13. Greenshiels

Greenshiels was located on the east slope of the Watch Hill, 3km NW of Newcastleton on the Long Gill, a tributary of the Black Burn, which flows into the Liddel Water. The Greenshiels Armstrongs had as their neighbours, the Elliots of Hartsgarth to the north and Copshaw to the SE, with fellow Armstrongs to the South at Puddingburn and to the West at Arkleton. It is possible that the Greenshiels Armstrongs operated the lookout on the Watch Hill, and were responsible for reporting raids to the surrounding communities.

Thomas – in Greenshiels – (fl.1535)

Thomas is named as being "in Greenshiels" and not "of Greenshiels," meaning that he simply lived at this community and was not the laird.

Thomas, noted as "*Thomas Armstrong in Greneschellis*," was listed as taking part in a night raid on 27 July 1535 upon "*John Cokburne of Ormistoune*," at his lands of Craik in Roxburghshire. Here, Thomas helped in the thieving away of seventy oxen and thirty cows, and for good measure three men servants of Cockburn were also spirited off. The prisoners were relieved of their possessions, leaving the poor men naked. The outrage was taken seriously on 30 October 1535 at a court case in Edinburgh, where Thomas was requested to attend alongside his fellow gang members which included Thomas Armstrong, 7th Laird of Mangerton, "*Sim the laird*" of Whithaugh, and John Forster alias "*schaik-buklar*" (shake buckler – a buckler was a small shield), sixteen names in total. Those named were accused of cattle stealing, taking prisoners and "*stouthreif*" – and were all denounced as rebels.

On 21 February 1536 more charges came to light when Sim the Laird was brought to trial in Edinburgh. Thomas was named as riding alongside Alexander Armstrong, called "*Evil-Willit Sandy*," during the Craik raid of 27 July 1535. And taking part in another foray on 28 October 1535, in which the farm town of Howpaslot (Howpasley) was set on fire and sixty cattle were stolen from Robert Scott. The trial ended in Sim's execution, the fate of Thomas is not known.

14. The Side

The Side was on the west bank of the Liddel Water, above the settlement of Ettleton – which has now disappeared with only the graveyard remaining. The Side as its name suggest, sits on the side of a hill – on the south eastern slopes of Kirk Hill. Kirk Hill has an Iron Age hill fort upon its summit, the area having a long history of habitation and ritual despite its upland and windswept outlook. Mangerton lay below in the valley, 1.5km to the east on the opposite bank of the Liddel.

Today at the Side, nothing can be seen of a tower, if there ever was one, though the remnants of a farmstead can be worked out amongst the ditches and mounds, overgrown with grass and rushes. At least three buildings can be traced, a kiln-barn, a complex of small enclosures and a circular sheep *"stell."* Traces of rig cultivation within field boundaries show a basic agriculture was being undertaken on terraces. The Armstrongs of the Side would have had more than beef to put into the pot.

Christopher of the Side – (fl.1528)

Christopher was possibly the father of *"Jock o' the Side."*

Christopher was once used as a bargaining tool by Henry Clifford, the 1st Earl of Cumberland, in a negotiation to round up a gang of Lisles. The situation came about when Clifford *"had in his hands* [at Carlisle] *some of the hedesmen of the Armesstrongges."* One of these was Christopher, and their detention was of concern to the Mangerton Armstrongs. A gang of Lisles under Sir William Lisle had been making a nuisance of themselves since August 1527. Using the Debateable Land as a base they had been harrying Northumberland, especially the property of Sir William Ellerker. The Armstrongs often rode with them, the gang growing as it attracted "broken men" through their successes and the lack of opposition. The English authorities could not track down the Lisles, and Angus spoke up for Scotland stating they were not within his bounds. King Henry then lost patience with the Lisles and declared them rebels, indicted for high treason. The hope was that the Lisle outlaws would be handed over to the authorities of England by the Armstrongs, and in return they would obtain the release of Christopher and others. The Armstrongs did not go ahead with the offer. King Henry instead made plans for the Earl of Northumberland to overrun Liddesdale and burn all the houses. This threat was sufficient to bring the Lisles seeking atonement. Eighteen of the gang appeared on the 26 January 1528, all in penitent mode in their shirts, and with halters around their necks. Northumberland was not in a merciful mood; they were all hanged, drawn, and quartered – except for one.

✳✳✳

John (Jock) of the Side – (d.c.1606)

John of the Side was the nephew of Archibald, the 8th Laird of Mangerton. His mother was the laird's sister, and was called Sybel Downie of the Side (another source names her as Dinah). Jock would have been a regular visitor to Mangerton and a frequent face on forays.

The earliest reference to Jock is from around 1550 (this of course could be his father), when recorded as John of the Side ("*Gleed John*") in a complaint against him that was submitted in a petition to Bishop Aldridge of Carlisle. He does not appear for another dozen years in the archives, until as a signatory to a bond – "*Jhon Armstrang of the Syd, with my hand at the pen*," authorising the handing over of an Armstrong as prisoner to the Laird of Ferniehirst in Jan 1562-3. Jock was an active reiver during the 1560s. He is included in William Maitland of Lethington's *Complaint* of 1567:-

> *He is weil kend, John of the Syde,*
> *A greater theif never did ryde,*
> *He never tyres*
> *For to brek byres*
> *O'er muir and myres, ou'r guid ane gyde*

On one such raid during this period, Jock bit off more than he could chew, and set off a catalogue of events which resulted in him going from a low-key reiver to literal fame. The raid was into Northumberland, and for some unrecorded reason it did not go to plan. Something went disastrously wrong; the raiders were badly mauled and repulsed, with Michael of Winfield slain and Jock captured. Jock was taken to Newcastle, manacled in fifteen stone of Spanish iron, and placed in the tollbooth awaiting trial and a possible hanging. There had been a man murdered during Jock's foray, and if the finger could be pointed at him, justice would be swift and exact. One less Armstrong of the Mangerton grayne would be a blessing for the English Border.

Jock was a valued member of the Mangerton household, a family who would never allow a fellow Armstrong to be executed if they could help it. The situation was gearing up for a dramatic rescue attempt, and a venture that would subsequently become immortalised in ballad form within the century. By no fault of his own, Jock became the subject of one of the most famous of the border ballads, "*Jock o' the side*." The earliest version of the ballad is from around 1592, when it appeared in the manuscript "*Percy Folio*." The first printed edition of the ballad was published in Hawick in 1784, in George Caw's "*Poetical Museum*." The book describes the ballad as "*long admired by the people of Liddesdale and its neighbourhood*." Francis James Child (1825-1896), the American ballad collector, called the ballad "*one of the best in the world, and enough to make a horse-trooper out of any young borderer, had he lacked the impulse*."

The ballad "*Jock o' the Side*," is the swashbuckling story of the rescue of Jock Armstrong from Newcastle prison. The ballad starts with the lines:-

NOW Liddesdale has ridden a raid,
But I wat they had better hae staid at hame;
For Michael o' Winfield he is dead,
And Jock o' the Side is prisoner ta'en.

For Mangerton house auld Downie is gane,
Her coats she has kilted up to her knee;

Then up and spoke her Lord Mangerton –
"What news, what news, my sister to me?" –
"Bad news, bad news! My Michael is slain;
And they ha'e taken my son Johnie."

Sybil expected the worst for her son, and sought to use her connections with the Laird of Mangerton to obtain his release. She had lost Michael, and was determined not to lose Jock also. Great distress was felt at Mangerton...

The lords they wrang their fingers white,
Ladyes did pull themsells by the hair,
Crying "Alas and well-a-day!
For Jock o' the Side we'll never see mair!"

The laird was sympathetic to Sybil's plight; he stated "*Ne'er fear, sister Sybill... Three men I'll send to set him free.*" Mangerton then organised a rescue mission, putting together a small but tight operation involving his best men – two of his sons the Laird's Jock and the Laird's Wat, plus Hobbie Noble to act as the guide. Hobbie was an Englishman, born and bred in Bewcastle. He had been banished from England due to his misdeeds and was taken in by the Mangertons as one of their own. Hobbie had an expert knowledge of the English frontier, and would be invaluable for navigating across the land at night. Mangerton had everything planned down to the finest detail, and gave the three their orders...

Your horses the wrang way maun be shod,
Like gentlemen ye mauna seem,
But look like corn-caugers ga'en the road.

Time was of the essence, there had been a man murdered when Jock had been captured, if they pinned this on him he would be hanged. Disguises were made up, the three dressing as cadgers (itinerant merchants), an inconspicuous style and a neutral trade that would not arose any questions or hold-ups. The horses were made ready, with horseshoes shod in reverse, designed to leave no incriminating trail behind. Hobbie was mounted on *"his grey sae fine; Wat on his auld horse, Jock on his bey,"* and together they rode for the River North Tyne. A fourth horse for Jock was taken along, that was probably ladened down with corn to complete the disguise and avoid suspicion.

On reaching Cholerton ford (Chollerford) on the Tyne, the group stopped to cut down a tree to make a ladder. By the light of the moon they cut *"nogs"* on each side of the trunk, which would hopefully enable them to scale the walls of Newcastle. The Tyne was then crossed without mishap and the walls of Newcastle reached. Staring up at the stark sandstone rough hewn wall, the little band undid their secret weapon – the wooden ladder. As in all good adventure stories, the ladder was found to be too short. The ballad describes the scene as – *"And down were alighted at the wa'... They fand their stick baith short and sma."* The tree was *"three ells"* (2.82m) to low. This was a major problem, which potentially could have scuppered the mission. The same problem was to dog the "Bold" Buccleuch around thirty years later, when on the mission to rescue Kinmont Willie from Carlisle Castle. It has to be wondered if the incident really happened or was added later by the ballad writer just for dramatic effect. Measuring wall heights was clearly not in the Armstrong guide book. The wall could not be scaled but luckily there was a plan-B; to use brute force. Locating the nearest town gate, the three crept up on the gatekeeper, leapt out and strangled him. Newcastle was entered. The three made for the castle which was stealthily crept into – but where to find Jock in the darkness? The rescuers called out:-

"Sleeps thou, wakes thou, Jock o' the Side,
Or art thou weary of thy thrall?"

And a familiar voice spoke back...

"Aft, aft I wake – I seldom sleep:
But whae's this kens my name sae weel,
And thus to mese my waes does seek?"

Jock did not recognise the voices, and unlike Kinmont Willie, he was not expecting to be rescued. The Laird's Jock introduced the party...

"For here are the Laird's Jock, the Laird's Wat,
And Hobbie Noble to set thee free."

Jock was in disbelief and remarked back...

"Now haud thy tongue, my gude Laird's Jock,
For ever, alas! This canna be;
For if a' Liddesdale were here the night,
The morn's the day that I maun dee."

Jock was in a rather immobile state within his cell when the Laird's Jock called, locked and manacled...

"Full fifteen stane o' Spanish iron,

The Laird's Jock told him not to have fear, and swore to set him free – *"Work thou within, we'll work without."* Two doors were then broken through, before Jock's cell was reached and opened. Jock had to be aided out of the prison and down the tollbooth stairs to the awaiting horses. Jock had problems getting onto his horse due to the chains, having to sit side saddle. The ballad comments:-

The exit went swift, with the four riders speeding back towards the Tyne. Unknown to the party, the escape was soon discovered and a posse of twenty was put together, and was hot on their tail. On reaching the Chollerford for the second time that day, they found that the Tyne had risen rapidly and to record levels. An elderly local resident commented that he had never seen the Tyne in such a flood before. The Laird's Wat was overcome with cold feet at having to re-cross the Tyne, and was all for giving up. The Laird's Jock though was made of sterner stuff, and he put the back-bone back into the group. He bodily picked up Jock, complete with fifteen stone of iron attached, and waded into the swollen river. The Laird's Jock with extreme effort swam across the ford, followed by Hobbie and Wat, taking a lead from his example. On reaching the opposite bank, the party looked back to see the Newcastle posse drawing up – as in all great rescue stories, an escape in the nick of time. The Land-Sergeant knew the game was up, and refused an attempt to cross the ford. The Land-Sergeant called across the mountainous water, *"Ye the pris'ner may take, But leave the irons, I pray, to me,"* wanting to salvage something from the situation. A request which the Laird's Jock rejected, he would do no such thing. The cry went out again for the Armstrong's to leave the fetters behind, to be met from the Laird's Jock a witty and triumphant reply that he would use the iron to make into horseshoes for his mare.

The remainder of the journey was trouble free, arriving back safely to Liddesdale and a celebratory punchbowl at the laird's table at Mangerton. Jock was brought to his own fireside and a relieved wife, none the worse for his unexpected journey. Contemporary records of this event happening have not survived, but a letter dated 1 September 1599 offers a second hand testimony. It reads... *"In the reign of the king's mother John Armstrong called the laird's Jok and Hob the nobill came to the prison of Newcastle and broke up a postern gate and took out John Armstrong called John of the Syd, their kinsman and no fault with it by England but only punished their own gaoler for his sloth."* This would place the rescue between 1561 and 1567, during the reign of Mary, Queen of Scots.

Jock of the Side reappears again a few years later, not through his own actions this time, but when national politics came to visit him. In November 1569 a rebellion of several Roman Catholic Lords broke out in the north of England. Their goal was to restore the old religion and to liberate Mary, Queen of Scots. The rising though lacked popular support, and was soon put down, sending the rebel Lords into panic as they now became hunted figures. Scotland was unsafe, but there was Liddesdale, the traditional haven for fugitives. They would have thought long and hard about putting their destiny into the hands of the Armstrongs, but Elizabeth's mercy was the only alternative. The move was only temporary, a hideout in the hills until an overseas exile could be organised. In the depths of winter their choices were limited, caught between a rock and a hard place. Around one hundred fled into Liddesdale, with Charles Neville, 6th Earl of Westmoreland and Thomas Percy, 7th Earl of Northumberland leading their retinues into the Debateable Land, dodging Lord Scrope's patrols on the trail north.

Entering Liddesdale on 21 December, they were met by Jock of the Side and Black Ormiston – an unruly pair as could ever be imagined. The identity of Black Ormiston is not known, he was referred to as a Teviotdale man and *"an outlaw of Scotland, that was a principal murtherer of the king of Scots."* Translated, this meant that he was present at the death of David Rizzio in March 1566, acting on orders of Lord Darnley, and was one of those who savagely plunged their daggers into the queen's secretary at Holyrood Palace. He was also a follower of Bothwell, having a foot in both camps according to personal gain. Black Ormiston acted as the guide to the party, and led everyone north east towards Mangerton. The fugitives were still in danger as the Earl of Sussex knew where they had gone, and would do all he could to obtain their capture. Sussex was confident he could use the reiver's weak point – money, and buy a betrayal of confidence to land the earls back into his hands. Sussex wrote – *"Their whole trust is upon three or four mischievous thieves and men full of treason... they shall be had by corruption, though the Queen pay dear for it."* Moray, the Scottish regent, also wanted the rebels caught and handed over to Elizabeth.

After only one day in Liddesdale trouble arose in the form of Martin Elliot of Braidley, a powerful laird in upper Liddesdale, who acting under a pledge from the Regent Moray, rode out with a force of three hundred lancers to confront the earls. A face to face situation happened that could easily have turned nasty, but neither side was in a mood for fighting. Both sides were reluctant to fall out and came to an agreed bloodless solution, for the earls to be out of Scotland within twenty-four hours... or else. The threat was very real. Black Ormiston and Jock made their own arrangements to cater for the fugitives. The Earl of Sussex wrote to Cecil on 22 December 1569 describing how *"my lord of Westmoreland changed his coat of plate and sword with John of the Syde, to be more unknown."* Disguises were essential in their new home. This would have left Jock of the Side in possession of the earl's fine clothing, and no doubt wore the garments on occasion, looking the full dandy at the laird's table at Mangerton on his next invitation.

Black Ormiston moved the two earls into the Debateable Land as ordered, Northumberland's wife, Anne Somerset, Countess of Northumberland, however was left behind. The Countess was exhausted, and was in no fit state to walk to the Debateable Land. They had ridden into Liddesdale the day before, but the local Liddesdale men had stolen their horses within the day. The Countess accompanied by three others, had to stay for a short spell in the house of Jock of the Side. Jock's reaction at having such important guests in his house can only be imagined, and if he made any preparations before having a lady enter his humble abode. The Countess was rather unimpressed to say the least on Jock's house, describing it as *"a cottage not to be compared to many a dog kennel in England."* It is interesting to read the description of Jock's house. The question can be asked – was there ever a tower at the Side? The type of house that the Countess stayed in would have been typical on the Border. These cottages could be built in less than a day, and were of no loss if destroyed in a raid. Why build a house for luxury and permanence, when the neighbours could burn it down the next day. The dwelling most likely had a turf roof, which had fire proof properties, and had undressed stone walls. Inside was dark and smoky, with an earth beaten floor and a hearth against one wall. Westmorland's disguise worked well, dressed as a Borderer in Jock's clothes, no run-ins with Scrope's troopers occurred and they reached the stronghold of Hector Armstrong of Harelaw, who would provide refuge. Hector though had secondary motives, personal profit, and did not care about his new guest's wellbeing. As quick as he could, Hector handed Northumberland over to the English authorities. The Countess meanwhile was holed up in Jock's hovel. Black Ormiston returned to the Side and stole all the Countess's jewels – so much for the myth of Border hospitality and honour.

There was one ray of light in this dark grubby un-gentlemanly affair – enter the figure of Sir Thomas Kerr of Ferniehurst. Sir Thomas was an avid supporter of Mary, Queen of Scots, and was a Roman Catholic. He came to hear of the earl's plight and saddled up his riders on a rescue mission. With no interference, the Kerrs entered Liddesdale and picked up both the Countess and the Earl of Westmorland. The encounter is one of high romantic legend when Kerr reached the Side, and freed the Countess. Jock probably made himself scarce at this instance, not wanting to tangle with such determined troopers. They were both soon back at Ferniehurst Castle and finally safe from the Liddesdale outlaws. The pair survived the outcome of the rising, but had to take ship for Flanders and a life of exile.

Jock does not crop up in the archives until the following century – when *"John of the Syde"* appears in a list of the Scottish outlaws of Liddesdale, dated 18 April 1601. The list of outlaws was those who came under the Laird of Buccleuch's charge which His Majesty had commanded to be given up to Lord Scrope and Sir Robert Carey, and contained the names of the recent murderers of the March Warden, Sir John Carmichael. It is impossible to know for sure if this John was the same Jock that was sprung from Newcastle jail thirty-five odd years before. It may of course be his son, but it could be a sixty year old Jock still up to his old tricks. In the same document for the West March, *"Syme and Lantie Armstrangs of the Syde,"* are listed – possible sons of John, who were wanted for the murder of Sir John Carmichael.

The last documentary reference to John comes at the end of 1606, when he is named amongst three hundred others in a list of declared outlaws. The law had finally caught up with John, with a deportation or execution lined up – a possible victim of Jedburgh Justice.

✳✳✳

Christopher of the Side – (fl.1597)

Christopher of the Side was a brother of *"Jock o' the Side"* and a nephew of the 8th Laird of Mangerton. He is listed as one of the principle chiefs on the Border in John Monipennie's document of 1597. Under *"LIDDISDAIL,"* he is named as *"Chrystie of the Syde,"* alongside the Laird of Mangerton and the Laird's Jock. Christopher being named by

Monipennie suggests that he led the family and took a major role in the raiding and functioning of Armstrong society. Christopher was the senior brother of the Side, taking precedent over Jock. He was probably the first born son and took his father's name.

✸✸✸

Lancelot of the Side– (fl.1601)

Simon of the Side – (fl.1601)

Simon and Lancelot both appear in a document dated 18 April 1601, on a list of those wanted for the murder of Sir John Carmichael the West March Warden, in the year before. They are named as *"Syme and Lantie Armstrangs of the Syde,"* and are probably brothers, perhaps the sons of either *"Jock o' the Side"* or Christopher of the Side, his brother. The death of Carmichael came as a shock to the authorities, who hunted down those responsible with a great energy. The fate of the brothers is not recorded, but judging by what happened to the other murderers of Carmichael, they faced a grim end.

✸✸✸

Robert of the Side – (c.1648)

Robert, *"called Syd,"* is recorded on a list of moss-troopers in around 1648. He may have been related to Lancelot and Simon of the Side.

✸✸✸

15. Puddingburn

The tower of Puddingburn once stood on a narrow promontory between the confluence of the Dow Sike and the Stanygill Burn in the shadow of Tinnis Hill. Strangely, there is no burn in the area named "Pudding," or even a hill or landmark of a similar name. The Pont's map c.1595 calls the tower *"Stainygil,"* which makes more sense with a landmark nearby of this name. The term "Pudding" derives perhaps from the Scots word for a frog, *"puddock / puddy,"* – the area is marshy and a good habitat for the creatures. Or more interestingly, from "pudding," an oatmeal stuffed intestine. With some imagination, perhaps this was a place where pig intestines were cleaned and soaked in running water during food preparation – and then laid out to dry on the banks of the burn. Puddings were known as a source of food for medieval peasants, and the reivers would have regularly eaten them. The puddings came in two forms; the white pudding made from oats and suet, and seasoned with salt and herbs; and the black pudding, which was similar with the addition of blood. And not forgetting the haggis. All could be eaten cold, saving the need to burdening themselves with pots and pans. A ready meal for a raid could be rolled up into an intestine for ease of carrying, and if wanted hot, be fried upon a breastplate placed on a fire.

The Armstrongs of Puddingburn had some excellent neighbours, with fellow Armstrongs 1km to the north east at the Side and yet more Armstrongs at Whisgills 2km to the south; a viper's nest indeed for those brave enough to enter. Puddingburn was provided with its own ready-made army of desperate cut-throats, and was always primed for the attack or defence. The peak of Watch Hill 5km to the north warned the Armstrongs of intruders, with a rabbit warren landscape of cleuchs and peat hags to hide out in or to mount a timely ambush. And if the heat became too much, there was always the Tarras Valley 5km to the west, a morass of bog and scrub that was the favourite hiding place for the Armstrongs. Dominating the landscape at Puddingburn, is Tinnis Hill, 1km to the west, a sacred place of ancient power, taking its name from the Welsh *"Dinas,"* meaning a stronghold or a place of refuge. Surrounded by hills and bogs, with only the one entrance into the valley, the Puddingburn Armstrongs were a tough nut to winkle out – a high place where cattle could easily be corralled and defended, the perfect reiver's lair.

The Puddingburn Armstrongs came to the attention of the authorities in June 1583 when it was noted that the Bewcastle garrison was in no fit state to resist the depredations of the family. To build up the defences, fifty of Her Majesty's soldiers were requested from Berwick – with all to be well horsed and armed, and able to not only help keep watch, but also to ride and follow the local lances wherever they were required. Their job was to defend the country from the Armstrongs of Puddingburn, Whithaugh and Mangerton, and also the Ellwoods (Elliots), who joined with them to reive and steal in their own country, even up to the very gates of Edinburgh. This was an overly ambitious task at the best of times, and can be assumed to have only scratched the surface of the problem, which was permanently underfunded and always playing catch-up. A document from 1584 provides an update on the situation on the Border. The arrival of soldiers from Berwick was achieved, with a hundred foot lying at Kershope ready to assist and *"keep down the Armstronges of Tinnes alias Puddyborne, the Whithaches and Mangertouns, and Elwoods."* It is interesting to notice the Puddingburn Armstrongs being named alongside Mangerton and Whithaugh. Mangerton and Whithaugh were the two most troublesome graynes of the Armstrongs, for Puddingburn to be included in the roll of dishonour suggests that they had an equal capacity for destruction and mayhem.

Today, little remains of the tower. The tower met the same fate as the others in Liddesdale, and was knocked down. The stones from the walls were put to a more productive peaceful use, and formed into a sheepfold. A small part of the tower though can be seen today, which measures 6.6m x 5m with a maximum height of 1.5m. Within the 1.3m thick walls a single window looks out.

✳✳✳

John – "The Laird's Jock" of Tinnisburn / Puddingburn – (b.c.1518 – d.1599)

Jock was the second eldest son of Thomas Armstrong, the 7th Laird of Mangerton (1479-1549), from where his "Laird" name tag originated. Archibald, his elder brother would go on to inherit the family chieftainship and become the 8th Laird. The Laird's Jock though played an important role in his own right, his name appearing as a signatory on various bonds and marriage entries between the years 1569 and 1599, as well as being an active rider and leader. When Jock's father died, he did not inherit the title of chief, and continued to be known as the *"Gude Laird's Jock,"* or more formally as John of Tinnisburn.

He was a popular figure and possessed the hearts of the Liddesdale folk through his courage and generous nature. He was also physically strong, with a heroic form and was noted for taking part in contests of strength where individuals could show off their prowess. Jock was an expert with the two-handed sword and unrivalled at single combat. No one, Scots or English could get the better of Jock in combat; he was the champion of the Borders in swordsmanship, unbeatable with his great double edged blade. Jock had been passed down the sword from earlier generations. The sword gained a sacred aura of its own, tempered with the blood of its victims and the spirit of its previous owners. Only those seen as worthy could yield the sword. An ancient magic was captured within. The sword was used as an image upon the graves of the Armstrong chiefs, drawn around as a template and carved into the stone for eternity with a ritual power. Folk memories of the Danish Viking Siward Bjornsson were conjured up in the strong arm of Jock and his blade, bringing alive the Norse legends for a new audience.

Jock was married to the daughter of Anton Armstrong of *"Wylyave"* (Williava) in Gilsland, England. Thomas Musgrave recorded Jock in his survey of 1583, and noted his marriage, concerned at the cross Border alliances that stemmed from the union. It was illegal to marry without permission across the Border, and Jock had committed this very March Treason. The Laird's Jock would gain allies for raids and an ear on information which could mean all the difference between life and death. The complex web of alliances gave the authorities countless headaches, with attempts to try and understand and defuse the powder keg of explosive families. Jock's in-laws were a dangerous bunch. Anton Armstrong's son, Edward, was reported as *"a great thief and maintainer of many others about him,"* by Lord Eure in June 1587. Edward's daughter was married to John Charleton of the Bower, another freebooter and noted as *"a great thief*," which added to the web of intrigue. Jock gained strong contacts deep into England to his benefit, and the loss for others.

In the same document, Jock is mentioned as dwelling "*under Denyshill besydes Kyrsope in Denisborne*," which reads in modern spelling as – "Tinnis Hill besides Kershope in Tinnis Burn." He had at least two sons:-

1. John – (c.1570/80s)   **2.** William of Greena – (k.1599)

The Laird's Jock was a well known and active reiver; he also found fame outside of the usual criminal circuit of Truce Days and bills – in the literary world of the border ballads. John Armstrong of Puddingburn Tower, alias the Laird's Jock, has the rare privilege of featuring in not only one, but two of the border ballads – "*Jock o' the Side*" and "*Dick o' the Cow*." The ballads though works of fiction, provide a fascinating glimpse into Jock's life. They have to be studied with historical caution, as the tales they weave may of course be total fabrication, with artistic license emphasising drama. However they capture the essence of the period and at the core, the main story has a high probability in being correct.

Jock of the Side was a neighbour of the Laird's Jock, the Side being the nearest dwelling to Puddingburn. Jock would have been a familiar figure, they were also related – the Laird's Jock was the uncle of Jock. The close family connection to the Laird of Mangerton ensured that mountains would be moved if it was necessary to protect one of their own. The Armstrong's of Mangerton could not tolerate this incarceration. The Laird of Mangerton was the mastermind behind putting the rescue mission together, the story of which is the subject of the ballad of "*Jock o' the Side*." Mangerton called the shots, as the ballad enfolds...

Three men I'll send to set him free,
Well harness'd a' wi' the best o' steel;
The English louns may hear, and drie
The weight o' their braid-swords to feel.

Jock set off together with his brother and Hobbie Noble on their mission. The ballad paints him in the heroic roll, with Walter adding the counter balance. The physical strength of the Laird's Jock is displayed several times; when the brothers grabbed the gate porter and – "*His neck in twa the Armstrangs wrang*," and then breached several doors to discover Jock in his cell. On the return journey, it was the Laird's Jock's strength which saved the day, when he picked up Jock in his shackles and bore him to the opposite bank of the Tyne. The party all reached Liddesdale safely and lived to fight another day. A great celebration at Mangerton was no doubt held, with copious feasting. The Laird's Jock would be busy for the next few days with his souvenir of the adventure, in making horseshoes from Jock's shackles. A second version of the ballad adds the aftermath of the rescue – in true reiver style...

And now they are fallen to drink,
And they drank a whole week one day after another,

The second ballad, "*Dick o' the Cow*" does not have the same anchor of providence in fact as the first, though is no less fascinating. The ballad as the name suggests involves cows, though it is interesting to note that the cow referred to is not a proper cow, otherwise the ballad would have been known as "*Dick o' the Kye*." The cow in this instance probably refers to the hut in which Dick lived. The surname of Dick is never revealed, and was probably not another Riding family, though he was in regular contact with Lord Scrope in Carlisle.

"*Dick o' the Cow*" is the tale of a raid into England by William Armstrong and John Armstrong, two sons of the Laird's Jock. They rode deep into England, travelling 45km across the Border and descended upon Hutton Hall just north of Penrith. Raiding the property, they found the laird "*the wiser man*" than themselves, who had prudently locked up his livestock for safety. He "*had left nae gear to steal, except six sheep upon a lee,*" which the Armstrongs had to satisfy themselves with. The six sheep though did not satisfy the Armstrongs desire for plunder, having travelled so far they thought more was deserved. The brothers then turned their attention to Dick o' the Cow, a man they had passed on the journey south and thought to be "*an innocent fool,*" but he had "*three as good kyne of his own*" – and was well worth a second look. The Armstrongs arrived at Dick's house and broke down the walls to lose out his three cows. To add insult to injury, they also impudently stole "*three coerlets off his wife's bed.*" Dick must have watched on in stunned silence, powerless to intervene.

In the morning when the day grew light, the full extent of the theft became clear; "*the shouts and crys rose loud and high*" from Dick's wife. Dick halted his wife's tongue with the promise that he would return the stolen cattle, and set off to seek his "*lord and master,*" to request a hot trod was made. This individual was Lord Scrope, though exactly which Scrope it was, is not made clear, as the year the incident took place is never mentioned. Henry, Lord Scrope, was warden from 1563 to 1593 and his son Thomas for the next decade – Henry though, seems the most likely figure of the two for Dick's lord and master. Dick explained to Scrope "*Liddesdaile has been in my house this last night, and they have tane my three kyne from me.*" Scrope refers to Dick as "*my fool,*" suggesting that he had a jester type roll at Carlisle, and gave Dick his permission to leave and obtain his property back himself. It is not clear why Scrope did not assist, and call out his troopers on a trod. Instead he gave Dick instructions that he was to only steal from the man that stole from him, and no others – or he would be hung from Harraby Hill as a common thief.

Dick then journeyed to Puddingburn on a solo cold trod; indicating that he knew exactly who was responsible for the attack on his house. Arriving at the tower, he was faced with the daunting site of "*thirty Armstrongs and three*" in residence, and openly approached the wasps nest with only a naive appeal to decency as his weapon. Boldly (and stupidly) he faced up the Laird's Jock and made his complaint on "*your man Fair Johnie Armstrong*" and "*billie Willie,*" explaining how "*they have tane my three ky frae me*" the previous night. Those gathered gave their responses, with the two Armstrongs responsible for the theft being the most vocal; John suggested "*we'll him hang,*" and William "*we'll him slae.*" An unnamed Armstrong forwarded the idea to "*nit him in a four-nooked sheet, give him his burden of batts, and lett him gae.*" Being beaten with wooden bats was the best of a set of unpleasant options on offer; luckily the Laird's Jock was of a more gentlemanly nature, "*the best falla in the companie.*" Dick was offered a seat in the Great Hall of Puddingburn at the laird's table for dinner, which he agreed to. At the banquet he was served a piece of his own cow's "*hough*" (hock), which he could not stomach to eat. With a weary heart, he abandoned any plea for Armstrong justice and fell back instead to cunning.

Dick unwanted, found himself as a guest of the Armstrongs. After feasting he was put up for the night in an "auld peat-house," a token of hospitality designed to both be civil and show who was boss. Before retiring, Dick was careful to observe where the key to the stable was kept – "*Above the door-head they flang the key,*" and made a mental note to return later when everyone was asleep. He had earlier seen the stables, and thought "*There's a bootie younder for me,*" forming a hope that he could gain entry and remove some beasts as compensation for his loss. He was not a prisoner, and could easily walk out of the peat-house at his leisure; the Armstrongs had no fear of him, he was just a fool after all.

In the wee-small hours, all went to plan, there were no guards and Dick managed to pick up the stable's key unseen and enter the building. Inside "*there stood thirty horse and three,*" Dick decided he would steal just two of the horses, reckoning this was fair exchange for losing three cows. He was thinking ahead to justify the situation to Lord Scrope, not wanting to go beyond his promise and be accused of being a thief. To give himself the best possible chance of escape, he tied the remaining horses with a "*St Mary's knot.*" This type of rope work was not what it sounds, and certainly could not be undone by the Armstrongs. A "St. Mary's knot" meant to cut the ham strings of an animal. The scene must have been grotesque in the extreme, and captures the desperateness of the situation. With blood and shrieking horses all around in the dark, Dick leapt onto his selected mount, then taking a second in his hand – "*And out at the door and gane is Dickie.*"

The reaction to Dick's escape and handicraft on the following morning can be imagined – "The *shouts and cryes rose loud and high.*" The bloody horror was enough to traumatise even the hardened Armstrongs; a furious rage erupted which demanded an instant and deadly revenge. The Laird's Jock exclaimed "*Dick o' the Cow has been in the stable this last night, and has my brother's horse and mine frae me.*" Dick's choice of horses to thieve was not accidental, shaped as a personal attack on the Armstrong leaders, and with an added vengeance in having the whole family horseless – the Border would have peace from Puddingburn forays for a while. Angers were fierce at Puddingburn, and denied the means of pursuit grew to a boiling point. Only one horse had survived Dick's handiwork, a bay horse belonging to Jock that was not in the stables at the time of the slashing. Jock loaned his horse to his son John, who spurred after Dick. Before heading off, Jock also loaned John the padded-jack off his back, a two-handed sword, and the steel cap on his head. Jock then warned John that his horse was "*both worth gold and good monie; Dick o' the Kow has away twa horse, I wish no thou should no make him three.*"

John made good progress and caught up at Canonbie Lee. John was an experienced fighter, closing the distance John threw his spear at Dick, striking him on the jerkin. The jerkin took the power of the blow without being penetrated, and its wearer was unhurt. Dick lacked the fighting skills to tackle the reiver, and knew with terror what could only come next. John unsheathing his sword rode in for the kill. Dick reached for his own sword, and turned in the saddle preparing as best to deflect the oncoming blow. What occurred next was an unexpected display of military skill, *"Dickie could not win to him with the blade of the sword, but he feld him with the plummet under the eye."* Dick struck John a lucky blow with the pommel of his sword, sending him sprawling from the saddle.

Victory went to *"the prettiest man in the south country,"* who remarked *"I had twa horse, thou has made me three."* Dick was surprised at his victory; expecting to have been cleaved in two, he had actually despatched a skilled reiver. Dick then took John's *"twa-handed sword that hang lewgh by his thigh,"* plus jack, helmet and horse. With an increased load, Dick returned to his *"lord and master"* at Carlisle, pleased with himself at his triumph. Lord Scrope took a double take at his fools exploits, however he was not happy on Dick's actions despite admiring the bravery – *"Now Dickie, I shall neither eat meat nor drink. Till high hanged that thou shall be!"* Scrope disliked the fact that Dick had broken a promise, and stole from the Laird's Jock, a person who had done him no harm. Dick explained how he came about to having the Jock's three horses, *"I wan him frae his man, Fair Johne Armstrong, hand for hand on Cannobie lee."* He then presented his sword, jack and helmet – *"I have a' these takens to lett you see."* Scrope mulled over the evidence, and decided Dick was telling the truth. He offered Dick twenty pounds for John Armstrong's good horse, and added *"one of my best milk-kye, to maintain thy wife and children three."* Dick turned down the offer of twenty pounds saying he would sell the horse at Mattan Fair, and asked for thirty which Scrope accepted.

Leaving Carlisle Castle, the first man that Dick ran into was Ralph, *"Bailife Glazenberrie,"* the brother of Lord Scrope. *"Welcome, my brother's fool,"* Ralph greeted Dick, asking where he got John Armstrong's horse from. A similar conversation then occurred as with Lord Scrope, resulting in Ralph offering Dick fifteen pounds for one of Jock's horses, and his best milk-kye, to maintain his wife and children. Again Dick refused the offer, and raised it to thirty pounds, which Ralph agreed to, paying all in good gold.

Dick returned home in triumph, with the tension over he gave a little dance for joy, laughing loud and leaping on high. Despite being the "fool," he had outwitted both his foes and master, and had kept the best horse of the three for himself. Dick had trod a thin line just inside the law, and had returned an un-heroic hero. A clever fool who had outfoxed the best, and not only lived to tell the tale, but profited. His wife would be more than happy at the outcome, he had to show her *"three score of English pounds for the three auld coerlets was tane of her bed,"* and two good *kye* to replace the three stolen. And for his pains there was a bonus *"white-footed naigg"* from the Armstrong stables to himself.

The ballad however concludes on a negative tone, with Dick o' the Cow afraid that he had caused the Armstrongs so much offence that his life was in permanent danger. Such a belligerent family as the Armstrongs would surely have a vendetta out to get him. The ballad ends on the verse...

But I may no longer in Cumberland dwell;
The Armstrongs the'le hang me high:

What happened to Dick after the dust had settled? He had rattled the cage of the Border's most destructive family; he could only but have an unpleasant ending. No happy ever after with his wife and two new cows and horse. He relocated to the Pennine foothills, but this was only a temporary respite from the Armstrongs, who eventually tracked him down several years later. There are two grizzly versions of what happened to Dick once he fell into the Armstrong's clutches. One source says that the Armstrongs plunged him into a large pot of boiling water, and another says they tore his flesh from his bones with red-hot pincers.

In October 1582 a complaint was made by Sir Simon Musgrave, the Constable of Bewcastle, upon Jock, together with Simon, the 9th Laird of Mangerton and "Sim's Thom" Armstrong and their accomplices, *"for burning of his barn, wheat, rye, oats, bigg, and peas, with L. 1000 sterling."*

Jock was arguably the most troublesome of the Laird Mangerton's sons (he had at least seven), as he was requested to attend a meeting at Whithaugh Tower to sign an assurance on 20 December 1584. Sir John Forster took the pledge, recording *"the Lards Jock assures for hym selfe his tennents and servands as the rest of his surname hathe done."* Forster would have hoped with the assurance, to have ended Jock's reiving activities, though in the bottom of his mind he could have only hoped for a temporary breathing space. As expected, Jock could not resist the life of crime and soon broke his assurance. In July 1586 a complaint was made by Thomas Musgrave, Deputy Warden of Bewcastle upon John and *"Dick of Dryupp and their complices"* for thieving *"400 kine and oxen, taken in open forrie from the Drysike in Bewcastle."* Dick of Dryhope was Jock's brother, and perhaps he was responsible for gearing up Jock for the foray. And a similar raid happened again in September of that year, when Andrew Rootledge of the Nuke (near Bewcastle) complained upon *"Lard's Jock, Dick of Dryupp, Lancie of Whisgills, and their complices for... 50 kine and oxen, burning his house, corn, and insight 100 L. sterling."*

In February 1588, a complaint was brought upon the *"Lairds Jocke,"* in a bill found filed for Liddesdale by the Commissioners at Berwick. The complaint was made by the Laird of Prendicke and Henry Collingwood of Ryle and their tenants of Ingram and Reavelie. Jock was charged alongside Andrew Armstrong of Whithaugh, Hector Armstrong of the Hillhouse, Jock Armstrong of Kinmont, George Armstrong of Arkleton, John Bateson called *"John of the Score,"* and another 500 men – *"who ran a day foray and carried off 600 kye and oxen, 600 sheep, 35 prisoners and insight worth 40L. sterling, on 23 June 1587."*

The Laird's Jock had at least two servants, two of whom were fellow Armstrongs, Mungo and Jock. Mungo and Jock were also active reivers, and are both recorded taking part in a foray at Candlemas in 1588 on Heathery Burn, and having a complaint made upon them by William Fenwick the English Deputy Middle March Warden and Mathew Armstrong. They followed the raiding lead of fellow Armstrongs, David *"Bangtaile,"* Jock of the *"Holles,"* and Andrew *"Bungell."* They were billed for stealing *"37 wedders"* in April 1590, held at the Bells Kirk. Jock is named as a main chief in Liddesdale within John Monipennie's publication in 1597 on the principle clans and chiefs of the Borders. He is named alongside the 9th Laird of Mangerton and Christopher of the Side. The three were all related and would have raided together.

Jock's son William, eventually left the Tinnis Valley and took up residence at Greena Tower, becoming a land owner in his own right along the Border with England just below Greena Hill. William though did not get on well with his neighbours the Fosters, a short distance away on the opposite side of the Liddel Water. Tension rose to a level and he was challenged to a duel by Foster of Stanegirthside in 1599. William accepted the challenge which filled Jock's heart with pride; his son was following in his old father's footsteps. William asked his father to be loaned his two-handed sword, as his family honour was at stake. With mixed emotions Jock passed the sword over, the relic would give William a great advantage in the fight Jock thought – but if he lost, the sword was to be presented over to Foster as a prize. The duel was contested at Tourneyholme on the east bank of the Liddel Water, where it was met by the Kershope Burn. Jock was suffering an illness and was bedridden on the day of the fight, but still insisted on being present. Jock was wrapped in blankets to keep warm, and against the protests of his daughters, he made the journey south. Jock took up his place to watch the contest, sat upon a shaft of stone, which was later named the "Laird's Jock's stone." The two combatants walked onto the thin strip of land, waiting to have the rules of the fight read out. Foster was not going to play fair. Treacherously before William could draw his father's sword, Foster whose sword was already drawn, took a thrust and pierced William causing a killing wound. The duel was over and Foster had won. It is said that Jock let forth such a wail of despair that it was heard echoing throughout the dale. He had lost both his son and prized weapon – and the lands of Greena were now in Foster's hands. He continued in sorrow long after the sun went down, the cries growing fainter and fainter. Eventually friends and relatives prepared Jock for his travel home, were tradition says he died on the journey a broken man.

Simon (Sym) – of Puddingburn – (fl.1597)

Simon was probably related to the Laird's Jock, and was at least an active member of his gang. Simon came under the beady eye of no other than King James VI, in 17 November 1597 when he brought his carefully crafted wrath to bare onto the Border. He wisely wrote to Henry Leigh – *"As some of the broken men and malefactors within this our West March, have refused to enter and submit as directed by our Council, we have resolved to passe forward in proper person uppon them with fyre and sword upon Tysday next the xxii th day of this instant, to their exterminacion and wreike."*

James writing from Dumfries requested of Leigh, *"that yow will be in a redynes with some sufficient force, to remaine at the Mote of Lyddell upon Tysday next, at twelve howres, for hawlding them in at that syde,"* in concurrent with the king's plans to pass through Annandale on a mission to capture outlaws. The king remarked on hearing that Leigh had in his hands *"some of the most vyle and notable theives of Annerdell,"* and also *"one Sym of Puddingbourne, whilk was taken read hand in their thirtice deedes*." James was keen to get his own hands onto these prisoners himself, individuals who with *"mischeivous mischeifes"* had committed a great *"hurte of the good subjectes of beith the realms."* James sought Leigh to use his own power in the absence of Lord Scrope as warden, to deal with the outlaws and advised – *"ye woll ether cause they notorious lymmers be delivered to ws to be hanged, or ye woll cause hange them your selfe."*

Whatever came of the king's determination to have Simon hung, he was still raiding three years later. In a Declaration by Henry Leigh dated 12 April 1600, he describes Lord Sanquhar being chased twice in one day by the Laird of Johnston, who was aided by Simon. Leigh reported *"Sim of Puddinge burne was abroad with his guard of theeves, to rob the passengers to the fayre, and I was loath to fall in such handes."*

16. Whisgills

Whisgills was a village located in the Tinnis Valley, a third of the way up Whisgills Edge on the east slope of Tinnis Hill. Tinnis Hill lends its name to the valley, standing stark and proud demanding the viewer's attention; the most prominent landmark in the area. It comes as no surprise to find that the hill was a place of ancient power, where on Windy Edge Bronze Age tribes buried their chieftains in chambered cairns, and erected standing stones to their gods. When the Armstrongs arrived in the valley, the significance of the hill was long forgotten, but its shape and presence on the landscape continued to have a spiriting influence. It is not known if a tower stood at Whisgills, but bastles and other strongholds must have been present. Whisgills was on the west bank of the Tinnis Burn, a tributary of the Liddel Water, with the Armstrongs of Puddingburn their nearest neighbour to the north. The valley must have been a busy place, with the hoofed traffic of reivers setting off on raids, and coming back with livestock to hold and distribute.

Eamont of Whisgills – (fl.1583)

Eamont is documented taking part in a raid into Bewcastledale, the favourite hunting spot of the Armstrongs, over the days of 5-6 October 1583. The gang was named as containing the "*Lard of Maingerton, Lard of Whithaugh, and Eamont Armstronge of Wisgills, with their complices to the nomber of 40 persons of Lidsdall.*" Eamont was riding alongside the two main power houses of the Armstrongs; the gang was relatively small but contained a destructive force beyond its size. Their first target was Rowy and Dand Rowtlege of Bewcastle on 5 October, who later made a complaint on the spoliation caused. The gang thieved away "*xxx kyne and oxen, all the insight of ii steadings.*" The Routleges resisted the raiders thieving their livelihood and must have fought back, as there was several persons recorded badly hurt. The Routleges were known as the target that every man preyed upon, giving the impression that they were free game for every reiver to thieve from. But judging by the injuries sustained, they could put up a spirited defence on their home turf. The family were once a predatory force based in Liddesdale and Teviotdale, but had been pushed south to Bewcastle during the "Rough Wooing," where they eked out a precarious existence.

On the following night another foray was made in the same area, which hit two targets in Bewcastledale. Again a gutsy one sided resistance was put up, but left several Routledges wounded as the Armstrongs rode off with sixteen cattle, twenty sheep, ten goats and all the insight that they could carry. The Routleges were fighting a battle they could never win, and this kind of damage was something the family could not endure every year. It was losing family members killed to the Armstrongs which probably deterred the Routleges from fighting back in the future, giving the impression that they were a soft target. And resulted in a decision to let any reiver take what they wanted, becoming the prey of everyman. Better a poor man than a dead man would have been the thought. The castle of Bewcastle under Christopher Musgrave should have given the Routleges adequate protection, but a lack of funds, manpower and corruption watered down the garrison's effectiveness.

Lance of Whisgills – (fl.1587)

Lance is documented making a raid down to Gilsland together with his neighbour from Puddingburn tower, John Armstrong ("*the Laird's Jock*"), and Richard Armstrong of Dryhope. The bill was recorded as:- "*Andrew Rootledge of the Nuke complains upon Lard's Jock, Dick of Dryupp, Lancie of Whisgills, and their complices for 50 kine and oxen, burning his house, corn, and insight 100 L. sterling.*" – September 1587.

✻✻✻

17. D'mainholm

D'mainholm was situated 0.5km north of the confluence of the Tinnis Burn and the Liddel Water, a strategic site looking over the frontier and the warden's gathering site of Tourneyholme at Kershopefoot. There once was a village at D'mainholm (*"Demayne Holme"*), with only a farm steading remaining today on the site.

✳✳✳

Thomas – "Symes Thom" – of D'mainholm – (c.1580s)

Thomas was the son of Simon, which Simon this was, is frustratingly absent as he may have been a son to Simon, the 9th Laird of Mangerton or a cousin. Looking at the company that he kept, Thomas was possibly related at a high level to the Mangertons. The stronghold of Thomas is recorded as *"Sim's Thoms"* on the *"Aglionby Platt"* (a map of the Borders from an atlas that belonged William Cecil, Lord Burghley, made by Edward Aglionby and dated December 1590), and was placed opposite Mangerton Tower on the west bank of the Liddel Water. This however was an error of the draughtsman, which was an area occupied by the Side; D'mainholm sat further down the valley.

Thomas was with a gang of three hundred Liddesdale riders in 1580 (see Lancelot, Laird of Whithaugh – page 133), when they ambushed a hot trod of Scotts and Gladstones that was heading home after an unsuccessful attempt to get their stolen livestock back. Thomas's involvement in this clash led him along with several others, to be denounced as rebels. In 1582 Thomas raided with the main Armstrong lairds. In June he rode alongside Lancelot Armstrong, the Laird of Whithaugh and his son Simon, plus John of Copshaw in a raid in which Martin Taylor was murdered by the reivers. The bill was documented as – *"Matthew Taylor, and the poor widow of Martin Taylor, complain upon Old laird of Whithaugh, Young laird of Whithaugh, Sims Thom, and Jock of Copshawe for 140 kie and oxen, 100 sheep, 20 gaits, and all the insight, L.200 Sterling."* And in October a charge was laid against Thomas for taking part in a raid alongside Simon, the 9th Laird of Mangerton and his uncle John. The bill read – *"Sir Simon Musgrave, Knight, complains upon the Lard of Mangerton, Lards Jock, Sim's Thom and their complices, for burning of his barn, wheat, rye, oats, bigg, and peas, with L. 1000 sterling."* Musgrave was the Constable of Bewcastle, and this audacious attack on his property would have been an embarrassing affront.

Thomas turns up in the 1583 list made by Thomas Musgrave on the Border Riders, which suggests his status as a troublesome character and a leader of lancers, adding weight to Thomas being a relative and possibly a son of the Laird of Mangerton. He is listed under the category for *"The Lord of Mangerton and his frendes, and theire allyaunces with England."* His entry reads *"Thom Armestronge called Sims Thom, dwelleth in the Demayne Holme by Lendall syde, and maryed Wat Storyes daughter of Eske, called Wat of the Hove ende."* Thomas's marriage partner was of interest, noted as residing in Hove End, which was in England and created a potentially dangerous alliance – best to be forewarned.

Thomas took part in a large 300 man day foray into Tynedale at Michaelmas 1584. The foray contained Willie Armstrong of Kinmont with his gang of *"The Bairns,"* plus Hector Armstrong of the Hillhouse, Clement Croser (*"Nebles Cleme"*), and Davye Elliot (*"The Carlinge"*). The Liddesdale raiders lifted an impressive tally from the Milburnes of the Keam and Tarset, taking away *"forty score kye and oxen, three score horses and meares, 500 sheep, burned 60 houses, and spoiling the same to the value of 2000L. sterling and slaying 10 men"*.

Thomas is finally recorded in 1588 when raiding on a much smaller scale than before, riding with a mixed gang of Elliots and Armstrongs against an English Armstrong (possibly in Gilsland):- *"John Armestrong complains upon said Will of the Steill, Martin's Arche, Martin's Dande, Hob the tayleer, Thome Armstrong 'Smys Thome', &c. for stealing 6 kye and a bull, and insight 3L. 6s. 8d., the first Satterdaye in Lente 1588."*

18. Greena

Greena Tower was located 1km south of Greena Hill on the west side of the Liddel Water, on gently sloping pastureland. The Liddel at this point was the actual Border with England. The tower measured about 10m by 7m and was probably named "Greenhaugh" originally. The stronghold was also noted as Grina and Grenehag tower. The Aglionby Platt map of 1590, named the tower as the *"Lard o' Jockes Grenehag,"* placing the Laird's Jock of Puddingburn / Tinnisburn as the tower's original owner. The Laird's Jock probably built the tower and chose the location carefully, having the stronghold on the borderline to give advance warnings of English raids and to intimidate the Fosters on the opposite side of the river.

William of Greena – (k.1599)

William was a son of the Laird's Jock, and grandson of Thomas Armstrong, the 7th Laird of Mangerton. William took over the tower of his father as his own residence, moving down from the Tinnis Valley at an unknown date, providing excellent intelligence and defence for his grayne and others.

Directly opposite Greena, and 140m into England was Staingarthsyde, a bastle owned by the Fosters. Staingarthsyde was also known as Stonehouse Tower, and not to be confused with Stonegarthside Hall 2km to the NE. The Foster neighbours of William gave him constant problems; just a stone's throw away they were too close for comfort. The Liddel Water separated the two strongholds, which had a ford allowing access to and from the Border, but friendship never flowed between the two families. As the families witnessed the constant traffic of raiders and stolen cattle across the ford, arguments occurred. Trust could never be developed and a festering resentment built up.

Tensions grew between the Armstrongs and the Fosters, which boiled over with violence threatening. In order to defuse the situation, a duel was organised to settle the matter once and for all. The prize for winning was to take over each other's tower; big stakes which illustrates the levels of animosity between the two families and the attempt to hold back from a full blood feud. It was thought better to risk one life than have a feud with many innocent lives being lost. A time and place was set – to be fought at the Tourneyholme 3.5km north. This was an area that was used for the warden's Truce Day and for tourneys, trials of combat and sporting feats. Rules were set, and William requested his father's sword to fight with. The date of his duel is difficult to pin down, as there are two possibilities – 1583 or 1599. The 1583 theory comes from a document which mentions William as *"Will Foster of Grena"* from that year, suggesting that he was the tower's owner in that year. The second date comes from a ballad of the event entitled *"Will a Grenah's Death."* Ballads can't be taken as factual of course, but the traditional story may hold elements of truth. The ballad ends with the death of William's father, and as this was in 1599, it provides a second and more plausible date for the duel.

On the day of the duel, William's father came to watch, taking a seat on a large pillar. He was sickly and had come against the wishes of his daughters. The ballad provides a witness (however unreliable) on how the duel went, when "*Foster of Stongarthside*" faced up with "*Armstrong of Greenah.*" Duels were not necessary to the death, with a first to draw blood often being taken as the victor. This duel though did not go along with the normal convention of rules...

By fraud did Foster gain the field:
Ere Greenah's sword was drawn,
He unawares did thrust him through,
Base coward! with his brand.

Foster cheated in the duel, and ran through William with his sword before he even had the chance to take it out of its scabbard. The Laird's Jock was distraught with grief and could not be consoled. Greenha was handed over to Foster, together with the Laird Jock's sword, which was a family relic and of spiritual importance. The return journey back by the Laird's Jock was grim indeed, and he died on the journey.

The loss of William was commemorated by a stone erected on the site he was killed. The stone was named the "*Will o' Greena's stane*" and was possibly the same stone that the Laird's Jock sat on to watch the fight. Today only a fragment of the stone remains, and sits a 100 yards east of its original site. It lies on its side and measures 0.6 m in length by 0.3m, with a sub-square at the base.

19. Whitlawside

The tower of Whitlawside appears on the Aglionby Platt of 1590, named as *"Sime of Whitesside,"* and was located 0.5km upstream of the Whitlawside Burn, which flowed into the Liddel Water. There is no sign of the tower today, which sat adjacent to the current farmhouse, 4.5km SW of Kershopefoot.

Simon – "Wanton Sim" – of Whitlawside – (c.1560s/1600s)

It is not known what Simon was *"wanton"* over – whether he was sexually promiscuous or of a cruel and violent nature, but the name suggests he was a reiver of unbridled passions.

Simon is first recorded in a document dated 15 December, 1567 from the Scottish Parliament in Edinburgh, where he found himself up to his neck in an impossibly difficult situation. The Master Robert Crichton, advocate to King James VI, acting under the Regent Moray, produced a judicial summons of treason and forfeiture against James Hepburn, 4th Earl of Bothwell, James Ormiston of that Ilk, Robert (*"Hob"*) Ormiston, Patrick Wilson, William Murray, and Simon Armstrong, alias *"Wanton Sim,"* and a Frenchman named Paris. It is not known what Simon had done to deserve his name included within the list, but the reason can be assumed that he was a follower of Mary, Queen of Scots. Simon was possibly at the Battle of Carberry Hill on 15 June 1567, in support of Bothwell, which would explain his unpopularity with the new Scottish court and the calls of being a traitor. Those named had been called to attend on three previous occasions, to answer the summons of treason raised against them; and none showed up. The Council then decreed and declared that each one of them had incurred diverse crimes of treason, and should have all and sundry of their goods moveable and unmoveable confiscated, and be held perpetually by His Highness. The rebels were to *"underly the pane of tressoune and hieast punischment destinat of the lawis of this realme, and nevir to bruik armis, honouris, offices nor digniteis within the samin in tyme cuming."*

Simon survived the threats of treason, and kept his land and status within Liddesdale. He appears as large as life and unscathed within Thomas Musgrave's list of the Border Riders in 1583 – named under the heading *"The Armstrongs of Melyonton quarter and their allies with England,"* with the entry – *"Sime Armestronge, called Whetlesyd, marryed two English women – the fyrst was Robin Fosters daughter, the other Thome Graymes daughter called little Thome."* Musgrave was careful to record marriages across the Border. Simon had two such marriages, and chose the surnames of his closest neighbours both times, the Fosters and the Grahams. The two sets of in-laws provided some very useful intelligence and co-operation. There was a live-and let live attitude along the border line of the Liddel Water in certain places.

Simon is named within the *"principall Clannes, and surnames"* on the Borders within John Monipennie's manuscript of 1597. Under *"LIDDISDAIL – Merietoun quarter,"* three chieftains/heidsmen are named together, which suggests they were all part of the same gang, with Simon named as one of them.

1. *Archie of West burnflat*

2. *Wanton Sym in quhitley side*

3. *Will of Powderlanpat*

Simon is last mentioned in 1607 (as *"in Quhitliesyd"*), when listed alongside his son Ninian and other Armstrongs, when charged with trying to prevent James Maxwell and Robert Douglas from taking possession of the Debatable Lands.

✳✳✳

Simon – "in Whitlieside" – (c.1640s)

There is a Simon *"in Whitlieside"* recorded in the 1640s, who was possibly a son or grandson of *"Wanton Sim."* This Simon had all the traits of his reiving ancestors, and took full advantage in the breakdown of law and order during the Great Civil War. Simon's residence was most likely not the tower house of *"Wanton Sim,"* this having been knocked down, but a farm steading – probably constructed from the old ruins. Simon's house at Whitlawside was a centre for criminal activity. It is stated that he made his house *"a rendezvous for resetting and entertaining all the fugitives, outlaws, and moss-troopers that come either from England or Ireland, or are upon the Borders of Scotland."* He held regular "trysts" on his property; these were markets for the disposal of stolen cattle.

He is first mentioned in 1642, listed among many Borderers who were wanted for theft and other crimes. Three years later, the archives report a scene that could easily have come from fifty years earlier – when Geordie of Kinmont, Old Sandy's *"Hutchen,"* and Will and Francis of Woodhead, were accused of stealing fifty *"kye"* and oxen from Thomas Chatta of Swinburne Park in Northumberland. In another raid Simon led a gang that stole *"four score"* (eighty) of sheep from *"the Ruken, in Ridsdale."* The owners though managed to get their livestock back, when Simon and his followers carelessly left the flock unattended near Kershopehead to go and find food.

Simon is recorded in prison in 1646, incarcerated in Selkirk where William Scott wrote to Francis, 2nd Earl of Buccleuch asking if he would speak up for his liberty. The request was successful, and he was ordered to be released by the king, but there was a forfeit – he was banished from the Borders.

20. Harelaw

Harelaw Tower was located 5km NE of Canonbie, on the upper flats of Harelaw Sike, north bank of the Liddel just below the slopes of Harelaw Pike. The family were at the entrance of the Liddel Valley, and witnessed the coming and goings of numerous raids. The warning beacon upon Harelaw Tower must have had frequent use, informing the Mangertons and Whithaughs to the north of impending trouble.

✳✳✳

Hector (Ecky) of Harelaw – "with the Cuts and the Grieves" – (c.1560s/80s)

Hector's father was George Armstrong of Ailmure, and his grandfather was Thomas, 5th Laird of Mangerton. Hector was the head of the family at Harelaw, and had at least four sons – Hector, William, Thomas, Ninian, and one daughter. Hector has one of the most colourful of reiver nicknames; the question has to be asked of the cuts – is he delivering them or receiving? And the grieves; is Hector making his victims feel sorrow, or is he in sorrow – or does the term grieves refer to body armour for the shins, to lessen the risk of cuts?

Hector is named within the 1583 list compiled by Thomas Musgrave on the Border Riders, seen as someone to keep a close eye on. He was recorded within the section *"Hector Armstrong of the Harlawe and his friends and allies,"* such was his notoriety that Hector had a list all for himself and his brood. He was named as *"Hector Armestronge called ould Hector"* within the document. His sons were also mentioned – *"Wille Armestronge called Hectors Wille"*... *"Thome Armestronge called Hectors Tome"* and *"yonge Hector."* Hector of Harelaw had at least three brothers, Patrick, George and Edmund (or Edward). George was a tenant in Raltoun (Gingles) and later settled in Cumberland where he became the founder of the House of Willieva (anciently called "Willieaway") in Gilsland. This branch of Armstrongs appears to be the only English Armstrongs who were engaged in reiving.

Marriage partners within the Harelaw stronghold came under close scrutiny, as the Border was so close at hand at only 1km away on the Liddel Water. Having an English wife was a sensible precaution to keep the family as safe as possible. Hector's son, *"yonge Hector,"* was married to *"Fargus Graymes daughter"* of the Mote, and a daughter was married to a William Graham of the Fauld. This gave the Armstrongs strong allies on the English side of the Esk, providing advance warning of attacks and a trouble free route for their own forays south. Hector was an active raider, and his brood of sons all followed in his horse's hoof prints.

Hector had at least one narrow escape on his forays; when returning from a raid an angry hot trod caught up with him. His life was saved by Sir Thomas Percy, 7th Earl of Northumberland who was present, and was eternally indebted to. A few years later, in the autumn of 1569, the Earl of Northumberland and Leonard Dacre of Naworth (former Deputy Warden of the West March), led a rebellion of Catholic Lords in England. The rebellion was in the cause of the recently abdicated Queen Mary of Scotland, and therefore was taken as a serious threat to national security by the English monarch and parliament. The rebellion was badly co-ordinated however and was speedily suppressed by Sir John Forster and Henry Carey, 1st Baron Hunsden, Governor of Berwick. With the status-quo resumed, Queen Elizabeth could relax, but she wanted the rebel Lords rooted out of her realm, and the threat removed permanently. What remained of the rebel Lords and their followers, were labelled as traitors, their lives as good as forfeit – the only immediate solution was to flee north into Liddesdale and seek sanctuary. Scotland was reluctant to welcome the Lords, but Liddesdale was known for being populated by outlaws; and a few extra rebels would surely not endanger the political balance – and may even be welcomed as brother criminals.

The two earls and their entourage then journeyed into Liddesdale – Charles Neville, the Earl of Westmorland and the Earl and of Northumberland, plus his wife Anne Somerset, the Countess, hoping to find hospitality amongst thieves. Entering Liddesdale on 21 December, Harelaw was one of the first communities that were come across, and the party ran into Hector, Black Ormiston, and John Armstrong of the Side. It is probable that Northumberland sought out Harelaw on purpose, thinking that he would be welcomed by Hector, which was the safest method of entering Liddesdale and avoid being casually robbed. After listening to the earl's predicament and wishes, Black Ormiston acted as the guide to the party, and led them to their chosen destination of Mangerton Tower, where the earls hoped to become guests of the Armstrong chief and be given temporary refuge until a boat to Europe could be organised.

An audience with Archibald Armstrong, the 8th Laird was held. The earls pleaded their case to receive his protection and hospitality, and it probably would have been granted but for the untimely arrival of Martin Elliot of Braidley and his lancers. Martin was acting under a pledge from the Regent Moray, who wanted the English Lords out of Scotland, fearing the political fall-out if they remained in the country. Worried of the backlash and spotting an opportunity for profit, Black Ormiston stepped in as the unofficial spokesman for the party, and suggested he escort the group back the way they had just come. Black Ormiston's action was not inspired by charity, with darker thoughts entering his mind on the possibility of handing over the rebels to the English authorities for cash. Westmorland and Northumberland were given sanctuary at Harelaw, an act seemingly inspired by Hector wanting to repay his debt for Northumberland saving his life. The earls would not have expected any betrayal by their host, and were glad for the moment of respite to gather their breath. Hector though, had an evil glint in his eye. Whatever Hector's attitude to Northumberland was at the start, he came to see the earls as a way to make some easy profit. Perhaps encouraged by Black Ormiston, Hector felt beyond the law at Harelaw with his secret guests, and planned to use them as if they were the spoils of a foray. The Countess of Northumberland was luckily not present at Harelaw, she had taken ill on the journey (possibly a cold since it was the winter), and was given instead lodgings inside Jock of the Side's hovel.

Hector alerted agents of the Regent Moray to inform them on his transaction, and all was agreed upon. On Christmas Eve Hector separated the two earls, isolating Northumberland from the main party to make it easier for him to be passed over to the authorities. Hector then promptly sold on Northumberland. A lot is made of the reiver code of honour, if it ever existed – but here it was severely lacking; no tradition of hospitality for the earls was given – and morally worse since Northumberland had previously helped Hector when his life was at risk during a raid. Northumberland was passed onto Hunsdon in England, and from there was taken to York and beheaded as a traitor. Did

Hector have a guilty conscious at betraying someone who had once helped him? Family came first with the reivers and money second; but there was also a sense of right and wrong within the Riding society, and betrayal was something that was very much looked down upon.

Westmorland remained in the keeping of Hector, and fearing a similar fate to Northumberland sent out secret messages to organise a rescue. One attempt was made by the Forsters and some Scottish riders, but was chased off. Westmorland eventually managed to escape, and received sanctuary with Scott of Buccleuch at Branxholme Castle. The Countess would eventually escape, when Sir Thomas Kerr of Ferniehirst and his follower's rode chivalric into Liddesdale and rescued her. For good measure, Westmorland was also picked up from Branxholme, and the two were united safely back at Ferniehirst Castle. Stories of adventure were swapped by a warm fireside, and preparations made for a life of exile in Flanders.

Hector profited little from his betrayal of Northumberland, with karma about to hit in more ways than one. On 23 January 1570 the Earl of Moray was assassinated in Linlithgow, an event which required some celebration from the Kerrs who were pleased to see him go. Teaming up with Buccleuch and Westmorland, they rode off in open foray to England, and with a special satisfaction they paused on the journey at the house of Hector's, and to Westmorland's delight they set fire to its roof.

And more was to come. Hector's standing within the Armstrong community dropped. His act of treachery saw him becoming ostracised by society, and he fell into disgrace and poverty. Hector's conduct even became a proverb on the Borders; to say "that he had put on Hector of Harelaw's coat"... or... "taking Hector's cloak" – was a byword for an act of betrayal. It is claimed that Hector of Harelaw lived to be over a hundred years old, but in the era before birth registration, age was not always certain – and the exaggerating of an old age would have been common when life expectancy was short. Hector was an amazing character to have endured the many cuts and grieves attributed to his name, and to live so long. Hector spent his last days with the Grahams of Eskdale, whom he had connections with through his sons marriages. Shunned by his own community he probably died in bed, looked after by the charity that he had once denied a Northumberland lord and his lady.

Hector had the following sons:-
1. Hector – "*Yonge Hector*" – (fl.1583)   **2.** William – "*Hectors Wille*" – (fl.1583)
3. Thomas – "*Hectors Tome*" – (c.1580s/1600s)   **4.** Ninian – "*Ecktors Rynion*" – (c.1590)

Hector's sons grew up next to the main high-way of the Armstrong reivers, and coming as no revelation, followed in their father's footsteps. The sons grew up in the shadow of Hector's cloak; with their father dishonoured the sons were eager to shape out their own niche within Armstrong society.

A son of Hector, Thomas (called "*Eckis Tom*"), is named within a set of complaints by Lord Forster in May 1584. Thomas took part in an open foray to the "*Slymefoote*" on the Middle Marches and helped in the stealing of three hundred head of cattle and forty horses, leaving thirty shielings on fire. He was accompanied by a rogues gallery of around one hundred Elliots and Armstrongs – including Francis and Hob Armstrong of Whithaugh, various Armstrongs of the Gingles, Dick Armstrong of Dryhope, Edie Ellott of the Shawes, Willie Ellott of Thorlieshope, Davie Ellott "*the Carlinge*," Hobbie Ellott of the "*Burneheades*," and not forgetting Clement Crosier alias "*nebless Clem*." Sandie Hall of "*Yerduppe*" forwarded the complaint.

Ninian, another son, was ordered to appear at the Bells Chapel on 13 April 1590, on two bills for crimes committed in the Middle March. He appeared before William Fenwick, the deputy warden for the English Middle Marches, and Thomas Trotter, the deputy Keeper of Liddesdale. Ninian was riding with a mixed gang of Elliots and Armstrongs, with some added Crosiers – a cross section of the worst cut throats in Liddesdale.

1. "*The Larde of Troghwen, James Hedley of the Garret sheills and others, complain upon Alexander Ellott of Falleneshe, Renyon Ellott of Dodburne, Will Ellott of Fidderton, Arche Ellott of the Hill, James Ellot his brother, Hobb Ellott of the Burneheades, Davie 'the Carlinge', Hobbe Ellott 'Hobbe bullie', Robin 'the taillor', Renyon Armstrong son to Ector, Thome Trumble of Hoppisburne, Davie Laidlea 'Cuddis Davie', Quintins Arche Croser, Eddies John Croser, Rowie Croser brother to 'Nebles' Clemye, and 100 others, for a day foray and reiving 100 kye and oxen, 5 horses and meares, lynn clothe   worth 10L. sterling, slaying 2 men and taking 2 prisoners, on 19 May 1589.*"

2. "*Percevell Read of Trowhen complains upon Will Ellott of Fydderton, Alexander Ellott of Fallon, Rynion Ellott of Dodborne, Robin Ellott 'the laird of Borneheades', Hob Ellett 'Hob bullie', Davye 'the Carlinge', Rynione Armestrong 'Ecktors Rynion' of the Harelawe, and 80 others for an open foray at Trowhen on Whitsond Mounday 1589, and reaving 51 kye and oxen, 3 horse and meares, 60 yards of lynne clothe and killing 2 men, which is alredie agreed fyled and sworne by the sight of iiii Englishe-men and iiii Scottesmen.*"

A document titled "*Brief of outrages, &c., done by the prisoners from the Hairelawe in Scotland*," dated June 1601, produced an interesting insight into the Armstrongs of Harelaw. The main subject of the document was Thomas Armstrong, called "*Ectors Thome the elder*," who is referred to as "*manifestly a chief councillor of his 'names men', &c., of Hairelawe, in all the robberies, murders, &.C., for the last 14 years, specially in last Lent in Gilsland*." He was accused of resetting at his house "*with great joye*," two wanted reivers named as "*young Ector, Willes Thome &c, his 'steale fellowes'*." Another outrage was recorded, on how Thomas had kidnapped four Hendersons from Brampton and "*kept them close*" as prisoners. He had fixed their ransoms, and was expecting the money to roll in, but payment was slow with "*only part whereof is paid*." Thomas had short patience, and rather than give more time or lower the amount wanted, he resorted to violent means. The document relates what followed next – "*To get the rest of the Hendersons to pay, he killed or caused to be killed, one Patton Henderson the eldest of them, while prisoner in his house, whereby the other three to save their lives, paid what they could, but must beg to get the greatest part yet unpaid, and are reduced from a good estate to utter beggary.*"

The following year Thomas stole at Midsummer a white gray mare belonging Thomas Sandforth of Howgill, and held the horse in his possession for around a month until John Forster of the Oxclose in Gilsland, took the animal back to her owner. The action resulted in Thomas's father, Hector and the Armstrongs of the Gingles, trying to kill Forster, and threatening Sandforth for taking his own horse back. It was noted at the time, that all of the beasts inside Thomas's "*byer*," or most of them, "*were challenged as stolen from Englishmen in Lent last, and it is apparent he was one of the riders then.*"

Within the same document, a grandson of Hector (son of William) is recorded within an itemed list of crimes, appearing four times, and named as "*Thome Armestrang otherwise called Ectors Willes Thome Scottes-man.*"

1. "*He was at the spoil of the towns of Teming and Westhall in Gilsland, and of Thomas Crawe of the Holme there.*"

2. "*Also at the spoil of Adam Robinson at Almerie holme near Carlisle, also took away his wife and in unmanerly maner did abuse her.*"

3. "*Was also at the spoil of Brampton, Irthington, and elsewhere in Gilsland – and at the hership of Crosby barony.*"

4. "*Lastly – By the oaths of many true Englishmen it is plain that the goods taken from these 'illdoers' lones' were robbed from Englishmen, and it is 'most probable' that they are all notorious thieves, insolent malefactors, stealers, and resetters, contrary to their own King's commandment.*"

It is interesting to note in item two, Thomas was reported as abusing a woman. This could possibly be interpreted as rape, and is the only reporting of such a crime within the Border Calendar Papers. It has to be wondered at how common this crime was, and what justice there was for the victim in this male dominated society?

✱✱✱

Patrick (Pawtie) of Harelawe – (c.1580s/1600s)

Patrick is recorded in the 1583 list of Thomas Musgrave, within the section headed "*Hector Armstrong of the Harlawe and his friends and allies*" – his exact relationship to Hector is unclear.

Patrick was requested to attend four bills against him for "*West March complaints against Buccleuch, &c,*" committed during the period June – Sept 1596. It is interesting to note Patrick being regular partners in crime with Simon and John of Calfhill.

1. "*The tenants of Whitehill, lately Christofer Dacres esquire, now his son's her Majesty's ward, upon Sime and Joke Armstronge al as 'Calfehills' Pawtie of Harelawe, Ekie 'braidebelt', Willie of Briggomes, Willie 'Kange', with 100*" *men, for burning 6 tenants' houses, and steadings, with goods worth 200L. sterling, and taking the six tenants prisoners."*

2. *"George Hetherton of Hawehills, Roger Hetherton, &c., upon Jocke of Monkbehirst, Simes Arche, Pawtie of Hairelawe, Jocke and Sime Armstrongs of Calfehill, Willie and Geordie Yrwen alias 'Kanges', with 16 persons, burning his houses and insight worth 200L. sterling, taking 40 kye, &c., 10 horses, &c., 40 sheep and 'gaite'."*

3. *"The tenants of Walton, late Christofer Dacres esq., upon said Sime 'Calfehill', Pattie Harelawe, &c., with 200 men, for taking 80 head of cattle, 20 horse and 'naiges', and household stuff worth 200L. sterling."*

4. *"The tenant of Thornby more the late Christofer Dacres, upon said Sime and others 'last above written' with 100 men, who burned 10 houses of habitation, 20 out houses, goods moveable and unmoveable, taking some prisoners and detaining them, with 4 score kye, &.C., 20 horse, &c, and insight worth 100L. sterling."*

Patrick took part in the murder of Sir John Carmichael, Warden of the Scottish West March on 16 June 1600. He was a member of the gang organised by Ninian ("*Sandies Rinion*") Armstrong of Ralton / Auchinbedrig, who ambushed the warden at Raes Knowes when he was travelling to attend a Warden's Court in Langholm. Thomas Armstrong ("*Ringans Thom*"), a son of Ninian, fired the deadly shot, but all of the gang were tarred by the same brush and became wanted men. Patrick and his fellow gang members headed into Graham territory on the Esk to lay low until the searching stopped. The Scottish authorities though were determined to get their men, and English help was requested in the hunt. Carmichael was a popular and conscientious warden, and his murder caused outrage, seen as an attack on the government itself. A new steely determination was gained to sort out the reivers. This was the third March Warden who had been killed; it was time to say no more to the senseless killings. Involving the English wardens in the search for Ninian and his gang paid off, as a letter by Lord Scrope relates on 29 November 1602, reporting from Carlisle to Cecil on the demise of Patrick:-

"Lest the Scottish King should write otherwise, I think good to signify, not long since 8 score of Scots and outlaws came to burn our town called Stenton, half a mile from Carlisle, but were 'well bett', and some horses killed and hurt: they spoiled some houses at Drumhewgh, and then some of the Bishop's tenants of Linstock. Hearing they were in a tower of the Scottish Armstrongs, I sent and burned up the door, killed Petti Armstrang, a notorious thief, outlaw, and murderer of Sir John Carmichael the warden, and took Johnston, who stole 1000 marks sterling from the King's merchants of Edinburgh."

21. Rowanburn

The modern village of Rowanburn sits 1km north of the English Border (the Liddel Water) and 1km to the east of Canonbie. It is not known exactly where the stronghold at Rowanburn stood. Modern Rowanburn was built as a coalmining village in around 1810, and is not necessarily the site of any 16th century community. A tower may have stood at any point along the Rowan Burn, from Rowanburn Head to Rowanburn Foot. An interesting feature on the landscape is Battle Knowe at Todsykehead, just five hundred metres to the south west of the village, where human bones have frequently been dug up.

✳✳✳

Thomas of Rowanburn – (c.1580s/90s)

Thomas is named within Thomas Musgrave's document of 1583 on the Border Riders, under the title of the "*off-spring of 'ill Wills Sandy'*." He is named as "*Thome Armestronge of Rowenborne*," and to be selected by Musgrave suggests that he was a freebooter to be wary of. In the same document beneath Thomas's name is recorded another inhabitant of Rowanburn, "*Gorthe* [George] *Armestronge*." George's marriage to Jeme Taylor's daughter of Harper Hill was also noted.

Thomas appears in the Border Calendar Papers on three separate bills; all incidents were in the same month – November 1592. November was the busiest time for the reivers, getting in the cattle before they were slaughtered for the winter. It is interesting to note Thomas's riding companions, William Armstrong of Kinmont, which suggests the raids were by the gang "Kinmont's Bairns," and that Thomas was a member.

1. *November 1592 – Roger Bulman of Skailby, uppon William Armstrange called Kynmontes Willie, Christie Armestrange called younge Christie of Barneleishe, Thome of Rowanburne, &c., for taking 11 kye and oxen, 4 'stottes', a 'whye', 2 mares, and mutilating the complainer.*

2. *Thursday, 16th November 1592 – The said James and John Tailler, upon said Kynmonts Jock, young Will of Kinmont and Thome of Rowanburn with 24 persons, for coming in myde afternone to Bolton fell and taking 30 kye and oxen, one brown 'rackinge' [pacing] mare, and hurting divers in peril of death.*

3. *Wednesday, 25 Nov. 1592 – James Tailler of Boltonfell foite, and John Tailler his brother, upon Kynmontes Jocke, younge Will of Kynmonte, Willie Kange, Geordie Kange, Richie Kange, and Thome of Rowanburne, for 10 sheep, 2 'gaite' and their insight.*

Alexander of Rowanburn – "Lang Sandy" – (ex.1606)

Sandy as his name suggests was "lang" – standing over six feet tall. There is little record of Sandy up until he took part in the murder of the Scottish West March Warden, Sir John Carmichael, on 16 June 1600. He was though a prolific criminal, as a comment by the Scottish Privy Council in 1606 remarked that Sandy *"has ever been a common and notorious thief, trained up from his youth in reif, theft and oppression according to the accustomed trade of the wicked and unhappy race of his father's gang and branch."*

Alexander and his colleagues were at the forefront of Carmichael's policing, and as such they held a deep bitter grudge against him. It is sad to think, and an indictment of life on the Border, that a person as efficient and popular as Carmichael would be targeted with such venom. But he was getting in the way of the Armstrong family reiving businesses, and his removal was seen as a necessity. Sandy signed up, becoming a member of the select group of around twenty – a murder squad who planned, set out, and killed Carmichael. Sandy did not pull the trigger which committed the murder, but he was guilty by association.

Sandy is named in a document dated 18 April 1601 on the *"Scottish outlaws of Liddesdale,"* which listed various outlaws under the Laird of Buccleuch's charge, who were now the responsibility of English officials to root out. Sandy was named amongst those who had taken part in the murder of the Warden Carmichael, a bad omen for all those involved. The implications of this new move meant that crossing over the Border to escape Scottish justice was no longer a safe tactic. It did not take long to capture the ringleaders of Carmichael's killers, with "Ringan's Tom" Armstrong being caught a few weeks after the request for English help. Thomas was taken to Edinburgh and executed at the market cross on 16 June 1601. The speed and brutality of the event would have taken Sandy by surprise. Sandy was probably sheltering with the Grahams at this moment in England, but his bolt hole was about to be closed as King James wrote to Elizabeth complaining that the Grahams were giving refuge to these outlaws.

When Queen Elizabeth died on 24 March 1603, the Borders burst into a seven day period of mayhem that was to become known as "Ill Will Week." Sandy was amongst the thousands or reivers who set out in an estimated two hundred forays. He accompanied his fellow Armstrongs of Rowanburn, including Ninian of Auchinbedrig, and rode into Cumberland looting and going as far south as Westmoreland, North Yorkshire and County Durham. For his troubles, Sandy was named in a list of 113 men on 23 July of that year. Named and shamed, this would have been a paper exercise a year earlier, but now it held dangerous implications. With the queen's death a new era had been entered, Sandy and his ilk were now fish out of water. A new tactic to eliminate the outlaws was being employed by the Border Commissioners – old crimes were being re-examined a second time in order to get convictions. This development was of a grave concern for Sandy and his family. He had once been charged for murder, and murder was a capital offence. All it would take was for the case to be reopened and he was a dead man. Sandy was not to stay at liberty for long. The authorities had an excuse to hang him on his presence at the Carmichael murder. Nothing would stand in their way, with the determination and the resources to get their man, and the power of two united Kingdoms behind them. The search for Carmichael's killers went into 1605.

Sandy was eventually run to ground and taken to Edinburgh for a show trial. He was tried on 13 February 1606, in a case that was biased from the very start. He was accused by John Bothwell, the Commendator of Holyrood House, who was the son-in-law of the murdered Carmichael. Sandy was named as being a part of the gang under *"Thom Airmstrang, sone to Sandeis Ringane, and otheris,"* numbering up to around seventeen persons that committed *"treasonabill Slauchter"* upon *"Sir Johnne Carmichell of that Ilk, knycht and Warden of the West Marches."* A summary of the attack was read out describing the attackers as part on foot and horseback, and armed with *"hagbuttis and pistolettis, lance-stalffis and utheris wappinnis."* Sandy had no actual involvement in the killing of Carmichael, but his presence was the issue. Sandy admitted his guilt but *"declarit him selff to be innocent of ony uher haynous crymes, except the foirsaid innocent Slauchter,"* which he professed *"wes brocht upoun against his will."* His only defence was that he was forced to take part in the murder by his fellow riders. The evidence concluded – *"And the said Alexander Armstrang wes airt and pairt of the said crewall and tressonabill Murthour, he being than upoun the ground with his complices, att the committing of the said ungodlie fact."*

Sandy was also accused on a second item – *"for commoun Thift, commoun Ressett of thift, inputting and outputting of thift, fra land to land, fra countrey to countrey, baith of auld and new."* The charges were for two crimes, that of theft and reset. Reset was the buying and selling of stolen goods, a business which encouraged reiving and was viewed as being an accomplice to the outlaw's crimes. The verdict of the assize was read out by James Johnstone, Chancellor, who found Sandy guilty – *"culpabill and convict of airt and pairt of the crewall Slauchter and Murthour"* of Carmichael. He was also found culpable of common theft and common *"ressett"* of theft. The sentence was as follows – *"To be tane to the mercat croce of Edinburghe, and thair to be hangit upoune ane gybet quhill he wes deid; and all his movabill guidis to be escheit and inbrocht to our souerane lordis use, for the said crymis."*

There is a tradition that ascribes Sandy Armstrong as the composer of one of the best known Border poems – "Armstrong's Goodnight," penned on the eve of his execution. Sir Walter Scott though places the writer as "Ringan's Tom" Armstrong, who was known to be the minstrel of the Armstrong clan.

"Armstrong's Goodnight"

This night is my departing night,
For here no longer must I stay;
There's neither friend nor foe of mine
But wishes me away

What I have done through lack of wit,
I never, never can recall;
I hope you're all my friends as yet;
Good night. And Joy be with you all.

Sandy ended his life on the market cross gibbet in Edinburgh, where "Ringan's Tom's" body once hung a few years earlier. He was buried in an unmarked grave on the town's Burgh Muir, another victim of King James's pacification of the Borders. When the dust settled, there was probably not one adult male Armstrong left in Rowanburn, with the wives and children of the missing men-folks having to fend for themselves as best they could. All his goods were forfeit to the crown, bringing an end to Armstrong power at Rowanburn. The new monarch, King James I of a United Kingdom, granted Sandy's lands jointly to James Maxwell and Robert Douglas, who were officers of his household.

Sandy is said to have had eleven sons – all were hung at various places and on differing dates. There were winners and losers on the Border in 1603, with the Armstrongs of Rowanburn falling into a catastrophic ruin.

✱✱✱

Ninian (Rinian) – "New Maid" of Rowanburn – (ex.1605)

Archibald – (fl.1603)

George (Geordie) – (fl.1603)

David – (ex.1604)

William – (ex.1605)

Ninian was the father of Archibald, William, David and George – and must have been related in some way to *"Lang Sandy"* of Rowanburn. Will and Archibald helped *"Lang Sandy"* when he took Thomas Watson of Duston prisoner, hoping to get a share in his £35 ransom. A list compiled on 23 July 1603, contained 113 wanted men, and amongst these were Ninian and his sons. Another list a few months later contained 157 names, with David, George and William mentioned. The net was tightening in on the Rowanburn Armstrongs.

Branded onto a wanted list, the Rowanburn clan feeling the heat upped sticks and moved into England to live out in safe houses. David was the first of the family to be captured. In 1604 he was apprehended and charged for a particularly violent crime spree which left five individuals dead. The reason for the killings is not mentioned; they were not attached to any reiving activities, suggesting revenge – the settling up of old scores. The trial was on 2 March 1604 in Edinburgh, where David was accused of the *"airt and pairt of the Slauchter"* of John Johnstone of Tundergarth – and for *"airt and pairt of the Slauchter"* of Robert Currie, servant to the Baillie of the Water of Leith. Three masons at the *"Oisleris-hous"* (Ostler's House) in the Leven, who were with Currie when he was cut down, also became embroiled in the action, and were slain in a similar fashion. Perhaps as a way to cover his tracks, David set fire to the building, and this was added to his crimes. The assize passed the verdict of guilty and David was hanged.

Ninian and William were to have their own experience of the same justice in the following year – when on 12 March 1605 – "*Ringane   Airmestrang, callit New-maid Ringane, and Will Airmestrang of Rowan-burne,*" were requested to stand trial at King James's pleasure. They were charged with "*contravening the Actis of Parliament,*" and the crimes of "*ressetting and assisting*" the King's rebels. This was classified as March Treason, giving a safe house to wanted criminals. The two Armstrongs were charged of helping "*Johnne Murray of Stable-Gortoune* [Staplegordon], *Cuddie of the Bankhous, Cristie of Langholme, Andro of the Langholme and Johnne Baittie of the Scheill, fugitives and outlawis.*" The verdict of the assize came from "*the mouth of Johnne Weir of Clowburne, chancillar,*" who pronounced Ringan and Will to be culpable of the crimes above written. The sentence came by "*the mouth of James Henrysoun, dempster of Court,*" the Justice-deputy, who read out – the "*saidis Ringan and Will to be tane to ane gibbet besyde the mercat croce of Edinburgh, and thair to be hangit quhill thay wer deid; and all thair movabill guidis to be escheit, &c.*"

Father and son were hung in Edinburgh's High Street, at the Market Cross next to St. Giles Cathedral. King James had been on the throne for only two years, and this public display was to show the Royal authority in action – the day of the reivers was now over. All goods and property of Ninian and William were fortified to the Crown, their bodies taken to an unmarked grave on the Burgh Muir – a brutal end to a brutal cycle.

Ewesdale

22. Arkleton

The tower came into the Armstrongs hands in 1537 when Robert, Lord Maxwell gave it to Ninian Armstrong. Nothing of the tower remains today; it once stood in the landscaped garden of the current Arkleton House, built in the early 19th century. The tower was on the banks of the Arkleton Burn, a tributary of the Ewes Water, protected on three sides by high boggy hilltops; and with an easy escape route in emergencies of an up-and-over Auldshiels Hill, and into the Tarras Valley to hide out.

George – ("Renyens Geordie") of Arkleton – (fl.1587)

George (the son of Ninian) took part in a large scale raid on 30 August 1583 into the Tarset Valley. He is named in a complaint as *"George Armestronge, called Renyens Geordie, and his sons, of Arcleton in Ewesdale,"* riding alongside William Armstrong of Kinmont (he was possibly a gang member of Kinmont's Bairns) and the Armstrongs of Gingles, and other accomplices to the number of three hundred (see p289/290).

George's presence was required at Hermitage Castle on 15 December 1584, when Sir John Forster wanted assurances for good behaviour signed. Along with the Elliots of Redheugh, the day was attended by *"Arche Armestrange of Arkilton, George Armestrange of the same, in like manner."* To be selected for a pledge of assurance suggests that George was a troublemaker of international status. Three years later George was back raiding, having a complaint laid upon him by the Laird of Prendicke and Henrie Collingewood of Ryle, and their tenants of Ingram and Reavelie. George was part of a gang that included *"John Armestronge called 'the Lairds Jocke', Andro Armestronge of Whithaugh, Ecktor Armestrong of the Hilhouse, Jock Armestronge of Kynmoth, John Bateson called 'John of the Score', and other 500 men, who ran a day foray and carried off 600 kye and oxen, 600 sheep, 35 prisoners and insight worth 40L. sterling, on 23 June 1587."*

<u>The Gingles of the Ewes Valley</u>

The House of Gingles were not only located in Liddesdale, but also in Ewesdale – situated at Glendivan and Kirkton. John Monipennie recorded in his report from 1597, a list of *"The names of the principall Clannes, and surnames on the Borders not landed, and chiefe men of name amongst them at this present."* Contained within the list for *"EWISDAIL – Armestrangs of the Gyngils,"* were:-

Ekke of the Gingils

Andrew of the Gyngils

Thome of Glendoning

23. Kirkton

A map of 1590 by Edward Aglionby shows a tower named *"Ecki of Gingles."* This tower was at Kirkstile, on the south side of the Kirkton Burn and the west bank of the Ewes Water. Here was the hamlet of Kirktoun and the Nether Kirk of Ewes, which loaned its name to the community, stemming from a church dedicated to St Cuthbert and was first mentioned in 1296.

✱✱✱

Hector (Ecki) of Gingles – (c.1580/90s)

Hector was a son of *"Ill Will's Sandie,"* and brother of William of Kinmont. Hector was probably the same *"Ekke"* named by Monipennie in 1597, and the same "Ecki of Gingles" featured in the Edward Aglionby map. Hector was a member of William of Kinmont's gang – "Kinmont's Bairns," and is recorded raiding with them on 18 August 1583. A complaint on the gang was made by John Rowtlege of the Stoneknowe, and placed upon *"Kinmontes Jock and Ecky of the Gingles, with their complices* [for] *xii kyne and oxen."*

Hector is included within Thomas Musgrave's list of the Border Riders in 1583, coming under the section of *"The Armstrongs of Melyonton quarter and their allies with England."* Hector was named first in the list (*"Hector Armestronge of Chengles"*), suggesting that he was the head of the family and the main trouble maker of the Gingles. He had at least four brothers:-

1. *Thome Armestronge his brother marryed Gourth Routlishe daughter of Shetbelt*

2. *Elle Armestronge his brother, marryed John Fosters daughter of Krakrop*

3. *Eme Armestronge his brother*

4. *Arche Armestronge his brother*

Two of Hector's sons had wives from England, a Foster and a Routledge – producing useful allies.

24. Glendivan

The tower was named in Edward Aglionby's map of 1590 as *"Tho: of ye Jingles."* Blaeu's Atlas of 1654 calls the stronghold *"Glendouin,"* which ties in with the present name of Glendivan. There is no trace of a tower today at Glendivan; the tower was probably located about 300m to the SE of the modern farmhouse on the south side of the Glendivan Burn, nestled between Hog Hill and Bittlestone Height. Two km to the south of the tower, a hill called The Watch served as a look out for raiders. A balefire once sat on the hill's summit, to be lit on the approach of the warden's men or English outlaws – to give warning of either a fight, or flight into the Tarras Moss.

Thomas of Gingles – (c.1580s/1600s)

Thomas was possibly the son of Andrew of Chingills, who was a son of Alexander, 6th Laird of Mangerton. Andrew was referred to as *"Andro of the Gingles,"* and was recorded in 1494 stealing cows along with his father. Andrew died at Kirktown, the village just opposite Glendivan. Thomas was probably the same *"Thomas of Glendoning"* (Glendenning) in John Moniepennie's report of 1597 – and gave his name to the tower noted in Edward Aglionby's map. Thomas was a neighbour of Hector Armstrong of Kirkstile, who resided on the opposite bank of the Ewes Water just an arrow shot away.

Thomas and Hector at Kirkstile, plus "Andrew's Thom" (the son of Andrew of the Gingles) were recorded raiding together in 1583. The raid was big scale, organised by William Armstrong of Kinmont who pulled in his Bairns to form a gang of three hundred riders. They rode in an open day time foray; such was the strength of the gang, that darkness and secrecy was not an issue. The raiders carved a swathe of spoliation up the Tarset Burn, plundering a series of bastle houses:- Redheugh, the Black Middens, the Hill House, Water Head, the Comb (*"Keyme"*), the Starr Head (Shilla Hill), the Bog Head and the Highfield – raising fire and burning as they went. The gang masterfully stole and drove away 400 head of cattle, 400 sheep and goats, and thirty horses. A large haul of insight was also taken from the houses, to the value of £200. The locals fought back as best they could, but this was always going to be a losing battle. The Armstrongs cruelly slew and murdered six people, and maimed another eleven, before taking away thirty as prisoners. Complaints to the English March Warden were of course forthcoming, with Bartrame Mylburne of the Keyme, and Gynkyne Hunter of the Waterhead speaking up for the devastation.

A son of Thomas of Glendinning and his brother Christie took part in a one hundred rider strong raid alongside the Armstrongs of Whithaugh and fellow Armstrongs of the Gingles, in an open foray which came to the attention of Sir John Forster in May 1584, after a complaint issued by Sandie Hall of Yerduppe. Perhaps in response to this raid and certainly others similar, Thomas, together with Hector of Kirkstile, were ordered to attend a Truce Meeting at Hermitage Castle on 15 December 1584, and make their assurances before Sir John Forster promising good behaviour. In 1616 an Andrew *"of the Kirktoun"* and Thomas *"in Gingillis"* were present on the assize that convicted John Scott (*"Jok the Suckler"*), for sheep stealing, common theft and reset of theft. Scott was a known low-life rascal, who narrowly missed the gallows in the previous year when he turned King's evidence after committing a particularly evil crime. Pitcairn's "Criminal Trials," refers to the case in April 1615 as *"unparalleled even in the annals of Border or Highland revenge"* – a crime which even shocked those used to the horrors of Jedburgh Justice.

The crime in question was instigated by the Lady Scott of Howpaslot (today called Howpasley, which lies 20km to the south west of Hawick), who sought revenge on a dispute over land ownership. She had recently lost the possession of traditional Scott lands to Sir James Douglas, 8th Baron of Drumlanrig, which roused an intense fury. She could not stand the thought of the Scott family heritage being lost, and vowed that the Douglases would never profit from their newly acquired possession. Lady Howpaslot consulted with her friend Jean Scott of Satchels on a plan of revenge. A fiendish idea materialized, if the livestock of Douglas was destroyed, perhaps the Douglas family would give up possession of the land – but how to achieve this? The two ladies decided the best way to accomplish their goal was to visit Hawick and root out some low-life characters who would undertake their devilish deed on their behalf. Feelers were put out to locate a gang of devious Scotts; their first recruit was Lady Howpaslot's personal servant, William Scott of Satchels, but more were needed. William no doubt helped in the finding of other suitable cut-throats within society's murky depths. Money was offered, inducing four miscreants to come volunteering their services. A meeting day was set up at the market cross in Hawick, where Lady Howpaslot put together her hit squad – enticing William Scott, Ingram Scott, Walter Scott, George Scott (and his dog "Hyde-the-bastard") and "Jok the Suckler," to come crawling out of the woodwork. Three days later the motley crew rode out on an overcast night up the Borthwick Water, passing Eildrig to reach their destination – Cleuchside, where Drumlanrig's sheep were lying in their pens. Then began the barbarous act of slaughter and maiming; using swords and other weapons the gang proceeded to slay sixty of the sheep, of which forty had their heads struck off. The scene would have been a horrific butcher's yard to those who witnessed it the following morning. The manner of the cruel act was almost too gruesome to be related. Full of abject repulsion, the hunt was immediately out to find the culprits. James Douglas, a follower of Drumlanrig, tracked down George Scott as a possible suspect, but lacked the evidence to obtain a conviction. Feeling the law closing in, Jock turned informer. With Jock's testimony, George, Walter, and Ingram Scott were apprehended and taken to Edinburgh to be tried – and were hung on 20 February 1616, for the offence. It was alleged that "Hyde-the-bastard" also took part in the slaughter, but was found not guilty. If Jock thought he was off the hook, he had another thing coming. Jock was such a nasty character and serial thief, that the authorities could not let him go. They dug out a set of earlier crimes that he had committed, and got in a new jury of fifteen members (nine of which were Armstrongs) who had him sentenced, found guilty and hung *"in ane gibbet,"* at the market cross in Edinburgh on 21 June 1616.

25. Flask

Flask Tower once stood 4km north of Langholm, on the east bank of the Ewes Water. Flask was well protected by the surrounding hills, nestled below the aptly named "The Watch." The inhabitants of Flask had an easy escape route if an armed force marched up the Ewes Valley, a short journey up the Terrona Burn and up and over Hog Fell, and the Tarras Valley was entered with its maze of bogs and impenetrable scrub woods.

Archibald of Flask – (fl.1605)

Archibald was one of thirteen, named as *"Archibald Armestrang of Flaskholme,"* who was accused of burning Langholm House at a trial in Edinburgh on 11 January 1605 (see page 249). The incident had occurred in September 1581, with the issue thought dead and buried; however there now was a United Kingdom and old cases were being dug out to punish those responsible anew.

On 24 July 1605, Archibald, alongside Ingrie (Ingram) Armstrong in Inzieholme, was accused of *"Dilaitit of airt and pairt of the tressonabill Raising of ffyre, [within the House of the Langholme] burning and destroying thairof, pertening to Harbert Maxwall of Kavense: Taking of the said Harbert captive and prissoner: Schuiting of hagbutis and pistolettis, &c."* To ensure their compliance with the law, Archibald Beattie, Burgess of Dumfries, acted as surety for Archibald and Mathew Findlasoun of Killeyth for Ingram. A *"Fyve hundreth merkis money"* fine was placed to persuade the accused to not abscond from the legal process.

The outcome of the case is not recorded. Archibald avoided execution for the time being, recorded amongst a set of Armstrongs as *"of Flascolme and Barnegleis"* in 1607, when charged with attempting to stop Robert Douglas and James Maxwell from taking possession of the Debatable Lands.

Wauchopedale

26. Stubholm

Stubholm was located on the northern side of Warb Law (Wurbla Hill), immediately below the confluence of the Wauchope Water and River Esk, adjacent to the town of Langholm.

***

Hector (Ecky) of Stubholme – (fl.1583)

Hector is noted in Thomas Musgrave's list of 1583 on the Border Riders, within the category *"The Armstrongs of Langholm and their allies with England"* – and was recorded as *"Hector Armestronge of the Stobham."* Hector was someone that the authorities had to keep an eye upon. A complaint was made upon Hector by Christopher Bellman of Hedderswoode, when he raided his property on 2 September 1583, alongside Jock Armstrong of Kinmont. Hector was recorded in the complaint as *"Ecky of Stubbholme,"* and was charged for thieving *"XX kyne and oxen, and three horses and their insight."*

He had at least one son, Richard, and was grandfather to Archie Armstrong, who would go on to gain fame and notoriety as the "fool" of the wisest fool, King James VI/I.

***

Archibald of Stubholm – (b.1586 – d.1672)

Archie of Stubholm was one of the most remarkable of all the Border reivers, going from an unknown common freebooter, to rubbing shoulders with the highest and mighty in the land. He managed to not only survive the brutal suppression of the Riding families in 1603, but emerged as one of the new elite of the Stuart Age. Archie was born at Stubholm. His father was "Sandie's Ekke's Richie" – Richard Armstrong, the son of Hector and grandson of Alexander. There is no information on Archie's youth, with a mystery on where the talents that he later displayed came from. As an Armstrong, he grew up to be a natural horseman and trained in the use of the lance and sword. He was noted later as taking part in jousts, a skill that he would have picked up at Tourneyholme, Kershopefoot, where feats of strength was a common past time.

Archie's reiving career was short, starting at around 1602 when he was about sixteen years old. There is no record of Archie taking part in any raids, however a traditional story and a poem by Rev. John Marriott (1780–1825), *"Archie*

Armstrong's Aith" (featured in *"The Minstrelsy of the Scottish Border"* by Sir Walter Scott), relates a foray by Archie onto his neighbour's land that went wrong, and transported him into becoming one of the most well known and celebrated figures of his day. The raid in question was small scale, with Archie riding out alone and taking a single sheep to replenish the larder. He was unlucky in being spotted by the sheep herder and a hot trod followed, with Archie being chased back to the very door of his house, running in with the dead animal over his left shoulder. Archie's wife was aghast. It is interesting to note Archie as being married within the poem; this of course could be artistic license. Archie was married at least twice, the name of his first wife is not known. Archie silenced all questions on what he had been up to and asked for her help, or the consequences could be dire. A panicking blur of action ensued.

> *"Now haud your tongue, ye prating wife.*
> *And help me as ye dow;*
> *I wad be laith to lose my life*
> *For ae poor silly yowe."*

He had only minutes to conceal the beast, and hid the animal in an empty cradle, *"And smoored it wi' the claes."* The covering of the sheep with clothing was done just in time, as the sheep herder, government law officers and troopers forcibly entered the house. Archie went into an act to distract those searchers away from the cradle, pretending that the dead sheep was his child. A verse in the poem has Archie quietly singing to the sleeping infant as he rocked it with his hand.

> *And saftlie he began to croon,*
> *"Hush, hushabye, my dear."*
> *He hadna sang to sic a tune,*
> *I trow, for mony a year.*

Archie tried to throw the officers off the scent by taking an oath to dull their suspicions that he was a sheep stealer. He stated that the Devil would have him if he were lying – And if he was found to be false...

> *"May I be doom'd the flesh to eat*
> *This vera cradle halds!"*

He beckoned the party to have a thorough search...

> *"And if ye find ae trotter there,*
> *Then hang me up the morrow."*

The officers gave Stubholm a complete top to bottom inspection and no sheep was found.

> *They thought to find the stolen gear,*

They searched baith but and ben;
But a' was clean, and a' was clear,
And nae thing could they ken.

The poem has those searching giving up and leaving Archie in peace. Archie had got one over on the authorities, and with relief the dark humour of the reiver flowed through the house. Archie had broken his vow not to lie, and would have to make amends and right the wrong. The poem ends on a happy note with Archie obeying his oath and eating the contents of the cradle. The poem though is missing the next part of the story, the link which propelled Archie from being a petty thief and into fame and fortune. The story continues beyond the poem. The officers were puzzled at finding nothing at Stubholm, and as they were leaving one of the party took a casual glance into the cradle to see Archie's child, and saw a dead ewe looking back. Archie was caught red handed and was charged for sheep stealing – he would be surely hanged.

Archie was taken to Jedburgh for trial and appeared before King James VI, who was holding a justice aire. He was found guilty of theft and sentenced to hang. At the execution a Bible made a key appearance for the reading of the 51st psalm, which was often called the "neck verse" – comforting words for the soul about to be departed. Archie had a quick and sardonic sense of humour, often macabre, and even though he had been condemned to die he kept a level head making a lightness of the situation. Getting the king's attention, Archie pleaded his youth and lack of education on wanting a delay on the execution, stating "*I have but recently heard of the Bible, and am desirous, for my soul's sake, of reading through the precious volume. Would your Majesty's grace be pleased to respite me until I have done this?*" The Armstrongs were famous for their lack of concern of the Church, thinking nothing of burning them down. James was a very religious man, ruling by God's divine law. The subject struck deep into the monarch's mind, this was a request he could not easily deny being a Godly king. Archie saw a pause in the king's actions as he was giving the matter some thought and added with a smile, "*Then de'il tak me an I ever read a word o't as lang as my een are open*!" The king saw something in his character that was pleasing and commendable. Archie's youth and eagerness to learn the Good Book impressed James. The king then made Archie an amazing offer; to enter his Royal service and become employed at court as the King's Jester. Archie jumped at the chance; he would have been a fool to turn it down, and became the fool of "Christendom's wisest fool."

James was arguably the most unusual monarch that Scotland and the United Kingdom have ever had. He was unique in that he never fought any wars, and ruled the country purely by the pen. Well educated and eccentric, he inherited nothing of his mother's legendary Stuart charm. He had a strict Scots Calvinist upbringing, undergoing a rigorous programme of education by his tutors, which would stay with James as an adult. He displayed a high level of precociousness and intelligence from an early age, and had a court of sycophants to agree on his every word. A contemporary description by Sir Anthony Weldon is worth quoting, giving an insight into James's character and hints on how it influenced Archie:-

"He was naturally of a timorous disposition, which was the reason of his quilted doublets: His eyes large, ever rolling after any stranger came in his presence, insomuch, as many for shame have left the room, as being out of countenance: His beard very thin: his tongue too large for his mouth, and made him drink very uncomely, as if eating his drink, which came out of the cup of each side of his mouth... His legs very weak... his walk was ever circular, his fingers in that walk ever fiddling about his codpiece."

James was famous for his toilet humour and crude tastes, which Archie shaped his act towards, eager to please the king. James in public lacked finesse at holding back good manners, and with his overly large tongue and no inhibitions, was something that guests to the Royal Court were shocked to see. A good fool was exactly what James needed, a foil to complement and accompany his life. Archie tailored his jokes and entertainment to suit the king's personality, and became an asset when the king was entertaining in public. The Court Fool was traditionally the king's constant companion, and James and Archie developed a close friendship. James had a great love of wildlife, with a particular obsession with lions. He also enjoyed horse-racing and bred horses with the finest Arab blood; something that Archie took a particular interest in, which recalled back to his youth and the race course at Langholm, where he no doubt was a frequent visitor. Archie was given the typical costume of the jester, brightly coloured which harked back to the Middle-Ages, complete with hood and sewn on bells. He was expected to entertain audiences with juggling, acrobatics, songs, music, storytelling, slapstick jousts, magic and jokes. It is not sure to what extent Archie had all of these skills, but he excelled at jokes, using the contemporary people and events around him as the material for comedy. Archie's acid wit and popularity with the king made him many powerful friends and a few enemies.

Archie was in office as jester no more than a year, when news came of Queen Elizabeth's death in 1603. His life was about to change dramatically, as Archie was now the first Royal Fool of the new United Kingdom. James eagerly packed, and took Archie along in his large entourage which crossed the Border and set up a new residence in London. As court jester, Archie was Gentleman Groom of the Chambers and had the king's ear. He was in a position of great influence, and gained a secondary income from bribes given by those who wanted him to arrange an audience with the king. Archie was forever the reiver, looking out for any money making scheme, using his privileged status to the full.

James did not enjoy ceremony, and his welcome in London made him uncomfortable – he commented, *"God's wounds, I will pull down my breeches and they shall also see my arse."* Drunkenness was rife within his new London court, and a fool would have been the ideal companion to help James settle in and make sense of it all. James had a rocky relationship with Parliament, who objected to the manner in which he showered his favourites with money and titles. Archie of course took the awards that James presented eagerly, attention that inflated his ego to a dangerous level. Archie became presumptuous, insolent and mischievous as success went to his head. Due to the patronage given, jealousy mounted and Archie became disliked by other members of the court. Archie's saucy and subversive wit also caused more dislike, as he used the traditional privilege of the jester to state blunt truths to the full effect.

When explored closely, the details behind Archie becoming the court jester appears rather random and unorthodox. Employing a common low grade thief into such a high status job; surely there must have been more deep hidden motives behind it all? It is a fascinating question to ask, did Archie also double up as a secret bodyguard? With good evidence James had every reason to be worried about assassination and kidnap. There had been numerous attempts over the years to either abduct, shoot, dethrone or blow up his Royal personage – going from the Ruthven raid in 1582, to various attacks by Francis Stewart, 5th Earl of Bothwell, and the most recent in November 1605 by Guy Fawkes. There could have been no better recruit for a body guard than a Border reiver. James's court was full of Scots, and Archie would have been familiar with the various machinations that went along with it, having an inside knowledge on who was who. And being a "Fool," who would suspect Archie listening in on conversations, or having the knowledge for politics, or the skill of battle – Archie held both.

As a part of the monarch's court, Archie met many of the countries important characters. He knew William Shakespeare, and may have been written into some of his plays as a character. The drunken porter in Macbeth, Lavache the clown in "All's Well That Ends Well," and Feste the clown in "Twelfth Night," all show shades of being based on Archie. Macbeth was written with the interests of James in mind, and Shakespeare perhaps picked Archie's brain for suitable ideas and information for the play. The witchcraft scenes were included for James's enjoyment, as he was fascinated by the subject, and even wrote a book on the topic.

The king was generous back to Archie for his services; in 1611 he was granted a pension of two shillings a day, which a month later was re-granted for life. Almost every year James presented Archie with an elaborate new uniform. Archie would have looked the peacock at every function, the centre of attention of the great and famous when guests of the British Crown. He was granted a patent to produce tobacco pipes in August 1618, an odd subject for James to favour, since he had a huge aversion to smoking. Archie took advantage of the influence he acquired at the English court and often stretched it too far, becoming over familiar with the royal family and noblemen in his service. In 1612 when at the Newmarket races, he pushed his freedom of expression too far and it backfired. Archie caused a childish quarrel between James and his eldest son, Henry, when he stated that the prince commanded a greater popularity from the public than his father. A bickering of jealousies broke out which tarnished the days atmosphere. The friends of Henry, who witnessed the event, took their revenge on the fool's impudent meddling by tossing him *"every night they could meet him in a blanket like a dog."*

Archie's foolery once resulted in him being challenged to a duel. Archie had insulted a famous knight called Sir Thomas Parsons, which comes as no surprise, and Sir Thomas demanded the satisfaction of a "mock combat" on the celebration of Ascension Day to settle the matter. A letter written on 24 March 1613 by Sir Henry Wotton, the Provost of Eton College describes how the encounter proceeded... *"Towards the evening a challenge passed between Archie and a famous knight, called Sir Thomas Parsons, the one a fool by election, and the other by necessity, which was accordingly performed some two or three days after a tilt, tourney, and on foot, both completely armed, and solemnly brought in before the Majesties, and almost as many other meaner eyes as were at the former; which bred much sport for the present, and afterwards, upon cooler consideration, much censure and discourse, as the manner is."*

Sadly there are no accounts on how the encounter went; it can be presumed that Archie won. The contest illustrates that Archie was a skilled fighter, every inch the Border reiver, and capable of taking on the best.

In 1617 James made his first and only visit to Scotland since 1603, and Archie accompanied as usual. Archie was greatly courted and flattered on the tour, which added to inflate his already large ego. On the journey through England, the boroughs of Coventry and Nottingham honoured him with gifts of clothing and money, which included *"one Portugall ducat."* James, never one for ceremony, was made a guest of honour across Scotland, and noticed the marked differences in the wealth and clothes between the Scottish and English. When James was hunting near Aberdeen, Archie was admitted together with the other royal attendants into the town, where he was given the Freedom of the City of Aberdeen.

The English poet John Taylor (1578 – 1653), who dubbed himself *"The Water Poet,"* despised Archie, and took the opportunity in his works to show his disdain. In the introduction to his pamphlet *"Praise, Antiquity, and Commodity of Beggary,"* in 1621, a mock dedication reads to, *"The bright eye-dazeling mirrour of mirth, adelantado of alacrity, the pump of pastime, spout of sport, and regent of ridiculous confabulations, Archibald Armestrong, alias the court Archy."* He refers elsewhere to Archie's *"nimble tongue, to make other mens money runne into your purse."* Taylor disliked Archie for his avarice and venality. He compares Archie to previous fools John Scoggin (c.1470 – 1490), jester of Edward IV, and William Sommers (d.1560), the jester of Henry VIII – to whom Archie is the Nero or Caligula to their *"good Augustus."*

When James died in 1625 Archie's career did not die along with him, he continued to be the jester of the next monarch, Charles I. Archie was already familiar with Charles; he had accompanied Charles before he was crowned on a diplomatic voyage to Spain in 1623, on a secret mission to negotiate a marriage with the Infanta Maria. Archie was actually against the marriage plans, but insisted that he was included in the retinue. Also on board was George Villiers, 1st Duke of Buckingham (1592 – 1628) a favourite of James, alleged to be the king's lover. The two did not get on well, with a growing animosity which clouded an already tense visit. Just before setting out on the expedition, Archie created for himself an *"extraordinarie rich coate,"* and asked permission to take a servant along to wait upon him. Complaints began to be showered upon Archie before the boat had even left the harbour. "The privy-chamber gentlemen" complained bitterly on the favours bestowed upon Archie, a favouritism that the other passengers were not allowed.

On arriving in Madrid, Archie turned on the charm and soon ingratiated himself with the Spanish royal family. Archie's fools act was popular with everyone, bridging languages and culture; a mixture of acrobatic performance and mime. He performed for the Spanish court, where his brand of physical comedy went down well. The attention Archie received goaded him into behaving with unprecedented arrogance. On 28 April 1623, Archie dictated a letter to James, were he described receiving the Spanish king's favour – *"To let your Majesty know, I am sent for by this King when none of your own nor your son's men can come near him."* A report from James Howell writing from Madrid on 10 July 1623, described *"Our cousin Archy hath more privilege than any, for he often goes with his fool's coat where the Infanta is with her meninas and ladies of honour, and keeps a-blowing and blustering among them, and blurts out what he list."*

Archie pushed his humour and charm to the maximum, and managed to even get away with jokes to the infanta on the defeat of the Spanish Armada and on the Pope. Archie was a big hit, especially with King Philip IV and was made warmly welcome. Archie was the most popular of Charles's entourage, more so than Charles himself, gaining access into the private world of the infanta far more readily than the prince. Favours were returned; Philip IV granted Archie a pension, the arrears of which he received in 1631 amounting to £1500.

Archie's fellow companions were not spared his obnoxious behaviour. He quarrelled openly with Sir Tobie Matthew, one of Prince Charles's attendants at a public dinner, who had become unable to endure his blunt taunts no longer. Buckingham was concerned at Archie's open critical comments on the entire expedition. Archie expressed his severe disapproval of the marriage plans to Buckingham's face, which caused him embarrassment. Buckingham declared that he would have Archie hanged, to which Archie replied, "*dukes had often been hanged for insolence but never fools for talking.*" A marriage agreement looked a long way off in being signed. Archie was quick to give it a "told you so" type of reaction, wrapped up as a jest. He dared to speak his opinion to the duke, and blamed the lack of progress on the truthfulness amongst the concerned parties. Buckingham also fell out with Gaspar de Guzman, the Count of Olivares, the Spanish chief minister, with a personal quarrel erupting. Archie though got on well with Olivares, who gave him a "*rich suit.*" The marriage arrangements did not go well either, with Charles and the Infanta not getting on; she thought Charles was little more than an infidel.

The mission was an embarrassing failure. It was hoped both for the infanta to be betrothed to Prince Charles, and for an alliance with Spain, but everything fell through. The Infanta demanded that Charles convert to Roman Catholicism before any wedding took place, and that was never going to happen. The Spanish king also insisted on the toleration of Catholics in England and the repeal of the penal laws, an issue which the UK parliament would never agree to. Charles returned without a bride, arriving in London to an enthusiastic and relieved public, glad to be home. Charles and Buckingham felt tarnished by the experience, and pushed a reluctant King James to declare war on Spain. Archie on the other hand, had an amazing trip, all the more richer and coated in adulation.

Archie returned to the news of the death of his brother, James, who died in 1624 without children. Archie also had a sister, Agnes, who married William Grimes and acquired one hundred acres of land in Ireland. Buckingham's demise was near; he had a habit of making himself unpopular, and in 1628 things came to a head and he was assassinated by a disgruntled army officer. Archie as usual could not resist a final dig, commenting "*the greatest enemy of three kings is gone.*" In that same year Archie had his first recorded child, Philip, born on 25 November, named after the King of Spain. Archie retained his old office when Prince Charles became King Charles I, and even increased his standing. Charles equally appreciated Archie's services and showered him with generosity. He granted him life pensions and a thousand acres of land in Ireland.

In 1630 Archie published his first book, entitled "*A Banquet of Jests: a Change of Cheare. Being a collection of modern Jests, Witty Jeeres, Pleasaunt Taunts, Merry Tales.*" Archie dictated the words for the book as he was illiterate. The book had a second part added in its third edition in 1633, and a fifth edition appeared in 1639. The book must have sold well to have had these new editions made. This collection was one of the earliest joke books in Britain. Most of the jokes obviously have dated, appearing stale or difficult to understand lacking the context and references to current affairs and characters, but some are worth a chuckle or two – and worth quoting:-

A man on the Gallowes

"ONE that saw a poore fellow, in a very cold morning, upon the Gallowes in his shirt, and after a short confession ready to be turned off the ladder: Alas poore man (saith he) I much pitty him; he hath stood so long yonder in the cold, that I am affraid hee will goe neare to catch his death."

A Horse Stealer

"A FELLOW for stealing a Horse, was apprehended, arraigned, convicted, and executed: when a stander by asking, why the man was hanged, it was answered, for stealing a horse. Nay, saith the other, no such matter; he was hanged for being taken: for had he stolne an hundred horses, and not beene taken, he might have lived many a faire day."

Despite Archie's popularity and ability to entertain, he was making more and more enemies, and only tolerated because he was a favourite of the king. Trouble was always brewing. The final straw came in 1637 when Archie's outspoken acidic wit went a joke too far when saying grace in Whitehall at which William Laud, the Archbishop of Canterbury was present. Laud was England's most eminent churchman, one of the king's trusted advisors, especially on matters of religion. Archie saw Laud as a figure to be openly vilified and ridiculed. Matters in Scotland were coming to a head regarding religion. Charles and Laud were trying to bring the separate Churches of England and Scotland closer together by introducing a new Book of Canons and a new Book of Common Prayer into Scotland. There were no consultations with either the Scottish Parliament or Kirk. Presbyterian Scots were outraged, seeing the proposals as an attack on their national and religious identity. A movement against the Laudian reforms was gaining momentum, which Archie was aware, seeking to poke fun at the Archbishop's interference in Scots affairs. Allowing Archie a voice at Whitehall with Laud listening, together with a captive audience of nobles and politicians, was too good an opportunity to miss out on – for the delivery of some choice wit.

Archie, as part of the devotion for the Grace, burst forth with the unscripted *"All praise to God, and little Laud to the de'il!"* This was a word play joke too far; Archie was sarcastically suggesting that Laud should go to the Devil. And at the same time made a cutting remark on Laud's small stature, he was only five feet tall and bitterly resented this being pointed out. In one sort sentence Laud was shamed and embarrassed. Archie had been so used to jesting with kings and princes, that he had become complacent on the effects of his words on people's feelings. In expressing too openly and boldly his contempt for Laud, Archie brought about his own downfall. That archbishops should be subject to the criticism from the fool was not to be tolerated.

The final nail came in the jester's coffin when Laud was on his way to the Council Chamber at Whitehall a few days later, when Archie spotted Laud and could not help himself catching up and unleashing a further taunt. Laud was assailed by Archie's Doric tones, *"Wha's fule noo?"* ("Who's fool now?") – And the question, *"does not your Grace hear the news from Stirling about the liturgy?"* This was referring to events sparked off by a riot in Edinburgh on 23 July 1637, when Jenny Geddes flung her prayer stool at the Dean of the High Kirk of St Giles in Edinburgh when he tried to read from the new prayer book for the first time. The protests were growing into a campaign of petitions, with the denouncing of the Laudian liturgy. Archie felt self gratified at his direct criticism of Laud, but he had bitten off more than he could chew in taking him on. All of this was too much for Laud to bear, he made an official complaint to the Council and Archie was sentenced the same day. Archie was summoned before the king, were he pleaded the privilege of his coat, but in vain. Laud wanted Archie to be brought before the Star Chamber at Westminster, and deliver a full humiliation as pay-back. This motion was thwarted by mediation of the queen; he still had some friends at court. The archbishop ordered that Archie should be carried to the porter's lodge, and *"to have his coat pulled over his head and be discharged the king's service and banished the king's court."* This was carried out, with Archie stripped of his power, and was no longer under the protection of the monarch. Archie's replacement was Muckle John, who never achieved the same heights or notoriety as the king's court jester.

The swift change in his status would have come as a shock for Archie, no more applause, patronage or favours were coming his way. He was pushed off the stage with nowhere to perform. Inconsolable and in a dark mood, he wandered London thinking on what to do next. On his wanderings a week after his dismissal, he was met by the writer of the "Scout's Discovery" at the Abbey of Westminster, who described Archie as *"All in black. Alas! poor fool, thought I, he mourns for his country. I asked him about his coat. O, quoth he, my Lord of Canterbury hath taken it from me, because either he or some of the Scots bishops may have use for it themselves, but he hath given me a black coat for it, to colour my knavery with; and now I may speak what I please, so it be not against the prelates, for this coat hath a far greater privilege than the other had."*

Archie was never going to be out of money with his investment in pipes to fall back on and pensions. He remained in London for a number of years after his disgrace setting himself up as a money-lender, his wealth had enabled him to become a large creditor. Archie was a merciless lender, operating harsh methods to obtain the repayment of his loans. Many complaints were made against him to the Privy Council and House of Lords for his sharp practices. In 1641 with relish Archie heard the news that Laud had been imprisoned in the Tower of London for treason (and was beheaded in Jan 1645). Archie could now speak up with impunity on whatever scandal he pleased, no longer a member of the Royal Court, and speak up Archie most certainly did. He enjoyed a personal revenge that same year by publishing a small pamphlet entitled *"Archy's Dream; sometimes Jester to his Majestie, but exiled the Court by Canterburies malice."*

Around this time he moved to Arthuret in Cumberland and became a considerable landowner. Perhaps tired of the city life and wanting a return to his roots, Archie became a respectable gentleman and had the funds to live a luxurious life. The parish register of Arthuret records the baptism of *"a base son"* (illegitimate) Francis, to Archibald Armstrong on 17 December 1643. A second entry was made, for Archie's marriage to his second wife Sybella Bell, on 4 June 1646.

In 1660 there was a second book printed, allegedly to have been written by Archie Armstrong, published in London and titled, "*A choice Banquet of Witty Jests, Rare Fancies, and Pleasant Novels.*" It was advertised as a body of work never published before by the deceased Archie, however Archie was very much alive in Cumberland and could never have been the author. The publisher was using Archie's name as a marketing ploy to make sales.

Archie Armstrong died in 1672, and appropriately was buried on 1 April – All Fools Day. His travels came to rest at Arthuret Church, 1km to the south of Longtown. The present church at Arthuret dates from 1609 and is dedicated to St. Michael and All Angels. It was built on the orders of King James, after the monarch had received reports of the local people being without faith, virtue or regard for any religion. No memorial of him in the churchyard survives today sadly, but the site of his grave is easy to locate, near to an ancient cross which is thought to have been erected by the Knights of Malta in the 14th or 15th century. Archie had an extraordinary career as a Royal Fool, amusing two monarchs and having the privilege to witness important events in British history at close hand. A simple petty reiver had come far – the King's Jester poking fun at the authorities in an unimaginable way that his forefather's could never have thought possible, and getting paid for it too. A reiver for the 17th century; loud and proud – succeeding to a great prosperity when many other families struggled and collapsed.

27. Calfhill

The Calfhills were one of the most troublesome graynes of the Armstrongs. The tower of Calfhill (Calfield / Cawfield) once stood on the eastern slope of Naze Hill 1.5km west of Langholm, next to the Back Burn, a tributary of the Becks Burn which flows into the Wauchope Water. The site of Naze Hill seems impossibly steep to build a tower upon, but a natural shelf was found on which to construct. From their eagle like eyrie, the Calfhills would be safe from all but the most determined attack, and be able to survey all that they commanded.

The Calfhills were active reivers, with Bewcastle being one of their main happy hunting grounds. Dicks Grayme of Bewcastle and the wife of Quinting Rowtledge were typical victims – they made a complaint upon the *"Armestranges of Calfhill"* in November 1592 for a raid on their steadings. The Calfhills were charged *"for taking 60 kye and oxen, 40 sheep, a horse, his insight, and cruelly killing said Quinting."*

John (Jock) of Calfhill – (c.1580s/90s)

John was named in Thomas Musgrave's list on the Border Riders in December 1583, within the section on *"The Lord of Mangerton and his frendes, and theire allyaunces with England."* John is listed as *"Joke Armestronge of the Caufeld dwelleth on the Cawfeld, not marryed in England."* John was married to a Scots lady so proved less of a threat than other Armstrongs. He had at least one brother, George.

John was first recorded in trouble with the authorities in 1582 when riding along side *"John's Christie"* and *"young Cristie"* of Barngleish, Hector Armstrong in Stubholme, Ninian (*"Sandys Ringane"*) Armstrong and John of the Hollows. This motley crew descended upon the farms of Deuchar, Montbenger and Whitehope, taking away what they wanted. The following year he turns up in a document on the *"Raids on the West Marches by Liddesdale"* from 19 July to 6 Oct 1583. The complaint upon John was made by Dick Rowtledge of Kirkleventon, who was raided by *"Jock Armstronge called Kynmonth* [Jock]*, Jock Armstronge of the Calfhills, Jamy of Cannonbie, with their complices* [to the] *nomber of xx persons."* This was probably the "Kinmont's Bairns" in action, placing John as one of its gang members. The gang got away with *"xx kye and oxen, two naiges, all his insight."* The raid was of a brutal nature and it was noted *"At this heirshipp Dick Rowtledge and his sonne were maymed and wounded in perill of death."* It comes as no shock that Dick Rowtledge made his complaint and a wonder if he survived his horrific wounds to rebuild his life on the compensation fines that were charged.

The Routledges were a common target for John. John is recorded four times at one court session at Berwick, on bills of England found foul (guilty) for the West Marches of Scotland. Three of the raids were upon the Routledges, living up to their nick-name as *"everyman's prey."* The *"breviate of the bills"* contained the following:-

1. *Jan 1582. Thomas Rootledge of Todholes, and his neighbours complain upon Kynmont Jock, Eckie of Stubholme, Jock of Calfhill, and their complices 40 kine and oxen, 20 sheep and gaite, a horse, insight 300L.*

2. *Jan 1582. Dick's Rowie Rootledge, complains upon Kynmount Jock, Jock of Calfhill, and their complices 30 kine and oxen, a horse, insight and spoil 60L.*

3. *Sept 1582. James Rootledge and his neighbours, complain upon Geordie Armstrong of Calfhill, and Jock his brother, with their complices; for 100 kine and oxen.*

4. *Nov 1586. Cuddie Taylor and his neighbours of Hullethirst (against) Young Christopher Armstrong of Awghing gill, Jock of Calfhill, Eckie's Richie, Willie Cany (Gait Warden) 60 kine and oxen, 4 horses, armour, and insight 200L sterling.*

Interesting to note one victim of the Armstrongs – "*Dick's Rowie Rootledge,*" perhaps this figure was the son of Dick of Kirkleventon who was maimed in the later raid by John in 1583. Having found one soft target, John would be sure to return yearly.

The Calfhills could not resist being involved in the rescue of Kinmont Willie Armstrong in 1596 from Carlisle Castle. Lord Scrope records three Calfhills in a letter on 14 April 1596, pointing the finger at them as amongst the principal assailants in the rescue. They are named as – "*Jocke, Bighames, and one Ally, a bastard.*" Interestingly it shows a connection between Calfhill and Bigholms – indicating a spread of the family along the Wauchope Valley.

A final raid is recorded in the "*West March complaints against Buccleuch*" between the dates June – Sept 1596, when the tenants of Whitehill were the unfortunate target. John was accompanied by Simon, another Armstrong from Calfhills (certainly related), plus "*Pawtie of Harelawe, Ekie 'braidebelt', Willie of Briggomes, Willie Kange, with 100 men.*" The gang raked much havoc being charged "*for burning 6 tenants' houses, and steadings, with goods worth 200L. sterling, and taking the six tenants prisoners.*"

✱✱✱

William – "Geordie's Will" of Calfhill – (c.1588)

The son of George Armstrong, he is documented twice within the Border Calendar Papers – on both occasions when raiding into Gilsland.

1. "*February 1588. Malle Blackburne of Darmontstead in Gillesland, against Wille Armstrang son to Geordie of Bigholms, Wille and Syme of Calfhill, Alie of the Syde, for 94 sheep, 1 naig, 3 oxen, insight 20L. sterling.*"

2. *"Thursday, 21 Aug. 1589, Gillesland. – Mathewe Blackburne of Darmontstead against Wille Armstrong son to Geordie of Calfhills, &c., for 6 old kye and oxen, 30 sheep and his insight 6L."*

✽✽✽

Simon (Sym) of Calfield/Calfhill – (k.1601)

Simon was the most dangerous of the Calfhills. Such was the level of Simon's notoriety that he came to the attention of the Scottish king. James VI singled him out to Henry Leigh, hoping to put an end to Simon's reiving ways. Leigh wrote to Scrope on 25 November 1597, stating that James *"complains much of Sim of Calfhill, and in good earnest would gladley have him to hang or that your lordship would hang him."* The king declared it was *"a great sinne to save him who haith cut the throtes of so many poore people,"* seeking help from the English Border officials.

Sym was possibly married to a daughter of Fergus of the Mote, an English Graham. He is first mentioned in trouble with the authorities in February 1588, when Malle Blackburne of Darmontstead in Gilsland placed a complaint against *"Wille Armstrang son to Geordie of Bigholms, Wille and Syme of Calfhill, Alie of the Syde, for 94 sheep, 1 naig, 3 oxen, insight 20L. sterling."*

By 1596 Sym was a serious nuisance; within a set of West March complaints against Buccleuch for the period June – Sept 1596, he appears on four separate bills...

1. *"The tenants of Whitehill, lately Christofer Dacres esquire, now his son's her Majesty's ward, upon Sime and Joke Armstronge al as 'Calfehills' Pawtie of Harelawe, Ekie 'braidebelt', Willie of Briggomes, Willie 'Kange', with 100 men, for burning 6 tenants' houses, and steadings, with goods worth 200L. sterling, and taking the six tenants prisoners."*

2. *"George Hetherton of Hawehills, Roger Hetherton, &c., upon Jocke of Monkbehirst, Simes Arche, Pawtie of Hairelawe, Jocke and Sime Armstrongs of Calfehill, Willie and Geordie Yrwen alias 'Kanges', with 16 persons, burning his houses and insight worth 200L. sterling, taking 40 kye, &c., 10 horses, &c., 40 sheep and 'gaite'."*

3. *"The tenants of Walton, late Christofer Dacres esq., upon said Sime 'Calfehill', Pattie Harelawe, &c., with 200 men, for taking 80 head of cattle, 20 horse and 'naiges', and household stuff worth 200L. sterling."*

4. *"The tenant of Thornby more the late Christofer Dacres', upon said Sime and others 'last above written' with 100 men, who burned 10 houses of habitation, 20 out houses, goods moveable and unmoveable, taking some prisoners and detaining them, with 4 score kye, &.C., 20 horse, &c, and insight worth 100L. sterling."*

On 18 April 1601, a document on the Scottish outlaws of Liddesdale was draughted. Amongst the names contained was *"Sym Armstrang of Caffeild,"* now officially branded an outlaw. Another dozen Armstrongs were named, all under the Laird of Buccleuch's charge, who now at King James's command, were to be given up to Lord Scrope and Sir Robert Carey and their deputies, *"as neither Buccleuch nor his deputies will be answerable for them."* The Scottish March Wardens were not succeeding in keeping the peace, with a frustrated monarch seeking an English solution. James sought English military arms and assistance in controlling the Scottish reivers, for too long the Scottish wardens had struggled under-funded with little to show for their effort. A change of tact was needed and the English officials were only too pleased to help. Elizabeth was not in the best of health and they knew who would be taking over as the next monarch. Sir Robert Carey was the queen's cousin, was more than eager to oblige and commented, *"He warrants us her Majesty's officers to take revenge on either side of the Border."*

A month later Simon showed his respect for King James's wishes, by totally ignoring him – and went raiding into England. Simon's gang burned a village and took away four or five prisoners to hold for ransom. Carey was responsible for the area that was spoiled and sent Henry Woodrington, one of his deputies, on a mission of part reprisal and part to free the prisoners. Carey now had new powers given to him by the Scottish king and was keen to try them out. Carey describes in a letter to Cecil on 13 May 1601 on what occurred:-

"This last week the Scottish outlaws, having done their utmost on the West March, have begun with me, and burnt a small town in my charge adjoining the West March, taking 4 or 5 prisoners away.

Having the King's warrant, I directed my deputy, Harry Woodrington, with 300 horse, to enter Scotland: who has burned the houses of 3 chief offenders, with great store of cattle and sheep also, and rescued the prisoners. Many of these outlaws are set on foot, for he brought off near 20 of their best horses. The offenders themselves lyes in bogges and wooddes, so that none of them could be gotten. This is their first attempt on me, and the first revenge I have taken. They may likely provoke me further, but knowing the Queen's mind, and having the King's warrant, I will not suffer the poorest under my charge to be overrun.

I have power enough, and will weary them with their own weapons for the King of Scots, besides his first letter, has sent me another to approve it, which I herewith send you – praying you to return both by your first occasion to send northwards."

Woodrington had sufficient man-power for the task, with three hundred riders. They rode confidently into Liddesdale and knowing who was responsible for the raid, rode directly to target the houses of the chief offenders. The Armstrongs had prior warning of Woodrington coming, with their chain of hill top watches and beacons springing into action. This allowed the Armstrongs to find refuge before the troopers arrived, leaving the area seemingly deserted. Carey stated in his memoirs that *"The outlaws themselves were in strongholds, and could no way be got hold."*

The English prisoners were tracked down and rescued and for revenge, Woodrington rounded up as many cattle and sheep as he could find. To deter future raids Woodrington also collected twenty of the Armstrong's best horses and satisfied with their work the English troopers then withdrew. Simon was close by sheltering within a stone bastle or peel tower, observing the action through a slot window to his extreme infuriation. Simon was overcome with a mix of red rage and blind valour – what happened next was a piece of classic chivalry straight out of a border ballad. Luckily for posterity, Carey recorded what occurred next in his memoirs – "*But one of the chief of them, being of more courage than the rest, got to horse and came pricking after them, crying out and asking, 'What he was that durst avow that mighty work?' One of the company came to him with a spear and ran him through the body, leaving his spear broke in him, of which wound he died.*" Carey goes on to explain that the lone attacker was "*Sim of the Cathill,*" and the trooper that turned around to take him on in a duel was "*Ridley of Hartwesell* [Haltwhistle]." The Ridleys and the Calfhill Armstrongs were at feud, which explains why a Ridley would choose to spur their horse around, and with a levelled lance go into the charge. Simon wanted revenge and a Ridley bravely rose to the bait. The death of Simon would go on to be immortalised in the ballad "*The Fray o Hautwessel,*" which describes how "*John Rydly thrust his speir Reet thro o' the Cathill's wame*[stomach]."

Woodrington had no further incidents on the return journey and on passing the recently raided village – "*The goods were divided to poor men from whom they were taken before.*" Simon's death would have to be avenged of course, the Armstrongs knew no other way. Carey concludes the incident in his memoirs, "*This act so irritated the outlaws that they vowed cruel revenge, and that before the next winter was ended they would leave the whole country waste, that there should be none to resist them…They presently took a resolution to be revenged on that town.*" Carey knew trouble was to come and was prepared for any Armstrong fall-out. He told Cecil "*I have power enough, and will weary them with their own weapons,*" fully expecting to be provoked further.

Simon's slaying demanded the death of yet more Ridleys – such was the state of the Border society. But at last a solution to the cycle of slaughter was in place under the capable hands of Carey. Carey managed to obtain bonds from at least the Whithaugh Armstrongs and reined in an immediate revenge response. Two years later Carey was riding for Edinburgh carrying the ring of a deceased Queen Elizabeth to symbolically present before King James – the end of the Border and its bloody feuds could not come quick enough.

✳✳✳

Archibald (Archie) – (c.1600)

The main record on the life of Archie comes in the form of the border ballad titled "*Archie o' Ca'field.*" Literature though is never the best evidence on documenting history and can't be trusted, but the tale told and the characters named within can be taken as factual in some form. There is a possibility that Archie is the same "*Sym's Archie of Cowfield,*" who appears in a list of fugitives from a law court held in Hawick on 26 August 1605. If correct, this would identify Archie as the son of Simon and places the events of his life into the late 16th century; a life that was well endangered by 1605 – and mostly likely over.

The ballad's narrative is similar to "*Jock o' the Side*," and is so similar that it can be considered that sections were copied and/or influenced from it. The story then is of a rescue mission – Archie has been captured and imprisoned within the tollbooth of Dumfries; the ballad unfolds the trials and tribulations of his escape. Whilst "*Jock o' the Side*" had the Armstrongs as the heroes, this ballad has John Hall (possibly Hall of Newbigging) named as the main character – "*The luve of Teviotdale aye was he.*"

The rescue party was thirty men strong...

"Ten to hald the horses' heads,
And other ten the watch to be,
And ten to break up the strong prison,
Where billy [brother] *Archie he does lie."*

The journey to Dumfries was not without its dramas, when a black mare lost a shoe at Murraywhaite on the banks of the River Annan. A smith had to be tracked down and have a hasty shoe fitted in the "*mirk*" of night by candle light. Riding speedily they reached the Dumfries port, where five of the party dismounted to hold the horses and another five acted as watchmen. The tolbooth was then approached and calling out, the cell of Archie was located; he was requested to "*Work thou within, and we without*" and would soon be free. As with "*Jock o' the Side*," Archie was found chained up and had to be carried down the tolbooth stairs and mounted upon a black mare. Dumfries was exited without problem, but the chains around Archie were a hindrance. The party stopped at the same blacksmith as on the journey in, calling out – "*'A smith! a smith!' then Dickie he cries;*" asking to have Archie's irons removed.

The smith had barely filed through the first iron shackles, when Simon, a member of the party, spotted danger approaching...

"O dinna ye see what I do see?"

"Lo! yonder comes Lieutenant Gordon,
Wi' a hundred men in his cumpanie;"

The authorities were after them, removing Archie's shackles would have to wait and a quick escape was required. The River Annan had to be crossed in order to reach safety, but as in all good adventure stories, "*it was flowing like the sea.*" A flood had happened behind the rescue party, as in the same way the River Tyne had flooded behind the Armstrongs in "*Jock o' the Side.*" With little debate, the party swims across the river, with no mention of the heavy chains dragging Archie down. On the opposite bank, the ballad has a heroic Hall issuing the classic boast of many a reiver...

The Dumfries posse did not follow, with Lieutenant Gordon concerned on the loss of the shackles. Gordon calls across the water *"Throw me my irons... I wot they cost me dear aneugh."* In response, Hall shouted back that he would have the shackles for himself and make them into a plough. Another offer to Lieutenant Gordon was made, this time by Archie, to cross the river and join them for a celebratory drink of wine – a proud and defiant Armstrong cock-a-snook at authority.

The party returned for home safely, with Archie declaring...

28. Bigholms

Exactly what type of stronghold this was is not known, a big house of sorts. As the term "tower" is not applied the building could have been a block-house or of the bastle type. The house was 6km to the SW of Langholm, on the Bigholms Burn just off the Wauchope Valley. The Bigholms were in regular contact with Simon Armstrong, 9th Laird of Mangerton and had family connections to Calfhill.

✳✳✳

George (Gorthe/Geordie) of Bigholmes – (c.1580s/90s)

William – "Geordie's Will" of Bigholmes – (c. 1580s/90s)

George and William were father and son, and belonged to the Mangerton grayne. George is named in Thomas Musgrave's list of December 1583 on the Border Riders. He comes under the section *"The Lord of Mangerton and his frendes, and theire allyaunces with England,"* and his entry reads – *"Gorthe Armestronge of the Bygams dwelleth on the Bygams, and marryed Will of Carlilles daughter."*

William is recorded raiding twice in 1588, both forays heading to the Armstrong's favourite hunting ground of Bewcastle. The bills read as follows:-

1. *"February 1588. Malle Blackburne of Darmontstead in Gillesland, against Wille Armstrang son to Geordie of Bigholms, Wille and Syme of Calfhill, Alie of the Syde, for 94 sheep, 1 naig, 3 oxen, insight 20L. sterling."*

2. *"November 1588. Margaret Forster of Allergarth, Bewcastle, against Pawtie of Harlawe, Wille of Biggams, Wille Kang, Dick of Dryupp, Jock of Calfhills, &c., for 18 kye and oxen and her insight, 5L. sterling."*

George or William possibly took part in the rescue of Kinmont Willie in 1596, named as "Bighames" in a list of those present on the raid. A final raid was recorded in that year, contained within the *"West March complaints against Buccleuch"* for the dates June – Sept 1596. William was complained upon by Christofer Dacre and the tenants of Whitehill when he took part in a one hundred strong raid. William was named as *"Willie of Briggomes"* and rode aside Willie "Kange" Irvine, Hector Armstrong (*"Braidebelt"*), Pawtie Armstrong of Harelaw, and Simon and Jock Armstrong of Calfhill. They stole goods worth £200 sterling and burned six houses, returning home taking six of the tenants as prisoners.

29. Langholm

Langholm was a market town and had its own castle. The castle was built at the strategic confluence of the Rivers of Ewes and Esk on the edge of the town. Today there is little to be seen, only the south wall of the stronghold still stands, upon a raised rectangular platform of rubble overgrown with turf and long grass. The wall is 9.2m long by 6.0m high, with a narrow rectangular window gap in the centre, and two short return walls at each end. The castle once had a protective barmkin, and probably a wall that stretched from one river to the other. The castle was abandoned in about 1724.

***

Christopher of Langholm – (b.c.1505)

Christopher was the son of Alexander 6th Laird of Mangerton, and brother to Johnnie Armstrong of Gilnockie. He was married to the daughter of Arthur Graham (son of William "Lang Will" Graham) of Canonbie. He was responsible for the building of Langholm Castle, a political sign of the Armstrongs expanding their power out of Liddesdale and making a new base in Eskdale. He had at least one son, John of Langholm.

Christopher is mentioned within the *"Ballad* of *Johnnie Armstrong"* – A sad parting verse given by Johnnie of Gilnockie just before his execution in 1530:-

"God be withee, Kirsty, my brither!
Lang live thou Laird of Mangertoun!
Lang mayst thou live on the Border-syde
Or thou see thy brither ryde up and doun!"

***

John of Langholm – (c.1580s/1600s)

John was the son of Christopher of Langholm, the nephew of Johnnie Armstrong of Gilnockie; who had at least two sons, John and Christopher. Langholm came under the control of John 8th Lord Maxwell, who leased many properties to the Armstrongs. Maxwell held the post of Warden of the West March on two occasions during the 1570s, a situation which caused jealousy and a power struggle with the Johnstones. Maxwell garrisoned the castle at Langholm with his troopers, and this became a target of the Armstrongs in 1581. Perhaps prompted by the Johnstones to aid them in their feud with the Maxwells, the Armstrongs attacked Langholm Castle. John took part in the raid and set fire to the "House of Langholm," a malicious foray with damage of Maxwell estates its only goal. He brought along his two sons on the foray, John and Christopher, who were aged eight and four respectively. John would have thought it a good idea to initiate his sons into the reiving life at this young age. Langholm was an easy target and relatively risk free, a good place for the brothers to see their father in action and to prepare them for what lay ahead.

John's involvement in this outrage went unpunished until the death of Queen Elizabeth I. With a new monarch old crimes were looked at anew, and when possible the perpetrators were to be punished. On 11 January 1605, John, together with his two sons were summoned to attend trial in Edinburgh to answer for their actions at Langholm twenty four years earlier. The full list of those on trial reads as follows:-

Archie Airmestrang, the Mercheand, in the Hoilhous   *Ingrie Airmestrang, in Inzieholme*

Niniane Armestrang, in Tortwne   *Johnne Armestrang, in the Hoilhous*

Cristie Airmestrang, thair, callit Nanse Cristie   *Johnne Michelsoun, in Tortwne*

Johnne Thomesoun, in Dwmescheil-burne   *Archibald Armestrang of Flaskholme*

Archibald Armestrang, callit Nanse Archie   *Mathow Twrnour in Hoilhous*

Niniane Airmestrang, callit Roweis Niniane, in Murthome   *Johnne Couthird*

Cristie Airmestrang, sone to the Guidman of Langholme (Johnne Airmestrang)

The group were accused – "*Dilaitit for airt and pairt of the tressonable Burning of the House of the Langholme; and taking of Harbert Maxwall of Cavense captive and prissoner: And for the thiftious steilling of certane horse, nolt, scheip, gait: And burning of certane coirnis, pertening to the said Harbert, Alexander Bell in Eikinholme, Williame Bell in Gallosyde and George Irwing in Holmeheid*".

The pursuers of the case were its four victims, Herbert Maxwell, Alexander Bell, William Bell, and George Irving. They found Archie Armstrong "*The Merchant*," Agnes Cristie Airmestrang ("*Nanse Cristie*") and Anneis Archie ("*Nanse Archie*") to be "*Innocent of the crymes lybellit*." John, known as "*the Guidman of Langholme*" and "*Johnne Airmestrang of Langholme*," appeared separately on the 11 January 1605, which implies he was the ring leader of the operation. John had the same offences read out to him as the earlier group, but more detail was gone into. The accusations were broken down into several items, showing the burning of Langholm House to be a more destructive raid than it first looked, and that John was the main instigator behind it.

"*Dilaitit of airt and pairt of the tressonabill Raising of fyre about Harbert Irwingis hous in Murthholme, and burning ane grit pairt thairof: And lykwayis for airt and pairt of the tressonabill Raising of ffyre at the Castell of Langholme, and burning of ane grit pairt of the barnes, byres, stables and uther office-houssis of the said Place of Langholme: And burning of the haill insicht pleneissing being thairin; togidder with thre barnes full of beir and corne; and xxiiii stakkis of corne, Handing in the barne yaird; and fourscoir dargis 1 of hay, with ane kilnfull 1 of malt.*"

The "beir" mentioned above, noted as inside the burning barn, was not alcohol but barley. An ancient type called bear/bere; a four to five row barley that was hardy and well suited to the poor acidic soils of the Borders. A "darg" was the measure of work that one man could accomplish in a day; the raiders destroyed eighty days' worth of hay, which must have been a serious blow to the community.

Other charges flew thick and fast...

"And for airt and pairt of the thiftious steilling of threttie nolt, with sax or sevin horse and naigis, furth of the said Place of the Langholme: Quhilkis all and sindrie guidis, geir, coirnes, horse, nolt and remanent guidis, pertenit to Harbert Maxwell of Kavense."

"And siclyk, for airt and pairt of the tressonabill usurpatioun of his Maiesteis authoritie upone him, in taking in of the said Harbert Maxwall of Kavense captive and prissoner; and transpoirting him in Ingland, at the tyme foirsaid."

"ITEM, for Burning of Williame Bellis house in Gallowsyde, with tua barnes full of beir, and tua stakkis of aittis standing in his barne-yaird: AND for the thiftious steilling fra him of tuentie nolt, threscoir scheip and tuentie gait, &c."

"ITEM, for Burning of Alexander, Richerd and Fergie Bellis houssis in Dikinholme, and steilling threscoir nolt, tua hundreth scheip and threscoir gaittis."

"ITEM, for Burning and destroying of David and George Irwingis duelling houssis in Holmeheid, with sax barnes full of beir and corne, and aucht roukis of corne, standing in thair corne-yaird, and tuentie dargis of hay; committit the tyme foirsaid; upoun set purpois and provisioun. Sir James Johnnestoun of that Ilk of Dunskellie, knight, as cautioner, unlawit and amerciat in the pane of ane thousand merkis money."

With the amount of crimes placed at John's door, he would be lucky to escape the gallows. The *"Justice adjudget"* announced the verdict on the said *"Johnne Armestrang of Langholme."* He was to be denounced as a rebel and put to the horn, with *"all his moveabill guidis to be escheat."* John, banished from Scotland, would have to seek a new life elsewhere. He may have laid low with his Graham or Forster relatives in Cumbria, went to the Low Countries as a mercenary, or sought a new life in Ireland.

✳✳✳

John of Langholm/Hollows – (b.1572/3)

Christopher – (b.1576/7)

Robert of Langholm – (fl.1596)

John and Christopher were brothers, the sons of John of Langholm, and their grandfather was Christopher of Langholm, the brother of Johnnie Armstrong of Gilnockie. Robert was related to them, possibly being an uncle or brother.

John and Christopher were present at the burning of Langholm House in 1581, and were aged eight and four respectively. It is unlikely if they had any part in the spoiling of the building, only present at their father's bidding. The glow of the burning building can be imagined, illuminating the two young boys as they stared in excited wonder at the destruction. This would be the world they were being brought up into, an initiation into the fire and steel life of the reiver. Their presence on the raid illustrates the young age at which reiver society was introduced to the outlaw's offspring – A harsh heritage indeed.

Both John and Robert were involved in the rescue of Kinmont Willie from Carlisle Castle. John was reported being seen the day before the rescue on Saturday 12 April, at a horserace meeting in Langholm. John was referred to as the "*goodman* [of Langholm]*... young John Armstrong,*" and later dined with several Grahams and "*Buclugh at the Langam.*" Robert, recorded as "*Roby of the Langholm,*" was named as one of the "*principal assailants*" in a document by Lord Scrope on 14 April 1596, on the rescue.

Almost exactly one year after the Kinmont rescue, John was in trouble with the authorities for riding on a foray with the very same Kinmont. At Carlisle on 28 April 1597, by "*ordre of the lordes commissioners for Border causes, betwixt the lordes wardens of the West Marches of England and Scotland*" – John was indented to appear regarding West March bills against Scotland. The complaint was made by Thomas Musgrave, Captain of Bewcastle, against "*John of Langham*" and "*Will Kynmont.*" This raid may have been one of the earliest outings of "Sandie's Bairns," a gang of reivers put together from various members of "Kinmont's Bairns." They were charged for stealing "*24 horse and mares,*" and took away Musgrave as a prisoner to be ransomed later for £200 sterling. The raid also lifted another sixteen prisoners and did much slaughter; Musgrave was obviously enraged by the whole experience. The bill was found "*Foule by confession,*" and was referred to the commissioners for "*tryall of the trodd,*" and fined "*400L*".

John and Christopher's past came back to haunt them on 11 January 1605 when they were named amongst thirteen people, accused of burning Langholm House in 1581. They were named as "*Johnne Armestrang, in the Hoilhous* (Hollows Tower)," and "*Cristie Airmestrang, sone to the Guidman of Langholme.*" The authorities were digging up old offences in an attempt to remove troublesome reivers from the new United Kingdom of James I – and had netted two small fish. Arthur Scott of Newburgh and "*Gemilscleuch*" (Gilmanscleuch) acted as a pledge and surety for the two brothers, with "*Johnne under the pane of ane thowsand pundis, and the said Cristie under the pane of fyve hundreth pundis,*" should they refuse to comply with the law. The young ages of John and Christopher were a favour in their avoiding the charges. It was stated – "*the said Johnne of the age of viii yeiris, and Cristie of the age of foure yeiris; and sa war nocht doli capaces* [capable of mischief]; *and be the law of this realme, can nocht be put to the tryell of ane Assyse.*"

The authorities were hoping that the old charges would stick, no matter how thin the case may be, and result in their execution. Declared to be in their minority and too young to be tried, the charges were dropped – the brothers were free to go.

30. Munkhurst

Munkhurst Tower once stood on the east bank of the River Esk, 4km NW of Canonbie, its nearest neighbour was Hollows Tower, the peel built by Johnnie Armstrong of Gilnockie. The tower was known under several different names and spellings; Monkeby, Monkbehirst, Mumbiherste, and Mumbie – ending in the present as Nether Mumbie. There is no trace of any stronghold today, as the castle was destroyed and the stones were used to build the adjacent farmhouse.

Alexander of Monkbehirst – (c.1540s/60s)

Alexander is first documented in 1541, known as *"at Monkbyk... in Liddersdell,"* within an English complaint. He was alleged to have given reset to some English rebels – George Purdom, Jamie Purdom, George Waugh and Thomas Waugh. There is an Alexander mentioned within the Register of the Privy Council in 1569, which is possibly the same Alexander.

John (Jock) – (k.1596)

John is mentioned in a list of West March complaints against Buccleuch, when he took part in a raid around June – Sept 1596. John was tried alongside *"Simes Arche, Pawtie of Hairelawe, Jocke and Sime Armstrongs of Calfehill, Willie and Geordie Yrwen alias 'Kanges',"* and sixteen others. The gang had a complaint made upon them by George Hetherton of Hawehills and Roger Hetherton for *"burning his houses and insight worth 200L. sterling, taking 40 kye, &c., 10 horses, &c., 40 sheep and 'gaite'."*

John was present at the raid on Carlisle Castle to free Kinmont Willie Armstrong. He was to suffer for his involvement in the venture. Lord Scrope had endured humiliation and a loss of face; someone would have to pay and the Armstrongs were in his sites. He was determined to claw back the lost prestige and hopefully show those who had challenged his power that such action would never be tolerated. A warden's rode into Armstrong country was then what the doctor ordered. Nobody had been killed in the Kinmont raid, but Scrope felt that he had to turn a firm hand onto those responsible and have his hurt pride avenged. Scrope set off on a warden's rode in response to the raid, he writes with gleeful satisfaction to Burghley afterwards on 15 July 1596 informing him on its outcome – *"I had taken some who were at the breaking of this castle, an attempt was made this night, but the men employed found only empty houses which they burned, bringing back 3 or 4 Armstrongs prisoners not of the greatest accompte – yet some requital for their burnings and taking prisoners every night this week in Gilsland."* During the rode, one of the Armstrongs was killed – Scrope adds more detail on the incident; *"Jok Armstronge of Munkhurst, onne who was at the breache of the castell, hapened to be slayne in this nights roade."*

John was cut down by Scrope's troopers with no explanation given. Warden's rodes were a law to themselves, the Armstrongs would get little legal comeback on John's death. John's death can be assumed to have been due to his involvement in Kinmont's rescue, the troopers taking the opportunity to make a token example on one of Buccleuch's riders. The slaying could be classed as a piece of judicial murder, with all evidence quickly buried. John was unlucky to be an Armstrong at the wrong place and the wrong time.

31. Hollows

Hollows stands on the west bank of the River Esk between Canonbie and Langholm. The tower was originally called Gilnockie Tower and built by Johnnie Armstrong, but became renamed the "Hole House" due to the basin of land (the "hole") which sits amphitheatre like to the north. The hollow was caused by the quarrying of stone to build the tower, which made a defensive feature in the process. In time "Hole House" became corrupted into "*Hollas*," and then into its present form. The tower was burned by Sir Christopher Dacre, the English Warden in 1528, and further destruction was caused by English raids in the 1540s. The damage required extensive repairs, making the tower that later generations inherited not exactly the same building which Johnnie Armstrong left on his final journey to meet the king.

The stronghold is a typical peel tower in construction, with a barrel vaulted ground floor, three floors above, and a garret with parapet walk-way on the roof flanked by crow-stepped gables. A beacon lantern sat perched like a church belfry on the apex of the southern gable, which probably saw more use than any other bale-fire along the frontier. Single gun-shot loops situated on each side of the tower except the east, gave a suitable protection and deterred any foe from advancing to close. A courtyard with stabling was probably located to the east of the tower. Today, the tower looks very much as it did in its heyday. Reroofed and made inhabitable in 1979/80, Hollows stands as arguably the best example of a peel tower in all of the Borders. And more surpringly, considering it belonged to one of the worst Riding families – a wonder it survived intact when so many others were knocked down.

✳✳✳

John – "Jock of the Glen" – of Hollows – (b.1545 – d.c.1628)

John was the son of Christopher Armstrong ("John's Christie"), and lived in the tower that was built originally by his grandfather, the infamous Johnnie Armstrong of Gilnockie. Johnnie built the tower in around 1526, but did not get to enjoy his new home for long however, when in 1530 he raised the anger of King James V and was executed. John is first documented in 1579, noted as "*Johnne Armstrang of Hoilhous*," appearing alongside his father before the Privy Council on the matter of a feud with the Turnbulls of Bedrule.

He is first recorded raiding in 1582, when accompanied by his father and brother Christopher on a foray to Montbenger, Deuchar and Whitehope. John is mentioned in the 1583 list made by Thomas Musgrave on the Border Riders. John is listed under the Armstrong grayne of Langholm. He is also noted for his marriage choice, having an English wife, the daughter of "*Riches Dick*" (Richard Graham) of Batlinglees. The entry reads – "*John Armestronge of the Hollus, marryed Walter Graymes sister of Netherby.*" The Grahams of Netherby were only 7km away, English neighbours who were essential for the Armstrong communication system. The chain of warning beacons leading into Graham country helped the Armstrongs of the Hollows several times out of tight scrapes.

John first came to the attention of the March Wardens in April 1590, when he turned up at the Bells Kirk charged on two bills. The warden himself was one of those bringing the complaints forward. William Fenwick, the deputy Middle March Warden of England and Mathew Armstrong were the complainers in both of the two bills against John. The name "*Jock Armstronge of the Holles*," was read out for a raid at Lammas 1587, upon Heathery Burn in which John's gang lifted four cattle and a horse. He was accompanied by Davie Armstrong "*Bangtaile*," and Andrew Armstrong "*the Bungell*." The second charge was for a raid to the same place, but a year later at Candlemas 1588. Again John was accompanied by Bangtail and Bungell, and also two servants of the Laird's Jock who tagged along – Mungo and Jock Armstrong. The gang were charged for stealing thirty seven "*wedders*" (castrated male sheep).

John is listed within John Monipennie's publication from 1597, recorded under "*ESKDAIL – Johnes*," and named together with two others. It is interesting to note that these three chiefs come under the title of "*Johnes*" and not a location. This was perhaps the name of the gang, so called after John of the Hollows.

1. *John Armstrang of Hoilhous*

2. *John Armstrang of Thornequhat* [Thorniewhats]

3. *Wil Armestrang of Tennishill*

John took part in the rescue of Kinmont Willie Armstrong in 1596. In a letter by Lord Scrope on 14 April 1596, he names the principal assailants on Carlisle Castle, with "*young John of the Hollace and one of his brethren*," amongst them. A second document confirms Scrope's list, written anonymously on 24 April 1596 by "*Richies Will*" Graham. Graham was hoping to avoid the political fallout of the rescue, and wrote to "*pleaseth your lordship to ken this the truth of the takinge out of Kynmont... There came frea the Langholm with him younge John and Kirste his brother*."

John paid the price of his helping out on the rescue of Kinmont. The embarrassment and shame of the rescue required some hard action of revenge to save face by the English authorities. An example of this appears in a document dated Aug 1596, named "*A note of suche slauchteris, stouthis, refis and oppin oppressionis as have bene committit be England upoun the West Merche and Midill Merche*." Amongst the various raids, one was taken out on the Hollows – "*Item. The Captain of Bewcastle, with 500 men of the Middle and West Wardenry, came 6 or 7 miles within Scots ground, and carried off 300 ky and oxen and 24 score sheep, perteining to Johnne Armstrang of the Hoilhous*." This was undertaken as a warden's rode, which were at times no more than legalised reiving. Thomas Musgrave, the Captain of Bewcastle, was authorised by Lord Scrope, and mustered what amounted to a small army giving him the power to do anything that he wanted. Punishing the Armstrongs who rescued Kinmont was on the top of his list.

Thomas Musgrave again punished John of the Hollows for the Kinmont raid a month later. John become the fall-guy that year for taking out various frustrations upon. Musgrave wrote to the English Privy Council on 9 September 1596, describing the aftermath of a hot trod that he had just recently returned from. He was helping the "*pooermen of Bewcastill*" to have their belongings returned, but failed in the attempt. Musgrave did not want to return home empty handed, and recalled an earlier letter from the Privy Council which stated "*if no justice could be had otherwise, I might recover the worth of their goods as I cane*." Here was the justification for some legalised theft. Musgrave took this as a green light to make a free for all grab at John's livestock – *"Wheron with my kinsmen and friends, I took from John Armstrong of the Hollus, the leder of thes incurcions, somme vi or vii scor of cattill, and made restitution to the poor men."* Musgrave's men stole 120-140 head of cattle from John and handed them over as compensation to the Bewcastle tenants. John was a known reiver and had carried out frequent raids into Bewcastle, and the Kinmont affair had given the opportunity for retribution. When looking at the thefts, the actions of *"Richies Will"* Graham can be understood; by playing the shrewd card of turning informant to please the authorities, he avoided a similar backlash.

Taking pledges was one of the methods that wardens employed to keep the peace on the Border. In 1597 lists were drawn up with names demanded by Scotland and England to be handed over, and John for sure was included. John had recently been making himself a highly visible pest in the Bewcastle area, becoming a prime catch. The document demanded John amongst the West March pledges, to be delivered to Sir William Bowes, at the west ford near Norham on the 25 June 1597. John must have been viewed as one of the worst reivers in the Scottish West March to have received the summons. John was placed under the charge of Richard Lowther, who gave him an assurance for himself and his family's good behaviour. This arrangement was never going to hold up, with Lowther writing to Cecil on 30 June 1599, to explain the situation on the ground. John can be seen to have not ceased his raiding, and to have taken out a foray upon Musgrave as an act of vengeance for having his cattle stolen by him three years earlier. The letter is worth quoting in full...

"It appears by the inclosed, that the Armstrongs Scotsmen, have not only given up assurance with the Musgraves for former injuries and harm done them without reason, as they alledge; but in revenge, this day ran a foray with 60 horse and foot in Bewcastle, taking the captain's goods &.c. 60 head of cattle, 6 horse, 100 sheep and gayt, killed one man and hurt others. Which I doubt will cause further combre to this March; the rather, as I am informed that insolent persons are thereto animated by letters lately sent from Edinburgh. Therefore I humbly intreat your honor to hasten the lord warden's repair home.
Carlisle. Signed: Richard Lowther"

Contained in the same document was a letter from John Armstrong to Lowther, which gives an interesting counter view to Lowther's claims – it reads...

"Your worship understands when we met you, I was desyrand your worship to cawse the Musgraves to done reason, and at your worship's desire I have done no harm to no Englishman, and caused all my friends to forbear sensyne. I now write to let your worship understand that I will be no longer under assurance with the Musgraves, for give I wald, it might come to my reproafe, for there is some sayes, give I wald not have dischardged with your worship, they wald not forbeare them that hes made faultes. Therefore I thought meet to dischardge my self of my promisse, and give that I do in tymes comynge for your good will and honor, I have the maire thanke to receyve at your worshippis handes. I doubt not to have your good countenance; for I take God to my wytnes that I wold have tane les nor reason of them. I would you took my discharge in good part, and consider my case howe ewell I hawe bene used without faulte done to them.

. . . Off the Hollowse the xxviii of June 1599. Your frend to use lefully.

Signed: John Armestrange of Hollowse."

An observation was made on the letter, that the writing was *"perhaps too good for a border rider;"* implying that someone else wrote it, and that John was not an educated man. There is no reason to assume that John could not write, and he was indeed the letter's author. The usual Border confusion of claim and denial was at work, making it impossible for the March Wardens to bring proper justice to bear.

John had the following children:-

1. Andrew – (1576-1671) – He died in Brookeborough, County Fermanagh, Northern Ireland.

2. John William – (b.c.1578) – He married Ann Kendrick.

3. Robert – (b.c.1582)

4. William – (b.c.1582-1625) – He married Alice Dunn in 1614, London, England, and died in Newport News, Virginia, USA.

5. Henry – (b.c.1584)

✹✹✹

William of Gilnockie – "Christie's Will" – (1565 – 1646)

Andrew – (1576 – 1671)

Andrew was the son of John of Hollows – William was a brother of John of Hollows. William was married to Margaret Elliott c.1600, and lived at *"Aughingill"* (Auchengyle) near Chapelknowe. They both belonged to the Langholm grayne of Armstrongs and were involved in the families raiding business with close ties.

The two relatives saw up-close and personal the catastrophe which hit the Armstrongs in 1603 when King James brought fire and steel to the Border, harsh actions to finally pacify and eradicate the reivers and their society. William and Andrew must have been more than worried as the net closed in on them, with various friends and relatives strung up by Jedburgh Justice, left right and centre. Old crimes were brought out to justify executions, and new ones punished with instant hangings. In 1604 William left Scotland for Ireland taking his nephew Andrew with him. It is not sure if William was forced out of the Borders due to the king's plan to be rid of the outlaws, or he saw no future in staying and fled to live with friends – the latter seems the most likely scenario. They resettled in County Fermanagh, finding fellow Scots to help them create a new life. The Armstrongs took up residence in the village of "Brooksboro" (Brookeborough), which was originally called Aghalun, having once been under the rule of the Maguire Clan. Hugh Maguire, Lord of Fermanagh died in 1600, with his lands going to the Crown, creating opportunity for new ambitious Scots. The village changed hands after the 1641 rebellion when it was given to the Brooke family, and was renamed "Brooksboro" after Sir Henry Brooke, who was granted the village in 1666.

The two Armstrongs fared better in Ireland than the Grahams would do two years later. In 1608 many Graham families were shipped out to the new Ulster Plantations that King James had just set up after the "Flight of the Earls" in September 1607. The Crown seized all of this un-ruled land and gave it to the new English and Scottish settlers to form a pro-United Kingdom colony. Roscommon was a main destination for the Grahams, where many settlers arrived to find poor quality land, wild bogs, no trees to build farms and a lack of finances. William and Andrew were luckily living in Fermanagh, good farming country with pasture for livestock. They also found help in the local Scottish communities that were already in place. They may have taken up a military career initially, with Enniskillen Castle close by and a divided population with a history of rebellion.

Perhaps due to financial reasons or boredom, William was back in the Scottish Borders again in 1630 and back into trouble. He stole two horses during a marauding expedition and was imprisoned in the tolbooth of Jedburgh facing the famous Jedburgh gallows tree. All was not lost for William; he had a stroke of good fortune in the passing figure of the Earl of Traquair, Lord High Treasurer. Traquair was by chance visiting the district, and enquired on the reason for William's confinement. The prisoner told him that he had got into trouble for stealing two halters, and would be hung for this. Traquair was astonished to hear that such a trivial offence had landed him the death penalty, and asked if there were other crimes that he had committed. Reluctantly William acknowledged that there were two more – at the end of the two halters were two delicate colts. The bold humour pleased Traquair who took a shine to William, and decided to intervene on his behalf and seek a suitable release. Traquair was successful and saved William's life. William became heart-felt devoted to the earl for his assistance and vowed to help him in future in any way that he could.

In around 1642 that opportunity came along, when the earl was up for trial in the Court of Session, Edinburgh, for a lawsuit against him. The episode became the subject of a border ballad, entitled *"Christie's Will,"* and featured in volume three of Sir Walter Scott's "The Minstrelsy of the Scottish Border." It is unknown why William was in Scotland at this time, but the reason can be assumed to be the Civil War that had just broken out between the three Kingdoms. William took it upon himself to pay back the debt, and decided to kidnap Sir Alexander Gibson, Lord Durie, who was the judge of the Court of Session. William knew that Durie took regular exercise on horseback at Leith Sands, and this relative seclusion would give him the ideal space to pounce. William took his chance and grabbed Durie; he was blindfolded and then whisked off to the tower of Graham, on the Dryfe Water near Moffat.

Durie was kept in a dark room, his imagination going wild thinking himself to be in the dungeon of a sorcerer. For three months Durie was kept in this solitary confinement, as William waited for the time when Traquair was released. Durie's friends assumed that he was dead, thinking he had been thrown by his horse and swept off to sea on the tide. The lawsuit was eventually solved in the favour of Traquair and with his release, William released Durie. Durie was taken at night blindfolded, and without speaking a single word, William placed Durie down at the Frigate Whins, a common near the sands of Leith at the exact same spot from which he had been taken twelve weeks earlier. Durie was bewildered as he regained his bearings and walked into Edinburgh, his friends stunned at his arrival having mourned his loss. It must have made a strange scene, the meeting of Durie with his friends and having to explain his absence –

he was convinced that he had been spirited away by witchcraft. Durie had been replaced by a new judge; his successor was in for an interesting shock. The truth of the ruse eventually came out, with those involved seeing the comical side of it all. William joined the army of Charles I soon after and was to have another high adventure.

Again the Earl of Traquair was behind this escapade. The Great Civil War was in progress, with William on the Royalist side. Traquair gave him a mission, to take a package of documents of the highest importance to His Majesty the King at London. The task was a difficult one, with the Scots Covenant army in the way and eager to prevent any Royalist communication between the king and his Scottish friends.

William arrived at London safely and delivered his papers without mishap. He now had to return home, a journey made all the more hazardous as the Parliament forces were aware of his presence and aimed to catch him. William negotiated with skill the route from London to Carlisle, but ran into problems when crossing the flooded River Eden. He was half way across the bridge when Parliamentarian soldiers suddenly closed a trap, emerging from both ends of the bridge at once. He was cornered, with nowhere to go but up. William then spurred his horse over the bridge parapet and into the swollen water, the current taking them down to the Stanners/Stanhouse, where with difficulty he gained the northern shore after casting off his long wet cloak. The soldiers for a moment were struck dumb by the spectacle and forgot to fire. A handful of eager soldiers ran to the rider-side, but were deterred when William pointed his pistol at them, forgetting that the gun had recently just been in the water and would not fire. The pause enabled William to get a head start on the rest of the soldiers, who pursued him to the Esk and a second flooded river. Here, he received his second soaking of the day in swimming across. He was not pursued, and once upon the opposite river bank, he turned around and cried out a taunt in true Border style to his pursuers, to come across and drink with him. The soldiers declined; concerned that William was now in friendly territory. William was one of the very last Border freebooters, following in the footsteps of his great grandfathers – who lay approvingly not far away.

Andrew's life was no less adventurous; he also joined the army of King Charles I. The Great Civil War that had began in Scotland, broke out in Ireland in 1641, and pulled both Andrew and William into its sphere. William returned back to Ireland, living at Maguiresbridge after his escapade in England, primed for more action in this new conflict. Both Andrew and William did well in the army, which comes as no surprise considering their reiver background, and both reached the ranks of officer. Andrew was in the army for seven years and gained a great reputation as a leader. Andrew would have played an active part in the military actions to end the rebellion. William joined the forces of Robert Monro's Scots Covenanters / Anglo-Scots settler's army, who marched out to take on the Irish Confederates led by Owen O'Neill. The two armies met on 5 June 1646, and fought the Battle of Benburb. The battle was a victory for O'Neill, and in the Scottish rout, William was killed.

Andrew survived the wars and came to settle in the village of "Brooksboro." The house in which William and his family lived in Brookeborough still remains today, and over the fireplace can be seen the Armstrong crest and motto, "*Valida Manu.*" The house can be considered the first home of the Armstrongs in Ireland. The family and next generation or two lived and died in Fermanagh, with the next century tempting many to the USA and adventures anew.

The exact location of William and Andrew's graves are not known for sure, though they probably lie in the old Churchyard of Aghavea, 2km away from Brookeborough. The cemetery holds the burials of several of William's relatives, at least two of his nine sons, Edward and Alexander – and also three of his grandsons (sons of Edward), John, Francis and James.

William's children were:-

1. William – (b.1600) – William of Hightower. Died in Enniskillen, Ireland.

2. Thomas – (1603-1693) – Married in 1645 Brooksboro, Ireland – Died in Londonderry, Ireland.

3. Edward – (1604-1650) – Called "Edward from the Border." He was born in Brooksboro, and died at Terwinney, Ireland. Married c.1625 to Mary Maguire, in Brooksboro, Ireland. He was a captain during the Civil War in Ireland.

4. Robert – (b.c.1608) – Born in Brooksboro, Ireland. Married Jane Burton. Died Longfield, Ireland.

5. David – (b.c.1610) – Born in Brooksboro, Ireland

6. John – (b.1612) – of Longfield, Ireland.

7. Christopher (b.1616)

8. Simon – (b.c.1628) – Born in Brooksboro, Ireland

9. Alexander – (b.c.1631-d.c.1721) – Died at Carrickmakeegan, Leitrim, Ireland. Married c.1695 to Frances Dalziell, Terwinney, Ireland.

32. Gilnockie

Gilnockie Castle was situated on the east bank of the River Esk 2km north of Canonbie. The site of the castle was chosen well, on a promontory in a bend of the river with natural steep slopes on two sides down to the water. An external ditch was added to cut off the neck of the promontory, creating a well defended area measuring 61m by 36m. Little is known about the castle, which contained a late medieval fort measuring about 40m by 36m. There are no stone walls or masonry to be seen today, with only earthworks and a bank measuring 7.5 m thick and 1.8m high visible. A bridge crosses the Esk adjacent to the castle, which was not present when the castle was in existence.

Gilnockie Castle oddly, is not marked on any maps from the 16th, 17th or 18th centuries, and not until the ordinance survey map of 1856-59 does the stronghold's name turn up. The omission of the castle on maps is difficult to explain, but there are two possibilities – the castle was either raised to the ground and disappeared before the maps were produced, or the tower was renamed. The 1590s map of Timothy Pont show a stronghold called Nether Thorniewhats sitting in the area where Gilnockie Castle should be, suggesting the castle simply changed names.

✻✻✻

John (Johnnie) of Gilnockie – (b.c.1480 – ex.1530)

Johnnie Armstrong is arguably the most famous of the Border reivers – An almost legendary character who has come to symbolise the image of the romantic reiver. Epitomised as the classic outlaw, Johnnie is cast in the heroic mould, standing up defiantly to authority with a bold courage and a gentlemanly honour – a King of all he surveyed. Ironically it was Johnnie's demise which brought him the eternal fame, rather than his deeds – when a young king decided to flex his royal wings, and transported one of the Border's greatest thieves into immortality. As with several other reivers, Johnnie was made the subject of one of the border ballads – which has the apt title "The ballad of Johnnie Armstrong." Ballads of course cannot be taken as historically accurate, however in the case of Johnnie the ballad attributed to him has been accepted as mostly factual, and elevated him to an iconic status. Whether Johnnie deserves this accolade is open to debate, which makes the reality behind his life difficult to disentangle, but all the more fascinating to investigate.

There is not much known about Johnnie, what can be teased from the evidence is that he was probably the most successful reiver of his time. Johnnie was the second son of Alexander, 6th Laird of Mangerton and brother to Thomas, 7th Laird of Mangerton. This connection brought Johnnie close to the seat of Armstrong power, with access to the lancers from which he would build his empire of misrule. His brother Thomas, was older and held the real Armstrong power, but Johnnie had the greater charisma and drive within the family. Johnnie through his personal actions came to be viewed as the leading Armstrong, the clan chief in all but name.

After the Battle of Flodden, Scotland had a new monarch, James V, who at the tender age of seventeen months was too young to rule. The absence of a firm hand on government allowed many outrages on the Border to go unchecked. Johnnie took full advantage on the lack of policing and co-operation, and raided at will. Most reivers of any notoriety had a nickname, and Johnnie was no exception, being known as "*Johnnie the Strong*," and "*Black Jok*" – names that seem earned, and would have struck dread across the frontier. He was married to Elizabeth Graham (b.1506), a Scottish Graham in around 1523 and had at least two sons.

1. Christopher – (1523-1606)   **2.** Thomas

Johnnie's main source of income and annoyance was from racketeering, in which it is said (by Lindsay of Pitscottie) that from the Borders to Newcastle, every man from any estate paid him tribute to be free of his trouble. His blackmail business instilled a hardship on people's lives, driving many into poverty. The penalty for not paying his illegal rent would be a visit from Johnnie's heavies, who turned up unexpectedly and set fire to the poor soul's house, adding homelessness to the already asset stripped farmer. Johnnie was a big time gangster, and together with his gang was virtually untouchable as he made his regular cross Border missions. Johnnie's hunting ground stretched across Cumbria and Northumberland, and with pride it was stated that he never molested any Scottish people. Wherever Johnnie went, he was always accompanied with twenty four able gentlemen, all well horsed. Having this constant entourage illustrates Johnnie's status within Armstrong society, whether real or imagined. He saw himself as Armstrong royalty and at the top end of the tree. He was a figure which commanded respect from his followers and cast an intimidating power upon his victims. Johnnie took great pride in his appearance, and probably dressed heads to foot in black as the current fashion dictated. Looking well attired was important to Johnnie, and he certainly had the wealth to buy the finest of fabrics and keep up with the latest European trends.

Johnnie is first heard of on 25 August 1525, when he was granted lands in Eskdale and Dumfriesshire by Robert, 5th Lord of Maxwell. Later that year his name appears as the "signatory" on a bond of man-rent to Lord Maxwell "*at Drumfres, the second day of November, the year of God 1525 – John Armstrang, my hand at the pen*." Maxwell was the Warden of the Scottish West March, an influential figure who gave Johnnie his protection and a level of legitimacy. The documents signed in 1525 gave Johnnie the tenancy of lands around Langholm, the office of the Keeper of Langholm Castle, and the agreement to serve Maxwell in war and peace. Signing up Johnnie to the land would have benefited both Maxwell and Johnnie. Maxwell was ensured that Johnnie did not raid his own cattle and was gaining Johnnie's lancers as an ally. And Johnnie was also happy with the arrangement, obtaining Maxwell's protective might, and the hope that Maxwell turned a blind eye to his illegal business activities.

The Armstrongs made their first moves into the Debatable Lands in 1518. Johnnie seeing the opportunity for new lands jumped at the chance and built a tower at Hollows in 1526 between Canonbie and Langholm. Johnnie was a wealthy man with his very own lucrative protection racket business; this was his way of upgrading, moving to a high status tower to show off his affluence and physical power. All travellers crossing the Border could not fail to notice who the boss was. He now had a home in keeping with his wealth and power. This placed Johnnie onto the very edge of the frontier, with Graham friends just a few kilometres away in England. The stronghold though became instantly contentious with England, who claimed it was illegally built within the Debatable Land. Johnnie on the other hand refuted the allegation; the tower would stay and became the cause of many simmering disputes.

There is confusion to where Johnnie Armstrong actually lived; the most popular location is at Hollows Tower on the west bank of the Esk, and another named as Gilnockie Castle, 500m further to the SE and on the opposite bank of the Esk. It would be assumed that Johnnie lived at Gilnockie Castle, as it loaned him his title, however Hollows Tower is often referred to today as Gilnockie Tower, and also claims to have Johnnie as its most famous residence. The situation has caused historians a great puzzle, with the exact nature of Gilnockie Castle difficult to pin down. When Johnnie came to live in the Debateable Land, he either moved into this Gilnockie Castle directly, meaning that it already existed – and then proceeded to build himself a new tower at Hollows. Or he may have never lived at Gilnockie, only moving to the Esk once Hollows had been built. There is a small possibility that Johnnie built Gilnockie from scratch – and Hollows was a later addition. It is feasible that Johnnie had two towers; he did have the finances and the men to garrison them, and a brood of children awaiting towers in their own name. The title of Hollows though would take precedence over Gilnockie in importance. Johnnie wanted a residence to display his power and status, and Hollows was designed to do this – a more suitable home for a robber baron than Gilnockie Castle.

Nothing today remains of Gilnockie Castle. There is a thought that the name Gilnockie Castle is purely a recent attachment given to the site in a romantic tradition, but medieval earthworks illustrate that the area was once a very defensible stronghold. There are though some convincing clues that the site was indeed Johnnie's castle. The *"New Statistical Account Volume 9,"* compiled by the minister of the parish of Canonbie in 1836, provides the best information for the site being at least a castle, and that it was thought of belonging to Johnnie. He describes Gilnockie as *"situated near the eastward of Hollows bridge, upon a situation, which in natural beauty cannot be equalled in Scotland. It is in the form of an oblong square, extending in front about 60 feet in length, and at each end of the squares about 46, the height may be estimated at nearly 72 feet. It has two round turrets with loop-holes at each of the east and west angles, and is built of red sandstone, though now roofless, it must have been in former times a building of considerable strength."* The named Hollows Bridge was probably Gilnockie Bridge, built in the 1790s across the Esk (replaced in 1961); although another Hollows bridge was situated 0.5km further to the west on the Braid Burn. The construction of Gilnockie Bridge took some of its stones from the castle. One stone had upon it the initials "J.A." inscribed, and the image of an oak tree – the monogram of Johnnie together with the family emblem.

Gilnockie Castle was built in a very strong defensive position as would be expected. The castle sat upon a steep slope with a loop in the river protecting three sides, an ideal base camp for Johnnie's racketeering. Gilnockie Castle was either destroyed in the raid of 1528, or shortly after his execution in 1530, or in 1547 during the "Rough Wooing," and its name became lost from the landscape. Hollows Tower on the other hand still stands today, but dates from a later period as it was rebuilt after extensive damage in 1528 and the 1540s. The footprint of the tower though would be from Johnnie's time, and many of the stones from the original tower were incorporated in building the most current stronghold.

As a scourge of the Marches, Johnnie was most successful in cultivating his image at home. Johnnie stated that he only raided in England, and did not harm his fellow countrymen, a claim that does sound plausible. Archibald Douglas, 6th Earl of Angus held great influence in Scotland at this period; in 1526 he was appointed Lord Warden of the Marches and guardian over King James V, making him one of Scotland's most powerful men. Johnnie was reluctant to upset Angus, and signed a pledge for his good behaviour ensuring his compliance to the law. Johnnie may have abstained from raiding his Scottish neighbours out of fear of reprisal from Angus, rather than any patriotic sentiment or nationalism. Angus wanted to suppress the disorder and anarchy on the frontier which he feared could cause a war with England, and obtained a three year peace treaty with England. The treaty may have curtailed Johnnie's activities as it set out new laws to stop the cross-Border thieving of timber, granted safe-conducts for travellers, redress for the victims of robberies and the surrendering of criminals.

Despite the restraining effects of Angus and the Maxwells, Johnnie and the Armstrongs continued to be a national menace to England. Johnnie felt safe in Eskdale, with no need to fear attack from behind, and with his allies and watch posts, he could intimidate or out think any danger from the south. Johnnie built up his own followers forming a private army, which contained besides Armstrongs, many Elliots, Irvines, and Littles, obtaining a formidable reputation. He levied with flourish, blackmail over a considerable swathe of northern England. This flamboyant display of martial power however, was to be Johnnie's undoing – this type of force was supposed to be only in the hands of the monarchy, how dare a man such as Johnnie yield a similar status?

Moving so close to the English Border and his increase in missions, made him an unwanted addition to the area. It was as if an outsized rat had moved into the kitchen, the equilibrium of the English West March had been knocked out of sync. Johnnie had the Grahams as his neighbours, several of which were his in-laws and aided him in his illegal activities. The Grahams were the greatest racketeering family on the Border, and Johnnie would have fitted in just nicely.

Johnnie may have been involved with the Lisles in 1527, when that family joined in an alliance with the Armstrongs. The combined force raided into Northumberland however, the local inhabitants put up an unexpected resistance and gave the marauders a bloody nose. Several of the gang were captured and warded in Newcastle awaiting trial. Johnnie may have been one of those captured – or perhaps was amongst the rescue mission which was despatched later to release the prisoners. The rescue was a success, with nine being released. The Lisles threw in their lot as being English subjects and lived with the Armstrongs as broken men. The Lisles had nothing to lose and became magnets for other similar desperados. A reiver confederacy formed, with Sir William Lisle becoming the leader of the over-all gang. He made his first mission an attack on the property of Sir William Ellerker, with many Armstrongs in attendance and possibly Johnnie.

Another foray followed shortly, which had serious implications for Johnny, as it resulted in King Henry writing to James V expressing his concerns on the raiding, and obtaining permission for his English officers to enter Scotland and suppress the outlaws themselves. The Lisle's reign of terror soon came to a halt when a reward of one hundred marks was placed on Sir William Lisle's head. Henry Percy, Earl of Northumberland, demanded the handing over of the rebels otherwise he would bring destruction to Liddesdale and spoil every house. If Johnnie was a member of the Lisle's gang, the threats would have made him leave, and put a good deal of distance between their associations. Leaving the Lisle's confederation was a wise move, as the rounding up of the outlaws promptly followed. Fourteen of the gang were seized, ambushed at the village of Felton, a mixture of Lisles and Armstrongs. Justice was swift; they were taken to Alnwick in January 1528 and executed. Sir William followed later that month. Johnnie was careful not to be tarred by the same brush.

Encouraged by the reversal in fortunes for the outlaws, William, Lord Dacre (newly appointed as the Warden of the English West March), decided to continue in the battle – with the Lisles neutralised, it was the turn of the Armstrongs. Dacre desired to have the Armstrongs cleared from along the Esk for good, to push out all of the inhabitants and destroy their buildings. Dacre mustered an ample force for the expedition in February 1528, amounting to 2,000 riders which illustrates the scale of the problem that he was about to tackle. Dacre required this large number of soldiers in response to the expected Armstrong threat. A letter from the Earl of Northumberland in 1528 to London stated that *"the Armstrongs muster three thousand horse,"* and named Gilnockie (alongside Mangerton and Whithaugh) as *"enemies of the King of England, and traitors, fugitives and felons of the king of the Scots."*

The force was organised in secret, hoping to surprise and take Johnnie Armstrong, plus Sim the Laird, and others as prisoners. Everything looked good on paper, but no sooner than the English were setting off from Carlisle, an English Storey was relaying the details back to Johnnie. The balefires were lit, and the Debateable Land was primed and to horse. Johnnie led his followers south, accompanied by other Armstrong lairds and their allies. The gathered riders were all born to the saddle and knew the land intimately. Dacre and his troopers rode straight into a hornet's nest, with the Armstrongs pricking at the flanks of Dacre's men with their lances. Barriers were possibly put up to channel the invaders into single file, and fords were guarded to become ambush points. The Armstrongs used the land to their advantage and avoided a pitched battle. A series of bloody and well directed skirmishes entailed, which took its attritional toll on Dacre. Dacre's forces were mauled and bashed, slowing the advance to a halt – and with moral cracked, they were driven tail between legs back to their starting point.

Dacre wanted those responsible for the leak of his invasion into Armstrong territory caught, and sent out officials to search. The officials returned with Richie Graham of Arthuret, the son of Lang Will of Stuble, as their chief suspect. Richie was innocent of course, but as he had an Armstrong wife, was accused of having mixed national allegiances and passing on the information due to family loyalties. Richie was being made the scapegoat for Dacre's anger at failure. With chains fettered around his ankles, Richie was taken to Carlisle Castle on 23 March and indicted for treason – his future looked bleak.

Dacre though, was not beaten yet by the Armstrongs, he was soon plotting another expedition in March and had learned lessons on what to avoid. Dacre was now on the war path, he had been humiliated once there would not be a second time. Another expedition was mounted that same year, and on this mission Dacre was accompanied by an artillery train.

This expedition had greater success than the last, but again there was a security leak when Archie Graham, who was sympathetic to the Armstrongs, overheard the plans from a soldier, and passed the information on to Sandie Armstrong, who in turn told Johnnie. Dacre was happy at the progress of this second invasion, which encountered little or no resistance. Dacre was unaware that as he ventured north, Johnnie did the opposite, taking his Armstrong lancers south in a circuitous route over the moors and into Cumberland. Dacre suspected that his large force had intimidated the local inhabitants into a state of passivity, with the Debateable Land emptying itself of Armstrongs as he advanced – seeking the safety of the hills. With the opposition gone, Dacre would take great pleasure in destroying the Armstrong towers. The tower of "Ill Will" Armstrong was arrived at, and with considerable labour was cast down. On reaching Hollows a similar procedure of demolition was followed, Dacre lined up his cannons and open fired, pummelling the structure into rubble.

With the mission complete, a contented Dacre had his artillery train limbered up and returned to Carlisle, however the gloss of his satisfaction was soon tarnished and dented when he discovered what Johnnie had been up to whilst Hollows was being reduced. Johnnie had been given sufficient warning of Dacre's approach, but rather than attack Dacre or flee, he opted to abandon Hollows to its fate and make his own invasion. Johnnie and his followers formed into their raiding array and rode across the Border arriving at Netherby, which they plundered and set on fire. Their next target was a mill at Gilsland belonging to Dacre, which Johnnie and his gang took great pleasure in spoiling and returned with forty prisoners and a large head of cattle. Johnnie's cunning was more than a match to Dacre's brute force.

Dacre's mood took a further dip when he received the news that Richie Graham, who was languishing in Carlisle Castle awaiting his execution, had escaped on Sunday 29 March. The castle was a secure place to confine a prisoner, but a recent change in how Richie was held allowed him to break out. Sir William Musgrave, the under-sheriff, had a humanitarian streak and allowed Richie to attend church services and eat in the dining hall freely. He also had his chains taken off. Richie used this liberty to communicate with the outside world and planned his escape. At a pre-arranged time Richie approached a *"privy postern,"* and jumped out through to land in a field outside of the main walls. He was met by a colleague holding a horse, and mounting up he casually cantered off to freedom.

The loss to Dacre's property together with the audacity of Johnnie Armstrong went towards convincing both the Scottish and English governments to appoint commissioners to look into Border affairs. King James V wanted the renewal of a peace treaty with England, and Johnnie and the Liddesdale Riders were a serious obstacle to this deal. A solution was found when a proposal was made by England, to exclude Liddesdale from any peace treaty. This was agreed upon, allowing England to enter Liddesdale legally when tackling the outlaws. The Liddesdale reivers were now fair game by both Henry VIII and James V, there was now no hiding place – the happy hunting days for Johnnie and his gang were coming to an end.

Apart from the attacks on Dacre, there are no records of Johnnie taking part in any reiving raids, but there are frequent forays documented in which Johnnie possibly took part in. In May 1528 eight villages were destroyed in Cumbria on one fearful night, and on another raid seventy livestock were lifted and eight people slain. Retaliations were made against the marauders; Christopher Dacre, the English deputy warden, made a warden's rode against the Routleges in an attempt to stem the flow. The Routleges fled into the Tarras Moss for safety, with Dacre driving away their livestock. The mission culminated with a descent upon the homes of Johnnie Armstrong's sons, which were all set on fire. On the national scene, in September 1528 King James finally escaped from the clutches of Angus, and took up his full Royal power as monarch. Angus's influence in Scotland was falling fast, much to Johnnie's delight, having led at least six destructive expeditions against the Armstrongs. In May 1529 Angus fled Scotland to seek refuge with Henry VIII, an event which gave many Armstrongs a cause for celebration. Johnnie though was premature in his jubilation, Angus may have been devoted and fiery in his attempts to pacify the Border, but King James was a different kind of animal. James had a ruthless side which had not yet been experienced, and held a new enthusiasm to rule that would soon be released on the Kingdom. With Angus now gone, James was keen to put his ideas into practice after being held in check for so many years – he wanted *"to put gude ordoure and reule apoun thame, and to stanche thiftis and rubberis committit be theiffis and tratouris."*

In 1530, James at the tender age of seventeen, decided to flex his royal power into the Borders, and show his subjects that they now had a monarch on the throne that meant business and would not tolerate anymore disorder and crime. James was determined to pacify the Borders and ordered an expedition to be undertaken. He intended to *"proceed to the sharp and rigorous punishing of all transgression upon the borders"*... and to *"gar the rush bush keep the cow."* James desired to create a peaceful state of affairs; a reiver free Border where the only type of force required to stop a farmer's cow from straying would be a rush bush. This was of course naive thinking, from a youthful mind that had yet to tackle full on the reivers. The king had fresh ideals, and at his inexperienced age had not yet developed the cynicism of his elders regarding rule on the frontier. He was a believer in the divine right of kings, and was confident that all that it would take to bring the outlaws to heal was a firm hand.

James ordered an expedition into the Borders in the spring of 1530, which was under the command of his half brother, James Stewart, Earl of Moray. James was probably not present, but had briefed Moray fully on the goals and expectations of the venture. The success of Moray's expedition revealed to James the scale of the problem, making a second venture needed. Before setting off, James removed those lords and lairds that he thought responsible for the lack of law on the Marches. In an unprecedented round up, which began with the worst offender, the Earl of Bothwell, James ordered the detention of those he thought a barrier to his progress. James called a meeting of the Council on 19 May 1530, to discuss his expedition of pacification. The meeting included only the one Borderer, the provost of Lincluden, and it was decided that James would lead the venture, and make a great triumphal procession of hunting, feasting and law making.

With the go ahead, James put together an expedition with great energy, a magnificent show of power numbering as high as six thousand. Part police force and part sporting – the venture was designed to be both political and pleasurable, and at the same time to bring shock and awe to all the Borderers, both rich and poor. James knew the names of some of the most prolific offenders and targeted his route in their direction. Details on the royal progress are limited, and can be assumed to have been a mixture of summary executions and taking bonds of assurances. James also made time and space for relaxation, and for allowing the population to see their monarch. He summoned the earls of Argyll, Atholl and Huntly to his camp for a spell of hunting within Ettrick Forest. The area was rich in deer, where the party bagged an impressive total of 360 animals. The king's ardour in pursuing the outlaws seems to have dropped during the distraction of the sport, with a general reduction in ill feeling towards the thieves. James wrote a warm and friendly letter to Johnnie Armstrong from his encampment, and despatched it south in preparation for his visit in July, a taste of which is captured in the *"Ballad of Johnnie Armstrong."*

The King he wrytes a luving letter,
With his ain hand sae tenderly,
And he hath sent it to Johnie Armstrang,
To cum and speik with him speedily.

On receiving the invitation, Johnnie felt honoured and pleased that his status within the Border community had been recognised. Judging by the "loving" angle of the king's letter, only a positive joy can have been taken from the correspondence. The letter contained the king's wishes for Johnnie and his supporters to attend a royal audience at Carlenrig in Teviotdale, and probably included the option to join in with some deer hunting and other sporting activities. It is not sure if the fates of William Cockburn of Henderland and Adam Scott of Tushielaw were known to Johnnie, as the writing was on the wall on what outcome the reivers faced if they displeased the monarch. Johnnie though had no reason to fear the king, as stated earlier he had committed no crimes in Scotland and had the protection of Maxwell looking after his interests. Henderland and Tushielaw had preyed upon their neighbours, so were justified in being executed, but Johnnie was innocent regarding Scots law. Presumably a safe-conduct was offered to Johnnie, he was a master criminal after all. Pardons were also offered to all of those attending which clinched the meeting, having their life of crime in England wiped clean from the Royal slate and clemency given. Feasting and merriment was to be the theme of the meeting, and Johnnie was excited at the prospect. The earls of Argyll, Atholl and Huntly had already attended the king's hospitality, and now it was his turn. The new king was treating Johnnie like an earl, this was a great change of attitude, and the future interactions looked bright. Perhaps this Stewart monarch, the fifth of the line, was someone who the Armstrongs could trust. Johnnie summoned his main supporters, asking them to rendezvous at Langholm and to come clothed in their finest attire. They were meeting the king and had to dress like princes, fine wine and dining lay ahead.

The king meanwhile continued with his leisurely way south. He was at Peebles on 2 July and at Yarrow two days later, entering Teviotdale on 5 July. Carlenrig lay 14km south of Hawick, and sat between the Elliot strongholds of Binks and Falnash. On arriving, the royal progress set up their tents in the triangle of land made by the River Teviot and the Frostylee Burn, near to Teviothead and made themselves at home. The invitation of the king struck a chord with the Armstrongs. Depending on which source is taken, Johnnie gathered 36 (Lindsay of Pitscottie) or 48 (Bishop Leslie's 16th century chronicler) followers to make up his gallant company. They included two of his brothers, George and Robert, and many non Armstrongs – Scotts, Grahams and Elliots amongst them. The mood was celebratory as the various lairds and headsmen arrived at Langholm. As they waited on their scheduled time to meet the king, the company enjoyed some jousting on the holm of Langholm, and probably drinking and merriment. They were all pleased to be seeing the king, and turned out in their finest – the reiver equivalent of their Sunday best (as if the Armstrongs ever attended church). There was talk amongst the Armstrongs on welcoming the king back to Gilnockie in a return gesture of generosity, where they would feast on *"kinnen"* (rabbit), capon and *"venison in great plenty."* The high mood continued as the group left Langholm for Carlenrig. The prospect of forgiveness from the king for the family's blackmailing business, and crimes of reset and theft were looked forward to. They would be able to sleep sound in their beds thereafter without the fear of the monarch's wrath coming to hang them. The carnival atmosphere of the Armstrongs was not to last however, receiving a short nasty shock when they finally came face to face with James.

The meeting with the king took place as planned at Carlenrig, next to a 15th century chapel dedicated St. Mary the Virgin, a holy site that was about to witness an outrage of moral injustice. Johnnie would never have entered James's camp unless he felt one hundred percent secure. He rode in with all the pageantry that he could muster, perhaps with banners flying and the flourish of a trumpet. All was smiles, but rapidly displeasure and scorn was the mood. The king's feelings towards Johnnie can only be guessed at, and whether he intended to have Johnnie executed from the very start is not clear. There are two versions on what happened next; one that he was ambushed on his journey and taken to the king already a prisoner. And the second by Lindsay of Pitscottie, which states that the king only made up his mind on how to deal with the Armstrongs once they had met – and this sounds the most plausible. Pitscottie writes – *"He came before the king, with his forsaid number richly apparelled, trusting that, in respect of his free offer of his person, he should obtain the king's favour. But the king, seeing him and his men so gorgeous in their apparel, with so many brave men under a tyrant's commandment, frowardly turning him about, he bade take the tyrant out of his sight, saying 'What wants that knave, that a king should have'?"*

The evidence points towards the king as having no intention to harm Johnnie. First impressions are always important, and Johnnie's was an entrance that was one of the most provoking in history. James believed Johnnie to be little more than a bandit, and here he was dressed better than himself. The ballad states – *"When Johnnie came before the King, He weind he was a king as well as he"*... and was described as follows:-

> *John wore a girdle about his middle,*
> *Imbroidered ower wi' burning gold,*
> *Bespangled wi' the same mettle,*
> *Maist beautifull was to behold.*

> *There hang nine targats at Johnie's hat,*
> *And ilk ane worth three hundred pound:*

It is interesting to note the £300 *"targets"* hanging from Johnnie's hat. A *"target"* was a tassel, and made from gold or silver to have cost so much. If the ballad is correct, then Johnnie carried a value of £2700 on just his head, a phenomenal price tag. The value of Johnnie's entire clothing can only be guessed at. It is no surprise that the king was aghast at Johnnie's appearance. James remarked – *"What wants that knave that a King suld have, But the sword of honour and the crown!"* There was no sign of the normal reiver attire of quilted jack and steel bonnet, all bedecked in their courtly finery, the best fabric that money could buy. Silk bows, lace embroidery, jewellery, pearls, gilt, velvet and gold – the trappings of gentry and worn by criminals; the ill gotten gains of thieves being flaunted in the eyes of the monarch. James's blood boiled in seconds, an instant rage at the impudence and implications of all he surveyed. Johnnie introduced himself to the king with a dialogue that is captured in the ballad:-

> *"May I find grace, my sovereign liege,*
> *Grace for my loyal men and me?*
> *For my name it is Johnie Armstrang,*
> *And subject of yours, my liege," said he.*

To the backdrop of Carlenrig Chapel, the sorry sham of a trial took place. The king took the roll of judge, jury and executioner, and no witnesses were called forward to testify guilt or innocence. James was stubborn in his opinion, he wanted Johnnie executed, and there was to be no room for negotiation. A hostile rant escaped from James's lips which came as a shock to the Armstrongs...

> *"Away, away, thou traytor, strang!*
> *Out of my sicht thou mayst sune be!*
> *I grantit nevir a traytor's lyfe,*
> *And now I'll not begin wi' thee."*

There was no possibility of Johnnie fighting his way out of this ticklish situation; he would have to fall back on the reiver's famous sharp wit, and hope that he could talk his way back to safety. The king's reply was not what was expected – and a desperate dialogue ensued. Johnnie made great offers to the king on what he would receive if he spared his life – fine horses, the fighting services of twenty four bold men, the profits from twenty four wheat mills and the rents from his blackmail business.

"I'll gie thee all these milk-whyt steids,
That prance and nicher at a speir,
With as mekle gude Inglis gilt
As four of their braid backs dow beir."

"Grant me my lyfe, my liege, my King!
And a great gift I'll gie to thee;
Bauld four-and-twenty sisters' sons,
Sall for the fecht, tho' all should flee!"

"Grant me my lyfe, my liege, my King!
And a bony gift I'll gie to thee;
Gude four-and-twenty ganging mills,
That gang throw a' the yeir to me."

"Grant me my lyfe, my liege, my King!
And a brave gift I'll gie to thee;
All betwene heir and Newcastle town
Sall pay thair yeirly rent to thee."

All of the offers fell on deaf ears, with James repeating the same words over and over again...

"Away, away, thou traytor, strang!
Out of my sicht thou mayst sune be!
I grantit nevir a traytor's lyfe,
And now I'll not begin wi' thee."

Johnnie changed tact on his lack of success; he swore his loyalty and then protested that he had never robbed in Scotland or committed any crimes against his fellow Scots. He offered to bring his majesty any subject within England, duke or baron of his choosing, within any stated day to his person; dead or alive. This was no idle boast, and which probably did Johnnie more harm than good. James was concerned at not provoking a war with England, and here was one of his subjects offering his services which could potentially cause a breakdown in Anglo-Scots relations, with great loss of life and property.

The offers fell flat; James was determined to hang Johnnie and was in no mood to bargain. Lindsay of Pitscottie records Johnnie's final dignified retort as he was being led to the gallows, which has become the stuff of legends... *"He seeing no hope of the King's favour towards him, said very proudly, 'I am but a fool to seek grace at a graceless face. But had I known, sir, that you would have taken my life this day, I should have lived on the Borders in spite of King Harry and you both, for I know King Harry would down-weigh my best horse with gold to know that I were condemned to die this day'."*

The "Ballad of Johnnie Armstrong" reflects a similar sentiment, and contains one of greatest put-downs in literature, aiming at James the lines...

"To seik het water beneth cauld ice,
Surely it is a greit folie;
I have asked grace at a graceless face,
But there is nane for my men and me!"

He knew the game was up, and this was the end of his gallant company. In the ballad Johnnie says his farewells, which makes tragic reading; to his brother Christopher, son Christopher and his home at Gilnockie.

"God be withee, Kirsty, my brither!
Lang live thou Laird of Mangertoun!
Lang mayst thou live on the Border-syde
Or thou see thy brither ryde up and doun!"

"And God be with thee, Kirsty, my son,
Whair thou sits on thy nurse's knee!

The ballad ends with the sombre lines... making no doubt on the author's opinion of the event.

Ropes were then flung over the boughs of stout trees within the kirkyard, making gallows for the unfortunate Armstrongs. Johnnie and his followers without the basics of a trial were promptly hanged. It can be considered that the group had it coming to them, whether they were taken by treachery and murdered or not. It was a case of spontaneous rough justice. Bishop Leslie's 16th century chronicle documented the event as follows:- *"The King passed to the Borders with ane great Army: where he caused forty-eight of the most noble Theives, with Johne Armestrange their Captain, be taken; who, being convicted of theft, reiving, slaughter and treason, were all hanged upon growing trees."*

Not all of the gallant company were executed. One of the party was selected for special treatment, Sandie Scott *"a prowd thief,"* who had been reported as burning down a house which contained a woman and her children inside. In a case of poetic justice, logs were obtained and Sandy himself was burned alive. The death of Sandy, horrific as it sounds, should remind those who give Johnnie Armstrong and his riders a heroic gloss. Those who were executed no doubt were responsible for countless murders and despoiling of property and people. Six (another source says 12) of the men were spared execution, being kept as hostages, and would have had to endure the terrible scene, but at least their lives had been spared; or so they thought. The hostages were taken to Edinburgh and after a show trial all were hanged a few months later. Johnnie's brother Robert was amongst those who were hung, his other brother George though was spared. George was the only member of the party to return home; there was no obvious reason for not executing George as he was no better or worse than the rest of the group. The king pardoned George, reserving him to be kept alive so that he could return to Liddesdale and inform on what had happened. James wanted to traumatise the Armstrongs into submission, and force home strongly what occurs to those who defy the royal authority. Also within George's pardon, James wanted to leave a door open for forgiveness and coming back into the royal fold.

There is a legend that says another Armstrong survived the tragic affair, though of course has to be taken lightly. Archibald of Mangerton, a brother of Johnnie, supposedly managed to slip away and escape the king's soldiers as they closed in to apprehend the outlaws. Archie in great alarm rode back to Gilnockie and alerted his family, taking them off to the standard Armstrong bolt hole of the Tarras Valley. After the executions, the royal progress descended upon Gilnockie to finish off their pacification, and probably tore down the castle. A member of the king's party came across Johnnie's stables and fancied one of the horses for himself, a suitable trophy over their victory upon the thieves. The new owner of the horse got the shock of his life when he mounted, as the animal sensing danger went into automatic pilot mode, and took its rider off at full gallop to safety – to the Tarras Valley. The rider tried in vain to control the horse, which eventually came to a halt at the very place where Archibald and his family were hiding. Archibald was cutting wood for a fire when the horseman came into view, with little fuss he swung the axe and with a single blow, killed the rider.

The hangings were a foul deed foully done – a cruel betrayal. Lindsay of Pitscottie, within his *"History of Scotland,"* written within thirty five years of the event, records sympathy towards Johnnie – *"After this hunting The King hanged Johne Armstrang, Laird of Kilnokie, which many Scottish men heavily lamented, for he was a redoubted man, and as good a Chieftain as ever was upon The Borders, either of Scotland or of England."* The reality of Johnnie Armstrong and his gang should be kept in mind however, as they were master criminals and would stoop to violence at the drop of a hat. Johnnie's alleged patriotic activities against England are often brought up in his favour, but it was probably Maxwell's pressure which prevented Johnnie from raiding in Scotland. If Johnnie could have made a profit in Scotland from reiving, he would have done so for sure. He was certainly not missed in England, a chronicler recorded his passing with the words *"the Englisch people were exceeding glade when they understood when they understood that John Armstrong was execute."* His death would have been regarded in the same way as that of Al Capone's in the U.S.A. The demise of Johnnie is recorded in Pitcairn's Criminal Trials, though for some reason they have got the date wrong. The official justiciary record is brief and lacks all details of the trial as expected – as there was none. It reads with a simple stark grimness as follows...

Apr. 1. – John Armstrong, "alias Blak Jok", and Thomas his brother, Convicted of Common Theft, and Reset of Theft, &c. –Hanged.

The brevity of the entry goes to prove that the ballad was correct in saying that Johnnie had no trial. The lack of information plays a silent witness to there being no jury or judge present. And the mistake on the date of the execution being wrong implies that the record was filled in on hind-sight and by someone who had no knowledge of what had happened. It is interesting to note the crimes of Johnnies, common theft and reset (selling of stolen goods). There is no mention of blackmail, though this was not regarded as a crime until later in the century. Paying blackmail was illegal, but asking for it was not. As if reacting to the foul deed, nature put on her own display. The trees on which the Armstrongs were hung all withered and died. The ballad captures the scene:-

The trees on which the Armstrangs deed

Wi' summer leaves were gay,

But lang afore the harvest tide,

John Leyden captures the same image in his poetic fiction "Scenes of Infancy," from 1803...

Where rising Teviot joins the Frostylee,
Stands the huge trunk of many a leafless tree,
No verdant woodbine wreaths their age adorn,
Bare are the boughs, the gnarled roots uptorn.
Here shone no sunbeam, fell no summer dew,
Nor ever grass beneath the branches grew,
Since that bold chief, who Henry's power defied,
True to his country, as a traitor died.

The Armstrongs had taken a blow to their power, however if James thought he had ended the families reiving activities on the Border he was sorely wrong. James was mistaken in thinking his heavy handed justice would force the Armstrongs into obeying the Royal will, in reality the opposite happened. What little loyalty to the Crown that the Armstrongs held was extinguished, leaving a bitterness that could only begin to be healed after a spot of vengeance. In disgust at the betrayal and fear of further Royal persecutions, many Armstrongs migrated across the Border into Cumberland and lived in exile for a number of years. The Armstrongs had strong links through inter-marriages with the Grahams, and would gain a welcome hearth. They resumed their reiving and black mailing activities with a new vigour, free from the Scottish monarch's gaze. They made frequent return predatory raids into Scotland, and now that they were residing in England, had the protection of the Border against capture by James.

After removing the Johnnie Armstrong problem, the king's progress was not over; the procession turned east and travelled 6km to Priesthaugh on the Allan Water. The purpose of this journey is not recorded, but can be assumed to have been a meeting with the Elliots. Priesthaugh was in the possession of Robert Elliot of Redheugh, the clan's chieftain, who was a character that James desired to be brought under his control. Nothing is documented on what happened next, which indicates that Robert heard about the execution of the Armstrongs, and wisely failed to keep his Royal appointment. James returned to Edinburgh on 24 July, where he remained for the rest of that year. The consequences of the king's meeting with the Armstrongs were a public relations disaster. Many of the Border barons turned against James, rejecting his authority. James with irony came to be known as the "Prince of Lothian and Fife." Many Borderers lost trust in their king, becoming alienated to the House of Stewart. James would live to regret his treatment of the Armstrongs, when in 1542 he ordered his army on an invasion of England and came unstuck at Solway Moss. The Armstrongs refused to take part in the action, and as an insult they looted the retreating Scots army. Revenge was done for Carlenrig. King James died three weeks later from a fever brought on by grief it was said. James died thinking this was the end of the line of the Stewarts, and may have paused for thought on his treacherous treatment of the Armstrongs at Carlenrig Chapel, wondering if divine intervention was punishing him for his cruel murders.

There is a theory that Robert, Lord Maxwell, was responsible for Johnnie's death. Prompted by the idea that he was jealous of Armstrong power and goaded James's impetuous temper into a flame, persuading him to eliminate some of his rivals. Maxwell received on 8 July all of Johnnie's property and possessions just a few days after his death, which adds the motive for his actions. This conspiracy theory can be discarded, as Maxwell had granted those same tenancies to Johnnie some years earlier, and Maxwell was not present at Carlenrig, currently held a prisoner at the king's command.

The story of Johnnie Armstrong quickly made its way into literature and folklore, his death being the stuff of legends. Sir David Lindsay of the Mount wrote in his "A Satyr of the Three Estates," within a decade of the hanging, mentioning a knavish dealer in relics who is already peddling...

> *Ane coird, bath gret and lang,*
> *Quhilk hangit Johnie Armstrang.*
> *Of gude hemp, soft and sound,*
> *Gude halie pepill, I stand for'd,*
> *Quha ever beis hangit with this cord*
> *Needs never to be droun'd.*

Sir Walter Scott in "The Minstrelsy of the Scottish Border," observes that *"the common people of the high parts of Teviotdale, Liddesdale, and the country adjacent, hold the memory of Johnie Armstrang in very high respect."* Johnnie is well on his way to becoming a heroic Robin Hood-like figure. Moving into the 20th century, John Arden turned the familiar tale into a historical drama in three acts of Scots dialect prose. He added verse and songs and produced a play "Armstrong's Last Goodnight," which was first performed in Glasgow 1964, and was published in the following year.

The church at Gilnockie is now gone, which once stood in the centre of the old kirkyard. A plaque has been erected as silent testimony to the murder within its grounds, and in the adjacent field a single standing stone marks the mass grave of Johnnie and his followers. The manner of Johnnie's death created a great sensation; he was a great and notable thief, with a long and well earned name for terror. He reigned over the English West March as a virtual uncrowned monarch and lorded over his lawless clansmen. Johnnie's death was mourned by few, except for friends and kin. The method of his passing propelled Johnnie into immortality and a type of fame that was never expected; but the proud peacock within him would have surely enjoyed.

33. Canonbie

Canonbie was a village on the banks of the River Esk just above its confluence with the Liddel Water. The village was the main population centre within the Debatable Lands, settled by the Armstrongs, Grahams, Elliots and Bells. The Aglionby Platt map of 1590 has two towers illustrated which are associated to Canonbie and of interest; labelled *"ffrancie of Canobie"* and *"Davy of Canobie."* The towers were named after their owners, with the surnames of both Davy and Francis sadly lacking. Davy's tower is placed on the west bank of the Esk, and Francis on the east, adjacent to Halgreen.

Canonbie gets a mention within the poem *"Marmion"* by Sir Walter Scott, published in 1806. Canto V covers the exploits of young Lochinvar, who steals the hand of the bride of Netherby Hall, and is chased through Canonbie making good his escape in a high Romantic fashion.

> *There was mounting 'mong Graemes of the Netherby clan;*
> *Forsters, Fenwicks, and Musgraves, they rode and they ran:*
> *There was racing and chasing, on Cannobie Lee,*
> *But the lost bride of Netherby ne'er did they see.*
> *So daring in love, and so dauntless in war,*
> *Have ye e'er heard of gallant like young Lochinvar?*

✳✳✳

Thomas of Canonbie – (c.1578)

David – (c.1578)

James – (fl.1583)

William – (fl.1583)

Thomas was the father of David, James and William. David was held as a pledge by Robert Keith, Commendator of Deer in 1578, to ensure the good behaviour of the family. Thomas was possibly a son of ill Will's Sandie. The three sons of Thomas are mentioned within Thomas Musgrave's list of the Border Riders in 1583, coming under the section on the *"Offspring of 'ill Wills Sandy'."* They are named as:-

1. *Dave Armestronge, called Dave of Kannonby, marryed Patyes Gorthes Grams doughter*
2. *Wille Armestronge his brother*
3. *Jeme his brother*

$$* * *$$

David (Dave) of Canonbie – (fl.1583)

William (Wille) – (fl.1583)

James (Jamy/Jeme) – (fl.1583)

This family group of Armstrongs, David and his two sons, turn up in Thomas Musgrave's list of 1583 on the Border Riders within the section on the *"Offspring of 'ill Wills Sandy'."* The marriage of David Armstrong was of interest to Musgrave, noted as – *"Dave Armestronge, called Dave of Kannonby, marryed Patyes Gorthes Grams doughter."* A marriage to a Graham was problematic for the West March Wardens of England, as the Armstrongs could use their family connections to slip easily across the frontier.

James, alone crops up within a set of bills for the period 19 July – 6 October 1583, on the subject of *"Raids on the West Marches by Liddesdale,"* to address a raid in which he took part in. The complaint upon him was made by Dick Rowtledge of Kirkleventon, who together with his son, *"were maymed and wounded in perill of death,"* at the herschip. The bill went as follows:- *"Jock Armstronge called Kynmonth* [Jock], *Jock Armstronge of the Calfhills, Jamy of Cannonbie, with their complices* [to the] *number of xx persons* [for] *xx kye and oxen, two naiges, all his insight."*

$$* * *$$

William – of Canonbie – (fl.1642)

William's name, noted as *"of Cannabie,"* surfaces within a list of accused thieves who were to be apprehended and tried in 1642. The motley crew of Armstrongs and other surnames were not reivers, just common brigands, and the short change from the criminal class of society.

34. Woodhouselees

The tower sat on the west bank of the River Esk, just opposite where the tributary Liddel Water joins – Canonbie was 2km to the south and Sark Tower 6km away to the West. Woodhouselees was built by Alexander Armstrong (Ill Will's Sandie), the father of Kinmont Willie. Alexander had done well out of his association with England, becoming a pensioner to King Henry the Eighth and was given lands in Cumberland as a reward for his good service. The Armstrong's popularity in England would explain why they were tolerated so close to the Border in the 1540s, a state of affairs in which Alexander was keen to exploit and construct his legacy in stone and prop up with his sons. Woodhouselees was in a strategic position at the Esk-Liddel confluence, and from its bale-fire the Liddel Valley could be given advance warning of incoming raids. Woodhouselees was an excellent hub of communication for the Armstrongs. Those coming and going through the Liddel Valley could be checked and monitored, and the general north-south traffic of kings, lords and armies observed.

As the place name suggests, the stronghold was originally of timber construction, possibly a block house. There is no proof that the tower was upgraded to stone, but there is a small quarry SE adjacent to the site, a possible source of material for a peel. Today all that remains of the site is a circular gravelly mound, with a flattish top, measuring about 20m in diameter and 1.5m in height, about 250m SW from Woodslee House. The circular cairn could be all that is left of a collapsed log framed clay bonded house. Or perhaps this is not the side of Woodhouselees at all, but is located on the site of the modern Woodslee House.

The tower's name was spelled in several different ways. Noted as "*Woodhously*" in Pont's map of c.1595, and "*Withisleis*," in the Aglionby Platt map of 1590; and intriguingly the stronghold was known as the "*Site of Kinmont Tower*," within the 1854-1858, Ordnance Survey, six-inch 1st edition map of Scotland. This raises the question of where did this second title of Kinmont come from? A source for place names often came from the nearest geographical feature, which suggests that the rising ground behind the junction of the Liddel and the Esk was called Kinmont. Perhaps the name derived from the French, "Mont" (Mount/Hill), and kin, referring to kinsman / family. Putting the two together, we have the mount of the Armstrong family, which sums up the territorial ambitions of ill Will's Sandie – poised at the edge of one valley and looking into another. There is an actual place in Annandale called Kinmount, but this originates to the Carlyles who were granted a charter by William de Brus in the 12th century. The property was owned by the Douglas Family from 1733, being renamed Kenmount, the ancient seat of the family of Douglas, of Kilhead. The present Kinmount House was built in 1812 for John Douglas, the 6th Marquis.

Another possibility is the Old English word "*Cynemann*" – meaning a royal man; but surely outlaws were never going to be the king's men. A more plausible theory comes from the name deriving from the Middle English word "*Kineman*" – the occupational term for a cowhand. If this is the correct origin, then with immense irony one of the greatest cattle thieves was named after herding cows. Taking the same "kine" (cow) idea further, the raised area of the mount could have been used as a viewing platform to count cows as they were driven past into Liddesdale – and the name

"Kine-mount" developed. The location was geographically ideal for splitting up reived herds and taking stock of what had been looted.

On the opposite side of the river was the tower of "*ffergus grame*," depicted on the 1552 map of Cumbria, as a tower called "*ye mote*," and on the Pont's map as a house called "*The Mote*." This was probably a stone tower rather than a wooden motte, taking its name from a nearby Norman motte and bailey. Fergus of the Mote became a great friend of the Armstrongs, and was probably a regular guest at Woodhouselees. He had a large family of eight sons; with the most notable being Richard of Brackenhill who held a great blackmail racket and took part in the rescue of Kinmont Willie in 1596. He also had at least two daughters, one married into the Armstrongs of Calfhill and another married young Hector of the Harelaw. Another relation, Andrew of the Mote, was part of the initial team who put together the Kinmont rescue, and would go on to betray them all – much to the annoyance and threats of violence from Brackenhill.

✳✳✳

Alexander (Sandy) – "Ill Will's Sandie" – "Evil Wullet Sandie" – (c.1530/50s)

Sandy was the son of William ("Ill Will") of the Gingles, and judging by his nick name "*Evil wullet*," inherited his father's bad temper and cruel nature. He was contemporary and an associate to Johnnie Armstrong of Gilnockie, the two can be imagined to have been great friends. And both desired property in Eskdale. Alexander was possibly one of the first Armstrongs to move into the Debateable Land in around 1518. The construction of a tower at the river confluence was dynasty building, establishing the family name in the area. Woodhouselees was both strategic and political, an ideal base camp from which to spread the family influence.

Sandy, with good fortune was not present with his father at Carlenrig in 1530, an event which traumatised the family and reinforced their dislike of authority to a level of hatred. With his father and Gilnockie gone, Sandy's status within the Armstrong society increased, with many of the clansmen looking to him for leadership. The Armstrongs were curtailed for a few years after their main leaders had been cropped off. A concern that King James would make this type of expedition a regular feature of his reign was most worrying. The Armstrongs though regained their confidence quickly and resumed their raiding. The family were an excellent buffer with the English; King James would always want such hardy militaristic men on his frontier, an excellent deterrent to the casual invader. Sandy always fostered a mistrust of the Scottish government and a deep animosity for the English, which he passed onto his brood of sons. He rebuilt Sark Tower and used stone to create a more substantial axe and fire proof building.

Sandy, recorded as "*Evil-willit Sandy*," was listed on 21 February 1536, at a trial in Edinburgh for two separate raids in which he had taken part in during the previous year. The first was for a raid on 27 July 1535, in which one hundred cattle were stolen from John Cockburn, the Laird of Ormiston, from his the lands of Craik. The raid also involved Thomas Armstrong, alias "*greneschelis*" (Greenshiels) and Robert Carruthers, both were servants of Simon Armstrong ("*Sim the laird*") of Whithaugh and certain Englishmen. The second foray was on 28 October 1535, with the raiders charged for "*art and part of the traitorous FIRE-RAISING and BURNING OF THE TOWN OF HOWPASLOT.*" Sandy was accompanied again by Thomas of Greenshiels, and various attached servants, common thieves and accomplices, plus the addition of Robert Henderson alias "*Cheys-wame*" (Cheese belly). On this occasion the gang lifted sixty cows and oxen belonging to Robert Scott of Howpaslot (Howpasley), and left the farm town in flames.

Strangely, Sandy was not the main concern of the authorities on these raids. The focus was on Simon Armstrong (Sim the laird) of Whithaugh, who was a thorn in the side of both Scots and English. Sandy was described within the documents as "*Alexander Armstrong, called Evill-willit Sandy, a sworn Englishman.*" It is interesting to read Sandy defined as being English; this was the typical reiver relationship to nationality in action – eager to change allegiance to suit family fortunes. Sandy resided in Scotland, but when on trial in Scotland he claimed to be English in the hope of avoiding a trial. If the English authorities pressed charges upon him, he would claim to be Scottish. Sandy was an expert at playing one side off with another. Simon of Whithaugh was accused of the "*art and part*" in giving treasonable assistance to Sandy and sundry other Englishmen. Helping reivers to commit their forays was classified as March Treason and the evidence was mounting to find Simon guilty. The verdict was given on the same day as Simon's trial, on 21 February 1536, he was found guilty and sentenced to be hanged. Sandy, the cause of Simon's treason, was free to ride away, seemingly unharmed by the accusations.

Sandy was eager to take English gold in 1543 as an "assured" Scot, when Sir Thomas Wharton came recruiting for lances to advance King Henry's political agenda. For the next few years Sandy raided his fellow Scots and profited well. He took part in the Battle of Ancrum Moor and swapped sides to avoid defeat – becoming Scots when he pleased. In February 1547, Sandy took part in Sir Thomas Carleton's raid into Dumfriesshire as a paid mercenary. During the campaigning which centred round Dumfries, Sandy took an active role. The campaign began well, but resistance under Maxwell caused concern and a strategic withdrawal. Sandy's advice was asked for by Carleton, on a suitable strongpoint to capture and occupy as a base camp for future operations – he answered with the suggestion of Lochwood Castle. Sandy was well placed to give such guidance, with great experience both on Border politics and warfare. Lochwood was the Johnstone family's chief seat and would be strongly held, though at present the castle was under garrisoned and Sandy thought a determined attack could gain entry without much difficulty. His choice was also based on a personal agenda, to settle old scores of bad blood between the Armstrongs and the Johnstones. Sandy and his followers travelled with Carleton's forces to Lochwood, reaching the tower an hour before dawn. The assault was professionally undertaken by a chosen squad of twelve men, who climbed over the castle's barmkin at night and captured the central keep by surprise in the morning. The castle was well supplied with food and would act superbly as an English bastion of political influence. Carleton returned to Carlisle soon after reporting to Wharton, and placed Sandy in command of the castle in his absence.

Sandy continued to play a role in the politics of England over the next few years. Tensions arose to boiling point between Scotland and England the following year, when King James V mustered a large army and ordered them south. Sandy probably received the king's summon to join his mighty host and took great satisfaction in tearing it up. James had executed his father; he certainly would not fight and possibly die for that deceitful monarch. The campaign ended in the disastrous defeat at Solway Moss, which Sandy probably watched with fascination on the opposite bank. Sandy saw the opportunity for plunder as the Scots soldiers broke ranks and routed back across the Esk, becoming overjoyed at the prospect of inflicting revenge upon James. The satisfaction can be imagined as Sandy and his followers took what they wanted from the supply wagons of James's army. Sandy no doubt added to his wardrobe and gained a few fine horses for his stable. James it is said, died of a broken heart a few days later, on 14 December at the age of thirty. Sandy took the news as divine justification for his sins. James would have to face a purgatorial payback for his wrong doings against the Armstrongs, a thought that put a wry smile on Sandy's face.

In August 1550 Sandy's loyalty to the English Crown paid off, when his tower at Sark came under threat from Lord Maxwell (Scottish West March Warden). The Debateable Land was in the process of being un-debated, when a commission was set up to make a permanent and visible border. Maxwell took the opportunity to be rid of certain Armstrong elements, those of which had a habit of being English when they wanted. Maxwell led a force into the Debateable Land to demolish all habitation, and Sandy's tower of Sark lay on their list. Sandy lacked the men to put up any protection, but had the time to contact the Council of the North for help, and they ordered Dacre to step in. Dacre did not want to create an international scene, and wanted to help Sandy, but at the same time did not want to offend the Scots. His solution was ingenious, he took his men up to Sandy's tower, and heaped it full of peat and turf within the barrel vaulted ground floor – and then set it on fire. The intention was to fill the tower with smoke and prevent it from being entered. The tactic worked, Maxwell arrived with gunpowder to raze the tower, and had to abandon his intended plans.

The Debateable Land was no more debated on 24 September 1552, when the "Scots Dyke" was completed. It was only 5.25km long and about one metre high, but the purpose was political not defensive. Those living along the dyke would now know if they were Scottish or English, though none would have cared much. Sandy, by one km, was now officially Scottish – but he would always be an Armstrong first and a Scot second.

Ill Will's Sandie had a large brood of sons, four of which – Ninian, Robert, Thomas and William, were known as the wildest of all the Armstrongs; an epithet which took a lot of beating and made the quartet of sons a truly terrifying bunch indeed. They were known to use Wauchope Castle as a hideout, which was in a bad state of disrepair and had seen better days.

Children:-

1. Herbert (Ebye) of Woodhouselees – (fl.1583)	**2.** William of Kinmont – (b.c.1530 – d.c.1605)
3. Robert	**4.** Ninian (Rinion) – Laird of Ralton (Gingles)
5. Christopher – "Sandy's Christie" – of Auchingavill	**6.** Alexander (Sandy) – of Gingles
7. Fergus – "Sandis Fergie" – of Kirtillheid (Kirtlehead)	**8.** David
9. John (Jok) – called "Wallis"	**10.** Hector of the Gingles
11. Thomas	At least one daughter

Herbert (Ebye) of Woodhouselees – (fl.1583)

Herbert was a son of Alexander Armstrong (Ill Will's Sandy) and brother of Kinmont Willie. He appears in the 1583 Musgrave list of the Border Riders, within the section titled *"Offspring of 'ill Wills Sandy',"* and named as *"Ebye Armestronge the goodman of Waddusles."* A goodman was a landowner who held his land from a feudal vassal of the king, and not directly from the Crown. Herbert probably took over the running of the tower when his brother William moved to Sark / Morton.

35. The Score

The Score sits on the east bank of the White Esk (a fork on the River Esk), between Clerkhill and Rennaldburn, near to Eskdalemuir. This location for the Armstrong's dwelling however poses some doubts, as it lies 21km NW of Langholm, away from the main Armstrong territory, and the Score was occupied by the Batison/Baty/Beattie family. There is a second Score though, which is more likely to have been the location of the Armstrongs stronghold, and is named within Thomas Musgrave's list of the Border riders in Dec1583, in which he describes the Esk and its feeding tributaries into England and the sea:-

"Eske is a fayre ryver, and cometh throughe Esdall, and is Scottishe, inhabyted with Battesons of Esdell, untill it come neare a placed called the Langhalme castill and meateth with the water called Use, which waters and dales are bothe my Lorde Maxwells untill it come to Canonby kyrke, and then the Armestronges and Scottishe Graymes have it untill it meete the ryver of Lydall at the Mote skore, where Fargus Grayme his howse standes."

The Mote was a stronghold owned by the Grahams, who were allied to the Armstrongs. They even had an oak tree on their coat of arms, in a similar form to that of the Armstrongs. It is possible that the Armstrongs developed a grayne at this English location, only a stone's throw away from their seat of power just across the Liddel at Woodhouselees.

John of the Score – (c.1590)

John attended a Warden's Truce Day at the *"Belles Kyrk the xiiith of Aprill 1590,"* appearing before William Fenwick, the deputy for the warden of the Middle Marches of England, and Thomas Trotter the deputy for Lord Bothwell, Keeper of Liddesdale. Under one of the Middle March bills for Liddesdale, was a raid that John took part in:-

"Alexander Hall of Wodhall and Thome Hedley of the Neatherhowses, complain upon Gawine Ellott of [?], Hobbe Ellott larde of the Burneheades, Will Ellott of Fidderton, John Ellott of Bohomes, Arche Croser 'Henhead,' 'Quintins Arche' Croser, John Armstrong 'John of the score,' for reaving 30 kye and oxen, 6 horses and mears, about 2 July 1589."

36. Morton

Morton Tower once stood on the east side of the River Sark, 1km north of the Anglo-Scots frontier and the Scots Dyke. The tower has went under several names, known as "*Mortoun*" on Pont's map c.1595, "*Kinmont's Tower*" on the Aglionby Platt map of 1590, and Sark Tower. There was a sizeable community at Morton, with a mill, blacksmith, church and farmsteads. The parish church of Morton was first mentioned in 1171, when its granting to Kelso Abbey was confirmed. Judging by the attitude of the Armstrongs to churches, it has to be wondered how it faired sitting within one of the greatest heartland areas for outlaws. Nothing can be seen today of the tower or church; the stones of which were used to build the Tower-of-Sark farmhouse.

✳✳✳

William (Willie) of Kinmont – (b.c.1530 – d.c.1605)

Better known as Kinmont Willie – William Armstrong of Kinmont is arguably the most famous of all the Border reivers. The Armstrongs were the Borders number one raiding family, and William was its most destructive member. He certainly deserved his reputation, a larger than life character who feared no one and raided on a grand scale. Even during Kinmont's day, his contemporary's held him in awe – and for good reasons. Kinmont rode from the front, and preferred to ride openly and by day. He was a charismatic leader who regularly led forays of three hundred riders into Tynedale on a routine basis. His targets were not single farms and steadings but whole areas; Kinmont operated on a big range leaving swathes of land in flames, taking away all that pleased him, including prisoners and slaying all that came in his way. His name would be a by-word for terror across much of the English West and Middle Marches, with villagers dreading the pounding of hooves and the glint of lances upon the horizon. Kinmont possessed a rare mixture of courage, strength and intelligence – which together gave him the attributes to hit hard and avoid capture at the same time. Kinmont planned his raids with an inborn instinct for detail; his successes built a reputation which formed a loyalty in his followers, and a desperate fear in the targets. He respected no authority, being a constant problem to both the Scottish and English monarchs – and was the curse of Henry, Lord Scrope, and later his son Thomas, as they struggled on how to cope with his depredations.

William of Kinmont was the son of Alexander Armstrong (Ill Will's Sandie) and the grandson of William Armstrong ("Ill Will"). The father of "Ill Will" was Thomas, 5th Laird of Mangerton, placing Kinmont high up the scale of Armstrong royalty. The exact date of Kinmont's birth is not known, but was between 1530 and 1540, with 1530 the most common estimate. 1530, if correct would be a symbolic date for his birth, as this was the year in which James V hung his grandfather, along with Johnnie Armstrong of Gilnockie. Kinmont always had a distrust of the Scottish monarch and authority in general, and it would be appropriate if he were born into this mind frame from the very second of birth.

Kinmont as a young man lived at the tower house of "*Withisleis*" (Woodhouselees) as a tenant of Lord Maxwell. Kinmont later moved to Sark Tower, which probably occurred on the death of his father. Kinmont's new home at Sark was sometimes referred to as Kinmont Tower, his title following him – with his old residence retaining the name of Woodhouselees. Kinmont's brother Herbert (Ebye) took over the tower's keeping on his departure, and was mentioned in 1583 as "*the goodman of Waddusles.*" Herbert married Katherine Dalston, and had at least three sons – David, Sandy and William. William was noted as living in England and "*enjoyeth that land that Kinge Henry the Eight gave old Sand Armestronge.*"

Family was everything for the reivers, and with the Armstrongs this was exceptionally so. On marriage, Kinmont had to be careful to choose a partner which would bring him and the Armstrongs useful profitable collaborations – that is if he had a choice at all. Love and romance could have been way down the list on who to marry, with his father calling all the shots, and he probably organised the very betrothal. William's choice of bride was a Graham – the daughter of Hutcheon Graham, which was the logical direction for a Border Armstrong to take, the Grahams being their closest neighbour and also English. William would obtain excellent inside intelligence on the activities of the English West March Warden, and hopefully advance warnings of approaching raids. He would also obtain a trouble free passage for his riders into England on forays through the areas of Hutcheon's influence.

A sister married George Graham (also known as Thomas Gorthe Graham) of Esk, and a daughter of this couple would go on to cause concern with Scrope, as she married Thomas Carleton, the Land Sergeant of Gilsland and Constable of Carlisle Castle. The unions were both mentioned within Thomas Musgrave's 1583 list of the Border Riders – "*Gorth Grame marryed Will of Kynmontes syster, and Thomas Carlton that seketh all the dispyte agaynst me, marryed his doughter.*" Further ties with the Grahams were obtained when a daughter of Kinmont married Fargus ("*Forge*") Graham, the son of William Graham ("*Ryches Will*"), whose father was Richard of Netherby.

Kinmont was hand-in-glove with the Grahams, and was on good terms with Thomas Carleton – which all added up to Kinmont having his feet firmly planted in both Scottish and English camps. He could be English when it pleased him, and Scottish when eluding Scrope. The link to Carleton spelled great danger to the English West March, were an alliance of sorts was formed with Kinmont which benefitted both parties. Thomas, together with his brother Lancelot, formed one of the most corrupt double acts on the Border. They even out did the Musgrave brothers (Thomas and John) for slyness and treachery, which took some devilish underhanded behaviour to achieve. The brothers were indeed dangerous men, and rose to positions of power and trust within the Border's law officers, a situation that increased the level of criminality they committed. Thomas Carleton would turn a blind eye to Kinmont's raiding, and give the occasional wink when danger beckoned – and in return, Kinmont agreed not to raid Carleton's property, and give him a cut of the plunder. It was not unknown for Scottish reivers to stop over at safe houses in England, and Carleton may have offered this to Kinmont. Carleton and Hutcheon Graham came into their own when Kinmont was captured in April 1596, and played key roles in obtaining his release – an event which catapulted Kinmont into eternal fame, and will be discussed later.

The earliest mention of Kinmont is contained within the "Register of the Privy Council of Scotland," where he is named as one of the principal members of the Armstrong clan. Under the date 22 October 1569, William, known as *"of Morton Tower,"* was entered as a pledge for himself and kin, promising to obey the wardens, and have Lord Maxwell as surety. Another entry on 5 March 1570, relates to Kinmont making a submission in respect of a feud between himself and Thomas Turnbull of Bedrule. Kinmont was said to have been *"the starkest man in Teviotdale,"* and was a man of great size and strength. William had his own gang of reivers, a group of loyal riders which he could call upon at any time to go out on a raid. His gang was called "Kinmont's Bairns," which at its core as the name suggests contained his sons, plus a host of broken men who had gravitated to Kinmont for protection, misfits cast into the Debateable Land. The gang had a paternal bond to their leader, which extended beyond Kinmont's own immediate family. This gathering of desperadoes was arguably the most destructive gang of reivers operating on the frontier. Kinmont and his sons brought together as many as three hundred men to their calling, and were the curse of the English Border. The gang raided almost at will deep into England, striking terror wherever they went, becoming known for slaying those who put up resistance.

From the documents that survive, William was first recorded taking part in a raid in about the Midsummer of 1579 – he was born to the saddle and would have been out on forays as soon as he could yield a lance. He was named in a complaint by *"Thomas Dod of Thorneborne, John Dod of the same, and Lyell Dod of the Blacklawe"* for taking part in a day foray alongside Syme Armstrong, the young laird of Whithaugh, Rynion and Eckie Armstrong of Tweeden, and another 400 men. This impressive raid of cut-throats was made up of Kinmont's gang plus at least one other from the Whithaugh grayne, resulting in a force that was unstoppable. The raiders lifted forty score (800) of cattle and a thousand sheep and goats – a considerable tally. And in the process of thieving, the Armstrongs slew Uswold Dode, who put up a brave but hopeless resistance to having his livelihood taken away from him.

Kinmont was middle-aged at the time of this raid and at the height of his power; backed by his sons and at the head of one of the Border's most successful gangs. Those who tried to limit or even halt the regular raiding had a whole stack of difficulties lined up against them. The size of the problem is illustrated in a letter from Scrope to Walsingham on 28 September 1583, composed when Scrope was fed up of the constant depredations. He made a complaint about the *"manye and almoste nightlie attemptates"* that had been committed in Bewcastle and elsewhere within his wardenry by the riders of Liddesdale and West March of Scotland – *"speciallie Kynmonte his sonnes and complices."* A large part of the problem was the lack of will from the Scottish authorities to bring legal action down upon Kinmont. Scrope commented on the Scottish raiders, who *"are neverthelesse at their pleasure conversaunte and in companye with the warden, and on no parte reprehended for their doynges."* Scrope was also severely undermanned and lacked the resources to do his job properly. He writes – *"I therefore pray you to hasten the supply of the 100 horsemen, the need being so great, and I will plant them in the best places for defence, also that money be sent for their pay from time to time."*

The English Border put up the best resistance it could against Kinmont's gang. A report on the "Rules for defence of the Borders" from June 1583, named *"Rokele Castle"* (Rushcliffe Castle), the farthest west of the Border strengths, belonging to the Barony of Brough (Burgh-by-Sands**)**, as a key point in the defences. Provisions were to be put in place, as kept in William, Lord Dacre's time, to have 100-200 armed guards out at night, especially on the fords and at ebb tide *"to prevent the thieves of Greteney, Redhawle, Stilehill and other the Debatable lands of Kinmowthes retinue, which commonly ride through the barony in the night to the in country."* The other great bastion of defence at Bewcastle was in a sorry state of affairs, and not exactly up to the job of stemming Kinmont's Bairns. A memoranda on the Borders from 1584 stated – *"Bewcastle in defenceless condition, owing to the feuds of the Graymes and Musgraves lately happened."* One hundred soldiers from Berwick were planned to be sent to Kershopefoot to assist in the keeping down of the Armstrongs and Elliots.

Kinmont features of course within Thomas Musgrave's list of the Border Riders compiled in 1583. William was listed under the heading of the *"Offspring of 'ill Wills Sandy'."* "Ill Will's" Sandy had such an impact on the English West March, that it was thought worthwhile to keep a wary lookout on his children. His offspring were sure to follow in his father's boots; this would lead to another generation of trouble – and multiplied by the number of sons. To be forewarned was to be pre-armed.

1583 saw Kinmont raiding down the Tarset Valley, carving a swathe of fire and theft along its length. The raid took place on 30 August and was large scale – Kinmont had the men and liked to flex Armstrong power. The raid left in its wake Bartrame Mylburne of the Keyme (The Comb) and Gynkyne Hunter of the Waterhead in Tyndale to make their complaints to the authorities. The complaint named Kinmont first, with more than a suspicion that he was the mastermind behind the raid. The raid was the Kinmont's Bairns in their full action attack mode – and described as; *"to the nomber of thre hundrethe parsons in warlyke maner ranne one opyn forrowe in the daye tyme, on Frydaie in the mornynge last, beinge the xxxth of August, in Tyndale unto certen places."* The main participants in the raid were named as – *"William Armestronge of Kinmowthe, Eckye Armestronge of the Gyngles, Thome Armestronge of the Gyngles, Thomas Armestronge called Androwes Thome, of the Gyngles, Johne Forster sone to Meikle Rowie of Genehawghe, George Armestronge, called Renyens Geordie, and his sons, of Arcleton in Ewesdale."*

The raid took the following route – *"the Reidhewghe, the Blacke Myddynes, the Hill howse, the Water head, the Starr head, the Keyme, the Bog head, the High feelde."* The devastation that the Armstrongs reeked was deep and all penetrating, the bill issued later captures the scene well – *"and there raysed fyer and brunte the most pairte of them, and maisterfullie refte, stale and drave awaye fowre hundrethe kyen and oxen, fowre hundrethe sheip, and goate, xxx horses and mears, and the spoyle and insyght of the howses to the valewe of towe hundrethe pounds, and slewe and murdered crewellie six parsons, and maymed and hurte ellevin parsons, and tooke and led awaye xxx presoners, and them do deteigne and keip in warlyke maner, myndinge to ransom them contrarie the vertewe of trewes and lawes of the Marches."* And with great justification, Bartrame Mylburne and Gynkyne Hunter sought out the March Warden and – *"Wherof they aske redres."*

One year later, the same Tarset Valley was targeted by Kinmont. Perhaps hoping for similar spoils to the last visit or having found the area a soft touch and with more to thieve – he led three hundred men on a day foray into Tynedale.

The victims of the raid were the same as before, with Jenkyn Hunter and Bartie Milburne of the Keam reliving the old horrors as before. They filed a complaint on the raiders, together with their neighbours Jarrie Hunter, Mychaell Milburne and Lante Milburne. The complaint was made upon *"Davye Ellot called 'the Carlinge', Cleme Croser called 'Nebles Cleme', Thome Armestronge called 'Symes Thom', Will Armestronge called 'Kynmothe',* [and] *Ecktor Armestronge of the Hilhouse"*. The gang *"took away forty score kye and oxen, three score horses and meares, 500 sheep, burned 60 houses, and spoiling the same to the value of 2000L. sterling and slaying 10 men – at Michaelmas 1584."* Having two such large raids back-to-back must have driven the inhabitants of Tarset to anger and desperation, fearing a winter of starvation – though redress was hopefully forthcoming for their losses. Fines were demanded from Kinmont's gang, but cash compensation could only go so far – the trauma for the Tyndale locals of losing loved ones, would be a more difficult problem to overcome. This was the stuff of nightmares; the problem was always going to exist, causing stress, fear and hyper-vigilance to infiltrate the community for years to come. Also in 1584, Scrope made an offer to Ker of Cessford to deliver him two Grahams who had been troublesome, in exchange for Kinmont and his son Jock. Cessford turned down the transaction.

Matters on the Scottish West March came to give Henry, Lord Scrope concern in 1585. He writes from Carlisle on 10 March to Walsingham on friction between the Earl of Morton (John 8th Lord Maxwell) and the Laird of Johnston. A feud was already in progress between the Maxwells and the Johnstones, but had recently entered a higher brutal phase with the addition of allies helping out the Maxwells, which included the Armstrongs. Kinmont had a son and a friend who were *"in warde in the pledge chamber"* in Dumfries, an arrangement made by Johnstone for the good behaviour of Kinmont and his family. Kinmont's involvement in the Johnstone-Maxwell feud was nil, hobbled by the pledges. This situation though had changed, both of the pledges had recently broke free and were presented before Morton, who set them at liberty, an action which Kinmont was grateful as can be expected. Johnstone no longer had a hold over Kinmont, who now allied himself to Morton. Scrope writes on the situation – *"By this meanes Kynmont and all his freindes bynde them selves to the Erle; and truelye I am perswaded that a great number of the borderers of that contrye will joyne them selves unto him against the Larde Johnston. So as great troubles are there lyke to aryse emongest them selves and suche as the Larde Johnston will be hardelie hable to susteyn without speedye relieff from the King. And I doubt his being able to have the borderers obedient to answer justice."* Scrope saw trouble coming, and ends on the ominous note, *"whereby evil doers will be encouraged."*

The predicted trouble was not long in coming, just a month away. Kinmont joined Robert "the Bastard" Maxwell (illegitimate half brother of John 8th Lord Maxwell), who led a force of four hundred into Johnstone territory in early April and targeted the Johnstone main seat of Lochwood Castle. Lord Henry Scrope reported on 7 April 1585, that the castle was taken and set on fire, and with irony how Lady Johnstone would now have *"a light to put on her hood"* – a touch of destruction that Kinmont may have been responsible for. The mayhem would continue; on 27 April 1585, Scrope wrote from Carlisle to Walsingham stating *"The troubles of the opposite borders doe still contynue and encrease, for even of late, Robert Maxwell with Kynmontes and their complices, have brent almoste foure skore howses of the Larde Johnstons his tenauntes and freindes, and have made spoyle of a great deals of victuall, catle, and insight. And albeyt the same was done xx myles within Scotlande, yet was there not any parson that made resistance."*

April 1585 was not all fire and steel for Kinmont, he did find space for social activities. Kinmont was recorded attending a horse race – noted perhaps by Henry, Lord Scrope, who was gathering information against Thomas Carleton. The document reads, *"On Easter Tuesday last at a horse race in Liddesdale, Thomas Carlton talked secretly with the Lairds of Maingertone, and Whithawghe, and Will of Kinmoth."* The race was probably held on the flats opposite Whithaugh Tower, where the village of Newcastleton sits today. Carleton wanted to sell a horse belonging Humphrey Musgrave to Mangerton, and was using the race as a ruse to have the horse legally in Scotland, and for Mangerton to see the quality of it. The horse was called "Bay Sandforth," and performed well, winning all the races in which it was entered. Mangerton liked the performance of the horse and bought it. Kinmont watched the races with excitement, wondering if he could do the same as Mangerton and purchase a similar fine animal. Carlton that night returned home to Askerton and the next day he *"ranne the bell of the Wainerigge."* Kinmont, together with his brother Robbe and other Scotsmen travelled with Carleton to Naworth and stayed overnight. The talk was all horses, which picked up the theme from Liddesdale. Kinmont and Carleton must have been friends, as he bid overnight in his castle, and was likely wined and dined in proper Border hospitality. On leaving Naworth, Kinmont gained an extra horse to his party, named "Gray Carver," which had once belonged to Lancelot Carleton. The animal was probably the topic of conversation over the past two days, after Kinmont had seen Mangerton buy a powerful horse. Perhaps Kinmont felt jealous and did not want to be out done, purchasing his own fast horse to keep up with his neighbours.

The violence against the Johnstones continued into May 1585, with the Armstrongs helping the Maxwells to spoil and burn the town of Lockerbie and a wide swath of land six miles across in Dryfedale. On 17 June 1585 Kinmont was present when Lord Maxwell besieged Bonshaw Tower belonging to the Irvings. A brave defence was put up in which two or three of the attackers were killed and four were wounded, resulting in the siege being lifted.

It was not only England that suffered at the hands of Kinmont and his Bairns, on one occasion the Armstrongs had the opportunity to take their thieving into the very heart of the Scottish government. In 1585 the Earl of Angus organised a campaign against the Earl of Arran, and raised a party of men planning to ride into Stirling and dislodge James Stewart, Earl of Arran, from his powerful influence over King James VI. The banished Lords from the Ruthven Raid of 1582 got on board, and soon had a motley crew of cut throats and desperados assembled. Francis Stewart, 5th Earl of Bothwell, Lord Maxwell (Earl of Morton), Lord Home and Ker of Cessford all joined in. Kinmont and his Bairns were only to eager to help out, invited to attend through Kinmont's association to Maxwell. This was just the kind of battle that Kinmont revelled in – a soft target, with little fighting and a lot of plunder. Stirling was not accustomed to the ways of the Border reivers, and would not have the defensive systems of hill top balefires, hot trods and bastle houses. Kinmont put out the muster for his Bairns, and put together his gang which included his seven sons, his brother Fergie, and ninety two others. Kinmont was also accompanied by Robert Makillwitty (MacVitie), who was referred to as his "writer." Robert was a legal clerk, and presumably held a position of some importance to be on the raid. Robert would have a firm grasp of the Border Law, and his sharp legal wits probably kept Kinmont on the right side of the law. Living on the Debateable Land, help to debate law cases was essential; a service which was essential to keep Kinmont out of the clutches of the warden. Kinmont's son Francis, could not write, so it is possible that Kinmont was also illiterate, and required a scribe to do his letters and official documents.

The purpose of the raid was political, but Kinmont had other matters on his agenda. Kinmont's riders joined Maxwell, combining to make up a force of 1,300 foot and 700 horse. They journeyed to meet up with the other rebel lord's and formed a small army numbering around 5,000 men – more than enough to intimidate the opposition. They camped for the night at St. Ninians on 1 November 1585, and entered Stirling early on the following morning. The occasion was a great thrill for the Armstrongs, to be in the very presence of the monarch. This would be the ultimate reive if they could pull it off. Here, the Armstrongs were under a mighty raiding force and at the seat of Scotland's power; they could basically do and take away whatever they wanted. David Moysie recorded in his memoirs that there was a *"great reaf of horsse and guidis be William Kynmonthe and his bairnis."* It is interesting to note Kinmont targeting specifically horses, and that no other individuals or clans are mentioned as reiving. David Hume the Scottish historian, documents that after the surrender of Stirling, the Armstrongs decamped and helped themselves to as many horses of their fellow allied invaders as they could lay their hands on. The Armstrongs were even noted as carrying off the iron gratings from the windows of houses, something that must have taken their fancy.

The casualty rate for the raid was reported by Moysie as *"thrie or four on baithe the sides,"* which is surprisingly low when considering that the armed riders were a possible danger to the monarch. The raiders caught Stirling by surprise, unknown to the moonlight foray of the Borderers; they would not have expected the clash of steel and the clump of a horses hoof in the wee small hours. The mission succeeded with Arran escaping by boat and King James pardoning the rebel Lords, giving them their forfeited estates back. Distrust of Bothwell and Scotland's unruly lords though would be a constant worry to James, an experience which was remembered and went towards shaping his later policies regarding the outlaws and war in general. With irony, James reaped revenge heavily upon the Armstrongs after 1603, perhaps from the seeds planted in the king's mind from that day. There was one new name on the block however – Kinmont; who was previously only known along the frontier, was now made infamous at the very centre of Scottish power. His name became a byword for violent crime. Kinmont was not a casual thieve, but a major robber baron, his status was there for all to see, with a new set of victims who had just become acquainted to his Bairns.

By 1587 Kinmont and his sons were at the peak of their powers, and had a small army at their command and beckoning. Such was the nuisance that they caused on both sides of the Border that King James was compelled to launch his own force to curtail Kinmont's raiding. James descended upon Dumfries intending to make an example of the Armstrongs and his ally, Robert Maxwell (half brother to Lord Maxwell), leading a royal progress that was lacking in nothing. James also intended to clamp down on Catholicism in the West March, which was beginning to make a dangerous revival. The Maxwells had connections to Spain, from where a great armada was sent in the following August to invade England. Kinmont's network of allies kicked into action as the king approached, and he was given advanced warning of the danger. Robert Maxwell considered Kinmont as a friend, and they stuck together in their collective danger. The forthcoming clash was too much to contemplate (possible political and military suicide), and putting discretion before valour, Kinmont and Maxwell took to the Tarras, and evaded the Royal wrath.

When Henry Carey, Lord Hunsdon took up the post of Warden of the English Middle March in 1587, he inherited the problem of Kinmont. On 18 October 1587 Hunsdon wrote from Berwick to Burghley reporting on a raid in which Kinmont had led – "*Syns my coming hither, their came 400 horse to Hawden brigges* [Haydon Bridge on the South Tyne] *and tooke upp the towne and burnt dyvers howsys.*" Hunsdon commented on the Scottish king as being "*verie angrey*" at the news. However later "*Wyll a Kilmott, who was the principall man,*" visited the king at his cabinet, where strangely there was not the expected reprimand. Rather than punish Kinmont, "*att his departur the King gave him 100 crownes.*" The award of 100 crowns explains much on why the Border was in a disordered state, at this treatment of a noted outlaw. With despair at the situation, Hunsdon summarised – "*What justis wee are to looke for att the Kinges hands, lett her Majestie judge! Their is no waye to bring them to any order but feare, and therfore if yt maie please her Majestie to send this 1000 men but for one monethe, I dought not but to bring them to justis – otherwise, nott.*" It is no wonder that Kinmont continued on with his criminal life, with the lack of a political will to rein in his gang.

Kinmont was involved in two raids in 1592...

1. Nov 1592

"*Roger Bulman of Skailby, uppon William Armstrange called Kynmontes Willie, Christie Armestrange called younge Christie of Barneleishe, Thome of Rowanburne, &c., for taking 11 kye and oxen, 4 stottes, a whye, 2 mares, and mutilating the complainer.*"

2. 17 Nov 1592

"*Walter Calverleye of the Holme Coltram, upon Kynmontes Jock, Kynmontes Wille, Christie Armestrange of Barneleish, and 27 persons for taking and keeping him prisoner, also a mare price 24L., 2 horses, 10L., a gold chain, jewels, gold, silver, writings and household stuff.*"

Kinmont took part in his largest recorded raid on 6 October 1593, when his gang combined with William Ellot of Lareston, Martin Ellott of Braidley and the Laird of Mangerton, who all together mustered a force 1000 horsemen strong. The raiders came from Liddesdale, Eskdale, Annandale and Ewesdale, making up a mounted army which was unstoppable. The reivers "*ran an open day foray in Tynedale and drove off nine hundred five score and five head of nolt, 1000 sheep and goats; 24 horses and mares, burned an onset and a mill, and carried off 300L. sterling of insight gear.*"

Lord Forster reacted promptly to the threat posed by the raid, he wrote to Burghley on 19 October 1593 describing the scene – "*Whereon I at once ordered the gentlemen of the country by special letters, to be ready on an hour's warning, and keep their usual watches day, night, and plumpe watches.*" Forster then sought immediate redress; this raid took the Border forays into a new terrifying dimension and needed to be brought to heal. Forster explains to Cecil his attempts to halt the mass Armstrong / Elliot intrusions... "*Hearing that the King was at Jedburgh, I sent my warden sergeant with letters to Mr Bowes the ambassador craving redress, and also sent my son Nicholas Forster to the King and council demanding justice, who appeared before them on Monday last and stated the facts. The King protested it 'was done contrary his pleasure', and his present visit to the Borders was to see justice done and good order kept, promising to send me answer on Friday next after."*

Forster was still asking for the immediate promise of redress to be made in 8 November of that year – stating in a letter *"therefore I require present delivery for the outrageous attempt, and that the opposite warden may be directed to hold meetings for mutual justice according to the treaty of peace and lawes of the Marches."* Forster felt frustrated at the lack of progress in obtaining a trial / fines for Kinmont's raiding, and probably suspected the king was delaying the redress on purpose, hoping that he would forget all about it. Border relationships had been strained, with Forster seeking better means of communication. Forster's request to increase vigilance on the Border started to show results the following year when, Lord Thomas Scrope received inside information which had the potential to catch Kinmont red handed. He wrote from Carlisle on 31 October 1593 to Burghley, explaining his recent exploit – *"On information sent me of an intended day foray to be made by Will of Kinmont and his complices on Monday last in Northumberland, I commanded my constable Thomas Carlton to lie in wait for their return ; but they not having held their journey, it fortuned that on his return homeward, he lighte upon two notorious evildoers to England – one an Englishman called Carrocke, the other a Scotsman nicknamed Bungell, and took them."* Kinmont probably had his own spies out, and got wind of Scrope's ambush plan and cancelled his raid. Scrope however was compensated for his work, in netting two other reivers of worth.

Kinmont was the number one reiver that Scrope wanted stopped. He was getting worried for the safety of the Border with winter approaching in 1594, which was the Riding season – another concern was that the Scots had not appointed an officer to attend warden meetings, which delayed the carrying out of justice. Scrope in desperation appealed directly to King James, asking if he would *"appoint an officer against him to provide for quietness till the evil of the winter be past."* James gave Scrope a helpful reply, stating that he would seek assurances of good behaviour from Kinmont. This proactive action by Scrope had a bad side effect however, as going direct to the king put Buccleuch's nose out of joint. Buccleuch had recently become the Keeper of Liddesdale, and took a violent exception at Scrope going over his head by-passing his authority. Scrope and Buccleuch were similar in character; both were young and ambitious, and saw themselves as soldiers. Buccleuch took the snub as a personal insult on his efficiency as a warden. There was little love lost between the pair, with a tension of resentment storing up that was sure to blow.

Scrope wrote to Cecil on 4 December 1594, to express his feelings:-
"Finding great delay in the King establishing an officer opposite, and also backwardness in redress, it seems to me good policy to provide for quietness till the evill of the winter be past. And it has been thoughte profitable to drawe an assurance (such as hath bin here accustomed in tymes of like necessitie) from Kynmont the cheife of the Armestronges of Scotland, who is a great clan or surname and suche as have and maye greate outrage her Majesties subjectes. This assurance for him selfe and surname is travelinge, and Kynmont had sent unto me a cattalog of the names of his branch and partakers to the number of 300 persons verie nere, who all shoulde be contayned within the assurance, if they might have such condicions as they tendered to acceptance. The motion of this assurance proceedinge from Kinmont upon his owne accorde, I thoughte meete to use for an advauntage to entretaine tyme – and therefore sent for the

Kinmont's reputation by 1596 was such that merchants in Edinburgh on hearing rumours that he was coming to sack their town, took evasive action in preparation. The merchants hurriedly cleared their shops and booths of all valuables that could be spirited away, and with great foreboding shuttered up to weather the storm. The approaching spectre of *"Will Kinmonde, the common thieffe"* and his gang of *"rank riders,"* was all a false alarm, but his very name was enough to send Scotland's capital into a panic. Scrope sought assurances from Kinmont as the way forward, and to bring the three hundred Bairns under control. Negotiations were undergoing, and Scrope felt hopeful at a positive outcome. He had a lot at stake, not wanting the repeat of another one thousand lancer raid descending. The outcome of the request for assurances did not reach any conclusion, and was interrupted by a diplomatic incident which both solved the situation and spoiled it at the same time – the capture of Kinmont in April 1596.

Kinmont would have went down in posterity as just one of the many reivers who raided big style; one amongst another fifty others – the Armstrongs of Mangerton and Whithaugh, the Elliots of Lariston and Redheugh. However one evening in the spring of 1596 catapulted Kinmont into folklore and legend, and guaranteed his name to be remembered as one of the Border's premier reivers. The event was of course his imprisonment and rescue from Carlisle Castle. The venture began innocently enough, when Kinmont attended a Truce Day on 17 March 1596 at Dayholme, 3km upriver from Kershopefoot. The Truce Day was hosted by two deputy wardens, Robert Scott of Haining for the Scottish West March – and Thomas Salkeld for the English West March. It is not sure if Kinmont was present just to observe the proceedings, give evidence or to be charged. Kinmont was easily recognizable and known to everyone; he would have strolled amongst the English officials secure in the knowledge that he could not be arrested. It was the law at Truce Days which gave all those present immunity from prosecution so that they could safely attend, lasting from sunrise on the day of the event until sunrise of the next. Rising tensions though were a common occurrence at Truce Days, as known thieves freely roamed in full view of their targets and those who were responsible for arresting the criminals. Both Scots and English attending, were hard pressed not to trade comments and insults, especially as alcohol was often present, on sale at stalls which were set up to provide refreshments. From what followed later, it seems most likely that Kinmont goaded the English party before heading for home, especially Salkeld, as he was the main authority figure.

The Truce Day ended without incident, and the various contingents headed for home. Kinmont trotted homeward accompanied by Robert Scott, the Scottish deputy warden, chatting merrily, parting company when they crossed the Liddel Water. Kinmont continued south west with three or four riders in his party, heading towards his tower of Woodhouselees where he intended to spend the night. Riding along the north bank of the Liddel Water, Kinmont was shadowed on his travels by Salkeld, who rode parallel on the opposite bank journeying into England. Verbal sparks flew across the river, probably a continuation from an earlier spate of insults. Kinmont would have given back more than he received, bating the English from his position of security. Kinmont had no respect for any national authority, and enjoyed venting his opinions across the Liddel, free in the thought that he could not be arrested. The idea to capture Kinmont must have been a spur of the moment decision, as the action was totally illegal. The opportunity to capture Kinmont was limited, as once the junction of the Liddel with the Esk was crossed, Kinmont would be at Woodhouselees and safety. The temptation of Kinmont being so close to the English, but yet so far, became difficult and then impossible to resist. Eventually Salkeld's men's patience snapped, with tempers flaring they seized their opportunity and splashed across the Liddel to give chase. It is not sure if Salkeld ordered the capture, but he probably gave it a nod and a wink, and a party of two hundred riders broke off from the main cavalcade and forded the river in haste. Kinmont was no doubt mounted on a fine horse, as he was an admirer of such beasts, and spurred off for the Esk in all the haste that he could muster. Salkeld's men were also well mounted and soon caught up, and after a short struggle, their tormentor was captured. Kinmont was bound and pinioned like a common malefactor, having his legs strapped securely underneath a horse to avoid him escaping. The party then escorted Kinmont to Carlisle, where he was taken to the castle and presented to Lord Scrope. And so began the most celebrated "incident" in the long and turbulent history of the Anglo-Scots Border.

Kinmont's capture became the subject of perhaps the most well know of all the border ballads – "The Ballad of Kinmont Willie," a piece of literature that took Kinmont from the Borders of the 16th century and into the wider consciousness. The ballad contains an exciting telling of his capture, incarceration and rescue. As a piece of literature it effectively gives the story of the rescue, however being fiction it can't be trusted as historical evidence. Sir Walter Scott collected the ballad when on his tours into Liddesdale, and printed the works within his "Minstrelsy of the Scottish Border" in 1802. The ballad has the extra problem of more than likely being tampered with by Scott, who added his own flourishes to the drama. The ballad is full of Scottish and Scott propaganda, but on the positive side it does capture the spirit and essence of the event despite being pompous in places.

The ballad starts with the opening verse...

O have ye na heard o' the fause Sakelde?
O have ye na heard o' the keen Lord Scroope?
How they hae ta'en bauld Kinmont Willie,
On Haribee to hang him up?

The scene was set, the three main characters except Buccleuch are named – and the danger at stake is made clear. Salkeld is made out to be the villain in the ballad's very first line – to be false. Here Kinmont is the bold, and not Buccleuch; and Kinmont faces the gallows, creating tension and the heroic. In reality Kinmont was not facing execution, the line added as artistic license, inserted to raise the level of tension. Kinmont's capture is retold in the second and third verse...

Had Willie had but twenty men,	*They band his legs beneath the steed,*
But twenty men as stout as he,	*They tied his hands behind his back;*
Fause Sakelde would never the Kinmont ta'en	*They guarded him, fivesome on either side,*

Wi' eight score in his cumpanie.   *And they led him ower the Liddel-rack.*

Kinmont was taken to the keep of Carlisle Castle, where he met Lord Scrope. Kinmont's reception in Carlisle can be imagined – with Scrope both thrilled and aghast at this windfall. Scrope knew what had just occurred was illegal, but he wanted to push his luck and try and nail a conviction on Kinmont, or at least obtain a pledge/bond of assurance while he had the opportunity. Words were exchanged between the two adversaries, as both sized each other up. In defiance of being captured, the ballad has Kinmont say...

"My hands are tied, but my tongue is free,
And whae will dare this deed avow?
Or answer by the Border law?
Or answer to the bauld Buccleuch?"

To be replied by Lord Scrope... And Kinmont's response:-

"Now haud thy tongue, thou rank reiver!   *"Fear na ye that, my lord," quo' Willie:*
There's never a Scot shall set thee free: *"By the faith o' my body, Lord Scroope," he said,*
Before ye cross my castle yate,   *"I never yet lodged in a hostelrie,*
I trow ye shall take farewell o' me."   *But I paid my lawing before I gaed."*

Kinmont had been taken during a Day of Truce, which broke Border Law, so technically Scrope did not have a leg to stand on legally in arresting him. An explanation on why Kinmont was taken was quickly made up; the Musgraves advanced a story that they were with Salkeld on that day, and went in pursuit of some outlaws who had just raided Bewcastle. A reiver called Blacklock was recognised and pursued, who ran to ground at the house of Peter of the Harelaw. The Musgraves approached the tower tenderly, where they discovered Kinmont Willie within to their surprise. Kinmont was alleged to have tried to raise the country against them with shouts of *"A Harelaw, a Harelaw."* The Musgraves felt themselves to be in deep trouble, in Armstrong country and with a chief Armstrong calling for help. In self defence the Musgraves stated that they were forced against their wishes to take Kinmont into custody and deliver him to Salkeld. The story seems possible, however it was totally made up – and was soon dropped as an alibi by Scrope. Scrope felt compelled to write up a more plausible report on 18 March 1596 to justify his apprehension of Kinmont, and to silence those who would be later shouting their complaints...

"How Kynmont was taken will appear by the copy of the attestation by his takers, which if true, it is held that Kynmont did thereby breake the assurance that daye taken, and for his offences ought to be delivered to the officer against whom he had offended, to be punished according to discreation. Another reason for detaining him is his notorious enmity to this office, and the many outrages lately done by his followers. He appertains not to Buccleuch, but dwells out of his office, and was also taken beyond the limits of his charge, so Buccleuch makes the matter a mere pretext to defer justice and do further indignities."

The excuse given by Scrope for this breach of Border Law is an exceedingly lame one. Scrope begins his letter with the question "if true," suggesting that he did not believe Salkeld's version of events, and that Kinmont was not guilty of any transgression on that day. Scrope claimed that Kinmont had broken the assurance on the day he was captured, but fails to say how he broke it. Surely if Kinmont had broken an assurance, Scrope would be exclaiming it loudly to everyone. And he made no mention whatsoever of the Blacklock story. There is no doubt that Kinmont more than deserved to suffer the utmost penalty of the law for his misdemeanours, but the same could be said about every other man who was present at Dayholme. If Kinmont had not felt safe at attending the Warden's Court, he would never have gone. There was an overwhelming desire by Scrope to deal with Kinmont once and for all. Border Law existed for a reason and was even extended to protect the greatest offenders when required. Salkeld had clearly violated the law, and Kinmont was entitled to walk out of the castle a free man.

As a prisoner, Kinmont was destined to be locked up within the dreaded dungeon of the keep. The keep was initially begun by Henry I of England in 1122, and finished by David I of Scotland in around 1135. Its solid walls of red sandstone fifteen feet thick where a formidable obstacle to any attacker. The castle's prison was on the ground floor; a windowless, airless dark and dank room which contained the ominous "licking stone," a stone which gathered moisture and was licked by the inmates to quench their thirst. Many a reiver would have spent their last hours on Earth languishing in this soul sapping confinement. To rescue Kinmont from this prison was beyond the capabilities of any hit-and-run expedition. Even if Buccleuch managed to get into the keep, the prison door was another obstacle to overcome, and the risk of alarming the castle garrison was very real. Once alerted, soldiers would be bearing down along the confined corridors blocking the exit of escape. It was a mission beyond the call of duty.

The rescue was impossible to mount with the resources that Buccleuch held however, there was a chance of hope as Kinmont was not your average prisoner. Fortunately Kinmont was not treated like a common criminal fit for the gallows; he was held in a type of house arrest within the castle's outer ward. The fact that Kinmont was treated in this manner is evidence that Scrope was intending to release him eventually when the political situation was right. Deep under, Scrope knew that a mistake had been made, but could not admit it for the current moment. He would seek to make the maximum damage with Kinmont, and play it by ear on his ultimate fate. Some myths about Kinmont can be removed about his imprisonment. Kinmont was never in danger of being hung at Harraby Hill as the ballad suggests, and he was not chained up. These were all lucky factors for Kinmont, making it possible for Buccleuch to rescue him; avoiding having to tackle the inner ward with its ditch, half moon battery, gate house and curtain wall. And lacking manacles, Kinmont could be spirited away fast and quietly.

A war of words soon erupted between Buccleuch and Scrope, as Buccleuch tried to secure Kinmont's release. Buccleuch's concerns also lay on the infringement on his own powers, a proud man of action who had recently been made Keeper of Liddesdale. Scrope tried to fob Buccleuch's complaint by stating that it was now too late for him to undo what was done, and matters now required the Queen's consent. Buccleuch eventually came up against a bureaucratic stone wall. It was the son ("young" Hutcheon) of Kinmont's father-in-law, Hutcheon Graham, who kick started the plan to take a rescue mission to Carlisle Castle, with a suggestion to Buccleuch; to attempt action were talk had failed. The help of the Grahams was essential for any rescue to have the slightest chance of success, as the route south for the Scots would pass entirely through Graham territory. The Armstrongs had been marrying into the Grahams for the past three generations, and a workable network of alliances had been laid in place to ensure smooth operations. The family link to the Carletons was also essential otherwise the final route from the Debateable Land and into the castle itself would have been impossible. It was Buccleuch who gave the green light to the rescue mission, and a small but select group of plotters sprang into action. An excellent network of connections and spies on the English side of the Border, reported back that the castle was surpriseable, which was welcome news to Buccleuch. The mission was on.

A meeting at Archerbeck sealed the rescue, where Buccleuch met up with the key players, a motley crew of Scotts, Grahams and Armstrongs – plus the Carleton brothers Lancelot and Thomas. Buccleuch learned from a woman spy (which could have been Kinmont's wife) that Kinmont was being held in a *"hous"* and not a proper prison or the castle keep, the news bid well for the rescue. The Carleton's had inside power and knowledge of Carlisle Castle, and without their help the plan would have been dead in the water. Thomas Carleton shared a dislike of Scrope, having been dismissed from his post as the Constable of Carlisle Castle that same year, and was eager to seek revenge upon him – this raid was the very antidote. Thomas may have been a secret accomplice on Kinmont's forays, making shady deals in return for his services. A day was chosen for the rescue – Sunday 13 April, and all retired with a promise to return on the day before the mission, choosing Langholm race course as the rendezvous point. Kinmont would be freed.

Preparation was everything. Kinmont knew that he was going to be rescued well in advance of the event taking place. The Carleton brothers had access to Carlisle Castle and rooted out those who could be of assistance to the plot. Buccleuch loaned a ring which was then smuggled into the castle and brought to Kinmont. Scrope was aware of the incident and wrote on 14 April 1596 to Henry Leigh stating – *"Also the sonne* [a Graham] *of one of them brought Buclughes ringe to Kinmonte before his losinge, for a token for his deliverance by him."* Kinmont's wife visited him also, a letter by Richie's Will Graham stated, *"There was never a turned done fornenttes the lowsing of Kinmont, but thur men was all counsel to it and causit Kinmontes wife, quha is Androwes sister, make it all with Kinmont within the howse."* Buccleuch's hit squad was mustered under secrecy, the less who knew about the raid the better. There would be no lack of enthusiastic and talented manpower to aid Buccleuch, Kinmont's own sons were obviously eager to be involved. Kinmont's gang were now leaderless, and his children without their father. Four of his sons signed up for helping out – John, Francis, George, and Alexander. Scrope found out about their involvement on 14 April and documented them in a list under the title of the principal assailants at the raid. Kinmont's Tower at Morton was used as a base camp to cache the necessary equipment for the rescue – ladder, crowbars, food, and weapons; and would be the gathering point for the bulk of the riders. The ring leaders though were to meet up with Buccleuch at Langholm race course, a location chosen so as to avoid suspicion. Nobody would suspect the Scotts, Armstrongs, Elliots and Grahams coming together in one field at the same time during a horse race, as being up to no good.

It was only ten miles to Carlisle from Morton Rig, where the Armstrongs prepared a late supper as the riders waited nervously on Buccleuch arriving. Around eighty riders were gathered in the rain, on an overcast "dreich" night with no moon to guide them. At around two am the call went out to saddle up, and with cloaks fastened, the party rode out into the mirk. The route was a straight forward case of following the Esk south, all obstacles in the rider's path having been neutralised. The party travelled in three groups; at the front was a reconnaissance party to scout the land ahead and check that the route was clear. This probably consisted of mainly Armstrongs. In this patriarchal society, Kinmont's loss was felt deeply by many Armstrongs, seen as a figure head. Every Armstrong able to ride a horse would have offered their services to help out. Behind the scouts came the assault party, carrying the ladders and other tools to gain access to the castle. And finally in the rear was Buccleuch himself, with the main body of the group. If something went wrong, the brains behind the operation had plenty of time to be warned and flee to safety. It was their necks that were on the line if captured, taking on a castle of Queen Elizabeth held untold risks. With a quiet air of confidence permeating the party, the riders crossed the Esk in total darkness – good practice for crossing the Eden later. The foray was one of the oddest that the Armstrong's had ever attended, their objective was not money or cattle – but a fellow reiver.

The journey went without mishap, thanks to the thorough planning by the Grahams. The main obstacle though came just before arriving at Carlisle – the River Eden. The bridge was an important crossing point, and as such had permanent protection against the outlaws. The bridge had armed guards and iron chains stretched across its width. The river would have to be crossed at another point; an intimidating prospect, shrouded in mist and in flood. The riders were required to dismount and swim across. The horses were perhaps left behind on the final approach. By this stage the rescue party had been reduced to a core hit squad, having placed two ambush parties to deter any pursuers after the raid.

It was two hours before dawn as Buccleuch reached the red sandstone walls of the castle, the driving rain swirling into his face. The rescue went into immediate action, with if the ballad is believed a ladder was brought up against the wall but was found to be too short. Not to be deterred, a postern gate was located and crowbars and hand-picks unwrapped and brought to play on the door's hinges. The sentries above on the battlements were oblivious to the work below, driven into taking shelter from the inclement weather, or more likely bribed by Carleton to look the other way. The popular version of events on what happened next is that the stone blocks which held the gate hinges were undermined and gave way, allowing the door to swing open. It is difficult to imagine the small team striking away for hours on the stone's mortar and not be heard; and would they have enough time before day break? Again, a more probable theory is another cash bribe from Carleton, and that the door was left unbolted. At least five rescuers entered the castle and ran across the inner ward to locate Kinmont's confinement. They had prior knowledge to where Kinmont was housed, and most likely had a guide to lead them there. Speed was of the essence, not wanting to engage in any unnecessary combat. The house where Kinmont was located and entered, where a brief scuffle occurred in which one of Kinmont's guards was wounded. The ballad narrates Kinmont being found, and builds drama with the prospect that Kinmont was due to hang that same day. A piece of fiction designed to raise the tension and construct the heroic.

<table>
<tr><td>And when we cam to the lower prison,</td><td>"O I sleep saft, and I wake aft,</td></tr>
<tr><td>Where Willie o' Kinmont he did lie –</td><td>It's lang since sleeping was fleyed frae me!</td></tr>
<tr><td>"O sleep ye, wake ye, Kinmont Willie,</td><td>Gie my service back to my wife and bairns,</td></tr>
</table>

The ballad's comment on Kinmont wanting to return to his wife and "bairns" has an irony that the writer was perhaps not aware of. Kinmont's bairns at this stage in his life referred to his gang, and his bairns were by 1596 all middle-aged men, not exactly helpless children. According to the ballad it was a rescuer named Red Rowan who took the honours of physically freeing Kinmont. There is no record of such a reiver existing, which casts a doubt on the character, suggesting he was fictitious. The ballad has Kinmont found in chains and has to be carried by Red Rowan out of the castle. The triumphant scene is painted visually in the mind, as Kinmont exits the castle to a flourish from a trumpet and lusty roars of defiance.

Then shoulder high, with shout and cry,   *"O mony a time," quo' Kinmont Willie,*

We bore him down the ladder lang;   *"I have ridden horse baith wild and wood;*

At every stride Red Rowan made,   *But a rougher beast than Red Rowan*

I wot the Kinmont's airns playd clang!   *I ween my legs have ne'er bestrode.*

Ignoring the ballad's version, the reality would be different but no less dramatic, with Kinmont running across the courtyard with no chains, keeping to the darkest areas in silence, to be spirited away and out of the postern gate – Success. An awaiting horse would be close by for Kinmont to mount, and a party of riders to deter any immediate pursuit was made ready. Wasting no time for rejoicing, the group returned for home keeping a high vigilance for Scrope's troopers, who were surely to be sent galloping out in a frenzy of anxiety. The use of the earlier placed ambush parties was not required. Scrope was paralyzed by the raid and was unable or unwilling to organise an immediate pursuit.

There is one final story to tell, though was most certainly just that, a tradition handed down and not based on any fact. As the party passed a blacksmith at Dick's Tree, located one km north of Longtown, Buccleuch decided to wake up the residents and have Kinmont's fetters removed. Sir Walter Scott, the author, was handed down the story on how the smith's daughter was roused at daybreak by a *"sair clatter"* of horses and shouts for her father. Receiving no response from the *"smiddy,"* Buccleuch checked the door and found it locked. To gain the attention of the blacksmith, Buccleuch levelled his lance and thrust the point through the window and into the living quarters. The gesture gained the necessary action. In the watery dim grey light of the morning, the girl followed her father to attend Buccleuch's party, and would remember the event clearly into adulthood. The girl observed *"more gentlemen than she had ever seen before in one place, all on horseback, in armour, and dripping wet – and that Kinmont Willie, who sat woman-fashion behind one of them, was the biggest carle she ever saw – and there was much merriment in the party."* The story of Kinmont having his iron shackles removed at Dick's Tree, though sounding convincing was probably false. Sir Walter Scott eagerly recorded the oral tradition as fact, with the narrative blending in with the heroic escapade and how he wanted to portray the Scotts. Scott may have embellished the story, or even made it up.

Buccleuch led the whole party back to Langholm as the sun was rising, where they returned to their previous day's occupation, giving the impression as if nothing out of the ordinary had just happened. It was advisable for Kinmont and his sons to avoid Morton for the next few weeks. An irate Scrope would surely be out for his blood – and any Armstrong in his way was at risk of an out of hand revenge attack. News of Kinmont's escape became international, and was seen as an example of the general decay on the frontier; a spiralling descent into chaos. Lord Eure wrote up a report on the state of the Border to the Queen on 17 April 1596, stating... *"I fear this weakness is over all the Marches – for proofe, on Mundaie last 12th Aprill, the Lard of Mangerton and other suche like, and as it is thought the Lard of Baclughe keeper of Lyddesdale, with a few horsemen, not fouertie as I here, come to Carlell and forceablie breake the place where Will of Kinmonthe, Scott, a notable offender against England, honorablie taken by the Lord Scroop, was taken away and earned into Scotland. This makes me fear they well know the weakness of the March or durst not have attempted such an action."*

Eure in his writing got Kinmont's surname wrong placing him as a Scott. This raises another problem on the Border for the officials, communication, and in knowing who they were dealing with. Eure echoed Scrope's claims that Kinmont was captured legally, and was hoping to pave the way for retaliation against Buccleuch and Kinmont; and with luck to be provided with reinforcements. The affair of Kinmont increased an unfortunate dimension to the problems of law keeping on the frontier; goodwill amongst the wardens and their officials. How could Scrope ever trust Buccleuch again – and face the Carleton brothers without animosity? The Borders went into a condition which was described as a *"tickle"* state, were wardens had no confidence in their opposite numbers and the only remedy seemed to be *"to doe one evill turne for another."* The wardens had joined the cycle of violence. King James now had someone to intimidate his minsters with if they disagreed with his views on matters of the Kirk – he could threaten to call upon *"Will Kinmond,"* and his *"Southland men"* to assist him and brow beat them into compliance.

Kinmont gained his freedom and immortality in ballad form, and Buccleuch became "Bold." The losers in the venture were the inhabitants of the Debateable Land, when Scrope full of rage, vented his frustration by sending out Captain Carvell on a raid with 2,000 men. This was undertaken under the banner of a warden's rode, but was clearly an illegal act of blatant revenge. Carvell stole 700 head of livestock and burned all the houses that he came across. Kinmont and his followers melted away into the hills until it was safe to return, but returned to a pillaged landscape. It was business as usual for Kinmont once released, though the remaining months of 1596 were quiet, laying low to avoid further antagonising the English authorities.

Kinmont was none the worse for his spell at Her Majesty's pleasure; he was soon back in the saddle and reiving as if nothing had happened. Almost one year to the date of his rescue from Carlisle Castle, Kinmont made a return to the town to answer for West March bills against Scotland. Kinmont was involved in two bills heard that day – *"Indented at Carliell the xxviiith of Aprill 1597, by ordre of the lordes commissioners for Border causes, betwixt the lordes wardens of the West Marches of England and Scotland as followeth."* The first case involved a complaint made by the Captain of Bewcastle against *"John of Langham, Will Kynmont, &c, for 24 horse and mares, himself prisoner and ransomed to 200L. sterling, and 16 other prisoners, and slaughter."* The bill was found *"Foule by confession"* and referred to the commissioners for *"tryall of the trodd, 400L."* Kinmont was found guilty, with a hefty fine heading his way.

In the second bill Kinmont was the victim. The bill does not state what the crime was, other than it was Kinmont making the complaint. It would take a brave, or rather a foolish man, to thieve from Kinmont. The bill read as follows – *"Will'm Kynmont against Sym 'Rydebefore' and Ranys Davy Grame. 'Rydebefore' dead, Ranyes Davye a fugityve."* The death of one of the culprits comes as no surprise in the bill; and no prize on guessing who caused it. Perhaps the two thieves had thought Kinmont a soft target after his spell in prison, his power broken – their assumptions were to be proven disastrously wrong. Ranyes Davye wisely became a fugitive; he would be a very nervous man indeed, constantly looking over his shoulder for the next few years. Armstrong vengeance was something with long arms and memory.

Kinmont was to receive more thefts to his property in that year. Scrope was itching to hit back at anyone he came across in the rescue of Kinmont, and if he got the chance to hit back at Kinmont within legal reason, so much the better. One such chance came along, which Scrope relates to Burghley on 25 July 1597, in a letter describing a raid in which six hundred riders from Liddesdale ran a day foray on the Bells in Gilsland, and took away two hundred head of cattle and forty horses. Scrope as his duty of warden entailed, formed a hot trod and was soon on the Scot's trail. The pursuit took them into Liddesdale, where the trail ran cold. Finding themselves unable to encounter the raiders and get their herd back, the trod hit on the idea to thieve a compensation herd on their return journey. The idea was probably Scrope's, as the trod veered away from the Esk and to the Sark, to the home of Kinmont Willie. With revenge in mind, *"they went to Kinmonth and took 300 horses and kine, which I ordered to be delivered to the poor people in Gilsland."* This was win-win for Scrope, not only was he addressing a crime, but was also gaining some self respect by striking out at Kinmont.

The tale does not end there, as the trod returned home by the Esk they ran into a party of Grahams who *"reft them all from"* – An ironic case of reivers being reived by reivers. The Grahams were perhaps allied to the Armstrongs, even related to Kinmont, such was the value of cross Border marriages. The Grahams may have returned all or part of the livestock to Kinmont. The Bells of Gilsland would have a lean winter coming ahead. During the rounding up of Kinmont's stock, Kinmont was netted also, much to the surprise of Scrope. Those present in the company, such as Edward Aglionby (Mayor of Carlisle), probably thought this action was what Scrope wanted, to have a second chance to enact justice upon this notorious outlaw. Scrope however thought differently, and let Kinmont go immediately. Once bitten twice shy, he certainly was not going to go through a second humiliation at the hands of Buccleuch.

Over the next few weeks the wrath of Scrope was at work again, which became so over the top that he again broke the Border Law. In August 1597 a set of outrages and wrongs committed by Lord Scrope and his deputy were reported as offences, and Scrope had to answer for them. Scrope was accused of *"Foraying away Will of Kinmont's goods from his own house"* during a *"heirschip."* Not content with the former injury, Scrope caused another raid on Will of Kinmont; *"burning his houses, spoiling his goods, and killing two men – conducting himself as though he were warden of both Marches, and imagining that he had commission from both princes to punish and ride on the disordered people of that border at pleasure."*

In the last few years of Kinmont's life, he no longer commanded his own gang of raiders, but was a member of a group called "Sandy's Bairns." Exactly who this Sandy (Alexander) was, has not been established, but they recruited widely and internationally. Kinmont's children were grown up and raiding in their own right and he was nearing seventy years old – time to hand the lead over to younger and keener Armstrongs. Kinmont though had not lost any of his old dash and would have taken a senior roll, possibly as mentor, alongside Sandy. Or perhaps not – Kinmont may have actually been the gang's leader, resurrecting the power of his father's name in an attempt to rekindle a new fire in the blood. John Monipennie records in his book *"Certeine matters concerning the realme of Scotland"* from 1603, Kinmont and his new gang. They surface within the section on the names of the principal clans, chief men and surnames on the Border in 1597 – and under *"Debaitable Land – Sandeis Barnes Armestrangs,"* three names are listed...

1. Will of Kinmonth   **2.** Krystie Armestrang   **3.** John Skynbanke

These where the main gang members of "Sandy's Bairns," a puzzle to why there is no one named Sandy within the group, unless the group took their name from their founder – the sons of ill Will's Sandie, which makes perfect sense. With the bairns of Kinmont fled the nest, perhaps he opened up his operations to a wider field of relatives and recruits. Kinmont was also one of Sandy's bairns, homage to his illustrious father.

Kinmont's tower became the site of a battlefield in the summer of 1600, when a warden's rode ran into unexpected Scottish resistance. Richard Lowther writing from Carlisle on 11 July 1600, relates the story to Cecil – *"yesterday morning being Thursday, a little before sunrise, with at least 200 well appointed horsemen, and 80 foot, ran a foray in Scotland above Kynmont tower, where the horse and the Scots met with many strokes, yet no deadly hurt, nor any goods brought away, as I credibly hear, saving that the common English people was in great danger of the enemy."* The fact that there were no major injuries during the clash suggests both sides put up a token fight, and there was no real life or death reason to brawl anyway. Lowther commented, *"These unauthorized rodes will give much discontentment to the King and his officer and produce disorder,"* unhappy that the skirmish had occurred. During the fighting, always on the lookout for opportunist booty, a mare and two horses were stolen by *"two or thre lymmers theifes from Thomas Sandford of Howgill."* The mare came under the watchful eye of Kinmont, who noted the horse as *"being a rynner."* Kinmont afterwards bought the horse off the stealers and *"rode upon the same."*

Amongst all the raids that ever took place on the Border, the series of forays which took place on 20 March 1601, stand out. The raid was undertaken by three hundred Scots riders, a mixture of families including – Armstrong, Bell, Beattie, Irvine and Johnstone. They rode in a *"warlike manner, in a day foray,"* into Cumberland and burned houses, barns, corn and insight around the townships of Newton of Irdington and Cammock. The land belonged to the Crown and was leased to Lord Scrope, which is perhaps why they were targeted, making a political point. The Scots lay waste the countryside, *"taking 20 horse and mares, 40 kye and oxen, 60 sheep and gaytte, with prisoners and mutilating others."* Kinmont was not named as taking part in the raiding, but was involved despite his advanced years, riding out with the Sandy's Bairns gang. Once the smoke had died down and darkness was setting in, Kinmont set off on two more forays, not content on his days work. Teaming up with Christie Armstrong of Barngleish, and the Irvine Kangs (Davy, Will, and Geordy), the gang numbered "*7 score Scotsmen*" (140), and set out to raid the Queen's township of Scotby. A complaint was later made by the tenants on the gang "*for burning, and taking prisoners, besides 60 kye and oxen, 50 horse and mares, &c.*"

The tally added to the day's foray, but yet Kinmont and his gang were not satisfied. They were not far from Carlisle, a target too tempting to ignore. Sandy's Bairns were keen to cause further chaos, perhaps encouraged by Kinmont who was always looking to make a nuisance of himself. The final outrage of that night was about to take place and was as flamboyant as it was destructive. The raiders were said to number 130 persons, ten less than the previous raid, who presumably did not want to take part, content on their earlier takings. Amongst their number were two "*Inglish disobedientes,*" Thome Carlton and John Carlton. The gang rode into the township of Rickergate, a suburb of Carlisle and targeted the bridge which crossed the River Eden – where the gang "*brack and cutt upp the postes that conteyned the yron cheyns (made for the keepeing and streingth of Eadenbrigg by night).*" It was normal practice on the Border to chain off bridges at night to deter reivers from driving off cattle. Kinmont and his gang were clearing the way for getting their plunder home by the most direct route. Once achieved, the gang then took pleasure in terrorising the inhabitants, "*and cutt app their doores, toke prisoners, &c.*" It was reported that some of the raiders came to the city walls near the castle crying, "*upon them, upon theym, a Daker, a Daker a read bull, a read bull.*" The "red bull" that was shouted out referred to the family coat of arms of the Baron Dacre, who was responsible for building Naworth Castle. The raiders audaciously called out their names like war cries – "*Johnston, Armstrang, Bell and Carlyll,*" which forced the citizens in their "*defencyve arrayes, for to repayre to the walls, and the beacon to be sett in fyre, for the warning of the wardenry.*" The sight of a burning beacon was the signal for the gang that the raid was over, a mounted host would soon be on the scene. Kinmont and his motley crew of cut throats then crossed the Eden Bridge for a clear ride home.

Kinmont is last heard of on 4 January 1603, in a letter by Scrope to Cecil. Scrope refers to a follower of Kinmont named Johnstone, who had robbed the King's merchants of Edinburgh of £1000 sterling, and "*Sandies Renion;*" both were named in the murder of Sir John Carmichael the late warden, and both were seen in Kinmont's house. This would make Kinmont guilty of reset, the crime of sheltering known criminals. Scrope adds, "*This Kinmonde since his release, has spoiled the 2 towns of Heskettes*" – which arguably was Kinmont's last raid. Low and High Hesket, located 15km SE of Carlisle, have the unfortunate privilege to be the recipient of Kinmont's final foray in around 1602. Kinmont was not recorded taking part in "Ill Week," when in March 1603 the entire Border erupted in a frenzy of raiding. Kinmont was either too ill to become involved, or was not noticed amongst the hundreds of other outlaws. "Ill Week" was a phenomenon in which Kinmont could not have resisted, and if he had an ounce of strength left, he would have rode with the best of them.

The ultimate fate of Kinmont is not known, but after decades of thieving and dishonour, he probably died in his bed. In dying peaceably and on his terms, the old scoundrel had triumphed and flourished over adversity. When totalling up the value of head of livestock and insight that he reived over the years, Kinmont was arguably the most successful reiver ever. He was an Armstrong first, and lived true to his families principles, always managing to stay one step ahead of those who would cause harm.

Kinmont was buried in the churchyard of Morton Old Parish Kirk, in the hamlet of Morton. Nothing is left of the kirk today, but the churchyard remains, and within the tombstones are several generations of later Armstrongs of Sark. There is no visible sign of Kinmont's grave, and was thought lost, however in the late 19th century a full length grave stone was uncovered just below the surface and was found to bare the strong arm of the Armstrongs. Could this be the last resting site of Kinmont Willie? A field visit a century later rediscovered the same grave which lay beneath a thin covering of turf. The field team found a thin rectangular slab of red sandstone, which bore the inscription of a cross pattée in a double circle at both ends. In the centre of the stone was the symbolic Armstrong arm, a left arm stretching out towards a saltire, and a martlet sat to the left. There was no name on the grave, but the carvings indicate strongly that here lies Kinmont Willie Armstrong. The martlet gives a pointer towards the graves owner, being the symbol of the Armstrongs of Sark. The saltire is also of a particular interest, and either refers to Scotland, or the Johnstone family, with the Johnstones the more fascinating candidate. The Johnstones were once the mortal enemy of the Armstrongs, but here both Armstrong and Johnstone are linked together for eternity, and upon one of the Johnstone's most feared adversaries. Perhaps Kinmont had laid the foundations of peace with the Johnstones just before he died. His grandson would after all marry a Johnstone, changing times indeed.

<u>Children of Kinmont</u>

1. William ("Young Will") of Kinmont – (d.c.1607)

2. Alexander (Sandie) – (c.1580/90s)

3. John (Jock) – "Kinmont's Jock"– (c.1570/1600s)

4. George – "Kinmont's Gorthe" of the Gingles – (ex.1611)

5. Francis – "Kinmont's Frauncis" – (c.1580/1600s)

6. Thomas – "Kinmont's Thome" – (fl.1583)

7. Ninian (Ringan) – (c.1585)

8. At least one daughter

Kinmont was proud of his sons, and made them the backbone of his raiding, naming his gang of reivers after them – "Kinmont's Bairns." Out of all Kinmont Willie's offspring, Jock was the most destructive; a chip off the old block in the full mould of his father. Jock first appears amongst the records in 1579 when together with his father, he signed a bond of man rent to John, Lord Maxwell. Jock had at least two sons, John (*"Black Jock's Johnnie"*), who married Catherine Graham c.1582 – and William of Sark, who married Enid Johnstone.

Jock is first recorded on a raid in 1582, documented as *"Johnne Armstrang, callit Castellis, sone to Will of Kynmonth."* He rode alongside his uncle John (*"Jok"*), *"callit Wallis,"* John Armstrong of Hollows, John (*"Jock"*) of Calfield,

Hector Armstrong in Stubholme, Ninian ("*Sandeis Niniane*") Armstrong, and Christopher ("*John's Christie*") Armstrong and his son "*young Cristie*," together with their servant Willie Irving – who raided the farms of Montbenger, Deuchar and Whitehope.

Jock crashes big time into the reiving scene in 1583, when he was charged for four separate forays into the West March of England:-

1. 18 Aug

"*John Rowtlege of the Stonknowe uppon Kinmontes Jock and Ecky of the Gingles, with their complices for xii kyne and oxen.*"

2. 26 Aug

"*Richard Sowrebie and Jeffrey his brother uppon Kinmontes Jock, yong Christofer Armestronge sonne to Johnnes Christie for xvi kyne and oxen, and three horses and mares, and their insight.*"

3. 2 Sept

"*Christopher Bellman of Hedderswoode uppon Jocke Armestronge, Kinmonth Jocke, and Ecky of Stubbholme for XX kyne and oxen, and three horses and their insight.*"

4. 6 Oct

"*Dick Rowtledge of Kirkleventon uppon Jock Armstronge called Kynmonth Jock, Jock Armstronge of the Calfhills, Jamy of Cannonbie, with their complices to the number of xx persons for xx kye and oxen, two naiges, all his insight. At this heirshipp Dick Rowtledge and his sonne were maymed and wounded in perill of death.*"

It comes as no wonder to find four of Kinmont Willie's brood featuring in Thomas Musgrave's list of the Border Riders in December 1583. They featured under the heading of the "*Offspring of 'ill Wills Sandy';*" and were named as follows – "*Joke Armestronge his sonne; Gorthe Armestronge his brother; Frauncis Armestronge his brother; Thome Armestronge his brother.*"

The appointing of the Laird of Ferniehurst (Warden of the Middle March) as the new Keeper of Liddesdale in 1584 did not alter the Armstrong's misrule on the Border. Henry Lord Scrope wrote from Carlisle to Walsingham on 22 December 1584, commenting on the recent raiding – "*But even on Frydaye last, Kynmontes Jock and his complices of the West Marche of Scotland under the Larde Johnston, have ridden emongest the Trembles within Pharnyhirstes wardenrye, and have spoyled and taken awaye foure skore head of nolte, and halfe a skore of horses, besydes the kylling of fyve or six parsons Scottishmen.*" Scrope could not see an end to the thieving – he added "*This bolde attempt emongest them selves, in myne opynyon will hardlie be reformed; so as what face of justice soever be made to us warde, there is no hope the same shall comme to good effect.*"

There is only one record of all of Kinmont's sons riding together with him on a raid; in November 1585, when on the mission to Stirling Castle organised by the Earl of Angus against the Earl of Arran. One of Kinmont's sons, Alexander, served at Langholm Castle in Maxwell of Newlaw's Troop of Horse, and would have ridden alongside the Maxwells supplying his expertise in the saddle. The seven sons took part in the great raiding taking particular care to select quality horses and provide the gang with new fast mounts.

Jock was next in trouble again in 1587, when he took part in two large scale raids alongside the main Armstrong lairds. This was the full Armstrong power in action – an unstoppable machine. The bills were issued by the Commissioners at Berwick; the first on a complaint by the *"Laird of Prendicke and Henrie Collingewood of Ryle and their tenants of Ingram and Reavelie,"* for a raid on 23 June 1587. The complaint was made against *"John Armestronge called 'the Lairds Jocke', Andro Armestronge of Whithaugh, Ecktor Armestrong of the Hilhouse, Jock Armestronge of Kynmoth, Georg Armestronge of Arcleton, John Bateson called 'John of the Score', and other 500 men, who ran a day foray and carried off 600 kye and oxen, 600 sheep, 35 prisoners and insight worth 40L. sterling."*

The second raid was reported by William Maughen and Thomas Hynde on behalf of *"43 persons of her Majesty's tenants of Haddingbriggs and Rattenrawe."* The complaint was made upon the Laird of Mangerton, the young Laird of Whithaugh and *"Jokkie Armestronge of Kynmett,"* who along with six hundred men burned fifteen houses and took twenty four prisoners on 6 October 1587. During the raid one of the tenants had his hands cut off; a horrific injury which can be imagined was caused by an Armstrong swinging his back-bladed sword against a tenant trying to defend their property. The raiders were charged for *"reaving their chattels and insight gear, worth 900 L. sterling."*

The autumn of 1592 was a busy year for Jock, who is documented four times within the Border Calendar Papers. Two of the bills were for raids when accompanied by his brother William and one when on a raid with his father present. The fourth entry was a letter from Lowther to Burghley commenting on Jock who had recently taken a prisoner.

1. Thursday, 16 Nov 1592
"The said James and John Tailler, upon said Kynmonts Jock, young Will of Kinmont and Thome of Rowanburn with 24 persons, for coming in myde afternone to Bolton fell and taking 30 kye and oxen, one brown rackinge [pacing] *mare, and hurting divers in peril of death."*

2. 17 Nov 1592
"Walter Calverleye of the Holme Coltram, upon Kynmontes Jock, Kynmontes Wille, Christie Armestrange of Barneleish, and 27 persons for taking and keeping him prisoner, also a mare price 24L., 2 horses, 10L., a gold chain, jewels, gold, silver, writings and household stuff."

3. Wednesday, 25 Nov 1592
"James Tailler of Boltonfell foite, and John Tailler his brother, upon Kynmontes Jocke, younge Will of Kynmonte, Willie Kange, Geordie Kange, Richie Kange, and Thome of Rowanburne, for 10 sheep, 2 'gaite' and their insight."

4. 28 Nov 1592

"I doe hears that young Mr Caverly of the Holme (who was taken prisoner by Kynmontes Jocke, and others conteyned in a bill I sent to your gwd lordship) ys come home, but in what sorte, for this present I cannot advertishe your good lordship."

As expected Kinmont's children eagerly gathered to help their father to escape from Carlisle Castle in April 1596. Lord Scrope on 14 April 1596, names *"Kinmontes Jocke, Francie, Geordy, and Sandye, all bretheren, the sons of Kinmont,"* as amongst the principal assailants at the raid. Further confirmation on the involvement came in an anonymous letter to Scrope (from *"Richies Will"* Graham) on 24 April 1596. It read – *"Right honorable lord, pleaseth your lordship to ken this the truth of the takinge out of Kynmont... There came frea the Langholm with him... foure sonnes of Kinmontes and iiii of his men."*

Jock's troublemaking skills came to the attention of the authorities in the following year, when he was chosen as the ideal candidate to be removed from the Scottish West March and held in safe keeping away from doing harm as a pledge. The request was demanded, and Jock had to deliver himself to Sir William Bowes on 25 June 1597 at the west ford near Norham. Jock obeyed the summons. Sir Robert Carey referred to *"Jok of Kinmontes,"* and the *"principal Gingles,"* as being the chief riders of the Scottish West March, in a letter to Cecil on 28 July 1601. He went on to add with relief that Jock and the Gingles riders had given *"bonds for themselves, friends, &c, not to offend, and that each of them would enter on 10 days' warning unconditionally."* Carey now had what he wanted, *"assurance of quiet hereafter."* Carey with satisfaction told Cecil, *"so I have brought the west part of my charge to such quiet as not often seen."* The Armstrongs had been brought to heal at last it seemed, but old habits died hard.

An interesting document dated 26 February 1607, issued by James Maxwell and Robert Douglas as "servitors to his Majesty," bring up two sons of Kinmont when recording their tenants in the Debateable Land. Francis is mentioned, referred to as *"Kinmont in Monbieherst,"* and William as being deceased. With William having passed away, his widow was of note to Maxwell and Douglas; they scribed – *"Blench Irving relict* [widow] *of umquhile* [deceased] *young Will of Kinmont in Mortintour"* into their records. It is interesting to note that William had married an Irving, perhaps this was organised by Kinmont, diplomatically undertaken to patch up the action at Bonshaw Tower from 1585. Also in 1607, George ("Kinmont's Gorthe") was charged with threatening the life of James Johnstone of Westraw. The authorities were closing in on George, he was eventually charged for another crime and taken to Dumfries in October 1611, where he was convicted and executed. George had a son Christopher, "Geordie of Kinmont's Christie," who was charged with the murder of John Johnstone of Fingland in 1600. He was luckily acquitted.

Grandson's of Kinmont Willie

William – of Kinmont and Sark – (b.1602 – d.1658)

William was the son of "young Will" of Kinmont and was married to Janet Johnstone. His marriage to a Johnstone may have been a method to obtain good interfamily relationships, to solve years of bitterness and feuding from the previous century. He led the Armstrongs successfully into the new Stuart Age.

William is first recorded in 1636, when he issued a complaint on the English Border Commissioners for being wrongfully detained by them. William's family history must have made him a figure to watch, with the legacy of his grandfather making the Border officials wary of his offspring causing trouble. The authorities expected the worst from William, and they were right to be suspicious. He was listed as a fugitive in 1642, named in a list alongside his brother John, though for what reason was not given.

He had at least one child, a son William, who is named on a list of "Mosstroopers," compiled in 1648. There is a possibility that William and his son William were involved in the murder of Edward Charlton of Antoun Hill and three other Englishmen in 1645, in a brief skirmish after thieving eighty cattle in Northumberland. William died on 10 June 1658 and was buried at Morton Kirkyard under an expensive tomb erected by his widow, illustrating his high regard amongst Armstrong society. William's grave was once mistaken for that of his more infamous grandfather, though that error has now been corrected. William's tombstone is of the rectangular slab type and supported by four short stone pillars. The upper surface has intricately inscribed upon it the following words:-

Heir lyes ane worthie person calit William Armstrang of Sark who died the 10 day of June 1658 aetatis suae 56... Jenot Johnstoun relek to the desised persn put up this monamente in Anno Domo 1660

Man is grass to grave he flies
Grass decays and man he dies
Grass revives and man does rise
Yet few they be who get the prise

Armorial bearings are inscribed centrally, showing the Armstrong bent arm holding a sword, and two family coats of arms are contained within shields. The first escutcheon is for the Armstrongs of Sark; three pales, with the centre pale bearing a martlet in sinister chief. The second is the heraldry of William's wife, a saltire in chief, with three woolsacks, and a heart in the middle base. Below the heraldry sits carved a skull and crossed bones, an hour glass and the phrase "*Memento Mora.*"

John – of Kinmont and Sark – (c.1642)

John is included within a list of Borders fugitives dated 1642. He is named as *"Johne of Kynmont called Johne of Sark,"* and appears alongside his brother *"William of Kynmont."* In a latter document from 1649, he is referred to as John *"called Kinmonth of Sark."* He was married to Katherine Graham, daughter of William Graham of Plomp, continuing the Kinmont tradition of marrying Grahams.

George – (c.1645)

George was the cousin of William and John, the son of Francis of Kinmont. George was recorded in a list of Borders fugitives in 1642, named as *"sone to Francis of Kynmont."* It is not mentioned what George did to become a fugitive, but the date of 1642 offers a clue. At this period Scotland was involved in civil war, the conflict brought about a breakdown in order, a situation which many Borderers used to their own advantage. George probably could not resist the temptation to loot.

George became a moss-trooper, an armed brigand which brought echoes of the earlier reiver times. It is interesting to wonder if George was inspired by his grandfather to ride out, or even if he wore his grandfather's helmet and armour – and maybe had his lance, and sword. Sword's held symbolic power, as mentioned earlier with Siward, often passed down from generation to generation like family heirlooms. Such a sword at George's side would have filled him with pride and courage, and an element of superstitious luck in the form of his grandfather as a guardian angel watching over him. The moss-troopers were not reivers, but emulated them in many ways. George would have been thrilled at the thought that he was copying his grandfather, sampling the free life on the high hills, and getting a glimpse of a past that should have been his. Armstrongs were fighters not farmers and now was the time to reclaim his harsh heritage.

In 1645 George was recorded taking part in an expedition which sounds very much like a reiving foray from fifty years earlier. The entry reads – *"Symon Armstrang, called of Whitlisyde, Geordie Armstrang, called of Kynmount, Hutchen Armstrang, called Old Sandie's Hutchene, Will and Francis Armstrangs, called of Woodhead... did steal out of Meikle Swinburne Park, in Northumberland, fyftie kye and oxen, pertaining to Thomas Chatta, in Swinburne."*

George took part in another raid with Simon of Whitlawside later that year, documented in a successful foray – *"Syme Armstrang of Whitlisyde, and his partners, did steal out of the Ruken, in Ridsdale, four score of sheep."* This raid had an unproductive ending however. When the gang brought their plunder back through Tynehead, and along the back of Flights-fell, they stopped at Cashope-head (Kershopehead) to search for food. The Armstrong gang saw no reason to put a guard on their stolen herd feeling secure in their home turf, and had failed to realise that the owners of the sheep had been following them at a discrete distance, echoing the trods of old. The Redesdale men catching up, were amazed to see their sheep in full view and with none of the brigands around, and used the opportunity to get their flock back. When the marauders returned, they found their booty was gone; it would have been interesting to listen in on who blamed who, as the arguments and excuses erupted.

During this period, the Armstrongs of Kinmont were very active as brigands, and feature frequently in all complaints within the Border. In a typical list from 18 November 1645 (on those outlawed for the non-appearance at the Justice Court of Jedburgh, before the Earl of Buccleuch), out of the forty seven persons named, sixteen of them were Armstrongs. The Kinmonts together with their accomplices, to the number of sixteen men, with possibly George present, made another foray into Northumberland in around 1645, and stole *"four score kye and oxen"* from the lands of Punder-shaw. The theft resulted in a pursuit by the land owner, Cuthbert Hearon, who mustered about sixty of his friends and servants into a marshalled posse. Hearon followed the robbers into the Debateable Land and caught up with them, prompting a prickly reaction from the Armstrongs. John Armstrong of Parkknow, and his brother Geordie, fired their pistols at Edward Charlton of Antoun Hill, who took fright and naturally fired back with his carbine. The pistols missed their mark, but Charlton's aim was clear and he hit John Armstrong. John fell to the ground and did not get up; a call for revenge went up – *"whereupon the whole crew of Kinmonts and the rest of the country people did rise."* An angry mob gave chase to Charlton, who fled for his life. The chase went on for two miles, until Charlton was overtaken and caught. He was brought back to Burnmouth in Liddesdale, and the news that John of Parkknow was dead. On hearing the information, four of the Kinmont Armstrongs leaped upon Charlton and murdered him. A small scale skirmish erupted in which another two of the pursuers were slain and a third was left for dead.

Once the Civil Wars were over, the moss-trooper was no more, and the Armstrongs had to put their lances finally away. There was no space for their services once the national conflict had ended. There would always be criminals on the Border, but never again on the scale of the reivers – and the brief reign of the moss-troopers.

37. Barngleish

Barngleish was a tower situated on the Hall Burn, a tributary of the Sark, just outside of the Debateable Land, 3.8km north of the Scotch Dyke. Today a farmhouse of the same name sits on the site.

✱✱✱

Christopher (Christie) – "John's Christie" or "John's Pope" – (1523 – 1606)

Christie was from a fine line of fighting Armstrongs. His father was the infamous Johnnie Armstrong of Gilnockie, who met his death at the hands of King James V in 1530. And his uncle was Thomas, 7th Laird of Mangerton. His mother was Elizabeth Graham. He followed in the family tradition and also married a Graham, Catherine (b.c.1530), the daughter of Will Graham of the Fauld. Christopher was also known as the "Elder of Langholm," to differentiate from his son, also named Christopher.

He had at least seven sons:-

1. John of Hollows – (1545-1628)

2. Christopher – "Young Christie" of Barngleish and Langholm – (1562-1604)

3. Robert (Rowe) – (b.c.1564)

4. William of Gilnockie – Called "Christie's Will" – (1565-1646) – Died in Ireland

5. Graham – (b.1567)

6. Gregory – (b.c.1569-1650) – Died in Plymouth, Maine, USA

7. David – (b.c.1571)

Christopher initially lived at Hollows Tower on the Esk, and later moved to Barngleish and then Langholm. Johnnie of Gilnockie was granted the lands in 1525 in exchange for a bond of man-rent from Robert Lord Maxwell. Gilnockie did not hold the lands for long, executed in 1530. Christopher was about seven years old on his father's death. The manner of which, was the stuff of nightmares, and may have traumatised the youngster for years. The *"Ballad of Johnnie Armstrong,"* has a verse within it that sadly refers to the infant Christopher – with Johnnie sending a parting word. On Johnnie's death, Barngleish relapsed back into the hands of Maxwell, with the Armstrongs temporarily subdued by the loss of so many chieftains. Johnnie's brother, Christopher of Langholm may have stepped in to raise Christopher, teaching him to be a fine horseman and to have no trust with the Stewart monarchy.

Christopher became one of Wharton's assured Scots in 1543, taking part in many raids against his fellow Scots. Christopher led a raid into Annandale in 1543, probably aimed at the Johnstones and undertaken with English gold and Maxwell blessing. Christopher was dwelling at Langholm Castle during this period with his son Christopher and handed over the stronghold to the English in 1545. This was for money; the English proceeded to garrison the castle as a base of operations. The castle was retaken by the Scots in 1547, when Arran led a force south fighting back against

English atrocities. The Armstrongs though remained assured Scots until the following year, when French reinforcements and the death of King Henry turned the tide.

Christopher was granted back Barngleish (appointed Bailie in 1552) in 1557, in a bond of man-rent from John 8th Lord Maxwell. In 1562 Christopher was given further land by Maxwell, granted the castle of Langholm, and appointed Keeper "*of the hous and place of Langholm*." The Armstrongs had a good relationship with the Maxwells, one in which required Christopher to return the favour and on occasion help the Maxwells in their long standing feud with the Johnstones. This relationship was all good in theory, but became unstuck in August 1579, when Johnstone took over the West March Wardenship. Johnstone wanted to defuse the Armstrong threat, and deprived Christopher of the wardenship of Langholm. The Armstrongs were furious and would not allow this change to go ahead lightly. Maxwell ordered Johnstone to hand the castle back over before 20 September 1580, with implied threats of violence if he refused and a power struggle began. The Armstrongs were impatient for action and acted before the date-line expired. Led by Christopher's son (Christopher) and John of Hollows, they attacked the castle in Aug 1580, destroying the barns, corn and doing much damage. The impulsive action by Christopher was disapproved of by Maxwell; now with the new title of the Earl of Morton and he claimed Langholm for himself. The double dealing move was met with Armstrong anger and resistance. The dispute is captured in a letter by Henry Scrope on 30 Sept 1581, to Burghley informing, "*On occasion of a disorder lately committed by one Christofer Armestrang, 'Johns Christie', and other Scots fugitives, in burning and spoiling about the Langholms, and taking prisoner Herbert Maxwell the captain, the Earl of Morton so terming himself, the warden, demands delivery of certain English borderers who were present, and intends on Tuesday or Wednesday next to seek for the fugitives*." Scrope had words with the Scottish king and Ker of Cessford on the raids, holding a meeting with Morton/Maxwell on the raid and publicly promised in future to deliver to the warden those who broke the peace. Scrope was also determined to deliver the current thieves in his prison awaiting trial to Maxwell if found guilty. Matters were finally settled by Lord Maxwell (recently deposed as Morton) in 1585, who took the castle and installed his own men and gunners as a garrison. Scrope wrote to Walsingham on 17 June of that year telling him that the House of Langholm was in the keeping of "John's Christie" – Christopher was back in charge of the castle. This falling out with Maxwell may explain later why the Armstrongs aided Johnstone at the battle of Dryfe Sands.

Other raids were noted during this period. In 1579 Christopher came before the Privy Council to answer charges on a family feud with the Turnbulls of Bedrule. His son John "*of Hoilhous*," John "*in Thornyquhat*" and "*Cristie Cavert*" were also mentioned within the enquiry. And in 1582, "*John's Christie and 'young Cristie'*," father and son, led a foray containing a servant Willie Irving, Hector Armstrong in Stubholme, "*Sandeis Niniane*" Armstrong, John ("Jock") of Calfield and John of Hollows. The gang were noted as raiding the farms of Montbenger, Deuchar and Whitehope.

As a son of Johnnie Armstrong, Christopher makes surprisingly very few entries into the archives for misdemeanours. Perhaps he led a reiving free life – but more probably he was an excellent raider and was just never caught. His son on the other hand was very much a tear-away and active freebooter. Christopher reached the fine old age of 83, a testimony of having the best light cavalry in Europe as protection and good strongholds to use as bolt holes. Christopher's life however was to end violently, he had survived into the Stuart Age successfully, to fall when peace came to the Border. His son Christopher only lived one year into the new era; the Armstrongs were not going to do well it seemed under the United Kingdom of King James I.

Christopher in his advanced age was not seen as a threat by the authorities however, he was noticed giving reset to wanted outlaws. Christopher came to the attention of Sir Wilfrid Lawson, who was one of the Border Commissioners put in charge of hunting down the fugitives. A big and unpleasant task, but at last the law officers had the men and the power to undertake their duties successfully. Christopher was suspected of sheltering several outlaws in his house, these being:- " *Sandie Grayme alias Geordies Sandie, a fugitive, who fledd for his offences from the said comissioners, and that George Armestronge alias George of Kinmonth, one condemned to death (who brake his Highnes gaole) with Wm Grayme alias Cockplay, and with divers others fugitives usuallie recett by the said Christopher Armestronge alias Barneglease at his howse.*" It was now time to send the soldiers round to inspect Barngleish.

John Musgrave at Carlisle was given the task of apprehending these fugitives. He held a warrant from his Highness's Commissioners of the Middle Shires of Great Britain to search within both Scotland and England for outlaws, prison breakers and fugitives. Musgrave received an intelligence report on the Sunday night of 21 September, stating that "*Geordies Sandie, and Geordie of Kinmont with divers others,*" were currently sheltering at Christopher's house. This was the tip off he was waiting for, a golden opportunity for Musgrave to make a clean sweep and bag several outlaws at once. There was no time to lose, Musgrave mustered his command of twenty horsemen, and set off with full authorization to pursue and bring the fugitives back to Carlisle for trial. Musgrave was not expecting any trouble from Christopher, but those he was giving shelter to were certainly a danger. Sir William Seton wrote to Lawson on 4 October 1606, saying on Christie that since 1603, he has "*never herd any complaint, neither on your side nor on ours.*" Musgrave stated a word of caution – "*I knowinge the said Christopher of Barnegleesse was and had bene a notable and great theefe a longe tyme and murderer within the kingdome of England, and for some of his offences condemned to die and reprived.*"

Musgrave and his troopers rode out that night for Barngleish, arriving in the early hours of the morning hoping to make a surprise entry. They lay hidden outside, adjacent to the tower's locked door, primed to spring into action once they were opened at dawn. There was no resistance as they pushed in, meeting a sleepy and confused Christopher. The Armstrongs were roused from their slumbers and guarded in the courtyard, as the party did their work "*and searched the howse and found none, yet findinge in the same howse the gunn of the said Geordies Sandie.*" This discovery changed the angle of Musgrave's visit, from one of apprehending at least two wanted fugitives, to arresting a suspect guilty of reset. The gun was the proof that Musgrave needed; he later stated to Sir Wilfrid Lawson, "*I could and can duelie prove that the said Barnegleese did usuallie recett the said outlawes and fugitives. I did command the said Barngleesse to make him readie to go to Carliell with me to answere his faultes and offences before his Majesties Comissioners.*" Musgrave sent all but two of his soldiers away to search the other houses and barns in the area, on the off-chance that the fugitives were still close-by. Christopher was probably annoyed and bad tempered at the intrusion of his home, eager for the troopers to leave. With the tower searched, he went back indoors accompanied by twelve women and descended a flight of stairs. Musgrave followed, and on catching up "*the said Barnegleesse and 2 women*" *did violentlie thurst me with the help of one man... into a vault at the foote of the said staires, and got the utter doore bolted.*" A scuffle ensued involving the two soldiers and all of the women, with Christopher crying out "*Kill them.*"

Musgrave recorded what happened next in a report, as the incident required investigation – "*Whereupon and being sore assaulted by the said Barnegleesse and his brothers soone, with the help of the foresaid women, I was forced in safeguard of my owne life and the other 2 of the souldiers to give a blow to the said Barnegleese into his body with my dagger wherebie he fell downe.*" Musgrave gave Sir William Hutton more details on his struggle with Christopher, stating "*that he was forced with his breast (both he and Barnegleesse haveinge hould of his dagger and seeinge the point towards Barnegleesse) to thrust with his whole bodie upon the pomell of the said dagger to help his hands withall, and so did thrust him into his bodie.*" More soldiers entered the room on hearing the crys – "*and seeinge me bleedinge did give the said Barnegleesse more wounds, whereupon with the first strooke he died, and I saved myself with the rest of my companie.*"

Sir Wilfrid Lawson, acting as Commissioner of the Middle Shires, wrote to the Earl of Salisbury, Secretary of State in London, on 5 October, "*marvelling*" that they had not been informed sooner about "*the truth of that accident,*" taking Musgraves version of events as a real telling of the event. There is an interesting postscript at the end of the letter which noted that "*Barneglesse hath been an evill doer long and of late thought to be a great recetter of fugitives.*" Salisbury however, had already received a letter from an unknown source which detailed him all of the relevant information. This letter is recorded within the Cecil Papers, dated 25 September, 1606 – titled "*The Slaughter of Christopher Armstrong,*" and endorsed by Salisbury, it reads:-

"*Upon the said day or thereabouts John Musgrave of Plumpton came to Christopher Armstrong's house at Barngleich by the break of day in search as was alleged of some outlaws, especially of one Sandie Graham called Georgdies Sandie; and entering with open doors after search finding no faulter nor fugitive they took Christopher himself, being a responsible man, and had laid in sufficient caution for his good behaviour. After his rendering, thinking to be carried to some of his Majesty's wards, they in most cruel form murdered him upon their own particular and old quarrels, to the great occasion of breaking of the Borders and special contempt of his Majesty's officers, and to their own great slander, who under pretence of his Majesty's service seek nothing but to revenge their own grudges.*"

The letter illustrates the view in Scotland on the motive on Christopher's death; there was a firm belief that he was murdered in an act of revenge. There were reports from Sir William Seton in Dumfries, who had heard Musgrave boast on what he had done. Seton wrote to Lawson on 4 October asserting that the killing was premeditated and inspired by Sir William Hutton "*who had some particular grudge and malice*" against Christopher. He complained that the country was scandalized at what had happened. Needless to say, Musgrave denied any fowl play and stuck to his previous story on the death being self defence. Musgrave was not charged with murder, his report accepted as an accurate version on the death.

$$***$$

Christopher – "The Younger Christie" – (1562 – 1604)

Christopher was the son of Christopher "John's Cristie" Armstrong of Barngleish and Langholm. Father like son, Christopher learned the reiving trade well. Christie was described as a *"theefe, and a Scottchman,"* by Thomas Carleton on 2 December 1597, and followed in his father's footsteps as a leader of reivers and head of the family, although his father outlived him. Christie was married c.1567, to the daughter of George (Gorthe) Graham of Esk. The marriage to a Graham brought Christie deep networking connections into England, essential for his family's safety. His father-in-law, George Graham, was married to a sister of Kinmont Willie Armstrong, a union which later pulled Christie into one of the Border's most adventurous and romantic episodes at Carlisle Castle in 1596.

Christie was a neighbour of William Armstrong of Kinmont, with Morton Tower 2.5km to the south. Christie would not have been able to resist the pull of this charismatic individual, becoming a member of the Kinmont's Bairns gang. He is first recorded on a foray in 1582, when riding to Deuchar, Montbenger and Whitehope, alongside several other notable Armstrong cut-throats. A document which covered 19 July – 6 Oct 1583, entitled *"Raids on the West Marches by Liddesdale,"* captures Christie again riding with the Bairns on a foray on 26 August 1583, and lifting twenty six cattle and four horses, plus insight from the brothers Richard and Jeffrey Sowerby. Christie was well known enough by December 1583 to be listed within Thomas Musgrave's report on the Border Riders, coming under the *"Armstrongs of Langholm."*

Christie's involvement with Kinmont's Bairns, probably led him to being labelled a "broken man." His name was included in a list of *"the principallis of the brokin men of the West Marche"* in November 1586. To be known as a "broken man" meant that Christie was without a responsible head or chief. This suggests that he had left the comfortable fold of legality and was living as an individual on the fringes of society. On 16 March 1588, he was wanted as a pledge for his father and the *"rest of thair branche,"* to be handed over as a bond for good behaviour. He is reported on 17 October 1588, when under caution by John Carmichael, and was held in ward in Edinburgh's tollbooth for *"attemptatis committit aganis England."* As a broken man, Kinmont perhaps took him in for protection. Reiving society revolved around a "heidsman" to give order and safety, and Kinmont ran one of the biggest gangs in the area, making him an attractive figurehead.

Christie made a foray into Graham country on Sunday, 25 January 1589, resulting in a complaint made upon him by *"Wille Grame of Slelandes in Leaven."* The target was a virtual neighbour of Christie's father-in-law, and perhaps he was behind the raid, hoping to gain from the spoils. Christie rode alongside *"Geordie Kang, Watte Corry, Hebby and Jock sons to 'Priors John,' Syme of Fingland."* They lifted from Graham *"10 kye and oxen, 4 young nolt, and his insight."* And for good measure nine Englishmen were taken away as prisoners to be ransomed later, and Geordie Hetherton (Dog handler for Lord Scrope) had his *"slowthounde,"* (blood hound) stolen – an embarrassing loss which would hamper any hot trod in future.

Christie is recorded in November 1592 in a complaint made by Roger Bulman of "Skailby" (Scaleby), when accompanying Kinmont and his gang. He is named as *"Christie Armestrange called younge Christie of Barneleishe,"* in the bill and a third rider is also mentioned, *"Thome of Rowanburne."* They were charged *"for taking 11 kye and oxen, 4 stottes, a whye, 2 mares."* During the raid Roger Bulman came onto the wrong end of the Armstrong's swords, *"mutilating the complainer."* Another raid followed on 17 November 1592, with Christie riding alongside Kinmont's Jock and Willie – plus twenty seven others. They lifted a mixed haul – *"a mare price 24L., 2 horses, 10L., a gold chain, jewels, gold, silver, writings and household stuff."* The theft of *"writings"* is an interesting item to note, was this writing paper / ink / pens, or books? Many reivers were illiterate and stole mainly to feed their family, Kinmont is going beyond this and into the world of learning, and maybe even literature. Walter Calverleye of the Holme Coltram was responsible for making the complaint, and was well justified at having the grievance as the gang had recently kept him a prisoner. A year later, Christie was at the Battle of Dryfe Sands in 1593.

Christie took part in the rescue of Kinmont Willie from Carlisle Castle in 1596. It was a natural reaction for the Barngleish Armstrongs to rally to the assistance of Kinmont, a strong bond of friendship probably developed over the years. This was viewed as part of the reiver code; the two families were literally as thick as thieves. Lord Scrope lists *"Christie of Barneglish,"* on 14 April 1596 as one of the principal assailants. An anonymous letter written ten days later to Lord Scrope confirmed the information. *"Richies Will"* Graham was responsible for the unsigned document, and had seen Christie with Buccleuch – describing *"Kirste of Barngleis and Rob his brother"* as riding out that night.

In the fall out over the rescue, Christopher's marriage oddly came under the spotlight. The marriage was noted by Thomas Carleton in a letter to Burghley on 2 December 1597, who describes Christie as being married to the daughter of *"George Grayme an Englisheman dwellinge uppon Eske."* Carleton was also married to a daughter of George Graham, and this relationship was of a concern to the authorities, especially in the aftermath of the Kinmont affair. Carleton had recently been accused of allying with the Grahams, an accusation that he wished to quash – even though it was true. Carleton was as crooked as they came. Carleton was trying to distance himself from the Grahams, and deflect any blame for his part in the Kinmont rescue away from himself and onto the hands of others – Christie made a suitable scapegoat. He explained that Christie was the main ally to the Grahams and not himself, as Christie had been married to the Grahams for much longer. He wrote on Christie commenting, *"he indeed married my wife's eldest sister, long before I married; but his lordship greatly wrongs me in saying I was the means of allying him with the Graymes, I never did it, or what needeth the same? For he is sister's son to Robert Grayme of the Fawlde, a principall Grayme of Eske, and hee married George Graymes daughter, another principall Grayme, about 30 years since, and what needeth better alliaunce with them?"*

Christie, along with all of the other participants of the Kinmont rescue survived to tell the tale. In 1598 Christie joined Kinmont's new gang, a bunch of marauders called Sandie's Bairns. Christie's new reiving spree with Kinmont soon led him into trouble with the authorities. Two years later he surfaces in a document entitled *"Outrages by the Scots,"* named when riding with Kinmont. The outrage in question was big scale and outrageous indeed, on the night of 20

March 1600 the gang descended upon Scotby town-ship, where a complaint was put forward by the Queen's tenants. The bill was against – *"Christie Armstrong of Barnleyce, Will Armstrong of Kynmont, Davy, Will, and Geordy Kang, &c., 7 score Scotsmen, for burning, and taking prisoners, besides 60 kye and oxen, 50 horse and mares."* The Kang's were a vicious branch of the Irvines who lived close by, 5km to the NE at Auchenrivock, and with Kinmont's experience, the gang was unstoppable. After plundering Scotby the gang attacked the suburbs of Carlisle, riding up the Rickargate in an act of defiance, striking the doors of the houses with lance and sword in their passing. The gang cockily approached right up to the walls of Carlisle. The Armstrongs were well and truly back.

Christie is named by himself on 8 May 1602 by John Musgrave, when he was described as *"One principal man, Christy of the Barnleische"* to Lord Scrope. Christie was ordered to be delivered to a *"Mr Sympson"* (Scrope's deputy), as a pledge for redress. This action may have come about from Christie's very public display of disrespect for authority at the walls of Carlisle two years earlier. The redress was to be heard at the next wardens meeting on 10 June at Gretna Kirk.

Christie was not to live much longer, dying in 1604. The reason for his death is not recorded, but the date of it suggests that he was hung (either in Carlisle or Dumfries) as part of the Border pacification. The authorities had certainly enough evidence on him, with no need for Jedburgh Justice.

Christie had the following children:-
1. Christopher – (b.c.1581-1604)   **2.** Alexander – (b.c.1599)

38. Auchinbedrig

Auchinbedrig lies 8.5km west of Canonbie in the Debateable Land, a stronghold 0.4km south of Solwaybank farmhouse. The area is flat, well watered good pasture land, with the tower on the north bank of the Ned's Beck (a tributary of the Cadgill Burn). In Aug 1596 the building was described as *"a hous of ressonable strenthe,"* after resisting an assault by English troops.

***

Ninian ("Sandies Rinion") of Ralton / Auchinbedrig – (c.1600)

Ninian was a brother of William Armstrong of Kinmont and son of Alexander ill Will's Sandie Armstrong. Ninian originally lived at Raltounburn (Ralton Burn) in Liddesdale, a tributary of the Liddel 1.5km to the north of Newcastleton. Ninian later moved to Auchinbedrig, where he built a tower house. Ninian had at least six sons, Andrew, Archibald, Hugh, Lantie, Thomas and Walter.

Ninian, living in the Debateable Land was in line for trouble with England. He was attacked twice by Thomas Musgrave, the Captain of Bewcastle and Captain Carvell, who commanded the Queen's garrison at Bewcastle. The first incidence involved 2,000 men under Lord Scrope's special warrant, which meant that this was a warden's rode. Ninian and his brood must have caused sufficient damage to the Western English March to deserve Scrope's attention. The Armstrongs of Auchinbedrig were made of stern stuff, the tower was assaulted, *"but being valiantly defended, they drew off."* Giving up on the tower, Musgrave turned his attention to the Armstrongs livestock *"and farraged the bounds, driving away 200 nolt."*

A second attack occurred and was documented within the West March bills against England on 28 April 1597. This assault was not the work of a warden's rode, having all the haul marks of a malicious opportunist theft. Musgrave may have been on a hot trod and lost track of the quarry, and just thought to seize the Armstrongs property as compensation. Or perhaps he had unfinished business to attend to, after the previous year's expedition to the tower. He had no authority to raid Auchinbedrig, and a complaint was issued on Musgrave, Captain Carvell, and William Hutton by Ninian for the theft of *"30 score kye and oxen, 20 horse and mares, 30 score sheep and gayt, insight of 20 houses, 1000 marks, a horse 40L."* The bill was found foul by the confession of Captain Musgrave and he was fined £2000.

In 1598 Sir John Carmichael was made the warden of the Scottish West March, a move which many on the Border disliked. Carmichael was well qualified for the job; he had already been a deputy warden and also Keeper of Liddesdale on previous occasions. He was one of those rare characters on the Border – honest. Carmichael was also very good at his job, cracking down on the activities of the reivers, and it was this factor which made him an enemy of the Armstrongs. Adding to Carmichaels alleged bad points; he was not a Borderer himself, which became a source of resentment with the reivers, viewing him as an interfering outsider. He was a symbol of authority who lefts its mark, and therefore was seen as a troublemaker that the outlaws could be well rid of. Ninian and his sons had many runs in with Carmichael. It was only a matter of time until something snapped.

The trigger for the break down in their relationship happened on June 14 1600, when Ninian attended a Warden's Truce Day at Gretna. Carmichael was there as the Scottish West March Warden, with Richard Lowther taking the roll as his opposite number, the English deputy West March Warden. Ninian was probably present to answer for a misdemeanour by himself or one of his many sons. Ninian felt the hackles rise when he saw Carmichael at Gretna; for here was a man who was out to punish the Armstrongs, with an agenda to hit hard the family at every opportunity. Ninian was accompanied by several of his sons, and pitched a tent to have comfort for the day's events. Tables and chairs were set up, with food and wine served. Ninian was a Border headsman and travelled in style, with all his needs catered for. Armstrong power was made clear and flaunted in the faces of the wardens. When Ninian's back was turned, one of Carmichael's staff decided to play a practical joke on him. He sneaked up to where Ninian had his camp, and located his personal area finding his sword. The official then pulled the sword from its scabbard and poured an egg yolk down into it, sliding the sword back in. Later in the day, Ninian had reason to draw his sword, probably on the goading of an English official, and when he went to draw the sword, he found it stuck solid. The egg yolk had bound fast the sword blade into the scabbard, making it impossible to pull out. Smirking English officials gathered to watch, including Carmichael, and all laughed. Ninian became incensed, full of shame and rage, how dare they treat a Border headsman in this disrespectful way. Ninian swore that the next time his sword left its scabbard it would be feared and respected.

Ninian's sons gathered around him, and in their mutual spite a plan was formulated to obtain revenge on a grand scale – to assassinate Carmichael. It was common knowledge that in two days time Carmichael would be travelling to Lochmaben from Langholm to attend another Warden's Court. This sparked an idea amongst Ninian and his gathered brood, with them visualizing apprehending Carmichael on his travels and slicing him into collops. Here was the perfect place to get his revenge, alone and on a bleak moor with no witnesses. Six of Ninian's sons bought into the idea, but more assassins were needed to come on board. They had a full day to organise a proper hit squad, word was put out across Liddesdale, and for those interested to meet up at Mumbies, 4km NW of Canonbie on the following day.

Mumbies was central for everyone, and "*at ane meeting at the futeball*," the finer points of the ambush was laid out. The match provided an excellent cover for their plotting, with Carmichael just 5km to the north unsuspecting in Langholm. The game was played and enjoyed, and afterwards around twenty names were signed up to take part in the assassination. Amongst those gathered, Thomas (Ninian's son), became the natural ring leader of the group, with Adam Scott "*the Pecket*" and Willie "Kang" Irvine volunteering as enthusiastic henchmen, eager to share in the glory of cutting down a cocky March Warden to size. The final arrangements were gone over, with the group agreeing to rendezvous on the following day, setting "*Blerieheid*" as their trysting place. A third of the gang was made up of Ninian and his sons, making the group a close knit affair of family and friends. The gang members were named in a trial on 14 November 1601:-

1. Ninian Armstrong of Auchinbedrig   **2.** Thomas (Son of Ninian)

3. Hugh (Son of Ninian)

4. Lantie (Son of Ninian)

5. Walter (Son of Ninian)

6. Archibald (Son of Ninian)

7. Andrew (Son of Ninian)

8. "Rob's Sandy" Armstrong

9. Syme Armstrong of the Side

10. Lantie Armstrong of the Side

11. "Lang" Sandy Armstrong of Rowanburn

12. Patrick (Pawtie) Armstrong of Harelaw

13. Rob Scott

14. Adam Scot – "The Peck"

15. Thomas Tayler – "The Laird"

16. Willie "Kang" Irvine

17. Will Graham of the Yaidfauld

18. William Foster of the Bakstangill

19. [?] Nickson (Man to Sandy Inglish)

20. Unknown

The meeting up on Monday 16 June went according to plan, with everyone armed and ready for the fray, dressed in jacks and steel bonnets, and carrying lances and hagbuts. The gang journeyed to the selected ambush point at "Colonheugh" (7km west of Langholm); this was probably the point where the Collin Burn crossed the Lockerbie-Langholm road. The gang settled down to wait until Carmichael was spotted, taking up their positions, possibly in more than one place so that they could surround their target. The trap was set.

At 2pm their quarry was spotted, there would be no negotiation. Hagbuts were made ready and shots rang out. The ragged volley missed, sending Carmichael into alarm. He managed to spur his horse into action, riding off in all the haste and skill that he could manage, convinced that death was the alternative. The gang pursued and a desperate chase developed. Carmichael careered off the track and onto moorland, but got only as far as Raes Knowes 1.5km NW in the rough terrain, where the gang came in range allowing Thomas to pause, load and fire his hagbut. A single shot hit Carmichael, knocking him out of the saddle – dead. The gang gathered around the still body and robbed the corpse, looting horse furniture, fine clothes, coins and jewellery. The body was unceremoniously slung over the crupper of Willie "Kang" Irvine's horse and taken west by the gang to Lochmaben, where a symbolic political gesture was made of the deceased Carmichael. As a final insult, the body was dumped at the site of the proposed Warden's Court. The statement was loud, proud and bold – and also suicidal, as the gang members were recognised. They had kicked over a hornet's nest, but did not recognise the significance of their actions until a few months later.

Having so openly broken the law and having this gang of outlaws put together, the ring leaders were eager to pick another target before disbanding themselves. The gang had expanded to eighty members after Carmichael's murder. They selected another position of authority – Carlisle; the castle itself was too big to tackle but Stanwix just outside was a different matter. Adding insult to injury the gang descended upon Stanwix and lifted every horse in sight. The raiders did not stay long and completed their sweep of the area by riding through Linstock, the home residence of the Bishop, adding yet more disrespect to authority. Richard Lowther was a witness to some of the night's activities and wrote to Cecil on 23 June 1600, filling him in on the recent raids made by Ninian and his sons, which arrogantly rode to the very walls of Carlisle. He stated:-   *"Since the untimely death of Sir John Carmichael, those wicked persons his kyllers, Sandys Rynyon with his sonns and dependantes, have not only rydden within the baronie of Burgh (and from thence toke ten nagges), but also have associate themselves to an insolent company of Armstranges and Yrwyns, specially the Hollases and Kanges, men of the lyke wicked disposicion, with the nomber of fourescore persons on Thursday last at night came to a place called Holme end within the baronie of Lynstock, brack a house and toke certaine goodes which was rydded, hurt one man: the followers put them to flight, took 6 horses and one of them prisoner."*

Scrope wrote to Cecil on the same topic on 26 July 1600 – *"That those thieves (while the lord bishop of Carlell was preching at Stannikes which is but a fleet shott from Carlell) had made an open forraye, and taken away all the nagges that belonged to that poore towne, 30 in number and the said men, 80 in all, had ridden on the Bishop's tenants of Linstock, about a mile distant from this city, and stolen all their cattle wherat the lord bishop is very sore troobled. Also these men (the principal murderers of Sir John Carmichael), took all the cattle the lord bishop's brother Adam had whose wife they beatt, and wounded pitiouslye."*

The gang's logic was probably to gather hay while the sun shined, and then to lay low. It was now time to go too ground. Ninian and his cohort were hoping that memories were short, and that the shooting of Carmichael would eventually be filed under yet another Border murder and be forgotten about. The gang headed for safe houses in Graham territory, satisfied that they had taught a lesson to both the Scottish and English governments, on not to mess with the Armstrongs. The murder caused an outrage in Scotland and a diligent search was made. James VI even became involved in the hunt, writing to Queen Elizabeth complaining that the Grahams were sheltering the killers. The Scottish authorities had trouble in catching those responsible for the crime, resulting in English help being asked for. A document dated 18 April 1601 was issued which contained *"The names of them that ys fugetyves for the slaughter of Sir John Carmichell late warden."* Amongst those for the West March were *"Ninian Armstrang in Auchinbedrigg, with Thome, Hew, Lantie, Waltir, Archie, and Dand, his sons."* It was hoped that Lord Scrope and Sir Robert Carey and their deputies would have better luck at tracking them down than the Laird of Buccleuch and his deputies. Eventually the authorities had success – one of Ninian's brood was netted on 17 September 1601, by Sir James Johnstone of Dunskellie, the Laird of Johnston, who captured Thomas ("Ringan's Tom"). He was executed two months later.

The death of Thomas was a deep blow to Ninian and a sign of the changing times, with co-operation on the Border finally arriving between the Scots and English authorities. A taste of what was to come when King James took over a united kingdom. Ninian was soon back making mischief in Scotland, choosing the Laird of Johnstone as his target. Johnston writes to John Musgrave from Lochmaben Castle on 29 November 1601, relating the incident with Ninian – *"Complaining that while he was at Court, his mill of Corrie was burnt by Sandies Rynyon, &c., who are reset by Geordies Sandie and two others. As he cannot believe Musgrave will oversee them within his bounds, craves early redress."*

The attack on the mill was Ninian's revenge on a dead son, a clear warning to Johnstone on what would happen in future if he continued to prosecute his family. The "Geordies Sandie" mentioned by Johnstone in the document was Alexander Graham of Kirkandrews in Cumbria on the Esk, a friend of Ninian's, and the location was where he and his sons where hiding out. Another document sheds more light on this, written by John Musgrave to Lord Scrope on 7

December 1601, confirming that indeed the whole clan of Armstrongs were living with the Grahams on the banks of the Esk in English territory. Musgrave stated that *"Geordies Sandie, Davie Grame of the Milleis, and Fergus Wille"* were *"resetting Sandies Rynyon and his 'bayrns'."* Musgrave added that he heard with credibility that *"Sandies Rynyon, &c, were reset at Geordies Sandie's house last Wednesday night."* It is interesting to note from this document that Ninian had a whole gang operating from out of Graham country, known as "Ninian's Bairns," a title based on many of the gang members being his sons and other relatives. Ninian was a father figure in more ways than one to the gang. The three named Grahams were said to be guilty of the crime of *"reset,"* which held the maximum sentence of execution. Musgrave added that Ninian's gang of Bairns were at *"the hership of Bengall"* also, a destructive force that needed to be winkled out of the Esk. On 25 May 1602, another foray occurred, observed by George Nicholson (the Queen's agent) who reported that the outlawed Armstrongs *"have the last week ridden upon the Laird of Johnstone's lands, and carried away some of his goods, and the other Armstrongs would not rise to follow the rest, which the Laird takes evil, and intends to take amends as he may. This I hear, and I do fear they will in the end get life."*

Johnstone was frustrated that Ninian was out of reach from Scottish law, and now three Grahams had just been added to the list of criminals. John Musgrave as Land Sergeant of Gilsland was the man to bring the Grahams to justice and close this Armstrong bolt hole, with Johnstone expressing a step up in gear and some pro-active action. Unfortunately for Johnstone and luckily for the Armstrongs, Musgrave had a personal reluctance to tangle with the Grahams. In September 1600, an attempt was made on Musgrave's life by a group of Grahams in Brampton, an experience which dampened his enthusiasm to help. Musgrave was therefore at feud with the Grahams, a conflict which he could never rise to challenge and was hoping if he left the Grahams alone, they would do the same. Johnstone therefore did not receive the action that he wanted from Musgrave and contacted Lord Scrope requesting that he help with the problem of Ninian and his marauders. Scrope was a different character to Musgrave, and was on good terms with Johnstone, he eagerly agreed to assist. Scrope wrote to Cecil on 29 August 1602, from Carlisle giving an update on his actions – *"I have as he requested, burned their resetters' houses in Bewcastle; but will surcease till he has burned those on his side who have spoiled our March."* The burned houses mentioned where those of the three Grahams, which would serve both as a direct warning to others who harboured reivers and to end Bewcastle for the time being as a safe base for Ninian and his gang to operate from. The hunt continued in Scotland for Ninian; Scrope also reported on the progress of this on 29 August in the same letter – *"The Laird of Johnston being now at Langholm to revenge Carmichael's cruel murder by Sandie Rinion and his sons."* The noose was getting tighter; in that same year Ninian's house was thrown down by the King's orders, and George Sandie Grahame was captured by the English and delivered up to the Scots. Ninian was a marked man, his Bairns had been effectively neutralised, denied a base camp. One last hurrah though remained, during "Ill Week" in March 1603 – and after which life would never be the same again. There is no record of what happened to Ninian and his brood, they were either hung or fled into exile to Ireland.

It is a sad reflection to make, that if Carmichael had not been murdered, he would have brought a stable hand to play in the politics of 1603 during the unification of the two Kingdoms. He could have helped in the transition from the reiving culture to peaceful farming on the frontier. His advice may even have stopped Jedburgh Justice being inflicted, and the years of brutal pacification. His murder only hardened attitudes towards the reivers, and his very death perhaps unwittingly brought on the end of the Armstrongs as a power.

✳✳✳

Thomas – "Sandy Rynyons Thom"/ "Ringan's Tom" – (ex.1601)

Thomas was the son of Ninian *"Sandy Rynyons"*Armstrong, nephew to Kinmont Willie, and was known as a minstrel. Thomas appears to have had a crime free life, or at least he was never caught – until 16 June 1600, when he joined in with his father and brothers in the murder of Sir John Carmichael, the Warden of the Scottish West March.

The murder of Carmichael was not a spontaneous act, but carefully planned. Thomas's father was humiliated at a Warden's Truce Day at Gretna, and gathered in his brood to plot revenge. All of the family were affected by Carmichael's efficiency as a warden; his removal was something that everyone eagerly agreed to. Thomas appears to have been the catalyst on the murder plot, and may have prompted his father into putting a gang together to take out Carmichael. They would have to act quick as their window of opportunity was limited. Carmichael was travelling to Langholm on the following day, and then onto Lochmaben on 16 June, this would be their chance to strike. After enjoying a game of football at Mumbies on Sunday 15 June, the gang set off *"all bodin in feir of weir, with jakis, steilbonettis, lances, hagbuttis,"* to slay a warden. Carmichael came into view as expected on 16 June, with the gang straddling the road to Lochmaben ready in ambush. Carmichael managed to evade the initial attack, taking off north-west to escape capture. The gang pursued and caught up with Carmichael on the slopes of Raes Knowes. Confronting Carmichael, Thomas took the roll of executioner, levelled his hagbut and shot the warden dead.

On the day after the murder, the authorities had already worked out who the killer was. Richard Lowther wrote to Cecil on 17 June stating, *"Yesterday about two of the cloke Sire John Carmychell ridinge from Annon to the Langhome, in his waye ther was xviii men, wherof xvi weere Scottes men, and two Englishmen, providid in jackes, laid in waite for him, and chaissed him and kilde him with a gonne. He that shote him was a Sonne of Rynyon Armstrange callyd Thom. Ther they spoyled him, and from thence he was carred before a Scottesman on horsebacke to Lochmaben he that carrid him was Wille Kange."* Lowther was in a low mood after the shooting, he lacked the men to offer a safe guard to the population. He added in his letter *"I cannot keep this March, for now the thieves will ride,"* and with a sad resignation to the reality finished off by saying *"This is the therd warden they have kild and taking prisoner in Scotland."* Nothing was going to improve and more wardens would for sure die in future.

The Scottish king also got in on the act, appalled at the audacity of having one of his warden's murdered. He wrote to Lord Scrope on 20 June 1600:-
"We dout not bot ye have hard of the recent accident buitcheing the barbarous and wyld murthour of our warden the Laird of Carmichaell, committit sa neir your boundis be Sandeis Ringanis sonnis, certane utheris of the Armstrangis and thair associattis raittit thevis and lymmeris... will (na dout) tak occasioun to seik refudge within the boundis of

James wanted Scrope to search for and apprehend Thomas and his fellow murderers, and to stop anyone giving "*ressett*" (refuge) to them. The Armstrongs had fled into England for safety, and were beyond the King's justice. The correspondence went thick and fast, as both the Scottish and English governments motivated themselves in a rare moment of cooperation to apprehend this group of villains. Scrope and his colleagues saw the new Stuart Age dawning soon, and wanted to influence the next English / United Kingdom monarch. The border would be gone, and futures could be made and lost on the lead up to that momentous event.

Thomas and his brothers were eager for more action. Thomas together with Willie "Kang" and Adam Scott (the "Pecket"), had taken over the command of the gang, with Thomas the ring leader. The gang descended upon Stanwix with nothing to lose, and stole horses from under the walls of Carlisle within the ear shot of power, while the Lord Bishop was preaching. The next stop was Linstock, the residence of Henry Robinson, the Bishop of Carlisle; targets chosen to warn the symbols of authority not to dare tackle the Armstrongs. The Bishop's cattle was lifted and his sister-in-law was hurt, perhaps deliberately so. The scale of these crimes demanded a robust response, with an unusually eager will to catch the gang, especially Thomas as the killer of Carmichael. A document dated 18 April 1601, on the subject of the Scottish outlaws of Liddesdale, lists those wanted in the West March, and Thomas was named. Lord Scrope and Sir Robert Carey were given legal permission to enter Scotland and come after him and his brothers. This was something new and unexpected; Thomas no longer had a safe bolt hole in England. The searching paid off, Scrope reported with satisfaction to Cecil on 17 September 1601, "*Johnston has taken one of Carmichael's chief murderers, and gone with him in great triumph to the King where doubtless he shall be executed.*" This individual was Thomas, who had been pursued by Archibald Carmichael of Edrom, brother of the slain warden, and run to earth where he was captured by the Laird of Johnstone.

Thomas was brought to trial in Edinburgh on 14 November 1601 – on the same day as fellow gang member Adam Scott (Adie the "Peck") was also tried. His prospects did not look good, relatives feared the worst. Thomas was the Border's most wanted criminal, the case could only go one way. He was accused of the "*the crewall, tressonabill and schamefull Slauchter*" of Sir John Carmichael, a capital offence and would be executed if found guilty. Thomas had little chance of coming out of Edinburgh alive; this was going to be a show trial in the Capital. The case was read out as follows – "*Sir Johne was to keip Court at Lochmaben, upone the morne thairefter, being Monunday, att thair trysting place of the Blerieheid, quhair thay lay att waitt for the said vmq Sir Johne Carmichellis thay altogidder sett upoune him at the Rae-knowis, schott thair hagbuttis att him, and thairwith maist schamefullie, crewallie (and) tressonablie schot the said Sir Johne Carmichell throw the body, and slew and murdreist him thair; upoun sett purpois, provisioun and foirthocht fellony."*

The verdict came from the mouth of George Ferrie, portioner of Restalrig, Chancellor, who pronounced and declared the said *"Thom Armstrang to be culpabill and convict of airt and pairt of the tressonabill and crewall Slauchter and Murthour foirsaid."* The sentence was read out as follows – for... *"Thom Armstrang to be tane to the mercat croce of Edinburgh, and thair his rycht hand to be strickin fra his arme; and thaireftir to be hangit upoune ane gibbett, quhill he be deid ; and thaireftir, to be tane to the Gallows on the Burrowmure, and thair his body to be hangit up in irne cheinis; and all his movabill guidis to be escheit, to our soverane lordis use."*

Prior to execution Thomas had his hand chopped off, a symbolic punishment as it was the same hand which pulled the trigger and caused Carmichael's death. There may have been another reason, as reivers were known to have an "unblessed hand." This allowed the reiver to kill without a guilty conscious; Thomas could commit no more wrong doings in Heaven. Thomas was hung alongside Adie Scott ("The Peck") at the market cross in Edinburgh. Adie was spared his hand being chopped off however. Once dead, his body was taken south to a second gallows located on the junction of East Preston Street (known as "The Gibbet Loan") and Dalkieth Road (the modern A7), on the edge of the city's Borough Muir and hung in chains. The chains was another symbolic gesture, and according to Robert Pitcairn, editor of the "Ancient criminal trials in Scotland," 1833, this was the earliest example ever recorded in Scotland of such a punishment. The atrocity of the crime and the dignity of the person murdered warranted the display of Thomas's corpse to the general public. Thomas's hanging body was used as a physical deterrent to other potential criminals, and also to reassure the public that justice was being done, that criminals were being caught and dealt with effectively. Today, Preston Street Public School (built in 1896) sits upon the site was of the gallows – and the grave of many miscreants, including at least one Armstrong.

39. Catgill

Catgill was located 2km to the West of Morton Rig, on the banks of the Cadgill Burn, which runs into the River Sark.

George of Catgill – (fl.1592)

George is recorded within one bill contained in the Border Calendar Papers, dated from Oct-Nov 1592:-

"The inhabitants of Etterby, complain upon the Yrwens, called the Kanges upon the Stankhewgh, Geordie Armestrange of Catgill and others, for taking 3 nags, and hurting 6 persons of said town."

40. Auchengyle

Auchengyle was located 4km to the west of Sark Tower, called *"Auchingeil"* on Pont's map.

✳✳✳

Christopher – "Sandy's Christie" / "Sande's Creste" – (c.1580s/90s)

Christopher was a son of Alexander (Ill Will's Sandie) Armstrong. He was a brother of Kinmont Willie, and would have shared many raiding experiences with him. Christopher later became a member of the reiving gang Sandy's Bairns. Christopher is first mentioned in 1580, when he was detained for a while within Blackness Castle; listed among other Borderers who were to be presented to the Privy Council. He was released later that year by special warrant.

Christopher was listed within Thomas Musgrave's document on the Border Riders in 1583, coming under the title – the *"Offspring of ill Wills Sandy."* He is recorded as *"Creste Armestronge called Sandes Creste."* Marriage arrangements were also noted by Musgrave, with a daughter of Christopher marrying a Foster from *"Kyrsope"* (Kershope). The entry reads – *"Rowe Foster marryed Sandes Creste Armestronges doughter."* This marriage was probably arranged by Christopher to gain a useful alliance. Christopher also appears in the publication made by John Monipennie in *"anno Domini, 1597,"* on the names of the principal clans on the Border. Christopher is listed under the *"Debaitable Land,"* and interestingly he is categorised by the gang that he rode with – *"Sandeis Barnes Armestrangs."* The gang contained three chief riders, who were named as...

1. *Will of Kinmonth*   **2.** *Krystie Armestrang*   **3.** *John Skynbanke*

Christopher probably shared in the command of this gang with his brother, Kinmont and John *"Skinabake"* Armstrong, who was probably a cousin.

✳✳✳

41. Williava

This grayne of Armstrongs appear to be the only English Armstrongs who were engaged in reiving. They were founded by George Armstrong in Raltoun, who was a brother of Hector of Harelaw. Williava was spelled in many wide and wonderful variations – Wulyevva / Willieaway / Williava / Wylyave / Willyeaver / Williavey / Wooleva. Williava no longer exists on any modern maps and was located in the Askerton quarter of Lanercost Parish. The area centred itself around Collin Bank, Side and High House, 2km SE of Bewcastle.

✳✳✳

Anton of Willieva – (fl.1541)

Anton was an English outlaw, who came to develop strong ties and alliances with Liddesdale. He most likely had marriage links across the Border and was probably put to the horn for his raiding in England, making him seek refuge with his Scottish namesakes. He is recorded in 1528 as being a tenant of Dacre, and had escaped to Liddesdale having committed robberies, murder and sold horses into Scotland.

In 1541 Anton led a large force of Liddesdale riders across the frontier on a foray into Bewcastledale. Anton must have risen to a high rank amongst the Armstrongs for him to have been given the command of a gang. The foray came at a tender time on the Border, with King Henry angry at the constant raiding, and James V had recently snubbed him at York by not showing up at a planned meeting. Tension was mounting to the brink of war. Anton and the Liddesdale riders rode into Bewcastle and set fire to several barns and the house of John (Jock) Musgrave, the deputy Constable of Bewcastle. Amongst the smoke and chaos, seven Fenwicks were struck down dead. The destruction came as an affront to Thomas Wharton, who had assured Henry that the Borders were *very qwyett*." Henry was furious and war came a step closer – he would have an army mustered by the following summer – the "Rough Wooing" was about to be unleashed.

✳✳✳

Ambrose of Willieva – (k.1531)

Ambrose was amongst several Armstrongs who captured horses belonging John Musgrave, deputy constable of Bewcastle. A response was forthcoming from Bewcastle, when five serving men issued from the castle under the command of John Ingram and Richard Musgrave, sons to John Musgrave. What happened next was reported by Sir

John Lowther in a letter to the Lord Chancellor on 16 October 1531, as the clash caused some controversy. A skirmish followed, and *"In the fray Ambrose Armstrong was smitten by John Musgrave the younger with a spear through the body, and died immediately."* The Musgraves wisely fled to the castle of Bewcastle, chased by the Armstrongs hot on their heels. The Musgraves only just managed to get back to safety, John Musgrave would have been taken if the drawbridge had not been drawn up. It was a near run thing and if caught revenge was ready to be instantly administered. Justice was demanded by the Armstrongs, as they gathered before the castle. Standing defiantly, Anthony Armstrong (possibly Anton of Willieva) shouted out in protest to complain on the slaying of Ambrose. He demanded in the King's name, that the felon should be forthcoming and be handed over; but Musgrave from the walls denied his authority.

✳✳✳

Edward – "Antons Edward" – of Williava – (c.1600)

Edward, the son of Anton, lived at Wintershields Tower ("Wyntersheles"), also known as "Anton Edwards Tower." The Armstrongs in England were in general a peaceable lot, living around Gilsland and keeping to themselves. Edward however was an exception to the rule. He was one of the few recorded English Armstrongs who turned to the life of reiving. Edward kept ill-reputed company and may have been sucked into reiving through his association with the Charltons and Armstrongs of Mangerton.

Edward's daughter was married to John Charleton of the Bower, an active reiver and follower of Edward Charleton, Laird of Hesleyside. Charlton had gathered around him various *"lewed and evil persons of name as followers, and lived in a waist place distant from greate plenishing, where he might with the Scots greatly hurt his neighbours"* – not exactly the most sociable of son-in-laws to have. Edward's father, Anton, was married to John Armstrong, the Laird's Jock of Puddingburn, who was the second eldest son of Thomas Armstrong, the 7th Laird of Mangerton. This marriage provided a link between Edward and the Liddesdale Armstrongs, a connection that Edward would use later when wanting a safe place to flee in 1596. It is possible that the Laird's Jock used Williava as a stop-over base on his forays, and that Edward took part in them, or at least assisted in their planning and obtained a cut of the plunder.

In 1591 Edward was named within a list of seven Armstrongs who were indicted for the murder of John Armstrong alias *"Cokespoole."* It is worth naming those he was charged alongside with, as they could be the thieves that he was later alleged to have maintained about himself...

1. Edward Armstrong of *"Willyeavide in Gilsland alias Anthons Edward"*

2. William Armstrong alias *"Andro his Will"*

3. Rynion his brother

4. Richie his brother

5. Andrew Armstrong alias *"Ingrams Andro"*

6. John Armstrong alias *"Stowluges"*

7. *"Gresaland Armestronge"*

It is interesting to note that Edward's name comes first in the list, suggesting that he was the ring leader. And the other six Armstrongs may have been members of his gang. The reason why John Armstrong was murdered is not explained; as if reivers needed an excuse to kill someone. Was John a local Armstrong that the group fell out with, or a Scottish Armstrong who had crossed the Border on a raid?

Edward became a thorn in the side of the English authorities due to his dealings with the Scots reivers, and would eventually throw his hand in with them. Lord Eure writes to Burghley on 8 February 1596, warning on the new dangerous status of Edward – *"Antone Armestrange alias Antons Edward, has lately since my coming fled out of the West March into Liddesdale, and is offered living by Baccleuch."* Lord Eure described Edward on 8 June 1597, as *"a great thief and maintainer of many others about him."* John Charlton meanwhile, was captured and charged with March treasons, which normally would be the end of a reiver's career. Charlton though had the good fortune to come under Lord Eure's authority, a more humane warden than the previous Sir John Forster. Eure saw the positive side in Charlton; he thought that if Charlton was honest, he could do good service. Eure gave Charlton the chance to redeem himself and offered him a roll in the garrison at Hexham under the Queen's pay. Charlton agreed, but before the time came to join up, Charlton broke out of jail and fled north to be with Edward. Eure wrote to Burghley on 8 June 1597, about his disappointments in Charlton – *"I took good bonds for his behaviour... but the fellowe returned to his former follie."* Eure always saw the better side of humanity and had not given up on Charlton. He was contacted by Edward who was making means for the return of his son-in-law, with promises *"that he would keep quiet, having secretly satisfied the parties offended."* Eure was eager for Charlton to return and not to be driven into a Scot's riding gang, vowing not to indict him for any murder or burglary.

Charlton can be assumed to have returned to Hexham, he is not heard of again and perhaps spent his years constructively policing the Marches. Edward though was still a thorn in the side of the authorities. As he was organising Charlton to be returned, Edward received a request that he was wanted as a pledge by Scotland for the assurance of his good behaviour. The warden's knew exactly who the trouble makers were, and having Edward under a type of house-arrest was a harmless and cheap way of keeping the peace. Sir William Bowes, the Queen's ambassador to the King, was the organiser behind the exchange. Edward was *"to be delivered at the west ford near Norham the 25 June 1597 at 10 hours before noon."* When the exchange time came, something must have gone wrong as Edward was not handed over. A document by Henry Leigh to Scrope dated 19 January 1598, has the interesting quote – *"Antons Edward whose Sonne your lordship hath in howld. But Edward offers to enter at all times to your lordship, his life being saved, and I doubt not, if it come to delivery indeed, he will be as ready as he was."* Scrope was in possession of Edward's son as an assurance, he must have been taken when Edward did not show up. Edward was anxious to have his son released, swapping himself for the pledge if necessary. His life being saved is a curious mystery, which may contain the reason why he missed the Norham rendezvous. The name of his son is not given, but may have been Thomas as Edward is recorded in 1606 as having a son of this name.

Nothing more is heard of Edward until 1606, when Lord William Howard, known as *"Belted Will,"* was employed to track down and apprehend the Border outlaws. Howard kept Sir Wilfrid Lawson informed regularly on his progress. He wrote to him excitedly on 9 January 1606, reporting on his latest catch. Howard was hoping to net Anton's Edward Armstrong; he drew a blank, but flushed out of the woodwork his son Thomas and two others. Howard wrote with relish, *"I have been away fishing, and took as many as I could get. I was in hopes to have taken Anton's Edward himself, but for want of a better was glad to take his son Thomas and Jock Stow Lugs."* He proceeds to describe galloping after the three outlaws whom he pursued from Naworth through the night to the border of Yorkshire, where he netted them all. Delivered to gaol a fortnight later were Thomas, written as *"Anton's Edward's Tom Armstrong,"* Christopher Urwen (Irvine) alias Gifford Carleton and John (Jock) *"Stowlugs"* Armstrong. Stowlugs was an earlier gang member of Edward. It is interesting to see Christopher Irvine giving a false name of Carleton in an attempt to try and throw the authorities off his trail. Howard clearly enjoyed his job, with achievement he asked Lawson if he found the matter sufficient to have all three outlaws hung – and was given the go ahead.

Anne Armstrong – (fl.1667)

It is not known exactly where Ann came from (possibly Williava), but she is one of the rare known female outlaws. She ran with a gang of Cumberland outlaws championed by William Oglethorpe and possibly led by Archie Little, operating from Bewcastle. The gang are recorded raiding in 1667, when they attempted to steal a white mare and foul at Wooler, but were chased off. The following day, the gang had more success and lifted five great beasts from Long Witton (12km to the west of Morpeth). On the return journey, the gang drove the cattle by Wasoow Shield, to the house of Thomas Scott of the Doddbogg (in North Tyne), and then to Charlton of the Bower, who offered them a place to rest overnight. Charlton was concerned for the safety of Ann, which suggests a posse was on the gang's tail. She was persuaded by Charlton to change clothes to avoid being recognised and captured. To help Ann out, Charlton sent one of his followers to obtain some man's clothes, which were stolen from the house of John Martin of the Riding, and delivered to Edward Charlton of the Newton, near Bellingham. When the gang arrived at Newton, Anne change into the clothes, and also deposited her stolen plunder (taken from Barwith house) for safe keeping – two old pieces of gold, three gold rings, a silver bodkin and a green petticoat with silver lace. Danger must have been close at hand for Anne to have left behind such valuable items, planning to collect them once the crisis was over. The rest of the journey was uneventful, with a successful end to the foray. Anne returned eventually to Newton, and when she asked for her stolen loot back, Charlton refused, threatening to turn her over to the justice of the peace if she demanded them. Anne was forced into abandoning her ill gotten goods. Honour among thieves had not changed, in a piece of roguery which was as old as the hills.

42. Woodhead

Woodhead was a bastle house 1.5km SW from Bewcastle in Cumberland, first mentioned in a survey in 1603 and noted in the possession of a John Armstrong. It was built in the late 16th or early 17th century, from grey and calciferous sandstone rubble, with walls 0.75 metre thick, and had a slate roof (excellent fireproof qualities). The stronghold was reconstructed as a farmhouse in the beginning of the 18th century. It is not known if the Armstrongs were living at Woodhead before 1603, which brings up the question if they were originally Scottish or English. The Woodhead Armstrongs could be Scots who moved south seeking a peaceful agricultural existence after the dismantling of the reiver society. Or were English, having a long history of habitation on the site. There is no evidence that the Armstrongs of Woodhead went reiving.

✳✳✳

Francis – of Woodhead – (c.1645)

William – of Woodhead – (c.1645)

Francis and William were brothers. They appear together in 1642, recorded as being *"of Wodheid,"* in a list of those declared as fugitives. The brothers were moss-troopers, desperate men taking advantage of the disorder caused by the Civil War to make a quick profit.

In 1645 they both rode alongside Geordie of Kinmont, Old Sandy's Hutchen and Simon of Whitlawside in a raid on Swinburne Park in Northumberland – and stole 50 cattle. Riding in the company of these Scottish Armstrongs suggests that Francis and William had Scottish roots.

✳✳✳

South Tynedale

43. Housesteads

The Roman fort of Housesteads (15km NW of Hexham, in Bardon Mill Parish) made an excellent ready-made home for the reivers. The stones provided building material, and the fort itself made a superb corral for livestock. The fort was built in stone around 124 CE, soon after the construction of Hadrian's Wall two years earlier.   Rectangular in shape with rounded corners, with a gate on each side, the fort joined Hadrian's Wall on its north face. The location was dramatic, situated on a high exposed ridge overlooking Knag Burn Gap. Before the arrival of the Armstrongs, Hugh Nixon, "Stealer of cattle and receiver of stolen goods," was noted as the tenant of Housesteads farm in 1604. On the south wall of the fort within its 1.5m thick walls, a bastle house was constructed, and a corn drying kiln was inserted into the gate's guard chamber. The area was wild and desolate, and became a no-go zone for traveller.

Housesteads was of an interest to others besides thieves. William Camden (1551-1623), the antiquarian / historian / topographer, desired to visit the site as part of his research on the archaeology of Britain. Camden had travelled other sections of Hadrian's Wall however; he skipped the Housesteads section, fearing the *"ranke robbers thereabouts."* In 1600, he described the area as being wild and dangerous, with the fort close to "Busy Gap," a natural pass in the ridge which was noted for the coming and goings of thieves; a favourite place for gatherings (trysts), herding cattle and the forming of raiding parties. The term Busy Gap lends its name to the Northumberland outlaws – who were known as the "Busy Gap Rogues." Such men were barred from entering Newcastle's guilds and doing any business in the town. The presence of the robbers with irony had a positive effect for later archaeologists, as they deterred farmers from setting up homesteads. The Roman Wall was heavily cannibalised by the locals as a cheap and easy form of quarry, used to build houses, dykes and barns – but the Northumberland thieves kept such people away.

Nicholas – (ex.1704)

William – (c.1700)

Thomas – (c.1700)

These three Armstrongs were brothers, and belonged to a notorious branch of the family living in Northumberland. They were from Scotland originally – *"But their misdeids they were so great, They banished them to the English syde."* The story of this Armstrong family sounds familiar and predictable. The family could not fit into the peaceful life as farmers and were exiled. The land they chose was one of the last bastions for the Border cattle thieves and other miscreants – at Housesteads. The Armstrongs were first recorded at Housesteads in 1663, with Nicholas Armstrong buying the farm in 1692, only to have to sell it again in 1694 to Thomas Gibson of Hexham for the sum of £485. They remained as tenants after that date, with a family branch taking up residence at Grandy's Knowes, adjacent to another Roman ruin – Vindolanda. The family were well-known as a band of horse thieves and cattle rustlers, who used the old fort as a place to hold their stolen beasts. It was reputed that every male member of the family was at some point a "broken man," formally outlawed and exiled by either the Scottish or English authorities. Housesteads may have become a last sanctuary for the last of the cattle thieves on the Border.

The theft of livestock was a profession which long lasted with the Armstrongs, going on for at least a century after the end of the reivers. In 1700 William and Thomas stole a horse, an act which was observed by their neighbour, William Turner of Cringledykes. Fearing that Turner would report the brothers to the authorities, they threatened to shoot him. After second thoughts and not wanting to risk a murder case on their hands, the brothers resorted to brutal and bloody intimidation – they cut off Turner's right ear and a part of his cheek. And to avoid Turner from reporting the assault, they cut out his tongue. Enough of Turner's tongue survived to enable him to tell his full story to the court, reporting the criminals in all their hideous glory. At the trial Nicholas Armstrong stepped in to defend his brothers, accusing William Lowes of Crow Hall, in South Tyne, of having instigated the brothers in their attack on Turner. According to Nicholas, Turner was trying to steal a horse from the Common, and encouraged the two Armstrongs to halt the theft. Lowes denied the charge.

The outcome of the trial is not known, but times were changing and the writing was on the wall. Nicholas was hanged in 1704 and his brothers fled to America.

Miscellaneous Freebooters & Moss-Troopers

George – (c.1500)

Hector – (fl.1502)

Edmund – (fl.1502)

These three Armstrongs were brothers from Liddesdale. George was probably the senior member as he was demanded as a pledge by Patrick, Earl of Bothwell, in 1498, to guarantee good behaviour for the family. The effects of George being locked up may have curtailed the clan's raiding, but once released, George resumed the family business. In 1502 he stole a stallion from the Earl of Lennox, a very bold theft which was committed in Edinburgh of all places – not exactly the normal hunting ground for the Armstrongs.

All three were recorded raiding together in that same year when charged for the burning and pillaging of Borthwickshiels. The case came before King James IV, who was visiting the Borders in early November, and was at Jedburgh on the 5th, 11th and 15th of that month, holding court and administering justice. On the 15th, George, Edmund and Hector, appeared before James on his command to answer for the *"burning of Bothnichelis and the hereschip of 300 sheep, 60 oxen and cows, 20 horses and mares, and sundry goods."* Another crime in 1502 is recorded, which possibly involved the same three Armstrong. The three brothers were named as Edward Armstrong ("Edward" may have been a spelling mistake for Edmund), George in Raltoune and Hector, who were accused of plundering Robert Ker and his tenants from Elereif in Ettrick Forest. William and Edward made pledges to satisfy the parties.

George had a daughter married to William Elliot – a useful partnership to the north and possible new lancers.

***

Archibald – (d.c.1520)

Archie was the chief of an Armstrong family grayne, though which one was not recorded. He was an active reiver, whose career came to a rather unpleasant end when he was caught thieving at Haughton. Haughton Castle dates back to at least 1373, fortified by Gerald Widdrington who built upon an earlier 13th century hall. Although it was owned by the Widdringtons, the Swinburn family currently lived in it. Archie was caught attempting to round up a herd of cattle in the meadows close to Barrasford, but was overpowered and incarcerated within the dungeon at Haughton Castle by Thomas Swinburne.

Swinburne had a lot on his mind when Archie was locked up, with a meeting planned in York to see Cardinal Wolsley foremost in his thoughts. Swinburne set off on his journey and clean forgot to leave instructions about the care for his prisoner, with no provision to supply food or water. He also forgot to leave the key for the cell, having taken it along accidentally hanging from his belt. On the third day of his journey and almost reaching York, Swinburne noticed the key, and put two and two together. With alarm he realised his mistake, and with all haste he galloped for home. Arriving back at Haughton, Swinburne enquired "How fared the prisoner?" – fearing what the answer would be. Archie had been dropped into an "oubliette," a bell-shaped prison with no proper door, an airless pit with no light or sanitation. The servants replied that they had heard moans and screams for a few days, but the noise had since stopped. Swinburne unlocked the dungeon and found a horrifying sight. He was too late – the prisoner was dead. It was macabrely noticed; in desperation Archie had gnawed the flesh from his own arm.

This was not the end of Archie, a few months later his ghost haunted the castle. Dreadful shrieks were heard coming from the dungeon. The cries and moans of Archie could be heard nightly, echoing around the castle and even out into the countryside going as far as the village of Barrasford. The screams would keep awake at night Swinburne and his staff plus the residents of Barrasford, driving many to despair. After months of sleepless nights, the villagers demanded that action be taken. Swinburne brought in the Rector of Simonburn to exorcise the ghost; and reading from a large black-lettered Bible, he banished the trouble making spirit. No more noises were heard from Archie, and for peace of mind, the Rector left behind the Bible from which he had read during the exorcism as a comfort for Swinburne that Archie was truly gone forever. All was quiet at Haughton; however Archie was to make an unexpected return visit many years later. The Bible of Simonburn was noticed to have become worn and was taken to London for binding; when its absence caused Archie to come screaming back to life, causing as much havoc as before. What to do? When the Bible had been repaired and returned, Archie's ghost naturally disappeared. The Bible laid the spirit of Archie to rest once again. Today Archie remains still at peace; however a local legend states that whenever a descendant of Sir John de Widderington/Thomas Swinburne sets foot inside Haughton Castle, the shrieks start all over again.

This was not the last Border reiver that Haughton would see. In 1541 a mixed gang of Armstrongs, Crosiers and Elliots descended upon the castle and broke into the castle's barmkin using ladders, injuring the keeper in the process. They could not gain access to the main keep, but the courtyard was plundered. They stole nine horses and goods worth £40, making a clean getaway.

✳✳✳

Roger Armstrong – (ex.1528)

On the 21 January, 1528, Roger together with Archibalde Dodde, Harry Noble and William Charlton of Shitlington Hall, entered the Bishopric of Durham gaining another five to their number, and robbed many persons in the neighbourhood of Woolsingham. For good measure they carried away the priest of Muggleswick with them as a prisoner, who was hoped to bring later a suitable ransom. On their return homeward, the nine reivers ran into trouble when the South Tyne River became flooded. The normal quiet routes by ford were impassable forcing the group to use the safer, but more dangerous bridges. Time was getting short also, with a hot trod on their tail. After a quick discussion the gang headed to Haydon Bridge; where as the name suggests stood a substantial stone bridge. They reached the bridge safely, and just in time as the bailiff of Hexham and the constable of Langley Castle with their followers were closing in. To the horror of Roger and his colleagues, the bridge had a gate across its width which was barred, chained and locked against them. There was no time for finesse, they would have to abandon their plunder and horses and run for it. Vaulting the gate they ran across the bridge hoping to disappear into the moorland on the far shore. The priest of Muggleswick must have watched with amusement as he was made a free man. As the hot trod arrived he probably pointed the way, wishing the posse well as their sleuth hound caught the scent and went in for the kill.

With a blood hound on their trail, the gang possibly scattered to make several trails for the hound to follow, wishing upon hope the hound did not single them out. The gang did not get far, with mounted troopers breathing down their necks. Outnumbered, a desperate skirmish broke out in which Charlton and James Noble was slain. Roger and Archibalde Dodde were taken as prisoners (Harry Noble and five others escaped), to be tried at a Warden's Court held at Alnwick on 27 January. They were both found guilty, with Roger hung in chains near to Newcastle and Dodde at Alnwick. The bodies of Charlton and Noble were not exempt from the gallows, their bodies were collected and also hung in chains; Charlton at Hexham and Noble at Haydon Bridge. Four decomposing reivers would serve for a while as a visual threat to deter further raids.

✱✱✱

John Armstrong – "Jony in Gutterholis" – (ex.1536)

John is recorded as coming from the wonderfully named "*Gutterholis*" (Gutter-Hole), the description imagines not the most cleanest of places. As John is termed "in" Gutterholes and not "of," he can be thought as not the property owner. The location of Gutterhole is not known, and was likely to have been a simple hut or cob type house. He appears only once in the archives, within Pitcairn's Criminal Trials, when sentenced in Edinburgh on 13 March 1536, alongside fellow criminal Christopher Henderson, for "*common theft, Reset of theft, Outputting and Inputting, in England and Scotland: And of art and part of treasonably inbringing Englishmen, common thieves, and traitors, within Scotland, and committing common Hereschip and Stouthrief, Murder, and fire-raising.*" A long series of offences which could only have the one outcome – "*To be drawn to the gallows and hanged as traitors: And all their goods, moveable and unmoveable to be escheated to the King.*"

✱✱✱

Anthon – (fl.1547)

Anthon was a Scottish mercenary who took part in Sir Thomas Carleton's campaign in February 1547 into Dumfriesshire. The venture was part big scaled raid and part invasion – the final stages of Henry VIII's "Rough

Wooing." Anthon was present for personal gain, accepting English gold to thieve from his fellow Scots. Carleton was acting officially for the English Crown and hired the Armstrongs with glee, eager for the help in subduing the enemy and lining his own pockets. Dumfries was the main base for Carleton's occupation, where Anthon spent time enjoying the fruits of the land. The only town in the district which put up a resistance was Kirkcudbright, and a force was despatched to capture it. Anthon was involved in this action, hoping to share in the spoils of the sacked town.

On reaching Kirkcudbright, the town put up a spirited defence, surrounded by dykes and barred gates. The assault began one morning, with arrow and musket shots exchanged from the battlements. Carleton could make little headway, with no advancement from his lines. During the various assaults, a curious incident occurred when a woman approached the outer dykes and *"came to the ditch and called for one that would take her husband and save his life."* The lady must have had a low opinion on the town's defences, convinced that Carleton's men would soon storm the gates and pillage the town. She feared for her husband's life and thought it was better to negotiate a deal, rather than trust to the fate of war. Anthon heard her plea and returned an answer – *"Fetch him to me and I'll warrant his life."* The women returned back into the town and with arrows flying overhead, she *"fetched her husband, and brought him through the dyke, and delivered him to the said Anthon, who brought him into England and ransomed him."* Even during the heat of battle, both sides knew the terms of engagement. This was a strict humanitarian transaction, though for Anthon it was purely business. He would make money from the exchange; and why not – this was why he was at the walls of Kirkcudbright, not for the vanity of any king or lord.

The lady's fears though were for nothing, as a relieving Scottish force under McLellan of Bombie arrived, and forced Carleton to lift the siege and withdraw.

✳✳✳

Mungo – "Flie the Gaist" – (fl.1579)

Mungo had a complaint against him made by the bailie of Hexham for stealing from Medhope near Hexham in 1579. He was accompanied by Niniane Armestrang, called *"Gaudee,"* from the Whithaugh grayne.

✳✳✳

Lancelot (Lancie) – "Bonybutis" – (fl.1580)

Lancelot has one of the most intriguing nicknames amongst the Border reivers – *"Bonybutis."* The meaning of his alias is easy enough to understand, but exactly what made these boots bonny, and how did he obtain them? Perhaps he reived them from some English lord, or had his wife add adornments to his existing riding boots. This illustrates the pride in appearance that some reivers followed, Johnnie Armstrong of Gilnockie being the most famous example. Reivers also lifted cloth besides their normal haul of cattle, why would a reiver not dress in the fashion which they pleased? The clothes made the man and wealth was often displayed in how you dressed. A successful reiver would look very dapper indeed and be proud to show off this fact.

It is not known exactly were Lancelot resided, but it was within Liddesdale. He was recorded amongst the Armstrongs who ambushed the Scotts and Gladstones at Whithaugh in 1580.

***

Quentin – "Pawtonis Quintene" – (fl.1582)

Simon – "Geordies Sim" – (fl.1582)

Quentin was the head of a gang, who accompanied by *"Sym Armstrang, callit Geordeis Sym,"* and other Armstrongs and Littles, raided the farm of *"Hairhoip"* (Harehope) in Tweeddale in 1582.

***

Ninian (Ringan) – "Gaudee/Gawdie" – (c.1583)

Ninian was related to the Armstrongs of Whithaugh, and was named as *"Rynyon Armestronge called Gaudee"* within Thomas Musgrave's list of the Border Riders in 1583. He took part in a raid with Mungo, *"called Flie the Gaist,"* and stole horses from Medhope near Hexham in 1579.

***

Richard – "Carhand" – (fl.1583)

Richard is interestingly known as *"Carhand,"* a term which is a variation on the modern corrie-fisted, meaning to be left handed. The word originates from the Kerr family, who were famous for being left handed. Left handedness would lend a great deal of advantage in a sword fight, when blows and thrusts could be delivered upon an opponent from unexpected directions. He crops up named as *"Riche Armestronge called Carhand,"* in Musgrave's list of the Border Riders in 1583, under the *"Armstrongs of Melyonton quarter."*

***

Simon (Sym) – (fl.1583)

Simon is recorded taking part in a raid on 6 August 1583, and stealing two horses from *"Hobb Tweddale of Orcharde house."* Simon is referred to as *"Sym Armstrong sonne to Hugh Harden"* within the document.   Harden may refer to

326

the location of the same name, a settlement / tower house in between the villages of Mains and Castleton on the Liddel Water.

✳✳✳

Andrew – "Bessies Andrewe" – (fl.1583)

Andrew obtained his nickname unusually from his mother, and not his father – Elizabeth. On 21 August 1583, Andrew together with Simon Armstrong, 9th Laird of Mangerton, stole six "*kyne*" and oxen from Davy Bell of Overdenton.

✳✳✳

Archibald – "Sandies Arche" – (c.1583)

Archibald, the son of Alexander, surfaces within Thomas Musgrave's list of 1583 on the Border Riders. He is named as "*Arche Armestronge, called Sandes Arche*" within the section on the "*Offspring of 'ill Wills' Sandy.*"

Archibald found himself in trouble twice in 1589 – the first time was when on a mixed foray of Armstrongs and Elliots:-

"*William Loren complains upon Robert Armstrong 'Robine the taillor', Rinion Armstrong of Tweeden, Mathew Armstrong, Adam Ellott son to Davie of Dunlies, Alexander's Arche Armstrong, &c. for coming to Trewhit the 26th January last* [1589], *breaking Robert Storie's house, taking away a black mare price 4L., money and insight 5 marks, carrying said Robert prisoner to Scotland, and keeping him.*"

And the second, when riding along with a gang of Whithaugh Armstrongs:-

"*Edward Shaftoo of Bavington complains upon Hob 'the Taillour', Arche Armstrong son to the 'owld' laird of Whithaugh, Robine Armstrong of Whithaugh, Alexanders Arche Armstrong for stealing 18 oxen, a bull and 7 old kye, a horse and a meare, about 8th September last.*" [1589]

✳✳✳

Archibald (Arche) – (fl.1589)

Rowland (Rowy) – (fl.1589)

In March 1589, William Armstrong and his tenants made a complaint against Davie Little of Glenyar, Davie Bell of the Water of Milk, and Rowy and Arche Armstrong sons to the "*Cockers,*" for stealing six horse and mares – A case of Armstrongs thieving from Armstrongs.

***

Robert (Hob) – "Red nebb" – (fl.1589)

Robert received his interesting nickname for having a red nose – "*neb*" being Scots for nose. Perhaps Robert was fond of the spirits, producing his own brand of Liddesdale whisky.

Robert was from Liddesdale and is recorded taking part in a raid on "*about St. Luck's day 1589*" (Saint Luke the Evangelist – 18 Oct). The foray was to Blackcleugh, Kirkhaugh, near Alston; the raiders being a mixed gang of Armstrongs and Elliots – "*Andrew Armstrong son to the Larde of Whithawghe, Francys and John Armstrong his brothers, of Whithawghe, Arche Ellott of Clentwood, Hob Ellott, Gib Ellott his brother, Marting Ellott called 'Martinges Gib', James [?], and old Will Ellot of the Steile, George Simpson, John Ellott 'longe John', Andrew and 'red nebb' Hob Armstrong.*" The gang reived forty "*yowes*" and ten "*hogges,*" and disappeared back into Liddesdale. The locals though were a spirited bunch and bravely organised a "*lawful trode,*" to get their livestock back. The trod successfully caught up with the raiders, but came off the worse. Tackling the Armstrongs and Elliots was always going to be a difficult task at the best of times, a task which the trod was unprepared for. All of the trod was captured. There are no reports of any deaths or people being wounded, implying that the reivers took the trod by surprise and intimidated them into surrendering. The trod together "*with their horses and furniture,*" were taken as prisoners and ransomed for £180 sterling.

Robert (Hob) – "Hob the taillour" – (c.1589)

As Robert's nickname indicates, he was a tailor, and known for his skills and trade within the Armstrong community. Looking at the lists of plunder stolen by the reivers, cloth was a common item. Such cloth would have provided the raw materials for the Border tailors to ensure their inhabitants were well kitted out. It gives the impression that the Armstrongs were a fashion conscious family, when considering Johnnie Armstrong made the king jealous on his flamboyant attire in 1530. And this eye for clothes may have continued with the Armstrongs into later generations. As kings of the saddle and all they surveyed, the reivers would have wanted to give a visual impression of their power and wealth, and what better way than to have fine clothes.

It would have been thought that Robert led a sedentary life, one of the few Liddesdale men to have a legitimate business. However the reality could not be further away from the truth. Between the years 1588-90, Robert is documented in a frenzy of raiding. Robert was first recorded in 1588, taking part in two forays:-

1. "*John Armestrong complains upon said Will of the Steill, Martin's Arche, Martin's Dande, 'Hob the tayleer', Thome Armstrong Smys Thome, &c. for stealing 6 kye and a bull, and insight 3L. 6s. 8d., the first Satterdaye in Lente 1588.*"

2. *"The said John Heron complains upon Whyntins Arche, Edward Croser alias Adey Farlamdes, Adams John, and the Taylour, for stealing 12 horse and meares about Michaelmas gone twoo yeare 1588."*

The following year he was billed for two more:-

1. *"The same* [Lord Forster, March Warden] *upon William Dugles of Yarnside, Eddie Ladley 'great leges', Robine Armstrong 'Hob the taillour', Thomas Trumble of Hoppesburn the younger, Jock Sheile of the Kirkeknowe, for stealing 11 kye and oxen, a black mear, insight 5L. sterling, Wednesday before 'Our latter Lady daye in harvest'* [15 Aug Feast of the Assumption of Mary] *1589."*

2. *"Bartrame Forster upon Thomas and Raiphe Eansley of Cleethaughe, Andrew and William Frisell sons to the Laird of Overtoun, Jocke Rotherford of Edgerstoun, Davie Ladley of the Sonnye syde, Martine Croser late of Baxtoun lee, Clement Croser his son, Robert Armstrong 'Hobb the taillour', Eddie Ellott son to Davie 'the Carling', for reiving from Wood burne 12 kye and oxen and insight 5L. sterling, at 'Mertlemas'* [11 Nov] *1589."*

Another dose of charges were placed before Hob at the Bells Kirk from 13-19 April 1590, for Middle March Bills, &c. Liddesdale. The Truce Day court was presided over by William Fenwick and Thomas Trotter. The two officials had their work cut out with the quantity of bills to plough through and the thieves to process. Robert was called up to answer for four raids, the deputies must have been sick of him by the end of the week. Robert would have chalked up quite a hefty bill in fines to pay up when he returned back to Liddesdale. But he could always thieve the money owed later in the year, or ask his fellow Armstrongs for a loan.

1. *"William Loren complains upon Robert Armstrong 'Robine the taillor', Rinion Armstrong of Tweeden, Mathew Armstrong, Adam Ellott son to Davie of Dunlies, Alexander's Arche Armstrong, &e. for coming to Trewhit the 26th January last* [1589]*, breaking Robert Storie's house, taking away a black mare price 4L., money and insight 5 marks, carrying said Robert prisoner to Scotland, and keeping him."*

2. *"The same complain* [Warden and the tenants of Middleton Hall] *upon William Dowgles of Yerneside, Eddie Ladelie 'Greteleges', Hobe 'the Tayllor', Thomas Trumble of Hoppesborne, younge Jocke Sheile of Kyrknowe, &c. for stealing 11 kye and oxen, a black mear, insight worth 6L. sterling, the Wennesday after Our Ladie daye in harvest 1589."*

3. *"Raphe Anderson of Davisheile, complains upon Robert Armestronge, called 'Hob the taillour', Clement Croser of Borneheades, Rychard Armstronge called 'Dick of Dryupp', Rynione Armestronge his brother, and others, for stealing 6 oxen, and taking John Anderson prisoner and ransoming him the morrow after St Luke's day* [18 Oct] *1589."*

4. *"The said John* [Heron] *complains upon Edward Elloit son to Davye, Robert Armestrong alias Tayler, for stealing 5 horse and meares about Martinmas last 1589."*

It is interesting to note, those that endorsed the bills used the Saints Days to record dates of the forays concerned. The 16th century life revolved around the seasons and a part of this was celebrating the life of Christ and his disciples. Life was short and hard, with the various annual festivals bringing a splash of colour and relief. At the Truce Day there was another reiver present who had the same nickname as Robert – Robert Elliot – alias *"Robine Ellott – the taillor."* He was charged for taking part in an Elliot foray on the Halls of Girsonfield and Otterburn at Martinmas 1589. It can be wondered if the two tailors knew each other and perhaps shared patterns. The two may have ensured that the Liddesdale reivers when they rode out were very dapper indeed. Cloth was an item that reivers occasionally stole. On Whitsun Monday 1589, a mixed gang of eighty Armstrongs and Elliots ran an open foray to Percival Reed's land of *"Trowhen"* (Troughend) in Redesdale, and amongst the usual booty of cows, oxen and horses, they also lifted *"60 yards of lynne clothe"*. Perhaps some of this cloth wound its way into the hands of the two Roberts. Robert was actually present on at least one raid when a quantity of cloth was stolen. The foray again was down Redesdale, with several targets hit on 19 May 1589, which included the Laird of *"Troghwen"* (Troughend – Percival Reed yet again), James Hedley of the Garret sheills and others. Hob rode aside a mixed gang of Elliots and Crosiers, including such rakes as Davie Laidlaw *"Cuddis Davie,"* Hob Elliot *"the Bullie,"* Davie *"the Carlinge,"* and one hundred others. They ran a day foray and reived *"100 kye and oxen, 5 horses and meares."* Amongst the plunder and slaughter (two men were slain and two taken prisoner), *"lynn clothe"* worth £10 sterling was picked up. It is interesting to think on Robert spying out the cloth on the raid and taking it as his personal plunder; returning back to Liddesdale to tailor up the fabric into various jackets and breeches – perhaps to rig out the Elliot and Armstrong chieftains in the latest European fashions.

Robert's last raid was recorded on 8 September 1589, riding with Arche Armstrong, son to the *"owld"* laird of Whithaugh, Robine Armstrong of Whithaugh and Alexander's Arche Armstrong. They were complained upon by Edward Shafto of Bavington for *"stealing 18 oxen, a bull and 7 old kye, a horse and a meare."*

John – "Skynbanke" / "Skinabake" – (c.1580s/90s)

John was related to ill Will's Sandie – and was named in Thomas Musgrave's list of 1583 as an offspring of that family. He was listed as *"John Armestronge called Skinabake,"* though his connection to Ill Will was not mentioned. John was a chief / headsman within the reiving gang *"Sandy's Bairns."* The gang appears within John Monipennie's publication in 1597, which sought to name the principal clans, surnames and chiefs on the Border. John is named as named as *"John Skynbanke,"* and his fellow gang members were no less than William Armstrong of Kinmont and his brother Christopher. It has to be wondered if one of them held the overall command of the gang, or they shared the responsibility.

Andrew – "The Bungell" – (c.1590)

Andrew was a servant to Simon, 9th Laird of Mangerton, a job and obligation that led him into many a misadventure. Andrew first surfaces at the Bells Kirk in April 1590, to answer for Middle March bills put before him by the deputy wardens William Fenwick and Thomas Trotter. There were two complaints made on Andrew, both by William Fenwick and Mathew Armstrong. The first complaint was for stealing from the "*Heatherie burne*" (Heathery Burn near Stanhope), two oxen, a "*stote*" (bullock), a four year old cow and a brown mare, at Lammas 1587. Andrew was charged alongside David Armstrong ("*Bangtaile*") and Jock Armstrong of the Hollows. The second complaint was against the exact same gang, who were joined by Mungo and Jock Armstrong, two servants of the Laird's Jock. The Laird's Jock was the son of Thomas, 7th Laird of Mangerton, giving the raid the feel that the main Mangertons were too busy, away on other business and sent their servants off instead on this separate mission to fill the pot. It is interesting to think that these two raids were inspired by a lack of meat for the servants to serve. And that an annoyed laird sent his servants away on orders not to return until they could bring back some cattle. The target was the same as before, the Heathery Burn; the gang must have remembered rich pickings from the previous year and struck a second time on Candlemas 1588. They were charged for stealing thirty seven "*wedders.*"

In the document entitled "*Gilsland complaints against Liddesdale*" dated 24 October 1595, "*Andro Armstrong, the bundgell,*" was named as taking part in a "*hearshipp at Tredermayne*" on 12 September 1595. The raid was led by "*Watt of Harden*" (Walter Scott – known as Buccleuch's right hand man), and featured John Henderson of Hoghyll, Andro Henderson, Hector Armstrong of Tweeden, Hob Ellott the Laird of Burnhead and three other Elliots. The gang was charged "*for 60 kye and oxen, and 6 horses and mares.*"

✳✳✳

David (Davie) – "Bangtail" – (c.1590)

David has one of the most curious of reiver nicknames, the reasons behind which can only be guessed. Was he a gay reiver, or the name an insult / joke on his masculinity? David was as tough as any other outlaw, and appears to have had a mischievous sense of humour, keeping in tune with his non-war like name. David is recorded taking part in two raids in the company of Jock Armstrong of the Hollows and Andrew Armstrong "*the Bungell*" at a Truce Day in April 1590, at the Bells Kirk. In the first foray they lifted "*twoo oxen, a stote, and a whye of fowre yeare old, a broune mear, at Lammes 1587,*" from "*Heatherie burne.*" On the second raid they had Mungo and Jock Armstrong along also, servants to the Laird's Jock and stole thirty seven sheep from the same location of Heathery Burn at Candlemas (2 February) 1588.

The last decade of the 16th century saw a great decay in the Borders, when the reivers were at their most untouchable high. The Bishop of Durham summed up the mood when writing on 7 August 1595, to Huntingdon from an assize in Durham. He stated "*that the outlaws of both Borders, and other notorious thieves, are determined to make this bishopric an open spoil and prey, to the impoverishing of the poorer sort, and endangering such of the better sort as are able and willing to repress them.*" The Bishop made recommendations to combat the reivers – these included having the Border officers in better readiness to resist and pursue the thieves or to stop suspicious passers-by, and asking the Privy Council for extra forces. Having the March Wardens observe more duly the days of truce, and execution of justice was also required; *the neglect whereof has bred wonderful boldness in the Scots.*" In the same document, the Bishop relates an amusing incident which took place at the assize in Durham. David was one of those to be tried and was rather reluctant at least, to be brought forward to the bar. The Bishop writes...

"Whereof a great prezumpcion at the bar this presente Assizes, was publiqely shewen by one David Armstrong alias Bangtaill, a Scot, and a notorious owtlaw, who being apprehended and brought in by Mr William Fenwick of Wallington upon your lordshipes commanndement, arrained and found guiltie of eight severall felonies, feared not to threaten Mr Fenwick, that though he were the best beloved gentleman of his clan, yet his heeles should be lifted and turned up to the sky for bringing him, being a Scot, to be tried here before us! Also that he the said Armstrong would kis the bar when he went from yt, and vow that never any Scot should be so brought in and dealt with againe."

It is interesting to see the word "clan" written to designate a Border family, lending evidence that the word was not only used in the Highlands of Scotland. And an amusing vision the document makes of an upside down "Bangtail," and a wonder if any law was passed to make it a crime to invert a Scotsman. A big part of the problem in keeping law on the Border was corrupt Border officials. Lord Eure came across this phenomenon when he became Warden of the Middle March and noticed William Fenwick, the Keeper of Tynedale and Henry Woodrington being in open association with the Scottish reivers. He writes to Burghley explaining the situation on 20 November 1595...

"The combination of the Scots thieves and the Northumberland gentlemen increases. The two principal gentlemen of worth in the country being with me, to whom I imparted how hateful it was to her Majesty that her subjects should make such unlawful compacts for their private safety, and refuse the open course of justice for redress: yet notwithstanding Mr Henry Wodrington and Mr William Fenwick have of late entered assurance with the Burnes lord Sesforth men, and Armestronges Bangtailes freindes."

Only "Bangtail" is mentioned amongst all of the other potential Armstrongs. He was operating at a higher diplomatic level, paying government officials to turn the other way and entering deals of mutual protection.

✻✻✻

Alexander – "Hebbies Sandie" – (fl.1592)

In November 1592, Rowtledge of Comecrocke made a complaint upon *"Sandie Armestrange called Hebbies Sandie, Willie Wawghe his man, Fargasies Willie of Kirkleheade, for taking 20 sheep, 20 'gaite' and 6 kye and oxen."*

✻✻✻

Thomas – (fl.1596)

Thomas was one of the planners behind the famous rescue of Kinmont Willie Armstrong from Carlisle Castle in 1596. He was at the meeting at Archerbeck on 7 April 1596, which fleshed out the embryonic rescue idea into something that could actually be pulled off. Thomas was in the same room as Walter Scott of Buccleuch, Walter Scott of Harden, Richard Graham of Brackenhill, and the two Carleton brothers Thomas and Lancelot. He was the only Armstrong present at the meeting, suggesting his importance within the Kinmont grayne. Thomas had an ear to the conversations with Buccleuch and the rescues operational details.

Reiver society was one of close family bonds and it would come as a shock to the Armstrongs when Thomas became an informant on the rescue. Thomas is not recorded as taking part in the mission, but he knew exactly who were involved. It was this information that he hoped would deflect Lord Scrope's anger when it came, away from himself and his family. As soon as the rescue was over, Thomas travelled down to Carlisle where he basically betrayed his colleagues. Thomas knew he was doing a risky thing with his life on the line, but must have felt a greater risk from Scrope to become a turncoat. Thomas was first questioned officially on 25 April, together with Andrew Graham, a fellow informant; examined by Lord Scrope and Sir Robert Carey. This was the first of four separate investigations, Scrope would have rubbed his hands with glee, hoping to gain irrefutable evidence and pin down some of the rescue party to a trial and conviction – saving face on the castle break-in.

Two interviews happened in May. On 2 May Lord Scrope, the Bishop of Carlisle and John Middleton (justice of peace for Cumberland), were employed to do the examining. Scrope writes to the Council that same day on his meeting with the two informers – *"concerninge the breckeinge of Carlisle castle, and they both being sworn, do affirm that one Thomas Carlton, Launcelatt Carlton and Richie of Breckenhill with others, did agree and sett doune the plott how the castell shoulde be brocken, and that Thomas Carlton did undertake to make the watchmenn of the saide castell shewre."* A second followed with the informants coming before the Bishop of Durham, Sir William Bowes, Dr Colmer and Mr Slingsbie.

A final investigation was held on 26 July, were both Armstrong and Graham came before Scrope, the Bishop of Carlisle and John Middleton; and – *"plainly affirmed their former evidence touching the breach of Carlisle castle, and release of Kinmont, and utterly denied that I had used any hard dealing to them."* Nothing became of Thomas's betrayal. The obvious happened; he had broken the trust of a group of powerful and ruthless cut-throats, and would pay the penalty. Richard of Brackenhill organised a group of his heavies, and together with Jock *"Stowlugs"* Armstrong and some assistance by Carleton's followers, a brother of Thomas was seized and murdered. The implications of this were loud and clear, to speak up would result in certain death. Thomas withdrew himself as a witness on the Kinmont rescue. Scrope wrote to the Privy Council on 9 August 1597 giving them an update on the new situation:-

"The said Armstrong, within the last 14 days has heard of the murder of his brother Rinion Armstrong near to Askerton castle where Thomas Carleton dwells, and has been sore troubled in mind, and in manner distracted: so I have had

moch to do to appease him in his sayd furie, and now (I thanck God) he is in som reasonable sorte recovered: yet not very aide at this tyme to travell... The said Andro Grame and Thomas Armstrong have not charged the Carletons and Grames with any offence, except conspiring for breaking Carlisle castle and taking out Kinmont... Carlisle – Signed: Th. Scroope."

✳✳✳

Thomas – "Boutfute/ Boltsfoote" – (fl.1596)

James – "how neif" – (fl.1596)

These two were brothers. Thomas was summoned to the tollbooth of Berwick on 2 February 1596, coming before the commissioners. His bill was one amongst 125 Scots and 210 English, a busy productive session, it went as follows:- *"The Laird of Belyster upon Tho. Armstrong alias 'Boltsfoote' for 4 stirkes and a oxe, referred to assise."*

Later that year, Thomas and James appear together contained within *"Cessford's Roll of Wrongs"* of August 1596. The document was *"A note of the slauchters, stowthis and reiffis as hes bene committit be the inhabitantis of the East Wardanrye of England, upoun the inhabitantis under Sir Robert Kerris office."* A real mouthful; the list contained forty nine crimes with the two Armstrongs turning up on the third – it reads:- *"George Chesholme 'hird' to Sir Robert Ker slain by Thom Storie in Killaime, Thom Armstrang 'boutfute,' Jame Armstrang 'how neif,' his brother, in plain daylight."* The Armstrongs had killed a herdsman of the Cessford chieftain, not exactly the wisest of moves. Sir Robert was noted for his ruthless and murderous nature; the Armstrongs would not sleep well over the next few days, expecting a vengeful Ker lance to come their way at any moment.

✳✳✳

Hector (Ekie) – "Braidebelt" – (fl.1596)

A complaint was made upon Hector by the tenants of Whitehill for taking part in a large one hundred-man raid, in which six houses were burned and goods worth £200 sterling and six prisoners were taken. The raid was brought to court on West March complaints against Buccleuch for the period June-Sept 1596. Another five of Hector's co-raiders were also present – Sime and Joke Armstronge of Calfehill, Pawtie of Harelawe, Willie of *"Briggomes,"* and Willie *"Kange"* Irvine.

✳✳✳

Alexander – "Hebbys Sandy" – (fl.1596)

Alexander was named ("*Sandy Armestronge son to Hebbye*") in a document by Lord Scrope in April 1596, as one of the principal assailants at the raid of Carlisle Castle to rescue Kinmont Willie. Sandy was on the night raid with Buccleuch and was accompanied by two of his followers, a part of the small core who was chosen to enter the castle and extricate Kinmont. Sandy's involvement was reported by "Richies Will" Graham, an informant who wrote an anonymous letter to Scrope on 24 April 1596. Graham wrote "*Right honorable lord, pleaseth your lordship to ken this the truth of the takinge out of Kynmont*"... stating that Richie Graham of Brackenhill and "*Ebes Sandey was the first that ever brake the hole and come in about Kinmont.*" Sandy was in Scrope's sights for an arrest after his betrayal by Graham. Scrope was eager to save face on the embarrassing episode and now had a name to search for on his warden's rodes.

✳✳✳

Archibald – "Ebbies Arche" – (ex.1601)

Archibald was possibly a brother of Alexander "Hebby's Sandie," the sons of Herbert. Archibald took part in the rescue of Kinmont Willie in April 1596 – and was a victim of Scrope's rage after the event. Scrope's anger and need for revenge was dangerously real after Kinmont's escape. Archibald was tracked down and made a scapegoat for Scrope's failings on the break-out. Archibald lacked the connections that the likes of Buccleuch and the Carleton brothers had; Scrope would make a token example of Archibald. Archibald was the only member of Buccleuch's rescue party to face trail and be executed. From such a death it can be seen why informants came forward to speak up and betray Buccleuch and his party.

In August 1601, Scrope was compelled to justify four charges against him by the Scottish king. The third charge was concerned about Archibald and was titled "*For the suppressing and executing of 'Ebbies Arche'.*" The king had thought Scrope was acting too heavy handed on Scottish affairs and wanted some explanations. Scrope wrote back on the death of Archibald:- "*He was a known chief actor in taking Kinmont out of Carlisle; and committed many murders, &c. here lately: justice for which being deferred, there was good reason to take him. Our good people are murdered and taken and in spite of the King's commands and Johnston's promises, kept in chains, and fed like dogs most inhumanly: so this complaint seems but to hinder justice!*"

✳✳✳

John (Jock) – "Stowlugs" – (ex.1606)

John has one of the most fascinating of all the reiver nicknames. "Lugs" is the Scots word for ears and "Stow" is to slice/lop. The image brings a deep cringe, John had both of his ears either part missing or totally cut off. The reason for this missing body part is frustratingly absent, but a war wound can be considered not to be the case. A dagger could take part of an ear off, if a reiver lost his steel bonnet in combat (a sword blow would be too much – damaging the head also), but to lose both ears is rather improbable. A more grizzly supposition is that the ears were cropped off as a

335

punishment. There is a later precedent and record for such a punishment occurring; in 1684 James Graham of Claverhouse severed the ears from James Gavin's head (with his own shears), a tailor from Douglas, for being a Covenanter. What could John have done to deserve such mutilation? The reason is sadly not passed down, but a possible suggestion can be made that John was a hitman and this was an act of pay-back. A cruel revenge of sorts does seem the most likely explanation.

In 1591, John was one of seven Armstrongs who were indicted for the murder of John Armstrong alias *"Cokespoole."* The group were all named in a document with Edward, "Antons Edward" of Williava, heading the list, hinting that he was the group's leader. Williava was in Bewcastledale, which suggests the entire party came from the same area. The facts behind the murder of *"Cokespoole"* are frustratingly missing. Was he murdered by the seven Armstrongs when they went on a foray? As the killing was termed a murder, it can be considered that *"Cokespoole"* was not a reiver. No one would mourn one less outlaw. If the seven Armstrongs were reivers, they would surely have stolen plunder to be accounted for, but none is mentioned. The situation then could either have been a revenge killing, or one out of anger / jealousy / politics, or a paid assassination.

Another murder happened five years later, which came about in the aftermath of the rescue of Kinmont from Carlisle Castle. The rescue caused great humiliation and anger from Lord Scrope, who was responsible for the security of the Queen's property. Sword rattling and threats followed, and in the wake of the blames and arguments on who was responsible, three informants came forward to supply information – Andrew Graham, William (*"Richie's Will"*) Graham and Thomas Armstrong. One of the informants, Thomas Armstrong, at an interview on 2 May, with Lord Scrope, the Bishop of Carlisle and John Middleton – pointed out that Thomas Carleton, Lancelot Carleton, Richie of Brackenhill and others, agreed to and set down a plot on how the castle should be broken into. This was dangerous information; Thomas had to be stopped from giving his witness testimony.

John was not involved in the rescue of Kinmont, his branch of the Armstrongs were from Gilsland and too far away from the route travelled by Buccleuch and his party. Secrecy was an important factor on the rescue; spreading those helping over a wide area could have compromised the venture, increasing the risk of it being found out or betrayed before it started. John though had connections to elements of the Kinmont rescue, with links to the Grahams and Carletons. John's help came to be required when Brackenhill and the Carletons wanted Thomas Armstrong, the informer to be silenced. John was probably a hired thug, brought in to do the dirty work and would have looked a terrifying character. John was the stuff of nightmares; it can be imagined, his figure arriving late at night with a levelled pistol or rapier, his earless face grinning as he professionally undertook his mission. Brackenhill organised the murder squad and brought John on-board, and with the assistance of Carleton's followers they set off to kill. Thomas Armstrong was not the target, slaying him was too obvious and would arouse the suspicions of Scrope causing more political fall-out. The gang chose Rinion Armstrong instead; a brother of Thomas. The gang caught up with Rinion near to Askerton Castle; Askerton was where Thomas Carleton dwelt, and no doubt he played the role of guiding the murderers to their target. The poor unsuspecting and innocent Rinion had no chance, and was cut down. John is the only named person in the murder, perhaps he was the sole assassin, his hand behind the killing weapon. The murder had its effect, Thomas was *"sore troubled in mind, and in manner distracted"* by the death, expecting rightly that he would be next. Thomas wisely withdrew himself as a witness. Within reiver society, betraying someone was taken seriously, and if that betrayal could lead to the gallows, the clans would rise. The other two witnesses on the rescue of Kinmont also pulled out, allowing Brackenhill and the Carletons to escape any trial or recriminations.

When 1603 came and the Union of the Crowns, John's days were numbered. As a known killer, he would be hunted down by the Border Commissioners and executed. Lord William Howard was on the case, and with great zest he rose to the challenge of tracking down the outlaws. On 9 January 1606, Howard wrote to Sir Wilfrid Lawson with relish updating him on his latest conquest. Howard, using the fishing metaphor related how he had been away hoping to catch as many outlaws as possible. His target was Anton's Edward Armstrong, but instead he flushed out his son Thomas, Christopher Irvine and *"Jock Stow Lugs."* Howard describes Jock as *"the last but not the least in villainy. I desire you to keep him as a jewel of high price."* Howard recounts eagerly the chase, how he galloped at the heels of the outlaws – riding all night in pursuit with his servants and followers, chasing them to the confines of Yorkshire where he seized them all. Howard took great satisfaction at capturing *"Stowlugs,"* and asked Lawson with macabre humour *"if you find matter sufficient to hang the two, hold up your finger and they shall be delivered."* And delivered they were, with all three hung within the month.

Thomas – "The Merchant" – (fl.1609)

Thomas, known by his nickname "The Merchant," must have successfully moved from a life of theft to that of trade. He may have been related to Archibald Armstrong *"the Mercheand, in the Hoilhous* (Hollows Tower)," who took part in the burning of Langholm House in 1581 and was brought to trial for it in 1605 – though the nickname similarities may just be a coincidence.

He was accused of murder however in 1609, which hints at the company he kept were not exactly gentlemen and that he still held onto the Armstrong trait of killer/attack despite domesticity. Thomas reported as *"Thomas Airmestrang callit the Mercheand,"* was charged for having *"airt and pairt of the Slauchter of umq James Somervell in Eirdhoussis."* He was ordered to stand trial for murder in Edinburgh on 31 January 1609, alongside *"Andro Airmestrang of the Langholme, Ebbie Airmestrang of Kirktonehill, James Airmestrang of Cannabie, and Johnne Murray, myller in the Cruikis."* The men were all acquitted, being found *"innocent of the said cryme."*

***

Hutchen – "Old Sandie's Hutchene" – (fl.1645)

Hutchen was the son of Alexander Armstrong. He was one of the many Liddesdale men who became moss-troopers during the Great Civil War. In about 1645 he took part in a raid with Geordie of Kinmont, Simon of Whitlawside, and

Will and Francis of Woodhead, onto Swinburne Park in Northumberland, where they lifted fifty cattle. In that same year, Hutchen along with others of the same clan broke into the house of Rev. Thomas Alane (Allan), the minister of Wauchope Kirk, and maliciously beat him and his wife up *"verie pitifullie."* They departed taking two horses away, hoping to sink into the shadows and have their violent depredation lost to memory.

With the Civil War in full flow, Hutchen probably thought he had got away with his nasty crime. However, Francis, 2nd Earl of Buccleuch had just that same year been appointed Justiciar, and the incident had fallen into his more than capable hands. Word reached the ears of Hutchen that the minsister intended to report his assault and robbery to Buccleuch, a prospect that filled him with dread. Buccleuch had the power to hold court over Eskdale, Liddesdale, the Debateable Land – and Wauchope came under his legal authority. What was to be done? Such was the fear that the earl generated, who was now the master of the lands of that parish, a plan was needed or it would be the gallows for him. Buccleuch had recently returned from England, and had fought against Charles I at the Battle of Marston Moor, a gang of moss-troopers would be of no match against him. A cunning plan was hatched by Hutchen and his fellow Armstrongs, an idea to hand back the stolen horses and hopefully those responsible for stealing them would be forgotten about. Word was put out in England to find a hard-bitten individual who had no fear and the brass-est neck possible. Such a person was tracked down, Perse Howme – *"a notorious outlaw, and as great a moss-trooper as themselves."* Hutchen intended Perse to take the blame for their theft, and was no doubt handsomely paid to do so. Perse agreed to the plan and acted as if he was the criminal responsible for the theft. He was given the horses and departed, sending a ransom letter to the minsters stating that he openly avowed that he would *"never have so much as a hare of one of his horses tailes againe, unles he did give him fyve pounds sterling."* It was hoped the minister would pay the ransom and all would be settled, with no need for Buccleuch to turn the parish upside down with his troopers. There is no record on what happened next, which can be assumed, ended quietly for Hutchen, and with Perse back in England several pounds sterling better off.

As soon as one problem was put to bed, another raised its ugly head. Hutchen went on another raid, and on this occasion he was accompanied by Rob Donaldson, in Reedbank upon Esk. Everything went well initially, but on reaching Catheugh and Cringlefold they became disturbed. When searching for a target in the dark, they were surprised by Elliot of the Park, Henderson of Catheugh, plus Matthew Robson and his brother, who had just returned from an excursion into the Debateable Land in pursuit after some cattle of their own which had been stolen. They had a sleuth-hound with them and bristled with menace, a daunting party to tangle with. Hutchen and Donaldson skulked off into the dark to find an easier target, and lifted three-score sheep from Carshope (Kershope), unaware that a sleuth-hound was leading a posse after them. The pair felt satisfied at their nights work when heading home, but the sound of barking sent shivers of alarm. Encumbered by the slow moving sheep, Hutchen and Donaldson were soon overtaken by their pursuers, and were forced to leave the sheep and make a desperate flight in hope of escaping. The hound however, was not put off by the darkness, and with scent alone led the pursuers forward with a new energy. The trail never went cold and the two rustlers were ultimately run to ground at Bruntsheills (Bruntshielbog / Hill – 5km SE of Langholm), on the edge of the Tarras Valley. Outnumbered and cornered, Hutchen and Donaldson were taken captive, and received an unexpected leniency. After a brief detention, their captors let them go. The reason for their release was not disclosed, and was even a puzzle to those recording the incident later. Hutchen and Donaldson may have convinced the posse that they intended to give up their crime spree. They were after all not reivers, but opportunist thieves. And with the civil war in progress, perhaps they were encouraged to take their energies and need for excitement elsewhere.

John – of Parkknow – (k.1645)

George (Geordie) – (c.1645)

John and George were brothers, and were friends with the Armstrongs of Kinmont. When the Great Civil War erupted in Scotland in 1639, they took the opportunity of the disorder caused to line their own pockets and became moss-troopers. The brothers are recorded taking part in a raid in 1645 with the Kinmont's, making up a gang sixteen men strong. The gang rode into Northumberland and stole from the lands of Punder-shaw eighty head of cattle. A spirited defence of the property was made, Cuthbert Hearon the land owner, mustered his friends and servants, and followed in pursuit of the robbers emulating the old hot trod tradition of forty years earlier. The gang headed for home, going into the Debateable Land, unaware of Cuthbert and his posse on their trail. On sighting Cuthbert's force, the moss-troopers went into defensive mode, John and Geordie drew their pistols and fired a shot each at Edward Charlton of Antoun Hill – and missed. Charlton having been attacked responded in the only way possible, he pulled out his carbine and levelled it at John Armstrong – and pulling the trigger, John fell dead. The death of John changed the dynamics of the affair and revenge was wanted. A disorganised scramble of horsemen raced south, with Charlton fleeing for his life. Charlton was captured and could expect no mercy from the Kinmonts.

***

Bibliography

Anonymous. *The New Statistical Account Volume 9,* William Blackwood, Edinburgh, 1836

Armstrong, A. *Archie Armstrong's Banquet of jests*, W. Paterson, Edinburgh, 1872

Armstrong, J.L. *Chronicles of the Armstrongs*, The Marion Press, London, 1902

Bain, J. *The Border Papers: Calendar of letters and papers... Vol. 1&2*, Her Majesty's Stationary Office, London, 1896

Brewer J. S. *Letters and Papers, Henry VIII* – Her Majesty's Stationery Office, London, 1875

Borland, R. *Border Raids and Reivers*, Thomas Fraser, Dalbeattie, 1898

Brown, P.H. *The Register of the Privy Council of Scotland, Vol.8.* H.M. General Register House, Edinburgh, 1908

Cadwallader, J.B. *The History of Northumberland*, Elliot Stock, London, 1895

Carey, R. *Memoirs of Sir Robert Carey, Earl of Monmouth*, James Ballantyne and Co, Edinburgh, 1808

Carlyle T. J. *The Debateable Land*, W. R. McDiarmid & Co., Dumfries, 1868

Durham, K. *Border Reiver 1513-1603*, Osprey Publishing Ltd., Oxford, 2011

Eliott, A. *The Elliots – The Story of a Border Clan*, Charles Thurnam & Sons Ltd., Carlisle, 1986

Fraser, G. M. *The Steel Bonnets*, Barrie & Jenkins, London, 1971

Fraser, W. *The Annandale family book of the Johnstone, Earls & Marquises of Annandale*, Edinburgh, 1894

Hyslop, J & R. *Langholm as it was*, Hills and Company, Sunderland, 1912

Jeffrey, A. *The History and Antiquities of Roxburghshire and adjacent districts*, J. F. Hope, London, 1857

Johnstone, C. L. *The Historical Families of Dumfriesshire and the Border Wars*, Anderson & Son, Dumfries, 1878

Lindsay, R. (of Pitscottie) – *The History of Scotland*, Edinburgh, 1728

Marsden, J. *The Illustrated Border Ballads*, Macmillan London Limited, London, 1990

McLeish, N. *Borderline Cases*, Alba Publishing, Jedburgh, 2000

Monipennie, J. *Certeine matters concerning the realme of Scotland*, A. Hatfield, London, 1603

Ogilvie, W.H. *Saddle for a throne*, R.M. Williams, Adelaide, 1952

Oliver, J.R. *Upper Teviotdale and the Scotts of Buccleuch*, W. & J. Kennedy, Hawick, 1887

Pitcairn, R. *Criminal Trials in Scotland, 1488-1624*, William Tait, Edinburgh, 1833

Reed, J. *The Border Ballads*, The Athlone Press, University of London, 1973

Robson, E. *The Border Line*, Frances Lincoln Limited, London, 2006

Scott, Sir W. *The Border Antiquities of England and Scotland, Vol 1.* Longman, Hurst, Rees, Orme, & Brown, London, 1814

Tough, D.L.W. *The Last Years of a Frontier*, Oxford University Press, GB, 1928

Watson, G. *The Border Reivers*, Robert Hale & Company, London, 1974

Glossary

Abstinence – Armistice or truce

Assurance – A promise of support

Avower – One who bears witness to the guilt of his fellow countrymen

Backbilling – Malicious retaliatory billing

Bairns – Children

Band/Bond – A mutual agreement or oath (Not restricted to a promise of good behaviour)

Barmkin – Walled enclosure, round a tower, used for the protection of cattle

Bauchled – To be accused or challenged for breaking a word, faith or bond

Bedstock – Bedstead

Bigging – The act of building

Billing – Laying a bill of indictment

Billy – Brother

Blackmail – Illegal rent, equivalent to protection money

Brand – Sword

Branks – Halter

Broken man – Men without a responsible head or chief (not necessarily an outlaw)

Brokers – Agents

Bruiking – Possessing

Byre – Cowshed

Cairting – Playing at cards

Cleare – To declare guiltless

Cleugh – Narrow valley

Coddis – Pillows

Cold Trod – The pursuit of reivers to get stolen goods back when the trail was cold

Dag – Hand gun

Darg – A unit of measure, the amount of work which one man can accomplish in a day

Daur – Dare

Double – Restitution which was twice the value of the damage proved.

Durance – A strong, hard-wearing cloth

Fauld – Sheepfold

Fause – False

Fecht – Fight

File – To avow the truth of a bill of indictment

Fostyone/Fustian – Coarse cloth

Fouled/Fyled – Found guilty, case proved

Fray – Conflict/Fighting

Gar – Make

Gavlocke – Iron crowbar

Gear – Property/goods, including livestock

Gleed – Red-hot iron

Grayne – Branch of a surname

Hackbut – Handgun

Heidsman/Hedesman – Chieftain, often the head of a gang of reivers

Heirschip – Plundering, harrying

Heugh – Hollow

Holm – River meadow

Horn (to put to the) – To outlaw

Horse furniture – Saddle & bridle etc. of a horse

Hot Trod – The immediate pursuit of reivers to get stolen goods back

Insight – Household goods

Jack – A padded jerkin used as body armour

Kye/Kine – Cattle

Kyfe (Coif) – Close fitting cap

Laird – Petty land owner (Not the equivalent to a Lord)

Lang speir – A lance

Law – Hill

Lifted – To thieve

Limmer – Rascal or rogue

Loun – Rogue

Loup – Leap

Mail – Rent paid on a property

March – A division of the Border for administration purposes

Mirk – Dark

Muckle – Large

Neb – Nose

Nolt/Nout/Nowte – Horned cattle / bullock

Oistis – Parties of armed men

Patlett – Neckerchief

Pensil – Small pennon or tapering flag

Pledge – Giving of hostages (an important element in the administration of Border laws)

Plump watch – A reinforced watch, often when a raid was imminent and at a strategic point

Prick – Raid

Pricker – Light horseman, scout, armed with a lance

Pullyn – Poultry

Quo – Said

Railes – Night dress

Rank Rider – Marauder, raider

Recetting / Redress – Receipt of stolen goods, or harbouring a robber or other offender

Reif – Robbery, plunder

Rode – Raid

Rype – Rob

Sark – Shirt

Sawfie – Allowance for expenses, equal in value to the damage proved

Scumfishing – The practice of using burning peat to smoke out the occupants of a tower house

Sheyld – The summer hut of a Border shepherd

Shifting – Making do, providing

Shooting (A Day of Truce) – Not meeting the opposite officer on the agreed day

Siclyk – Suchlike

Skurrouris – Scouts

Sleuth dog – Bloodhound

Sorning – Forcibly billeting oneself upon a person or his lands

Speire – Inquire

Stell – Sheepfold

Stot – Bullock

Stouth – Plunder

Straik – Sword thrust/stroke

Summering – Pasturing cattle on the uplands in summer

Surname – Family or clan

Swire – A high hill-slope

Syke – A marshy hollow, ditch, trench

Threaplands – Debatable lands

Tickle – Uncertain, difficult to handle

Toom – Empty

Trews/Truce – Meetings of opposite Wardens on the frontier for the administration of justice

Trod – Pursuit

Tryst – An appointed place of meeting

Vilipended – Held cheap or of small account

Wamb – Stomach

Warden – The governing officer of a March

Warden's rode – A punishment raid on suspected reivers

Watches – A system of observation points on hilltops, tracks and bridges to warn of danger

Wedder – Castrated male sheep

Whye / Quey - A young cow

Yett – A wrought iron lattice gate

Rulers of the Two Kingdoms

Scotland

James IV	1488 – 1513
(b.1473 – k.1513)	
Queen Regent	1513 – 1515
Margaret Tudor	
Regent Albany	1515 – 1523
John Stewart	
2nd Duke of Albany	
James V	1528 – 1542
(b.1512 – d.1542)	
Regent Arran	1542 – 1554
James Hamilton	
Duke of Chatellerault, 2nd Earl of Arran	
Queen Regent	1554 – 1560
Mary of Guise	
Mary I	1561 – 1567
(b.1542 – ex.1587)	
Regent Moray	1567 – 1570
James Stewart	
Earl of Mar, 1st Earl of Moray	
Regent Lennox	1570 – 1571
Matthew Stewart	
4th Earl of Lennox	
Regent Mar	1571 – 1572
John Erskine	

17th Earl of Mar

Regent Morton   1572 – 1578
James Douglas
4th Earl of Morton

James VI   1578 – 1625
(b.1566 – d.1625)

Charles I   1625 – 1649
(b.1600 – ex.1649)

***

England

Henry VII   1485 – 1509
(b.1457 – d.1509)

Henry VIII   1509 – 1547
(b.1491 – d.1547)

Edward   VI   Never reached maturity
(b.1537 – d.1553)

Regency Council   1547 – 1549
Edward Seymour,
1st Duke of Somerset

Regency Council   1550 – 1553
John Dudley,
1st Duke of Northumberland

Mary I   1553 – 1558
(b.1516 – d.1558)

Elizabeth I   1558 – 1603
(b.1533 – d.1603)

Timothy Pont's map of Liddesdale – c.1595

Copy Right – National Library of Scotland, Edinburgh

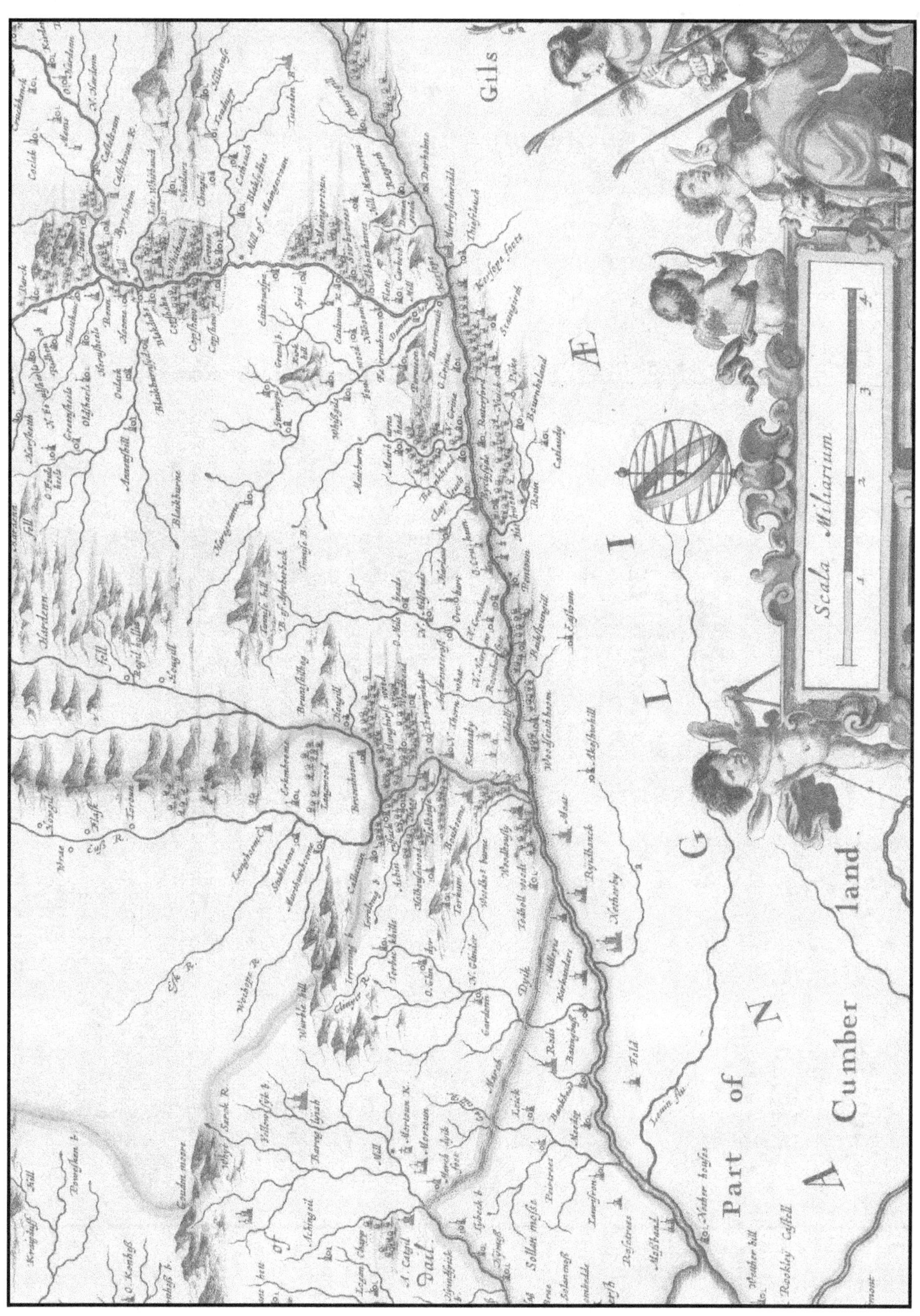

347

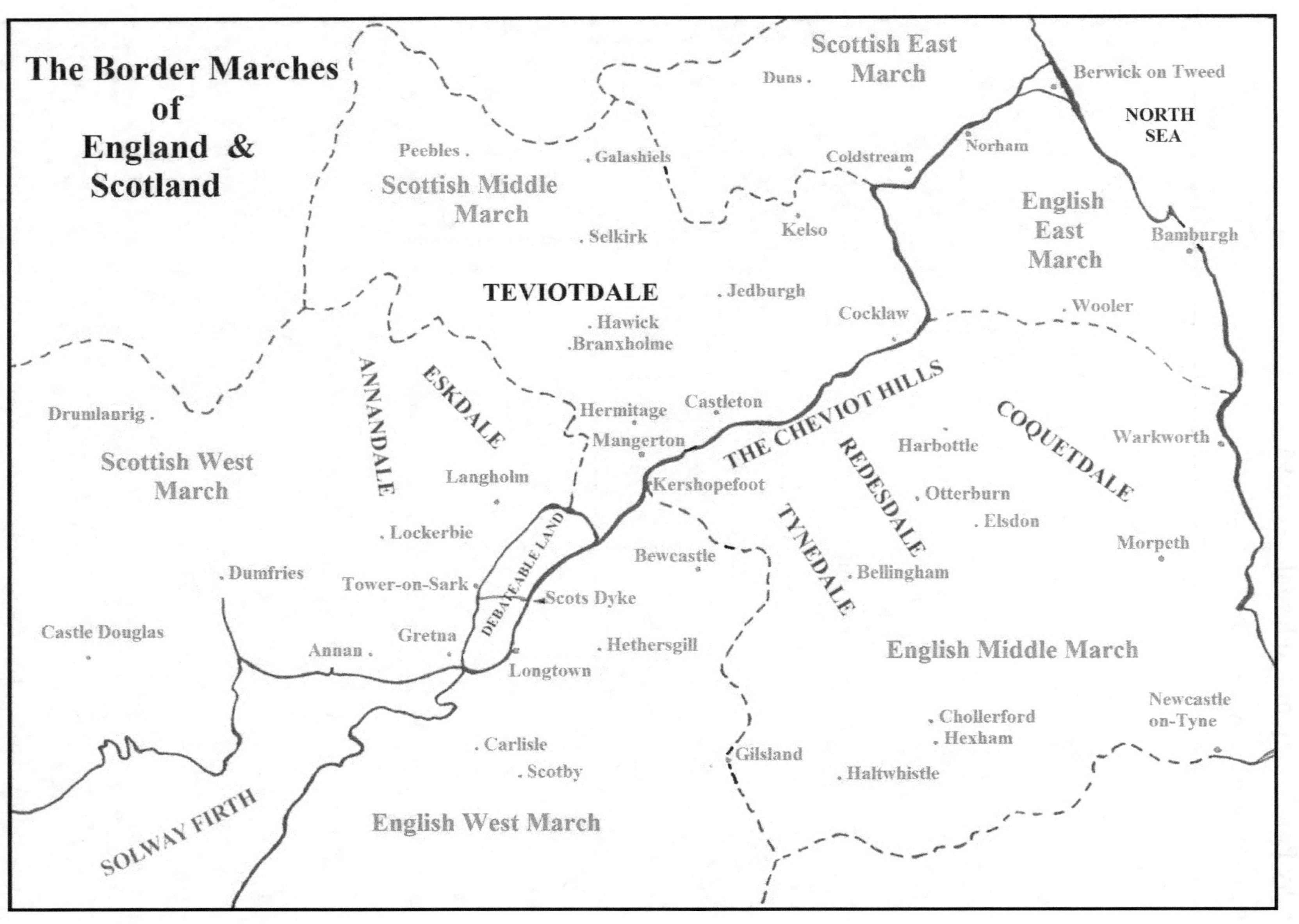

The Border Marches
of
England &
Scotland
NORTH SEA
Berwick on Tweed
Bamburgh
Warkworth
Newcastle on-Tyne
Morpeth
English East March
Wooler
Norham
COQUETDALE
Elsdon
Otterburn
English Middle March
Scottish East March
Coldstream
Harbottle
Chollerford
Hexham
Duns
REDESDALE
Haltwhistle
Kelso
Cocklaw
THE CHEVIOT HILLS
TYNEDALE
Bellingham
Jedburgh
Galashiels
Selkirk
Castleton
Kershopefoot
Gilsland
Scottish Middle March
TEVIOTDALE
Hawick
Branxholme
Hermitage
Mangerton
Bewcastle
Scots Dyke
Hethersgill
Peebles
ESKDALE
Langholm
DEBATEABLE LAND
Longtown
Carlisle
Scotby
English West March
ANNANDALE
Lockerbie
Tower-on-Sark
Gretna
Drumlanrig
Scottish West March
Dumfries
Annan
SOLWAY FIRTH
Castle Douglas